GF Newma[n] ... [prod]ucer, novelist and creator of the [...] [Judg]e John Deed. His first novel, *Sir, You Bastard*, was an instant bestseller, while *Law and Order*, his televison debut, changed the way criminal justice is portrayed on television and caused questions to be asked in the House of Commons. Further groundbreaking television followed, which he wrote and produced: *The Nation's Health*, *Black and Blue*, *The Healer*, and *New Street Law*. He lives and works in London, Edinburgh and Gloucestershire, where he's built a completely ecological house with his partner, two rescued dogs and an elderly horse.

'Newman's latest magnum opus, *Crime and Punishment*, is a roll-call of Britain from the 1950s to the 1980s, a *Sopranos*-meets-*Eastenders* underworld saga that consumes lowlife and highlife alike and spits out both with the same bad taste . . . This is a rumbustious, violent, cynical and yet frighteningly credible romp through the underbelly of three decades of British history . . . At a time when British identity is increasingly swamped by American influences, this is an unashamedly unselfconscious bath in a wholly English underworld. There is even a glossary to help with the language'   *The Times*

'This is a true gangster novel with thrills, spills and more twists and turns than Spaghetti Junction . . . if you like crime thrillers, his book will not disappoint. It delivers exactly what it promises'
Edinburgh Evening News

'More accurate and entertainingly written than much of the fiction that masquerades as books in the true crime section . . . well-written and researched'   *Sunday Express*

'This London gangster novel . . . goes straight for the jugular with a sex and violence-fuelled four-generation history of a dodgy East End family . . . it's certainly a page-turner and Newman possesses both a solid feel for time and place and the 'nouse' to tie the Bradens' trials and tribulations into postwar British history . . . Cushty'   *The List*

Also by GF Newman

GF Newman's

CRIME AND PUNISHMENT

Quercus

First published in Great Britain in 2009 by Quercus
This paperback edition first published in 2009 by

Quercus
21 Bloomsbury Square
London
WC1A 2NS

ISBN 978 1 84916 012 4

Printed and bound in Great Britain by Clays Ltd, St Ives plc

10 9 8 7 6 5 4 3 2 1

AUTHOR'S NOTE

This fictional history of crime relies on real incidents and real people. For both the major and minor named criminals, policemen and politicians, I have borrowed from their real-life activities as depicted in newspapers, court reports, biographies and autobiographies. None of these people or their families co-operated in any way with this book and it follows that a number of the scenes involving these criminals are also fictional.

All the other characters, including Brian, Jack and Joey, are entirely fictional and bear no resemblance to any living person.

BOOK 1

PROLOGUE

The moment he heard the terrible sound coming from his granddad Brian pissed his pants. It was like an animal being killed. Seeing little piglets slaughtered in Hoxton market didn't scare him, but Granddad was the strongest man alive – drunk or sober, Tiger Braden could beat anyone, Nan always said. Here he was, carrying on as if trying to frighten someone or not be scared himself. Sometimes Brian did that. Now he kept dead quiet and still.

The pee cooled on the inside of his leg and he wanted to cry. Instead he bit his lip to stop himself, like when he saw the Nazi parachute bombs floating down and didn't know where to run. He didn't move from behind the handcart in Sullivan's yard, or dare to breathe in case his mum heard him. If she found him, she'd be as cross with him as she was with his granddad. She always told him not to go out on his own after dark because of the German night-bombing. He might not get to a shelter in time. There was a shelter in their backyard. It was scary in there and you were all alone. He didn't like being alone.

Brian pressed his head against the wooden spokes of the large steel-rimmed wheel of the builder's handcart and tried not to look, but he couldn't stop himself.

When his mum arrived home early and came up to the small back bedroom and found Granddad sitting on the bed Brian shared with his uncle Jack, she started shouting. Nan left him in Granddad's care while she popped out to sit with Auntie Alice, who wasn't well because Uncle Jim was posted missing by his regiment. That was a long while ago and Auntie Alice still wasn't well.

'What you doing with him?' his mum demanded. 'What? What, you filthy sod?'

'Oi, watch that tongue of yourn,' Tiger Braden snapped, veins popping up in his muscular neck. His nostrils flared so you could see hairs like grey worms in his nose. 'We're only having a natter, ain't we, son? What's wrong with that?'

That made Mum angrier. She yanked her father up with such force it surprised him. She wasn't small, and Granddad wasn't weak, not like Brian's dad. She dragged her father down the stairs, calling him a filthy sod again and again, saying she wouldn't put up with him starting his nonsense with her son. Granddad was shouting. 'Shut your mouth, you daft cow! A mad cow's what you are, an' no mistake.'

Brian jumped out of bed to see what was happening. Mum often exploded like this, but her anger never usually lasted. Now it seemed like an incendiary that wouldn't die down. He pulled on his short, grey-flannel trousers and got into his plimsolls, then leaned over the banisters. They were arguing in the narrow, dimly lit hallway below. Mum dragged Granddad towards the front door, all the while slapping and punching him. Granddad threw up his arms, trying to protect himself, but didn't hit her back. Brian's dad didn't say anything, except an exasperated, 'Cathy,' as if trying to calm her as he followed them out. The situation wasn't getting calmer.

Sullivan's building yard at the end of the street was open to Goswell Road and next to their locked coal yard – coal was in short supply. Sensing something terrible was about to happen, Brian hoped someone would get the rozzers* or even a fire warden – like they did in the pictures – but there in the yard they couldn't be seen from the road behind the heaps of sand and piles of bricks. No one around there ever called the cops to anything anyway. Life wasn't like in the pictures, Nan always said.

'Hold him! Hold him!' Mum was screaming as she grabbed a metal reinforcing rod that was twisted like a stick of barley sugar.

* see Glossary on pp. 695–7.

Dad could barely hold a cat, much less Tiger Braden. With an arching motion Mum struck Granddad on the side of his head. Slowly the thin covering of flesh seemed to tip down over his ear like the wet, peeling wallpaper on some of the walls of bombed houses. Brian gasped.

'I put up with your nonsense all them years, Dad. You're not starting it with my boy!' Another blow struck Granddad, causing a louder scream. Mum shouted, 'You won't ever do that to anyone again, you rotten, filthy bastard. I won't let you ever again. I won't!' Brian's dad reached out as if to stop her, saying, 'Cathy, Cathy,' in the same quietly exasperated tone. Mum was growing more hysterical and took no notice as she landed another blow straight down on top of the old man's head. There was a crack, like a lightbulb exploding. Then the screaming stopped. His dad let Granddad slip from his grasp and crumple to the ground like a sack of spuds he was no longer able to hold.

Held-in breath burst out of Brian now on a long sob. Instinctively he knew what the stillness and silence meant. Sometimes he saw dead bodies being pulled out of bombed houses, but he'd never seen one of his own family dead. His mum gave no sign that she'd heard him. All her attention was on Granddad. 'I hate you,' she was saying. 'I hate what you done to me.'

She raised the iron bar to hit him again where he lay still and helpless-looking, but Dad caught her arm. 'That's enough, Cathy.' He never really fought or argued with Mum. He was ill a lot in his earlier life with TB, so wasn't strong. He'd lost his family to illness or something in Austria, but he never talked about it.

Mum dropped the metal bar, all her anger gone. She turned and looked straight at Brian and gave him a tight smile, as if to say, What're you doing here? Still Brian didn't move, except for his trembling limbs. Mum came over and unhooked his bloodless fingers from the spokes of the wheel. She didn't tell him off for being there; she didn't even tell him not to say anything to his nan or Uncle Jack. Brian knew he mustn't: if he did, there'd be big trouble. He was scared to death of that, and even more scared that he would accidentally tell someone.

'We'd better get you out of them trousers,' was all Mum said.

She picked him up and carried him with ease, even though he was nearly five and heavy for his age. She pulled him close to her and left the yard without a backward glance.

Brian tried to look back but she pulled his head round. His dad was right behind them. Brian still couldn't breathe: the air was being crushed out of his lungs by some great weight and he thought he might die.

When they were back at Nan's house, no one said anything about what happened in Sullivan's yard. His mum got him out of his wet trousers and stood him in the worn glazed sink in the scullery behind the kitchen. She washed his legs – the water from the brass tap was ice cold and stinging; she dried him with a rough towel. 'I have to do it properly, or you'll get chapped.'

'Goodness, what you doing up still, Brian?' Nan asked when she came in a little while later.

'He was having a bad dream, weren't you, love?' his mum answered.

Brian wanted to tell his nan it wasn't a nightmare, or not the sort you woke up from, because he was awake and still in it. But he knew Mum would kill him if he did. He shivered and clung to her. She was all he'd got – she reminded him of that over and over again. 'And you're all I've got, Brian.' What about Dad? he wanted to say. His dad still wasn't well and perhaps he was going to die like some of his friends' dads. He tried not to think about that in case it made it happen.

When Brian was sipping the cocoa his nan had made with powder from the Rowntree's tin, Uncle Jack came in looking as though he was already the world boxing champion instead of just training. 'What you doing up, m' ol' china?' he said. 'Piss the bed?' He dropped his boxing kit on a wooden chair.

'Leave him be!' his mum snapped. 'He's just going up, aren't you, lovey?'

'Oh, Mum, do I have to?' Brian didn't want to be upstairs on his own in the dark. At that moment he wasn't sure if what he'd seen had really happened, and only just stopped himself asking if Granddad was still at the pub.

'You won't ever be world champion you don't get plenty of sleep,' Jack said cheerfully.

'I've got a brother daft enough to get his brains bashed out,' Brian's mum said. 'I don't want my son doing it too.'

'You won't say that when I win the title,' Jack said.

She laughed, slipped her arm around his waist and gave him a squeeze. 'Course I won't.' Normally she didn't get on with Jack. He was too like Tiger Braden, she said. Maybe things would change now.

'Did your dad look in at the gym?' Nan asked.

'He stuck his head round the door. Said he was coming home.'

'Home to the George, more like,' Nan said, and started clearing up.

Suddenly there was no air in the room and again Brian couldn't breathe.

'You all right, my darling?' Nan asked.

'Course he is.' His mum put her hand on his chest and rubbed in a circular motion – she did that with Vick when he was chesty. He didn't know if he wanted her doing it now, but he didn't move away.

His dad was sitting at the kitchen table, dabbing at a permanent tea stain on the oilcloth. Why didn't he say something? Brian tried to speak but his throat started to close up. His tongue seemed swollen and wouldn't let him form words. Perhaps his dad would tell Nan what'd happened and why, but he was silent. Brian knew with a deep, gnawing certainty if Dad didn't say anything now, he never would. He and Dad were scared of Mum. Now he remembered how he'd felt when he walked across the thin ice on deep, dark Wapping Basin. It began to crack and the silt and slime below had tried to suck him under. He mustn't let Uncle Jack find out what

Mum did. His temper was worse even than Granddad's, and he was much stronger. But not as strong as Mum.

She picked Brian up and offered him around the family to be kissed goodnight, Nan first, then Dad and Uncle Jack. Finally his mum kissed his lips and said, 'You're safe now, lovey. I won't ever let anyone hurt you.'

Brian looked around the room, hoping one of them would save him from the dark and the picture in his mind of Granddad cold and still in Sullivan's yard. No one dared to in case they got the same treatment. He clung to his mum. One day she might do the same to him if he upset her.

ONE

The wail of the sirens made Brian Oldman's ears ring when they started at three o'clock sharp. Car hooters and bus horns, whistles and football rattles joined the din. When it stopped, a long cheer went up from the crowds on the street. This was the start of the Festival of Britain that would, they had been told, 'usher in a brand new beginning for everyone after the years of austerity and hardship following the war'. A barrel of beer was wheeled up on a handcart and everyone cheered again, Win Booker's mum doing a knees-up because she was happy to be alive. Some of the neighbours had gone up west to Buckingham Palace to see King George, Queen Elizabeth and the princesses at the head of the procession to Westminster Abbey. Life would be different from now on, Clement Attlee said on the wireless after the chimes of Big Ben struck three. They wanted to believe him. The crowd went wild, cheering and shouting, shaking hands and hugging, even people who didn't normally speak to each other. At last things would get better.

'You wouldn't have thought we'd won the war, Brian,' his nan said. 'We certainly didn't win peace under this bloody lot.'

Brian didn't know what she meant. But now wasn't the time to ask: whistles blasted again and people were throwing confetti and streamers over the Sullivan brothers as they rolled out a big papier-mâché model of Britannia on one of their handcarts. They had several lorries now and were busy building houses for the LCC.

'It's like they won the pools,' Brian's mother, Cath, said. 'The shoddy way they been throwing up them houses. 'S daylight robbery. They must have pots of dosh stashed away. Serve 'em right if someone robbed 'em.'

Just mentioning the Sullivans, who owned both the coal yard and builders' yard made Brian shiver. He refused to go there and always crossed the road to pass their place. Sometimes he wondered if his mum had forgotten what had happened, but then she'd do or say something that told him she hadn't. Now everyone was joining in with a huge snake-like dance that was winding around the corner into his street. Neighbours ran to the front rather than waiting for the end to appear. Others raised their glasses or teacups in a toast to the dancers.

More streamers sailed through the air. A bright pink one wrapped itself around Brian's tall, straight-backed Nan, Gracie Hill. She called herself that, even though she wasn't married to Billy Hill. She was strong-jawed, with dark hair and determined, handsome features. Her face showed the resolve that you knew would see you through any crisis. That was how Brian felt about her. She laughed as she carried a large enamel teapot out of her terraced house, whose door opened directly on to the pavement. She stepped into the roadway to the trestle tables that stretched the length of the street. She set down the teapot, among the plates, freed the streamer and twirled it around Brian, who was eleven now and slightly overweight. 'Come on, love,' she said, and pushed him ahead of her to join the snake, her hands on his fleshy hips. The man behind her clasped her hips, and all the while Nan's friend Eve Sutton, from number forty-seven, plonked her fat fingers down on the piano, which Brian's uncle Jack and his best friend Bobby Brown had dragged outside.

People fell about laughing in confusion when they had to kick their legs out on the third step as the song directed. They kicked different ways and almost fell over. Brian got separated from his nan and suddenly Win Booker was hanging on to him. 'Where's Jack?' she asked.

'I dunno.' Brian wriggled free of her to look around, as if he was helping her spot Jack. He knew his uncle wouldn't want her to find him. 'She'd ruin a bloke when he's in training,' Jack told him once. 'Know what I mean, Bri?' Brian didn't, but he pretended he did. He knew it must have something to do with the fact that neither his mother nor Nan liked Win. They thought she was no good.

Gracie was pouring tea into an assortment of cups for the adults when Brian found her again. 'They survived the German bombs,' she said, referring to the best, cabinet-kept china, 'but I'm not sure they'll survive this lot.'

There were too many people for them all to have a place at the table so the children sat at it and the adults pulled armchairs or sofas from their parlours. Women like his nan, in Sunday-best with a pinny wrapped around them served men in the armchairs or fussed around the table. They made sure everyone had something to eat and no one got more than their share. Some kids were grabbing food as if they were starving. The table was laden with sandwiches, mostly fish paste, but there were a few with ham or corned-beef, which went in a flash. There were homemade cakes, too, and tarts with shop-bought jam.

A well-groomed seven-year-old, hair slick with Brylcreem, in a stiff grey-flannel suit that was slightly too small for him, grabbed a sandwich from a passing server to add to the cake and two other sandwiches on his plate. The raw hand of a pale, thin woman shot out and slapped him hard, making him drop the third sandwich back on to the serving plate. That was Brian's aunt Alice: she was stopping his cousin John making a pig of himself. John was always being pulled up sharply by his mum. She was trying to make him into a better person, someone who wouldn't offend God – she had turned to God in earnest when her husband didn't return from the war. 'She's enough to make you take to the bottle,' his nan sometimes confided to him.

'He's all right,' Gracie said. She'd seen John's shame and stroked the side of her grandson's face to comfort him. 'Leave him alone.'

'He mustn't grab, Mum,' Alice said firmly. 'It's not Christian.'

'He's only a youngster.' She held out the green enamel teapot to her elder daughter. 'Here, more tea's wanted. It's Christian not to let these people die of thirst.'

She winked at Brian as Alice went away without another word. As soon as her back was turned Gracie put more food on John's plate. He glanced around in alarm.

'No, I mustn't, Nan. I mustn't,' he said.

'Don't worry about that, my darling,' Gracie said. 'You eat while you can. Brian, look after him. Make sure he gets his share.' That was his nan's credo, always making sure her own got their fair share, plus a little more. She ruffled Brian's hair, and immediately he flicked it back into place. Bobby Brown was always knocking off stuff and boxes of Brylcreem was part of one load. He had given them each a jar to celebrate the Festival of Britain.

'Nan, can I have some beer? George Foreman's got a glass and he's only a year older than me,' Brian said.

'Won't do no harm. Ask your dad or your uncle Jack. Tell 'em I said.'

John Redvers looked up at her hopefully. 'You can when you're a bit older, lovey,' she told him.

Win Booker came over with a plate of sandwiches. The tight top the eighteen-year-old bottle-blonde was wearing drew yearning looks from older men and tolerant smiles from their worn-out wives. 'We're running out of bread, Mrs Hill,' Win said. 'All that what Dad got from the Tip-Top's gone.'

'Mrs Thompson's old man brought a ton of it, too. I'll go and have a look,' Gracie said, and went away.

Win caught Brian's arm. 'Did you tell him I was looking for him? Did you?' she said.

'Tell him yourself,' Brian said. 'He's over there.' He nodded through the crowd to a group of young men hanging around the lamp-post as he picked up an empty glass. He saw her eyes settle on Jack Braden. She only had eyes for Jack. He was dark and handsome, his plaid shirtsleeves rolled up over muscular upper arms. He was the handsomest man in the world, Nan said, and ·

Brian couldn't disagree, especially as his mum said so, grudgingly, too. He wished his dad, Joey, was more like him.

Win Booker had got it bad and was throwing herself at Jack, his nan said. Brian understood what she meant – he'd felt like that for a while about Mr Rush, his teacher. He was tall and had leather patches on the arms of his jacket, smoked a pipe, rode a BSA motorbike and seemed to be all the things his dad wasn't. He felt a bit sorry for Win Booker, but he wasn't going to tell his uncle because he knew Jack wasn't interested in her. Jack's wavy dark hair and violet eyes were like a magnet to women but, right now, he was only interested in becoming the light-heavyweight world champion.

Brian went over to the young men and held out his glass to Bobby Brown, who had a quart bottle of Watney's brown ale. Jack stuck an arm round his nephew's shoulders. Brian liked it when he did that; it gave him goose bumps and made him feel part of the gang. Because of his age he was always left out and he wanted to be grown up so he could go around with Jack. His nan always told him it would happen soon enough.' But today was special so he was included and Bobby Brown was giving him beer. Brian watched the white foam rise up the glass.

'Steady on, Bobby,' Joey Oldman said. 'You'll make him sick.'

'Da-ad! Nan said I could.'

'He's all right,' Jack said. 'We're celebrating, ain't we? A drop of brown won't do no harm. 'S like lemonade.' He winked at Bobby.

Brian waited to see if his dad would go against Jack. He didn't. People didn't often argue with Jack, only his mum sometimes. Brian gulped the beer as his dad looked away, accepting defeat. Even though he'd wanted it, with its bitter taste of iron, he wanted his dad to argue just once, and insist on things being done his way. But he didn't, just as he didn't that night in Sullivan's yard.

'What you doing? You drunk?' Bobby Brown jumped back as Brian's glass smashed on the pavement.

'No harm done,' Jack said, kicking the broken glass into the gutter. 'Get yourself another pot.'

Eve Sutton, having exhausted her repertoire of tunes, launched back into the conga, a real crowd-pleaser. Another snake was forming. Brian saw Win Booker join it and look their way as if longing for Jack to come over. She pulled an old man's hands off her bum and on to her hips. Straightaway they slid down again. Bobby said, 'Dirty old sod!' Jack and the others laughed. Win blushed as if she thought they were laughing at her.

Brian's mum, Cath, who had the same dark good looks as her brother and Nan, came past in the snake. Every time Brian saw her unexpectedly his heart pounded. It did now as she reached out for his dad and pulled him into the dance that was bumping along. She tried to pull Jack in, too, but he resisted her – not many did.

Bobby gave Brian a new glass and splashed beer into it. He took another swig, although the taste wasn't any better. Really, he would have preferred Tizer.

'Oi! Don't you get him drunk, Bobby,' Cath said, as she shimmied past, Dad in front of her.

Bobby gave her a tipsy grin and raised his glass. 'Nan said it was all right, Mum,' Brian called after her, but his mum was disappearing, his dad in front of her.

It was then that Win Booker captured Jack. Her red, work-worn hand shot out and seized his. It must have taken a lot of courage but she wasn't letting him go.

'She's got you now, Jack!' Bobby jeered.

Jack winked back at him. 'It's a knockout,' he said, and thrust his glass at Brian. Win reached around and moved Jack's hard stevedore's hands off her waist and on to her bum. She looked up at him and smiled. Brian drank some beer, wishing he was in the dance line but too shy to push in. He saw his nan pull his cousin John across the road to join in. John couldn't do it properly, and Auntie Alice wouldn't do it at all. She stood on the pavement, frowning. Dancing was the devil's way of making people more sinful than they already were, she would say. Her iron-grey hair was pulled back like wire against her head, making her face tense and painful to look at.

After the conga's grand finale, Jack came back to the safety of his friends, but Win, emboldened now, tugged him in the opposite direction. 'Come on, Jack,' she said, 'you can help me cut some more sandwiches. They're running out.' She wasn't letting him go as she headed towards her house, Bobby and the others calling after him.

Suddenly Brian felt sick. The beer was rising in his throat, then settling back into his stomach. He didn't want to throw up in the street in front of all these people because his mum would be cross with Jack, Bobby and his dad for letting him drink too much and then he'd never be in the gang. He longed instead to be with Jack. Only he could protect him.

The stench of decayed fish and rat urine hung in the Bookers' kitchen. Mr and Mrs Booker didn't get on. They fought a heck of a lot and Mrs Booker would sometimes come flying along the street to Jack's house for his dad to stop her old man leathering one of the kids or laying into her. Since Tiger Braden's death, when Sullivan's yard had taken a direct hit from a V2 rocket, Jack had assumed that role.

Today the smell was mixed with gas from the cast-iron stove and made Jack's nostrils twitch. Mr and Mrs Booker had been arguing when a pan of fish got tipped behind the stove and left there, both of them refusing to clear it up. There were fat stains up the yellowing distempered walls, while food and empty paste jars littered the table. Jack's mum worked hard to keep their scullery clean – you could eat off the floor almost. In the Bookers' house he wouldn't have wanted to eat off the table.

'What you gonna do now we got them new opportunities the government was on about, Jack?' Win asked as she squeezed past, pressing her stomach into him. She reached for another loaf of bread and started to slice it. 'D'you wanna scrape a bit of marge on them? Not too much.'

Jack found a dinner knife and started to spread bright yellow Stork margarine far too thickly over the slices. 'No, like this,' Win said, putting her hand over his to guide the knife.

'I'm gonna have a shot at the world title,' Jack said. He thought of little else. 'I'm ready. I just need a chance.'

'Pigs'll fly, my dad says.'

'What does he know about it?' Jack wouldn't let her dampen his confidence. 'I'm better than Freddie Mills any old day. I could lick him easily. I just need a chance, that's all.'

'I wanna get right away from this street,' Win said. 'Everyone talks about me.'

'Who does?' Jack didn't want to be drawn into this conversation, but Peewee, his trainer, had told him that only dummies stood by and said nothing.

'They all think I'm a bad lot. Dad walloped me again last night, the rotten sod. I'll kill him one of these days.'

'You should've called me. I would've come.'

'Would you?'

He would've gone because no man should take his belt to a girl. Win was fully developed, but being three years older than her, Jack still thought of her as a girl – one he'd known all his life.

'You should see the welts on my bum. I'll show you if you like.'

She lifted her pleated cream skirt to her thigh, revealing a suspender. Jack's breath quickened and his cock began to stiffen, even though he knew it was bad for his training regime. As if sensing his rising urgency Win kissed him hard on the mouth. He felt something like an explosion behind his lips and cheeks, similar to the tingling sensation he experienced when he took a punch in the face, only much nicer.

'Not here,' she said, 'in case someone comes in. We'll go in our air-raid shelter. I'll show you what he done to me.'

She brushed against the swelling in Jack's trousers as she took his hand, then pulled him out through the scullery door. They crossed the narrow yard, past the privy and an empty chicken run to the rusting corrugated-iron shelter. Jack's mind held a single thought right then.

The air raid shelter was small, dark and crowded with junk accumulated since the war. Iron-framed bunks, rusting jerrycans, broken chairs, bits of pushbikes, piles of newspaper. No one ever went near the place, other than to add to the pile. The thick, undisturbed air smelled of pee and damp.

Inside, Win lifted her skirt and undid her suspenders. She eased down baggy cotton knickers to show Jack the vicious welts across her buttocks. 'Do you want to feel them? You can. Go on.'

Jack hesitated, scared of what was happening to him, afraid he was going to come right there and then. Win took his hand and laid it on her bum. The pressure he was feeling worsened.

'Do you want to do me?' she asked, in a trembling whisper. 'Do you? You can, if you like.'

Whatever the consequences, whatever his mum or his sister might have said about Win Booker, Jack lacked the will to resist. His hand plunged into the sticky wetness between her legs. 'Oh, Jack,' she sighed.

Oh, strewth, his mind cried as her fingers found him. He was ready to let go at any second and would if she didn't stop. In a flurry of clumsy movements they got her knickers off and his belt unfastened, along with his fly buttons. His brown cord trousers were barely down over his knees, along with his woollen pants, when Win's hot hand clasped him. He didn't know how he got inside her and worried that it would all be over before he was aware of doing anything. Only the sharp, stinging pain as he entered her stopped him ejaculating immediately. His foreskin tightened over the helmet of his cock, feeling like it was going to tear as it strangulated and cut off the blood supply; then moments later an explosion of sensation swamped the pain and left him moaning Win's name.

Then Win was saying, 'Quiet. Be quiet! Someone'll hear. Me dad might come. He'll go mad.' She sounded angry, or maybe she was just scared.

Jack felt good, as if he'd done something really worthwhile. It was a milestone inasmuch as it was his first time and he was pleased he didn't disgrace himself and come over her leg, like Bobby Brown did on his first go. But he was dissatisfied somehow, irritated that it hadn't been better than he'd imagined. The pain from his foreskin robbed him of a lot of pleasure. He supposed it would get better. He remembered his training regime and what Peewee had said about allowing his energy and stamina to run out through the little bean when you played around: 'When you get to the sixth round and can hardly get out of your corner at the bell, you'll wish you'd left the little bean in its pod.'

As Win pulled her knickers on she wouldn't look at him, and he was embarrassed now, tidying himself up. They slipped out of the shelter separately, Jack going quickly through the yard and out into the rear alleyway to skirt around the houses to the street. He wasn't any good at making sandwiches anyway.

Old Bill was at the street party in the rotund shape of PC Tony Watling. He'd been forever chasing Jack Braden and Bobby Brown, but he was friendly enough today. Jack knew the policeman would still nick them if he got half a chance. They were like that. Over the years PC Watling had given them a few clips around the ears, but now he smiled benignly and unfastened some of the chrome buttons on his new-style uniform, perhaps as a concession to the party; his mac remained folded neatly over one arm as if he didn't trust the cloudless blue sky.

His other arm was round the shoulders of a young boy, Tony Wednesday. He was the same age as Jack's nephew, John Redvers: they'd been born on the same day, but there the similarity ended. Watling's charge was from the orphanage and didn't have the advantage of a mother like Alice to guide his every move. John was pink and over-fed; Tony was thin, sallow and hungry-looking, his clothes old, patched, and a bit too small for him. Although he had the uncared-for look of a hand-me-down kid, he did have

PC Watling to keep an eye on him, a big advantage for a boy like him. The policeman had found him as a newborn baby in a wooden butter box on a doorstep while he was out on patrol one Wednesday night. No one had claimed him or had been identified as his parent. There were hundreds of kids like him, their mothers having taken up with servicemen only to be abandoned when they got pregnant.

Despite Eve Sutton's unflagging efforts on the piano, the atmosphere changed with the arrival of the man in uniform. Everyone was suddenly alert and watchful, sending notes of caution on the street telegraph.

Jack approached the table, indifferent to the copper, as his mum rushed a cup of tea into the policeman's hand.

'I'm not after your Jack,' PC Watling said, 'not today, missus. I'm off duty.'

'I didn't think the police were ever off duty,' Gracie said, not lowering her guard.

'I been down this street so often looking for your boy, I thought I'd join your party – like family. If I'm welcome, that is.'

'Today everyone's welcome, Mr Watling. And your nipper,' she said, turning to Tony Wednesday. Her eyes flitted nervously to Jack, who winked at her.

This was just the sort of day the police or military would come looking for him and Bobby Brown, but Jack knew he could outrun them. He and Bobby had refused to answer their call-up for the army. Instead of going to their medicals they'd done a bunk, Jack because he wanted a shot at the boxing title, and Bobby was too busy with the black-market.

'This boy's as near as I'm going to get to family, I dare say,' PC Watling said. 'I take him out when I can. They don't get too many treats down at the orphanage.'

'You're a kind-hearted man, Mr Watling,' Gracie said. 'You'd have made a good father. You hungry, young man?' She didn't wait for him to respond. 'Of course you are. Let's get you some proper grub.'

She smiled at PC Watling and took the cup and saucer from him. 'You'll want something stronger than tea as you're off duty.'

Ray Thompson, one of the neighbours, shoved a quart bottle of Whitbread Pale Ale into the policeman's hand. 'A glass would be useful,' PC Watling said.

'Why you looking so pleased with yourself, Jack?' Gracie said. 'You look like the cat who's been at the cream.'

Jack wanted to tell her – he wanted to tell everyone – but said instead, 'I can still run faster than any flat-footed copper.' He grinned at Tony Wednesday, but the boy was only interested in the plate Gracie was putting food on. Suddenly he snatched a fairy cake, stuffed it into his mouth whole and swallowed it.

'Them nuns at St Joseph's must starve you. You look after him, John,' she said to her grandson. 'He hasn't got no parents. I'd best sort some more sandwiches.' She turned away and Tony Wednesday stuffed more food into his mouth. Jack watched him, fascinated – he hadn't seen anyone so hungry since the war.

'My mum says you shouldn't stuff your face,' John Redvers told him. The orphan boy's adam's apple bounced twice as he forced the food down his gullet. 'It's not Christian.'

''S your mum a nun?' Tony grabbed another handful.

Jack laughed.

'What's so funny?' Cath asked as she joined them at the table. 'Didn't you see that copper? Or were you too bloody busy with Win Booker?'

'What do you mean?' Jack's cheeks started to burn. 'I was helping her make some more sandwiches.' He wondered who else had seen them.

'We'll get fat on those, I'm sure!'

Cath and he were too alike to get on, but he mistook her concern for tenderness and put his arm around his sister's shoulders. 'He's off duty.'

'Who's this he's brought? A gannet?'

'That's his nipper.'

Tony was still chucking food down his throat.

Jack glanced about: he needed to know the lie of the land in case he had to run. He saw Bobby with his arm around PC Watling's shoulders. Both held pint glasses as they sang, 'On top of Old Smokey . . .' Jack went over to them.

'Here he is,' Bobby said, flinging his other arm around Jack and slopping beer over his plaid shirt. 'The next light-heavyweight champion of the world.'

Bobby believed it wholeheartedly and was as pleased when Jack won a match as if he'd won it himself.

'World's champion dodgers. That's what you two 'erberts are,' Watling said. 'What a merry dance youse two've led me and no mistake.' He undid the rest of his buttons. He was getting hot and red in the face from the beer.

'Well, that's all over now, Mr Watling,' Jack said good-naturedly. 'We got a fresh start, didn't we?'

'It's the Festival of Britain, son,' the policeman replied, 'not a bloody amnesty. The Kate still wants you and, by golly, they'll have you sooner or later.'

'No! No, don't be silly,' Jack said, shock causing his voice – already on a slightly high register for a man – to go higher. 'Mr Attlee said this was a new beginning for us all.'

The policeman laughed, as if the joke was on Jack. 'Don't talk wet. You can't believe what cunting politicians say, especially not Labour. The army'll find plenty for you to do, son.'

Jack felt winded. Suddenly his title fight was no nearer than it had been when he was dodging the police.

Bobby Brown didn't have a fearful bone in his body. He laughed. 'The squaddies'll have to learn to run a lot faster, then, won't they? And you, chum.' He raised an eyebrow at Watling.

'Jack,' he said, as the policeman wandered off to find his charge, 'what d'you do to Win Booker?'

'Nothing! What d'you mean?' – guilt in his voice.

'Your aunt Alice said something about seeing you from the

scullery window. Win's old man got hold of her and marched her straight indoors. D'you charver her?'

Jack was torn between telling his best friend the truth and going to see if Win was all right. Her old man might be giving her another leathering. If he did, Jack would sort him out – even though he was related to the mad twins from Whitechapel. He told himself Win wouldn't want the whole street knowing. And he didn't want his mum to know – or his trainer.

Such concerns instantly became unimportant. The atmosphere on the street changed as if a wind had blown in the heat of Africa. Heads turned and people moved towards a shiny black Vauxhall Velox came along the road, honking its horn. It was a deep, urgent sound.

With a rush of excitement Brian ran past saying, 'Uncle Jack, Uncle Jack! It's Granddad Billy. He's out of clink!'

'He could have stayed there for all I care – an' he ain't your granddad, Brian,' Jack snapped.

But Brian was gone, along with most of the other mugs who wanted to find out what the fuss was about. Nothing, was Jack's conclusion. Billy Hill would still be as much of a show-off as he was before he went to prison. He always needed an audience and there were always plenty willing to oblige.

'We ought to see what he's got to say for himself,' Bobby said.

Jack didn't know what people saw in the chump, and especially his mum, getting hooked up with a bloke like that after being married to his dad. Tiger Braden would've seen him off any day of the year. And despite Billy Hill's reputation, Jack knew he could see him off, too. He didn't want the man coming back from Pentonville to tell him what to do. He wouldn't stand for that from anyone, much less Billy Hill.

TWO

Brian shoved through the crowd towards the car with a proprietorial air. People blocked his path, wanting to be near it too. Why didn't they understand that family members got special privileges? Now Granddad Billy stepped out of the front passenger seat of the four-door motor-car, waving some bottles of champagne clenched between his fingers like a milkman. His broad smile showed his large teeth, topped off with a pencil moustache. Handsome was what Nan called him, and the other women in the street seemed to think so too. He wore a chalk-striped double-breasted grey suit and brightly polished shoes, with a fedora hat tipped over his left eye, the way they wore them in gangster films.

'You lucky people,' he said expansively. 'Look who's home and look what he's got.'

The neighbours cheered like they did for the King and Queen when they visited the street after the war. Granddad Billy was more popular around here than either of them.

'I was driving along, minding my own business,' he announced, 'when I saw this fall off the back of a lorry – honest to God, Officer!'

The audience roared and Billy started passing out the bottles.

'Charlie, get some more of them out here. These people look thirsty to me – tea ain't no good.'

A younger man in a loud-checked sports jacket with wide shoulders got out from behind the steering-wheel and dragged wooden boxes off the back seat. His name was Charlie Richardson and something told Brian he'd be seeing a lot of him. Right then, though, he had eyes only for Billy, who suddenly brought more glamour and magic into their hard, dull lives than the entire

...tival of Britain. Brian knew he wanted to be part of that magic. He didn't care what his dad said about getting an education and making something of himself. All he could think about was how Granddad Billy had changed their lives. Two years ago he'd gone to prison for ram-raiding a Mayfair jeweller's. When Billy pulled off a job everyone he knew benefited. Nan said he was the most generous man and that was why she had 'married' him. She wasn't really married to him because he was already married – and Uncle Jack was dead cross about it.

'He puts the Sullivans in the shade,' a neighbour said. 'And that daft Britannia they made in their yard.'

Suddenly Brian was trembling. Immediately he tried to turn his thoughts from his granddad and the terror of that night in their yard to when Nan first brought Billy to the house.

It was hate at first sight for Jack, who was waiting in the kitchen, poking the fire in the range with its oven one side and a hob for boiling pans on the other. He tensed, the veins on his neck and forehead sticking up under his skin when the front door banged and he heard Nan giggling like a girl. The man's voice was deep, reassuring and a little thick with drink. 'Steady she does it,' he said. That was Billy Hill, and Nan giggled more. Cath shot Jack a warning look but said nothing.

Billy Hill was younger than Nan, but she was very good-looking still, like a film star. Both of them were a bit the worse for drink and almost any little thing set them off laughing as they stood in the narrow kitchen, facing Jack, Cath and Joey. Alice was in the scullery with baby John. How they all came to be there, Brian wasn't sure. Alice and John didn't live at Nan's; Mum and Dad and he did. There was a housing shortage still, despite Mr Attlee's promises that his government would build more homes. If they were it wasn't around them, apart from a few prefabs. No one seemed to get around to repairing the damaged houses either.

'What's this? The welcoming party?' Billy had said, attempting to salute.

'Behave yourself,' Nan said. 'This is my family, all I've got, God bless 'em.' She gave Brian a kiss. 'What are you doing up so late, lovey?'

'He couldn't sleep, could you, love?' Cath said.

'I'll take him up,' Joey said. 'Come on, son. I'm a bit tired myself.'

'That's Joey,' Nan said. 'He's my Cath's other half.'

'I bet,' Billy said, staring at Mum.

Brian's mum looked like the women in the magazines she read whenever she got the chance. People said how well she took care of herself. She was always changing her hairstyle and complaining she didn't get new things.

'Don't go on my part,' Billy said. 'We're not stopping, are we, Gracie?'

'Jack, be a good boy and pop the kettle on. Make Billy a cuppa while I go and change.'

'Maybe I should come and help you, Gracie,' he said, and they laughed.

'You behave yourself, or I'll call a copper.' That made them laugh even more. Brian had no idea what was so funny.

Jack didn't say a word, but kept poking the fire, his face like a thundery day, dark and angry. Something else Brian didn't get: why Jack wouldn't want Nan to go out and have a good time. She'd hardly been out since his granddad had died.

She was downstairs, changed, in no time, certainly not enough time for the kettle to boil and Jack to make tea, even if he intended to, which he didn't. Not even time for Joey to put Brian to bed, which he hadn't wanted to do either. No one wanted to leave Billy Hill.

Nan came back in her best red dress, which hadn't been out of the wardrobe in a long while, except when Brian got it out and put it on without anyone knowing. Anyone except his mum, that was. One day she'd found him in Nan's bedroom with it on but hadn't told anyone. It was their secret and she kept it locked away with the other one.

'Do you want to come with us, Jack?' Gracie asked.

'There's plenty of room in the old jalopy,' Billy said. 'You can show us the hot spots.' He winked at Gracie and his smile broadened.

Jack said nothing, disapproval written all over his face.

'Well, you needn't look so glum, chum,' Billy said. 'I ain't kidnapping her. Although I might. Look at her! Ain't she a picture?' No one answered so he winked at Gracie again. 'I don't think our Jack likes me, Gracie.'

Suddenly he was 'our Jack' and that didn't please him either.

'Of course he does. He's just a bit shy, aren't you, love?' Nan said, and tried to stroke his face. Jack shrugged her away.

'Well, that's all right, then.' Billy laughed. He said exactly what he liked whenever he wanted to say it. 'Don't wait up for us, son.' He leered, and pushed Gracie out of the room and along the hall. His car was outside, the engine still running.

If they hadn't gone Jack might have clocked Billy. Brian couldn't remember having seen him so angry before, and it was worse because he didn't say anything. He was tense enough to start a fire. Could Jack have put it on Billy? Brian wasn't sure. Jack was a great boxer but Billy was hard and wiry, with wide shoulders in his gabardine suit. He was older than Jack, the only man in the family apart from Joey, who didn't seem to count. It was always Jack the women turned to. Until then Jack had had his mum's undivided attention. She cooked and cleaned for him, and mended his clothes. He didn't have to lift a finger. She cheered when he won his fights at the local gym; she wept for him in August 1949 when he was called up for National Service. Later she encouraged him to go on the run rather than into the army; so did Cath. Both of them were cross with Joey for being too scared to take Jack's medical in his place: the army would fail him, as it had before, because of his childhood TB. But Auntie Alice was cross with Jack for not going into the army – she thought it was his duty.

'I've already lost one man in my life,' Nan said. 'I'm not losing another, not even to the army. Have a thought for someone else,

Alice.' She lied when the police came looking for Jack after he failed to appear for his medical.

The more Nan saw of Granddad Billy, the more Jack loathed him. He couldn't understand why no one else could see what he saw in him. When Nan and Granddad Billy were out together, Jack would lie awake in bed next to Brian, waiting for their return. If Billy didn't leave until morning Jack's mood was murderous.

'He's a bad lot, that one,' Jack said, as he listened for any sound through the thin walls of the house.

'Why? What's he do?' Brian asked, unsure what Jack meant. Granddad Billy always brought him things they often couldn't get because of all the shortages. There was plenty of sugar and meat in the house. He'd always bring sweets, and gave Brian a model of a green Bentley sports car.

'He's a thief. M' dad wouldn't have put up with the likes of him for two minutes. Nor should I. I wish my dad was here now.'

Fear crept over Brian and made him shake. His secret bore down on him. He knew he could never tell on his mum – but what if it just slipped out?

'What's wrong with you?' Jack said sharply. 'Keep still.'

Brian didn't say a word and prayed he never would.

There was nothing Jack or anyone else could do about Billy. Nan was gone on him. His mum said most of the other women around there were too. Billy Hill was so glamorous and had such a big reputation. Everyone, from Stepney's Mile End Road to Soho's Old Compton Street, knew him. Wherever he went people called out to him and he'd call back, giving them advice, telling them how to solve their problems. Sometimes he solved things directly, going straight to the heart of the problem. Often it was something wrong with those narrow, crumbling houses without front gardens. Billy would go along to the rent office or threaten the landlord and within hours the problem would get fixed.

'What's so special about that?' Jack challenged. 'M' dad was like that, fighting everyone's battles. He'd help anyone.'

'He would,' Gracie conceded. 'That's what attracted me to him. He was like Billy in that, God rest him.'

Was his granddad resting, Brian wondered, or was he angry about what had happened? Perhaps he was plotting revenge. Brian didn't know how the dead took revenge, but somehow they did because his mum was always threatening to come back and haunt the people she was angry with. Perhaps his granddad was haunting her.

What was most appealing about Billy was the excitement that surrounded him, the danger. He was a robber who drove vans into jewellery-shop windows and made off with the loot before the coppers could arrive; he robbed GPO vans loaded with registered letters and even factory pay-rolls. People treated him like he was Robin Hood because he was always on their side, never with the bosses or people with money. The war had provided him with plenty of muscle, young men deserting from the army mostly. Sometimes they came to the house too. Brian saw their bulging arms when their sleeves were rolled up. He was fascinated by them, just as he was by Jack's hard, fit body.

Jack didn't want to be a member of Billy Hill's gang, and was at a loss to know what to do. When Billy moved in, Jack moved out, upsetting Gracie and making Billy cross because she was upset. That was one thing Billy Hill couldn't fix and it gave Jack a little of his power back. Jack took a room across the street with Nan's best friend, Eve Sutton. She had three daughters but only one was left at home. Brian saw Jack every day and carried information back to Nan, even after his parents moved to the next street, into two rented rooms with a scullery and a shared toilet. After the German bombs, and with skinflint landlords saving their money, there wasn't much available for rent. When Billy's luck finally ran out and he was sent to prison, Jack moved back to his mother's house. So did Brian and his parents when rain came through their roof and the landlord was slow to repair it.

*

After his stint inside Billy didn't come back to live at the house but took up with a nightclub hostess, who was younger than Gracie. During one of his flush periods Billy had bought Nan her house, for which he paid £190 – rainy-day security, he told her. He was a rogue, but a practical one. None of the jewellery he gave her was stolen, as the police discovered when they came looking for him after his last raid.

Why he came back here instead of going to his fancy woman – as Auntie Alice called her – no one knew. They didn't ask or care because they were glad Billy was back. 'You lucky people!' he bellowed. It was his current catchphrase.

'Your mum's old man's outa clink!' Bobby Brown called to Jack, unable to keep the excitement from his voice.

'He's just a muggins, Bobby,' Jack told him firmly.

'He's still outa clink.' That was all that seemed to matter to Bobby, as he joined the crowd around Billy's car, trying to push to the front. 'I'll have one of those.' He grabbed a bottle of champagne from Charlie Richardson and undid the foil and wire. The cork flew out with a loud pop and everyone cheered. They were in the mood to cheer anything, especially when it was connected with Billy Hill. Somehow, without even trying, he brightened the world. Brian glanced at Jack, wondering what he'd do now.

'He's a mug, Brian, that's all,' Jack said, but, like everyone else, he was drawn to Granddad Billy.

'You look like you're getting hold of a bob or two, m' ol' china,' Billy told Bobby, as he ran his finger and thumb along the lapel of his suit jacket. 'You didn't get that out of a Christmas cracker.'

'Always one step ahead of the law, that's me,' Bobby said, puffed up with pride.

'They told me crime doesn't pay.' Billy turned to his audience, who laughed obligingly.

'I got something that will, Guv'nor.'

'Well, keep it dark, son, and I'll buy you a lamp.'

His attention went to Cath, who was pushing through the crowd. She threw her arms around him. 'Billy!'

He gave her a lingering kiss on the lips. 'That's better than a pound out the till.'

Brian glanced at his dad, who came through the throng behind his mum. She never kissed him on the mouth.

'You've lost weight, my darling,' Billy said, holding Cath at arm's length to inspect her.

'You should've let us know you were getting out,' Cath said. 'We'd have got up a welcoming party.'

Her sense of humour sometimes deflated tension, but it was Billy who got the laugh when he turned to the crowd and said, 'I thought this was it.' He let their appreciation die away before he turned to the car. 'I got something for you, darling.' He pulled out a party dress, shook it and held it out to her. She seized it and held it against herself. It was organza and taffeta, with many more yards of fabric in the underskirt than Utility permitted. It stood out in wide hoops and Cath twirled around, showing off the dress that her husband could neither afford nor find the opportunity to buy for her. It was too much for Joey and he left, squeezing his way out of the throng. Cath glanced after him and called, 'Joey!' but he didn't hear. She turned back to Billy, clearly torn. Brian hoped she'd go after his dad, but she didn't until Granddad Billy nodded, encouraging her to do so.

'You lucky people,' he said, for no particular reason. 'Charlie, get some more of them bottles open.'

Corks popped and champagne frothed into glasses, cups and jam-jars. Brian captured some, and found he didn't like it any better than beer. He knew he'd have to persevere with drinking: it was what grown-ups did all the while and he wanted to be grown-up.

After a moment he noticed that the buzz had dropped and his nan was making her way forward with that scruffy St Joseph's kid. She let go of his hand as Billy caught sight of her. It was like the boring bits in the pictures after Tarzan had killed all the spear-chucking blacks and then went on to kiss Jane. But Gracie wasn't a girl. Billy took off his felt fedora. His hair needed trimming and was turning grey. 'Gracie, my darling, you get prettier and prettier,' he said.

'Oh, you haven't lost any of your blarney, Billy Hill. You must be Irish.'

'See my finger's wet,' he said, licking his right forefinger. 'See my finger's dry.' He wiped it on his suit jacket. 'I'll cut my throat if I tell a lie.' He pulled the finger across his neck. There was an awkward moment when neither moved. Perhaps Gracie was wondering why he hadn't gone to his floozy. No one was more tense than Jack: Brian could see he was wound up like a spring. After a long moment Billy and Gracie moved forward together. He swept her into his arms and kissed her, a much gentler kiss than the one he'd given Mum, Brian noticed.

Eve Sutton struck up 'You're Just In Love' on the piano, and Billy swept Gracie into a slow waltz, holding her close. Others drifted over to watch, and Billy was in his element, the centre of attention.

'You'll have to watch your Ps and Qs now the guv'nor's back.' PC Watling refilled his glass from a champagne bottle. His face was red and blotchy now, his eyes glazed.

'He ain't my guv'nor!' Jack snapped, then turned to Brian, who was persevering with his champagne. 'That's enough. You'll be sick.'

Brian leaned against his uncle, feeling a little tipsy. 'What's Ps and Qs?' he asked.

His uncle was dismissive. 'Don't worry about that, Brian. I'll sort him out.'

Brian tried again. 'I love you, Uncle Jack,' he said.

'Don't talk wet,' Jack pushed him upright. 'What you talking about? You'd better stick your fingers down your throat and make yourself sick.'

Brian was determined not to do that. If he was put to bed he'd miss everything and be cast back with the kiddies. He squared his shoulders as if nothing was amiss and saw an older, stooped man in a three-piece suit and a Homburg step up to Billy and shake his hand. Granddad Billy greeted him as he did everyone, like a best friend.

'You've been getting more than your share, Frank,' he said.

'You don't look so bad yourself. Been on the Riviera?'

'Brought the bubbly back to prove it.' He held out an open champagne bottle to Frank Cockain, a racetrack bookmaker. He'd make a book anywhere he could take a bet. He pulled a sour face and popped a Rennie tablet into his mouth. 'It gives me heartburn,' he said, 'along with those mugs who think I owe them a living for letting me breathe.'

'I heard Jack Spot's been making a nuisance of himself.'

'You heard right. And those clowns out of Whitechapel – they act like they own the world.'

'I'll sort them out,' Billy said. 'Just let me find my feet.'

'You'd best be quick about it. They're getting too big for their boots.'

Now Tony Wednesday trotted up to the car to see what the fuss was about. Kids of all ages were hanging around the Vauxhall, watching enviously as John Redvers sat in the driver's seat, wrenching the big black steering-wheel this way and that, making car-engine noises with his thick lips. They waited with a mixture of fear and awe, not daring to get in themselves. Although cars were becoming more common, a ride in one was beyond their expectations. The braver ones risked patting the fat round mudguards.

Tony Wednesday fought his way to the front, shoving aside much bigger kids. 'Here! What you doing in that car?' he said with a mixture of surprise and authority.

'It's my granddad Billy's.'

The words were scarcely out of John Redvers's lips when Tony Wednesday flew at him. 'You liar! You said your dad died in the war! You said!' He tried to pull him out of the car, but John clung to the wheel. Tony was stronger, though, and eventually released his grip to protect himself. They crashed onto the pavement, with

Tony on top. The other kids were shouting, 'Fight! Fight!' as they cleared a space for the pair to wrestle. As one of the older boys Brian might have been expected to stop them, but he let them get on with it. He didn't like his cousin, who was a mummy's boy and told tales to Auntie Alice. Tony Wednesday and John were a pretty good match for each other physically, but it was instantly apparent which one was streets ahead in the survival game.

It ended in tears when Tony banged his opponent's head on the kerb and John let out a great yowl. Then Uncle Jack and Brian's mother were pushing through the onlookers along with Gracie and Billy, wanting to know what was going on.

'He did it!' John sobbed. 'He said my dad wasn't dead and hit me.' He sobbed harder.

'Smack him back,' Billy advised, 'a big fella like you.'

That was all the encouragement John needed to fly at Tony, who swung wide at him, the blow catching the side of John's head.

Finally the policeman stopped it. 'Oi! That's no way to behave!' he said, clipping Tony round the ear. 'You're with nice people now, not that bloody rough house from the orphanage.' Then both boys were crying.

'You ought to be ashamed, Mr Watling,' Gracie said, stepping in, 'picking on him like that.'

'He's not hurt. A clip round the ear's the best medicine in my experience.'

She wasn't listening. 'Come on, lovey,' she said, putting an arm around Tony.

'You have to let them sort it out themselves,' Billy said. 'Kids always fight.'

'We don't want any of that, Billy,' Gracie said, 'not today.' She was the only person there who'd dare to put him in his place.

As if realizing he was onto something here, Tony Wednesday said, 'I only wanted a go of the car. I ain't got no mum or dad, I ain't.' He squeezed out another tear.

'I know you haven't, lovey,' Gracie said.

Gracie might have adopted him there and then if Billy hadn't intervened.

'Charlie, give 'em a spin in the old jalopy,' Billy ordered. 'Go on, you little buggers, and don't wee on the seats.'

'Not you,' PC Watling said, capturing the now recovered Tony as he plunged for the car. 'Not till you learn how to behave proper.'

Without protest Tony hung his head.

'Ah, let him have a ride, Mr Watling,' Gracie said. 'There's no harm done.'

The policeman was buttoning his tunic, suddenly sober. 'He's got to learn right from wrong or he's down the road before we know it.'

'He's right, Gracie.' Billy nodded. 'You gotta keep kids on the straight and narrow.'

Now that Billy Hill had pronounced, with no sense of irony, the matter was closed. The car was full of kids and Charlie, the driver, was starting the engine. 'Don't you want to be taken for a ride, Brian?' he asked.

It was the last thing Brian wanted. Having entered, if only briefly, the adult world, he didn't want to be thrust back with the kids. He watched PC Watling leave with the orphan boy, a hand clamped on his shoulder. That was what happened to children, he thought. They were trapped in their small bodies. Brian was ready to break out of his. He followed them a little way along the street as the big shiny Vauxhall cruised past on litter-strewn Goswell Road, its horn honking. Kids hung out of the windows, cheering. Tony Wednesday glanced at the policeman, then turned to follow the car's stately progress. John Redvers was at the front passenger-seat window, jamming two fingers up at him.

PC Watling looked down at his charge and winked. 'Learn to box clever, son,' he said. 'Give them snooty kids a sly clip or a shove when their mums can't see you. Make it look like an accident, so there's no comeback.' He put an arm around Tony's shoulders.

That was what he would learn to do, too, Brian thought. He'd box clever and be sly to fit himself for adulthood in this new Britain, full of opportunities.

THREE

Shortages and austerity seemed to belong to a forgotten world now that Churchill's lot were running the country. None of that bothered Billy Hill as he swaggered through Tattersalls at the Kemptown racetrack in Brighton, one arm linked with Gracie's, the other round Cath's waist. Both women were wearing new dresses, courtesy of Billy, and looked like the real winners. As they moved to the ring where the bookmakers had set out their stalls, Billy spoke briefly to a large African man in a traditional costume of colourful, flowing robes. Brian was a bit scared of him, but the man was friendly enough to Granddad Billy. He was called Prince Monolulu and he tipped horses. 'I gotta horse!' was his catchphrase.

'Mugs pay him to tip the winner,' Uncle Jack explained.

Billy slipped a ten-bob note to the prince, who whispered a couple of names to him.

Only with great reluctance was Jack persuaded to go for a day at the races. 'Don't spoil it for everyone else,' Nan told him.

'Come on, Jack,' Cath said. 'It'll be fun.'

'We need some of that, right enough,' Brian's dad added.

Finally the two women pushed him out of the front door. Truth to tell, he was as caught up as they were by Billy Hill's big personality but would never admit it. Now he trailed in the guv'nor's wake with Bobby Brown, who imagined he was part of his gang. Joey was there too, looking after Brian who had begged his mum to let him come with them instead of going to school. It was only when Billy had stepped in and said, 'Of course Brian's coming. It'll be an education for him,' that she agreed.

'We'll get him some long trousers and a hat – people'll think he's the Clitheroe Kid.'

Brian listened to Jimmy Clitheroe on the wireless and read his strip in *Film Fun Comic* and, imitating him, protested, 'Hey, Granddad, I don't look anything like him!' Everyone except his dad laughed. Joey said nothing much as he walked behind with Charlie Richardson.

There was a line of bookmakers in the ring, calling the odds as the tic-tac men in white gloves signalled the changes in the odds that came out of the Tote and the bookies chalked them on their boards. They were colourful characters, some in loud-checked suits and brown bowlers barking at the punters, taking bets at great speed, calling them one after another, the clerks writing in their ledgers so fast that you could almost see smoke coming off their pencils. Frank Cockain was among them – 'Frank and Honest', the headline on his board shouted. He wore a dark grey three-piece suit although it was warm. Men were removing jackets and loosening ties, women taking off cardigans and wishing they hadn't put on their corsets.

'Give me a roaf on My Boy in the two o'clock,' Billy told the bookmaker, and peeled four pound notes off the roll he kept in the fob pocket of his suit trousers. Frank Cockain took the money and dropped it into the leather bag across his shoulder.

'Four on the nose My Boy two o'clock,' he said to Sam Forth, his clerk, who wrote it down and gave Billy his betting slip. 'What about something for the ladies?'

'They badly need a winner, Frank,' Billy told him.

'What do you suggest, Mr Cockain?' Gracie asked.

'Gracie!' Billy chided her. 'He's a bookie. You have to go to the likes of Prince Monolulu if you wanna tip.'

Frank took pity on her. 'A bob or two on Lone Star would see you right. He's a real pigeon-chaser, that one.'

And that was what she bet on, half a crown each way. So did Cath. Billy Hill rolled his eyes at the bookmaker as the bet was struck. 'It's lucky I got plenty. What d'you say, Brian? Do you fancy a house-to-let, son?'

Brian wasn't saying anything. The toes of Frank Cockain's boots curled upwards, like his dead granddad's had. The image of Sullivan's yard suddenly assailed him. He started to shiver in the hot sun, then jumped as his nan touched him. 'You all right, Brian?'

His mum put her hand on his head and pressed his face to her as if she knew what he was thinking. 'He's fine,' she announced.

'Eyes up!' Frank Cockain warned. 'Here's trouble.'

Three tough-looking men were pushing through the crowd, each wearing double-breasted chalk-striped suits with wide shoulders and trilbies. The top man was the bowler-hatted Jack 'Spot' Comer. He was in his early forties and wore sunglasses to hide a scar across his left eyebrow that ran over his cheek towards his nose. He stopped and rocked back on his heels, his thumbs hooked in his waistcoat pockets. 'My word, you do look well, Billy,' he said. 'Don't he look well? Stir suits you, my son. You should go back – soon!'

Billy smiled pleasantly. 'I been hearing a lot about you, pal, steaming ahead, nicking off everyone.'

Jack Spot seemed to grow taller. 'It don't do to let the grass grow under your feet.'

'You certainly haven't done that, Spotty,' Billy conceded.

'No one calls me that now,' Jack Spot said. 'You got my winnings, Frank? That deuce I had on Uncle Joe?' The odds were ten to one and the horse hadn't run yet. 'It's a stone ginger.'

It was a challenge to Billy as much as to the bookmaker. Most bookies accepted local gangs minding them, except when Jack Spot and his lads were on the turf: they collected from them all. A tense moment followed, both men waiting to see what the bookmaker would do.

Finally Billy smiled again. 'I'd take a funny run, if I was you, Spotty.'

'But you ain't me, are you? And don't call me Spotty. It ain't respectful.'

'Come off it, Mr Comer,' the bookmaker said, trying to lower the heat. 'I already paid the Brighton mob. Last I heard they were running this track.'

Jack Spot rubbed a thumb and forefinger together impatiently. 'They're a bunch of wide boys – about as wide as narrow tape!'

'Look, I can't pay them, the rozzers *and* you! I'd go broke.'

Spot laughed. 'Did you ever hear of a poor bookmaker, Billy?'

'Never in all my life,' Billy agreed. 'Let's have a look at what he's worth.' He stepped forward and peered into Frank's bag, then shrugged. 'He ain't holding, Spotty.'

The tension crackled again. This was a serious challenge.

Suddenly there was a chiv in the hand of one of Spot's heavies. As it came up to stripe Billy's face, Jack Braden jabbed him twice in the side of the head, so fast that no one saw the blows, only the man spinning and the cut-throat razor falling harmlessly on to the grass. Eagerly Brian grabbed it, then Billy took it from him, winking conspiratorially. 'I had a shave this morning,' Billy said, 'and unless you want one, Spotty, you'd better sling your hook.'

'You're pushing your luck. You ain't coming back and taking over,' Spot warned. He turned away to help his fallen minder, reaching into his waistcoat pocket. Billy stepped in and slammed a left and a right into Spot's kidneys, leaving him wondering where his breath had gone as the chiv hung impotently in his right hand. Deftly, Billy took it and put another stripe across Spot's cheek. Brian stared at the blood that dripped onto the grass – it had all happened so fast. Quickly his mum turned his face away.

'Mu-um,' he protested. He wanted to watch as Spot tried to hold his face together.

'The guv'nor's back,' Billy said, adjusting his jacket so that it sat square on his shoulders. 'You lucky people.' He gave a broad smile, then winked at Frank Cockain.

*

That night they celebrated in the pub at the end of their street. Too young to go in, Brian waited at the door with a bottle of Tizer and a packet of Smith's crisps, occasionally catching glimpses of the party as people went in and came out. He wished he really was the Clitheroe Kid, who wasn't really a kid and could go into pubs or anywhere else. 'Don't wish your life away,' his nan always said, when he complained that he wanted to do what grown-ups did. 'It'll go quick enough.' But not quickly enough for Brian.

The pub was bedecked with boxing posters and portraits still draped in black as a mark of respect for the King's passing. There were photos of the new Queen Elizabeth and one of Winston Churchill. Even he looked tired now as he struggled to justify the unpopular prescription charges.

As soon as Billy walked in all the customers' eyes were on him. They knew who he was and about his lucky escape that day. They followed his exploits, joined in with his celebrations, smiled at his antics, hung on his every word. What mugs, Jack decided, glancing across the table as Frank Cockain said, 'This puts you right back on form, Billy, my old flower.'

'It'll be like I was never off form.' Billy put his arm round Gracie.

She leaned closer to him, and Jack wondered what that meant. Was Billy planning to come back to the house? He'd been hanging around a fair bit since he'd got out, but hadn't tried to move back in and his mum hadn't said that he might.

'Here's the real hero of the day,' the bookmaker said, and raised his glass in Jack's direction. 'But for you, son, I'd have a stripe a mile wide around my face – and a thirty-bob whistle ruined with claret!'

Before Jack could wallow in the glory of the moment, Billy Hill claimed him, throwing his arm around Jack's shoulders. 'What a team we make! We'll knock 'em all into next Sunday, won't we son?'

Everyone in the bar was watching Jack now, waiting for his

response. He was being identified as Billy Hill's man, which wasn't what he wanted. 'There's only one person I aim to knock out,' Jack said, 'and he's Freddie Mills. All I need is the chance to do it. I'm younger, fitter and a better fighter than Millsy any day of the week.'

'You won't get a sniff at the title without a bent manager.' Billy spoke as though he knew everything about that world too. 'Set him straight, Frank.'

Frank Cockain raised a spiky grey eyebrow as if to indicate that Jack's chances were slim.

'I've done all right so far,' Jack said angrily. 'I've won every fight I've had.'

'Jack'll get there,' Cath put in. 'He's determined to get there—'

'On a tram – if he's got a tuppenny fare!' Billy mocked.

That did it for Jack. It was all he could do not to clock the flash monkey, but he stood up instead, ready to leave. His mum and sister exclaimed, 'Jack!'

'Why don't you leave the boy alone, Billy?' Gracie said.

But Billy caught hold of Jack and pulled him back onto the seat. 'Just listen for once. This man knows everyone in the fight game. Ask him. Right now you'll get his advice free, son.'

All eyes were on Frank Cockain, whose pink face seemed to glow with superior knowledge in the smoky atmosphere of the saloon bar. He placed his glass on the table so as to give the matter his full attention. 'Maybe he doesn't need my advice,' he said.

'Give it to him anyway, Frank – as a favour to me,' Billy said.

'You've got a good left, son – no, a great left,' the bookie told Jack, 'but, then, every tearaway this side of Deptford with a good left hook thinks he can be world champ.'

'I'll wipe the floor with Freddie Mills any day.'

'Maybe. But what about all the others you've got to knock out first?'

'I can take care of them, too,' Jack said. 'You just watch me.'

'He's plucky, Frank,' Billy observed, 'no doubt about that.'

'He'll need to be, and a lot more besides. Look, if I can do anything to help, Jack,' Frank Cockain said, 'I'll be glad to – for Billy's sake.'

If only he hadn't said the last three words Jack might have taken him up on his offer there and then, but he wasn't going to put himself in debt to Billy Hill.

Billy had different ideas. 'Pop down the gym, Frank. If he's as good as he thinks he is, I'll blow in Jack Solomons's ear – he's the top promoter,' he said. 'Between us we'll get him a shot at the title.'

However much pleasure that would give his mother and sister, both of whom sat there beaming at him, it wasn't going to happen, Jack decided. He'd sooner go into the army or carry on portering for Mr Thompson in Spitalfields Market.

Good as his word, Frank Cockain did look in at the gym, a converted bus garage off the Angel that still had oil stains on the floor with sawdust covering the worst. Pigeons crept in through the broken skylight in the pitched roof and roosted on the steel trusses. Occasionally the Garage, as it was known, served as a boxing venue for low-rent promoters, but it wasn't popular: it was too cold in winter and often too hot in summer. But that didn't bother Jack when he was training. He could beat anyone they threw at him, and when he was hitting his opponent, all that mattered was knocking him out in the fastest time possible. But he wilfully refused to learn that boxing was also about entertainment, giving the punters value for money. A swift, clean knockout was all he wanted.

He was aware that the bookie was watching his every move, and briefly lost concentration. His opponent hit him a series of lefts and a right cross that sent him spinning into the corner post. They were sparring in a roped-off area amid punchbags and punchballs. In this venue the ring stayed at floor level, another reason for its unpopularity – the sight lines were restricted, even from the benches that lined the walls below curling posters of past fights.

'No, no, no!' his trainer cried, and Peewee hurried forward on bowed legs to dive through the ropes with an agility that belied his seventy-plus years. He pulled Jack away from his sparring partner. 'What have you been doing?' he demanded. 'Poundin' your puddin'?'

Some of the hangers-on who were standing by the ring laughed. Jack glanced at his brother-in-law, Joey, who was watching with Brian. They didn't laugh. Jack wouldn't look in Frank Cockain's direction in case he was amused. Instead he shoved Peewee away and shaped up to his opponent.

Peewee thrust himself between them again, pulling them apart. 'The way you're shaping up, son,' he said, 'I could beat you. Boxing's about using your head as well as your fists. Concentrate on what he's doing. Anticipate his every move. His body'll tell you what he's going to do. Got that, nincompoop?'

'Yeah, yeah,' Jack said impatiently, wanting to get back at the other boxer and redeem himself in Frank Cockain's eyes. Before Peewee could climb back through the ropes to join the bookmaker, he sprang at his opponent like a tiger.

'He's got to listen if he wants to go the distance,' he heard Frank Cockain say.

'Anyone can have an off day, guv'nor,' Peewee replied.

'That's right. We could make a book on his having one – in the right sort of match.'

Not this one, Jack thought. I'll go all the way if the Kate don't claim me first.

At twelve stone ten, Jack was just two pounds inside the qualifying weight to box at light heavyweight, and his fight was second on the bill at Lewisham town hall. His opponent was a former US Army sergeant who had stayed in London after the war. He was ten years older than Jack and it showed. This fight wouldn't get him into position as a contender for the light-heavyweight world championship, and he wondered again how long he'd have to wait for a shot at it, how many old men he'd have to knock out, how long he could resist Billy Hill's help.

Billy was in the first row of spectators, and the buzz from the crowd was as thick as the cigar smoke as he waited for the seconds-away bell to sound the start of the third round. Jack could have put his adversary down in the first, but had been told to give them a show. His mum was there, with Cath and Joey. Bobby Brown was wearing a new whistle; he was a thief who was having a run of good luck. He'd got something else lined up and wanted Jack's help. Jack was reluctant to get involved, but Bobby had reminded him of how he'd helped him out in the docks where they had casual work as stevedores.

The bell rang and Jack was out of his corner and on his opponent before the other was off his stool. He hit him with a left and a left, then another. The mug certainly didn't see the right that put him on the canvas – perhaps he didn't have a Peewee to tell him how to read his opponent's body. The roar of the crowd was intoxicating and Jack could only imagine what it would be like at the Royal Albert Hall in front of a capacity crowd. Through the smoke haze he caught a glimpse of Frank Cockain, leaning over to Billy Hill and nodding approval.

Encouraged by the crowd, Jack tried to move in to finish his opponent as he struggled to get up. The referee pushed him back as he counted him out and raised Jack's arm. It was a popular decision. This was it as far as Jack was concerned. He didn't need Freddie Mills: he was ready for a fight with the reigning world champion, never more so. He was 100 per cent fit, mentally alert, fearless. Yet still he had to wait.

'You haven't got enough form for anyone to make a book on you,' Frank told him afterwards. 'It's not a charity, son. This game's all about making money for someone.'

'Mostly the promoters,' Billy chipped in. 'Then there's the bookmakers, the venue owners want a bit and last of all the boxers.'

'You have to be patient, Jack. Build up a bit more form.'

That was all he was ever told. Be patient.

*

Bobby Brown pressed Jack to get involved in his schemes, all the while dodging the army bods, who came looking for them – but never at the same time. Bobby would slip out of his drum and along the alleyway to warn Jack or vice versa. That was how he came to be dropping off the iron railings surrounding the railway sidings at the back of King's Cross, having earlier avoided the Military Police. Jack owed Bobby and could no longer avoid giving him a hand.

He lifted a side of bacon onto the fence. Bobby had wanted to nick a van so they could help themselves to a few dozen. To Jack's way of thinking that was real thieving, but he told himself this wasn't. The railway trucks were full of bacon and much more. Bobby jumped off the fence and reached for a side to lift onto his shoulder. 'Let's go again,' he said. 'We can carry two each.'

'It's easy enough,' Jack conceded. He knew a lot of people who could do with a bit of bacon. Getting into and out of the yard wasn't difficult.

'We can't leave these here,' Bobby said. 'Best get them away first.'

No sooner did they turn to head out along the alley when a torch beam caught the pinkish-grey bacon on their shoulders. They didn't know who the dark figure behind it was until he spoke.

'Got you, red-handed!' PC Watling came forward, wheeling his bicycle and keeping his light on the swag. 'I suppose that fell off the back of a lorry, did it? Well, I've waited a long time for you two.'

Neither Jack nor Bobby moved. Jack knew they could outrun Watling, even with the bacon on their shoulders. But the copper knew where they lived and had caught them thieving.

'What's it to be, Mr Watling?' Bobby challenged, as if they were in a position to bargain. 'You can't nab us both.'

This was yet another impediment to his boxing career, Jack realized. Six months inside, and he'd be finished. Afterwards the army would have him. The only way out seemed to be to top PC Watling – he didn't know where that idea had come from – but being topped himself for killing a policeman wouldn't make him world champ.

Then Watling offered them a way out: 'I like a bit of bacon myself,' he said. 'You don't get much these days, despite Churchill's lot promising to change all that.' The Tories had said there would be a swift end to the hated ration books but it hadn't come about.

'Why not cop one of these for yourself, guv'nor?' Bobby suggested.

The deal was done and Jack breathed a sigh of relief. Bobby heaved the side of bacon onto the policeman's handlebars while Watling eyed the one Jack had across his shoulders. 'My sergeant likes a bit too,' he said.

'So does my mum!' Jack protested.

Bobby lifted the bacon off Jack's shoulder and slapped it on top of the other side on the bike. 'What about us, Mr Watling?'

'You'd better nip over there again,' he said. 'I'll keep cave. Go on.'

In no time they were over the fence and into the yard. Jack waited at the open door of the dark goods wagon as Bobby appeared out of the gloom and slapped the heavy side of bacon on to his shoulder. Quickly Bobby dragged out another and offered it to Jack. 'That's enough,' Jack said, as his friend turned back for more.

'Just a couple – we got the perfect cover.' As a stevedore Bobby was fit and strong. They could carry two hundredweight apiece easily. He jumped down and threw his two sides over his shoulders. 'Close the door,' he said.

Jack wanted to leave it – and if they had, they might have been away before the night watchman appeared in the distance. 'Oi! You two!' he roared.

'I thought you said there weren't no night watchman!' Jack complained, as they tore off across the tracks, each with two hundredweight of meat on his shoulders. They ran round the end of the wagons through a gap where the next set of trucks wasn't coupled, and headed for the fence, their breathing laboured.

As the fitter of the two and not a smoker, Jack reached the fence first and threw his bacon on top of it. Bobby was struggling now and sweating, so he ran back, took one side from him, threw it on top of the fence, then did the same with the other while his friend hung on the fence like a wrung out rag.

'Come on!' the policeman hissed. 'Get over here.'

Jack could hear the night watchman's laboured breathing as he approached. He boosted Bobby over the fence, then pulled himself up just as the man's torch found them.

As Jack dropped down Watling stood on the crank of his bicycle, which was leaning against the fence, then on the crossbar to peer into the yard. He saw the old man fit to drop. 'It's all right, old man,' he said to him. 'It's the police. We've got them.'

'There was two of them, guv'nor,' the night watchman said.

'We'll take them straight to the Black Maria.'

Those words chilled Jack. What if this was a trick and they were arrested and the army was summoned to take them away? There'd be no boxing career.

PC Watling dropped to the ground and pulled down a side of bacon. He nodded to Jack to get the others. 'We'll keep these as evidence,' he said, and winked.

Around Jack's street it was often said that the police were thieving rogues, but he hadn't experienced it. This had been a real eye-opener.

FOUR

There was an atmosphere in Gracie's house you could have cut with a knife. Between Cath and Joey the tension rose and fell like the tide. Money, or lack of it, and the presence of Billy Hill were their main problems, and paradoxically Billy could have provided the solution. Recently Joey had had a medical check-up and the doctor had told him he should get away from the London smog or his TB would come back. Then he thought Cath was pregnant again – what a big laugh that was! Cath vowed never to have another child. Joey didn't want to stay in his poorly paid bookkeeping job at the fruit and vegetable warehouse but to start up his own business. He had taken advantage of the almost free education opportunities that the Labour government had introduced and was studying accountancy at night school. He wanted to stay in greengrocery, but Cath's wage from the garment factory, where she machined clothes for Marks and Spencer, was falling as the economy floundered. Money was always behind any discord between them, and they had heated conversations that stopped when anyone else came into the room.

'Why don't you ask Billy, Cath?' Joey urged, although he hated himself for suggesting it. 'He's got money to burn. You can easily ask him.'

'I don't know if it's right,' Cath said.

Joey knew the reason for her reluctance, but he had to ask. 'It's only a loan. It's a wonderful opportunity. The lease on that shop's dirt cheap. If I get it, I'll be made.'

'Then ask him yourself. Billy knows a good thing when he sees it.'

'Yeah, I bet he does.'

'What's that meant to mean, Joey Olinska?' She always used his family name when she was cross or caught out.

Joey didn't want to challenge her head on. 'He'd do it for you like a shot,' he said. 'Look at all the presents he keeps giving you. New dress, new coat, shoes, stockings. Anyone would think you were carrying on.' Convinced that they were having an affair, he wondered what that made him for trying to use his wife in this way.

'Don't talk daft,' Cath said. 'He's my stepdad, kind of.'

It was the first time that she had referred to Billy Hill in that way, and he wondered what she was up to. Not that bloody Billy Hill would have let any such relationship stand in his way. Perhaps if Cath asked him for the money, Joey thought, she'd feel indebted to him, which might lead to Billy getting more than he already was. Joey wondered if he could live with that.

'Maybe it ain't meant to be,' Cath told him, taking his arm.

Joey pushed her away and went out, feeling angry and resentful. He expected her to come after him as she sometimes did, to yield and do as he asked. He knew she pitied him, and while he hated it he traded on it. But in the matter of borrowing money from Billy, she wouldn't budge. Joey got on his old Rudge bicycle and pushed off along the empty street.

Mrs Booker was sweeping the pavement in front of her house and spoke to him, but he didn't respond. He was wearing his best suit and shirt for an appointment at Martin's Bank and he wasn't looking forward to it. He was going to the City Road branch, hoping to raise an alternative source of funding.

On Goswell Road, he got off his bike to look at the empty shop he wanted. There wasn't another greengrocers nearby. Handling fruit and vegetables would be the nearest he got to his doctor's advice to live in the country. Before the war Black's had sold boots here, and after her husband's death his widow didn't want to keep the business so she sold the stock, both sons having been killed on the same day at El Alamein. The dusty window display showed an advertisement for Wren's polish, a couple of laces and faded brown paper, curling off the wall. It was the perfect spot for a greengrocery, Joey was sure.

'What makes you think greengrocery is a viable proposition, Mr Oldman?' the bank manager asked from behind his desk. His drab cream and green painted office smelled of damp paper and stale tobacco smoke. A Gold Flake cigarette was burning in the overfull ashtray, the yellow packet close at hand. The smoke irritated Joey's lungs but he knew better than to say anything. 'There's not much profit in spuds and cabbages, is there?'

'People always need greens, Mr Griffith. 'S what keeps us regular.'

The bank manager pulled a face as if he found the subject distasteful.

'Things are getting better, Mr Griffith,' Joey said brightly, lacing the fingers of one hand with those of the other, then pulling them apart.

'I've seen not much evidence of it from this side of the desk,' the bank manager said. 'Credit controls remain tight, even under the current government. A hundred and fifty pounds is a great deal of money to lend to someone in your position, Mr Oldman. And there's your health. A bicycle and your word are hardly security, are they?'

'You'd have the lease on the shop, Mr Griffith,' Joey said. He felt small and foolish, and wished he wasn't there.

'It's been empty since the war, man. There aren't many fools around who'd want to take it off our hands if things go wrong for you.'

That was where the meeting ended. Joey was humiliated, but not defeated.

'Why can't you rob a post-office van and get the money, Dad?' Brian said. 'Granddad Billy does that all the time.'

'Don't be silly, Brian,' Cath said. 'Wherever did you hear that?'

'It's what everyone says.'

'Well, eat your tea and don't listen to them.'

'If Jack needed the money he'd have it soon enough. He gets the best of everything,' Joey complained.

'He's going to make something of himself,' Cath said.

'Oh, and I'm not? Is that it? I bloody well can if someone'll give me a chance.'

'Well, Mr Attlee's lot give you one, Joey,' Gracie said, coming in from the street. She went through and lit the gas ring in the scullery, then put on the frying pan with some lard in it. 'They let you go to night school for free.' She rapped on the window overlooking the backyard. Jack was out there, where he had been skipping non-stop since getting back from portering at the market.

'When I'm a certificated accountant, I'll show that bloody bank manager with his hoity-toity ways,' Joey said. 'You could make all the difference, Cath, if you was to ask Billy.'

'I won't and that's that.'

'Why don't you two give it a rest?' Gracie said. 'We got enough problems in this family with Alice going funny. God knows what'll happen to her little John.'

'She's not going funny, Mum,' Cath said. 'She's just got religious.'

'Well, I say my prayers every night,' Gracie replied, 'and I didn't join no Holy Rollers. It's not Christian the way they carry on.'

'You wouldn't know there was shortages still.' Cath watched her mum lift sausages, bacon and eggs from the hot fat on to a plate for Jack.

'He needs his strength. He's got another fight coming up.'

Billy Hill came in, with gold armbands on his shirt sleeves and braces, to hold up his trousers. His suit jacket was slung over his arm. He was spruced up and shaved, ready for action, having stayed in bed most of the day. He'd be out for most of the night. Joey resented the way he used Gracie's home as a doss house.

'Hello, gorgeous,' he said to Cath, and hugged her as if Joey and

Gracie weren't in the room. 'I swear this daughter of yours gets prettier every day, Gracie.'

'All my kids are good-looking,' Gracie said proudly, as she brought Jack's plate to the table. 'And their kids.' She stroked Brian's dark hair, then poured Billy some tea from the enamel pot under the cosy.

He took one of Jack's rashers and folded it into his mouth, then pulled on his jacket.

'Take five minutes and save your life,' Gracie said. 'I can easily do you some.'

'Can't stop, darlin',' Billy said. 'Got to see a man about a dog. Know what I mean, Bri?' He slapped Cath's backside to move her out of his way.

On the point of saying something Joey hesitated, but when he caught Cath's eye, he let the moment go.

'Be good,' Billy said, over his shoulder, 'and if you can't be good, be lucky.'

As likely as not they wouldn't see him for a week – perhaps never again – by which time the opportunity would have been lost.

'Billy!' Cath said, and started after him. Joey followed her as far as the door. He watched her with Billy as she reminded him about Joey's plans for opening the greengrocery. 'He's studying at evening classes down at the tech. He's determined to get on.'

'How's that gonna help him sell spuds?'

'What do you think? Could you help?' she asked.

'I wouldn't know a spud from a swede, darlin'.'

'Don't play silly buggers. No one's asking you to be a little shopkeeper. Joey'll do that.'

'I'd do anything for you, Cath,' Billy said, slipping his hand on to her tight buttocks and giving them a squeeze. When Cath didn't resist Joey smarted. 'Got a couple irons in the fire,' Billy said. 'Let's wait and see how they come out. That shop ain't going nowhere, is it?'

He was through the door and across the pavement to where

Charlie Richardson was waiting with a new cream-painted Humber. Half a dozen kids were hanging around it. He glanced towards the Booker's house – someone inside was shouting – as Cath joined him.

'He's off again,' he said, pulling her close and kissing her lips. 'We'll sort Joey out, darling.' He climbed into the car.

From the door, Joey watched as Cath turned away and walked back towards him. The shouting from the Booker's house was getting louder now.

'Perhaps we should knock on the door,' Cath said, as she joined him.

'We've heard them often enough.'

When they came into the kitchen, Jack was at the table. 'Why don't I ask Mr Thompson to give Joey a start at the market?' he said. 'That's healthy enough.'

'No one got rich working for skinflint Thompson,' Cath snapped. 'He pays you hardly anything.'

'I'm only casual.'

'Joey's going to start his own business anyway.'

'Did he find the lolly yet?' Jack asked, as if Joey wasn't there.

'He will,' Cath said. 'Somehow.'

'I could put the house up as security for the bank manager,' Gracie said.

Joey wanted to leap on her offer, but Jack cut him off. 'No. Billy gave you this for your own security. It's the only useful thing he's done, Mum.'

'Joey can't wait for him to pull another jewel robbery,' Gracie said. 'He might be dead before that happens!'

'Oh, you're so cheerful, Mum,' Cath said. 'You should be on the wireless.'

Someone hammered on the front door and they froze. Eyes went to Jack – was it was the MPs again? Then they heard Mrs Booker's voice: 'Gracie! Gracie!'

She hurried along the hallway and flung open the front door.

'Is your Billy here? He'll kill her this time – I swear he will,' Mrs Booker shrilled. 'I can't take much more! It's putting years on me.'

'Jack!' Gracie called back along the hallway, then ran into the street with Mrs Booker.

Murder was being done in the narrow house two doors along as Gracie, Jack, Cath and Joey pushed through the crowd of neighbours gathering outside. Jack ran into the house and along the hallway, which was hung with work clothes, following the screams to the kitchen where Mr Booker was laying into his daughter with the thick strap he normally wore around his white baker's overalls. Jack grabbed the belt mid-stroke. Surprise caused the older man to let it go. 'Pack it in, Mr Booker,' he barked. 'Just pack it in—'

There was no sign of that. Instead the older man threw a punch at him, which meant Win was able to scramble to the relative safety of her mother's arms.

'I'm warning you, Mr Booker,' Jack said.

'Don't you come it with me, sunshine,' Booker said. 'I know about your mucky little larks with my girl – and yours.' He nodded at Joey, taking him aback. There were no larks. He'd always been pleasant to Win, and things had only once almost got out of hand.

That statement unsettled Jack as much as Joey, distracting him, so Booker took his chance; he threw Jack up against the kitchen dresser, causing china to crash to the floor.

'Stop it – or I'll fetch Billy!' Gracie shrieked.

Booker paid no heed, so Jack caught him a straight left jab, which made Joey wince as if he himself had taken the blow. A right hook followed, then another left sent the larger man reeling into the cluttered table. Bottles and jars went flying. Still Booker refused to give up. He turned back gamely, arms flailing like the sails of a windmill, nose streaming blood. He stopped smack against Jack's fist. Then Mrs Booker pitched into Jack, screaming at him to stop as he hit her husband again. Her broken, dirty fingernails ripped his shirt and scratched his back. He threw up his hands as if to stop himself hitting her on the turn. 'You gone barmy or something?'

'You daft cow!' Gracie grasped Mrs Booker's matted cardigan and hauled her off Jack.

Joey knew there was nothing to be done for the Bookers. He wondered briefly what anyone would make of old man Booker's accusations against him and Jack. Cath would pick him up on it as a way to get back at him for needling her about Billy Hill.

In her tidy kitchen, Gracie dabbed iodine on the claw marks down Jack's flesh as Brian watched. He didn't move or even blink as he watched – until Gracie said, 'You're just like your dad, Jack, hard as nails. Never a peep out of him about anything.'

This worried Joey. Brian was far too influenced by his uncle, not all of it for the good. Also, he had noticed that any mention of Tiger Braden upset the boy. He suspected that his son was trying to blot out what had happened that night in the Sullivans' yard. He let his eyes find Cath. She would never talk about what had led to the events of that night. Joey wished he could do the same, but guilt wouldn't let him. He felt guilty for not topping the old bastard himself a lot sooner, and for not talking to Brian about what had happened and why.

Now Jack stood up and pulled on the clean shirt Cath had ironed for him.

How had Brian kept so quiet all this while? Joey wondered. Probably because he loved his mum and didn't want to hurt her. Maybe he was scared of her, too, like everyone else. One day it might come out; then there would be trouble and his son would never forgive either of them. As if she had sensed Brian's anxiety, Cath went to him, put her arm round him and drew him close. Brian smiled, and everything was all right in their world again. For now.

Jack neither knew nor cared how long Billy Hill's luck would last. He hoped it wouldn't be long, but he'd do nothing to hasten its departure. Billy was planning another robbery and pestering Jack to help. 'Nothing strenuous, son,' he said. 'Just be a bit of muscle on the street in case any of them have-a-go-joe types tries to make a fool of himself.'

Jack watched the well-padded landlord, Cyril Jacobs, with his ash-stained waistcoat, carry two gin and tonics along the bar to where an attractive redhead was sitting with her less attractive friend. Both women were in figure-hugging overalls and puffing Black Cat cigarettes. Cyril motioned across the tar-stained room to Billy, sitting in the corner with Charlie Richardson and his brother Eddie. The women acknowledged their drinks, raising their glasses to his health. Billy winked at the redhead and Jack tensed: his mum was being betrayed. He decided he wouldn't help Billy.

A canvas-covered van pulled up outside, a shadow falling across the frosted-glass windows. The driver came in wearing brown overalls and a cloth cap. 'Here's my man.' Billy beckoned him to the table. 'How're you doing, m' ol' china?' he said. 'What you having?'

'I'm all right, thank you, Mr Hill,' the driver said, and lit a Woodbine.

'All set are we, son?' Billy continued. 'All you gotta do is leave the engine running and Bob's your uncle. Eddie here'll do the rest.'

He nodded to the younger, more dangerous-looking Richardson, who stared truculently across the room and didn't acknowledge the driver.

'What if the busies come round asking questions, Mr Hill?' the driver said.

'You don't know the time of day. You just went into the shop to get a packet of Woodies.' Billy's laugh was reassuring to those around him.

Except Jack. He might regret not taking Billy's easy money, but if he got caught he'd have no crack at the title. He'd sooner hump vegetables for Mr Thompson in the market when he didn't get to bomp on stevedoring. He made his excuses. 'I got to go to work, Billy.'

'Work? That's a mug's game, son,' Billy said. The Richardsons laughed.

An hour later Jack was running with a hundredweight of potatoes on his back through the cavernous warehouse for one and a kick an hour. It might be a job for mugs, but it was good training, Jack found, for muscle tone and his breathing. He ran back down the ramp to where Bobby Brown was sitting on a stack of bagged spuds, smoking a cigarette. He was another offering Jack easy pickings.

'It's just sitting there in that rent office,' he said.

'Sounds like real thieving to me, Bobby.' Jack threw another sack on to his shoulder as if it was a featherweight. 'Not like nicking a bit of swag from railway trucks.'

'You could pack in the docks and this. You could train full-time.'

But Jack was scared – not that he might meet resistance at the rent office Bobby was planning to rob, he could handle that – but that he risked not getting his shot at the title. 'Ask Billy Hill.'

'I did. He said to be careful who I told in case someone comes copper,' Bobby said.

'Sounds like good advice.' Jack sprinted away with the sack, feeling the strain on his calf muscles as he propelled himself along at top speed.

'You make all the others look like loafers, Jack,' Mr Thompson said, as he stepped out of the little wooden office in his dust-flecked black jacket and bowler.

By the time he got back to Bobby, Joey had appeared with a sheaf of dockets. Despite his protests, he was now working at the warehouse. He could barely lift a carrier-bag of spuds, much less a sack, but he was good with figures and never got his sums wrong when it came to the tallies.

'What a brain he's got,' Mr Thompson said to Jack, but he never told Joey or gave him a rise.

'You're stopping a good man working, Bobby,' Joey said, with the air of responsibility that came from being in the office.

'He wears me out just looking at him.'

'We need thirty hundredweight of carrots on the bay for Clutterbucks this after.' Joey handed Jack the docket and headed back to the office.

''S dead easy, Jack. In and out. Must be two hundred quid left there on a Friday night.'

'I'll stick to boxing and a bit of fiddle,' Jack said, and boosted another sack of potatoes on to his shoulder. 'You coming to the fight tomorrow?'

'Yeah, I'm gonna bet against you. You'll be wore out at this rate,' was Bobby's parting shot.

As Jack stepped into the ring at the Goswell Road baths, he was at his peak. He wanted to rush over and put his opponent straight on the floor. Who cared about giving the punters value for money? Jack was convinced he did that just by knocking the other fellow out. Bam Bam Braden, someone called him. Two hits and they were gone.

The atmosphere was electric with anticipation as the audience waited for Jack to do what he did best. He was impatient to get started and looked into the audience to see who he knew. He recognized a number of people, but neither Billy Hill nor Frank Cockain was there – until a few moments later he saw the bookmaker coming down the aisle. He was with an equally familiar fat man who more than filled out his double-breasted suit, and whose even more familiar cigar was jammed into the side of his mouth, pushing out the fleshy cheeks. He wore no hat and wisps of thinning hair were slicked across his bald dome. Jack felt a surge of excitement. Jack Solomons was the top man on the boxing promotion circuit. If Frank had brought him here, he believed Jack was worth seeing.

'Don't let it go to your head, son,' Peewee told him, as he dug his fingers into Jack's solar plexus, helping him to relax the muscles.

At the bell Jack flew out of his corner and put three straight lefts on the side of his opponent's head, spinning him like a top.

The crowd loved it and roared when Jack stepped in with a right, then a left hook. The Irish boxer sagged against the ropes and the referee got between them. For a moment Jack thought he was going to stop the fight, but he stepped back and waved them on. A left, another left, then a right should have put the Irishman on the floor, but Jack realized this one had more stamina than some of the others.

Suddenly he caught sight of Billy Hill swaggering down the aisle to his seat, as if he owned the place, performing how-d'you-dos to half the audience. That wasn't a problem for Jack, but the redhead on Billy's arm, dolled up to the nines, was. Momentarily Jack lost concentration and an express train hit him, then another, and he was reeling. The crowd oohed with pain. This wasn't how it should be. Snapping back, Jack hit his opponent hard with his left, then again and again, aggressively, telling himself he was hitting Billy Hill. At that moment he wanted to kill him – he *would* kill him and show Mr Solomons just what he could deliver.

Billy reached over, tapped Solomons's shoulder, and said something to him that had the promoter nodding. Foolishly Jack glanced at him as the redhead whispered in his ear. The next thing he knew he was on his bum, not knowing what had hit him, his head singing, his muscles unresponsive to his commands as the referee began to count him out. He heard six and seven before he could get up. He struggled to his feet as another blow put him on the ropes.

Billy Hill was giving the Irishman the fight, Jack told himself. He could beat him easily and he wouldn't let Billy do this. He pushed through a series of stinging blows and found an opening for his left. It stopped the punishment he was getting. The right was blocked and his left came through again. From that point on he was hitting Billy, determined to do him a lot of damage.

The crowd was on its feet and roaring for him now. Left, right, left, right, the blows fell on the Paddy and down he went. The referee forced Jack back to stop him following through and hitting him on the floor.

Afterwards Jack strode along the white-tiled, echoing passageway, with overhead lights in wire baskets, his kitbag tossed over his shoulder. Anger boiled inside him. He met his trainer coming the opposite way and resisted the temptation to ask what was being said about his performance.

'You're wanted out front,' Peewee said.

Jack marched past him without a word. He stopped as he came into the main venue where men in brown overalls were collecting up the folding chairs and stacking them away. At first he couldn't see Frank Cockain or Jack Solomons, only Billy, who always dominated any conversation. The redhead was clinging to his arm, the only woman in a male gathering that roared with laughter at everything Billy said. Jack grabbed her arm and spun her round. 'Out,' he said, without letting go. Silence fell over the men, among whom Jack now saw Frank Cockain and Solomons. Having made his play, he couldn't back off.

Billy wrenched Jack's hand off the redhead. 'Half a mo', big shot. What you playing at?'

'I don't want her here,' Jack said. A red gauze seemed to drop over his eyes.

'You don't own the joint, son.' Billy wasn't stepping back. 'Carol ain't hurting you.'

'What you doing, carrying on with her?' There was no longer anything physical between his mum and Billy but, still, Jack didn't want Gracie treated so disrespectfully in public.

'Don't push your luck, buster. I ain't that punch-drunk Paddy you just put away.'

There it was! That was what they were saying and why they were laughing. Pride ratcheted up Jack's anger and he drove at Billy, catching him a glancing blow to the right side of his head, but enough to send him sprawling. Peewee, who had followed Jack out, grabbed him now, with Eddie and Charlie Richardson. Jack knew he could put all three of them away, but Solomons was watching, the cigar clamped between his fingers. Still he couldn't back off.

'You upset Mum,' he said. 'I'll top you, I will.'

'You and Monty's army,' Billy said, squaring up to him.

Jack was dragged outside. Frank Cockain followed him into the tiled corridor, bringing his bag.

'Are you a bit soft in the head, son?' he asked. 'Or did you think that little display would impress Mr Solomons? It was Billy who got him down here to take a gander at you. Mr Solomons isn't interested in hotheads with a quick temper. He can get them off any street corner in the East End. Your dad has all but talked him into promoting you.'

'Get it straight, Mr Cockain,' Jack said, his insides churning. 'He ain't my dad.'

The bookie tapped an old framed poster of Freddie Mills in his trademark two-fisted pose. 'That could be you up there, son. Mr Solomons reckons you're about a dozen away from a title fight.'

That stopped Jack. He looked to see if the others had heard this. Peewee was nodding like a rubber duck at the fairground. He was in on it.

'Don't cut your nose off to spite your face, Jack. Be guided by your old man – or whatever you want to call him.'

'It's what makes Billy what he is, love,' Gracie said. She was in the scullery, pouring hot milk into two cups. She brought them to Jack in the kitchen. 'It's part of his charm. Don't let him upset you.'

'I don't want him upsetting you, Mum.'

'Like the fools we sometimes are, we women think we can change men. He was like it before I took up with him, son. Trouble is, I fell for a charming liar. He's a tealeaf and a womanizer. How could I hope to change that?' She sighed. She looked more tired than usual, which worried Jack.

'He knows a lot of people, lovey, and I couldn't be more pleased he's helping you. Learn to use him – use anyone you can to get what you want in this life. If you don't, by golly, they'll use you, son. You don't want to end up one of the saps.' She put an arm round him and leaned heavily against him.

'You all right, Mum?' he asked.

'Fine.' She straightened up and patted his chest. 'You do as I say and you'll be as right as rain.'

Determined to get to the top, if only for his mum's sake, Jack put everything into his training. He even found an accord with Billy Hill, learning to use him as she had advised. Billy thought he'd won Jack's friendship, that Jack was joining his gang. It was easy to turn down the jobs he offered because Jack was training hard and winning fights, some of which Mr Solomons attended. All the while the big man was getting reports, taking an interest. That was what Jack cared about.

He ran eight or ten miles every day early in the morning before he went to bomp on at the docks for seven o'clock, then ran again after work. If there was nothing to do at the docks he'd train. Sometimes the ganger-man bomped on for him for half his money and let him go to the gym if they weren't busy. Jack always sprinted the last half-mile at record speed in a roll-neck sweater with a towel tucked around his throat.

Now he paused to catch his breath in his empty street, bending to rest his hands just above his knees. The milkman's horse was standing between the shafts of the cart outside number forty-eight while Mr Nicholls was inside. Some little kids were playing hopscotch on the pavement, which a girl who should have been at school was sweeping.

Two sandalled feet with white socks stepped into his line of vision. Win Booker was wearing a pretty floral dress that she was almost bursting out of, and at once Jack felt himself getting hard, despite his exertions. Ignoring his trainer's warnings, he had dipped his wick a couple of times in her air-raid shelter since he'd rescued her from her father. Now, in some cockeyed way, she seemed to think she was his girl, although he'd seen her out with other blokes.

'I lost my job again, Jack,' she said. 'That old cow at the canning factory kept picking on me.'

'You'll get another, Win. There's enough around.' There were for girls who were prepared to work as hard and sometimes better than men for a lot less money. There weren't so many for the men, just promises from the politicians.

'Dad went and told m' cousins about us,' she said. 'Ron and Reg said they was gonna sort you out.' She waited. 'Well, they may as well, I mean, you don't care about me – you don't take me to the pictures or nothing.'

'I can't relax my training, Win,' Jack said, not wanting to hurt her feelings. He knew he should tell her she wasn't his girl, but she was an easy poke.

'You could at least take me to the pictures,' she said.

That was a way out for him – and he could afford to ease off a bit. Peewee was always advising him to do so.

Sitting in the dark, watching Stanley Holloway and John Gregson saving a branchline railway from closure in *The Titfield Thunderbolt*, wasn't Jack's idea of entertainment – or Win's, for that matter. She seemed more interested in pressing her pillow lips to his at every opportunity, like most of the young couples in the back row at the Essoldo were doing.

During one dull sequence, Win whispered, 'Let's go to the air-raid shelter. Mum and Dad'll be in bed.'

They weren't: the light was on in the scullery when Jack and Win crept past the window and into the smelly shelter. Win seemed unaware of the surroundings or didn't care. Every sound of their lovemaking echoed in the dark space and Win was getting noisier with every quickening heartbeat. Jack wanted to tell her to shut up and considered putting his hand over her mouth. Finally he withdrew, which made matters worse: she cried out as if she was in pain. 'Oh, no,' she said. 'Don't stop – come on, Jack. Please.'

'I mustn't,' he said lamely.

'Come on. Nothing can happen what ain't already,' she said, and tried to pull him back inside her.

'M' trainer said I have to save my energy,' Jack told her.

'That's not fair.' Win shoved him away and wrenched down her dress. Then she tried one more time to rekindle the fire. Grabbing Jack's hand, she brought it to her wet crotch and pushed his finger inside her. It did the trick for her, and he could resist no longer. He found himself begging her to be quiet as she cried out, her entire body rocking and gripping him as if she would never let go. Sex was a lot easier since Bobby Brown had told him to push his foreskin back beforehand.

Afterwards he said, 'Look, I'd better skedaddle.' He was keeping a wary eye on the Bookers' scullery window. Without warning, Win burst into tears. He didn't know what made women do that in all and any circumstances, happy or sad. 'Look, there's nothing to cry about—'

'That's what you think, Jack Braden!' she said sharply, the tears gone. 'I'm pregnant.'

That simple statement winded Jack, who saw his ambition vanish with the yoke of domesticity: a wife, kiddies – it was rarely just one – and a house of his own.

'You can't be! Come off it,' he said.

'You do love me, Jack,' Win begged, 'don't you?'

The idea hadn't occurred to him. He liked her well enough – she was all right to take to the pictures – but he'd never thought she'd get pregnant.

As if she was reading his thoughts, Win said, 'Well, it happens. What d'you think happens? You stick it in without no rubber johnny? M' Mum says we'll have to get married. We will.'

Such insistence frightened him now. Why me? he wondered. And what would his own mum say? He couldn't tell her – or even Joey because he would tell Cath who would tell Mum for sure. He wouldn't tell Bobby: most of his friend's plans were harebrained at the best of times and only ever involved getting rich quickly. The person he most dreaded finding out was Peewee. The old man lectured him so often on the folly of loose women, the demon drink and pernicious tobacco, all of which, singly or together, had been the ruin of many promising young boxers. Jack didn't want to be a has-been before he had been someone.

Days later the worry of what to do gnawed at him, distracting him. Even Mr Thompson noticed when he did a couple of days' work at the fruit and vegetable warehouse. He came out of the office and caught Jack running through with half a hundredweight of cabbages on each shoulder. He waited at the end of the ramp, took off his bowler and wiped out the sweat. 'You all right, son? Is anything worrying you?'

Only the thought of Mr Thompson thinking less of him stopped Jack telling him the truth. He didn't want people saying he was a fool. 'I'm fine, Mr T,' he said, trying to sound cheerful.

'Best get off now – you're going training. Joey can move the rest of them cabbages – I don't think.'

'He's got brains, Mr T,' Jack said, defending his brother-in-law, and followed the boss's eyes across the warehouse to Joey on the loading bay, checking boxes off a lorry.

'He's quick enough, all right,' Thompson conceded. 'Too quick at times. I only gave him a job because I've a soft spot for your Cath – and now he's telling me how to run the place.'

'You might do well to listen, Mr T,' Jack said. 'He's got a lot of ideas about increasing profit.' Joey often talked to him about how the place could be run more efficiently but the boss wouldn't listen when he approached him.

'Get off training, lad. I want to see you with that world title one day.'

'It can't be soon enough for me.'

'You'll get it, son, and make us all very proud.'

Jack waited for Joey to finish, then hauled him outside. 'Don't get too clever around Mr Thompson,' he said, as if that was why he'd hung about.

People they passed in the market asked when he was going to get the title for them, which prompted him to press on with what he needed to ask his brother-in-law. 'What did you do when Cath told you she was in the family way?'

'I went up the wall. I was barely seventeen and I had all sorts of plans – I thought now I was in England I could go to college—' He stopped suddenly. 'You haven't gone and got some bint knocked up?' The answer was written on Jack's face. 'Oh, Jack, you silly boy.'

'What're the chances of getting rid of it?' Jack asked. Joey wouldn't know the answer to that but Jack knew who would. He just couldn't face telling her.

'Who's the lucky girl?'

'Win Booker.'

'Stroll on! Half of Hoxton's rattled a stick in that drain.'

But that didn't let Jack off the responsibility he felt towards Win.

'You'd best talk to Mum about it,' Joey said. 'She'll know what to do.'

Jack shook his head, shame colouring his cheeks.

The cat was well and truly out of the bag. Joey told Cath, who told his mum. She didn't judge Jack or tell him he was silly. Instead she talked to Mrs Booker and Win, and made all the arrangements.

A week later Jack was training hard in the gym on the five-foot punchbag, but he couldn't concentrate. He knew what was happening that evening. Suddenly his mum rushed through the doors, startling him. She was breathless when she reached him.

He panicked. 'What's wrong?'

She pulled him outside and held him tightly. 'You can't trust women, Jack. They're all the bloody same – out for what they can get.'

'W'as'up? Is Win all right?' Fear was creeping through him.

'She ain't your concern, son,' Gracie said. 'Not any more. The baby was a pongo – or would have been. Yes, a little piccaninny!'

'I don't see how,' Jack said, not grasping the significance of what she'd said. 'I mean, how could it have been?'

'I expect one of them black American servicemen paid her a call – maybe more than one,' Gracie added bitterly. 'She must think we was bloody well born yesterday. You'd've been a right mug if you'd have married the mucky little cow. You ought to have had more sense than to go with her.'

'But is she all right, Mum?' Jack asked.

'She lost a lot of blood. Serves her right. She'll live.'

Seven days later Gracie was regretting her words when it looked as if Win would die: the bleeding wouldn't stop.

Alice came to the house with John and pointed a boney finger at Jack. 'It's God's punishment on the wicked,' she pronounced. Everyone seemed to be in on the act now. It was a sort of family pow-pow.

'John shouldn't be here,' Cath said.

'He must know about the wickedness and sin in the world as well as the good,' Alice told her.

Jack glanced at his nephew. He seemed a lot younger than he was.

'It's human nature,' Cath said. She was well able to hold her own with Alice.

'Human nature is no more nor less than wickedness and sin.'

'That's all very well,' Mrs Booker piped up, 'but what about my girl?' She was ash-grey as she clutched a cup of tea in Gracie's kitchen. 'She needs a proper doctor after what you done.' There was a veiled threat in her words that made Jack want to sock her. His mum could end up in clink.

'Billy will know someone,' Gracie said. 'You make sure those towels are pressed to her, and keep her warm.' She set off straight away to find Billy Hill.

Jack followed her into the street. 'Why d'you always have to ask him?'

'We don't want the busies around,' Gracie said. 'We've had enough of them to last us a lifetime.'

'Peewee knows doctors. He won't say nothing.'

'You'll end up getting everyone's collar felt, Jack,' was Billy Hill's response when he came round in answer to Gracie's call. She'd gone to the phone-box at the end of the street. Billy wasn't at the number she rang, but someone knew where he was.

An hour or so after he'd gone, a slim, elegant man in a trilby and sunglasses got out of a grey Austin Healey car, carrying a neat leather Gladstone bag. He knocked at the Bookers' door. Afterwards he came to Gracie's house and she offered him a cup of tea, as she did all her visitors. He introduced himself as Stephen Ward, then glanced at Jack. 'Are you the father?'

'Not likely.'

'He's my Jack,' Gracie said. 'This is our Cath.'

'Is there anything I can do for you, Mrs Braden?' His posh accent made him stand out.

'A bit late at my time of life, Dr Ward,' Gracie said.

'Do call me Stephen. You did a very nice job with the girl, Mrs Braden,' he said. 'It's just unfortunate that she's what we call a bleeder.'

'You can say that again!' Cath put in.

The doctor smiled. 'If ever you want a bit of extra work I can send one or two girls to you. I'd have every confidence in you.'

'I'm glad to help out, but it would worry me to do it regular,' Gracie said, 'in case anything went wrong.'

Later that night Jack was still steaming over his mum having called in Billy Hill, instead of letting him solve the problem.

'God, you're so like your dad. He felt he had to help the world and its uncle. There was a man and a half . . . everything a woman could ask for,' she said wistfully. 'He never understood how to say no to people, Jack. People'd always call on your dad to help rather than the cops or a doctor, and look where it got him. A direct hit from a German bomb! At least he wouldn't have known about it, God rest him. Don't let your generosity stop you getting what you want. There'll be plenty like Win Booker trying to get their hooks into you, son. Learn to use people instead of letting them use you. Use me, use Billy, Frank Cockain, Mr Solomons – anyone. Make something of yourself. You got the talent and the looks.' She put her arms around him and held him tightly.

'You're the real champ, Mum,' Jack said.

'Just remember what I told you, son.'

Jack was determined that he would.

Finsbury Secondary Modern School for Boys was a raging inferno by the time the fire engines arrived and they couldn't get near the blaze. All the staff and most of the pupils burned to death. It was a mystery how the fire started and took hold so quickly. Only Brian knew the truth as he read the imagined story in the *Evening News*.

A piece of chalk hit the top of his head, accompanied by the cry of, 'Shot!' His teacher, Mr Harrisfield, had a lopsided jaw from a motorcycle accident. 'Pay attention, Oldman!'

Brian kept Finsbury Secondary Modern at the top of his list for razing to the ground, with most of the staff and other pupils. He hated it. He loathed getting up in the morning, putting on the rough dark blue uniform with the grey shirt and trekking there on foot. He was at the school because he hadn't passed his 11-plus. If he'd known what he'd be in for he might have tried harder at junior school. He resented the petty rules and restrictions, having to sit in damp, cramped classrooms for hours and, worse, being forced to do PT and games. He detested games even more than the school itself. He couldn't see any point in them – couldn't see much point in school at all. He wanted to leave as soon as he could but the stupid Labour government had put the leaving age up to fifteen when they were in office and the Tory government hadn't changed it back. The thought of another two and a half years of listening to teachers who only came alive when they were talking about what they'd done in the war weighed heavily on him.

The bell at ten to four was his reprieve, and as soon as it rang his head switched off. At times not much seemed to go in. He was self-conscious because he was too fat and different from most of the other boys – apart from the fruits and the mummy's boys and he didn't want to be associated with them. Brian had no idea how many boys knew what he was. Sometimes it felt like they all did.

'Oi, Oldman!' someone called, as Brian headed out through the main gates.

He turned. A lanky boy with spots was bearing down on him, in the company of three others. Roy Shepherd's acne lit up even redder whenever he was caught out or embarrassed. 'We're going to bash a queer,' he said. 'Wanna come wiv us?'

'No, I gotta get home,' Brian said lamely. 'M' Nan's not well, I gotta.'

'You queer an' all, Oldman?' Shepherd challenged. 'You get the same pasting he gets, 'you are.'

'Shut your gob, Shepherd,' Brian said.

'Yeah, you're probably queer an' all.'

'Go and squeeze your spots!'

'They ain't spots. 'S acne,' Shepherd retorted. 'I'd sooner have spots than be a queer.'

'I ain't no queerer than you.'

'Prove it, then. Come on, then. Bash Bill Flaps with us.'

Bill Foster, the queer in question, was called Flaps on account of his large ears. He was a pathetic copper's nark who never actually helped catch anyone. 'He's harmless,' Brian's mum had told him one day, when they passed him in the street, and he pointed at them and said, 'I've been told to look out for the likes of you.' He hung around on the corner outside Martin's Bank in Rosebery Avenue and reported to the police anything he decided was suspicious. Brian wondered if he'd reported them for taunting him: 'Queer! Queer Flaps opens his traps!'

'You bugger off, you cheeky perishers, 'fore I have you run in.'

'What you gonna run us in with? A bike?'

'I've been told to keep a lookout for your sort,' he said, and hurried along the pavement. As he went, Brian picked up an empty milk bottle off a doorstep and hurled it, hitting Bill Flaps squarely in the back. He was a good thrower with an accurate eye. The nark swung round, alarmed. 'You leave me alone,' he said. Tears welled in his eyes and his nose ran. 'Just leave me alone.'

'Queer! Queer!' The boys called, laughing at him. Brian joined in, but wasn't sure why.

'It doesn't make me a bad person,' Bill Flaps managed to say.

'It doesn't make me a bad person.' Roy Shepherd mocked, imitating his shrill voice.

They were hooting and laughing, causing Bill Flaps even more grief, when his guardian angels hove into view. Immediately he ran into the road to flag down the Wolseley police car. Shepherd and the others turned and ran, Brian too. No sooner did they gain the corner of Tysoe Street than they split up and went different ways. Brian turned right, went down to Farringdon Road and crossed into the lower end of Rosebery Avenue. There, he slowed and glanced back to make sure he wasn't being followed. It was then that his eyes alighted on a pair of shoes in the window of S. Heal and Son. They were black suede with thick crêpe soles and two buckled straps across the top. Brian was transfixed: he wanted them more than he'd wanted anything in his whole life. He wondered whether he dared to go into the shop without his mum.

'Rather nice, aren't they?' A softly spoken man had appeared at his side.

Brian spun round, thinking that somehow Bill Flaps had caught up with him, but it was a man in a brown button-through overall. 'Smashing,' was all he could say.

'I bet you'd be off down the Palais and dating all the prettiest girls with those on. If I had your good looks I would.'

Brian returned to stare at the shoes. He could try asking his mum to buy them, but he didn't know if she had twenty-seven and six to spare – or could spare it without his dad knowing. Joey would say that he'd had a new pair of shoes at the start of the school year. But these shoes weren't for school.

'You could try them on. Go on, be a devil!'

'No,' Brian said quickly. He couldn't buy them, and if he did try them on, he wouldn't be able to leave without them. 'I've got to go.'

The lower end of Rosebery Avenue wasn't on his route home from school but two days later he found himself outside S. Heal and Son again. The shoes were even more desirable now. Out of the corner of his eye he saw the man in the brown overalls step out of the shop and sidle up to him. 'Go on,' he said. 'You want to try them, don't you? I dare you to. You won't be sorry.'

He had to now, but there was still the problem of how he would pay for them. He couldn't ask his mum. She'd only remind him that they were saving every penny for his dad's business. And now that Jack had given up work to train full-time he couldn't ask him. Perhaps he could get the shop people to lay them away and pay them sixpence a week – but if he did that, it would take him more than a year to pay for them. Still, he had to try them on.

The shop was fairly dark and dusty-smelling. The Son of S. Heal, who told him he was called Stephen after his father, whose shop he'd inherited, plucked the shoes from the window – the only pair in the entire shop and they were a size seven. Stephen Heal crouched on the stool in front of Brian and pulled his foot on to the sole-shaped plate. 'You've got nice feet,' he said. 'Nice bones.' He smoothed Brian's sock with a firm stroking motion, then slipped his foot into the shoe, like the prince did in Cinderella. It was a bit loose but Brian didn't care. He thought they looked dandy and glanced up to see what Stephen Heal thought. It was then that he noticed the man's fly was open and he wasn't wearing underpants. He could see everything. Stephen Heal looked up and saw him looking, then glanced down at himself and laughed. 'Oh, I'd better not let him out of his cage, had I?' He got up and slipped into the back of the shop behind the brown velvet curtain.

Immediately Brian took off the shoes and stood up to go, but stopped. If he left, he wouldn't get the shoes and he wanted them, even though they were a size too big. He guessed that the shopkeeper hadn't gone in the back to button his fly. He'd met a few men like him. They seemed to be drawn to Brian like wasps to a rotting apple. Now the shoes were his for the taking. All he had to do was walk out of the shop with them, away down Clerkenwell Road and home. It would be easy because he wouldn't ever have to come past here again. Doubt made him hesitate. What if he was wrong about the bloke? What if he called the police?

A plan formed. Brian moved quietly across the wooden floor in his socks. He eased back the curtain and saw Stephen Heal, eyes closed, gripping his cock with one hand and a shelf with the other.

'I'm gonna tell my dad on you. He's a copper.'

Heal's eyes flew open. 'Oh, no. Oh, no, you wouldn't do that. Course you wouldn't, good-looking young man like you. Go on, be a sport.'

'He told me to be on the lookout and report people like you,' Brian said, thinking about Bill Flaps.

'Go on, you don't need to do that. Really.' He put it back in its cage and buttoned his fly hurriedly. 'Look, it'd be my word against yours, now, wouldn't it? I'm a respectable married man.'

'Oh, no, they'd believe me, all right. Especially if I say you made me do it to you.'

'Oh, and I thought you were a nice boy,' Stephen Heal said. 'You'd better get out of my shop right now. I don't want your sort in here.'

'If I go out without them shoes,' Brian said, 'I'll have to tell my dad what you made me do.'

Stephen Heal looked at him uncertainly. 'Well, they fit you like a glove and they looked lovely . . . Look, just take them and go.'

'What? You think I'm stupid? You'll have the police on me!'

'I wouldn't do that.'

'You'd better put them in one of your bags and give me a receipt.'

Stephen Heal thought about that. Suddenly Brian felt panicky. His muscles tensed, ready to run.

'Yes, you're definitely a policeman's son,' Heal said eventually. 'Only a policeman's son would think up such a despicable thing.'

He walked out past the curtain and put the shoes into a brown carrier-bag with 'S. Heal and Son, High Class Footwear' on it. He wrote a receipt for twenty-seven and six and gave it to Brian with the shoes.

That was Brian's first experience of wielding power over others through sex, and he was determined to exploit it. He'd get whatever he could out of being different.

It all looked like ending before it had begun. He was up in the bedroom he shared with Jack when his mum came flying upstairs. She was too quick for him and he didn't get the shoes under the bed in time. 'What are you doing with them?' she said. 'Where d'you get them?'

'They're Uncle Jack's,' Brian lied smoothly. 'I think he bought them to take Win Booker to the Palais. He's sweet on her still.'

'He ought to have more bloody sense,' Cath said. 'There's a bobby down in the hall. He wants to see you. What you been up to?'

'I never,' Brian said, with a tremor in his voice.

'Whatever it is, just say you didn't do it,' his mum advised.

Brian could feel the constable's eyes on him as he came down the stairs ahead of her, trying to act naturally. He was ready to say that Stephen Heal made him give him a wank, then gave him the shoes to keep him quiet, but that wasn't why the cop was here.

'We had a complaint about you,' the rozzer said. 'You and some other boys were roughing up Bill Foster, known as Bill Flaps—'

'I never,' Brian said, before the constable could finish.

'Who did, then? Someone did. Mr Foster gave us your name, and he knew where you lived.'

'Lots of people know where we live, Constable,' Cath said, giving Brian time to come up with his next fib. 'His uncle's about to become the world light-heavyweight champion.'

'I know Bill Flaps,' Brian said. 'I talk to him sometimes. He must have got me mixed up with someone else.'

'Where were you around four o'clock today?'

'He was here,' Cath said. 'I met him from school to get him some new shoes. Show him the shoes.'

No, Mum! Don't go there, Brian urged silently.

The policeman thought about it for a moment. 'Well, he's not all there up top, is Bill Flaps. He's definitely got a couple of marbles missing. But something upset him right enough.'

When the policeman had left, his mum gave Brian a conspiratorial smile that made him quake.

With seventeen pounds, nine-and-sixpence from a collection taken up among the stevedores in the King George V docks, Jack stopped work there to train full-time on the expectation that a title fight was in the offing. Billy promised it. Frank Cockain hinted at it. Mr Solomons said it was a possibility, but more hard work was needed – plus he had to put away a couple of other fighters first. But the opportunity never came. Believing with every fibre of his being that he was ready, Jack was almost exploding with frustration at having to wait. For how long? Until he was an old man and could only hit his opponent with a walking-stick? The Kate didn't make the wait any easier: the Military Police continued to show up at the house without warning.

He refused offers of money from Billy Hill, because of the strings attached, but scratched a living instead, selling stuff Bobby had knocked off. There was no problem finding buyers. A lot of goods remained in short supply, even though the last of the rationing had ended under Mr Churchill. People wouldn't wait for things any more, and the cheerful grin-and-bear-it of wartime was long gone. Goods were easily got through the likes of Billy or Bobby and the black-market was making crooks of everyone. Even people with cut-glass Mayfair and Kensington accents approached Jack for certain things.

The first thing he noticed about Billy Hill when he entered the gym with Bobby Brown was his suit, brand spanking new, so loud it shouted at you. Billy always wore good clothes. 'The best of everything, that's what I like,' he said, and enjoyed showing off what he'd got. Jack began to think he was in the wrong game. Bobby's threads weren't hand-me-downs either.

A couple of men in donkey jackets, hanging around in the gym out of the cold during their search for work, tapped Billy for the price of a smoke. He slipped them each a ten-bob note. Jack found it strange that no one seemed to resent Billy's luck. Eventually he came to the side of the ring, where Jack was sparring, and spoke to Peewee.

'He's working hard, guv'nor,' the old man said. 'He certainly is.'

'He needs to, if we're gonna take him all the way,' Billy said loudly, for everyone to hear. 'I could've gone all the way, Peewee. My problem was I liked the pop too much and the merry-hearts.'

'Neither's any good for you, Mr Hill,' Peewee said, and turned his attention back to Jack, who was slamming into his sparring partner, 'Ease up – he ain't the world champ. Switch to the bag.'

'Keep your shirt on,' Jack said.

Billy Hill joined him at the punchbag, leaning against the heavy leather cylinder as Jack pounded it. To Jack it was almost like hitting Billy and that was good.

'What you doing for gelt now you've quit stevedoring?' Billy asked. 'Ten bob here and ten bob there from a bit of black-market swag won't get you far. The army's still looking for you – they almost collared young Bobby the other day.'

'When? He never said.' He glanced at Bobby who was lounging on the bench reading the tissue and marking his racing selections.

'It was a close thing, Jack,' Bobby said, without looking up. 'I had to have it on my toes a bit sharpish.'

'You'll be outa luck if they get you before your big fight, son,' Billy told Jack.

'What big fight's that?' Jack said. 'I'm beginning to think you and that gasbag couldn't deliver a sack of coal.'

'Jack Solomons can place you right on the spot where you need to be. He's about the only one who can get you a shot at that title.'

Jack stopped hitting the bag and gave the older man a measured look. 'What'd you want, Billy?'

In this mood, Billy Hill always had some daft proposition for him. 'It'd mean a lot to your old man, God rest him, to see you win,' he said. 'Tiger Braden could knock 'em down like ninepins. I know I weren't exactly a good influence when I was around, but your mum was all the influence you needed. I always put plenty on the table, though.'

Jack said nothing.

Then Billy got to his daft scheme. 'I need a hand to sort out Jack Spot,' he said. 'It won't take us ten minutes. Then we'll set you up proper with Jack Solomons.' He winked at Bobby and walked away, as if it was a done deal.

'He means it, Jack,' Bobby said. 'You just stand there looking tough. That's all there is to it. Don't be a mug. Give him a hand.'

The swimming-pool and vapour baths off Westbourne Grove, where Jack Spot hung out, had closed because there was no coal for the boilers. When they opened again gas boilers had been installed, but by then a lot of people had bathrooms in their homes. Now the place was run-down, worn out – you wouldn't have known it was open. Maybe it was Spot's secret and he didn't want other people coming there. A poster warning of VD was displayed on the wall at the entrance. Another prohibited spitting and a third gave the opening times of the slipper baths, which a lot of call girls in the area frequented – they had no baths in their workrooms. The desolate atmosphere was made worse by the damp, cold air, which was filled with the smell of chlorine. It was as if people had got out of the habit of going out for a bath. Probably the weather was too cold. The Richardson brothers climbed out of the Humber with Jack and Billy, wearing light sports coats and open-necked shirts. Jack had on a donkey jacket someone had given him with 'Wimpey' across the back. Although he wasn't cold, the heavy coat made him feel good and stopped his muscles tensing.

'Keep the engine running, Bobby,' Billy said, and walked into the baths. Bobby Brown was no use in a fight.

Workers' Playtime was on the wireless in the ticket booth, and a comedian called Bob Monkhouse was telling some lame joke that had the factory hands laughing. Fat Cecil, the keeper of the baths, wasn't laughing as he read the *Sketch*. He glanced up as Billy slapped a shilling on the counter to get attention.

'Hello, Cecil,' Billy said. 'I heard Spotty's in.'

The doorman glanced first at Jack, then at the speaking tube that connected to the baths. 'I'm not sure, Mr Hill. I ain't seen him.'

'I expect he is,' Billy said good-naturedly. 'The dirty bastard needs a good scrub.' He reached through the window, tore off four tickets and took some towels. 'Don't even think about warning him,' he added.

Fat Cecil held Jack's eye and winked at him. Jack wondered what that was about, then realized the fat slug was a ginger-beer and raised a fist at him.

'Steady on, tiger,' Billy said. 'He ain't the enemy.'

Anger carried Jack up the stone stairs to the big vapour room where Spotty lay face down on the marble bench, looking less distinguished than he remembered. Last time they'd met, he'd been wearing expensive clothes and dark glasses. Now the ugly white ribbons of fat across his hairy back were on display. A naked man with a towel around his midriff was brushing him with a wad of raffia from a suds-filled bucket. Others could be seen through the steam doing the same to other men.

Billy stepped up and tapped the man on the shoulder, took the raffia off him and waved him away. 'Nothing like a nice relaxing shmeeze, Spotty,' he said.

Spot turned over, clearly alarmed. There was nothing he could do to save himself when Billy hit him squarely in the face with the bucket, cutting his eye. Suds spilled everywhere. Then Billy grabbed his soapy hair and smacked his face hard into the marble bench. 'We all get the hump with bookies, Spotty, specially when the gee-gees don't run like we want 'em to. But don't push your luck. Don't take the Michael.' He banged his head again, then again.

Spot was fighting for breath now. 'I'm gonna cut you so badly your mother won't know you,' he wheezed.

'At least m' dad does!' Billy said, and hit him again.

The blood spilling into the white foam excited Jack and he wanted to fly at the man too, if only for having a queer friend who'd winked at him. But it was all over. Jack Spot and his crew clearly didn't have the stomach for it – or so he'd thought, but then a naked man came at Billy with a chiv. He ran into Jack's fist as if it was a brick wall. Jack hooked him another into the throat with his right and the man hung in the air, buoyed up with shock. Billy prised the chiv from his hand, swivelled on the balls of his feet and put a stripe across the face of another man who rushed him. He stepped back as the man went down screaming – he didn't want blood on his suit.

'Lucky it wasn't your Hampton, son!' Billy laughed. So did the Richardsons.

How many of the other men taking vapour worked for Spotty, Jack didn't know. None chose to identify himself. He felt disappointed – he was keyed up, ready for a fight, and could have laid out any number of them.

'What a team,' Billy said as, outside, he danced down the steps. Charlie Richardson opened the car door for him. 'I'm thinking of pulling off Bobby's post-office raid. How about joining us on that one, Jack? Bobby's always kept you in mind. Right, Bob?'

'Be like old times, Jack,' Bobby said.

'It's not my line, Billy.'

Why he went on resisting, Jack didn't know, especially as he was now well and truly identified with Billy Hill's gang – if without the benefits that the Richardson boys obviously enjoyed: status, respect and plenty of money. Perhaps he was scared of getting caught and going to prison. Would that be such an ordeal? Billy took it in his stride.

Billy feinted a blow, which Jack made no attempt to counter, then grabbed him around the neck and hugged him across to the car. 'Spotty's well and truly finished,' he said.

'He's not dead,' Jack pointed out.

'Listen to him, will you?' Billy said. 'Save that killer instinct for the ring, son.'

Candles flickered in the saloon bar of the King's Head. The country was in the midst of a power crisis. They were always short of something and now it was coal. The miners were out on strike from the nationalized coal mines.

Jack ordered a light ale for himself and one for Bobby Brown, who was trying hard but still wasn't officially in Billy Hill's gang. Jack, who wasn't bothered, was finding it hard to keep out. Bobby needed his proposed post-office raid to prove successful.

'They ain't gonna keep us warm, Cyril,' Bobby said to the landlord, and lit a Gold Flake in the candle flame.

'Unless we get some coal soon, that's all there'll be.' He put their drinks on the bar and took the money from Jack. 'Is that big fight anywhere on the horizon, Jack? I wanna have a house to let on you.'

'I'm waiting for the announcement,' Jack said. 'I'm ready for whoever they throw at me.'

'According to Harry Carpenter in the *Mirror*, Sugar Ray Robinson's going all the way.'

'To about the third round if I have anything to do with it,' Jack told him. The landlord went off to serve someone else and Jack turned back to Bobby. 'Mum said you'd got hold of a bit of cheese.'

'So much I'm turning into a mouse!' Bobby said.

'How much is it?' Jack asked.

'Special price to you. Waste of time, the black-market. You should come after the real gelt with us.' He glanced across at Billy Hill and his men. 'The Kray twins ducked in earlier,' he went on. 'They was looking for you.'

'They know where I live.'

'And you know where their cousin Win lives!' Bobby laughed. 'You can't be thinking about the merry-hearts if you want that title.'

'Right now I want some of that cheese for Mum.'

It was an entire mature Cheddar, weighing half a hundredweight, that Jack had wrapped in a sack and balanced on his shoulder when he ran into Reggie Kray. Like his twin Ronnie, who was behind him, he was fit and muscular. They did a bit of boxing but were too emotional to get anywhere, especially Ronnie. Both men were quick to anger in the ring, which wasn't an asset to a boxer.

'Want a word with you, Jack,' Reggie said, like a man with something serious on his mind.

'Reg, Ron,' he said affably. They were so alike it was hard to tell them apart. Jack had never liked them – there was too much malice in them. Reg was the most even of the two, while his brother had a permanent scowl that always seemed to threaten trouble.

'You been carrying on with our cousin Win,' Reggie said. He usually did the talking for them both.

'No. That's long finished.'

'What, ain't she good enough for you?' Ronnie butted in, stabbing the air with a finger for emphasis.

'No,' Jack said. 'It's not that. I like Win. She's a laugh.'

Something about that enraged Reggie. Jack was watching Ronnie so when Reggie shoved him in the chest, he staggered back, dancing to keep his balance and hang on to the cheese. He didn't want it smashing on the ground. 'Pack it in, Reg, or you'll end up hurt.'

'Will you listen to this mug?' Heedless, Reggie pushed him harder. 'You deserve a good hiding, 's what we think,' he said, spoiling for a fight.

This was it, Jack knew. There was no avoiding it unless he turned tail and ran. He was thinking about doing just that, when Ronnie said, 'Your mum's messed her up an' all. She can't have kiddies now. She's a bloody butcher, your mum. She should get a job at Smithfield.'

'Leave her out of it,' Jack warned.

Reggie swung a furious left at Jack, his entire body signalling what was coming. Jack sidestepped as Ronnie threw a punch too. It smacked dully into the cheese, which was now off Jack's shoulder. He shoved it at Ron. 'Cop this!'

Ronnie hesitated, then dropped it on the ground and launched himself at Jack, who bobbed away and sent him staggering off the pavement, falling over a bicycle parked at the kerb into the empty road. Jack danced away from Reggie, who was getting angrier because none of his shots was landing. Jack could have kept it up all night and worn them out but he doubted that that would have the desired effect. They needed a lesson they wouldn't forget.

'Stand still, yellow belly!' Reggie yelled, his breathing laboured.

Suddenly Jack stopped and Reggie landed a punch, shocking himself. Neither he nor Ronnie knew what to do next. The fight seemed to have gone out of them. Jack turned away to pick up his cheese and the brothers rushed him – that was their style, he remembered. He swung round and bopped Ronnie's nose, which fountained blood. It had been a much harder blow than was necessary, but Ronnie Kray was one of those stupid geezers who didn't know when enough was enough. Jack hit Reggie with a left, then a right and another right, and he went down, but got up. Jack knocked him down again. That was it, as far as he was concerned. He helped Ronnie to his feet.

'You'd best try and get something cold on that, Ron, to stop the swelling.' He collected his cheese and brushed off the dust.

Neighbours piled into Gracie's kitchen where she was parcelling out wedges of cheese hacked off with the bread knife as they listened to Arthur Askey on the wireless.

'You should be the Minister of Supply, Gracie, not that twerp we got at present.'

''S my Jack what got it,' Gracie said proudly to her best friend, Eve Sutton, nodding at Jack, who was sitting in his dad's old chair in the corner reading *Boxing News*.

'We ain't had nothing this good in the Co-op. You're an angel,' she said, and chucked Jack under the chin as she left.

Suddenly Eve cried out, slammed the front door and ran back in with her cheese. 'Gracie! That busy's outside with them army blokes.'

Jack was out of the kitchen and up the stairs, ready to scarper through the bedroom window and over the outhouse roof almost before the heavy knocking had started. He waited tensely rather than diving straight out in case some of them had gone round the back. He heard his mum open the door to PC Watling, who pushed in with two heavy-booted MPs.

'I thought this lot had given up, Mr Watling,' Gracie said.

'That's not likely to happen, missus.'

He paused. Jack guessed he'd spotted the cheese. 'That looks like a nice bit of Cheddar. I do like a nice bit of Cheddar.'

Jack smiled. That was it, as far as their greedy beat bobby was concerned. He heard them all go into the kitchen. Gracie'd give them a cup of tea and a bit of cheese.

'You still visiting that nipper in the orphange, Mr Watling?' she asked now. 'Tony, wasn't it? You'd best take a chunk for him too.' Eventually they left, each with a generous parcel of cheese instead of Jack.

When he came back downstairs, his mum was astonished. 'Were you up there all that while? I'd've had kittens if I'd known. I thought you'd scarpered over the roof.' She laughed but then she frowned, worried. It occurred to Jack how unwell she looked. 'What's going to happen, son? You'd have thought the army would've given up on you by now.'

'They will, don't worry. When I get that title fight – if I get it.'

Jack shook his head. 'I'll be an old man before bloody Billy Hill pulls that one off.'

'You'll get it, son,' she said. 'I'll go and talk to him. It just wants Mr Solomons to get his skates on, that's all.'

That's all, Jack thought. 'He keeps on at me to help him out on that post-office job Bobby's got his eye on. Maybe that's what he's waiting for.'

'You won't get no title fight if you land up inside, son,' his mum told him, as she reached into the cupboard under the stairs for her coat. 'Thieving's all right for the likes of Billy and Bobby, but it ain't your game.'

'I get hold of meat and cheese,' Jack said, 'and anything bent what's going. Maybe I owe him.'

'Don't talk daft,' she said. 'What Billy's got to do is what any man would do for his family. Even though you ain't family.' She collected her handbag and went out of the door.

The path to his title opened up directly. Jack never found out what his mum said to Billy or what he said to Jack Solomons. He only knew that he had to step up his training. No late nights, no women, no beer. Solomons popped into the gym from time to time to check on his progress. He spoke to Peewee and seemed satisfied, but he never smiled or gave Jack the time of day.

Frank Cockain looked in more often.

'What's wrong with Mr Solomons?' Jack asked, as he stopped skipping and went over to the punchball. The bookmaker followed him. 'He don't never say a word to me. Just looks right through me when he's here.'

'He and Billy Hill had a few choice words, that's what,' Frank Cockain said. 'From what I can make out Billy threatened to do him some serious mischief unless he made you a front runner.'

'Did he?' Jack was amazed. 'And Mr Solomons went along with it?'

'I expect he didn't fancy having his fingers broken. And you won't get to be World Light Heavyweight Champ just yet, son – you got to put away some serious contenders before you meet Archie Moore. Billy's got a lot of clout in certain circles. Jack Solomons heard how he did that ponce Spot. I wouldn't want to cross him and neither does Solomons.'

Suddenly Jack saw Billy in a different light. Perhaps he wasn't such a bad fellow after all. He was curious to know just what he'd said to the promoter.

'I certainly didn't tell him the army's still tryna nab you,' Billy Hill said, when Jack caught up with him. 'That would have put the kibosh on it for sure.'

'Look, if you still need a hand with that post-office job,' Jack said, 'I'm your man.'

'Did I hear him right, Bobby?' Billy said, turning to his companion.

'That's what he said, guv'nor,' Bobby replied, like a straight man feeding a comic.

But Billy Hill didn't deliver a punchline. He put his arm around Jack's shoulders in a fatherly way. 'Stick to what you know, son,' he said. 'Mugs like Bobby and me can knock over post-office vans.'

'Come off it, Billy,' Jack said. 'I'll play fair by you.'

Billy Hill wasn't having any of it. 'It takes something special to climb into the ring with someone even half as good as Archie Moore. Get back to training. Just beat the brains outa them mugs. Then it's the title and we'll all make a packet.' He shaped up to Jack, who let him slip through a couple of light slaps. 'See that, Bob?'

'Maybe you should be taking on the next contender, guv'nor,' Bobby said, pulling a cheeky face.

Fresh fruit and vegetables were part of his training regime and Jack got plenty of both. Mr Thompson and the other Spitalfields traders made sure of that. Jack swung past every day on his run and always came away with some extra ballast. Sometimes Brian ran with him and he enjoyed the boy's company. He was with him today and they paused to listen to Joey on the dock, arguing with the driver of a lorry that was being unloaded. The count was wrong and Joey was refusing to accept it. Jack watched, surprised at how tough little skin-and-bones Joey was in dealing with people, even those twice his size. Mr Thompson was on the blower at the desk in the small office. It was littered with delivery dockets and order forms, all of which were covered with a thin film of earth from the potatoes. Once a week, Brian came in after school to sweep up for a bit of pocket money, but didn't make much impression.

'It might be government orders,' Mr Thompson was shouting to the party down the line, 'but it's not worth my while handling potatoes at that price. I thought the Tories had stopped all that. I don't give a bugger what the minister or anyone else says. They need shooting, the bloody lot of them.' He slammed down the heavy Bakelite phone with a satisfying crash. 'I'm going to make tracks,' he said to Joey, as he came in with his clipboard, wearing a three-piece suit and a bowler hat the same as the boss. 'Make sure Jack gets plenty of what's best.'

'Ken was short with his delivery again,' Joey said. 'The third time this week.'

'You're a Boy Scout, Joey.'

'Did you look at them figures I give you, Mr T?' Joey asked. 'If we do better, I might get a rise.'

'I can barely make ends meet as it is,' Mr T said, 'with spuds the price I'm forced to sell them at.'

'Well, fiddle's costing us about ten per cent of turnover.'

'What's all this "we" and "us", Joey?'

'That triple-docket system I showed you would stop all that. We learnt it at night-school. Keeps track of everything.'

'You know what they say, son, if you build a better mousetrap . . .' He started out of the door. 'Be lucky, Jack – and if you can't, be good.' He waddled off along the dock.

'These aren't mice we've got,' Joey said, 'they're bloody rats. He doesn't deserve to stay in business. He won't try new ideas.' His eyes lit on Brian. 'You should be at school, Brian. At least that's free.'

'Jack's taking me to the gym,' Brian said eagerly.

'That's real education, Joey.'

'A waste of time,' Joey snapped irritably. 'His mum don't want him missing school. We want him to make something of himself.'

That wasn't the problem, and Jack knew it. 'She's got the hump with you, Joey,' he said. 'You're always here, she says, like it's your business.'

'It will be one day. I'll buy the old fool out. I've got plans for my own business if Thompson's not interested in my ideas. It just needs a bit of money. I got the brains.'

'Did you ask Billy? He's always got plenty.' But Jack knew he was wasting his breath: Joey wouldn't ask Billy Hill the time of day – and who'd blame him? 'I could help out – there's a two-hundred-pound purse when I knock out Joe Bygraves.'

'First you have to do it,' Joey said, 'and you have to keep out of the army's way. They're practically camping outside Mum's these days. I s'pose they've heard about the fight.'

'You could still help me with that,' Jack said, 'if you went and took my medical instead of me. The army'd tell you to sling your hook right away.'

'Sling me straight in the jug, more like.'

'Come on, Joey,' Jack pleaded. 'Who'd ever know?'

'You could – easy, Dad,' Brian piped up.

'You just keep out of it and get to school or you'll end up like one of them gym flies.'

'Ah, Da-ad,' Brian protested.

Joey was unrelenting. 'Do what I say, son.' He turned to Jack. 'D'you think the army's stupid? They'll see you fighting. They're not mugs.'

'But I'd have the title, Joey,' Jack said, as if that was the answer to everything in his life and everyone else's.

'While I sit in clink. No, thank you.'

'He's a real chicken, your old man,' Jack complained, when he caught up with Brian. 'I hope you get to be more like your granddad than him.' When Brian didn't reply, he glanced round. The boy was leaning against a lamp-post shaking and white as a sheet.

'What's wrong with you?' Jack said. 'You seen a ghost or something?'

Brian tried to speak but no words came out. He ran off along the street, crashing past people like a thing possessed. Jack tore after him and overtook him easily. 'What is it, mate? What's wrong, Bri?'

For a moment he thought Brian was going to tell him but instead his nephew started to sob.

'Is he all right?' a woman sweeping the pavement in front of her shop asked.

'He's okay, ain't you, Bri?'

Brian sniffed his tears away and nodded.

'That's the ticket,' Jack said. 'We'll slip into the gym. Don't care what Joey says. You'll do all right.' He put his hand on the boy's shoulder and guided him away along the street.

Jack's excitement rose as his big fight with Joe Bygraves crept nearer. Now the day was almost upon him. He was at the peak of fitness – which worried Peewee in case he overdid it and lost his edge. All it needed was a sprain or a head cold, and flu was raging across the country.

'I won't catch a cold, Peewee,' Jack said, as he stopped in the sparring ring to adjust the laces in his gloves with his teeth. 'Joe Bygraves is the only one who's gonna catch cold tomorrow night.'

At that moment, watery sunlight poked through the skylight, putting Jack in a kind of spotlight. It was a good sign, he decided, as he watched tiny particles of dust floating in the rays. That's what he would do at Harringay Arena: he'd float round Bygraves so he wouldn't know which direction he was being hit from.

'This is it, Jack,' Peewee said, kneading the tension in Jack's deltoid muscles and pummelling them with liver-spotted hands.

'No more training. Take the night off, son, but no booze and no merry-hearts.'

'I'll try, Peewee. I'm ready for him. I can see him on the deck, knocked out in round one.'

'Give them a bit more than that for their money,' Peewee said. 'The wireless will be there, and the people from BBC television. It won't be much for the punters at home if it's, "Bam, bam, out for the count, Mr Bygraves."'

The thought of Freddie Grisewood commentating on the television troubled Jack. The army people might see it and stop him going on to get a crack at Randolph Turpin, the current light-heavyweight champion. Nausea flooded him, leaving him feeling weak. Perhaps Billy Hill could do something.

'The army's not gonna be there, Jack, or if they are, they'll be cheering for you like everyone else in the country – apart from that Joe Bygraves and his fat mum.' Billy laughed. 'Relax.'

Everyone was telling him to relax. Easier said than done. Billy was sitting at the bar of the King's Head with Carol, his girl. Jack was in such a state of anxiety he didn't even remember to resent this donah being there instead of his mum. She wasn't much older than him and spoke to him as if they were friends. 'We'll all be there, Jack, cheering for you.'

'Here,' Billy said, pulling a fiver off his roll and giving it to Jack. 'Take Mum up west tonight. There's a new Gary Cooper film on at the Empire. She always liked him.'

His mum was full of the same nervous anticipation as he was, standing at the board in the kitchen ironing and re-ironing his boxing clobber over and over. She didn't want to go to the pictures or anywhere else. The hours passed slowly. Jack could hardly sleep that night.

On the big day, powdery snow drifted down on a light north-easterly wind, settling in corners and along the neatly swept kerbs outside the houses in Jack's street. A new sort of anxiety crept in as he packed his kitbag. 'What if no one turns out for it in this weather, Bri?'

'I should coco!' Brian said. 'No one's gonna miss this fight in a million years.' He stood wide-eyed with admiration in Gracie's kitchen with his mum and dad. Alice was there too, with John, who was in his best suit for the occasion. Even though she didn't approve of boxing, she couldn't helping getting caught up in the excitement.

'I should be going with you,' Gracie said. 'My nerves'll drive me crackers. I won't be able to listen to it on the wireless.'

'It's only the weigh-in, Mum,' Cath said. 'The fight's not till eight o'clock. And how would it look, a grown man's mum going along?'

'What if that other fighter's mum is there?' Gracie retorted.

'I'll be all right, Mum,' Jack said, and put his arm around her. 'I don't even want you to come to the door with me. I know my way there – and to Harringay on the Underground!' He winked at Brian, who laughed at his joke.

'We'll be glued to that wireless,' Cath said. She threw her arms round him and kissed him.

'Not half,' Joey said. He'd abandoned his class at night school, a big sacrifice especially as he'd paid two shillings for it.

Jack caught Alice's eye and wondered whether he should give her a kiss too, but she made no move towards him so he made none to her. The gap was widening between them and he didn't understand why she had come.

'You'll knock spots off him, Uncle Jack,' John said. He stepped forward and offered him a little crucifix, glancing at his mum uncertainly. Jack took it and quickly put it in his pocket.

Jack slipped out the back way to avoid the neighbours who, despite the cold, were waiting at their front doors to wish him luck. He went along the alleyway, as he had many times to avoid the MPs, his kitbag on his shoulder. He slipped on the icy ground and did a little dance to get his balance. A sprained ankle would finish his chances. Win rushed from her gate at the end of her tiny yard, wearing only a thin, short-sleeved dress. 'Jack!' she said. 'I didn't mean to tell them. Honest, I didn't!'

He smiled, not quite catching what she said. 'You'll catch your death dressed like that, you silly girl. Where's your coat?'

She tried to pull him into their junk-littered backyard. 'Stay with me. Come to the shelter. It's warm – I got a paraffin stove.'

Of all the times to have a bit of meat! Peewee would go completely hairy at him even thinking about it. Jack didn't hear the alarm in her voice or see the fear in her eyes. Instead he chucked her under the chin. 'I've got a special date with Joe Bygraves. He ain't as pretty as you.' He walked away on the slippery surface, sensing Win still watching him. He didn't glance back.

A skinny dog was cocking its leg against the age-blackened wall at the end of the alley where it let out on to Goswell Road. It scampered away as two men in jackets, no coats, stepped into the mouth of the alley. Jack recognised Ronnie and Reggie Kray and was touched – they'd come to wish him well. Then he realized that that wasn't why they were there. 'Come on, you two,' he said. 'If you're looking to start anything, it'll have to wait till after my fight.'

Neither of them said anything, but Reggie glanced nervously at a black Rover that was parked at the kerb just below the alleyway. It was the only car on the street. A red Routemaster bus was approaching, snow swirling in its headlights in the afternoon gloom. Jack didn't connect the four men sitting in the car with himself or the twins until they leaped out and ran towards him. He recognized one as the Jack Spot goon who Billy had striped at the vapour baths, the wide scar across his left cheek clearly visible. There was something in his hand, Jack noticed now, as he approached, some sort of cosh. They all had leather saps. He was about to toss his bag at them and give them what-for when the Krays lunged at him. Ronnie caught him with a right hook while Reggie clamped his arms around him, forcing Jack's arms to his sides. He struggled and managed to free one arm as the first blow from the blackjack struck him in the left temple. It felt like a dull sting and he was relieved; he could handle this and still beat Joe Bygraves. But the pain that followed started to spread and seemed to paralyse him. Other blows landed on him in quick succession. Jack managed to get his fists up, but not a single blow did he strike back. Instead, he felt himself sinking under the weight of the blows, losing consciousness.

He steeled his mind, determined not to go under. Where were Billy and the Richardsons now? Didn't these mugs in the alley know he had a fight to win? Why wasn't he winning this fight? How could Joe Bygraves get in so many hits all at once? Why was he allowed to kick him? Kicking wasn't allowed. The referee should stop it. He wasn't doing so because he was bent. Frank Cockain said they were all bent. Jack curled into a tight ball, and eventually the blows stopped. He heard running feet and what sounded like car doors slamming. An engine roared and they were gone.

Next he heard someone saying, 'Jack. Jack. I'm sorry. I told them. I'm so sorry.' He tried to open his eyes. Only the right one worked. It was bloodshot and watery, and the lid wouldn't lift properly. He could just make out Win. You'll catch your death, Win . . . the words swirled away in the snow. Gotta get to the weight-in . . . no longer was he even sure the words came out past his cut and swollen lips.

With a supreme effort of will he got on to his hands and knees in the powdery snow. It felt like hot wires were being slowly dragged through his flesh. Blood dripped on to the white pavement as he crawled painfully towards the only life he was aware of at that moment, someone on the wireless somewhere singing, '*I'll never stand in your way . . .*'

'It's time everyone got back to work and Britain was great again,' Nan said angrily, when she came downstairs from taking Jack a cup of tea. 'If Winston bloody Churchill can't put a stop to all this bloody rock-and-roll nonsense and coffee bars they ought to find someone who can.'

'But, Nan,' Brian argued, 'you said the Tories was good for the country.'

'Better than the last bloody lot. At least we don't have to queue for every blessed thing nowadays. All Labour ever done was nationalize everything and make it worse. Except for the National Health Service. At least we can be ill now without worrying about whether we can pay for the doctor or going to the hospital.'

Brian went round to his nan's after school most days while his mum and dad were at work. She gave him his tea. He hated going there now in case he saw Jack, who he thought was the worst yellow coward. More than once, Brian had considered phoning the cops or the army to come and cart him off. If his nan found out about that, she'd be angry, although she was as fed up with Jack as any of them. He didn't speak much and mostly avoided people where he could. That suited Brian just fine. Jack wouldn't even help Granddad Billy pull a job Bobby Brown had set up and Bobby was supposed to be his best friend. He didn't say anything when he heard about Bobby getting nicked – a gang of GPO workers had collared him at the gates of the sorting office as he'd tried to run with some sacks of registered mail. 'Have A Go Joes' the *Sketch* called them. There were too many for Billy and the Richardsons to fight off so they'd scarpered, leaving Bobby to face the music. When Jack heard about it, he hesitated, then just shuffled away down the street. For a moment, he looked like he was going to cry. Brian felt ashamed of him.

Excitement breezed through the door in the shape of Billy Hill, who had come to meet the detective who was investigating the robbery. Now he told Brian to make himself scarce when he tried to hang around to hear what was being said.

Nan caught him by the neck. 'Out!' she said, and steered him through to the scullery to help her peel some spuds so Billy and the detective could talk in private. That was a laugh. With the paper-thin walls and the scullery door that didn't shut properly, Brian could hear every word they said. The cozzer was called Big Bill Trope on account of his size. He was heavy-set, with frog-like jowls and a lavatory-brush moustache. He didn't bother to take off his Homburg, with its dented crown and stiff upturned rim. 'He ain't got no manners,' Nan whispered.

'This was worth winning the war for!' Billy said, as he came in and made for the fire in the kitchen range. Brian didn't know what he meant. Perhaps he was talking about the rain – it had hardly stopped all spring.

'Well, I expect Mr Churchill will do something about it, Billy.' Detective Inspector Trope took a cigarette from his silver case and tamped the end before putting it into his mouth. He brought the flame from a silver lighter up to it and dragged deeply.

'He'd better bloody hurry up about it.'

'You seem to be doing quite nicely.'

Peeping through the crack between the lopsided door and the jamb, Brian saw Billy take a thick wad of notes from his jacket pocket. 'Fold that little lot onto your hip – see how it feels, guv'nor,' he said.

The detective wetted his middle finger and quickly counted the money. 'I can tell you for nothing, Billy – it's like betraying my own children,' he said, slipping the money into his pocket. 'It rankles with honest policemen, the way some of these spivs make so much money on the black-market. It makes you want to spit.'

'What about Bobby Brown? Can we claw him back?'

'Stroll on! You could have done if I was the arresting officer. It was all I could do to let the army take him instead of him going for trial.'

Billy sighed. 'Well, two years' square-bashing will make a man of him.'

'I'd say so,' DI Trope said. 'Take some advice, Billy. Lie low for a while.'

'I should coco,' Billy said. 'I'm moving in on the West End.'

Brian watched the detective go out into the hall. Now was his chance. He glanced at his nan and nipped out through the back door. He ran hard along the alleyway behind the houses and met the detective as he was coming along towards Goswell Road. 'M' Uncle Jack's dodging the army,' he blurted out.

'Well, keep it dark, an' I'll buy you a lamp, son.'

That was all he said, then he went off along Goswell Road. Confusion and disappointment chased through Brian. He'd thought the copper would arrest Jack, cart him off to the army and make a man of him – he wanted the old Jack back.

If I had a pound for every time I got offered a bit of fiddle,' Joey said, 'I could have started my own business.' He sighed. Maybe he was the mug.

'All you gotta do is look the other way while the lorry gets mysteriously unloaded,' the pot-bellied driver in brown overalls said to him. 'With a brainbox like yours, you could easily come up with the right number on the count. No one would know it was coming in short.'

Joey took a more egalitarian approach to fiddle. 'What about all those people who can't afford to operate on the black-market?'

'There's always gonna be them what go short, Joey,' the driver told him. 'Go and take a blow with a nice fag.'

'I don't smoke.'

Maybe he was stupid passing up the money, Joey told himself

afterwards. Was he going to work for someone else all his life? At this rate he would. He could have made enough to get going on his own twice over by now if he'd done as he was asked. Feeling a better, superior person for saying no to the bungs was no longer enough.

Joey parked his bike against the privet hedge in the tiny front garden, lifted the box of fruit and vegetables off the handlebars, and pushed open the front door. The house was dark and quiet. Cath worked hard in the clothes factory and saw no point in sitting up, burning electricity, waiting for him to come home.

The springs of the old iron bed creaked as he slipped between the warm sheets, trying to make as little noise as possible. He was surprised when Cath reached out and touched him. 'I thought you was asleep,' he whispered.

'It's about the first time in a month you've been home before Brian's up for school,' Cath said. 'I think you must be carrying on with some other woman.'

'Chance would be a fine thing.'

'Oh, would it now?' Cath began to stroke him. 'You haven't paid me any attention for I don't know how long.' Not surprisingly, she wasn't very keen in that department and Joey was excited by other things, but every so often she pressed herself on him.

'There's a lot of them about,' Joey said, his thoughts still on work as Cath propped herself on her elbow and looked at him. 'Chances, I mean. I got offered twenty smackers today.'

The gaslight beyond the thin curtains at the window lit Cath's strong features. Her nostrils flared slightly, making her look determined, and the bump on her nose seemed to give her strength of character. 'Well?'

Joey shrugged. He knew what was coming.

'There's a lot we could do with twenty pounds. It'd take me a fortnight or more to earn that much. Where do people get all that money?'

'They're not people, Cath,' Joey said. 'They're parasites.'

'A few like that and we could afford a deposit on our own house, Joey. Or are we going to be renting like this all our lives?'

'Wait till I get going on my own,' Joey told her. 'We'll have the lot.'

'While you just let all your opportunities pass you by?'

That rankled with Joey. He wanted his opportunity more than anything, but was scared to take backhanders in case he got caught. 'Ask Big Bloody Billy Bullshit for a loan to get us started,' he said angrily. 'He'd do it for you – wouldn't he just. And the rest.'

'And have you accuse me of carrying on? No thank you.' She threw back the covers and got out of bed, pulling straight her pink winceyette nightdress. He heard her stomp down the stairs. How or where she was carrying on with Billy Hill he didn't know, but he couldn't convince himself that she wasn't.

Later that week, Joey watched the pair larking around at Mum's house, Billy slipping his arm round Cath's waist and giving her an affectionate squeeze. 'Isn't she the best-looking girl in the world?' he said.

Gracie looked up from rolling pastry on the kitchen table. 'She certainly is.' She glanced towards Alice, who was in the scullery prodding clothes in the copper.

'You're putting on a bit of weight. Not in the family way, are you?'

'No fear. Joey wants to get himself started before that happens.'

'If you need any help in either department, I'm your man.' Billy laughed.

'Joey might have something to say about that.' Cath glanced at him.

That decided Joey. When the right opportunity presented itself again, he'd take a chance.

Opportunity came knocking a week or so later in the shape of a tax inspector called Selwyn Carruthers, who approached Joey. 'We've been watching this warehouse. There's a lot of shortages,' he said.

'No, there ain't,' Joey said, surprised. 'The books are all perfectly above board.'

'All perfectly cooked, you mean,' the inspector said. 'You could find yourself in prison before too long.'

'No. No. I haven't done nothing,' Joey insisted.

'We know who the real culprit is. That's who we'd sooner have.'

'Who?' Joey asked. 'Who?'

'As if you don't know. Your boss, Mr Thompson. He's been fiddling his tax for years. It's got to stop and we're going to stop it.'

There was the answer. They were going to continue their investigation until they had enough evidence against Mr Thompson and wanted Joey to help them. He hinted that Joey could take over the business if they found Mr Thompson was cheating. He wanted Joey to watch and report anything that was wrong. It would be a strain, more so for not letting on to Mr Thompson. Joey wasn't sure he could do this to his boss.

Whole days sometimes slipped past without Jack knowing the time or where it went or what he did. His thoughts would suddenly churn angrily, then they would subside. For no apparent reason, he would burst into tears – he would sooner have killed himself than be seen like that. At such times, there were people he wanted to kill and was afraid he might. Then he was afraid that if he did he'd swing for it. Perhaps he should see a doctor, like his mum suggested, but he didn't want to see anyone, except Brian. He was his only real friend, the only one he trusted or wanted to talk to, and he seemed to be avoiding him. He left the room whenever Jack came in. That hurt more than anything and, wanting Brian's friendship, he tried to snap out of these moods.

A strangely familiar sound rose up from the street to penetrate his thoughts. The hammering on the front door that followed told him it was the low-revving engine of an Austin Jeep, which MPs drove. Suddenly Billy Hill was in the room. 'Get your skates on, son! The MPs are here.'

For a moment, Jack didn't move. He no longer cared enough to run.

'Jack, what you doing?' Billy hissed.

Finally Jack put on his boots as his mum and Cath argued with the MPs in the hallway. Alice was with them, taking the MPs' side, which confused and delayed them as Jack slipped out and across the privy roof, down into the yard and out into the alleyway, hardly drawing breath. He glanced up and down. Mrs Westbrook, who lived next door, caught his eye and signalled him through her back gate.

From her upstairs window Jack saw two MPs enter the alleyway. He wondered how long he could go on dodging them like this. Maybe now was the time to give himself up and do his national service, like Bobby Brown. If he'd gone when they'd first called him up, he'd've been finished with the army long ago, still young enough to go after a boxing career. The thought depressed him and made him more angry. He seemed helpless to make any change in direction.

Jack felt guilty about borrowing money from his mum, and when she had said finally she wasn't holding, he'd felt even more guilty about helping himself from her purse after she'd left the room. Perhaps she knew. All she'd had was about seven shillings and some coppers. He considered taking it all, but took only two shillings and salvaged some of his pride that way.

It was just a loan, he told himself. It got him on to the bus and into Catford dog track. There, he hoped to see someone familiar enough to borrow from, but not so familiar that he had done so before.

He saw no one he knew and instead put the one and six he had left on a dog in the fifth and lost. He considered the Tote and wondered what his chances of robbing it were. One of the bookmakers in the enclosure would be easier. The most obvious choice was Frank Cockain, who was unlikely to turn him in. Somehow Jack felt this man owed him for his missing his fight with Joe Bygraves, who was now the number-one contender. Instead, he decided to try and borrow ten bob from him.

'Tuppence gets you on the bus, son,' Frank Cockain said coldly.

'I just need a few bob till I get back on my feet.'

It was a familiar refrain, and the bookmaker cut right through it. 'How you going to do that? You didn't even have the decency to show up for Peewee's funeral.'

Jack's head hung even lower than it normally did these days. He'd heard his old trainer was gone and felt real pangs of guilt about ignoring the man, but he couldn't face the boxing fraternity after his big disappointment.

'If ever a man died of a broken heart, it was Peewee. He lived to see you get that title. You let him down badly. You let us all down.'

'It wasn't exactly my choice,' Jack said, angry now. 'Give us half a bar anyway, for old times' sake.'

The bookie stared at him for a long time. Jack felt foolish. He knew he wasn't going to give him a brad and thought about grabbing his money satchel off Sammy, the clerk, and running.

'Don't even think about it,' Frank Cockain said. 'I'd put you away.' His attention went to a customer who brought his winning ticket up to the stand. Jack turned away.

Catford dog track was a small wooden stadium right outside the railway station, with a car park covered with holes filled with rainwater. It was run-down, with peeling paint. Jack waited there, looking for an opportunity, he told himself. He tried asking some of the punters for his bus fare, but none of them seemed to be winners. One threw his torn-up betting slips at him.

Fury surged through Jack when he saw the prosperous-looking bookmaker come out through the enclosure gate, rather than the turnstile through which most of the punters passed in their cloth caps. Sammy, who was as old as the bookmaker, was carrying their joint to a brand new Wolseley 6/90 saloon. A number of other cars were jostling to get out of the car park, but it was mostly bikes and motorbikes.

'Come on, Frank. Gimme ten bob,' Jack said, stepping up to them. 'I'll pay you back.'

'Well, I'll say this for you,' Frank Cockain said. 'You're persistent, or just plain fucking stupid.'

'Then gimme the bag, Frank,' Jack said, as menacingly as he could, 'an' you won't get hurt.'

'You think I wouldn't hurt if I lost all my poke? You don't know how much, son.' He paused to light a Capstan cigarette and shook his head.

This wasn't going as Jack had hoped. Maybe he really would have to hurt the old man. He was startled when Frank said, 'You got good-healing skin. There's hardly a mark on you. You thought about going back into training?'

Jack scoffed. 'I need the money.'

'Try working for it like we do, you fucking parasite,' Frank Cockain said dismissively. 'I've done collar all my life, son, and it wasn't to please you. I got you the best chance of your life and you weren't there. No one'll give you sixpence now. So sling your fucking hook and jump in the canal for all I care.'

His hostility winded Jack. He was unmoving as Sam closed the lid of the boot on their gear, then climbed in behind the wheel with the cash bag and slammed the door. Hope of getting this or any other money was fading fast.

'I'll tell you this for nothing,' Frank went on. 'There's a bit of wedge to be made from taking a dive, if you fancy it. People might pay to see you get knocked about.'

Jack turned away, tears welling in his eyes. He wanted to leave quickly before anyone saw him crying. He started towards the station.

'Wait a minute,' Frank said. 'Hold up.' He caught Jack's arm. 'I must be the world's biggest mug, but I like you, son. I always liked you. I hate seeing you like this. Here.'

That sounded like an offer of money and Jack turned back. Frank extended his hand with two sixpenny pieces. 'That'll get you on the bus and a cuppa tea when you get there.' Before Jack could take the coins he let them slide out of his hand into a puddle.

Anger boiled up in Jack. 'Pick them up,' he ordered, with the sort of authority he didn't know he possessed.

'I don't need them, son.'

'Pick them up,' Jack said again and took a step towards him, making the old man hop back.

'So you have got some fight in you, after all. That's good. For a moment I'd wondered.' He stooped and picked up the two silver joeys, then shook the wet off them. He nodded. 'Could you make anyone else do that? If you think you could, I'll give you a bit of work – worth more than ten bob. I need some help dealing with the local teddy-boys. Reputation ain't much good if people don't know who you are any more so you'll have to whack some of this riff-raff for your money.'

Jack felt his spirits lift for the first time in a long while. Then doubt assailed him. He found himself saying, 'You think I can, Frank?'

'Not looking like that. You're a sorry sight and no mistake.' The bookie walked to the car and opened the door. 'Sammy, give him a score,' he said.

'I'll give him my toe up his arse.'

'We'll chalk it down to experience if he's a wrong 'un. He needs a shave and a new whistle, or the rozzers'll think he's a footpad out to rob us.'

'That's exactly what he was planning to do, Frank. You might as well throw this down the drain.' Sammy complained in Jack's hearing as he counted off twenty well-thumbed green one-pound notes. He hesitated before handing them over.

'It's only a score, Sam. It'll get him out of the gutter. Then it'll be up to him whether or not he stays out of it.'

That was exactly where he was, Jack realized. He looked at the money in the bookmaker's hand. If it wasn't for living at home, protected by his mum, he'd be in an even worse state. Enough was enough.

Clothing, like most other things, had come off rationing under the Tories but good cloth was still hard to come by and you needed a tailor who knew someone who could get it, unless you went to Savile Row. Twenty quid wouldn't buy him much there. Instead he went to a man who struggled to make a living altering old clothes or taking them apart and redoing them. His small untidy fluff-filled workshop, that fronted on to Theobald's Road, was lit by a naked lightbulb that burned from the ceiling at all times of day.

Sammy Cohen, whose parents had suffered the fate of many Jews in the Russian pogroms, owned the business. He was tall and round-shouldered, with skin so grey it might never have seen sunlight. Round glasses magnified his eyes which were flecked dove-grey. His room was more like a rag-and-bone yard than a tailor's shop. The only thing that gave away its purpose was the felt-covered cutting bench, the dummy with a half-made jacket on it and the pressing bench with its brass steam cylinder. Clothes were piled everywhere. When Jack told the tailor what he needed, he ran the tape-measure expertly across his shoulders.

'What shoulders,' he sighed. 'I should have such shoulders. I'd be world champion too.'

'You didn't hear the news, Mr Cohen,' Jack said. 'I ran into some tearaways going to the weigh-in.' He realized that for the first time he'd spoken of it without feeling a crushing sense of regret.

Sammy Cohen rolled his eyes. 'Tell me about problems,' he said, obviously full of his own woes. 'I've got a sick wife and every wide-boy who passes my door thinks I should pay him for the privilege. I should go on breathing.' He paused to jot Jack's measurements on a torn-open Weights cigarette packet. There were plenty of those around as the small cigarette never left the tailor's mouth, except when he used the stub to light another. 'If I had such muscles,' he said, still noting figures. 'They swagger in here, like Nazi thugs, demanding a pound for this, or a deuce for that. They prey on us small shopkeepers all the while. How can we get our living when we're bled dry by such leeches?'

'You should go to the police, Mr Cohen,' Jack said. 'That's what they're there for.'

'Please. So we eat, we pay the rent. But now they take my little Leah, these people. I'll get a gun, Jack, and shoot them. I swear I'll kill these beasts.'

Jack saw how agitated the tailor was getting. 'You'd swing,' he told him.

'Should I care? Jack, you're not a father – I think you're not a father. God forbid you are. So I made a mistake. One mistake, maybe two. Times were hard in the war.'

'What did you do? Cut one trouser leg shorter than the other?'

'You mock me, son. Am I so wicked you should mock me?'

Jack felt chastened, regretting having made a joke at this man's suffering. 'What's the problem?'

'I took a little opportunity or two, dabbled on the black-market to help some customers. So I try to be decent. For this my life should be a misery?'

'Keep it nice and wide on the shoulders, Mr Cohen.'

'Ah, such shoulders, like Samson – they need showing off. And a waist like Delilah's. It's as it should be for a man. My money they can take. My Leah . . . They've made her no better than a common prostitute, my pretty little girl child. I pray to my God, give me courage to kill these men – but I'm a coward who fails his little girl.'

His hand was shaking so much he could barely write the figures on the fag packet. Jack caught his wrist and turned through the wraiths of smoke.

'Who are these people? They can't just take your girl. It's a free country.'

'Free? "You keep your trap shut, kyke, or go to prison," those twins tell me. The Krays, they terrorize shopkeepers from here to Mile End.'

All at once Jack couldn't breathe. Panic was crushing his lungs. He needed to get out of the shop fast in case he started to cry. He knew he might.

'Is this why we escaped the Nazis terror raids?' Sammy Cohen went on, catching hold of Jack to make his point. 'Jack, you're crying!'

Panic swamped him now as he tried to flee, but the tailor clung to him like a lover. 'What a man!' he said. 'What a man who can cry for my Leah.' Then he was in floods of tears too, and Jack's fear subsided as he experienced some of the pain this man felt. He knew he had to help him – but how? The righteous anger of this father gave him courage and might get him to the door. What then? He knew he had to start somewhere if he was ever to check the thugs who beset Frank Cockain, but he wasn't sure he could bring himself to go after the Krays.

The address from where Sammy Cohen's daughter was forced to operate was a Peabody Trust tenement that stood behind Old Street in Shoreditch: five red-brick blocks, with an open central staircase rising up four floors. Washing was strung across the paved courtyard on wooden posts between the building, no one apparently concerned about their neighbours seeing what they wore or slept between. Jack ducked under a greying sheet and approached a group of men lounging outside one of the blocks. There were three of them and he saw Ronnie Kray immediately. He tensed, gripping harder on the tailor's lead weight in his hand. From Ronnie's sudden alertness it was clear he had recognized him, and he straightened up ready for action. His two mates did the same. All of them were wearing trilbies and long jackets. A girl clacked past in high heels, seamed stockings and a tight skirt, but no one turned to watch her as Jack approached.

'Where's Leah Cohen?' Jack said, as though he wanted to give her an urgent message. He tightened his grip on the lead, afraid it would slip out of his sweaty palm.

'Who is it wants her?' Ronnie asked, his jowls falling over his high starched collar. His Cupid's mouth puckered into a smirk as he turned to his mates. They smirked too.

Jack held back, uncertain if he was ready to take on all three of them. His eyes flitted between them as he tried to assess who was the most dangerous. 'You got the donah – Leah Cohen. I want her.'

'Oh, why didn't you say? She's a bit busy just now.' Ronnie sniggered, then rubbed his fingers together. 'Let's see your money.'

'I want her now. Where is she?'

The two younger men stopped smiling and glanced at Ronnie like they knew they had trouble on their hands. One stepped into Ronnie and whispered something to him as if he didn't know who he was dealing with.

Irritably, Ronnie Kray brushed him away. His territory was being directly threatened and his hand dived into his trouser pocket. Before he could reach whatever weapon he carried Jack flew at him. His left came up in a feint, then his right with the lead in it drove into Ronnie's fat throat, sending a paroxysm of shock through his body. His mates stared in disbelief for a moment as excitement raced through Jack, making him feel alive for the first time in a long while, buoying him up as adrenalin produced more aggression. He hit Ronnie again and again, wanting to kill him for what he and Reggie had taken from him.

He pulled back now, because he knew he could, then grabbed the fat man by the lapels and yanked him round his left shoulder to smash his face against the wall by the entrance. One of the others jumped on Jack's back and got his arm around the throat. With piston-like energy, Jack drove his elbows into the man's ribs, knocking him off. Then the other man slapped him with a blackjack, a six-inch sewn piece of leather with a lead weight in the end, delivering a deadening blow. His energy began to leak away, like a torch battery running down. As the man swung at him again,

Jack ignored the pain and drove his fist into his face, uncertain how the blow connected or what damage it did. Following through, Jack hit him again with his left, and by then he knew he had hurt the thug. Neither Ronnie nor the other man moved.

Jack was trembling with exhaustion as he put his face tight into Ronnie's busted face. 'Where is she?'

The willowy, olive-skinned girl who sat on the double bed, which took up most of the space in the dingy, narrow room, was the most beautiful Jack had ever seen. She took his breath away and he fell instantly in love with her, not knowing if this was because of herself or because she was the means by which he recovered his manliness. At that moment he saw nothing else, not the fading floral wallpaper, the dirty grey curtains or the stained counterpane, not even the middle-aged man who was removing his trousers. Jack stood in the bedroom doorway unable to speak. Leah sobbed but didn't move, as if passively accepting this was the way her next client had arrived. He wondered if she was drugged. The middle aged man froze as if not knowing whether to pull his pants down or up. Right then, Jack could willingly have killed him for even thinking about violating this girl who was fifteen or sixteen.

He drew back his fist, met the man's eye and pointed to the door. The punter grabbed his clothes and briefcase and fled, trying to yank up his strides.

'Are you Leah?' Jack asked. She nodded. 'Good. Where's your clothes? Get them on, Leah. We gotta leave.'

'I can't,' she said. 'I can't. Look, they won't let me.'

'Get your clothes. We ain't got all day. Your dad asked me to come and get you.' He opened the dark satinwood wardrobe and found a dress hanging there, some shoes and a coat. None of them were right for her, they were too tarty.

'They'll hurt him,' Leah protested, as he dragged her onto the landing. 'They will. They'll kill him.'

Girls appeared from some of the other rooms, none as young

or pretty as Leah. They watched Jack pull her down the stairs, neither knowing who he was nor attempting to stop him.

As they reached the bottom stair the front door of the building flew open and Reggie Kray came at him with an iron pipe. The two men behind him were also armed. Ronnie was in the rear, his face raw and bloody. 'You're dead,' Reggie said.

I'm alive! Jack wanted to shout back.

In the narrow hallway, it was possible for only one person at a time to attack him and Jack felt he could have a good go at them – until Leah grabbed his left arm.

'No! Don't make it worse!' she shrieked, terrified.

Reggie Kray seized his opportunity and whacked Jack with the pipe as he tried to push Leah off. It was a glancing blow, but the second, straight across his left temple, stunned him and hurt like nothing he had ever experienced in the ring. His vision blurred, and he couldn't tell if he was seeing two Reggies or if Ronnie was crowding in for the kill. He swung his right at what he hoped was Reggie and connected with something solid, that immediately gave way and a girl-like scream followed. It was Ronnie making all the fuss as Reggie had been knocked against his brother's injured face. Jack swung again, driving Reggie harder into his twin, who went down, screaming even louder. The others dragged him away. Reggie ran too. They didn't return.

When he turned to get Leah, Jack saw four or five girls, some in flimsy slips, hanging over the banister rails along with tenants, who weren't on the game. Some were clapping. 'Now's your chance, if you want to leave,' he said.

'Get rid of the bloody lot of them,' a woman in a smock said, taking the fag out of her mouth and coughing.

Jack grabbed Leah's hand and dragged her outside half expecting an ambush. There was none.

Jack was a somebody again, with something worthwhile to sell, something people like Sammy Cohen wanted to buy: protection.

What he gave them back was pride, self-respect, and they thanked him for that, not only with the few quid they gave him but their friendship. When he swaggered along the street in his new wide-shouldered Prince of Wales check suit – for which Sammy Cohen wouldn't accept a single copper coin – people greeted him warmly, offered him tea or food, and asked his advice about all manner of things. It was good to feel wanted, and popularity made Jack believe he could do anything, take anyone on. But there was only one person he truly wanted to impress and that was Leah. From her, he received no acknowledgement. She was either not well or avoiding him. He wanted to see her, to know she was all right, and for her to know he was there if she needed him.

'She's upset with me,' Sammy Cohen said, when Jack asked again after Leah. 'She thinks I let her down. All men have let her down, Jack. I don't know what to do.'

'D'you want me to talk to her, Sammy? I'll do anything she wants.'

'What a man,' Sammy said. 'What a friend.'

Jack ached to be more to Leah, even though she was still so young. He'd have to go back into training to stop himself thinking about her.

As he stepped out of the tailor's shop, a mother with a young baby on her arm plunged across Theobald's Road to him. She complained about her landlord who wouldn't mend her roof, which was letting in the rain. Jack followed her to the St Pancras estate, others joining them to tell him about their problems. They went with him to the rent office.

The rent collector, Mr Wiggins, stooped badly, from carrying the heavy rent satchel over his shoulder. He got up from a battered wooden desk, which was dominated by the chained rent-book that he clutched to himself as if it would protect him from his tenants. An elderly clerk sat at a lino-covered counter waiting to take the money.

After listening to what Jack had to say, Mr Wiggins removed

the pipe from his mouth, revealing brown-stained teeth. 'It's no good you coming here like this, Mr Braden.' Jack's reputation warranted respect. 'If I've told her once, I've told her a dozen times. The estate can't deal with her leaking roof while there are rent arrears.'

'Be reasonable, Mr Wiggins. Her babies get wet when it rains.'

Jack's firm but unthreatening tone seemed to give the rent collector the courage to push his case. 'There's a simple solution,' he said, opening the rent-book and finding the appropriate page. He counted off the lines of missed payments with the stem of his pipe. 'She's seven weeks behind. We can't run a business on that basis.'

Jack reached over the counter, unbolted the flap, lifted it and stepped through. Wiggins shrank away. Jack put his hand on the man's shoulder to reason with him. 'We'll go over to her place now and take a look at the ceiling. You can see the buckets of water she collects.'

'Miss Johnson, ring the police at once!'

'They won't save you from a dusting, if that's what it takes.' Jack steered him towards the door.

Mr Wiggins clung to the counter flap. The tenants watched him.

'Let's be reasonable,' Wiggins said. 'Miss Johnson, try Mr Sullivan, the builder, first. Tell him it's urgent. Ask if he can come straight away.'

There was a solution to every problem, Jack found, if you took the right approach. His was always the same: physical presence and muscle. Now he was back on form and training again, he expected it to work every time. He enjoyed it when shopkeepers and strangers alike wanted to shake his hand as he passed.

Later that day, when the situation at the flats had been sorted out to Jack's liking, George Snelling, the butcher, pulled him into his shop. He cut and wrapped a piece of brisket for him. 'Your money ain't any good in this establishment,' he said, even though Jack wasn't offering any.

Brisket was a cheap cut and Jack made no move to take the parcel. 'A bit of rump would set Mum up a treat,' he said. 'She's not been too perky, these past few weeks.'

'Bit of flu, I expect, Jack,' the butcher said. 'There's a lot of it about. They reckon thousands died since prescription charges came in.' He went out to the back and returned with a piece of rump, then sliced off two thick steaks.

'At the rate you're going, son,' Billy Hill said, sliding into the brown-painted booth opposite Jack in the café he used on Gray's Inn Road, 'you'll get every house this side of the river repaired.' He turned to the chalk-faced Cockney who owned the café. 'Cuppa char, Alfie. Plenty of sugar.' He checked what was on Jack's plate. 'He's looking after you all right.' The eggs, sausage, bacon and tomatoes were swimming in fat.

He took a piece of Jack's toast, dipped it into one of the eggs and bit into it. 'Real butter, too. His daughter must be getting a wet bottom from you!' He laughed.

That offended Jack. 'What do you want, Billy? Isn't it a bit early for you?'

'No, I'm an early riser. Nice bit of schmutter you got on.' He reached over to feel the quality. 'I like a man who dresses well. I keep telling Eddie it means he's got places to go. Them two still dress like fairground barkers.' He glanced over his shoulder at Eddie Richardson, who was leaning against Billy's Jaguar, his brother behind the wheel, their shirt collars outside their jackets. Billy was right about them. The only place they'd go unnoticed was in this café or a scrapyard.

'You're a marked man since you put one of the twins in hospital.'

'Which one? I thought I hurt them both,' Jack said, and forked some food into his mouth.

'Fat Ronnie's pride's what you hurt most – and they're well teamed up with Jack Spot. All ponces together.'

'What am I s'posed to do? Start trembling?' Jack said.

'Good luck, son,' Billy said, as the café owner brought him his tea. 'He's getting too big for his boots again. I mean, I can't be everywhere. We should team up. Together we can sort that firm out once and for all. Albert Dimes wants to top him.'

'I thought a bit of thieving did you, Billy. Why you getting involved in the clubs and spiels in the West End?'

'There's a lot of money to be had. The Sabinis are gone, and the Malts, they can't even speak English! Why let Spotty bring the twins in and nick it all? Now's the time to hurt them bad, before they recover. We go over to Vallance Road and top them.'

'They'll get what's coming to them soon enough,' Jack said, 'if they show their ugly mugs around here again – and Spot. He can have their trouble any time of the day he wants it.'

'You talk tough, looking out for a few kyke shopkeepers,' Billy said, gripping his arm, 'but there's only one guv'nor, remember.'

Jack wrenched himself free. 'There is on this manor, that's for sure.'

Breakfast was over, but so, too, was the peace with Billy Hill. Jack knew it had been too good to last.

St Joseph's Orphanage weeped suffering from every brick, every wood panel and piece of polished linoleum. The big, dark forbidding building was run by blue-habited nuns of the Order of St Celia. They ministered to the boys until they were eleven when the brown-clad brothers took over until they left at sixteen. Many went straight into the army as boy cadets.

Tony Wednesday wished he could too. He hated every moment of his time there, and every person, whether nun, brother or fellow inmate. Twice he'd tried to run away and twice he'd set fire to the place. Each time he was caught and thrashed with a leather quirt. The first two beatings were administered by Brother Michael, the second two by Sister Morgan, who hit him far harder than ever the priests did. She was right at the top of his list of people to kill. He hated the way she sucked up to Tony Watling, the policeman, who came regularly to visit him, especially now that he'd been promoted to sergeant, acting like some angel of mercy ministering to his every need. Tony knew what was his most pressing need when he came here. Sister Morgan was always on duty and just going off each time he arrived.

Sergeant Watling arrived at the same time each week, never missing, carrying his folded Mackintosh over his arm and bringing a small brown-paper-wrapped package tied neatly with string. In it were sweets and bits of food, few of which Tony ever saw. The greedy Sister Morgan scoffed most of them.

'Anthony's not in our best books today,' she said, when she led Sergeant Watling and him along the dimly lit, panelled upper corridor to her office. She always referred to him as 'Anthony' when Sergeant Watling came, but as 'Wednesday' or 'boy' at other times. He was wearing too-short, too-tight shorts that chafed the inside of his thighs, but he knew better than to complain. When once he did, the sister told him that was because he'd wet-legged himself. He'd never pissed his pants, and hated her even more for that.

'He gets bigger every time I see him, Sister,' Sergeant Watling said. 'Goodness knows what you're feeding him.'

'They do take a great deal of feeding,' Sister Morgan said. 'It's all we can do to get enough nourishing food into them. This one eats like a gannet. I'd hoped a little more of your influence might have rubbed off on him, Sergeant.'

'I'll take him to a café and stoke him up a bit.' Sergeant Watling held out the string-tied packet. 'Some sweeties. Me and the lads at the station had a whip-round.'

'Say "thank you", Anthony.' Sister Morgan reached for it.

Tony turned his face away and lowered his head so she couldn't see into his eyes. One day she had seen something in them that had frightened her and she had beaten him for it. Now he was learning to hide his feelings, to disconnect them from the muscles in his face so that whatever he felt didn't show.

'Do you want to go out, son?' Watling asked.

'He doesn't deserve a treat, sergeant,' Sister Morgan piped up. 'He's been messing the bed. I'm sure he does it on purpose.'

Tony smiled inwardly, showing nothing on his face.

'Still no offers to adopt him?'

'Who'd want him, apart from a saint like yourself? He's the devil's own, this one, begot of sin—'

Tony slammed his head into her large, round belly. Instantly she boxed his ears, making his head ring. 'Behave yourself, or this policeman will lock you up,' she said. 'And it won't just be in the cupboard over there.' She pointed to the dreaded cupboard at the end of the room.

There were any number of such cupboards around the orphanage, some worse than that one. Other punishments were worse: all the children knew about the ones who disappeared and were buried in the rose garden. The cupboard Sister Morgan shoved him towards was for immediate restraint. It was empty, with a strong door, a lock and no electric light. At least there was a crack in one of the panels that not only let a little light through but allowed you to squint into the room. He didn't feel so desperate there, not like the isolation cupboard in the cellar. In there no light of any kind ever reached you, no sound, no contact of any sort until your release. All you got was a milk bottle of water and a heel of stale bread, with a thunderpot to go in if you couldn't hold it. No day or night existed in that isolation cupboard and Tony hated it more than anything on this earth. He'd been incarcerated there a number of times, listening to the rats scurrying around outside as they smelt the bread and tried to gnaw their way through the door or wall to get it.

With no will to stop himself, Tony hit the sister again. Perhaps he did have the devil in him.

'That's enough! There'll be no nice outing to a café for you.' Sister Morgan thrust him into the cupboard. Darkness descended as the door slammed and the key turned in the lock. Tony begged to be let out, but neither the sister nor Sergeant Watling responded. After a while, he quietened, his throat sore. The two adults were still in the office. He could hear their voices and felt better for their company, better still for seeing them as he put his eye to the crack in the panel.

'You're a saint, Sergeant,' the fat sister said, through a mouthful of sweets, 'truly a saint, bothering with this one as you do.'

'I don't have no family myself, as you know. Like you, all I got is the job.' He gave a little laugh.

'A true vocation.' She took out another sweet and popped it into her mouth. 'Yes, we're so alike, Sergeant.'

After a short silence the policeman said, 'You know, you could call me, Tony. Especially in here, like this.'

'I could, Sergeant. But it wouldn't do to be over-familiar, would it? In case we slipped up elsewhere.'

A nod signalled that he went along with that. There was another silence. Then, without a word, the policeman spread his Mackintosh on the linoleum-covered floor and unbuckled his thick belt. Sister Morgan turned the key in the office door. Then Sergeant Watling undid his trousers and let them drop. Sister Morgan turned back to him but showed no surprise at what she saw. At first Tony thought he was going to make her give him a wank, as some of the older boys made the younger ones do to them. Instead she lifted her stiff, rustling skirts, pulled down her large knickers and stepped out of them. Sergeant Watling moved in close and tried to kiss her, but she brushed him aside. 'We haven't got time for that,' she said. 'Just be quick.'

She lay down on his Mac, pulled up the front of her skirt, then wriggled to get the back out of the way too. Sergeant Watling knelt between her thick white thighs and fitted himself into the top of her legs.

Tony knew what they were doing and got very hot as he watched, his own prick starting to swell. Soon it would be his turn to get wanked by the younger boys.

SEVEN

A black cab arriving on their street was still a rare enough occurrence to get people wondering, and Jack watched out of its window as it drove along the empty road, the kids playing football with a tin can scattering. Usually a cab signalled that someone special was arriving.

He paid the driver and stepped down off the running board as Alice hurried out of his mum's house with a small cardboard suitcase and two brown-paper parcels. John lugged another case and a package.

Gracie chased after them, catching John's arm as if to stop them leaving. 'This is your home, Alice,' she said. 'What's wrong with you, going all that way?'

'My mind's made up, Mum. God helped me.'

'Well, I wish He'd bloody well unmake it, for John's sake.' Gracie turned to Jack. 'Try and talk some sense into her, son.'

'Come on, Alice,' Jack said, like his presence was enough to stop this departure. 'This isn't right. How you going to live up in Manchester with a ten-year-old son to feed and no man?'

'I'm nearly eleven, Uncle Jack,' John Redvers said proudly.

'So you are, John – what d'you want for your birthday?'

'We don't hold with personal frivolity,' Alice said. 'I've been called to do God's work, Jack. He will provide for John and me.'

'Well, at least let me give you a ride to King's Cross in the cab,' Jack offered, 'and a bit of walking-out money.'

'The Lord gave us sound legs, Jack,' she said, nudging John forward. 'We can walk.'

John looked forlornly at the cab. ''Bye, Nan,' he called back.

Gracie ran to him and planted a kiss on his cheek. 'You take good care of yourself, my love.' She kissed him again. 'Don't forget us, will you?'

'We don't go along with displays of personal affection,' Alice said sharply. 'John.' Her tone brooked no argument. John turned away smartly and hurried along the pavement with her, glancing at neighbours who spoke to them.

'What's she doing, Gracie?' Eve Sutton said, coming along the pavement. 'She joining the Sally Army?'

'Worse than that, Eve. Something called the Plymouth Brethren.'

'Oh, is she going all the way to Plymouth, then?'

Gracie didn't answer. She went back to Jack. 'What's all this religious stuff about, Jack? Where's it all going to end? I'm sure I don't know.'

'She'll come to her senses.'

The look Gracie gave him said she didn't believe it, and he wasn't convinced either. Getting more and more involved with her religious set was Alice's idea of coming to her senses. She was one person Jack couldn't persuade.

'Here, I swagged you some eggs,' he said, offering her the bag. 'They got brought straight up from the farm in Kent.'

'You're a good boy, Jack,' Gracie said. 'Why can't they all be like you? Our Cath and her Joey have got it just as bad.'

'What? Religion?' Jack said, surprised – Cath was too practical for that.

'Money's their religion. 'S all they think about – how they can get hold of it, what they'll do with it.'

'Well, you can't get far without it. Joey wants to make something of himself, Mum. You can't blame him for that.'

'He's got a good job. Mr Thompson'll look after him when he retires, of course he will.'

'I wouldn't count on it. Anyway, Joey's smart enough to run that greengrocery warehouse with his eyes closed.'

'He wants more than that. He wants to own it!'

'He should go in with Billy and stick up a wages payroll.'

'What about you, son? What's going to happen to you?'

'I'm doing all right. I make good money. I got more work than I can handle. Things are good, Mum.'

'What about the army lot? They'll catch you, one of these days.'

'They'd need Monty and half his army to do that. Frank Cockain says they'll declare an amnesty for all them what bunked off.'

'I don't know. I don't want to think about anything else happening to my children.'

She let go of Jack's arm and turned towards her front door. As she did so, her right toe stubbed a flagstone and she lurched forward, dropping the eggs. Jack caught her before she fell. 'Mum!' he said in alarm. 'What's wrong?'

Gracie moved her jaw but the words wouldn't come out. She tried again. The frightened look on her face worried Jack. 'It's nothing, son,' she managed, her speech slurred. 'I couldn't lift my foot but I'm all right now. Nothing that a cuppa and a visit from you won't put right.'

Neither put her quite right. Jack went and got Cath when she came home from work at the Co-op, where she was now assistant cashier, and she insisted on calling the doctor out. After all, it was free now.

'It's a mild stroke,' the Maltese doctor said, coming back downstairs from examining Gracie. 'There isn't a lot we can do for it. Plenty of bed-rest and visits from her children and grandchildren will work wonders.'

Brian practically moved in with her. Jack sometimes stayed over too, and thought nothing of it when Brian got into the bed they'd shared when he was younger. He was quite well developed, too well-developed to be cuddling into Jack's back now, and Jack sometimes felt what it did to his nephew. When one night he found himself getting aroused, it scared the daylights out of him. He stopped staying over and began to worry that he might have those tendencies.

*

'Joey!' a voice hissed, as if there was some big conspiracy. Sammy Cohen was on the cobblestones below the loading bay in front of the warehouse. 'Joey!' he said again, beckoning him. 'Do you know what that is?' he asked, pulling a printed blue note out of an envelope. It looked like a cheque.

'It's a Thomas Cook traveller's cheque,' Sammy told him. 'You can cash them anywhere in the world. I know a man who's getting hold of a load of them. He wants two thousand smackers for them.'

Joey glanced behind him, fearful that someone was listening. 'What can I do? I ain't got that sort of money.'

'You could make a fortune.'

'Why don't you?' Joey asked.

'Would I be asking if I had the readies?' Sammy Cohen said. 'Maybe we could take a piece of it. Make some real money instead of letting the Krays have it all.'

But Joey turned him down.

Then Mr Thompson dropped a bombshell that left Joey feeling so angry he could barely cycle home from the warehouse. When he went across a red light on Clerkenwell Road a beat bobby jumped out of nowhere and pulled him over. 'Fortunately there's not much traffic about, sir,' he said, having pointed out Joey's error. 'If there had been you'd be in Bart's. You just be careful in future.'

Joey said he would.

He pushed into the tiny, messy kitchen and stopped to listen to the silence in the house. Cath would be in one of two places – her mum's or her work. She was as driven as he was about work. What a mug, he was, he told himself. Joey, you're a prize chump.

The grill on the cast-iron stove wouldn't light. The gas blew out the first match, but the second ignited it with a bang. Joey filled the kettle from the single tap over the Belfast sink and slammed it on the stove, then lit the hob. The loaf which Cath always managed to cut so it tilted backwards to the board at a sharp angle wobbled as he tried to cut a straight slice. The knife slipped and cut his finger.

He stuck it under the tap. Unwashed dishes were piled in the sink and on the wooden draining-board. As his anger took hold, he knocked a cup, which smashed on the floor. With the dish-rag round his injured finger he tried to put the bread under the grill, but the pan's handle was hot and burned him. He yelled and dropped it.

'Gosh! What's all the swearing about?' Cath came in from the hall with a bag of shopping as Joey picked up the pan with the dish-rag.

'Why don't you get this place tidied up? It's a disgrace.'

'Well, bugger you,' she flared. 'I've been at Mum's most of the day. The doctor said she'd had another little stroke.' There was worry in her voice, which she deflected by going for Joey. 'A lot you bloody well care. Get out the way and sit down – I'll do that.' She took the grill-pan from him without a cloth.

'I don't want to sit down,' Joey snapped back. 'That's not the answer.'

'The answer to what? What's the matter?'

Joey had never known his mother, who died in childbirth with his stillborn sister when he was two. He was looking for a mother when he married Cath. She was two years older than him, but in some ways, he found more of a father than a mother in her: the love she gave was always conditional.

'Joey, what? What's happened? Tell me,' Cath demanded.

'Old man Thompson's selling up – that's what.' It was like the whole world of work and security he had helped to create was only an illusion.

'He can't. He can't after all you've done for him, the rotten sod. You put that business on a sound footing.'

'He needs to get out before the tax people get him. More fool me for not helping them,' Joey said bitterly. 'It's no good working for someone else. You're always their slave, making money for them.'

'Joey, we've been over this a thousand times,' Cath said. 'We haven't got the money to go out on our own.'

'The tax people said if he's put out of the business I'd have a chance of getting it.'

'Whatever they said, it'll still cost money, Joey.'

'I've been thinking about that, how we can double our bit of savings. The other day when Sammy Cohen offered me part of them traveller's cheques he was getting, I should've said yes.'

'What do you know about the black-market? And you know even less about traveller's cheques.'

'I know they're from Thomas Cook's, the big travel firm. He was doing me a favour.'

'You hardly know him, Joey – I mean, Jack helps him out, and he makes Jack's suits, but that doesn't mean he's a solid bet.'

'Sammy's as good as gold. He thinks the world of Jack.'

'He's a Jewboy. Why was he offering you all these black-market cheques?'

'He didn't have the readies,' Joey explained. Even though he'd turned him down before, now the situation was dramatically changed. Joey's livelihood, maybe his entire existence was being threatened. Why couldn't Cath see that?

'Whatever happens, you'll still have your job – someone's got to run that warehouse and there's no one better than you.'

'If my face fits. What if the new owner thinks it doesn't?'

'You're too good at what you do, Joey.'

'Too good at making someone else rich!' Joey spat the words out. 'Twelve hundred pounds he's selling it for. What a sap. Everyone gets rich but Joey Olinska.' Using that name shocked him into a brief silence. He hardly used his family name, not since the immigration official at the Port of London advised him to change it if he wanted to get on. He was seven and spoke little English when he arrived with Great Aunt Frieda, the only other surviving member of his family. She had died in the flu epidemic of 1936. Joey was fifteen, with a good command of the language by then, even though his schooling had ceased a year before. He had taken a job, one of the dirtiest in the East End, cleaning the dust and fluff from under the guillotines in a sack factory. It had meant crawling under the machines and dragging out the thick wodges of flock the knives made as they sheared through the jute. The air was choking and the particles irritated his lungs.

It was there he met Cath, a cutter, earning more than he was. She found him one day under the machine, passed out. If she hadn't seen him before she had started her machine, she'd have sliced through Joey's shoulder. She was the kindest person ever, Joey thought, and he soon fell for the raven-haired beauty. On more than one occasion she had told him not to be so daft, and that she was too old for him. Finally, when she had taken him home and her mother made him inhale Friar's balsam in a bowl of hot water with a towel over his head, Joey knew he'd found a family and that he would marry Cath. It was only a question of when. She had resisted while he persisted in his amorous endeavours and soon after he turned seventeen, she confessed to him she was pregnant.

'Then you'll have to marry me!' was Joey's immediate response.

Cath's father was dead set against it. Her mother argued fiercely in its favour: 'I'm not having a daughter of mine dropping a chavvy without a husband.' Joey held his breath and hoped. Still Cath's father would have none of it. Tiger Braden was how he was known around the docks, and he fought like one.

'You do something about it,' he told Gracie. 'You got rid of enough others in them circumstances.'

'Not my daughter. I'm not putting her through that,' Gracie said.

'Look at him. He ain't a man. He's a boy still.'

'You leave Joey be you rotten sod!' Cath cried, and flew at her father.

The old man smacked her hard around the side of the head, knocking her down. 'Don't you talk to me like that, you dirty little whore!'

He was about to hit her again, when Joey snatched up the poker from the kitchen range and raised it. Just then he wanted to kill

Tiger Braden. 'Touch her again, I'll brain you,' he threatened, but made no move to go further.

Tiger Braden gave him a steady look, then reached out with his left hand and grabbed the poker. He hit Joey across the face with his fist, knocking him down.

'Never threaten it, son, not unless you intend to follow through.' He threw down the poker. 'You're a good man for having a go over her – even though she ain't worth it. What sort of girl would let the likes of you get her in the family way? Strewth! You're welcome to her.'

There were so many times when Joey had wanted to kill that man, and that had been only the first. Although Tiger Braden gave his daughter away in the register office, he barely spoke to Joey afterwards.

Cath was eight months pregnant when, with no one but Joey in the house, she started having contractions. He wanted to fetch help, but she wouldn't let him leave her in case she died. Dying in childbirth terrified her. During the pains, and with waves of fear washing over her, Cath told him how much she hated her father: he had interfered with her from when she was a young girl, going right up to her marriage and beyond. Joey felt sick. Momentarily forgetting that his wife was in labour and his child was coming, he wanted to get that poker, seek out Tiger Braden and smash his head in, as he knew he should have done long before. Cath begged him not to let on, it would kill her mum if she found out. Right then this knowledge was killing Joey; later he'd rejoice at Braden's death, and revisit it again and again in his mind's eye with pleasure.

Too honest, too stupid, too naïve, too gullible, that was Joey Olinska, but he was about to change. The deal with Sammy Cohen would be the first of many. He and Cath would double their money, then double it again. He would work to the first principle of business: buy a piece of cloth for a pound, cut it in half and sell each for a pound. No one would pull the rug from under him like

Mr Thompson ever again. He wasn't yet done with that tricky sod, but would give the tax inspector all the information he could on him.

'The deal with Sammy'll be worth it,' he said. 'You'll see.'

When he saw Sammy Cohen coming up the wooden steps onto the loading bay, Joey knew immediately that something was wrong. This man's whole demeanour was like a GPO telegram – always bad news.

'The party getting the traveller's cheques for us got himself knocked off with them, Joey,' the tailor explained. 'All two thousand pounds' worth. He could hardly tell the rozzers he'd been saving up for his holidays.'

'What about my money, Sammy? That was my entire savings. A hundred and twenty-seven pounds!' His stomach was clenching and he was afraid he might have an accident.

'We had a little flutter, Joey, and it didn't come off. Next time we'll be lucky.'

'No – no!' Joey grabbed him in panic. The reality of his situation and Cath's warning against the enterprise flooded his mind. 'What'll I tell my missus?'

The tailor said nothing, just freed himself and walked back through the warehouse. Joey stared after him like someone demented. After a moment, he ran to the little toilet behind the warehouse, getting there just in time.

The calm with which Cath received the news astonished Joey. He was prepared for a big row. But Cath seemed preoccupied with Brian, who was parading in front of her dressing-table mirror in one of her dresses. In response to his concerns, Cath told him Brian would simply grow out of it. 'It's a phase boys go through,' she reassured him. Never having grown up in a family, and certainly not having experienced any sort of normal boyhood himself, he couldn't argue with Cath. He worried that what went on for so long between Cath and her father was affecting Brian, or what he'd witnessed in Sullivan's yard all those years ago. Joey couldn't begin to guess why it might have turned him into a nancy-boy, though.

'Here,' Cath said to her son, handing him a lipstick.

Watching from the doorway, Joey said, 'Cathy ...' in mild admonishment – he always called her Cathy in such circumstances. 'You'll make him a nancy boy.'

Defiantly, Cath applied the lipstick to Brian herself. 'Like this,' she said. 'Now press your lips together.'

'It's not my fault the bloke got nicked with our traveller's cheques. Sammy Cohen lost his money too, you know.'

'Oh, Joey,' Cath said, 'for someone so brainy, you can be dead slow at times. *Our* traveller's cheques – you don't know if they even existed. Did you see them? Of course not.'

'I'll find out. So help me, I will.'

Billy Hill was the man to discover the truth, and he wouldn't want anything in return, only the power such information gave him and the favour he would be owed. Joey was summoned to Holborn vapour baths where Billy sometimes got a massage. He seemed to enjoy summoning people and making them wait until he was ready to tell them what he knew. So Joey waited.

'Oh, there was Thomas Cook's traveller's cheques right enough, Joey,' he said, as he emerged from the building and walked to a smart new Jaguar parked at the kerb. The tough, muscular Charlie Richardson was with him. Eddie was lounging against the car in his leather blouson jacket. The window was open and the radio was playing Doris Day singing 'Que Sera, Sera (Whatever Will Be, Will Be)'. 'The bloke who was getting them for you did have them when he was pinched.'

'Why was he pinched?' Joey asked desperately. 'Why was he?'

'It was Sammy Cohen, whose collar the police was trying to feel as a favour to the twins – he's been dabbling since the war.'

'I'll shop them,' Joey threatened emptily, not knowing how he would go about it.

Billy Hill laughed. 'You're a mug, Joey. Look at us, son. Where do we live? On Easy Street. You know where that is? Where there's plenty to eat, plenty to drink and money to burn. Right, Eddie?'

'Couldn't be righter, guv'nor,' Eddie said obligingly, and glanced at his brother, who wrinkled his nose.

'Chalk it down to experience, son,' Billy said. '*Que sera, sera*, like the song says – right, muggins?'

He climbed into his car with the brothers and Joey watched them roar away. Muggins was about right. That was what he was. But his problem was that he liked and trusted Sammy Cohen like few other people.

EIGHT

In the deep-set doorway of a cycle shop, Brian shifted his weight from one foot to the other as he watched the entrance to the swimming-baths into which Jack had vanished a short while ago with Frank Cockain. A boxing tournament was taking place and Jack said they were fixing fights. He was unsure about going in after him on his own in case Jack told him to sling his hook. He couldn't bear that. In any case, he was old enough to go around with his uncle now that he'd left school. With the pocket money his mum gave him, he could walk in and pay his half-crown like any other punter – only he wasn't any other punter: some people recognized him as Jack's nephew, and that was all right because it sometimes meant he was given things for free; he enjoyed it more when they thought he was Jack's brother, which, in Brian's eyes, was more grown-up than being a nephew. In the window he noticed a poster for the latest Hercules sit-up-and-beg bike, showing a smiling black boy hurtling away from a lion. That was what he needed – confidence.

Finally making a decision to go in, Brian started across the road as a shiny grey Jaguar 2.8 approached and beeped its horn. He swung sound irritably as the car stopped. Billy Hill hopped out, with Charlie and Eddie Richardson.

'Going to see the fight, m' ol' china, are you?' he asked. 'Come on, I'll save you a tosheroon.' He walked past the fat woman in the booth with a wink. She smiled back, tore off four tickets and handed them to Brian as if he was one of Billy's gang.

Elation ran through him and he tingled. Then he worried that it might get back to Jack before he could explain how it happened. There was still bad blood between Billy and Jack. Jack was too independent, getting too much of a reputation for Billy's liking. People talked about Jack Braden, rather than Billy Hill, as the man who sorted out problems. These days, Billy was too busy knocking over bank messengers and being fancy in the West End to help anyone locally.

Brian held back a little as Billy strolled down the aisle between the chairs where punters were watching a black lightweight slug it out with a great white hope, Terry Spinks. They were putting on a reasonable show, but no one's fortune would be made: only half the seats were taken. Billy seemed to know a lot of the punters and the focus of attention swung to him as he greeted them. Brian felt even more self-conscious, especially when Jack glanced round from his ringside seat and fixed Billy with a look. Brian thought about diving into a seat to show he wasn't with them, but he wanted to be nearer Jack.

'Here he is, you lucky people,' Billy said, pretending he'd only just noticed Jack. 'Look who's here! The saviour of Hoxton himself!' Some of the nearby punters smiled as Billy ruffled Jack's curly hair. 'Only a tosheroon to touch the saviour and all your troubles are small ones.'

'Sit down and watch the show, Billy,' Jack snapped.

Billy stepped back, everyone's eyes on him now, not on the boxers. 'Hey, it's me, son, the guv'nor, not some old mug the cat dragged in.'

Frank Cockain glanced at his clerk, Sammy, as if to say, 'We may as well shut up shop.'

There was an empty aisle seat two rows behind Jack and Brian slipped into it. He waited out the next tense moments as Billy shaped up to Jack. 'We'll have a bit of sorting out here, shall we?'

'Why don't you turn it in, Billy?' Frank suggested.

'Who's gonna make me?'

'He's working for me. We're trying to get a living.'

'You're wrong there, Frank,' Billy snarled, the charm gone. 'He's working for *me* from now on – or he does his call-up.'

With that Jack sprang out of his seat and shoved Billy in the chest. The Richardsons closed in, ready for action.

'The best day's work you ever did was walking out on Mum,' Jack told him, loudly enough for others to hear. 'I don't have to worry about putting it on you no more.' Then he jabbed him with a left, too fast for anyone to see. Certainly Billy didn't see it coming as he was knocked back against the ring.

Eddie Richardson, the more hot-headed of the two, stepped forward. 'Pack it up, Jack,' he advised, 'or you'll get trouble.'

'Stay out of this. It's family.'

That presented Eddie with a dilemma. As a rule you didn't get involved in family matters, but he and Charlie worked for Billy. The atmosphere was electric. Now the boxers in the ring had stopped to watch, and the ref couldn't get them started again.

Charlie, the older and steadier of the brothers, stepped in. 'Then let's behave like it's family.' The words were barely out of his mouth when a right hook from Jack caught him in the side of the jaw and spun him. Then Jack let fly at Billy with a left and a right, before he shaped up to Charlie, who was recovering and reaching into his pocket for his blackjack. The punters were all on their feet now. This was a much better fight than the one they'd paid to watch.

But Billy stopped it. 'Turn it in, Jack,' he said magnanimously. 'These people have paid good money to be here tonight. They don't want to see you scrapping.'

No one dared contradict Billy, but no one agreed with what he said either.

Suddenly it was all over, and Billy left with the Richardsons. Brian found himself tagging on to Jack as he walked out of the building with the bookmaker, past some posters advertising wrestling.

'You'd better find another line of work, son,' Frank Cockain was saying. 'Your old man's put the kibosh on you doing any more for me.'

'He's not my old man, Frank,' Jack protested. 'How many times have I got to say that?'

'Well, I can't get between him and Spot while they slug it out over who runs the West End. I'd be out of business. I'm sorry, Jack.' There was a real feeling of regret coming off the old man. He reached into the bag Sammy was holding and offered Jack two fivers. 'There's a few bob for your trouble.'

Brian stood at Jack's side and watched the old man go. For a moment, he thought his uncle was going to cry – but he was too tough for that. 'Does that mean you're working for Granddad Billy now, Jack?' he asked.

'Him? Not on your life,' Jack said, as if it was the most natural thing in the world for Brian to be there with him. 'He's not a quarter the man your real granddad was. Tiger Braden would have put him away in two seconds.'

Mum and Dad put Granddad away in Sullivan's yard – the words were on the tip of Brian's tongue, waiting to be said. Then, finally, he would have rid himself of the horrific images that were always lurking in his mind, dragging him down. Unsure how to escape his thoughts, Brian said, 'Mum says Billy's got money coming out of his ears.'

'That won't stop him getting a good hiding one of these days.' Brian smiled as Jack put his arm around his shoulders and steered him away. The contact between them gave Brian a warm sense of belonging. He wanted more than anything to be with Jack's gang. But nothing lasted for ever, except the memory of that night his granddad was killed. It was all he could do not to tell Jack. But Jack would kill Brian's mum and dad, and he would have to help. Better to stay quiet.

The bell for 'time' caused not a flicker of an eyelash, much less a pause in the bar, which was still adorned with boxing pictures, none of which made Jack feel nostalgic. That life was behind him now.

'Come on, gents and ladies. Let's have them glasses,' Cyril, the landlord, pleaded. 'I'll lose my licence.' Still no one made any move to leave.

Win Booker was across the room. Jack had noticed her the moment he walked in. She looked like Diana Dors with her short, top-curled bleached hair, her large breasts pushing against her tight polo-neck jumper. She had given him a friendly smile as she returned from the ladies' to join the older man she was sitting with. Her glances his way told Jack that she and her bloke weren't getting on and he wondered if he should do anything about it. Someone had told him Win was now a laundress, but then no one ever had a good word to say about her. She was pretty in a brassy way – he wouldn't have minded helping her out tonight.

'Jack.' Sammy Cohen tapped his arm. Suddenly he remembered Leah, who he still thought about from time to time.

'Jimmy Jacobs said you was just what the doctor ordered. A money-lender giving *you* money! He asked me to give you this.' He offered Jack a wedge of money, which Jack tried to push away, but Sammy wouldn't let him. 'It's business, Jack. He's still in business thanks to you. Those teddy-boys haven't been back.'

'Cannon Street Road's a long way from here, Sammy,' Jack said. 'I can't look out for him regular.'

'So, we'll see what happens.' He closed Jack's fingers around the money. 'I hear you got some butter.'

''S five bob a pound,' Jack said. He knew the routine with Sammy and waited for his pained expression. 'I got instant coffee too. It's the latest from the States. You put powder in the cup and add hot milk.'

'It won't catch on, mark my words. Coffee you make in a pot.'

'All the coffee bars are going for it.' He had dealt with Sammy Cohen many times and knew this was how he negotiated. Talk about anything but the price. Get the buyer to like you. 'How's your girl getting on?' Jack asked.

'Her father should know?' Sammy said in disgust. 'The

government makes adult education available to everyone – it's free – but it steals girls away from their mothers. Such big ideas she gets from night school.'

The image of Leah Cohen, so desirable and pretty, still haunted him.

'Such an ungrateful girl. Now she wants to be a psychologist as well as a nurse.'

Jack nodded, his attention going across the bar as the man with Win Booker got up angrily and left.

'She's pretty – for a shikseh,' Sammy Cohen said, following his gaze. 'I'll take twenty pounds of butter at two shillings.'

'Not even for you, Sammy,' Jack said. 'The very best I could let it go for is three.'

'Such a businessman, Jack. Such a shrewd head. Drop it round to the shop.' He finished his drink and walked out.

Again Jack found his eyes straying to Win Booker. She smiled and came over to him. 'Walk me home, Jack?' she asked. 'M' dad's on nights.'

That was invitation enough for him to buy a half-bottle of Booth's gin to take back, but they didn't waste much time drinking. The bedroom in Win's house was colder than church and he made love to her in his vest under the counterpane. The clock next to the gin bottle read ten past one by the time Jack was done and he hadn't paused for a moment to think about Win's needs. His breathing was hard, hers calm and steady.

'I expect you woke half the bleedin' street.' She laughed. Jack suspected she was long past caring what people living in their street thought of her. 'You do like me a bit, Jack, don't you?'

'What d'you think?' He put his arm around her and pulled her close, feeling her breath on his neck. Suddenly the erection he remembered getting when Brian was curled into his back made him hot and uncomfortable. To dispel the image, he lifted her slip, put his hand at the top of her legs and eased them apart, then climbed on top of her again.

'Oh! Oh. Oh!' Win cried out, so loudly that Jack worried she'd woken the other half of the street. 'Oh, Jack, Jack . . .' She was clinging to him, her legs clamped round him as her body rocked.

A little later, he tried to ease himself off Win. 'I'd better make tracks.' She held on to him tightly. 'You'll always be my champ, Jack,' she said. 'You will. You're the only one who ever stuck up for me. He never did – he was always jealous when I went with boys. I'll kill him one of these days.'

'Who?' Jack said. 'Who you talking about?'

'Him, of course. That toe-rag who calls himself a father. He killed my mum, he did. She couldn't take it any more.' Mrs Booker, Jack knew, had died of cancer, but he didn't say anything. 'I'm gonna move to Cable Street over in Wapping. A friend's getting me a room there. You can look me up any time of day or night. I won't charge you anything.'

Despite being told she'd dropped the laundry for money these days her words still shocked him. She saw his look. 'Oh, you needn't be so surprised,' she said, and sat up. As she did so, the springs on the bed boinged and they missed the sound of a bicycle slamming against the wall outside, but not the door being tried.

'Oh, God!' Win cried. 'It's m' dad.'

'I thought you said he was on nights!'

Jack dived out of bed and into his trousers like a fireman. His next priority was his shoes and he'd just got them on when Ted Booker roared up the stairs and threw open the door. He was even bigger now than when Jack had last seen him and was wearing the familiar white bib-and-brace overalls. Removing the thick leather strap from round his waist, he closed on the bed. 'You mucky little whore,' he said, directing his venom towards his daughter. 'Your mum would turn in her grave if she knew—'

'I'm over twenty-one,' Win protested. 'I can do what I like.'

'Not in my house you don't. Not with this dirty bastard!' He lashed at Jack and the belt buckle caught him under the eye, cutting him and sending him off balance. He crashed into the dressing-table, scattering pots and face powder. Win screamed and scrambled off the bed, distracting her dad.

Recovering quickly, Jack shaped up to the baker, guessing he was giving away four stone. The difference was, he was fit. 'Pack it in now, Mr Booker, 'fore I hurt you.'

Driven by blind fury, Win's father grabbed him in a crushing bear-hug and squeezed and squeezed, trying to crush the life out of Jack. All Jack could do to retaliate was gouge at the other man's face, then bring up his knee into his groin. The baker fell back on the bed breathless and in pain.

'Go!' Win squealed. 'Before you have to kill him!'

She seized her father and held him as Jack grabbed his clothes and tried to run. Booker backhanded her, then threw himself at Jack again as he tried to get out through the bedroom door. Jack turned back, dropping his clothes, and let go a series of jabs. Bam, bam, bam. Booker was stunned. and fell against the dressing-table, where he grabbed a large white glass pot of Pond's face cream. He swung round with it and smacked Jack in the left temple, knocking him to the floor. Dazed, Jack lost all sense of where he was, but reached into his pocket for his flick-knife. The blade snapped out as the baker hit him a second time with the pot, which shattered against his head. He reached up and felt blood and broken glass in his hair.

After a few moments his head was clearing, and Win was screaming as her father laid into her with his belt. Staggering to his feet, Jack caught the strap and pulled him off balance. Win scrambled away. Jack tried to follow but the baker got him in another bear-hug. In his weakened state Jack could feel all strength being crushed out of him – until Booker gasped and crashed to the floor, releasing him. Then Jack saw his knife sticking out from between Booker's ribs. There was silence apart from his own heavy breathing.

It dawned on him slowly that Win had stabbed her old man. He couldn't pretend to be sorry. 'I think you've topped him, Win,' he said, checking to see if the baker was breathing.

'He was going to kill you, Jack.' They heard the familiar bell of a police car in the distance. 'You'd best scarper, before they get here.'

'Don't be daft – I can't leave you like this.'

'He had it coming. He did. Go.'

Jack hesitated, then picked up his clothes, pulling a sock from under Booker, and ran.

When he reached the empty street he thought about ducking into his mum's house two doors away, but he didn't want to worry her so he turned in the opposite direction – a wrong move. He hadn't gone twenty yards before a black Wolseley police car turned into the street, its bell ringing. There were several parked cars, including the new square-shaped Ford Prefect, but they were all too far away to hide behind. He tried a neighbour's door – no one would mind him popping through to avoid the rozzers – but it was locked. The police car braked and the two buttonmen sprang out. Jack knew neither and thought about fighting them, but decided to try to bluff his way out instead.

At the police station, a sombre, red-brick building with anti-shrapnel grilles from the war still fixed to the windows, the bluff ended when Sergeant Watling was called in. He was friendly enough and made sure Jack got a cup of tea with plenty of sugar and a bun from the afternoon shift that by two o'clock in the morning was more than a bit stale. Jack was grateful for it – he hadn't eaten since lunchtime.

'How about you look that way, Mr Watling,' Jack said, 'and I scarper?'

'I can't do that, son,' the old policeman said. 'Not any more. We won't put you in a cell, though. Not you, Jack. You can wait in there.' He showed him into the long, narrow charge room and left a young policeman to watch him.

There, Jack found a scarred wooden bench, which was shedding splinters, and a high wooden desk that you'd need to stand behind or have a high stool – there was no stool. The only other item was a clock that had been made in Colchester and had a loud tick. There were no windows, just a door at either end.

'That one leads directly to the cells,' the policeman said, seeing him look there.

Jack settled on the bench to wait. An hour passed with nothing happening. He counted every painted brick in the long wall opposite and suspected the policeman was doing the same. It didn't make the time go any faster. He inspected his grazed knuckles, then cautiously felt his blood-matted hair. The cut on his head would heal in a few days, as would the one on his cheekbone.

At last the door opened and a large man of about thirty came in. Jack recognized him immediately as Detective Inspector Ken Drury. He had been on Billy Hill's payroll until he'd got too greedy and started coming almost every other day for his wages. There was a deep cleft in his square jaw, like Kirk Douglas's, and his blue eyes seemed to be laughing and looked out of place with the rest of him. He was an inspector now and had gained weight with his rank. Sergeant Watling was right behind, carrying a heavy book with a chain attached to it.

'You're out of luck, duck,' Drury said. 'You've gone and killed that baker. It'll be the swinging job for you.'

'What are you telling me? I hardly touched him,' Jack said, suddenly fighting for breath.

'Well, you can't say the same about his daughter, Jack!' Sergeant Watling winked.

'What's happened to Mr Booker?' Jack asked.

'Oh, *Mr* Booker now, is it? As if you didn't know, duck,' Drury said. 'He died in the ambulance on his way to the hospital.'

Still he couldn't breathe. Jack looked at the older man, wanting him to say it wasn't true.

Sergeant Watling gave a helpless shrug.

'That's not the worst of it, duck,' Drury said. 'He named you as the one what stabbed him. There's nothing stronger than a deathbed statement. You'll swing all right.'

There was a long silence as the two policemen let that settle over Jack. He was wishing more than anything that he'd gone into the army and done his time when he was called. The thought of losing everything, the respect, the friendship, the money, his life, closed over him, like a suffocating blanket.

'You'd better have some more tea, son,' Sergeant Watling said.

'He'll need something a lot stronger than tea, Tony,' DI Drury said. Then to Jack: 'D'you want to make a statement, duck?'

'What? He cut my head. He hit me with a glass pot.'

'Is that why you killed him?'

'He was beating up Win. He'd been shagging her all her life.'

'Like half the street. Is that why you decided to top him, is it?'

'Yes,' Jack replied, confused. 'No, no, I didn't. I just tried to stop him hitting her and me. Look, does Mum have to know? I mean, she's not been well.'

'We had to send a policeman round there. The whole street knows, son,' Sergeant Watling said. 'I'll let you know when she gets here. Meantime, I'll see about that tea.' He left the room.

'So what about that statement, duck?' DI Drury asked.

Instinctively Jack wanted to defend himself, as he had done all his life, but that would mean saying Win had killed her father. In his mind's eye he saw her then, looking up from the floor, telling him to scram, trying to save him. So typical of Win.

'There's nothing more to say, Mr Drury.'

'If you've got an ounce of sense, duck, you'll make a full confession. We'll see if we can't reduce the murder charge to manslaughter. If it's argued in court that it was self-defence, you could be out in six or seven years.' He waited. 'What d'you say?'

Jack closed his eyes and leaned back against the wall. He was tired and his head hurt. He wanted Drury to go away. Maybe if he gave him a statement he would leave him alone. He found himself shaking his head.

'You're as thick as that piece of shit you call your old man.'

Jack looked up sharply, puzzled.

'Billy fucking Hill, that's who. You'll both end up in the same boat, if I have my way – at the end of a rope.' Then, to the young policeman, Drury added, 'Watch yourself with this dog turd.' He went out.

Jack closed his eyes and dozed, aware all the while of the ticking clock, his life running out. Mr Pierrepoint, the hangman, carefully fitted the noose around his neck and tightened the knot so he couldn't breathe– He woke with a start, gasping.

'Easy, son,' Sergeant Watling said. 'I brought you some tea and a bit of good news. That girl of yourn's put you in the clear. Said she stabbed the dirty old bastard 'cos he'd been poking her since she was a nipper.' He sounded angry.

'What's she gone and said that for? You believe her?'

'Well, the prints on the knife support her story. We only found one thumbprint of yours on the blade release. All the rest were hers. That's some donah you got there, Jack. Very brave.'

'What'll happen to her, Mr Watling?'

'She'll be charged with manslaughter–'

'No!' Jack protested. 'She should go free.'

'I got no argument with that, son, none at all. She'll be charged, then released, I daresay. I don't suppose anyone will want to spend time and money bringing it to court. Now we'd better get the police surgeon to take a look at that cut on your head.'

Next Drury was shaking him awake, telling him the police would hold him until the army came for him – 'Unless you want to do a deal, duck?'

'What sort of deal? Plead guilty to murder?'

'Don't be clever with me, or you'll be down in a cell for a proper thrashing before the army drags you off.'

'It ain't fair, them getting me like this.'

'That's my feeling precisely. You know, I don't like your old man . . .' He waited to see if Jack would react, and when he didn't, he went on '. . . and I know you don't, so why don't we get shot of him good and proper? Then we'll see what we can do about this little pickle you're in. You help me to collar Billy Hill, Jack, and you're free to go. You walk right out. No army, no charge. Nothing. A free man.'

'How could I do that?' Jack said angrily, feeling the forces of desire and revulsion in conflict and pulling him apart. He wanted so badly to walk out of that police station.

'We still want him for the Clerkenwell post-office-van robbery,' Drury said. 'I'm determined to put it on him, Jack. Help me, help yourself.'

Sick to his heart and disgusted that he was actually contemplating coming copper, Jack gave him a long stare, but didn't trust himself to speak.

'I know you don't think much of rozzers,' Drury said, 'and who can blame you? It's not a nice job we sometimes have to do. But I always try to be fair – play a straight bat.' He licked his lips anxiously. 'What do you say now, duck? There's the door. You're free to walk away, take your chances with the army – troops'll be going out to Suez if things get any worse. Think about my offer. Billy Hill has to go away.'

Jack folded his arms across his chest to hold in the voice that was trying to scream, 'Yes! I'll take the deal.' With a great effort of will he shook his head.

'I thought you'd respond like that, you stupid berk. Well, we'll hold off calling the army until the morning,' Drury said. 'We'll see if you change your mind overnight. I think you will, duck.'

Jack didn't get a wink of sleep. He spent the night wrestling with Drury's proposition. He tried to convince himself that Billy was ready for a fall, and that his mum, who still wasn't properly recovered, needed her son around. But he couldn't do it. Not even when Gracie arrived at the police station with Brian to talk to him.

'It's not you they want, Jack,' Gracie said, across the small table in the interview room clutching his hands in hers. She was looking tired and grey with worry. Jack wanted so much to give her what she asked – and Brian, who was in tears. 'Think about their offer, son. I know it's hard to trust a copper, but Sergeant Watling's a decent sort. Remember how he's kept an eye on that nipper in the orphanage all this while. Give them what they want, son,' she urged. 'Don't worry about Billy. He knows how to do time. You get your freedom.'

'Do the deal, Jack, for Nan's sake,' Brian begged.

Tears stung Jack's eyes. He was suddenly terrified that he'd never see his mum again if he didn't do as she begged. 'I can't, Mum. I can't come copper like that.'

Gracie pulled his clasped hands across the table and kissed them, as if, despite everything, she was proud of him. 'I'll sell the house, if I have to – sell all that tom Billy give me. We'll get you a top mouthpiece.'

All three turned as the door opened and two Military Policemen in brilliantly shined boots and glaring white belts and gaiters walked in, accompanied by DI Drury. Jack jerked backwards, as if given an electric shock. Gracie flew to them, Brian at her side. 'No!' she said. 'Mr Watling said you'd give us a chance to talk to him properly.'

'How long does it take to say goodbye?' the detective asked.

'You can't have him! You can't!'

'It's all right, Mum,' Jack said. 'Take her home, Brian.'

Gracie screamed as one of the MPs snapped heavy steel manacles on to Jack's wrists and turned a key to lock them.

Jack wouldn't look at her as they led him away. If he glanced back he might lose it – and that would haunt his army days.

NINE

The lead in his pencil snapped when he pressed too hard writing some figures, then on a second pencil. Joey Oldman was growing ever more desperate as the tax inspector's deadline for him to point the finger at Mr Thompson drew nearer. He wasn't worried about losing his job: with his head for figures and willingness to work hard, he could always find another, but that would leave him no better off. He knew how sound this business was and he wanted to buy it – whether from the Inland Revenue or Thompson. The problem was he didn't have the twelve hundred pounds that Thompson wanted for the lease and goodwill. Perhaps it would be less now the government had opened its investigation, but even half of that sum was too much for Joey to get hold of. He had to give up Thompson to the taxmen for whatever he could get out of it.

'Buying the business sounds like a lofty ambition, son,' Selwyn Carruthers, the tax inspector, said, sipping tea from his saucer in a café on Commercial Street across from Spitalfields. He was in his forties, an unsmiling man who never seemed to blink from behind his thick glasses. 'If you've got that sort of money, perhaps we'd want to take a close look at you too.'

'I haven't. I'd borrow it,' Joey said. 'And I could have stolen that amount twice over from Mr Thompson, the stupid old fool.'

'I think you're an honest man, Mr Oldman,' Carruthers said and poured more of his boiling hot tea into the saucer.

The porters who used the café did that – the tea was always too hot to drink and, on piecework, they were invariably in a hurry. Joey had never seen anyone like a tax inspector do it. Perhaps he was trying to fit in and not be noticed.

'It'll be ours to sell if we don't recover revenue to the tune of one thousand two hundred and forty-nine pounds, fifteen shillings. The fine on top could double that.'

'I don't know if it'd be worth that much to me or anyone else,' Joey said, as the man opposite continued to sip his tea, staring at him. He felt pressured by those unblinking eyes and his cheeks reddened. He didn't understand why he felt guilty. 'Give me a go, Mr Carruthers. At least that way you might get some of your money.'

Carruthers waited, his face expressionless. Then he said, 'Will you help the government to put your boss inside?'

Joey closed his eyes as if to help him avoid making such a decision. This was the moment of truth he knew would be coming from the minute he started along this path.

'No? Then how much would you consider paying?'

Without hesitating Joey said, 'Eight hundred pounds.'

'That's a lot less than the government's owed, but if you're prepared to get us information that assists our case we'll accept that price. Look, I'll delay making any move for, say, two weeks. If not, I'll recommend the government accepts no less than fifteen hundred pounds. That's a fair offer, son.'

Reprieve was a wonderful feeling, but it was short-lived. Joey went looking for the money from people he knew to avoid thinking about the second part of the deal. He swallowed his pride again and again, going back to those who had turned him down before. Most of all, he hated returning to the bank. Mr Griffith, the manager, with his Hitler moustache and too-tight starched collar, made him feel even smaller than he had before.

'So, tell me, what's changed, Mr Oldman? Has the man from Littlewoods Pools called at your door? Or a wealthy aunt died and left you a legacy?' He lit a Senior Service cigarette while he waited for Joey to answer. 'You people come over here, with your funny ways, and expect Martin's Bank to lend you money on your word.'

Joey hated this man more than he hated anyone for calling him 'you people', for making him feel like a thief. He wanted to tell him he was helping the government catch a real thief, that he'd been in England for more than twenty years, had learned the language and customs and loved the young queen. Instead he kept quiet, but he was determined to show the bank manager and all the others that he could make it to the top.

His mother-in-law didn't have the money he needed, of course. Neither did Sammy Cohen – the tailor's preoccupation was Jack, how he was getting on in the army, when he might have some leave to come and help him. The Hoxton boys, who worked for the Kray twins, were cutting up rough, making demands he couldn't meet. Finally Joey steeled himself to approach Billy Hill again. He could come up with the money easily, but anything legitimate seemed alien to him.

'Think about it for when you retire,' Joey suggested. 'I do the work, you count the lolly rolling in.' Then he changed tack. 'Do it for Cath's sake. It'll give her a bit of security.' They were in the Crown, which Billy used as his office. 'You like her, and I know how much she likes you. Do it for her.'

Billy glanced at the young woman with him. 'She's like a daughter to me,' he said.

That didn't stop her real father, Joey almost said.

'If it's such a good investment, son, try the banks.'

'They don't lend to the likes of me. Not that sort of money.'

'Then get a gun, Joey. There's plenty to be had still. Stick them up.'

'Don't think I haven't thought about it,' Joey said.

'That's the way,' Billy said, and laughed. 'Come and see me when you've got one lined up. I'll give you a hand.'

He winked and took the woman's arm and steered her out of the pub.

If Joey had been a drinker he might have drowned himself in alcohol, but even in his deepest despair he couldn't understand why men did this. Now, looking around the bar, he could see several men, a lot of whom were out of work, sucking pints and shorts like they were from their mothers' tits. They were losers and Joey didn't want to be associated with them.

Suddenly the door burst open and Billy Hill rushed back in. He reached inside his coat pocket, pulled out a large wad of notes with an elastic band round them and stuffed the money into Joey's shirt. 'Sounds like a shrewd investment,' he said. 'I'm in. Keep it dark.'

With that he leaped the bar, like Errol Flynn in *Robin Hood*, and disappeared out through the back. The landlord didn't bat an eyelid, not even at the sound of the bell peculiar to police cars. Moments later the door crashed open again and two uniformed policemen came in, with the tall, square-headed Detective Inspector Drury. 'Where is he? We know he came in here.'

No one bothered to answer as the police hurried through the room, fumbling with the bolt on the counter hatch, then going out at the back. No sooner had they vanished than Joey hurried to the gents'. He threw up in the single urinal with cigarette ends floating in it. The tiny space with its tar-stained cream wall began to spin and he pressed himself to the door to stop himself falling over, he was shaking so much. He reached inside his shirt and touched the money to make sure it was real. It was, and had a steadying effect.

Walking on air wasn't something Joey could ever claim to have experienced, but that was how he felt for the rest of the day. His instinct was to go to the warehouse and cement the deal with the taxman right away, but Cath thought differently. 'You should wait,' she advised. 'Don't look too keen.'

She held up the notes to the light to inspect the watermarks, then Brian counted the money, and recounted it. He handled the large white five-pound notes so often that Joey was afraid he'd wear them out.

'It's definitely all there, Dad,' he said, with a smile as bright as sunshine. 'Nine hundred and forty-one pounds and ten bob.' He started the count again, unable to leave it alone. Suddenly he looked up. 'Why did he give you an odd amount?'

'It must be to pay for legal costs,' Cath said.

'But why'd he give it you now,' Brian persisted, 'I mean, after he'd turned you down?'

'He changed his mind, Brian,' Cath said firmly. 'Billy's like that. Leave it alone.'

'Your mum's right,' Joey chipped in.

But now Cath's face was etched with worry.

'What's wrong with you?' Joey said impatiently. 'What d'you want me to do? Turn him down? Give it back?'

'Of course not. I want you to get a place of your own. I just don't want you to come a cropper.'

'It's not forged, is it, Dad?' Brian asked.

'No. How could it be? Forgery's not Billy's game.' Joey held up some of the notes to the naked lightbulb in Gracie's kitchen. A flypaper stuck with struggling insects hung alongside it. As far as Joey could tell, the notes were good. He collected them up, squared them on the table and banished doubt from his head. 'Maybe I should get on the blower to that tax inspector.'

Cath didn't say anything, which Joey knew meant something. 'I'd like to get it tied up,' he said.

'You gonna be able to squelch on old man Thompson like they want?'

'What's he gonna tell me when the government close him down because he's on the fiddle? "Sorry, Joey, I didn't think I'd get caught"? Not on your nelly. He won't give me or you or Brian a thought. He's just as likely to say it was me what was on the fiddle.'

There was no phone in the house so Joey fished in his pocket for coppers and the slip of paper with Selwyn Carruthers's number on it.

'How you going to say you came by so much?' Cath asked.

'I'll tell him people invested in me.'

'"What people"? he'll ask.'

'I'll tell him m' father-in-law's putting up the money.' Joey waited for her reaction. The face Cath pulled was enough. He almost panicked, feeling trapped with so much money – money that should be solving his problems, not making them worse.

'Perhaps I'll sleep on it. I'll talk to Sammy Cohen. The best thing might be to wait, salt it into a few different bank accounts then give the taxman a kite when we do the deal.'

The hammering on Gracie's door just before dawn was immediately incorporated into Joey's anxious dreams. He slept with one hand on the money under his pillow, fearing someone was coming to take it. Then Cath was shaking him and telling him the police were at the door.

'What do they want? Your mum's all right, is she?'

'I'd hardly think so with all their racket,' Cath said. 'Get up and see to them.'

With an effort, Joey pulled on his trousers and padded down the narrow stairs. When he opened the front door four policemen were standing there, three in uniform. The fourth was DI Drury, who didn't wait for an invitation but pushed straight in. 'You know what we come for, duck,' he said.

At once the colour drained from Joey's face and he felt sick. He could hear Cath at the top of the stairs telling Gracie everything was all right, that she should go back to bed, and Brian was there too, reassuring his nan. He had grown up so much and so fast since Jack had gone.

'Come on, where's the money, duck? If you don't tell us you'll get as much time as Billy's facing.'

Joey couldn't lie easily and certainly wouldn't be able to hold out under questioning.

'What is it you're looking for?' Cath asked.

The police didn't say. Instead they started to search the house. Downstairs first, in front of Joey, Cath and Brian. They began in the scullery, then went outside to the privy, and came back into the kitchen, where DI Drury pointed to things and the uniform policemen searched, opening cupboards and turning out drawers.

They found nothing suspicious – mainly because Jack was away and they weren't getting stuff on the black-market. Billy Hill had kept his distance since Gracie had been ill.

In the parlour, they found five gold sovereigns in a vase on the upright piano. Joey didn't even know they were there. Cath said they were her mum's rainy-day fund.

'She's going to need a lot more than that where her old man's going, duck,' DI Drury said, and tossed the coins back into the vase. 'It'll be more like a bloody blizzard. Search upstairs.' He nodded the constables on.

Blocking their way, Cath said, 'Give over. Mum's up there and she ain't well. It's bad enough you disturbing us at five o'clock in the sodding morning. Have a heart.'

For a long moment, Joey held his breath. Was the detective going to call off his men? Drury put a pipe in his mouth, struck a match to it, then clamped the box of Swan Vestas over the bowl to get it to draw. He exhaled a satisfying cloud of smoke. 'I'm sorry about your mum, duck,' he said. 'She's been through a lot, what with Jack and now Billy. It's enough to make anyone ill. But if I went back to the station without taking a gander upstairs I'd feel I'd neglected my duty. We'll try not to upset her.'

The money was still under Joey's pillow in what was Jack's old room and Joey knew it would be found in a moment.

On the landing Drury asked, 'Whose room's this?'

'Brian's – my son.' It was a small box-room over the stairs.

He followed two men into Brian's room, sharing their embarrassment when they found some women's clothing pugged up in a corner of the tiny wardrobe. Brian sprang forward, snatched it and went downstairs. Just then, Joey saw DI Drury and the other two coppers go into his and Cath's bedroom. Sweat trickled out from under his arms. He followed them in and watched as the men pulled back the counterpane, then the blankets one at a time, the sheet. When they reached for the pillows Joey stopped breathing. Breathe, he told himself, or you'll be a dead giveaway. They found nothing inside the pillowcases, the pillows themselves were intact. The police tossed them aside as they pulled back the bottom sheet. Where was the money? Perhaps it was a dream and he didn't have it after all. No, Cath must have moved it. But where to? There could be only one place – Gracie's room.

The policemen paused at the door and glanced at Drury, who brushed past them and approached the bed where Gracie was dozing. 'I'm sorry to disturb you, Mrs Braden,' he said.

Without opening her eyes Gracie said, 'It won't be the first time your lot's done it. What is it now?'

'We have to search your room,' he said.

'There's no peace for anyone, is there?' Cath said. 'C'mon, Mum. Let's get you up.'

She helped Gracie out of bed and put a crocheted shawl around her shoulders. 'You'd better take your hot-water bottle.'

'I'm fine, Cath,' Gracie said. 'I don't want that.'

'Yes, you do – to keep the chill out.'

'But it's cold,' Gracie insisted.

Joey wasn't sure what the detective read on Cath's face, but it made him turn to the bed. As Cath picked up the hot-water bottle to give it to her mother, he reached out and took it from her. 'It is – stone cold,' he said, and shook it. 'Empty too.' He unscrewed the cap on the glazed earthenware bottle and poked a finger inside. He smiled. 'It feels like some more rainy-day money. In fact, it feels like enough to see you through a bloody thunderstorm.'

The police weren't interested in Joey's story about Billy Hill investing in his purchase of the fruit and vegetable warehouse. Or that it was a legitimate business enterprise. They were only interested in Joey having the money, that he'd got it from Billy Hill and knew it to be stolen. What they couldn't prove was where the stolen money had come from. At the police station they persuaded him to make a full statement about how it came into his possession, promising that he wouldn't be charged with receiving stolen goods. Joey didn't question that or ask to consult a solicitor; he was just immensely grateful not to be charged. DI Drury, as good as his word, let him go.

As he walked down the steps of the police station, Joey's feet were like lead. Even though he was free of the law, he was back to square one with the warehouse. That was his first run-in with the police, and he wanted it to be the last.

Selwyn Carruthers was disappointed when Joey told him he couldn't offer for the warehouse, and even more so when he said he didn't have any information on Thompson's business that would help them.

'We'll be the best judges of that,' Carruthers told him. 'Don't think you've heard the last of this because you haven't.'

When Billy went to trial, Joey attended the hearing with a sense of inevitability. He felt helpless to change the course of events as Billy was sent down for two years. Billy turned in the dock and winked at him.

'He won't do two years, Dad,' Brian said.

'How do you know?'

'You always get a bit off for good behaviour. Granddad Billy knows how to play the game.'

The money that Joey felt was his wasn't returned to him. When he asked DI Drury about it, he said, 'Money, duck? What money's that?'

Two weeks later Mr Thompson was charged with tax evasion and Joey found himself working for the government until the warehouse was sold to the owner of the business next door for a mere two hundred pounds.

TEN

The canvas-covered three-ton truck stopped with a squeal of brakes outside the guardroom and Jack Braden jumped down with two other soldiers, fresh from the military detention centre at Colchester. The hardest part of his six months there was the cold. An east wind blew in off the sea making the old stone building a permanent igloo. Once the chill got into your bones it didn't leave them.

All three soldiers slammed to attention in front of the unblinking company sergeant major, each with his kitbag sitting alongside his left foot, parallel to his left trouser leg seam. The CSM ran his small round eyes over them from where he stood some ten feet away with a thin, slightly round-shouldered corporal. Why they were made to wait, unmoving, like this, Jack couldn't tell. Everything in the army seemed to involve waiting. His lips parted and he sucked in more air, thinking the problem was because they weren't standing straight or stiffly enough to attention. After six months of square-bashing at Colchester, Jack could drill and snap-to as smartly as anyone, even this little barrel-chested CSM.

Catterick Camp was an endless series of single-storied Nissen huts that probably hadn't changed much from when Baden-Powell was there in 1915. It was on the edge of Hipswell, which looked no less bleak to Jack than Colchester, with a lot of treeless countryside surrounding it. After a few minutes a young, good-looking captain approached and flapped a hand in a casual salute. The CSM stood to attention, his brightly polished boots smashing the ground.

'Which is he, Sergeant Major?' the captain asked. 'Identify yourself, Private Braden.'

Jack tried to be even more at attention than he already was. 'Sir!' he barked.

The young captain, who had a blond moustache that he stroked, as if putting it in place, stepped forward and inspected Jack. He didn't appear impressed. As he leant in closer, letting his cold, slightly bulging eyes check that he was up to the mark, Jack fought the inclination to smack him across the bridge of the nose with his forehead – the Colchester nod, favoured by the army prison inmates.

The captain flapped his hand again. 'Carry on, Sergeant Major,' he said, and strolled away.

The CSM stepped into the same space, his gaze harder, more critical. Jack didn't flinch.

'If it was my decision, son, you coming here,' he said, his face close to Jack's, his hot breath buffeting him with the smell of the rissole he'd eaten for lunch, 'I wouldn't give you house room. But our officer commanding is a tactician. A good one. He wants the best boxing team in the army. That means you boxing on his team. Toe the line, son, and before you know it you'll be a ticket-of-leave man. Home to see Mum and show your mates your glasshouse scars.'

Scars were something all but the most passive inmates of Colchester got aplenty. Fights, with any weapon you could get hold of, were frequent. There, Jack was obliged to fight for survival; now he was determined not to fight for the army.

'Corporal Jenkins is going to be your guide, your rock and your confessor,' the CSM said. 'If you have any complaints about the food, your bed or anything else that makes your life less than comfortable, just have a word in his shell. He'll make sure they're changed. Me, I wouldn't bother.'

There was no hint of a smile on his face, but Corporal Jenkins wore a smirk from ear to ear. He was loving every moment of this. He was the sort of bloke you'd punch holes through and not know you'd made a fist.

'Now, pick up your kit and double over to your billet. And I mean double.'

As they went swiftly across the parade-ground to one of the green-painted corrugated-iron huts, Jack saw the young captain speaking to a close-shorn, bull-necked squaddie, who seemed more relaxed and at ease around an officer than he should. The captain put a hand on his shoulder and grasped it in a familiar fashion.

It soon became clear to Jack why that was when he got inside the stark green-and-cream-painted Nissen hut with seven iron beds along one wall and seven along the other. A few soldiers, all younger than Jack, were cleaning their equipment as they listened to Charlie Chester's *Stand Easy* on the Light Programme over the Tannoy system.

'Get yourself a kip,' Corporal Jenkins said. 'Stow your gear, and stow it like a soldier or the whole platoon's up shit creek without the proverbial. Know what I mean?'

The soldiers stopped their work as Jack walked down the room, past the pot-bellied stove that was the only form of heating, to a folded bed. Some nodded, others just stared, as if he was from another planet. Jack took the end of the frame and pulled it sharply, telescoping it to its full length. Then he unrolled the stained mattress. The bedding was in a neat square pile on the locker. Colchester had taught Jack how to make a bed the way the army liked it.

As he was spreading and smoothing the blankets, the bull-necked squaddie who was so easy with the captain came into the barracks and strode up to him. 'That bed's mine, cocker,' he said.

'It was folded up,' Jack said.

'Yeah, but it's taken.' His neck wasn't the only part of him that was over-developed. He was thick and hard through the body, like a tree-trunk, and spoiling for a fight. Menace oozed from him, but Jack saw at once where he was weak. Bull-neck stood too far back on his heels rather than on his toes as a fighter should be if he was hoping to stay vertical.

Jack stopped unpacking, scooped up his gear and went across

the room to another folded bed. He pulled that one out and started to make it up. Bull-neck followed him. With a careful glance, Jack noted he was still back on his heels. 'Oh, you forgot to say, didn't you?' he ventured. 'That one's taken too. Right?' Without protest he picked up his kitbag again. 'Why don't you tell me where to put it? That would save us a lot of time.'

'You could shove it up your arse.'

'That's where you like it, is it?' Jack asked him, pumping his arm forwards and backwards. 'Plenty of stiffy up your bum, especially from officers.'

Laughter erupted, but died the instant Bull-neck looked round to identify the culprits. Then no one moved or even breathed as they waited for his response. It was for him to call it, but he no longer seemed in a hurry, even though Jack had insulted him in the worst possible way. Whether you were like that or not, the last thing anyone ever did was admit it. To do so left you open to ridicule, the glasshouse and dishonourable discharge.

'You yellow or what?' Bull-neck said, baring his teeth. 'Is that why you won't box, Braden?'

'Piss off, you fat nancy-boy.'

Jack turned away and tossed his bag onto the bed. As he did so he felt the young man grab his arm, strong fingers biting into the muscle.

'Let it go, Keffo,' a young voice from along the room said. 'He don't want no trouble. Nor do we.'

'Stow it, brownhole!' Keffo said. 'Let's hear what this shit-hot boxer's got to say. Well?'

Keffo tugged at him, putting himself right off-balance. As he came forward, Jack drove a straight left into his throat, paralysing his larynx and shutting off the air. He followed through like a runaway train, slamming another left and a right into the younger man before he hit the deck. He lay there, gasping for air and clutching his throat. The others stared in disbelief, mouths hung open as Jack stuck a booted foot across Keffo's neck. 'You didn't tell me where I could sleep,' Jack said, leaning down to rest his arm on his bent knee. Keffo thrashed around, unable to speak.

'Jack!' a familiar cry came from the doorway.

Jack glanced up as the scruffiest soldier in the British Army ran in. Bobby Brown tore up to him and slapped him on the back, dancing around him in excitement. They hadn't met since the army collared Bobby a year and a half ago. He was a Colchester graduate with only months left before his demob. They ignored Keffo, who was still under Jack's boot, even when Corporal Jenkins came hurrying over to them.

'You're on a charge, Braden,' the corporal said.

Jack grabbed him by the lapels and shoved his face into his. 'He started it.'

'You picked on the wrong fella here, Snake,' Bobby said. 'You wanna live to old age you'd better take a funny run.'

'All right, all right, as you were,' Jenkins gasped. 'Don't get snaky. No harm done. Stroll on. He's only decked our best hope for the championship.' He wriggled out of Jack's grip and smoothed his tunic, glancing about to check how the men responded to his climb-down.

'He's only shining the floor,' Bobby said. Some of the others laughed as Jack let Keffo get up. He was not in good shape, his neck red and swollen. Snake Jenkins and another man half carried him out to the MO.

Jack and Bobby had a lot to talk about. Bobby gave him the low-down on how to survive at Catterick, what the little wrinkles and fiddles were, but was more concerned to hear what had been going on outside.

'I'm more in the dark than you about that.'

'Talk about a lot going on, Jack,' Bobby said, as they strolled around the camp idly checking the security of the fence, hands in his pockets. 'We're missing so much out here, all sorts of opportunities. They'll be gone by the time we're demobbed.'

'Couldn't we just walk out?' Jack said.

'Now you're talking! We'll do it, dead easy.'

'You sure you want to? I mean, you almost done with the Kate.'

'Who cares? I want my share out there.'

'Get them hands out of your pockets, you sloppy, idle men!' The CSM's voice boomed across the parade-ground.

'Ballocks!' was Bobby's response.

They were put on a charge and doubled around the parade-ground under full field order for what seemed like a week. Jack was fit, so this presented him with few problems, apart from the boredom. Everything about the army was dull. Bobby, though, was struggling alongside him so he reached out to help him.

Two days later they were brought, one at a time, before the young captain, who was called Charles Tyrwhitt and ran the regiment's boxing team. He looked Jack up and down. 'Not an auspicious start to your life in the regiment, Braden,' he said, stroking his wispy moustache as he read his record in the buff folder before him. 'Life here could be very different for you, man. I heard you decked Private Kefford. To his credit, he didn't say what happened. He's looking forward to the return match.'

'What return match?'

'Don't speak until given permission!' the CSM barked, not a foot from Jack's ear.

'Why don't you box for us?' the captain said. 'It makes a lot of sense, from your point of view. Consider the advantages – I can't imagine you haven't.' He glanced down at the record again. 'Yes, the MO says here you're damaged but not without intelligence. An innate sense of leadership and authority. You're just the sort of man the army needs, Braden. Straighten yourself out and you could go far. You might even find yourself with some stripes.' He glanced at the CSM, who didn't move a muscle. 'We need leaders. You could lead our boxing team to victory. If you're up for that there'd be no square-bashing, no fatigues. You get double rations, extra passes to go home to your family. It's what your lot would call cushy.'

The way he said 'your lot' made Jack tense. He tried to breathe deeply and stay calm. He remembered Joey saying the bank manager talked to him like that. Were they some lower form of life?

'What have you got to say, Braden?'

It wasn't an invitation to explain himself, Jack decided, so he stayed silent.

'Are you daft? Or scared? Is that it? Afraid of getting hurt?'

Jack clenched and unclenched his fists.

'No, I don't believe you're scared, Braden. Your record states that you fought other prisoners in Colchester fearlessly, often taking the side of the underdog. That's not the coward's way. No, it's sheer bloody-mindedness.'

Again it was a conclusion.

'I can't order you but I will persuade you. By hook or by crook you'll be in that ring, slugging it out.' He punched the air with more excitement than skill.

'Permission to speak?' Jack said, and received a curt nod. 'I don't box no more. Not after I missed my big fight with Joe Bygraves.'

'Sir!' the no-longer-affable captain shouted. 'You will address me and all officers as "sir". Do you understand, you insubordinate man?'

He had nothing to say to this officer.

'Colonel Ruff, the OC, pulled strings to get you here so you could box on his team. I'm not about to disappoint him, so box you will.'

That was the start of the pressure. It was harder to resist his mates in the barracks, because whenever he was punished for not doing what the army had decided he should be doing, they got punished too. As a result Bobby Brown smartened himself up.

Finally it was Bobby who cracked. 'Look, you might as well box, Jack. Be like boxing fucking kippers with them clowns. For fuck's sake, you don't have to win nothing.'

'The thing is, Bobby, if I put the gloves on, I've had it. I lose the bigger fight. I'm not m' own man no more. Can't you see it my way? I can't break faith with m'self.'

'What about us?' was all Bobby said.

Out on the fieldcraft course, Jack ran at the ten-foot wall and pulled himself onto the top with ease, where he straddled it and looked out beyond the barracks to the fields and open countryside. Freedom. The odd field was ploughed, but most were grass and fog was closing in at a hundred and fifty yards. When he turned back, Bobby was attacking the wall, so he bent to haul him up by his collar. For all the punishing regime Bobby didn't get any fitter. 'You gotta give up smoking and drinking,' Jack told him.

'Then it'll be all punishment, Jack.'

'Don't help him, nincompoop!' Corporal Jenkins bellowed at the edge of the course.

They dropped down into the ditch on the far side of the wall and ran into a copse where there were simulated landmines. Halfway, Jack let the two soldiers behind them pass, then pulled his mate off the track. They darted at a right angle through the trees.

'Hey! There are ruddy great mines in here,' Bobby said.

'I couldn't find none last night,' Jack told him. 'Keep inside these sticks I laid out.'

The rudimentary path he'd marked led them out of the wood to the chain-link fence that was the boundary. Dumping their field gear, they scrambled over it to freedom. Jack breathed deeply and stretched as if the air was different on this side. They checked the empty road, then ran across it and through a ploughed field to a hedgerow, which gave them some cover from passing traffic. Jack glanced up and saw a plane in the clear sky. They could be seen from the air, but they'd be long gone before the army missed them or thought about wasting time and money on a search party. They ran hard for about half an hour, Jack's pace exhausting Bobby. At the busy A1 trunk road, which would take them to London, they were faced with two obstacles.

'We ain't gonna get far dressed like this,' Bobby said.

They didn't know how many soldiers might be walking about

legitimately, or if the army had already informed the police they were AWOL.

'We ain't gonna get far unless we get hold of a bit of lolly.'

'We can thumb a lift. People always stop for soldiers.'

'Yeah, but usually they're heading back to barracks, having spent their money or sold their rail ticket.'

'Some get lifts heading away from camp,' Jack argued.

'Too risky, my son,' Bobby said.

Two hundred yards along the road Jack pulled Bobby upright and straightened his uniform.

'What's the matter with you?' Bobby said, as Jack brought up his right hand in a smart salute. An Austin Jeep raced past on the opposite side of the road, heading, away from the camp.

'Who was in it?' Bobby asked.

'I didn't see, but they won't forget two mud-splattered squaddies on the road when the balloon goes up.'

They climbed a low fence, then went across a wide, closely grazed field. Eventually they came to a lane.

'I can't go on, Jack.'

'Well, go back, then,' Jack challenged.

Round a bend, about half a mile along the narrow, muddy lane, they stumbled on a farm track. Bobby Brown perked up. 'Wait here,' he said.

'What you gonna do?' Jack asked, as if he couldn't guess.

'Stay out of sight.'

Jack watched him run along the track, swerve to the left and jump a ditch, then a single strand of barbed wire on rotting fence posts.

How long was he supposed to wait? Jack wondered. He didn't have a watch, but Bobby was gone for ages. What if he'd been nicked? It would be no time at all before they found him. He emerged from the bushes, about to leave, when Bobby reappeared in civilian clothes, carrying a suitcase.

'What did you do with your uniform?' Jack asked.

'No one won't find it.'

'They'll put you back in Colchester for that.'

'Yeah, but they gotta catch me first. Here, cop this.' He gave Jack some money.

Jack counted it. Twenty-eight pounds. More than he'd seen in a long while. 'Where d'you get it?'

'The farmer's savings – they was under the mattress! Would you Adam-and-Eve it? Here, put this on over your uniform.' He pulled an overcoat from the suitcase, which had some food in it. They ate a real feast as they crossed another field towards railway tracks: a train would be safer than thumbing lifts.

Their first stop when they got to the Smoke was Bobby's auntie Gladys. She lived in a little terraced street behind the police station in Peckham. She was tiny and toothless, and showed no surprise at their appearance. 'How's your mum, Jack?'

'That's what I come to find out, Mrs Brown.'

'Good. It's about time the army let you go,' she said.

'Well, they didn't exactly wave us goodbye, Glad,' Bobby told her. 'Know what I mean?'

The bed she gave them was comfortable, with proper springs. It was a luxury, even though they had to share it. At least it wasn't in a room with fourteen others snoring and farting and crying for their mums. Jack didn't expect to be there long; he was planning to drift back to his old stamping ground north of the water, see what was going on and make his presence felt.

'It beats square-bashing, Jack,' Bobby said, across the kitchen table where they were eating one of his aunt's fry-ups. 'You know who's got a scrap-motor business around the corner? The Richardsons. It's on the Walworth Road. Keeps them outa trouble while Billy's away. We should look them up. They might put us on to a bit of fiddle.'

'Sounds good to me.'

'Beats square-bashing!' It was Bobby's current catchphrase.

It was the first time Jack had seen Charlie Richardson in a blue boiler-suit with black grease up his arms. 'It don't suit you, Charlie,' he said.

'The boiler-suit?'

'All this collar you're doing.'

''S good business, spare parts. Eddie organizes dragging them in here, I take 'em apart. Can you drive? There's good money for nicked motors.'

'I'll do some. I'll see how Mum is first, though.'

'Yeah. Mind how you go – the coz're bound to be watching her place,' Charlie said. He wiped some black oil off his muscular arms.

All the while he was in Colchester, Jack hadn't had any letters. Cath wasn't a letter writer, but he knew his mum would have scribbled a few lines regularly every week. Letters of an emotional nature, liable to upset the prisoner, weren't allowed by the censor. Every letter that was handed to him as he left the prison camp for the barracks at Catterick was of an emotional nature. All the envelopes were split carefully along the top, the letters stamped 'withheld'. Gracie's notes berated the army for taking him as they did. They told him little about her own health, but they got shorter and shorter, her hand less legible. Notes from Cath told him Mum wasn't well and she, Joey and Brian were moving back into her house; then, more alarmingly, she had informed him that Mum had had another stroke and was in hospital; she was grateful for the NHS as they wouldn't have been able to pay for so much treatment. In another letter Mum was out of hospital feeling better, and in the next she was back in.

His mum's street seemed quiet enough as Jack approached it. He saw a young woman manoeuvre a pram out of number twenty-eight. For a moment he thought it was Win Booker and saw an image in his mind's eye of her on the bedroom floor telling him to scram, trying to save him. He wanted to see Win as he watched this unknown woman totter away on high heels. Several motor vehicles were parked at the kerbside. One was a panelled delivery van, the others were cars. Nothing about them worried Jack – no one seemed to be waiting to pounce as he approached Gracie's house.

'My God, Jack!' Cath said, as she opened the door. 'What are you doing here? Are you soft in the head?' She yanked him inside, then shut and bolted the door. 'The cops were round here only this morning looking for you,' she said, leading him through to the kitchen where she switched off Max Bygraves on *Workers' Playtime*.

'They didn't waste much time, did they?'

'They ain't got nothing better to do with Billy away.'

'You heard from him?'

'About two lines, asking how Mum is.'

'It's something, I s'pose. How is she?'

'The doctor says she's got a tired heart, whatever that is. A broken heart, more like. She needs plenty of bed-rest so she's in hospital.'

'Can't she get that here? She'd be better off in her own home, looked after by people she knows.'

'It's not that easy. I mean, we're out all day and they got the staff to look after her properly. I mean, Brian could have done it but he's working now. He's got a good job in Blurton's in the Strand, the men's outfitters.'

'What about you?' Jack asked.

'I'm only here for my dinner. No, Jack, she's better off where she is – for now anyway – unless you want to look after her.'

'That's a laugh. Where is she? I'll pop in and see her.'

'Bart's – but you go careful, Jack. If they came here, they'll go there too as likely as not. That won't do her no good, you getting collared again. D'you want a bit of food? Joey still gets plenty from the warehouse.'

'How's Mr Thompson doing? Didn't he sell up after all?'

'Got nicked for not paying his tax. There's a new owner now, a company. They leave it all to Joey mostly. You'd think he owned the business – he practically lives there – only he don't get the profit. We're still saving – he's got his heart set on a little greengrocer's. He's seen a shop that's vacant around the corner,' Cath said nervously.

She jumped when Jack touched her wrist.

'Calm down. What's wrong?'

'Nothing. It's nothing.'

'Something is, Cath. I can tell. It's Mum, isn't it?'

'No. Mum's getting the best treatment there is. Her doctor's a top heart man – all free on the NHS. But the hospital's the first place they'll look for you – the local police will have told the army your mum's there.'

'I'll be careful. You sure she's all right?'

'Under the circumstances. I'll make you some tea.'

'What's happening to all them shopkeepers around here? Bobby Brown said they'd got a bit of trouble again.'

'I'll say. The Hoxton lot's moved back in with them Kray twins. No one does much about it. And the place Joey's got his eye on is in Clerkenwell Road. Stupid, really. Be hard enough making a go of things without having to pay them lot.'

'I'll have a walk round and sort a few out.'

'You worry about yourself, Jack.'

'So where did you get the schmutter?' Sammy Cohen said, when Jack walked into his workshop. 'Was it the rag-and-bone man what fitted you out? Can we do better than that?' He didn't take his cigarette out of his mouth.

'I'd hope so, Sammy, or it won't have been worth coming back.'

'So you're back for good? You can do something about this riff-raff that the police do nothing about?'

'I'll have a go,' Jack said. 'Mobbed up, are they?'

'With Billy Hill off the manor, they came back like a rash in summer,' Sammy said, not pausing from the fine stitching he was putting in along the lapel of a camel-hair overcoat. 'Jack Spot's an old man, but he has all these young Nazis – tearaways, they are.'

'Don't worry about them, Sammy.'

'So, God still answers prayers.'

'I wish He'd answer mine. How's your Leah?' Jack asked. 'I only came back to see her.' A picture of her slid tantalizingly into his mind. He still smarted at her rejection after he'd rescued her from the Krays and their little brothel on the Peabody Estate.

'Still training to be a nurse. "A nurse?" I ask. "Why a nurse?" She wants to help people, she says. "So be a doctor. A doctor's got degrees in knowledge."'

'Nursing's a good job, Sammy,' Jack said. 'Where'd you be in hospital without nurses?' He thought about his mum, and going to St Bartholomew's despite the risk. First he'd see Leah. She was training there. Maybe she'd know exactly how his mum was doing.

Standing back on the far side of the wide, cobbled square that was West Smithfield, in front of the hospital, Jack watched people coming and going for more than an hour as he waited for Leah to come off duty. It was too early for visitors. There was a lot of activity and he saw some police, but that didn't deter him. He looked for anyone who seemed to be standing around smoking or talking for longer than they should. A beat policeman walked past, and a black Wolseley stopped alongside him. The driver and the officer exchanged a few words, then the car drove off. Finally people were going in clutching bunches of flowers and yellow-orange bottles of Lucozade. Jack guessed it was visiting time and suddenly felt vulnerable.

Then he saw Leah emerge in a large starched cap, wrapped tightly in her cape against the cold. She had filled out a little and was more lovely for it. He walked rapidly across the square and cut her off. 'Leah,' he said.

'Oh, hello,' she said, as if she couldn't remember his name.

'How you been?' he asked.

Leah shrugged. 'Studying hard. I've got exams coming up.'

'You're gonna pass them,' Jack said. 'On looks alone you'd do it.'

'I don't think that's how it works, Jack.' She glanced up at him. 'I should get going. I've got to study.'

'Am I going to see you, Leah? I'd really like to.'

'I don't know. I've got a lot to get through,' she said.

'Maybe we could go to the pictures on Saturday. What's on at the Scala? D'you get Saturday nights off?'

There was a long silence, and when she didn't reply, he said, 'I'll wait for you, Leah. I don't care how long it takes.'

Leah nodded and turned away. Jack watched her cross the square towards a low building on the other side. Finally his attention went back to the main hospital building. Is it safe? he asked himself. He decided it was, and skirted the square to approach the steps at the south end. The covered walkway in front of the building was bounded by tall Doric columns and Jack trod lightly as he approached the main entrance, his eyes darting everywhere.

A man in a white coat passed him, then turned back. 'Jack! How are you?'

The familiar greeting caught him off guard and he turned instead of running. The man in the white coat smiled and signalled to two buttonmen at the main entrance. Before Jack could decide what to do, the policeman in the white coat had snapped handcuffs on to his wrists.

He shut his eyes and his stomach seemed to fall away. 'Could I just see Mum now I'm here?'

The policeman took off the white coat he wore over his uniform and nodded. 'If I let you and you gave us the slip,' he said, 'I'd be for it.'

'I won't.'

'Famous last words.' He snapped a second set of cuffs onto Jack's right wrist and the other half onto his own.

'Fourteen days in the guardhouse,' the OC said, sentencing him for absconding. 'Number-one diet. Bread and water.' He sat back in his chair in the adjudication room, took a du Maurier cigarette from the square maroon box and lit it. He drew deeply, his fingers stained browny-yellow with nicotine. 'There is an alternative, you know. If you put the gloves on you won't go into the guardhouse, and you can go to see your mother under escort. But you have to become a willing partner in bringing the inter-regimental boxing cup home to Catterick, Braden. The alternative is a life burdened by jankers, as your lot call it.'

'Your lot' helped Jack to decide immediately. He wouldn't do it, no matter how much jankers they gave him. When he shook his head he saw a look of contempt fall over the OC's face.

Square-bashing, spud-bashing, lavatory-cleaning, even white-washing coal fell to him. He accepted every order at the double from any insignificant NCO who chose to shout at him, including a puny lance corporal. He survived.

On the last day of punishment, Jack was doubled across to the gym, which took up a whole Nissen hut. It was warm, comfortable and familiar to him, with the equipment set up for boxing, the tangy smell of embrocation oil and sweat drying on freshly toned bodies. Suddenly he was back in the world of Jack Solomons, the promoter, Frank Cockain, the bookie, and Peewee, who had never once lost his belief that he could go to the top. There was no way that would happen now. He was twenty-seven and had left it far too late, even for the army.

Jack stood like a rock between the two lance corporals who'd doubled him here while the CSM put Roy Kefford through his paces in the ring. Straight away Jack saw that the boxer's balance was still wrong. How could they be so blind? Keffo might prove dangerous if he ever learned how to dance with his partner. Jack knew he could rectify the problem in a morning, but he didn't intend to become a trainer when he should have been world champion.

'Morning, Twinkletoes,' the CSM said, when he eventually turned to him. Other soldiers, all in boxing kit, smiled slyly, as if they were waiting to see what Jack might do.

He didn't do anything.

'Thirteen stone of pure mean killer there,' the CSM said, referring to Keffo. 'I can understand why a big soft nelly like you wouldn't want to go up against him. What are you, Braden? A big soft nelly? Let's hear it. "I'm a big soft nelly who's scared of this mean killer." Come on, say it.'

The others were laughing now, and anger finally got the better of Jack. He broke rank, ripped off his belt and tunic, then grabbed the first pair of gloves he saw, hoping they'd fit but not caring much as he heaved himself into the ring. This was what he was born for, he knew, and the twenty or so men in the gym surged to the ringside in anticipation of action.

Before he could pull on the gloves, Keffo rushed him, hitting him with a left, then another and coming wide with his right. The young boxer wasn't only off balance, he was angry, probably with a lot to live down. Jack knew the mug didn't have a chance. Rather than struggle to get the gloves on, he ripped them off and tossed them away. He hadn't even undone his shirt collar before Keffo was pressing home his advantage. He had youth and fitness on his side, and Jack's bread-and-water diet didn't help but Keffo walked almost blindly into a sharp left that broke his collarbone and stung Jack's fist. Seeing him teeter, badly unbalanced on those heels, Jack followed through with a series of rights to the body and a left cross that saw the regiment's best hope falling like a tree to the woodcutter's axe. The deck vibrated as he hit the canvas. There was silence from the onlookers. Keffo wasn't about to get up. Jack climbed out of the ring, picked up his belt and tunic and put them back on. Then, insolently, he stood to attention. He was breathing heavily, his jaw clamped.

The CSM strolled over to him. 'Someone's gotta replace him,' he said. 'You just got yourself elected.'

Jack didn't move a muscle. He felt his left hand stinging and knew it was swelling. Keffo was being brought round with amyl nitrate.

'The boxing team wants you, son,' the CSM continued, 'and, by golly, I'm going to make sure it has you. Or I'll rip off that fucking left arm of yours, jam it up your arse and use you for a lollipop!'

When someone or something was bigger than you and immovable, it was stupid to try to move it. Jack applied for compassionate leave – he knew he'd get it if he boxed. A letter from his sister was waiting for him when he got out of the guardhouse. Mum was going downhill rapidly in hospital. She needed a visit from him to lift her.

Following his application, Jack was called out after morning parade and doubled into the guardhouse by two lance corporals. He came to attention before Captain Tyrwhitt. The CSM held a clipboard with the names of applicants. Jack was one of several asking the army for something. All such soldiers were viewed automatically as malingerers.

He waited in silence for a few moments as Captain Tyrwhitt studied him from his chair, then got up and walked around the desk to look at him closely. He nodded approvingly. 'We're doing a good job here, Sar'nt Major,' he said. 'There's a big improvement in this man. He's beginning to look like a soldier at last. I dare say now he wants his reward.'

A smile slid across the CSM's face, then vanished. 'Compassionate leave, sir.'

'Oh, he's done that well, has he?'

It was all piss-taking, but Jack was determined to stay calm.

Captain Tyrwhitt went to the end of the wooden desk and turned the morning's list towards him as if he needed a reminder. 'Oh, yes. Mother in hospital. That would be it.' He nodded. 'Well, I'm pleased to inform you that we've been in touch with the hospital. Your mother's condition isn't nearly as bad as your sister painted it. She's conscious, stable and quite comfortable, I'm pleased to say.'

'Sir,' Jack said, on cue.

'So, you see, nothing warrants compassionate leave. If her condition were to worsen . . .'

'Please, sir, I would like to see her.'

'Well, of course,' Captain Tyrwhitt said, 'but you know the name of the game. It's co-operation. You scratch our back, we scratch yours.'

Jack was beaten or as close to it as he wanted to admit. Tension clamped muscles in his neck, his shoulders painful as he tried to resist, but instead it brought him close to tears. The last thing in the world he would choose to do was cry in front of these bastards, especially not an officer.

'But she's seriously ill, you stuck-up git. She is!' The words burst out of him.

'Sir!' the captain exclaimed. 'Address all officers as "sir".' He thrust his face menacingly close to Jack's. If he'd left it at that Jack might have co-operated. But the officer went a step too far. 'Are you crying, man?' he barked.

Jack's eyes were watering. He couldn't stop them.

'Good God, you snivelling cry-baby. Shame on you, soldier. Sar'nt Major, get him out of my sight.'

'About turn, quick—' The CSM started to turn round, clearly expecting to be obeyed.

Jack didn't move. The CSM grasped his arm. As he did so, Jack whipped round and drove his head into the tough, leathery face, splitting his nose.

'Guard!' Captain Tyrwhitt shrieked.

That was all the hapless officer managed before Jack wheeled and sprang at him. The captain's lean, angular body wasn't made for any sort of punishment, but Jack laid into him as though he was a punchball, landing a series of rapid blows before the regimental police piled into him. He floored one with a left hook to the throat, and headbutted another before four more boiled down on him and knocked him senseless with their batons.

ELEVEN

'This opportunity's too good to miss, Cath,' Joey said, smoothing out his rudimentary sketches of the layout of the shop he wanted to open. He moved the sauce bottle and cruet off the green-checked oilcloth on the kitchen table. 'Five hundred and fifty pounds is what it'll take. That's the lease, new shelving, a bit of paint and the stock. We could do without a paint job, I dare say, but a fresh look is best. We'd have to have a nameboard painted – J. Oldman and Son, High Class Greengrocers.' The excitement made him tingle. He was so close to achieving his goal, he could almost taste it. He saw himself in the shop, serving customers, enjoying it, pleasing himself rather than a boss. 'Have you talked to her yet?'

'No, she's not well enough,' Cath said, and went to get the bread out of the dresser for tea.

'You have to talk to her. It's not exactly robbing her. We'll just be using the house as collateral for the bank loan. I don't know why I didn't think of it before.' He waited for her reaction, and saw resistance in her busyness.

'You didn't,' she said finally, 'because we've only just found the deeds.'

'The thing is, Cath,' he said awkwardly, reluctant to broach the subject of death, 'if she was to pop off—'

'Joey, don't say that!'

'I'm not saying she's going to or nothing, but if she was to go, well, she'll have died in what's called intestate. No will means we couldn't use the house.'

Pausing and becoming surprisingly calm, Cath said, 'What if

she did and we'd already used it for the loan? What then? Do we have to sell up to pay it back?'

'No. She'd have given her permission for the full term of the loan until the bank is paid back. The house is just security, that's all,' Joey explained. 'In case we don't pay up.'

'Well, you seem to know all about it. How long have you been plotting like this, you cunning sod?'

'I'm not plotting, Cathy, just trying to get what's best for us all.'

Finally Cath agreed to talk with her Mum in hospital. Gracie was lucid although she'd had another stroke. 'I don't know,' she said. 'I'd better ask my Jack. He'll know more about it.'

'No, he won't, Mum.' Cath glanced at Joey across the bed on the long ward. 'Joey's been into it and the figures work. Jack won't know nothing about it.'

'Billy give me that house,' Gracie said. 'He wanted it as a bit of security for me. He's such a thoughtful, caring man.'

Joey almost laughed. Poor old deluded Gracie.

'We ain't seen hide nor hair of Billy since you been ill, Mum,' Cath said. Joey was about to say he was in gaol until he saw Cath's look. 'God knows where Jack is with the army. We don't hear anything from one month to the next. He doesn't even come to see you, his own mum.'

That was rather hard on the old girl, Joey thought, but said nothing. He knew what Cath was up to – and it seemed to do the trick. Gracie took up the pen and, with a shaky hand, signed the document the bank needed for the loan.

'I can't see how properties on that street can be worth so much money,' Sydney Griffith, the bank manager, said to Joey, as he countersigned the loan document. 'Two hundred and fifty pounds is a lot of money, but your business plan is sound.' He lifted his cigarette off the ashtray, drew deeply, then picked a thread of tobacco off his lip. He gathered up the loan document, which

Gracie had signed, and the deeds to the house, which he clipped into a folder.

This was the same man who had turned him down two years ago. The difference a bit of security made was a stark lesson in economics for Joey. He would manage on this loan even though it wasn't enough.

'I hope you're not planning to employ any of those coloured chaps the government keeps inviting over here to work,' Mr Griffith said.

'We've got enough help in the family, Mr Griffith,' Joey told him. 'Cath'll run the shop, and my boy Brian will help while I do the buying.'

'Very sensible. Keep the overheads low,' the bank manager said. 'God alone knows where we're going to house all these blacks, Mr Oldman. We can't find enough room for the Irish we have to put up with, but at least they're the same colour as us.'

Now that Joey had a secured loan, the bank manager was treating him like someone with whom he wanted to share his thoughts. None of them was doing Joey one bit of good until Mr Griffith said, 'Now cheap property to house those coloured folk would be a sound investment, old chap. Mind you, it would be some sort of trick to pull off. You'd have to get property cheaply enough and rent it to sufficiently large numbers of them to make it pay. They won't have the money for decent rent and the property will be worthless by the time the blacks have had their hands on it.'

'That sounds interesting,' Joey said, thinking only of his greengrocery shop. 'Any idea where you'd get such property, Mr Griffith?'

'All those slums out west – Notting Hill, Bayswater. Big old houses nobody wants because they can't afford the upkeep. I dare say no one would be too concerned about the blacks going there. We don't want them in the suburbs.'

The idea intrigued Joey, if only because he'd seen the power property gave him. It had made him someone with whom the bank manager was prepared to discuss a proposition. But with no means of doing anything about it, Joey had to be content with getting his greengrocery shop open.

'May it be the first of many, Joey,' Cath said, raising her glass of South African sherry to him.

'You really done it, Dad!' Brian said, with unconcealed excitement. 'That's smashing. With you owning a business, people'll look up to you.'

'I expect we'll get them Hoxton boys coming round for a drop,' Joey cautioned.

'"Those", Dad,' Brian corrected him, 'not "them".'

'Well you're very hoity-toity with your Strand manners.'

'Well, you get a better class of person around the Strand and the Aldwych. A lot of judges from the law courts come into the shop, and the barristers. Even Tom Driberg, the MP, comes in to buy shirts and underwear. Twice he asked for me to serve him.'

'He's right to pull us up, Joey,' Cath said, as she returned to rolling pastry on the kitchen table. 'We should try to improve ourselves. We're in business now with our own shop. Look at some of the fancy expressions Brian comes out with. Tell him what else Mr Driberg said, Brian.'

'He wouldn't be interested,' Brian said.

'Of course I would. I want you to make something of yourself, get some of the better things in life. There's plenty out there to be had still.'

'He told Brian he'd got a quick brain when he added things up in his head. He gets that off you, Joey. He said our Brian should think about going to university.'

'Steady on, Cath. Where would that sort of gelt come from, d'you think? I haven't even opened the shop yet. All I've done is borrow a ton of money and still I'm a bit short.'

'Mr Driberg said I could go for free under Labour's university-grant scheme,' Brian told him.

'What about the shop?' Joey was dismayed at the thought of losing his cheap labour. 'I've got to keep the overheads down, at least to start with. That means us all doing our bit.'

'Oh, I'll be there for you, Dad. But I'd have to study at night school, like you did, and pass some exams first. That's the only way you can get into university.'

'If you got the qualifications, why would you need to go to university? Are you sure this MP's all there, Brian?'

'He'd meet the right people at university,' Cath observed.

'First things first,' Joey responded. First on his list was getting the shop open. He'd given himself four weeks, but halved it and worked day and night instead. Ironically, the only carpenter he could find to build his shelves and display bins, with storage underneath to hold the sacks of spuds and carrots, was a black man called Joshua. He'd been a ship's carpenter on the *Ark Royal* and was glad of the work.

One day as Joshua was sawing some plywood, Joey said casually, 'Where do you live?'

'Notting Hill, sir. M' sister's family rent a couple of rooms there and I live with them.'

'Property's hard to come by, is it?'

'Even if you can afford it. There's nine of us living in them two rooms. We gotta bathroom on the landing we get to use and a kitchen – if you can call it that – we share with two other families. We always rowing about who use your food. There's no space in the rooms for food.' Joshua stopped working. 'One day I'll get my own house in a suburb, like Bromley or Orpington.'

It sounded to Joey like a pipe-dream. This man had been in England all his life, served in her navy during the war and still wasn't on the first rung of the ladder. 'Is that a dream most of your people have?' Joey asked.

'They're not my people, sir,' the carpenter informed him. 'No more than all Jews are yours.'

Joey laughed at that, but didn't tell him why. Now he had property and could employ someone less well-off, he was bracketed with those ranking among the chosen and he enjoyed it. That was where he was determined to stay.

'Somewhere decent to live is important, sir.'

The thought of how to make money out of these people's need for rented accommodation burrowed into Joey's brain like a worm. He could do nothing about it now, but he wouldn't forget it.

'I can't give up my job in Blurton's,' Brian said, alarmed. 'They need me. And I meet all those important people.'

'That's all very well, Brian,' Cath said. 'But you're needed here and there's an end to it. Family always comes first. If you haven't got family you haven't got no one.'

Reluctantly, Brian gave notice at the men's outfitters and went to work in the greengrocery shop. Joey was pleased as he was a great success with the customers. He was charming and they liked the nice manners he'd learned in the Strand. Joey was determined to teach him everything – how he sometimes got stuff off the back of someone's lorry, and made even more profit, but especially how he kept the books so it looked as if he was losing money.

Business was almost too good and Joey knew it couldn't last. One day a local tearaway came in with two of his pals. They were in fingertip drape jackets and had sideburns. They offered Joey a simple choice: 'You can fight or you can pay.' Despite the teddy-boy's high-pitched voice, Joey decided on the latter and felt ashamed of his cowardice.

'You can't pay them, Dad,' Brian said. 'It's not right. The one with the squeaky voice is Johnny Shannon, from Hoxton. Why don't you go to the cops?'

'Why don't all the other shopkeepers who give them a drop?'

'No police, Brian,' Cath said. 'We don't want the shop set on fire or smashed up. They'd do it.'

'Well, Jack would stop them if he was here.'

'Well, he ain't. So either your dad gets a razor and goes after those thugs or we pay. We're better off paying.'

Joey shuddered inwardly at the thought of paying for nothing.

The first few weeks it was two pounds out of the till and some apples. Then, when they saw how well the business was doing, their demands rose sharply. 'It's a tenner a week now, m' ol' china,' Johnny Shannon said, testing the sturdiness of the shelving, which was loaded with fresh apples and oranges. 'Oh, yeah, and a bit of fruit and veg for Mum.' He took a paper carrier-bag off the hook and handed it to Joey.

Joey pushed down his anger, with the faint hope that someone would stop this happening. No one did. He filled the bag slowly.

'They're bleeding us dry, Joey,' Cath complained at dinner, as they were going through the books. 'That ten pounds could have gone towards the loan, or your next shop.'

'I know, I know,' he said irritably. 'Try to look at it as a business expense. We write it into our balance sheet and pray for a miracle to rid us of these parasites.'

Joey knew whose help they needed, but it was a waste of breath to mention his name.

Instead it was Billy Hill who knocked at the door, out of gaol and less than his usual chipper self. 'I just need a few days to get back on my feet. Then I'll help you out,' he told Joey. 'I could start a little racket around here, undercut the teddy-boys. What would you say to a fiver a week?'

'It's cheaper than what I'm paying now, but five pounds is still too much for a legitimate business.'

'I got a scheme to make you plenty in that little shop and square away the bit of poke I get at the same time.'

Joey listened, fascinated, as Billy told him his plan. He wanted to put the money he got from robberies through the till to make it seem legal.

'Where d'you get that idea from?' Joey asked, tempted by the twenty per cent Billy was offering him.

'A Yank I shared a cell with in the Scrubs. He said the Mob put their dodgy money through their restaurants and make it legit. It's foolproof – I'd even pay tax!'

'What happens when the taxman suddenly sees all that money coming out of my little shop?'

'You think them robbers care? You pay your taxes.'

It was a good scheme, but Joey knew he wasn't brave enough.

'Your problem is, son, you're scared of your own shadow. Maybe I'll go and see Gracie, get the old girl to give *me* a loan on her house. After all, I bought it for her.'

Alarm spread through Joey at the prospect of his own loan somehow being undermined by Billy's plan. He decided to talk to Gracie himself, which meant going to the long-stay ward at Bart's the moment he closed the shop.

His anxiety was for nothing. Billy hadn't been anywhere near the place. Instead Alice and John were there.

'Alice!' Cath said, as they approached the ward and saw her waiting in the corridor. 'What? She's not . . .'

Alice shook her head. 'The nurses are changing her.' She was dressed in such a dark shade of grey it might as well have been black. Her hair was thin and entirely white. 'I came to get her to make peace with God before it's too late.'

'What?' Cath said. 'That woman's lived like a bloody saint. Look at you, all dressed up like you're going to her funeral.'

'It's important she leaves free of the bad ways of this world,' Alice said, pulling tightly at her scarf. It flew out of her hand onto the floor. Joey and John stooped to retrieve it for her. Her son got there first.

'You're getting to be a big boy, John,' Joey said.

'I know, thank you, sir.'

'Your mum's taught you nice manners.' He held out a bag of

pears he'd brought in for Gracie. 'Would you like one? They're South African.'

At Gracie's bedside, Alice said, 'I want Mother to join us in our new life. I've met someone and we're going to get married.'

'Good stuff,' Joey said. 'I like weddings – they're so hopeful.'

'First we must be accepted by the Brethren—'

'Oh. What if you're not—' Joey stopped abruptly.

Joey's question wasn't answered, as Gracie came out of her slumber and said. 'Jack?' seeing something in John that made her reach out to him. He was tall for his age and good-looking, like his uncle, with the Bradens' thick dark hair.

'Let go of your sinning ways, Mother,' Alice said urgently. 'Redeem this life before it's too late.'

'Don't talk so daft, woman,' Cath said, tugging her away from the bed. For a moment it looked as though they'd fight, but Cath turned back to her mother. 'He's on his way, Mum. Jack'll be here in no time.'

It was clear that Gracie felt she wasn't in need of redemption: she didn't reply to Alice. Cath told her sister unkindly that she'd sounded like a pawnbroker. 'They're always talking about redeeming – and charging you for the privilege.'

It was almost with disbelief that Joey watched the increasing stream of customers come through the shop. Brian chatted away easily with the older ladies, always remembering their names and problems, even offering them a remedy – more fruit. Sometimes he would give them a pear or a tangerine. They came back for more and told their friends. Reluctantly, Cath agreed to give up her job at the Co-op and came to work in the shop as he planned. On Saturday, they were so busy that Joey didn't do his books or go to the market, serving with them instead. At the rate they were going, he could open a second shop – he'd seen somewhere that had no competition nearby – and soon he'd need a van because he couldn't get all the produce on to his bicycle. Perhaps things were going too well. When you acknowledged that, something always went wrong, almost like he was tempting fate. One bright, sunny morning in their seventh week of trading, with fifty pounds almost paid back to the bank, Ronnie Kray came through the door. 'These are two of my associates,' he said, as if he was in business, his thumbs and index fingers stuck in his waistcoat pockets. They all picked up pieces of fruit, inspected them and tossed them back. The youngest of the three, who couldn't have been more than eighteen, picked up a banana and pranced around like a monkey.

'That's what you look like, without the banana,' one of Brian's elderly customers said. 'You daft sod.'

The young associate put the fruit back and grinned at Ronnie, who was quietly munching a pear, juice running over his fat lower lip and dropping on to his jacket.

'What can I get you, gents?' Joey asked.

'A pound out the till would be handy,' Ronnie said.

Bravely, Brian slammed it and removed the key.

'He's not very smart, is he, Joey?' Ronnie said, still eating his pear. 'You wanna put a notice outside: "Smart lad wanted". You need one.'

'You're wrong there, Mr Kray. Brian's very smart. So smart, in fact, that Tom Driberg, the MP, is saying he could go to university,' Joey said.

Ronnie dropped the pear core on the floor. 'Why's he need to go to university if he's so smart?' He grinned at his men, who laughed. Without warning he kicked a strut from under the corner of the vegetable display and potatoes poured onto the floor.

Brian charged over to him. 'If you don't sling your hook,' he said, 'you'll get plenty of trouble with Billy Hill.'

'Oh, you got big bad Billy pugged up here, have you? Where's he hiding? In that little cubbyhole out there, is he?'

After that, there was nowhere for Brian to go. Joey knew from Tiger Braden you should never make threats unless you can follow them through. Any threat he ever intended he'd keep locked in his head to act upon without anyone knowing, except the person who would feel the result. There was nothing he could do about Ronnie Kray right now, but the time would come when he'd see this fat, over-confident lout in his three-piece suit feeling sorry for himself. He didn't know when that would be, but it didn't matter. He was a patient man who would find his true place in the scheme of things. As yet he harboured only a loose idea of what that might be. He could never be a thug, like the Krays, commit robberies, like Billy Hill or boast about his exploits, like Jack. You had to hold that side of yourself in check if you were to succeed in this world. Joey would sit somewhere in the supply of things for any criminal enterprise, perhaps providing money, information or ideas. 'Give me the key, Brian,' he said to his son.

'Dad!' Brian protested.

Ronnie Kray puckered his fat lips at Brian, taunting him, as he reluctantly handed the key to his dad and went outside to serve a customer on the street.

Joey opened the till, took out a crisp five-pound note and reluctantly gave it to Ronnie Kray, who snapped it and smiled. 'What about my associates?' he said.

Each received a five-pound note. 'Fifteen pounds a week, Mr Kray, is a lot of money for a small business like ours,' Joey said. 'Five is the best we can do. We don't want any trouble. We don't want thugs or riff-raff coming through the door with their demands.'

'On my patch?' Ronnie said. 'They'd better bloody not.' He winked and left, the other two following.

Now Joey was aware of just how exposed he was. The more successful he became, the more the Krays would demand. That was how extortion worked. And if he got Billy Hill or Jack to do something about the parasites, he'd have to pay them. He would have to make himself indispensable to the criminals by supplying them with whatever they needed. That meant becoming rich.

*

RSM 'Tinker' Bell dominated Jack's life. He was the man who ran Shepton Mallet military prison. There were officers, of course, senior to him, but they controlled nothing. Tinker Bell filled Jack's waking and sleeping thoughts. The fourteen-pound sledgehammer with which he smashed Portland stone, brought in for the purpose, came down on Bell's head, mashing his brains, pulverizing and atomizing him. No one would tell him how long he had to stay on the rock pile. Spud 'Pongo' Murphy, an Irishman in name only, and black as the ace of spades, told him it would be until he was dead. 'You've beaten up an officer and five NCOs, man. The army ain't ever gonna forgive you that. They ain't forgiven me my transgressions.'

Soon after Jack's arrival at the Mallet, he and Pongo had fought and Jack had lost. In a haze of sweat and total physical grind, when every muscle in his body screamed with pain, he couldn't remember whether he had lost because the short wide black man was a better fighter or because he himself had been too exhausted to care. When he had arrived at Shepton Mallet broken and bleeding from the swamping he'd received at Catterick, he was given a medical by a doctor who reeked of booze, and a hot meal. He was allocated a cell with Pongo and put to work straight away. The army board ordered that he should spend the rest of his National Service doing hard labour. How he would get through it and survive, he didn't know. He didn't even know how he got through the day and there were days when he believed he wouldn't. On those days Pongo Murphy got him up and got him going, saving him from another beating.

Dragging him off his bed, as he did, Pongo said, 'Oh, brother, it's gonna get a lot worse than that rock pile.'

After breakfast – porridge, a thick slice of white bread with a dollop of margarine and a sausage washed down with a mug of sweet tea – Pongo worked alongside him, swinging his hammer with such ferocity that Jack almost imagined it was a competition. Not a stroke did he miss, and he never paused in his work until the staff sergeant in charge of the rock pile blew his whistle for the mid-morning and afternoon tea-breaks or lunch. There were no other breaks, not even to visit the lavvy, as Pongo called it. Prisoners collapsing at this collar were simply worked harder the next day. Death was the only escape. One collapsed and died there six days after Jack had started. He never even learned his name.

The stone walls of the prison in the centre of the town were high and forbidding. There was no running away from here. What lay beyond, Jack couldn't guess. He'd been ghosted in late at night so had had no contact with the town or its people. They would probably rather the prison wasn't there, but it had been since the early seventeenth century. It was full of the ghosts of men who had been hanged during the war, all American servicemen, all dropped by Pierrepoint the death bringer in the brick block jammed incongruously between the stone wings. The walls seemed to absorb no heat in summer and the windows let in little light. Jack was too tired to care.

'You're not here for your health,' RSM Bell was fond of telling them. 'You're here because you're fucking deviants, rapists, murderers, or worse. In other words, the scum of the world. My job is to make you so sorry for your sins you'll never sin again. Understand this. We're not out to make soldiers of you. Most of you are beyond that. We're here to punish you. Remember one thing, I enjoy my job.'

Pongo Murphy was a regular soldier, a good one by all accounts. He'd fought bravely with the expeditionary force in France and was evacuated from Dunkirk and honoured by the army – until he'd killed an officer in a drunken brawl over a woman, strangling him with his bare hands. He got eighteen years for manslaughter with hard labour. Some American officers from some secret unit came and offered him a way out during the latter part of the war. They were selecting dangerous prisoners to go on dangerous missions behind enemy lines, with little chance of returning. The deal was if they survived, they'd be pardoned.

'By then I'd had it,' Pongo told him. 'I turned them down flat. I'd got a total siege mentality, us and them.'

Jack was glad that Pongo ranked him among the 'us' and was therefore always ready to help him. When he collapsed on to his steel bunk bed at the end of those first days on the rock pile, unable to get up again, it was Pongo who had hauled him to his feet and saved him from a merciless beating. Some prisoners never returned from such punishment. Where they went, no one knew, but speculation was rife.

Survival was what mattered to Jack, but most days he was so weary he couldn't remember why, other than that he had to repay Pongo. Other days he knew he wanted to see his mum. On the rest he could sustain no clear thought. By the end of his second week, he knew that not letting the system beat him was reason to survive. Then he would see his mum and help Pongo. He wouldn't be allowed to visit Gracie until he had completed his entire sentence. He could receive no visits, letters or information from the outside world. For now, the army owned him, body and soul.

The rock pile was designed to break the hardest man. It never got any smaller, because each day a three-ton Dennis lorry trundled across the yard, which served as a parade-ground, and through a narrow archway to a smaller yard where it reversed and tipped a fresh load of boulders. This was psychological warfare. The hard-labour prisoners were to have no sense that they were winning, that there was an end in sight.

Rock-breaking was only their daytime job. After supper they had to prepare their kit for inspection before breakfast. There were serious consequences for the entire four-man cell if anyone failed.

Staff Sergeant Lambert was a large man of thirty-five who carried more fat than muscle. But with his swagger stick tucked under his arm, as he marched along the echoing stone corridor with three other staffs of the Military Provost's Corps to start morning inspection, he was king. The door of Jack's cell flew open and Staff Lambert filled the narrow doorway, letting his half-closed eyes trail around the room as if praying for a transgression. There could be none. The kits were neatly arranged at the foot of the bunks, blankets folded into tight box-like squares, all the sewn-on name tags in a line. Webbing was freshly cleaned and rolled, spare boots were brightly polished, the leather soles upturned for inspection, spare laces on either side in neat Catherine-wheel rolls. The mess tins, knives, forks and spoons gleamed.

'By your beds!' Staff Lambert barked. No one in the Provost's Corps ever spoke in a normal voice.

The four prisoners sprang smartly to attention. Even Tricky Dicky Dobbs, a young card sharp who'd got them into trouble a few times on inspection, was up to scratch.

As he stepped into the cell, Lambert's eyes settled on Jack. With his three-foot cane he lifted the corner of Jack's blanket square, held it for a moment, then tipped it over. Jack knew what would come next. With a violent slashing motion Staff Lambert wrecked the neatly folded kit, as he'd often done before. 'This won't do,' he screeched. 'Drop me in it with the RSM, and I'll double you till your cods drag on the floor.' He wheeled out.

There were only moments to get things right again before Tinker Bell came round for his weekly inspection.

'What a shambles!' was Bell's opening salvo as he walked into the cell. He was in his mid forties, and looked as hard as everyone knew him to be. His constant habit was to smooth his moustache, a habit most of the staff sergeants copied. All sported hair on their top lip. He turned to Lambert. 'Staff, I thought you said this was ready for inspection.'

'Sir.'

'It's like an 'ore'ouse.' His eyes wandered round the cell. 'No, 'ore'ouses are a lot tidier than this fucking tip.'

Clearly the tension building inside Dicky Dobbs was unbearable. He was twenty, thin and wiry, and didn't live on the rock pile: his sentence wasn't hard labour. Inwardly Jack groaned as Dobbs said, 'He wrecked it. He did.' Bell fixed him with a glassy stare. 'Complaints against my staff, musher?'

Standing at a diagonal to Dobbs, Jack caught his eye and gave an almost imperceptible shake of his head. But the signal wasn't small enough to get under Tinker Bell's radar. He wheeled. 'I might have known you'd be behind it,' he said. 'Complaints, son?'

'No, sir,' Jack snapped back crisply.

'No, sir. No complaints, sir. Everything's tickety-boo, sir,' RSM Bell mocked. Jack knew the words by heart. They never varied. 'Well, everything ain't tickety-boo. This place looks like a fucking knocking shop. Knocking shops in this man's army is against the King's Regs.' They were now the Queen's Regulations, but Bell hadn't noticed that. He slapped the small-print poster that was on the wall of this and every other cell. 'Staff, get these prisoners sorted. On the double.'

Getting them sorted meant missing breakfast and doubling around the parade-ground for two hours. The routine punishment was in addition to the rock pile. The casual brutality of the staff sergeants, who brooked no argument, ate into Jack's soul, causing anxiety to creep up on him, weakening his resolve to beat them. In this vulnerable state, worry about his mum got to him so badly that he had to ask about her, even though he knew what the answer would be.

After a day spent smashing rock, he found his tired mind returning again and again to his mother. Soon he convinced himself that her condition was worsening. 'I gotta speak to someone about her. I'm going mad here.'

'They won't be telling you nothing,' Pongo Murphy advised him. 'Don't be giving them no satisfaction.'

Jack knew he was right but he still had to ask.

'Permission to speak, sir?' he said, when RSM Bell came by at the end of the day and they were fell in, aching and raw from work.

Bell was a little more glassy-eyed than usual, which meant he'd taken a couple of whiskies already.

'The court-martial promised I'd be told how my mum is, sir.'

Bell nodded and stroked his moustache. 'Staff!' he shouted. 'Double this fucking shower away.'

'Sir!' Lambert barked back, even though there was only five feet between them.

Jack never received a single snippet of news from home.

No contact with the outside world – no newspapers or wireless – ensured that time lost meaning for prisoners at the Mallet. Spring followed winter, then summer came, but the days weren't marked, apart from Sunday. Then the chaplain held a church service and the hard-labour prisoners weren't taken to the rock pile. Instead they were allowed to do their laundry and extra work on their equipment. Jack barely knew what day or month it was, only that it was late spring, from the lengthening light in the evening sky. One day an unfamiliar staff sergeant approached and spoke to Lambert. 'Go and get some char and a wad,' he said.

'We could do with a cuppa, Staff,' Pongo said.

Instead of the punishment Jack expected to follow, the staff sergeant said, 'I expect you could, you black whoreson.' He winked at Lambert, who doubled away.

After a while, the new man wandered over to Jack and said, ''S that right your mum took a turn for the worse?'

'Did she? Where d'you hear that, Staff?' Jack asked, trying to hold down his anxiety.

'In the RSM's office,' the staff sergeant said. 'I think the hospital was on the horn to him. I thought it only right you should know – I'm not a vicious maniac like some of them. They won't tell you nothing.'

Without asking permission to speak, Jack said, 'I wanna see the RSM, Staff.'

All reasonableness was gone. 'All you'll see is chokey if you start that lark. Now get back to work.'

'No. I wanna see the RSM,' Jack insisted.

'Careful, Jack,' Pongo warned. 'Don't give them the opportunity to duff you up.'

'What d'you say, you grinning monkey?' the staff sergeant asked.

Jack ignored them. 'I'm seeing him.' Dropping his hammer, he sprinted away from the rock pile and headed out through the arch, ignoring Pongo's shouted warnings.

The RSM's office was in a red-brick building at the gate end of the main parade-ground. Jack hit the half-open door at a run, almost taking it off its hinges. He barely registered that it didn't slam back against the wall. Instead it was caught by one of the five large staff sergeants who were waiting for him, each holding a sock filled with sand. 'What's happened to Mum?' was scarcely out of Jack's mouth when the first blow struck him in the face, cracking his cheekbone. Lambert got in the second, on the side of his head.

'Good stuff, son,' Bell was saying. 'Your action makes this legal – necessary restraint.'

Blows fell thick and fast on his head, face and shoulders. Soon Jack felt himself sinking under the weight of them until he lost consciousness.

'You had us worried there,' a voice was saying, pulling open his painfully swollen eyelid. The torchlight hitting the retina was as painful as a pin stuck into the eyeball. 'He's still with us,' the voice said, and the light clicked off, giving Jack immediate relief. There was a clang as a door slammed. The familiar sound told him he was in an isolation cell at the Mallet. Consciousness drifted away again and he escaped briefly from the pain that even the slightest movement caused.

How long he lay on the cold stone floor of that cell, he didn't know or care. His dreams were filled with images of someone being carried out of his Mum's house in a cheap pine box, but he couldn't see who it was. All the while his father was urging him over and over to stop them, but Jack had no inkling of who he meant.

Eventually the pain lessened and his injuries healed. Broken bones left unattended – mostly for want of anything that could be done about a particular break – fused, the muscles flexed and strength returned, but Jack was left with no inclination to fight any of the men who had beaten him. Gradually he was brought back into the routine of prison and the rock pile. First there was inspection by a staff sergeant, then by RSM Bell. Jack scrambled to his feet when the block staff opened the door with a sharp 'Ten'shun!'

RSM Bell stepped in. 'Not good enough, soldier. Try again.'

'Ten'shun!'

Jack slammed his ammo boots hard on the concrete, feeling a judder through his spine.

'Better,' the RSM said. He looked at his clipboard as if for guidance as to why he was there. 'Some news about your mum.' His tone was flat, unemotional. He might have been reading from the bulletin on the clipboard. 'She passed away at oh three hundred hours yesterday. It comes to us all, son,' he added, as an afterthought.

If Tinker Bell hadn't said that, Jack would have held up at least until they were out of the door and he was on his own. That small kindly gesture caused him to lose control and cry. The army had broken him. All that the rest of his sentence did was strengthen his hatred of those who had done this to him. He began to plan how he might get even.

TWELVE

'Gracie would never have wanted this sort of lolly spending on her,' Joey said quietly, so the funeral director wouldn't hear. 'Forty-seven pounds, sixteen and six? It's daylight robbery.' He sounded as if he was in pain and Brian guessed he was somehow. Parting with money was as painful to Dad as having his teeth drilled.

'Shut up about money,' Mum hissed. She resisted his every suggestion about getting it done for half the price at the Co-op.

'There's a lot we could've done with that extra twenty pound,' Joey continued.

'I hope you're not such a tight wad when it comes to putting me six feet under, Joey Olinska.' She sounded even more bitter now.

'I could have stocked the new shop with that money. Well, near enough. I could certainly have got Joshua to fit it out.' Joey couldn't let it go.

'Without Mum and the money off her house we wouldn't have had the first bloody shop, much less the second.'

Brian turned his attention to the pallbearers as they lifted the coffin from the shiny hearse and carried it slowly through Kensal Rise cemetery to the open grave. He glanced at his dad, hoping he and Mum would stop arguing about money, at least until Nan was in the ground. Joey was in his best suit, shirt and tie. The whole lot had cost him twenty-seven shillings – much less than he would have had to pay in Brian's old shop – but saving money on his outfit didn't stop Joey worrying about the exorbitant cost of the interment. Mum had wanted Nan to go out in style so had ordered a solid oak coffin with real brass handles, while Tooke and Son's new Rolls-Royce hearse carried her to her resting place. That added to the price over their usual horse-drawn arrangement. Cath bought a new dress for the occasion from Gamages in Holborn. But Sammy Cohen had made her a coat as a peace-offering for losing their money on the dodgy black-market deal in traveller's cheques. So she was able to forgive him a little.

Her wishes prevailed over the funeral as they did in most other things. Brian hoped they would when it came to him going to university because Dad would be loath to lose his cheap labour at the shop.

Seeing Nan go into the cold, dark ground terrified Brian. He tried not to think about what was happening but then his granddad reached out of the grave to prod him. It was all he could do not to run. His mum squeezed his arm. 'She's better off now she's not suffering,' she whispered.

There were more men in black coats and top hats from the undertaker's than there were mourners, so Mum's argument that you had to do it right or people would think badly of you didn't make sense. Apart from close family, Nan's best friend Eve Sutton and her daughter Ruth were the only others present. Alice didn't come because Nan, she said, had died in sin.

'I'll never forgive her for saying that. Or for not turning up at her own mother's funeral. Billy Hill's not worth a light either.'

'Your mum was fond of him, Cath, and he did send a nice bunch of yellow Eternity roses. Mum would have appreciated them.'

Brian doubted she would in the light of Billy's absence. What would have upset her most, though, was Jack not being there. Her precious Jack was the only person she'd asked for as she'd slipped away.

Later, they were all having a cup of tea in the kitchen, Cath had made some ham sandwiches, but no one felt much like eating, except Ruth Sutton. As hungry as he was, Brian didn't want to eat just then in case he somehow got lumped together with Ruth in any way.

'It'll seem very strange without her, Cath,' Eve said, after one of the long silences that kept falling over them.

'She was the life and soul of this street, your mum. Do anything for you. I remember at the start of the war when you couldn't get a bit of coal, your dad carried an old railway sleeper home on his shoulder. Your mum made him give me half.'

'I remember that,' Joey said. 'You propped it up and fed it on to the fire whole.'

'Well, I didn't have no strapping man to saw it up.'

That image of his granddad not looking so strapping with his head bashed in popped up behind Brian's eyelids. It was followed by another, of Granddad sitting on the bed and touching him under the blanket. He started to shake.

'Brian?' his mum said. 'You all right, love?' She took his hand and put her arm around him.

That made Brian shake more. He tried to breathe deeply.

'He's upset about his nan, aren't you, lovey? He was ever so fond of her, weren't you, love? Couldn't do enough for her.'

Let me speak for myself! Brian screamed inwardly. To avoid his mother, and stop himself wondering whether Nan would find out the truth about Granddad now she was on the other side, Brian let his eyes slide over to Ruth. She was twenty, plump, and had dry, pastry-like skin. He didn't want to engage with her in case she thought he was interested. Even the idea made him blush, but he didn't look away. He knew that what lay elsewhere was worse. Ruth met his gaze, smiled and glanced away. Then her eyes came right back to his. She smiled again.

Brian blushed some more, and glancing away saw Joey ease back his cuff to check the time. His dad would be wanting to reopen the shop. He'd closed for the funeral as the undertakers hadn't been able to fit it in on early closing day. Brian knew, too, that he wanted to see how the second shop was progressing.

'It was a shame your Jack couldn't get here,' Eve Sutton said. 'I don't s'pose the army could spare him.'

Brian almost laughed. He knew his mum and dad were dreading the day Jack came back. After Nan's last stroke, and with her condition getting worse, Brian went with Cath to the War Office in Whitehall to ask if Jack could come home. The man they saw refused to give them any information, but said he would pass on Cath's request to the regiment at Catterick for Jack to get leave.

'He's not at Catterick,' Cath argued. Bobby Brown told them a friend had said Jack was doing hard labour at Shepton Mallet. Finally, when Nan wasn't expected to live, Cath and Brian had gone to Somerset on the train. Joey couldn't go because he couldn't afford to close the shop. Cath accepted this as she was equally keen to get money in and pay off the loan as soon as possible.

The cold-eyed officer who came to the gatehouse to meet them reeked of booze. 'You're correct in your assumption, Mrs Oldman,' he said. 'Your brother is here. Regrettably you can't see him and he certainly can't have leave. The regulations are quite clear on that.'

'But his mum's dying,' Cath had remonstrated.

'A message about her will be passed to your brother when it is appropriate to do so.'

'What the bloody hell is appropriate, Brian?' Cath exploded, on the platform as they waited for the train back to London. 'I'd like to kill those stuck-up gits.'

Nan died without any word from Jack. Cath was bitter about the army, but angry with herself for letting them fob her off. 'They shan't do it again. Mark my words. No one's ever going to fob me off ever again.'

From that point on, Brian noticed that she questioned everything, then questioned it again, especially the things he did. It wasn't enough for her to see rain falling to know it was raining: she had to feel it, too. It drove him mad. Every time he was out with her, she challenged things and embarrassed him. She checked his change out shopping to make sure people weren't diddling him, checked his adding-up in the shop if a customer queried anything. Again and again, the urge to kill her rose in him, but never more strongly than when he agreed to go to the pictures with Ruth Sutton. About a week after his Nan's funeral he'd met her in the street.

Ruth was on the pavement, her mouth open, watching some young boys play hopscotch. She folded her arms under her breasts, like her mother did when she stood to watch the world go by. 'Finished work, Brian?'

Reluctantly he told her he had.

'You going in for your tea now, are you?'

'Yeah,' he said, scuffing his foot down the crack between the paving stones.

'Got some new shoes from Dolcis,' she said. 'Mum had a Provident cheque for ten pounds. She got some too. And a coat.'

Brian looked down at her new high-heels. They didn't make her legs look any less fat.

'Stanley Baker and Patrick McGoohan's at the Essoldo tonight,' she announced, as if they were expected in person. ''S *Hell Drivers*. D'you want to go? I'll pay.'

That embarrassed Brian. The man was supposed to pay. 'I was going to the drill hall for Boys' Brigade. I gotta go,' he said.

'Any good?' was all Ruth wanted to know.

'All right.' There was no enthusiasm in his voice. *Hell Drivers* would probably be more interesting, but he enjoyed being with the boys at the drill hall. 'What time's it start?' he found himself asking.

Cath embarrassed him even more when she said, 'What do you want to go with her for?'

Brian didn't answer and hurriedly ate his tea.

'That Ruth's not all there up top, is she?'

'She's all right,' Brian said, enjoying taking the opposite position to his Mum, and defending Ruth. 'She offered to pay.'

'She can't get a bloke to buy the tickets!' Cath announced triumphantly. 'I never had to pay to go to the pictures with a man.'

'He should go,' Joey piped up. 'He has to start somewhere with girls, and Ruth seems harmless enough.'

Why would I want to go with one who was 'harmless enough'? Brian felt like asking. Instead he said, 'I'm not going anyway. It's Boys' Brigade tonight.'

There the matter rested and he slipped out of the house, but not in his Boys' Brigade uniform. He waited at the end of the street for Ruth and they walked to the Essoldo without speaking. Brian didn't have much to say to girls and knew nothing about the film. Even though he didn't have much money, he insisted on paying – he didn't want to be seen to let a girl buy the tickets. Even the cheap seats at one and ninepence would eat into his money. No one was paid a proper wage for working in the shop, but on Saturday afternoons, as Joey was cashing up, he usually slipped Brian a ten-bob note. Brian was glad of it, but it didn't seem much for working every day except Sunday.

'You got your keep to think about, son,' his mother told him.

Occasionally Brian helped himself to half a crown out of the till His tally was never wrong at the end of the day because a lot went in without being rung up.

They queued to get in and discovered they were missing the start of the B picture with Tyrone Power when the commissionaire came along the queue calling, 'There's one at one and nine, and two at two and three.'

Brian stepped forward, pulling Ruth with him, and grabbed the two seats at the top price so he could disappear into the dark before anyone recognized him.

The cinema was heaving and they disturbed people as they slid along to their seats in the second row from the back. Ruth took off her coat and put it on her lap, then opened her handbag, took out her cigarettes and offered Brian one. He didn't smoke, as a rule, because of Joey's lungs, and the Woodbine from the green and brown packet made him cough when Ruth gave him a light. A constant haze of blue smoke drifted up to the ceiling, caught in the flickering light of the projector. Everyone seemed to be smoking.

The ice-cream girl appeared before the main feature.

On his way back to his seat with ice-creams and a Kia-Ora, he met a boy he'd gone to school with, Roy Shepherd. 'You with that tart?' he said. 'You getting a bit, Bri?'

The blood rushed to his cheeks and Brian was sure everyone was staring at him – Roy Shepherd had spoken so loudly. Worse, someone might tell his mum. A wave of uncertainty swept over him and he considered hurrying out of the cinema, but Ruth was craning her neck to see him. She waved as he came up the aisle so he couldn't run.

'You jammy sod,' Roy Shepherd said. He still had acne.

During the main feature, Roy Shepherd kept turning to stare at him, no more concentrating on what Stanley Baker was doing than Brian was. At first he didn't notice Ruth's hand find its way into his lap. She clasped his hand tightly, then dragged it on to her lap. Brian started to sweat. The cinema was hot and he wanted some air. Everyone would see him if he got up on his own, so he didn't move. That was like an invitation to Ruth, who slid his arm round her back and leaned into him. She turned her face away from the screen and found his lips. He could taste cigarette smoke on her breath and strawberry ice-cream on her lips, mixed with lipstick. Ruth kissed him again, clinging to him. All Brian could think of was what people might say to his mum, and what Cath would say to him if she found out. She would find out. She always seemed to know everything he ever did.

Who told her about his 'deception', as she called it, she didn't say. 'Don't throw yourself away on the first girl what comes along.' She switched off the television, which had shut down for the night. 'With your looks you could have the pick of half the women in London. Eve Sutton's youngest isn't all there.'

Yes, you said that before! Brian didn't dare voice the thought.

'You can do better, Brian. You've got plenty of time.'

'Well, Dad wasn't much older than me when he got married.'

'You ain't gone and done something silly, have you?'

That was a laugh! Brian hadn't felt a thing with Ruth. Not even when her hand had brushed his knob accidentally on purpose in the cinema or when they stopped in the alleyway behind the houses and kissed again, much harder, and she encouraged him to explore her body. Even when she squeezed and touched him he didn't feel anything – although he didn't have any problems when he did it to himself.

A couple of weeks later he discovered there was no problem at all. He was in the shop on his own, serving one of his regular ladies, when he glanced up from sliding her potatoes and onions onto the newspaper at the bottom of her basket and saw a man walk past the window, looking in at him. A few minutes later, he came back the other way. He was quite old, maybe forty, quite thin, and wore a raincoat over a good tweed suit, even though it wasn't raining. He had on cycling clips although he wasn't pushing a bike. When he paused for the third time, Brian noticed he was limping and felt sorry for him. His Mac was belted at the back only. Finally he came into the shop, and Brian knew immediately that something was about to happen. The way he looked at him with his pathetic eyes, Brian would have given him anything – even a pound out of the till. But that wasn't what he was after. He didn't want fruit or veg either.

'Do you go across to the wasteground when you close the shop?' he asked, in a posh Irish accent. He said his name was Wilfrid, and that he was an actor.

Brian didn't usually go via the wasteground, where there was once a factory, but he would go that way today. He had been waiting for something to happen without quite knowing what.

When he saw Wilfrid step out from behind a foundation wall left standing on the weed and bramble-covered ground, he panicked. What if he wasn't an actor but a cop who was out to catch him? What would his dad say? But Brian knew he couldn't stop himself now.

'You're well endowed,' Wilfrid said, as he undid the buttons on Brian's fly and put his hand inside. Brian's breathing quickened with excitement. He throbbed and ached, and screwed up his eyes with such intensity he thought he'd go blind. The older man barely squeezed him before he shot his load. Brian sucked in his breath hard, trying to contain his excitement in this public place and draw out the pleasure.

It was all over in moment, or so Brian thought, until Wilfrid undid his belt and got him to drop his trousers and pants. The little man was enormous, he discovered, and for a moment Brian thought something would break. Then he realized he was hard again as Wilfrid's hand reached round. He'd never known anything nicer, and right then he didn't care if all the cops in London poured down on him.

Each day after that, he looked out for Wilfrid, hoping he'd come past the shop and signal that he'd be waiting on the wasteground. He wanted to do it again, and wondered if he'd imagined it. A month passed without even a glimpse of the other man and Brian felt increasingly desolate. He'd have to look elsewhere for his pleasure, even with all the risks it would bring.

There was little choice about closing on Thursday afternoons. His dad didn't want to, but all the other shops were shut, so there weren't enough customers on the street to make staying open worthwhile. On Thursday, Joey and Brian did the books. His dad was showing him double-entry bookkeeping, how to lose and write off stock due to supposed damage or produce supposedly going rotten. It was a wonder they made any money at all. There was another book in which all the money was entered that was never declared to the taxman. His dad noted down every penny he spent on anything. He didn't buy so much as a newspaper without putting it into the book. Brian couldn't see the point. When Joey got fruit and vegetables from drivers for cash in the market, sometimes for half or even a quarter of the price he'd have paid wholesalers, he registered all those transactions. He didn't tell anyone where he kept that book.

His mum was catching up with the housework in Nan's old house and baking in the gas oven in the back scullery. She didn't use the oven in the range for cooking now, just for heating the room and drying laundry. It was then that the worst of all possible things happened, as far as Brian's mum and dad were concerned, almost six months to the day after his nan had died. There was a faint knock at the front door. Joey glanced up irritably, finished his sum, then went to open it. They never left it unlocked nowadays.

Brian paused from the bookkeeping and listened to the voices in the hall. The second was strange yet familiar, and carried with it some inexplicable threat. Cath dropped the plate of fairy cakes she was bringing through for their tea when Jack stepped into the kitchen. He stared at them for a long while, as if he was meeting the wrong family. Finally he said, 'You lock the door now.'

'Can you wonder with all the thieves about?' Cath said.

'You're filling out, Brian.'

His voice was different, which was why Brian didn't immediately recognize it. It was deeper, with a harder edge. Jack didn't look directly at anyone, but off to the side. There were scars on his face where none had been before he went into the army, and his hair showed streaks of grey.

'Why didn't you let us know you were coming, for God's sake?' Cath said sharply. 'We'd have laid on something. There's nothing in the house.'

Joey picked up the fairy cakes and set them back on the plate. 'No harm done,' he said, taking, as usual, the line of least resistance. 'You could eat your dinner off them floors, the way your sister cleans the place.' He stood nervously, wringing his hands and twisting his wedding ring, round and round on his finger. Brian knew what he was thinking. 'Cath's right,' he went on.' We'd have got a bit in, Jack, if we'd known.'

'I've been doing training at the Boys' Brigade,' Brian said.

A long silence fell as the gulf between them widened. There was an atmosphere about Jack that Brian didn't understand. Instinctively he wanted to move away from him, but he couldn't.

'D'you want a cup of tea?' Cath said. 'I don't suppose the army grub was up to much.'

'You're right there. It wasn't worth a light.'

To Brian, they sounded like strangers speaking different languages to each other.

What did Jack want?

Brian knew that thought was uppermost in his mum's mind. His dad was probably wondering whether Jack would make them take money out of the shop.

Cath cut her brother a sandwich of thick white bread with cheese and pickle. He ate hungrily and drank three cups of tea using it to wash down food he'd barely chewed, all without saying a word.

'How long you been out of the army?' Brian asked.

'About a month.'

'A month?' Cath couldn't keep the surprise out of her voice. 'Why didn't you let anyone know? I could've made your old room up. It's there if you want it.'

'I've got a room,' Jack said.

'Was it tough in the army?' Brian said.

'I should've boxed. It would've been cushy for me then. Dead easy.'

'Why didn't you?'

Jack shook his head. 'Where's Mum buried?'

'Kensal Rise cemetery. We gave her a smashing send-off, Jack, didn't we, Joey? No expense spared.'

'No expense spared,' Joey repeated. 'Solid oak coffin, brass handles, the works. She even had a Rolls Royce to carry her to her resting place. I've got our little van outside. I'll run you up. You won't find her plot on your own.'

'No. Brian can show me.'

'Brian?' Cath sounded suspicious. 'Don't be daft. Joey'll run you up in the van.'

But Jack started out of the house, gesturing to Brian, who glanced at his parents, but felt compelled to obey Jack. He grabbed his jacket and ran after him.

They walked, Jack setting a fast pace, which at first Brian had difficulty in keeping up with. His uncle's truculent mood didn't lift as they strode through the streets, Brian still putting in extra steps. Neither spoke. After a while Brian asked, 'What are your plans, Jack? You gonna have another go at boxing?'

If he had any plans, Jack wasn't saying. A couple of people recognized him and greeted him along the four-mile walk. He sailed past as if they didn't exist. Eventually he asked, 'What d'you hear of Billy Hill? Does he come round at all?'

'He's back on his feet again,' Brian said, keen to give him some real news, hoping it might cheer him.

'He always was lucky,' Jack said. 'Things always fell right for him.'

'Not any more. He's scrapping with Spot. Spotty's little gang causes no end of problems to shopkeepers.'

'You have to pay him protection, do you?'

'Well, Dad gives the Krays a few quid every week.'

'Is Ronnie still fat as a pig?'

'I'd say so. He puts the bite on all the shops. They all pay up.'

'Up to his old tricks, is he? What if they don't pay?'

'I don't know, Jack. Everyone just gives him what he asks for.'

'Reggie's involved too, then, is he?

'Dad calls him the silent partner.'

Gracie's plot was neglected. 'Why's it left like this?' Jack asked, not pleased. He picked up bits of rubbish that had blown there, then threw away the dead flowers that stood rotting in a jam jar. Brian pulled up some weeds. He couldn't do anything about the long-uncut grass.

'Mum keeps saying she must come up with flowers, but there's always something urgent what stops her. We're opening a new shop. She's ever so busy with that,' Brian explained.

'Too busy to give the old girl five minutes.'

Brian spent most of his time in the first shop. They had two part-time assistants working for them, both of whom Joey complained about each time he paid them, telling them he wasn't sure how much longer he could keep them on, with business so bad. As far as Brian could tell business was never better. He resented being tied to the shop. His mother worked long, hard hours in the other, but that was her choice. 'You know how they got them shops, don't you?' he said aloud to Jack.

Jack stopped weeding and straightened. There was hurt and anger in his eyes.

'They used Nan's house when she was ill, so the shops are partly yours as well by rights.' Brian held his breath, heart thumping, not sure what he had started.

'D'you sell flowers?' Jack asked.

'On Saturdays Dad fetches a few bunches. We got two shops – well, three almost.'

Jack nodded. 'Bring a bunch of something nice up here for the old girl, if the profits can stand it. Even if they can't.'

'He asked about the shops' profits, did he?' Joey said, the pained look suggesting his acid stomach might be playing up. 'He wanted to know about our profit?'

'We should have taken a bit more trouble and gone up there,' Cath said. 'I said so often enough. She was good to us.'

'What if he wants some of the profit?'

'We'll tell him there isn't any, Joey. We're just getting started. Is he coming back?'

'He didn't say, Mum.'

'He will. Of course he will. He'll want his share of the house,' Joey said.

'That'll be difficult – for a while, at least. We ain't got it to give. Why did he wait a month before he showed up?'

'He's up to something,' Joey said.

'What's he been doing for a month?' Cath frowned at Brian, wanting an answer.

Brian shrugged. 'He didn't say nothing to me.'

'He must have said *something*,' Joey said accusingly.

'Well, he didn't, just that he was doing a bit of this and that.'

'Thieving, most likely.'

'As long as he doesn't come thieving round us,' Cath said. 'Trying to take all we've worked like blacks to build up.'

'But the house is partly his. Didn't Nan leave it for him as well?'

Joey chewed on that for a moment. 'He could go to a solicitor, find out what his true position is. That would put us in a bind.'

'Jack wouldn't give a solicitor the time of day,' Cath said. 'Would we be able to come up with anything for him, if he was to ask?'

'A couple of quid out of the till maybe, but he's bound to want more than that, isn't he?'

Cath said, 'You sure he didn't say nothing, Brian?'

'Well, I'll ask him when he comes round again,' Brian said, enjoying their anxiety.

'What did he say when he left?'

'I told you. We looked in at the gym. We didn't see anyone he knew, apart from some bloke called Rikki the Malt. Jack and him talked about the old days when his trainer was alive. He said he'd look Rikki up – he's got a spieler or something.'

'Is he coming back into us on the nip?'

They were terrified Jack would bleed them dry. And Brian hoped he would. This might be the way he could eventually get free.

THIRTEEN

Brian wasn't sure what Jack expected from his sister and her husband. The next time he turned up at his mum's old house to see them he didn't say why he'd come, but his presence made everyone uncomfortable. Brian saw that Joey was impatient to get on with his bookkeeping, and wondered how he would react if Jack asked to see the accounts. Did he have any right to see them? He would like to have known about that secret book himself, listing every penny of his fiddle. His dad's records were his religion.

'Does Jack want a look at the books?' Brian said suddenly, unable to stop himself. 'See how we're doing?'

'He wouldn't want to waste his time on that,' Cath said. The wicked look she gave him was chilling.

'You can if you want,' Joey offered, and stared at his son.

'Would it do me any good?' Jack asked.

'We ain't cheating you out of nothing, Jack. Everything has to be accounted for to the government,' Joey said. 'We're just about managing to keep our heads above water.'

Brian waited for Jack to come back about the books, but he didn't. Instead he said, 'Why didn't the other fella go to Mum's funeral?'

Brian was puzzled by that. It was as if Jack wasn't connecting to the steer he was giving him to the fiddle that was going on right under his nose.

'He always was a no-good ponce,' Cath said. 'Shoulda been him in the ground, not her.'

'He did give her the house,' Brian blurted out. 'That's how we got the business.' He couldn't resist going back to it, knowing how his parents felt. 'I mean, it's Jack's house too. Right?'

'We got every penny we could raise on the house tied up in the shops, Jack. Every penny's invested, trying to make a go of things.'

'Yeah, I get the message, Joey. There ain't no money spare. What about her bit of tom? That ponce give her plenty when he was ram-raiding jewellery shops.'

'We sold it, Jack. We had to. We didn't hear from you.' Cath wet her finger and twisted off Gracie's wedding ring, which she wore on her right hand, and held it out to him. 'That's all we got left. We had to sell the rest under the counter. We didn't know if it was knocked off.'

'We went to a solicitor, Jack. It was all done proper, like.'

Still Brian couldn't understand why Jack was taking this so calmly, why he wasn't shouting and swearing, demanding his share. If he did, that might mean the end to the shops and Brian's enslavement. He could go back to the men's outfitters and the class trade he found there.

But if Jack was ruminating on some alternative plan, he wasn't offering it. Instead he glanced at Brian. 'D'you want to look in at the gym?'

Brian didn't hesitate. He got his jacket.

'What about the books?' Joey asked.

'I can do them later with you.'

'Don't be late,' Cath said. 'You've got work tomorrow.'

As if he needed reminding.

'That sounds like regular collar, that shop,' Jack said.

'It is. I had a really good job in a men's outfitters.'

They walked out on to Goswell Road and turned east towards the boxing gym. When they passed Sullivan's yard, Brian didn't look in case his granddad saw him and pulled him in.

'What's wrong with you?' Jack said.

'What d'you mean?' Brian replied, quickening his pace to get ahead of Jack. If he told Jack that his mum and dad had murdered Granddad he'd be free.

'I s'pose he must be in there somewhere. Well, little bits of him,' Jack said, pausing at the entrance to the yard. 'Talk about poxy luck, catching a direct hit from a doodlebug.'

Suddenly it occurred to Brian that Jack or anyone else might not believe him about what happened to his granddad. No, they'd believe him, all right, but he wasn't about to tell.

'Nothing much changes, does it?'

'What d'you mean?'

Jack nodded across the road. There were still plenty of gaps in the lines of buildings on the streets of the City and the East End where bombs had taken out buildings. 'You'd think someone would build the houses, at least. People need homes.'

Weeds grew over the bombsites in the summer and buddleia sprouted out of the walls, then died back. Litter and rubbish collected there.

'Some of the owners died in the air raids. Others can't be traced,' Brian explained. 'There isn't much spare cash around to rebuild them, not speculatively anyway.'

He glanced at Jack to test his reaction. When there was none, he added, 'Tom Driberg told me that.' Apparently the name meant nothing to Jack. 'He's an MP I know. As a matter of fact, I know him quite well.' He didn't say what they had done while they were getting to know each other.

They lapsed back into silence, Brian longing to know what his uncle was thinking. 'He's making plenty of money from the shops, Dad is. He hides it.'

'Yeah, I wouldn't be surprised. Your mum too.'

'You gonna claim your share?' Brian asked, excited now. 'He pugs away a fair bit of cash.'

'That sounds like Joey. He was always careful with money. Where's he put it?'

There was an edge to the question. Having at last got his

undivided attention, Brian didn't want to lose it. 'He keeps two sets of books. He knows exactly what he makes. There's plenty of fiddle, Jack.'

'Is that right? How much?'

'Hard to say. As much of what he makes goes away in cash as what goes back to the shops.'

'But if you don't know where he keeps it, that ain't much use, is it?'

'He wouldn't trust the bank with it.'

'Then where does he keep it? You know, Brian, don't you?'

'Honest to God, I don't!' Brian said earnestly.

Without warning, Jack punched him in the side of the head and sent him staggering on to a bombsite on Goswell Road. Brian tripped over a low, moss-encrusted brick wall and went down, scraping his knee and banging his elbows. Before he could protest, Jack dragged him up and hit him again.

'What?' Brian couldn't understand why he was so angry.

'Don't be a mug, son. Don't tell anyone nothing about your business. Not even me. Understand? Don't ever say nothing. That's what coppers' narks do. Next thing you'll be telling someone like them.'

'I won't.' Brian was fighting back tears. 'I'm sorry, Jack. I won't do it again.'

There was nothing Brian could do or say to impress on Jack that he was on his side and always would be. Thoughts collided in his brain as he tried to understand why Jack was suddenly taking his parents' side when he only wanted to steer him to what was his due. He considered throwing his arms around him and embracing him, but Jack wouldn't like that. He didn't get the same feeling from him that came from the actor Wilfrid Bramble on their brief encounter, not even when Brian peeled off his shirt and vest at the gym and Jack admired how his body was developing. His casual observations didn't mean what Brian would have liked them to mean.

Now, watching Jack strip off and start whacking the punchbag, his body soon glistening with sweat, Brian felt as if he was at the seaside – all pleasure. He couldn't imagine any man being in better shape. Afterwards when Jack towelled himself dry, Brian wanted to touch his scars and take away the pain he believed Jack was suffering – Brian believed it was the cause of his uncle's sudden murderous rages.

The small, swarthy Rikki the Malt sidled up to them as they were watching a couple of young boxers sparring. 'Jack, m' ol' china.'

'D'you find out what Billy Hill's doing, these days?' Jack asked.

'No one ain't heard nothing. I did see that ol' dripper of yourn, Win—'

Bang! Jack hit Rikki again and again, putting him on the floor, bleeding. There was no fight in the Maltese club-owner, who reached feebly into his pocket and pulled out a flick-knife. Brian doubted he could have used it to cut up an apple, much less cut Jack, who took it off him as if he was a child. 'Be the worst day's work you ever did,' Jack said, his anger gone.

Brian was at a loss. How could a man be so angry one moment, then so calm? When he got really angry he sometimes shook for hours. 'What was that about, Jack?' he asked later.

'He was too flash for his own good. People have gotta know I'm back. That flash 'erbert Billy Hill will know all right. Rikki's been into him.'

Several times Brian missed work or shut up shop early and went off with Jack when he dropped in at the greengrocers. It was like truanting from school, and it gave him a thrill. Never once did he stop to consider the consequences. His dad talked about sacking him. Was that what he really wanted instead of taking over the business one day? Brian said he didn't care. His Dad and Mum were shocked as much as he was himself. He didn't think he could ever say that. Jack gave him courage.

One day he took some money from the till, closed the shop and got a cab to Wapping High Street with Jack. The prefabs that had replaced some of the bombed homes were cracked and covered with lichen, while stretches of derelict housing were still untouched and boarded up, many showing no evident signs of living, while others suggested an active business behind the soot-smudged fronts. Brian followed Jack on foot along the High Street, then to Cable Street. Brian had learnt that Jack never liked to be seen drawing up outside a place he was visiting. 'It lets anyone know you're about. If that cab'd dropped us here, we'd soon have some nark telling a copper.'

They pushed in through an open doorway between a cobbler's and a bag shop. Brian followed Jack up the worn stairs to a landing on the first floor where he rapped on one of two doors. The varnish on both was chipped and scarred through years of wear and the whole place might have been abandoned, but a woman's voice said, 'Half a mo'.' He glanced at Jack, whose face was expressionless. When the door cracked open, a middle-aged man hurried out and clattered down the stairs.

Not knowing what to expect, Brian kept close to Jack as they went through the door and into a bedroom that smelt of sweat and perfume.

'Oh, I don't see two at a time,' the woman said, hardly looking at them. Win Booker had aged, but Brian knew her at once. She didn't recognize them. Probably she didn't notice any of her clients.

'That ain't what we're after,' Jack said.

'If it's trouble you want, darling, my boyfriend can give you plenty.' She lit a cigarette and at last turned to him. The penny dropped. 'Oh, my Gawd! Jack! You daft bugger! Why didn't you say? Oh, Jack.' She threw her arms around his neck and kissed his lips. He didn't move until she reached up and touched his face tenderly. 'What have you done to that beautiful face of yours? What bastards done that to you? I'll murder them.'

'It don't matter.' He didn't like talking about what had happened to him in the army, but the scar across his face was testament to a thorough beating.

'If it ain't business, darling, I'll put the kettle on, make us a cuppa. Who's this?' she asked, lighting a gas ring that sat on the tiled grate and setting the kettle on it.

'Don't you recognize me?' Brian said.

'Give me a clue, darling. You ain't been up here to see me, I know that. I'd remember one as young and good-looking as you. I wouldn't let him go,' Win Booker said, and winked at Jack.

'He's our Cath's boy, Brian,' Jack said.

'So he is. Well, he certainly knows how to fill a shirt. And a pair of pants, I bet!'

Brian blushed. She looked so different from how he remembered that he might have walked past her in the street. Her hair was now bright ginger, her makeup like a mask. She pulled on a quilted pink housecoat and wrapped it tightly around herself, covering her large breasts and the dark stain of pubic hair showing under her flimsy negligée. Brian looked away.

There was a long silence as they waited for the kettle to boil. Was she wondering why they were there? Neither of them was looking for a poke. Win got started then with endless chatter about movie stars and there was no stopping her, the films she'd been to see, what gramophone recording artists she liked.

'I'm crackers about Frank Sinatra. He's one of my favourites,' she said. 'He could fly me to the moon any old day of the week. And Frankie Laine. Jack was always gonna take me dancing to the Locarno ballroom, weren't you? Never did.'

'What sort of trouble you getting these days, Win?' Jack asked.

'Oh, I don't get none much. Only from them bleedin' cousins of mine. I don't see nothing of them, of course, only their collectors, that young John Bindon and his tearaways. He always tries to cop a freebie. You mark my words, Jack, he'll end up a bad lot, that one.'

'Just mentioning of the Krays usually takes care of any

troublesome clients – mind you, they ain't ever here when it happens, or Bindon.' She poured them tea in chipped mugs like the one Brian and everyone else at his school had been given to celebrate the Queen's Coronation. 'One of my regulars even wants to marry me, would you believe? Every week he proposes.' She spooned sugar into the mugs. 'What you got in mind, Jack? I do know a couple of girls what have just started up. They need a bit of looking after. I bet they'd rather have you than the twins.'

Business was what they came for. Jack was having a lean time since he'd got out of the army.

On the way back to the greengrocery on Theobald's Road, they stopped at a pawnshop. Jack knew the owner, Manny Evans, a large, unsmiling man who stepped into the narrow booth at the side of the counter so that they could conduct their business in private. Jack offered him his mum's wedding ring. The pawnbroker remembered him and bemoaned the loss of a good light-heavyweight.

'Yeah, yeah,' Jack said, with a flash of anger. 'Don't give me that old bunny, just what the groin's worth.'

'Hold your horses, Jack,' Manny Evans told him. 'It's worth a bit more because it's yours, like. I'll hold it against thirty bob, see, but I won't write you a ticket so I don't charge no interest.'

'What's the catch?' Jack asked.

'I'd like to see you get back on your feet.' He examined the ring again. 'Mum's is it? I'll take good care of it for you.' He slipped it into a small buff envelope. 'You used to be so handy with your German bands. Still are, I wouldn't wonder.' Then, finally, he got to it. 'I'm getting a spot of bother with them twins, see. Think they own the place. Trouble is they ain't got no opposition.'

'You pay them protection, do you?'

'Hah, that would be something if it was a straight business transaction. Instead they bring all kinds of goods in here and expect me to give them the value and more. All knocked off. I don't mind for the right sort of stuff. I have to pay them well over the odds, though.' He paused. 'What would you say to thirty bob a week to look after things? Every week the same, Jack, rain or shine.'

Brian tugged at Jack's sleeve and pulled him aside. 'It's got to be more,' he whispered. 'We have to pay a fiver a week at each of the shops. It's got to be more, Jack.'

That was the first time he'd seen Jack smile since he'd come back from the army.

The price was finally agreed at seven pounds a week.

'That was like getting money out of a stone,' Brian said, as they stepped out of the shop.

'Manny Evans is a Welsh Jew. There ain't none tighter,' Jack said. 'You done good, Bri. You should do all our negotiating in future.'

At that moment Brian felt ten feet tall, as if he had finally found himself.

'I had a chat with Edna and a couple of the other girls, Jack,' Win Booker said, pulling on her outdoor wrap over her housecoat and shucking off her comfy slippers for some fancy high-heeled shoes to go with the seamless stockings. She led them three doors down the road to meet Edna, who was older than Brian was expecting for a new girl. She was with a client so they waited outside in the street.

'Too dangerous inside,' Win explained. 'The rozzers can get you if there's more than one girl in the house – they think you're running a brothel.'

'D'you get any bother with buttonmen?' Jack asked.

'Not really. You just drop them ten bob now and then. Or they want a feel. Policemen are no different. Some get the full works.'

Brian was embarrassed, but fascinated. This was a real education.

'It's the detectives you gotta watch out for. Them dirty sods'll steal everything you got. They'll have you go through the card, *then* collar you if you ain't got enough cash for them.'

'Any in particular what dips his beak?'

'They're all as bad as each other. If you could do something about them, Jack, you'll be my hero. Ron and Reg can't seem to do nothing for all their talk. Or won't.'

As far as Jack was concerned, she had thrown down the gauntlet.

Brian felt excited. Suddenly his uncle was being catapulted back to his old position as local hero. He wondered if this might lift his mood, dispel some of his anger. Whatever the army did to hurt Jack, he was now determined to hurt the world more. It scared Brian, but he wanted so much to be close to it, he tingled.

The room Edna worked from wasn't much different from Win's. Its faded red-and-cream wallpaper was turning yellowy-brown like the tired quilt on the brass bedstead. There was a battered veneer wardrobe and a dressing-table loaded with pots and jars.

Edna got down to business as if she didn't have a moment to lose. 'The twins send someone to collect off me every day, a young ponce called John Bindon. A right tearaway. I hate him, and I hate them. He takes it all and gives me back pocket money. Pocket money!' Edna was spitting. 'I'll kill that lousy bastard one of these days, I swear I will.' She blew cigarette smoke down her nose. Her teeth, with wide gaps between them, were nicotine-stained.

With a glance at Brian, Jack said, 'Half.'

Brian nodded, feeling the eyes of the two women on him, enjoying the confidence Jack showed in him.

'What do I get for that?' the older woman wanted to know.

'No trouble from anyone. I'll take care of everything for half of what you cop, Edna. I won't be away off the manor like them other mugs.'

'Is he really as good as you say he is, Win?'

'He'll suit you a treat, girl.'

Edna agreed, and Jack seemed to think he had a bargain too. Knowing something about the value of things, nicking as he did out of the shop till, Brian understood why she agreed so quickly: it would be so easy for her to cheat. He and Jack would have to be in the room all the time to know any different.

'Don't be a mug, Brian,' Jack said, as they went down into the high street. 'We'll be copping twenny, thirty nicker a week off her and her friends. You'll see. We'll be on Easy Street, as Billy Hill always says.'

All Brian heard was 'we'. Jack was including him in the deal. They were partners. He was afraid to push it any further in case Jack changed his mind. At last he had entered the adult world.

Later, when he told his parents about his arrangement with Jack, his dad went mad, and he didn't often get angry. 'Have you lost your marbles, son?' he shouted, as he paced around the kitchen. 'I had high expectations of you, Brian, a proper education – didn't that Mr Driberg say you should go to university?'

'It's not for the likes of us, Dad,' Brian protested. Going out with Jack was far more exciting than sitting in a stuffy college with dull books.

'The likes of us? The likes of us?' Joey's voice went up into a high register as his emotions stopped his words forming properly. For a moment Brian thought he was having a fit. 'What's "the likes of us"? Are we so different? Can't we have hope of our children bettering themselves? Talk to this idiot, Cath, for Christsake.'

'Your dad's been scrimping and saving, pugging up every penny he can to send you to college,' Cath said, 'and to send you in style so you won't feel uncomfortable.'

'That uncle of yours is a loser, Brian.' Joey was still angry.

'It's better than being a pokey little shopkeeper.'

The smack his mother gave him across the face shocked him. Would Jack have hit her back? Brian didn't. He ran out of the kitchen and up to his bedroom.

It was there Cath found him. 'Oh, Brian,' she said, and sat on the bed next to him. 'I've never seen your dad so angry. You've made him so unhappy.'

Why couldn't he have been that angry when you killed Granddad? Brian wanted to ask. Then none of this would have happened. He used the thought as a wedge between his mother and himself, enjoying the feeling of power it gave him. When she reached out to put her arms around him, he got up and moved away. He pulled the darts out of his dartboard on the wall which had an old picture of Humphrey Bogart and Lauren Bacall stuck to it. He threw them, aiming for the woman – she looked a bit like his mother.

When he went back downstairs, things were calmer and his parents extracted a promise from Brian that he wouldn't rule out going to university. 'At least talk to that nice Mr Driberg again,' his mum said.

That nice Mr Driberg wants me to bum him again. What do you think about that? And what would Jack think of it? Not much, he supposed. To keep the peace, Brian agreed to go back to his job in the shop. 'But we ain't going to pay for protection any more.'

'Oh lovely grub. We'll have the shop smashed up, the customers frightened away,' Joey said. 'That'll cost us a pretty penny and no mistake.'

'We're paying through the nose for nothing, Dad,' Brian argued. 'Jack can protect us.'

'Against them twins? Are you potty?'

'He's done it before.'

'They're too well organized nowadays. Everyone has to pay. Do you know someone who doesn't?'

'Jack can do it.'

'And you think we wouldn't have to pay him?'

'He's family, Dad. He wouldn't charge so much.'

With a saving in prospect, Joey came round to the idea. 'Could he manage it? You sure about this, Brian?'

How Jack avoided a direct sort-out with the twins, Brian wasn't sure, especially as he got bolder and trod on their toes harder. Perhaps it was because they were too involved in other areas of crime and couldn't keep track of it all. They used rentmen to collect their dues, and they weren't the dangerous fighters their employers were known to be. Apart from the good-looking John Bindon, who was young and prepared to fight anyone. He came into the shop for protection money when Brian was there on his own. Brian almost lost his nerve.

'Come on, pal. You know what I want.'

'We ain't got nothing for you this week. We ain't taken enough to pay the light bill.'

'What d'you mean?' Bindon was puzzled. 'I come to collect. You know the score. You know the twins. You gotta pay up. Right?'

'Take a funny run, John. We ain't paying you.' The lack of reaction from Bindon made Brian braver. 'Not this week. Not ever.'

'Then you're gonna lose a lot of business, pal.'

'We'll see. Here you are,' Brian took an old Savoy cabbage and slapped it into Bindon's large hand. 'That'll cost you sixpence.'

Bindon shoved it back at him and left the shop.

His parents laughed when he told them, until anxiety dropped over Joey like a shroud. 'What if they come and smash up the place? Oh, Lord, you've started something now, Brian. Let's hope Jack can stop it, like you promised.'

Brian shared his father's concern, but for a different reason. What if Jack really couldn't handle all the trouble that was piling up? Why were the twins waiting so long before responding? It was like the Phoney War he'd heard people talk about when he was a kid but had never understood till now.

A couple of days later Jack was across the road in Ernie's café, having breakfast, when Bindon came into the shop with two other men. Brian glanced over and saw Jack slip out and dart through the traffic. 'You'd better piss off back to Fulhan, *Mr* Bindon. I told you the other day, we ain't paying nothing,' he said as Jack stepped through the doorway. The three men saw him and hesitated.

'The twins ain't gonna put up with no trouble from the likes of you, Jack,' Bindon said. 'They want things nice and rosy. You know what the guv'nor's like if they ain't. He'll steam down here and smash the place up, just as likely. You'll have a lot of spuds with black eyes.'

Bindon's two mates laughed.

'This man's so funny he should be on *Workers' Playtime*.' Jack punched him in the throat. That was his speciality. Bindon panicked, trying to breathe.

'I s'pose it ain't that funny after all, John, is it?' Jack said. The other two did nothing. They waited uncertainly. Jack snapped open the till, took out a ten-bob note and stuffed it into the top pocket of Bindon's jacket. It was to become another of his trademarks for dealing with people. 'Here you are, son. Get yourself a ticket to Brighton – the sea air'll clear your throat. Either that or you come and work for me.' Now it was Jack's turn to laugh. No one else did – especially not Joey. When he heard what had happened he rushed round to the shop, full of worry about the trouble his brother-in-law might have caused.

'Youshouldaseenit, Dad!' Brian said, his words banging into each other. 'Jack really clobbered him. One punch. John Bindon couldn't move.'

'What's going to happen? Is Jack going to hang around the shop all the time? Are customers going to risk coming here to get caught up in a barny with the twins?'

'They won't come,' Brian assured him. 'They won't come.'

He reassured other shopkeepers, too. One by one they turned to Jack for protection at half the price, just as the girls did, and still the twins made no response. At first Brian sensed Jack wondering why. For his part Brian was longing for the Krays to come so he could watch Jack knock them for six. To help play his part, he went to the gym after work to build himself up. The look and smell of the male physique he saw there was some compensation as they waited for the inevitable.

FOURTEEN

The twins didn't retaliate. Brian guessed they were too busy getting involved with important people who were coming to their spielers and carpet joints in the West End. He was envious. Those were the sort of people he wanted to be with and he yearned for his lost friendship with Tom Driberg and the MP's Oxford chums who he rarely saw nowadays.

Jack didn't bide his time: he moved in on the Krays' territory that lay outside the West End. He walked into a club in Creed Lane off Ludgate Hill and announced he was taking it over. It was a real flop where printers and loading-bay hands from nearby newspapers played three-card brag, sometimes losing all of their hard-earned wages but unable to stop themselves. Brian was the youngest person in the place and stuck out like a sore thumb. Billy Jones, an ex-docker Jack knew from when he was a stevedore, ran the place. He said, 'Half a mo', Jack, he'll get us nicked. He's under age.'

'Shut up,' Jack said. 'He's as good as gold. And look at him, he'll smarten the place up.'

'It don't want smartening, Jack,' Billy Jones said. 'All this lot wanna do is spend their money on stupid, rotten hands. If any of them makes trouble, Bobby Ramsay knocks them spark out.'

'There've been too many fights. It's all gonna stop with me around.'

'What d'you mean? We ain't had no trouble hardly. I told you, Bobby deals with any upset.'

'He might do okay with these clowns,' Jack said, 'but I fought Bobby Ramsay twice when he was boxing professionally. Then he was at his best and fittest, but I knocked him out both times.'

'What is it you want, Jack? A pension?'

Reluctantly, Billy Jones offered him a tenner a week in advance. Inevitably it wasn't enough, not for being there most nights, and especially not when Jack saw how much money went across the three tables. 'How much d'you reckon they're making a night, Bri?' he asked.

They were in an all-night café, with spoons chained to the tables, at Ludgate Circus, having breakfast, before Brian went to open the shop. He was droopy-eyed – he'd been up all night and didn't feel like going to work. 'It depends what they're paying the dealers, and how much them dealers're stealing.'

'Are they stealing? How d'you know?'

'Where there's cash that isn't going through a till there's stealing, Jack. Dad says so, and he'd be the one to tell you. I'd say it was a oner at least, but Dad'd know for sure.'

'How could he tell unless he counts it?'

'He has a knack of looking at money and knowing right to the pound exactly how much there is. He could easily do a count on them tables.'

'They wouldn't stand for it. If they was stealing, they'd put the kibosh on it with him there.'

'They wouldn't know if Dad did it. He'd watch from across the bar. D'you want me to ask him?'

'I don't want to get involved in that, son,' Joey said, when Brian told him what he wanted. 'You'd be better off in night school learning something useful instead of wasting your time in a spiel.'

'Jack says it's an education,' Brian argued.

'How come my dim-witted brother isn't running the country instead of Mr Macmillan, if he's so smart?' Cath said impatiently.

'It's not a lot to ask, is it?' Brian said. 'He's family.'

'Why does he want this information?' Joey asked.

'He doesn't think he's getting enough of a pension out of the place.'

'Ten pounds a week is a lot of money, Brian – especially for doing nothing. Look how hard you have to work for what we give you each week.'

Brian almost smiled. With Jack, he more than trebled the few bob he got in wages, including what he helped himself to out of the till. 'You can bet they get a lot more. And Jack don't do nothing exactly. If that was the case why do they pay him?'

There was no answer to that.

'You can bet if they give him ten, the mark-up's a fifty fold at least.'

'Five ton a week!' Brian was startled. 'Oh, yeah, 's what I thought. Somewhere around there.'

That did it for Joey. 'Let's take a look. See if I've taught you anything.'

With no liking for drink and even less for its effect on people, Joey stuck out more than Brian in the spiel. Tea wasn't served, so he nursed a glass of brown ale but didn't take a single sip. He hardly blinked as he watched the cards go down on the table furthest from the door. There was no need for him to stay there all night – and he couldn't anyway because the smoke hurt his eyes and lungs. He, Brian and Jack were about the only people in the place who weren't smoking. The fat man behind the bar kept a cigarette in the corner of his mouth the whole time, only taking it out to dock the ash or light another.

'Brian's right,' Joey said, stepping into Ludgate Hill and sucking the cold night air into his lungs. 'They'll be taking nearer to a grand a week, I'd say. I only counted on one table. In an hour the house took over fifty nicker. The dealer palmed a couple of oncers.'

'The thieving whoreson!' Jack exclaimed. 'You sure?' He was about to march back in and stop it, as if it was his money.

'I'm sure. He's not that good at it. The owner must be a bit slow. He wouldn't steal from me if I was running the place.'

'D'you want to run it, Joey?' Jack asked.

Joey recoiled at the idea. But he was attracted to the money. If anyone knew how to skim, it was Joey.

'To be honest, Jack, I wouldn't know how to run a place like this,' Joey said, 'and I wouldn't want to get involved. It's illegal. I don't want Brian too involved either.'

'Dad!' Brian protested. 'I'm with Jack. Nothing's going to happen.'

'The sensible thing is for you to study. I thought you wanted to go to university.'

'You said we couldn't afford it – you're saving up.'

'You got to get some education at night school first. See if you've got what it takes. You're not going to find that out hanging around a spieler.'

'He's all right, Joey,' Jack said. 'This is an education, being my right-hand man. I couldn't manage without him.'

Suddenly Brian felt good about himself, and even more determined to stick by Jack.

'He's got an MP who offered to help him get to university,' Joey said. 'He must have seen something in him to do that. We'll find the money somehow if Mr Driberg can help him get a place.'

'It'd be a waste of time,' Jack told him. 'It was Brian who saw what this spiel was doing, him what saw that thieving bastard stealing my money. I was thinking of getting him to run the place.'

'How d'you know they'll let you run anything?' Joey demanded. 'Isn't it controlled by the Krays?'

'We'll see.' Jack winked at Brian. 'If you took it over for us, Joey, Brian could still get his education.'

It was the right approach. Brian knew his dad wouldn't pass up this sort of money for the sake of a little lost sleep, and that his mum wouldn't let him, each telling themselves it was for Brian's sake.

'You've got to go on with your education,' Cath said. 'You have to agree to that, Brian. We can't let Mr Driberg down.'

Brian wanted to laugh. It was a promise easily made. Neither of his parents would accompany him to night school, so Brian would slip away to meet Jack instead.

*

The first threat to their takeover at the spiel was a challenge from Bobby Ramsay. He was old and finished, Brian saw, as Ramsay came through the smoky gambling room and dug out Jack, who was sitting at the bar drinking a cup of tea. Tea was an immediate concession by the new management. They served it to the customers who wanted it, and a lot of them did, preferring to keep a clear head at the table and not go back to their newspapers reeking of booze.

'This ain't right, Jack, is it?' Bobby Ramsay said. At first his slurred speech made Brian think he was drunk, until he realized it was the result of blows to the head.

'Why's that, Bobby? Billy Jones'll make more from the place with me keeping an eye on the thieving hounds around here.'

'There's only one thieving hound what I can see, Jack,' Ramsay said gamely. 'We'd better go outside and sort this, hadn't we? Quiet, like.'

'It's gotta be here, so people know right away who's the guv'nor.'

Ramsay hesitated. He glanced at Billy Jones, who licked his suddenly dry lips with equal uncertainty, not wanting to start it himself. Finally the boxer said, 'I wouldn't want no trouble with you, Jack, but you don't want none with the twins, do you? It's up to you.' As he turned away, his whole body seemed to signal what he was about to do.

When he turned back Jack was there, his fist driving hard into Ramsay's throat. He went down, gagging for breath, as Billy Jones jumped on Jack's back. It was a move he should have made earlier if he was to give his own man a chance. Jack twirled about, trying to shake him off as Jones punched him in the side of the head and screamed, 'You're not nicking my business.' The fat man behind the bar produced a policeman's truncheon and caught Jack a glancing blow. Brian grabbed a pint bottle of Mackeson off the bar and smacked the fat man in the face. The bottle shattered on the bridge of his nose and he went down, yelling that he was blind.

Finally Jack freed himself and swung round to face Jones.

'Enough, Jack. This is silly,' he said, putting up his hands. Jack hit him anyway. There was no stopping him now. The second and third punches both caught the spiel-owner before he hit the floor.

When the dust settled, the place was empty. Everyone had gone. No one there seemed to share the excitement Brian felt during the fight.

The barman wasn't blind, but his nose was fatter than before and there was a lot of blood down the front of his shirt. The three men were like lambs now – perhaps because there was no longer anything to fight over.

'I don't know what Reggie and Ronnie are going to say when they hear about this,' Jones said. 'I mean, it was a nice little business. Now look at it. No one.'

'They'll come back,' Jack told him. 'They have to. They're gamblers.'

He was right: a few men drifted in on the second night after the fight, and on the third the place was full of the same familiar faces and Joey was complaining about the smoke. The working men who came there were addicted to all sorts of things, but especially gambling. Fleet Street printers were well paid, and even when they lost everything they couldn't stop, but tried to borrow around the table, sometimes succeeding. They were all the same, drowning in their addiction.

Journalists were no less enslaved to it. One night, a small rotund bald man, Percy Hoskins, chief crime reporter from the *Daily Express*, came in with man Jack recognized as Ken Drury, the bent detective who'd said he could keep him out of the army if he'd help put Billy Hill away. He watched then play a few hands of brag and win a couple of pounds. Then they came to the bar to talk to him, mostly about his boxing career. 'What sort of trouble you expecting from those other two tearaways?' Drury asked.

'What tearaways is that, Ken?'

'Come off it! This used to be the Krays' place, didn't it? Are they going to stand for you barging in? I don't think so, duck.'

'All I know about is what comes through the door. The working man wants a little flutter, where's the harm?'

'They been getting a bit too heavy for their own good,' Drury said. 'They've got some bird due. Your stepdad and Albert Dimes're having a lot of bother with them up west. Dimesy had a fight with that other fella, Spot – he's backing them. It's all gonna end badly.'

'The West End's for mugs,' Jack said. 'This does me.'

'If you can help put those two away, Jack,' Percy Hoskins said, 'my paper'd pay you a nice few bob. It'd be a good story and a public service.'

Jack glanced at Brian, but said nothing. He wasn't about to become a copper's nark, not even for the *Daily Express*.

Every time Joey went to the spieler anxiety gave him an attack of acid indigestion, so he tried not to eat before he set off in his little Austin 7 van. At the rate money was coming in, he'd soon be able to afford a proper car, open another shop and pay off the bank loan. He wasn't in any hurry to do that in case he had to give Jack and Alice their share of the value of the house. Not that either had indicated they wanted it. Jack was doing nicely with the spiel – Joey saw to that – and they never heard from Alice. She might have been dead for all they knew.

Soon, money from the spieler became a problem for everyone involved. It was profitable and well organized under Joey's stewardship: he watched the tables like a hawk. But the house dealers were friends of Billy Jones, and they continued to skim. Finally he realized they weren't doing it for themselves but for their former boss, who doubtless rewarded their loyalty.

'The fuck he does,' Jack said, when Joey told him. 'You're certain they're still at it?'

'Watch the table with me. Count the money going to the dealer, then what comes to us at the end of the evening,' Joey said.

With neither the patience nor the concentration, Jack couldn't watch for ten minutes, much less the whole night long, not like Joey.

'What did you make it, Jack?' he asked, in the early hours, when the last punter was going back broke to the *Daily Mail*.

'I don't know. I lost count,' Jack said irritably. 'I got more important things to think about.'

'This is important. You can see what's happening here, can't you?'

Jack couldn't, but wasn't likely to admit it. He waited.

'Why d'you think we ain't had any trouble from the twins?' Joey asked.

'Because they're busy up the West End fighting them other mugs for turf.'

'That's one possibility,' Joey said, enjoying the power his superior mind gave him. He would have liked Brian to see this and understand how a quick brain could defeat brawn every time. 'We're being taken for mugs. I think we're running this place for the Krays. They don't have to come anywhere near us to get their pension. It goes via the dealers and bloody Billy Jones.'

'I don't believe it. He wouldn't dare.'

'He'd dare, Jack, because you wouldn't know. You're too busy with other things to watch the tables. The one I kept an eye on tonight took ninety-seven pounds, give or take. He turned in forty-two pounds nineteen shillings, not even half. If they're all doing that, they're either very greedy, very stupid or over-confident. We're talking about just one table here Jack.'

'I'll kill them!' Jack exploded. 'I'll slaughter the whoresons and cut them up and feed them to Cole Collins's pigs out at Stoke Poges.'

'Have a quiet word instead, Jack,' Joey advised. 'That way we keep the money coming in.'

'But they're making mugs out of us, Joey. I can't stand for that.'

'Be a rich mug. Lock the door at closing tomorrow night and confront them. We'll search them if we have to, then give them the ultimatum. Either it stops or they get hurt.'

'It won't stop. Not unless they get hurt.'

'It'll stop, especially if they know we're watching them.'

Denial and bluster were the first lines of defence when they confronted Billy Jones and the house dealers the following night. All evening, Joey kept a close eye on another table and watched the same thing happen again and again. First the dealer palmed a few oncers for himself, then at the end totalled the same shortage as the other table the previous night. Joey smiled inwardly.

'That's not what I make it, Denis,' he said to the sweaty, red-eyed dealer.

'Well, it was me taking the money across the table, Joey. It's all there, son.'

'On a one-for-me, one-for-the-house basis, Denis?'

'I wouldn't do that, not with Jack running things. Straight I wouldn't.'

'You've got about five seconds to come up with what the table's short, Denis,' Jack said, pulling a meat cleaver from inside his jacket. 'If not, I'm going to cut off your index finger. See how you deal then.'

'Shut up, Jack,' Billy Jones said. 'Denis is as good as gold.'

Ignoring him, Jack started to count out loud.

Sweat poured out of Denis. The count didn't get to five before he slapped a roll of notes on the bar. 'I'm sorry, Jack,' Denis said. 'I'm sorry, son. I don't want to fall out with you.' He glanced over at Billy Jones, as if expecting him to speak in his defence.

'What about you two?' Jack said to the other two dealers.

They hesitated a moment then followed Denis's lead, dropping rolls of damp notes on to the bar. Joey nodded, satisfied, his face expressionless. Business was like a game of three-card brag where you could all too often read your opponent's hand on his face.

Without warning, Jack swung the cleaver, taking the index and top joint of the middle finger off Denis's right hand. Joey gasped and his gorge rose. Billy Jones's cry made him think he'd lost his hand, but he hadn't – just the contents of his bowel and his business.

He fled. Jack put the injured dealer into a cab and gave the other two a second chance.

'We should replace them, Jack,' Joey advised.

'They won't nick from me again, not now,' Jack assured him.

Joey wasn't convinced. 'What makes you think that? They're thieves who were stealing for the Krays. They'll steal for themselves. I can't watch everything.'

'Stealing's a fact of life, Joey. Everyone does it. But I've made sure we won't lose too much.'

It wasn't a philosophy Joey wanted to embrace, even though he knew his brother-in-law was right. Somehow he would try to interrupt the circuit, pay them more, give them a bonus for what they took, but never tolerate theft. From that point on, he kept his eye open for fresh talent, and it wasn't long before he found someone, a thin-faced, sharply dressed young man called John Bloom, who said he was a printer. From the neatness of his fingernails and clothes, though, Joey suspected he was probably a salesman at the Bourne & Hollingsworth department store. When they got talking he learnt he was on leave from the RAF with a year to go, having signed on rather than be conscripted. Joey liked him for his enterprise and eye for an opportunity. Bloom wanted to make a lot of money fast.

'You won't do that in the RAF,' Joey pointed out.

'I wouldn't do it in the army either. But there's opportunities in both if you keep your eyes open. The RAF is selling off a lot of its old planes. There are countries all over the world that want aircraft – bombers, fighters. If I had the money, I'd buy them up. What about you, Joey? Do you make that sort of money?'

Joey confessed he didn't.

'Those planes could convert to goods transport. People everywhere will be wanting goods.'

The best Joey could do for him was a job dealing while he was on leave. He was sharp and ran a fast game, increasing the turnover and the take by fifteen per cent. He asked Brian to spend time with the young man, but they didn't hit it off, both in competition for Jack's attention. It was Bloom who suggested putting in a roulette wheel. Joey knew instinctively that it would cause trouble, but Jack and Brian liked the idea. When Bloom went back to the RAF, they talked endlessly about bringing in roulette.

'What's roulette going to get you apart from the rozzers' attention?' Joey wanted to know.

'Some style, Dad,' was Brian's response.

'He's obsessed with bloody style! That, and following your brother in everything he does,' Joey said to Cath at breakfast one morning – a thick slice of buttered toast and a cup of tea. That was all he could take at four a.m.

Cath insisted on getting up and going to the market with him. Covent Garden was so crowded with lorries delivering from the country that at times you could barely squeeze a lettuce leaf between them, much less their Austin 7. But they managed it, shouting and swearing with all the other traders who wanted to bring their vehicles close to their suppliers. Sometimes it took them an hour or more to get out.

Cath remained more sanguine about their son and tried to reassure Joey. 'He'll grow out of Jack. He won't be so impressionable once he goes to university.'

'As long as he doesn't get his collar felt before he gets there. I'd hoped he'd pal up with John Bloom. There's a boy who'll make something of himself.'

'Well, the trouble you think's coming is the result of John's daft idea! Anyway, there's nothing you can do about that, Joey. Jack's ordered the roulette wheel and that's that. It'll probably be a big hit.'

But that wasn't Joey's concern. He prayed it would be a failure, although he'd spent close to two hundred nicker on the thing.

It was like a magnet. Punters stuck at it, trying to break the bank, until they'd lost everything. What the house took at the wheel far exceeded what it made at the card tables. Jack and Brian were thrilled, and constantly goaded Joey that his worries were for nothing.

One night a punter walked away with more than two hundred and fifty quid, which horrified Joey, until Jack said, 'They'll all think they can pick up that sort of lolly. It'll do nothing but encourage them.'

He was right. The following night the clamour at the table was ferocious as everyone tried to get on. The croupier, a thin man with a moustache and heavily Brylcreemed black hair, could hardly follow the bets, but Joey did. Two nights later the same man won another hundred and eighty pounds. The third time it happened, Joey was watching the table with every instinct on full alert. He saw the drag the croupier put on the wheel as he set the ball in play, caused it to stop on the red. His favoured punter had a wide spread of bets on red, too many for it to be other than a cheat.

'You sure of that, Joey?' Jack said, as the last punter went out broke and they counted their takings. They had still made more than three hundred pounds and Jack was pleased, but Joey knew it should have been more and felt physically sick at having been cheated.

'We're still making plenty, Dad,' Brian said.

'Don't be stupid, son!' Joey didn't like to speak to him in that way before Jack, but how else would he learn? 'This is our money they're stealing. How do we know they're not stealing it for the Krays?'

'How could they?' Jack argued. 'We know Bernard. He wasn't one of Billy Jones's mob here.'

'Two hundred quid a night would be a nice little pension if they are.'

That did it for Jack. The thought of his man working for Ronnie and Reggie Kray made him murderous. He wasn't interested in waiting to see if it happened again but went straight round to Bernard Hedges' gaff.

He lived in a Peabody Trust building in Earl's Court. Washing was strung across the yard and wooden clothes horses with smalls littered the landings. When Hedges opened the door, they saw he'd been counting money on the dresser in the tiny kitchen.

'You thieving whoreson,' Jack said, and whacked him, knocking him across the room.

'No, guv'nor, I can explain. That's my wages what I'm saving up.'

'Then I'm paying you too much,' Jack said. 'What's there, Bri?'

Brian counted the money. 'More'n six hundred nicker.'

Jack hit Hedges again and again, even though he continued to protest his innocence. When his wife and kiddies started screaming, it all came out.

'Tell them, Bern,' she said, as if that would spare him. 'You bloody fool, I knew it would end like this.'

Having satisfied himself that the twins weren't involved, Jack slammed the kitchen door on each of Bernard Hedges' hands. First one, then the other.

Had Joey eaten anything earlier that night he would have lost it. His stomach heaved. What made him feel worse was to see Brian enjoying himself. What sort of man was his son turning into? The same sort of monster Jack was becoming, the sort his granddad had been? Joey hated to be reminded of Tiger Braden, but whenever he was with Jack or saw how like him Brian was growing, he thought of the man. He wanted to get out of the rancid-smelling flat with Mrs Hedges, her four children and her husband all crying, out of this spieler business, out of Jack's life. He wanted to take his wife and son with him and forget they'd ever known him. But Jack insisted they go round to the address of Hedges' partner and mete out some punishment there too.

It was small wonder he hadn't been alerted as he only lived in the next red-brick block set back off Earl's Court Road and the Hedges family's screams must have woken most on the estate who weren't already up for work. The sky was light and the gas lamps were popping off when they climbed the stairs to the third floor. The door was opened by George Cornell, a wide-necked man in his late twenties with curly dark hair. Jack hit him, knocking him back through the flat, then again. Cornell's wife came flying out of the bedroom in her slip and launched herself at Jack. He hit her too, knocking her out.

'That's what comes of stealing. We don't like thieves,' he yelled, bending over Cornell.

Joey looked along the hallway and saw two young kiddies peering round the doorway, too scared to cry. He wondered briefly what they would make of this, then told himself he'd rather not know. He loathed violence, and feared that it would land both him and Jack in prison. How to get away? The question nagged at him. There was no immediate or easy answer. He was related to Jack by marriage and tied to him by criminal enterprise.

'You look tired, Joey,' Cath said, real concern in her voice. 'How long can you keep this up? You'll have to get someone else to run the shops.'

'No.' He was angry as well as tired. 'I'm getting out of the spiel.'

'Are you crackers? Look how much money it's making you.'

'So would robbing payrolls. This way I'll still end up in the same place.'

'How would you get clear of Jack?' Cath said. 'Turn him in?'

That idea had been running round Joey's head and now Cath gave voice to it as though it was the most natural response to the situation. But what Jack would do as and when he found out who had shopped him didn't bear thinking about. The image of Bernard Hedges' broken fingers was sharp in his mind.

He knew how torn Cath was over the money, and he felt the same. They were doing all right with each of their three shops paid for and making a profit, even though no such thing showed up in the books. There was a nice bit salted away with Sammy Cohen, the tailor, and a little in the bank. Despite what had happened with the traveller's cheques, he trusted Sammy more than the bank or a box under the floorboards. The taxman wouldn't get a penny of it. But doing all right didn't satisfy Joey's hunger to be rich. Only that would make him safe. For that reason, he couldn't let go of Jack. Not yet.

Then an idea occurred to him. Maybe he could get rid of Jack and run the spiel on his own with Brian. Then he wouldn't be such a target for the cops, or the Krays.

The opportunity presented itself when a familiar figure in a Mac and a trilby came into the shop. If he'd been less tired Joey might have identified him immediately, but it wasn't until he said that some of the shopkeepers had complained about Jack taking too large a pension off them that he remembered it was Drury, the detective. Now he was offering to do what he said other shopkeepers had alleged Jack no longer did for them. Joey wondered if he realized he was related to Jack. Or even if Jack had sent the man to test him.

'What sort of protection can you give, Mr Drury?'

'Well, for starters, duck, you won't get no one asking about all that bent gear you buy.'

Panic came at Joey – Jack wouldn't have thought of that. 'What bent gear?' he said, trying to keep the fear out of his voice.

'Got receipts for all this, have you?' the detective asked. 'We'd better have a look, hadn't we?'

He picked up a South African pear and bit into it, just as Ronnie Kray had done soon after Joey had opened his first shop. Perhaps the Krays had sent Drury.

Joey snatched a whole pile of receipts off the spike he kept under the counter by the till. With a bit of stretching they'd cover all the goods in this shop. Perhaps the detective wouldn't look further. 'What if Jack still wants his pension?'

'Well, the best thing you could do, duck,' the busy said, a confident smile spreading across his fleshy face, 'would be to pay him. And me, of course. I'm not a greedy man. You got to get a living like everyone else. What shall we say? A tenner a week?'

'I can't afford that!' Joey protested. 'Ten nicker to you as well as

Jack? D'you know how much that is a year? More than a thousand pounds. That's all my profit and more.'

'Come off it. With all you're taking out of that spiel along the road? I should coco. I bet if I turned your drum over I'd find bundles pugged away under the floorboards. I know what you kykes are like – don't trust banks. No, it can't be less. We got a lot of greedy policemen – especially in the city police. I can assure you they don't earn a thousand pounds a year, and they do a dangerous job. Not like sitting here in the warm selling a few Irish apricots.'

Sweat broke out on Joey's forehead. He still wasn't certain that Jack hadn't sent the policeman as a test.

Drury finished his pear and wiped his hands on the handkerchief he took from the top pocket of his double-breasted suit jacket. 'Well, if it helps, you can drop Jack out.' He laughed as if he'd made a joke. 'He don't need this bit of wedge as well as what he gets from that spiel.'

'Why don't you come and take it from him?' Joey struggled to speak. His heart was thrashing so hard it hurt.

There was a long silence. Finally the detective said, 'How much?'

'As much as a ton a week,' Joey said, and saw Drury lick his lips. 'You'd have to deal with Jack first.'

'For a oner a week we'd take care of the young iron too, if you want,' Drury said.

The words turned to ice in Joey's brain. He knew instinctively that Drury was referring to Brian and wanted to deny he was homosexual. Yet at the same time he wanted to interrogate the policeman and find out what evidence there was to support such a statement about his son. He resisted, deciding to bury it in the furthest reaches of his mind: it was merely an oafish copper's dismissal of anyone sensitive as a poofter.

Drury didn't say how he would deal with Jack, and Joey didn't ask. He simply passed over twenty sovs as a down payment.

'You did what?' Cath said, when he told her. 'Are you mad? How do you know he's not in league with Jack?'

Joey was relieved that all her questions showed concern for him rather than for her brother. 'He's desperate for money,' Joey said.

'Perhaps all rozzers are, if they don't earn that much.' She paused. 'How do we know we can trust him to put Jack out in the cold? And if he does, won't we have to deal with him? Perhaps we're better off with the devil we know.'

'Jack's getting to be such a liability with his moods. Think about it, Cath. At a oner a week, Ken Drury'd be a lot cheaper than Jack.'

'Who's going to deal with the rough house when them mugs lose their shirt?' Cath wanted to know.

'These coppers will. That's what we'd be paying them for.'

Each night Joey waited nervously at the spieler for something to happen. He watched Jack and Brian at the bar, chatting to an actor whose face was vaguely familiar from films he'd seen but whose name he couldn't remember. He couldn't concentrate on the tables. The dealers and croupiers might have been robbing them blind for all he could tell. Suddenly there was a commotion at the bar: Jack smacked the actor in the face and threw him out. 'He's a fucking nancy-boy,' he said, when Brian protested. 'I don't want nancy-boys in my place, Brian. It gets the joint a bad name.' Brian accepted what Jack had decreed.

How would Ken Drury have handled the incident if he was here, minding the place? Joey wondered. The fact was that this sort of thing wouldn't happen if he put the increasingly irrational Jack out to pasture. Joey was annoyed that Drury wasn't there, doing what he'd been paid for.

The waiting for the detective to act proved too much for Joey. He couldn't sleep, and his deep-set eyes retreated further into his bony face to become little more than dark hollows with a dull brown pool at the bottom.

'He's took you for a ride,' Cath said, over their cuppa and slice at breakfast one morning. 'I've a mind to find out which station he's at and go round there. It won't be hard.'

'We'll chalk it down to experience, Cath,' Joey said. 'It's a cheap enough lesson. Never trust anyone, especially not a copper.'

'Are you going to stop worrying about it now?' she asked. She put her hand on his back under his jacket and stroked him affectionately. That was something Joey had noticed more and more lately, little things she did, perhaps because Brian was slipping away from her as he fell deeper under Jack's spell. He enjoyed having his wife to himself, but worried that Cath might be grieving for the boy.

If Joey could have found a way to pay back the detective for his treachery, he might have relaxed. A feeling of helplessness flooded through him when Jack Spot walked into the spiel with the Kray twins, and he knew he'd been stupid to pay the copper anything. A buzz of anticipation followed the men through the dingy basement room. The only light was from the shaded bulbs over the card tables and the roulette wheel, and the unshaded one at the bar, but you couldn't miss the distinctive presence the Krays had. Knowing there would be trouble, Joey's instinct was to slip out and disappear, but he couldn't have got Brian clear too. So he stayed to protect his investment.

Although the games continued, no one was concentrating as Spot, his came-hair coat draped over his shoulders, and wearing his usual bowler, made his way to the bar. The only sound to be heard was the clatter of the ball on the roulette wheel. He greeted Jack expansively. 'Are these premises fully licensed, son?' he asked, removing his dark glasses to show he was joking.

'Scotch, neat, with a slice of lemon – right, Spotty?' Jack said.

'He's done his homework,' Spot said, in the direction of Reggie and Ronnie, who scowled like hard men in search of trouble. 'I like that. See what sort of business the wheel's doing, Reg. We might get a few of them in our West End spiels.'

The smaller twin hurried over to the table and lifted the wheel off its spindle, checking for weights underneath. 'It don't look bent. There ain't nothing on it.'

Spot smiled and glanced at Joey. 'Smart move, Joey. Give the punters a fair shake. Nice set-up. Before you know it, you'll have that ponce Billy Hill steaming in.'

'He'll get less than you. He'll pay for his drink.'

That brought another smile to Spot's face and he turned to show everyone in the club that he was amused. As he turned back, Jack laid a chiv across his left cheek. No one saw where it came from, least of all the twins. Ronnie's eyes bulged and he shrank away as Jack shoved Spot towards him. 'Get this rubbish out of here. You come back, you'll get worse.'

'You're dead, son,' was all Spot managed to say, as the twins pulled him out, his fingers clutching the yawning red gash across his face.

Throughout the encounter, Joey didn't move. His breath came now in short asthmatic gasps. The buzz of excitement around the room was like the VE Day celebration, punters clapping each other on the shoulder as if they'd won something. In a sense they had. It was their spiel; an independent validation meant their wheel was straight; there hadn't been a management takeover. Joey failed to share their optimism. 'Jack,' he hissed, 'what the hell have you done?'

'Did you see it, Dad?' Brian asked. 'Them twins was useless.'

'They'll be back, Brian,' Joey warned. He was shaking.

'He's right, Brian,' Jack conceded, then smiled. 'And when they come, we'll be ready for them. Along with any other mug what tries it on. Give everyone a drink, and an extra strong cuppa char for Joey,' he told the barman.

Right then Jack seemed to think he was invincible and swaggered around, accepting praise from punters. Unfortunately, that belief was still pumping him up a few days later when Ken Drury came down the steps of the spieler with another detective.

'Spotty sent you dirty whoresons, didn't he?' Jack set about them with a ferocity that shocked everyone. He used his fists rather than the chiv, hitting Drury in the face until his eyes

CRIME AND PUNISHMENT | 236

ballooned. Then he turned to his colleague, who put his hands up, not wanting the same. Taking no hostages, Jack laid into him anyway.

Whether they would have been spared if Jack had refrained from beating the second detective, Joey didn't bother to ask. He knew this was the end of the spiel. 'We gotta get out of here – now!' he told Brian urgently.

That wasn't what Brian wanted to hear. His eyes were so bright and alert with excitement Joey wondered if his intelligence had totally deserted him. 'Jack, the flatfoots are going to come in here and hammer us to death.'

'I don't think so, Joey. They were two thieving cops trying to row in.'

'Do yourself a favour and stay away from here. Let these others run things for a few days. See what happens.'

The next night Brian protested when Joey and Cath prevented him going to the spiel. 'Jack's expecting me,' he whined.

'It's over, son,' Joey told him, 'after what happened there. Use your head for Christsake, Brian. Jack all but killed those two policemen. If I was him I'd be on the train to Brighton, if not a lot lot further.'

Reason prevailed and Brian didn't go. The spiel was hit, as Joey had predicted. Four Black Marias turned up and police poured down the steps, arresting everyone in sight, including Jack, hitting anyone who moved with their truncheons.

The strange period of quiet following the raid inspired Jack with confidence rather than unease. The police were mugs: they couldn't even hold him. They didn't mention the beating he'd given those two dicks either. The twins knew better than to come near him now. They wouldn't want the same medicine. He decided to rename Jack Spot 'Tramlines', and laughed as he walked along Cable Street to check on the girls. The street was busy with traffic, a lot of it on foot or barrows as people ferried goods from one workshop to another.

He didn't notice the black Ford Consul parked at the kerb outside Edna's as he approached the scruffy brown door. There were many more cars and vans than horses and carts these days, but some of the latter were still around, delivering goods. Wagons from Watney's brewery at Mile End were most in evidence, with their huge shire horses. Jack watched one of a pair stop in the middle of the road to dump his packet, holding up delivery vans. As he drew level with the door, someone in the Consul tooted the horn at him. He turned and saw John Bindon in the seat next to the driver.

'We've already collected off her, Jack. I just thought I'd mark your card,' he said, and gunned the car away into London's foggy gloom.

Jack flew up the stairs and pushed into Edna's room. She was sitting sideways to him on the bed, blood seeping through her fingers where her hand was clamped to her cheek. 'Look what they sodding well done because of you!'

Hearing the familiar bell of an approaching police car, Jack didn't immediately connect it to this. Instead, he went to the drawer in the dressing-table and opened it. 'Did they get all your money, Edna?'

'What am I going to do now?'

'Put a paper bag over your head.' As the car stopped outside he ran out of the door across the landing and crashed open the door opposite. The room stank of stale tobacco smoke and human detritus. As he went, he kicked over a full chamberpot standing by the unmade bed, spilling the contents across the floor and staining the bottoms of his trousers. The smell was choking and Jack held his breath as he threw open the window. He could hear the buttons hammering at the door as he clambered over the windowsill and dropped into the littered yard below, tangling with an old bicycle and a galvanized-tin bath. The clatter was sure to bring the police to him, he thought, as he hobbled away.

The house Win Booker operated from had a telephone on the landing outside her door. Jack could hear it ringing as he stood in the red phone-box by Shadwell Underground station, feeling dangerously exposed. Finally a voice said, 'This is Shadwell double two four nine.' Jack detected no alarm in it voice so he pressed button A, letting his threepenny joey drop. 'Is Win there, please?' he said. 'Tell her it's Jack.'

'She's got a visitor with her. I'm sure she won't be long. Can you ring back?'

'Yeah,' Jack said.

Was it safe? He decided to walk round to Win's place and wait for her to finish. She did brisk business and had men in and out before they'd got their clobber off. Maybe he could pause a while to wiggle the little bean. He missed Win. She was a good sort.

The moment he started up the stairs to Win's room in the small terraced house he knew something was wrong. He didn't know what, but he couldn't turn and run. If he did, he was done for.

On the landing, he saw her through the open door, sitting on the bed, her housecoat drawn around her. She was smoking a cigarette – a Gold Flake, probably. They were her favourite. Suddenly she looked up. 'I can't see you now, darling, I'm busy.'

They didn't have that sort of relationship, and he wondered why she'd said it. 'Are you okay, Win?' he asked.

'Run, you daft sod! They're here!' she screamed.

He caught sight of Chrissie Lambrianou and his brother, then another man, who seemed to wipe Win's face, leaving a blood-red slit. Razor-handed. Two more came out of the room opposite. The choice was flee or be trapped. Jack smashed past one, knocking him over the banister as he crashed down the stairs and out of the door. He raced along Bigland Street, his eyes darting everywhere, and ducked down into Shadwell station. He took a train to Whitechapel, got off and took another back to Shadwell. Finally, he plucked up courage to check on the other girls he looked after. One by one he found they'd all been turned over, either by the twins or the police. He hadn't done much of a job in minding them. None of them had any money left, or a kind word to say to him.

Brewhouse Lane in Wapping, where the last of the women worked, looked like a gappy mouth, with only a few houses standing, most of which were in need of repair. Of the others, only the weed-encrusted foundations remained. As Jack emerged from the door of one, where Diana, a woman he minded, had told him to piss off, he saw a familiar face. A man in a cloth cap was taking more than a passing interest in him. Maybe he'd been around the boxing ring when he was fighting, but Jack wasn't going to take that chance. He quickened his pace and dropped down on to the high street, which was also run-down and shabby. No one had either the money or the inclination to clear the bombsites and repair the old houses here. No one wanted them now that council-built flats were becoming available, with inside bathrooms.

As he hurried across the street, Jack was almost knocked down by a man on a bicycle. 'Get outa the road, you moron!' the cyclist shouted.

Didn't he know who he was? But who was he anyway? Jack wondered, as he went into Wapping station. A nobody again.

FIFTEEN

The summons to attend the army medical centre at High Holborn turned Brian's legs to jelly as he read it in the hallway. His thoughts leapt to his uncle Jack. Going on the run was his best option. He didn't want to join the army – not even the prospect of being with all those young men tempted him. The blood drained from his face as he went to the kitchen and held out the letter to his mum, who was home from the shop, it being early closing.

'Brian!' Cath screamed. 'What on earth—'

.She shed real tears for the first time Brian could remember when she read the letter. He was in tears too. 'What are we going to do, Mum?'

'Your dad'll know.' She held him close. Brian was suffocating, but even that was better than the army.

'It's the law,' Joey said, as he studied the letter. 'He might have to go.'

'That's as good as useless!' Cath was beside herself. 'I know what you think, Joey Olinska. Well, the army ain't going to be the making of him. Anyway, he's needed here with us, helping in the shops. We can't do without him.'

'What about that MP from Maldon? Mr Driberg? Perhaps he can help.'

When Brian telephoned Tom Driberg he offered to help straight away and suggested he pop along to the House of Commons for tea and a chat.

At once Joey saw that the Labour MP wasn't expecting Brian to arrive with his parents, but he was charming just the same and made them feel as though no one in the world was more important. This was the sort of life Jocy would have liked to live, sitting in the Commons tearoom with Mr Driberg and people whose faces he'd seen in the newspapers or on *The Brains Trust* on the BBC. The MP Harold Wilson asked Joey and Cath if they would excuse him while he had a brief word with Mr Driberg. Joey remembered his resigning over prescription charges. Never in a million years did he imagined that he, a poor immigrant from Austria, could be in Parliament sipping tea with an MP.

He watched Driberg catch the older, shorter MP behind the neck in a familiar fashion, then playfully shove him on his way before he came back to the table and sat down. 'Have you thought any more about going to university, Brian?' he said, and took a bite of his toasted teacake, pausing to elegantly zip butter off his chin and up into his mouth. 'Harold's the man to talk to if you want to go. He'd have all you boys at university rather than in the army. At the moment university doesn't exempt you, of course, but who knows where we'll be in three years' time? Harold doesn't think we'll have a conscripted army by then.'

'Were you discussing it with him?' Joey asked, amazed.

'That's why we're here, Mr Oldman.'

'He's been studying hard, Mr Driberg,' Cath said, 'as well as working all hours in the shop. He's a good boy.'

'I hope you get some time off to be a naughty boy too, Brian,' the MP said, and patted Brian's leg. 'We'll need to look at your academic achievements since leaving school and see if we can't help to place you. Higher education is something to which Labour gives top priority. I'm not sure the same goes for Harold Macmillan's lot. We could ask him.' He glanced across the room to where the Prime Minister was having tea with Winston Churchill, who was eating a sandwich between puffing on a fat cigar. Joey didn't recognize the other two people with them, but was surprised the Prime Minister and Churchill looked so normal.

Brian's qualifications were nowhere close enough for him to

walk into college on his own merit, and Joey felt guilty that they'd neglected his education.

'Fortunately I have chums in high places at a couple of the so-called red-brick establishments,' Driberg said. 'Reading's a good university. I'm sure we can place him there.'

'Reading?' Cath said, with some dismay. 'That's miles away.'

'It's only an hour on the train,' Joey told her. 'He could be home most nights, certainly at weekends. The army could send him anywhere. But first we have to find the money.'

'That's something you'll have to talk over with Brian,' the MP said and winked at Brian. 'There are a couple of other small obstacles. Perhaps Mr Oldman and I could have a little chat about that.'

After tea, he suggested he showed Joey where the gentlemen's lavatories were. 'The vice chancellor of Reading will probably want five hundred pounds to take Brian – in cash. For that they'll overlook his lack of educational attainment,' Driberg said, as he walked with Joey along the corridor.

'Five hundred?' Joey almost added that he wasn't buying the place.

'I've got a solicitor who'll fix it all up for you. Arnold Goodman, an excellent fellow.'

'How much would he want?' Joey needed a figure.

'That would be between you and Arnold, Mr Oldman,' the MP said. 'How much do you value your son's education? I think no price is too high.'

'That's all very well, Mr Driberg. You're an MP with all life's advantages and privileges to fall back on. I only have the bit of money I've been able to build up by scrimping and saving and putting aside what I can.'

Sammy Cohen was holding seven thousand eight hundred and seventy-two pounds of Joey's rainy-day cash. This wasn't such a rainy day. Anyway, he could hardly hand over a pile of used notes to the college. They'd know straight away he was on the fiddle and, the next thing, the tax inspector would be visiting him.

Arnold Goodman advised him to borrow the money from the bank and slip it back out of the business. It would mean paying tax on that money. Life, Joey decided, was less than fair. But he liked the frank overweight solicitor with rubbery lips.

After much agonizing and discussion with Cath, the donation Joey finally settled on for the college was two hundred and fifty pounds, which patently failed to impress the lawyer when he went back to see him in his Fetter Lane office.

'While I accept that this is a lot of money, Mr Oldman,' Goodman said, 'I'm not sure it will quite do. Tom Driberg tells me you're quite wealthy.'

'Wealthy?' Joey said. 'I'd like an MP's regular wage.'

'Well, let's approach the matter another way. Which is important to you? Brian doing National Service and not getting an education Or going to university?'

'To be perfectly honest, we need him in the business. We can't do without him.'

'In other words you don't want him going away at all.' Arnold Goodman laughed, his triple chin wobbling. 'Now we know precisely what's wanted that makes it easier. What about Brian going to Monte Carlo with Driberg and his chums? Do you object to that?'

Joey's immediate thought was whether Cath would approve, but he didn't see that anything but good could come of it. 'The trip would be an education, I'd say.'

'He'd be mixing with the right people. The sort who'd be useful to him and you,' the lawyer said, and touched the side of his nose.

It was obvious, with hindsight, that Brian should fail his army medical and Joey was annoyed he didn't think of it or have a direct contact with those who arranged it. He paid a thousand pounds in cash to the lawyer and was even less happy when he considered how he might have got the whole thing done for much less.

'The Harley Street doctor gave Brian a five-minute examination and told him he has a heart murmur,' he explained to Sammy

Cohen. 'The army medical officer confirmed it and certified Brian unfit for service.'

'That's a smart lawyer you got, Joey,' Sammy Cohen said, as he pulled up the cash. 'I should have such a lawyer. A thousand pounds! As if these people haven't got enough money.'

Sammy was still running his tailoring business out of the little shop on Theobald's Road, pretending to all the world he couldn't make ends meet. Joey knew different. Sammy was as shrewd as he was careful, and as mistrustful of banks as Joey was.

'Will Brian earn this thousand pounds back for you in those two years, Joey? My Leah won't earn that much in two years as a nurse. What you could do with such an amount of money! My landlord here is not a nice man – half the space he takes from me, then doubles the rent. "Jewboy," he says to me, "I need your spare room." What spare room? I've got no spare room! "Someone needs the space," he says. "I only put your rent up by half instead of doubling it." This man Rachman, he knows how to push people out of their property. How to put up their rent. Follow him. Do what he does is my advice, Joey.'

'I'd need rent collectors, enforcers,' Joey pointed out. 'We don't have the muscle even if I got the properties.'

'Was Peter Rachman born with such people hanging from his mother's tits? He was not. So you learn, Joey.'

'Where's he buying this property?'

'Does he come here to have coffee and almond cake of a morning? Does he say to me, "Sammy, what's the best area to buy cheap, rat-infested houses to put the schwarzers and Irish in? He does not."'

'Then how would I follow his lead?'

'Doesn't he have rent collectors? They are like the man on the wireless – they don't stop talking. The boss is doing this, the boss is doing that, they say. West London is the place, Joey. Those big old Victorian houses on Ladbroke Grove were built for people with servants. Who can afford servants nowadays? They can be got cheap enough.'

'I thought about it a few years ago,' Joey said. 'How cheap we talking?'

'Two thousand pounds would get you a house on Ladbroke Grove that can hold up to twenty tenants. Maybe you cut rooms in half like Rachman. He has thirty, forty people in some houses, all paying two, three pounds a week, I should be ruining my eyes making suits. It's real money, Joey.'

'And here I am, spending a pile to keep my boy out of the army.'

With the cash in his pocket ready to give to the lawyer, Joey thought again about whether property was the right place to put his money. He decided to talk it over with Arnold Goodman.

'You're a smart fellow, Joey. See how it works out. I might put some cash in,' Goodman said.

For Joey, the exemption certificate that came in the post to Brian from the War Office confirmed how good his lawyer was. He found parting with money painful, unless it was for something tangible, like houses to let to blacks.

Cath took some persuading. 'I don't know, Joey. It's one thing for this Peter Rachman with all his money. What if the blacks don't want to rent the property?'

'They got no choice. You seen the notices, "No blacks. No Irish"? They'll always need rented property,' Joey said. 'We can at least take a look. No harm in that.'

'Once you get started on something,' Cath said, 'that's it.'

'I know this'll prove a sound investment.'

The area between Notting Hill Gate and Harrow Road seemed to be falling apart. The huge five- and six-storey houses were too big for anyone to cope with nowadays. The trees in the streets were a nice feature, but leaves and dog muck were unpleasant underfoot. The residents didn't seem to care about the neighbourhood. No one was out sweeping their steps or the pavement, as they did in Clerkenwell.

'Oh, no, Joey,' Cath said, from the van as they sat in it outside

St Peter's Church on Kensington Park Road. 'This isn't for us. You can't even get a cuppa anywhere.'

'We're not moving here,' Joey said. 'It's like Sammy said. You could park a good few blacks in them.' They watched a man come out of number eleven, Stanley Gardens. The front door was jammed open, off one of its hinges.

In most matters Joey was guided by Cath, but in this he knew she was wrong. With half the money he'd salted away, Joey went into a scruffy little estate office in Lancaster Road. They had two properties for sale, one on Ladbroke Grove, the other in Ladbroke Gardens. Joey's heart sank when he saw them.

'Everything was let go in the war, Mr Oldman,' the round-shouldered estate agent said. 'We can do a deal if you're quick off the mark, but someone else is interested. Not the type we like doing business with.' Joey started the process to buy number six Ladbroke Gardens for seventeen hundred pounds. Number fifty Ladbroke Grove was in a worse state and he agreed to pay twelve hundred and fifty for it. He knew who he would ask to tidy them up: Joshua, the carpenter.

Brian had been born to get poked in Monte Carlo. It was a world that his six-day drive through France didn't remotely prepared him for, putting up as they did in boring little places off the beaten track, having separate rooms and sneaking around for a quick shag as they did in England.

They stayed at the Hôtel de Paris across from the casino, and Brian was almost afraid to walk through the high-domed lobby, he felt so out of place. He tried to stop the porter taking his cases until Tom Driberg told him off.

Driberg came through from the adjoining bedroom as Brian was trying to knot his black bow tie. He was getting angry as he stood there in his socks without his trousers. He wasn't sure what trousers he should wear with a white dinner jacket. 'Black, of course, you ignoramus,' Driberg said.

He'd never get the hang of this dressing-up-for-dinner lark, or going gambling and drinking on some fat poof's yacht. Once he'd got his trousers on all they ever wanted to do was get them off him again.

'Let me,' the MP said, and fixed Brian's tie with ease. 'There, you look respectable now, even without your trousers on.'

How did you ever learn to do these things so quickly? Brian smiled and said, in his mind, Reward. He knew what was coming next.

'Reward,' the MP said on cue, lifting Brian's shirt front and pushing down his underpants.

He hadn't let him alone all the way down through France – in château, gîte, friend's house or the car. His appetite was huge, and Brian loved every moment, as he did now, as Driberg knelt before him, then afterwards when he forced Brian over a chair. The MP liked to believe he was meeting resistance that only he could overcome. One of his chums preferred the pretence of romance as he passed from room to room.

Things started to go wrong on the fourth night in Monte, as everyone called the place. Brian was in the casino, winning a large number of francs, when Driberg, who had been losing with Kim Philby, said they were going.

'Not yet, Tom. I'm on a winning streak,' Brian said.

'Huh! It amounts to about fifteen quid, I suppose.'

'It's bundles.'

'Don't be stupid. It wouldn't even buy your corn flakes at breakfast. Come on.'

'I'm gonna play out this winning streak.'

'Gonna do that, are ya?' the MP said mockingly. 'We're spending a bloody fortune on you, so let's get some value, shall we?'

'I thought I was on holiday with you, but all I am is your fucking pin-cushion.' Brian was so hurt he could hardly get the words out.

'Let's not have a scene. Leave with me now or you'll be thrown out.' With that, Driberg strode to the exit.

Kim Philby stepped into the empty space beside Brian at the table and put his arm around Brian's shoulders. 'He can be a vicious bugger at times. Look, you've won again, but you'll lose in the long run, old chum. We all do.'

That night, Brian stayed in Kim's room and in the morning he walked to the nearby heated saltwater pool in his tight white swimming-trunks, which his host said showed him off splendidly. He felt acutely self-conscious as he passed a couple of Englishmen with familiar faces. One said, 'Oh, isn't that Tom's petulant bit of rough?'

The heat in his face barely subsided when he plunged into the water. He thought about staying submerged and having someone rescue him. Instead he decided to take the train back to England. He slipped some five-thousand-franc notes from Driberg's drawer, packed and left the spoilt bugger. The money he'd won at the casino last night would have been more than enough for his ticket.

Something was wrong with his son, but Joey couldn't work out what it was. His mood had changed. Something had gone wrong in Monte Carlo, he was sure, and so saw the possibility of all his investment taking flight. Brian denied there was any problem and, as if to confirm this, he quoted the MP and his chums endlessly. They were all Brian's best friends now, it seemed. Joey thought this marginally better than his brother-in-law's influence but, even so, he was getting fed up with it.

'Tom says the country can't get enough workers,' Brian announced.

'Well, a fat lot Labour can do about it,' Joey said. 'No one's interested in what they've got to say any more, not since the mess they made when they were in office.'

'It's the Tories who're doing something about it, Dad. It's them what's having the country swarming with blacks. They're getting thousands over from the West Indies to do the work. Carpenters, brickies, nurses, all sorts.'

The look Cath sent Joey across the dinner table was full of her approval for his purchases. He hoped it wasn't too late to grab a couple more houses. He had the money.

Joey stared in disbelief at Sammy Cohen's cut and bruised face, but his only concern was for his missing money. 'That's all I got in the world, Sammy.'

'The twins came collecting. Now your Jack's out of it they came back for a pension. Somehow they knew I had the money pugged up. They made me get it.'

'No. They didn't! They didn't!' Joey yelled. 'You're lying! You're lying to me. I had over three grand there, Sammy. It was my cushion. How could they take it all?'

'They took mine too. I told them there'd be trouble,' the tailor said. 'They just laughed. The fat one said, "Trouble's our middle name."'

The world spun and Joey's breathing was laboured as a vice seemed to grip his heart. Sammy Cohen was standing in front of him but Joey couldn't hear what he was saying. Why didn't he do the right thing with his money and put it in the bank? Why hadn't he paid his taxes? He'd be skint – he'd rather be dead than that. What would Cath say? His head felt as if it was about to explode.

'How can you be sure the kyke didn't take it himself, Joey?' Cath was frighteningly self-possessed. 'If I thought he had, I'd kill him. I'd put a knife through his thieving heart.'

Joey knew what she was capable of and felt chilled. It was bad enough that they'd lost their cushion, but it would be far worse if they went to prison and lost the shops. It took a lot to convince her that the tailor was also a victim.

'Oh, yeah? Just what did he lose?' she demanded. 'We gotta find Jack. He'll get our money back, even if we have to give him half of it, Joey. It'll be worth it. He'll get all that back and more besides.'

Suddenly her brother was their saviour. And Joey knew they had no other option.

Finding Jack for his parents was a challenge Brian welcomed. It gave him purpose and direction. His trip to foreign parts had disturbed him and he wanted more than anything to pay Driberg back. Somehow he knew Jack would be part of that. A bit of him still wanted to be around those blokes, even though he knew in his heart that Driberg and his Oxford chums despised him. He would never be like them, despite using longer words and thinking about how he spoke. No matter how careful he was, his voice didn't sound like theirs, and he lacked the confidence that allowed them to speak to waiters in restaurants or nightclubs as if they owned them. Some places they did own, like a nightclub in Belgravia where they sometimes went. In the lavvy there Brian had heard Anthony Blunt snigger as he described him to someone as 'Tom's bum chum'. Brian had wanted to kill him – and could have done quite easily. None of them was worth anything in a fight. It was only their confidence that intimidated people. Brian wanted some of that, but he didn't know how to acquire it. Hanging around with them or going to Monte Carlo as the MP's bumboy wasn't enough.

His mum and dad were suffering for losing their money, but Brian struggled to feel sorry for them. He never knew they had so much and wouldn't have trusted Sammy Cohen with it anyway. Jack would put pressure on the twins and get it back, but Brian had no idea where he was. He tried some of the other shopkeepers, who mostly complained about Jack not being there for them and having to pay the teddy-boys again. Some had tried already to contact him. Short of going to the police and asking them, Brian didn't know where to look. No one at the boxing gyms had seen him in a while. Some said they thought he was south of the river, but didn't know for sure.

Bobby Brown, Jack's oldest friend, was in the snooker hall above Burton's tailoring shop in Lewisham Way. 'We could use Jack ourselves, if you find him,' Bobby said. 'We got something big going off in the West End. Someone as handy as Jack would be useful.' He was recruiting for the Richardsons. 'Someone said they seen him at New Cross dog track, working for that old bookie again.'

That was Brian's best lead to date.

'I can't say I know where he lives exactly, m' old china,' Frank Cockain told him. 'Loam Pit Vale some place, isn't it, Sammy?' The clerk confirmed it was, wrote something on a scrap of paper and handed it to Frank Cockain. 'A number for him – not that you can ever get him on the blower. You leave a message with some old merry-heart there. He seems to get them.' He gave it to Brian.

'Rodney two six eight nine,' a woman's husky voice said.

Brian pressed button A to let the money drop. 'Is Jack there? It's Brian, his nephew. I need to speak to him.'

'He ain't in, honey,' the woman said. 'Family, you say?'

After a lot of pleading, she cautiously gave Brian the address.

The decaying red- and yellow-brick house with a bow window and heavy net curtains looked abandoned. Only an ex-army BSA motorbike behind the privet hedge suggested otherwise. The large black woman who opened the door startled Brian. She was as friendly as she was nosy and plied him with questions about the family crisis that had brought him there so urgently. Brian gave the distinct impression that it was illness close to death. Indeed, the loss of so much money was like a death to his parents. That was enough reason for the landlady to let him into Jack's first-floor back room.

It had a sagging, unmade bed, with a faded beige candlewick counterpane, and a brown-veneered wardrobe with two nylon shirts hanging is it. There were some chipped cups without saucers on the hearth by a gas ring with a kettle and teapot, and on the mantelpiece, the means of making tea – a packet of Horniman's Red Label and an open can of Nestlé's condensed milk. Brian wrapped some of the thick, sweet, milk around a teaspoon and put it into his mouth. He realized he was hungry. As he looked about the place, he recalled some of the bedrooms he'd been in with Driberg and felt sorry that Jack was reduced to this. Even his bedroom back at his nan's old house was a palace by comparison. His mum had encouraged him when he'd wanted to redecorate, even though it cost money, and he used the ideas Driberg had suggested to him. Fleetingly, he wondered what it would be like to share a bed with Jack now.

Brian didn't remember falling asleep on the bed but woke with a start when someone came in and turned on the light. The bedspread was over him and his slip-on shoes were on the floor. He didn't know how. He was embarrassed as Jack stood looking at him, as if caught taking unfair advantage.

'What d'you want, Brian?' Jack said, as if he wasn't pleased to see him. 'Marisy said there was family trouble. Did someone die?'

'Worse than that, Jack,' Brian joked. 'Much worse.' He sat up and pulled on his shoes, then told Jack what the problem was. His uncle listened without speaking. Eventually Brian ran out of steam.

'Them twins are getting far too big for their boots,' Jack said. 'Someone ought to take them down a peg or two.'

'Now you're talking.'

'And I expect someone will before much longer.'

'Not if you don't do it they won't.'

'What the hell d'you think I can do on my own?' Jack sounded indifferent. 'Use your brains instead of your arse for once.'

Brian was shocked. He hadn't been aware that his uncle knew about that side of his life.

'I could help. I swing a hammer as well as anyone.' Brian wanted to impress him, but he couldn't, which depressed him more. If ever there was a moment when he regretted his nature, it was then. He wondered how Jack knew. Some snitch must have told him. He wondered how Ronnie Kray got such respect when he was the same way.

*

'Maybe I should talk to Jack,' Cath said, when Brian had reported most of his conversation with her brother.

'It won't do any good, Mum.'

'Then we'll all have to work a bit harder,' Joey said.

'How the fuck can we do that?'

'Oi! We don't want that language in front of your mum.'

Brian glanced at her apologetically. 'He may come round,' he said.

'He's such a selfish bastard. Never a thought about no one but himself. Let him rot in his little rat-trap with his coal-black landlady. He'd better not come round here again, trying to ponce what we've worked and skivvied for.'

Cath was spitting mad. She never liked Jack much. There was nothing Brian could do about that either. If he could somehow go after the Kray twins and get back the money, he would be restored in Jack's eyes. Brian decided to ask Granddad Billy to help.

He took a number nineteen bus into the West End, got off at Tottenham Court Road and ducked into Soho Square. Nurses in uniform were coming out of the Hospital for Women on the south side, wrapping their cloaks about them to keep out the damp air. He knew where he was going.

Billy Hill was at the end of the bar in a spiel over the L'Escargot restaurant in Greek Street. The *News of the World* had once called him the 'King of Crime' and he tried to look the part in a pale grey coat with a dark velvet collar, but Brian found he was talking to a very different man from the one he'd once known.

'I ain't got no time for them twins, Brian. They've gone and grabbed most of what me and Spotty had. That ponce didn't do nothing. We shoulda got together and stopped them. Instead we got a sort of truce. Now all we'd do is muck up business if I whack them. How much did they nick?'

'Over three grand.'

'Has your dad got that kind of gelt? What sort of mug is he, leaving it lying around in cash?'

Brian was disappointed. He wasn't sure if that was because he had found only the shadow of the gangster he had once known or because Billy had insulted his hard-working dad. 'Well, he's gonna end up richer than you,' Brian said.

'That's the spirit,' Billy said. 'With an attitude like that, you should get tooled up yourself, Brian. Get that fat poofter Ronnie first. The other won't do nothing. Be lucky, Bri. If you can't—'

Brian didn't wait for him to finish. He knew what to do.

The next day he took a pound out of the till and closed the shop for half an hour, while he went along to Smithfield Market where an ironmonger specialized in knives and cleavers for the meat trade. He bought an eleven-inch cleaver with a hickory handle for nineteen and six and took it back to the shop tied up in brown paper. There were many used he could put it to, splitting open crates of vegetables, chopping stalks off cabbage, taking the head off the odd rat that popped its nose in. The Krays would come at some point, looking for their pension, and maybe they'd get more than they bargained for. Brian swung the cleaver and sank it deep into the endgrain of a large block of wood they kept there. That was how he'd chop off the hand of whichever Kray reached for the till.

The thought amused him and he didn't see Jack step in.

'Someone could lose a few fingers with that,' he said.

'Yeah. Them twins for a start, if they show up,' Brian said, trying to sound as if he meant business.

'Why would they?' Jack said. 'They got bigger fish to fry.'

Brian wondered why he was there.

'It's no good sitting around hoping them mugs will come to you, Brian. Go after them. Hit them when they least expect it.'

'When's that?' Brian said keenly. He started to tingle as if getting sexually aroused.

The Krays were looking after a joint in Mead Street, just north of Old Compton Street, in Soho. It was in a basement, smarter than the place Jack used to run off Ludgate Hill but still a spieler. There were girls to distract or console the punters, a bit of music and two roulette tables. The familiar clatter of the ball hitting the wheel seemed to mesmerise them as they shoved chips across the baize and mostly didn't see them come back.

The spotter on the door recognized Jack and smiled as if he was a lost-and-found friend, then realized he wasn't – by which time it was too late. The signature blow Jack gave him to the throat left him speechless and helpless. Brian wanted to hit him with the cleaver he held inside his jacket, but his uncle stopped him. 'Save it for something really heavy, Bri.'

The twins weren't there, as Jack had anticipated, but they still looked after the place. He smiled at the croupier on the first table, then hit him a left jab and pulled open the drawer where the money was kept. Brian took out the notes and stuffed them into his pockets, dropping the cleaver. The punters shrank back as if it was a bomb. As he bent down to pick it up, a large man in a tuxedo stepped up. 'What's your bloody game?' he demanded.

'The wheel's bent,' Jack told him.

Straightening up, Brian shoved the edge of the cleaver against the man's throat. 'What you gonna do about it?'

'The twins'll be very upset indeed when they get here – they're on their way,' the minder warned, in a shaky voice.

'Well, they're taking liberties with these bent games.' Jack pulled the heavy wheel off its spindle and flung it on to the floor, denting the rim. He went across to the other table, Brian following, and as Jack plundered the takings drawer, he chopped the top off the wheel. Then they emptied the drawer below the bar.

The woman serving there did nothing to stop them. She folded her arms under her breasts, which were almost popping out of her low-cut dress. 'I hope you're going to leave some to pay my wages,' she said boldly.

'How much do they give you?'

'Only two quid a night.'

'You shoulda said a fiver – I'd've thought you're worth it.' He separated two pound notes from those jammed in his fist, gave them to her and winked at Brian. 'Only fair you get your bit. We got no argument with you.'

Jack made a point of not taking the money on the table, which belonged to punters. Brian wouldn't have thought of that, but grabbed the lot.

The whole raid lasted less than five minutes and netted them three hundred and eighty-one pounds.

Even though they'd have to make ten such raids to get back what Sammy Cohen had lost for Joey, Brian knew it was a start, and felt elated by their success. This was more fun than hanging around the public toilets in Leicester Square picking up a man and risking him being a copper.

The haul didn't go straight to his dad. Jack took his cut and gave Brian about half of what was left. They had a meal in a smart restaurant called Leoni's at the bottom of Dean Street. The place had crisp linen tablecloths and napkins, waiters in black tie and tails, and menus in French. Brian felt superior. Tom Driberg had taught him what such items on the menu were and in what order you got them. He indicated to Jack which knife or fork to use as his uncle grew irritated with it all. The meal cost them seven pounds, eleven and ninepence, more than a lot of people earned in a week.

'It's not exactly the fortune them Krays stole off us, is it?' Cath said disparagingly, when Brian handed over the cash. 'I'd like to know how much more of our money Jack thinks he's going to take. And why did you have to go to a fancy restaurant, spending all that dosh? Couldn't you have gone to Ernie's café in Theobald's Road if you was hungry?'

'It's a start, Cathy,' Joey said. 'A hundred and thirty-five pounds is a very nice start. Let's be grateful to Jack.'

'We'll find them Krays next time,' Brian assured her. 'We'll get the lot then, Mum, and more besides.'

'Well, you mind how you go. I don't want you getting hurt, not on my account. After all, it's only money, Brian.'

'Jack'll get it,' Brian said. 'Next time.'

Next time was the very next night. They waited till much nearer closing when more money would have been taken. They expected to find the twins in the first-floor Poland Street club over the print shop. The bouncer on the door didn't recognize them and wasn't going to let them in. He wanted to know who had sent them.

'We're friends of Ronnie and Reg,' Brian said, in his best punter's accent.

'Why didn't you say?' He unbolted the door.

'They in?' Jack asked casually, and hooked a left into the man's throat, putting him down gasping. That meant their exit wouldn't be cut off.

They went along the narrow hallway, lit only with a red lightbulb, and into the room beyond. Brian pulled out his cleaver. He needed it to cut the cigarette smoke, which was so thick you could barely see across the gaming room. He watched Jack closely as he peered through the haze, looking for the Krays. Brian was ready for action and prayed they were there. At that moment, he'd have happily chopped off either one's heads, but doubted he'd get the second after he'd done the first. They were said to be scared of no one, but Brian was sure that if anyone saw their twin brother's chopped-off head on the deck they'd run.

'Can't see them,' Jack said. 'Probably out spending Joey's money. Come on.'

Brian followed him. At the first of three roulette tables, Jack punched the croupier's throat. The man went down and Jack wrenched open the money drawer. 'This wheel's bent,' he announced.

'I'm winning! Is that why?' a drunken player said.

'Do your missus a favour,' Jack advised. 'Cash in your chips and go home. Oops, too late. There ain't nothing left in the kitty.' He stuffed the notes into his pockets.

'That does it, Braden,' a voice said out of the smoky gloom. 'The game's up.' The croupier at the next table was pointing a gun at him. It was a small .32 pistol, but impressive enough to silence everyone in the room. 'Put the money back or you'll get it.'

What happened next caused Brian to freeze with terror. Jack stepped towards the man with the gun, defying him to fire it. The atmosphere was like ice fracturing on a pond. It was all he could do not to shout at Jack to stop being so stupid when he found himself hurling the cleaver under-arm at the croupier. It hit him squarely in the middle of the chest, startling him and causing him to drop the gun. Some punters let out shocked gasps. Now Jack punched the man and knocked him down, dragged him up and hit him again. Another minder ran forward and hit Jack on the side of the head with a leather sap. He went down and another blow followed.

This wasn't going to plan. Brian scrabbled across the floor and found the cleaver, then the gun. It went off, the bullet ripping harmlessly into the floor. Silence fell over the place.

'No, you don't,' Brian said, pointing the weapon. 'That's enough. Just give us the money. Give it here.'

Jack hauled himself up and hit the minder again. 'I'm Jack Braden,' he announced, for those who might not have worked it out. 'Tell them ugly twins they're going out of business until I get back all the money they nicked off Joey Oldman.'

They took more than five hundred and fifty pounds from the drawers, again leaving the punters' money on the tables. They wrecked the roulette wheels and were gone.

Brian whooped with delight, waving the gun and the cleaver, as they ran out into Poland Street.

'I done them blind. Did you see, Jack? Did you see the way I did it? Bang!'

'Yeah. Now put the tools away. What if you'd killed someone?'

Jack's question had a sobering effect and Brian shoved the pistol into his pocket, the cleaver down the front of his trousers. 'That would've been too bad,' he said, with a display of bravado as cold sweat trickled down his spine. Without Jack seeing, he slipped the gun out of his pocket and dropped it into a dustbin, one of several outside a haberdashery business.

'Let's hit another of their joints,' Jack said.

All Brian wanted to do was be sick. He took some deep breaths, trying to calm himself. 'Maybe we should wait,' he said.

'For what? A foggy day? Strike while the iron's hot. Just don't go shooting no one, Tom Mix.'

The place they picked was on the other side of Oxford Street. No one in the dive on Charlotte Street had heard about the Poland Street raid. No one even challenged them. There was no sign of the twins or Jack Spot, who was notionally the spieler's boss. They went through the same routine, Jack knocking the croupier down as Brian smashed the roulette wheel and turned over the second table. He took the money out of the drawer: two hundred and ninety-one pounds.

'You missed the real big pot,' Eddie Richardson told Brian, when he came into the shop.

Brian wondered what this villain wanted. Why was he coming to see him and not talking to Jack? He and his brother were establishing themselves south of the river and didn't pal out with Billy Hill any more.

'They got a little safe under the bar in Charlotte Street. That's where they keep the week's takings.'

'We didn't know that,' Brian said.

'Well, of course you didn't. You hadn't done your homework. Always do your homework, Charlie says. You know what you're in for then.'

He spoke with a strong South London accent, and was a bit older than Brian, quite good-looking with curly dark hair and broad shoulders. Brian liked such men.

'Where's Jack?' Eddie asked, when the rush of customers had

gone. There was always a rush first thing. 'Where's he living, these days?'

'Didn't you do your homework, Eddie?'

'All it means is them twins'll come after you when they can't find Jack.'

That possibility hadn't occurred to Brian. Somehow he'd imagined that, because their greengrocery business was legitimate, they'd leave them alone.

'Who's gonna look after things here if Jack ain't around? Me and Charlie could look after you for a few bob.'

'I thought you lived across the water?'

''S easy enough popping through the tunnel. We do it all the time with our pinball machines. How do I get hold of Jack?' he said, as if he'd forgotten he'd already asked that.

Brian gave him a look.

'Tell him Billy wants a word.'

'I thought he was gone,' Brian said. 'What you doing running his errands?'

'It suits Charlie for now.' Eddie didn't say why.

'Did Eddie tell you what he wanted?' Jack asked, when he showed up later to get things started again that night.

They found Billy Hill in a pub in Windmill Street off Shaftesbury Avenue. He greeted Brian with a hug, and Brian enjoyed being the centre of attention, but he saw straight away what Billy was doing: he was trying to lay claim to them now his grip on things was slipping.

'You're so fit, so good-looking, you must break all the girls' hearts,' Billy said. 'You still doing some boxing?'

'I do a bit of weights,' Brian said.

'I hear you been knocking them mugs in the West End for six, you and the Cisco Kid there.' He nodded at Jack. 'What you having to drink, son? Drop of Scotch?'

Brian still had no liking for booze. 'Brown ale, ta.'

'Not a ginger beer?' Billy Hill said, and winked at Charlie Richardson, who was at the bar with Eddie.

Brian coloured.

'What about you, Jack? You a ginger-beer man too?' The Richardsons laughed. Brian was scared Jack would start something and wished he'd kept the gun. He reached into his jacket and gripped the handle of the cleaver.

'Your boy said you wanted a word,' Jack said, pointing at Eddie with the baseball bat he was carrying. 'What about?'

'Oh, can't you guess?' Billy Hill said. 'You're causing a bit of upset in the West End. It's gotta stop, son, or there'll be trouble.'

'It ain't your trouble unless you want to make it yourn.'

'Things have settled down nicely. Spotty's looking for an easy life, and me and the twins rub along. If their places get hit, it won't be long before they think we're behind it.'

'Well, you ain't, and there's an end of it,' Jack said.

'It ain't doing me any good. That's a racing cert. Just do us all a favour, and knock it off. I mean, you and Brian ain't exactly Monty's army, even if you have got guns.'

'It's easily sorted, Billy,' Jack told him. 'Them twins steamed in and nicked over three grand off Brian's mum and dad. 'We get it back, we stop. Don't we, Bri?'

All Brian could do was nod. He was thinking how much he'd like to whack Billy Hill and end his nonsense. His hand stayed inside his jacket on the cleaver.

'That's out of order. No one mentioned that, Charlie, did they?'

'Not a dicky bird,' the older Richardson said. He was slightly shorter than Eddie, with a patient manner. Brian knew he was dangerous in a fight, but reckoned on Jack being able to knock him down.

'We'll have a word, make sure it goes back. Meanwhile, no more trouble on my patch or you and me will fall out.'

'Well, I look forward to that,' Jack said.

When they left the pub, Jack and Brian went straight to the

nearest joint Jack knew the twins were operating in Berwick Street. On one side of the road there was a bombsite where winos lit a fire and cooked vegetable scraps they cadged from the street traders. On the other side the buildings, pockmarked, had survived intact. There was a mixture of small enterprises, many in the rag trade, some to do with the film business, which was situated one block over in Wardour Street. At night it was full of punters looking for easy sex, or easy money, which was never easy or cheap in the spielers. The spiel over a button and buckle shop was quite smart and nicely decorated. To Brian's surprise, Spot was in there with his wife, Rita.

'You can sling your hook, for a start,' Spot said, on seeing Jack.

'You owe us three grand, you mug,' Jack said.

'You'd better look up the twins. They took your gelt. You got their address?' he asked, as if he was trying to be helpful.

'Yeah, and their number. And yourn, you mug.'

'Don't you threaten my husband,' Rita said. She was blonde, with yellow tombstone teeth, Brian noticed, as she shot off the stool at Jack with claws extended.

Jack punched her. 'Tell her to shut her gob and keep it shut. Brian!'

Brian ran across the room brandishing his cleaver and chopped the head off the single roulette wheel. He hit the startled croupier in the face with the flat of the blade, causing the punters to shrink back as if they thought he'd cut off the man's head – his nose was fountaining blood. Brian wrenched open the money drawer and grabbed the notes, lots of them. As he was stuffing his pockets, a minder ran through and hit him with a baseball bat.

Brian sank to his knees, wondering what had happened. He couldn't see clearly, the room going in and out of focus. He was aware of a struggle at his side, then the minder was on the floor beside him and he was being dragged to his feet.

'You got more front than a number-nine bus, son,' Spot said, from across the room where he was holding onto his wife, who was screaming at Jack for hitting a woman.

'I told you to shut your old cow up,' Jack said.

'You pair've got plenty of trouble coming. Your old man too, Brian,' Spotty threatened. 'I'll be round with the twins to sort you all out. Mark my words. It's war, you mugs.'

'I told you,' Billy Hill said, marching around the dusty floor of the shop Brian served in. Joey and Cath were there too. It was early closing. Joey and Brian were meant to be at home doing the books. 'Didn't I tell you? Where is he? Where the fuck's Jack?'

'I don't know, Billy,' Brian said. 'Honest. If he ain't at his digs, I don't know.'

'He'd be an even bigger mug if he went there. You two have really gone and set the cat among the pigeons. You ought to have more sense than let him, Cath,' Billy Hill said, ignoring Joey.

'Those thieving sods took our money,' Cath said defiantly. 'We want it all back, Billy, every penny.'

'Well, it ain't coming back. No one's going to make any money now. All I want is a quiet life. The twins are hitting places we look after.'

'You shoulda stayed retired.'

'That don't matter. You hit them, they hit back. Next the punters flee. How's that going to get your bloody money back?'

'Somehow it had better,' Cath said, 'or I'll start after them. Then they'll have trouble.'

There was silence.

Joey enjoyed hearing Cath talk to this villain like that, dominating him as she dominated her husband and son. An idea occurred to him. 'We should go and see them,' he suggested. 'Do a deal.'

'What d'you mean, a deal?' Billy Hill asked, clearly surprised.

'A deal deal. Reach an agreement with them so we can each walk away with something.'

Billy Hill thought about it. 'What's on your mind, Joey?'

'Arrange a meeting. Some place where we can talk.'

'We can't be seen to be weak or they'll walk all over us.'

'We want our hard-earned money back!' Cath persisted.

'Cathy,' Joey said, exasperated, 'it's a negotiation. We get what we can. They give what they can. That's what negotiations are.' He might have been talking to a child. Cath was smart and shrewd but emotional, and emotion was no good to anyone in situations like this.

Joey couldn't concentrate on anything as he waited for word on the meeting. He tried to analyse why he was so jittery, and realized it was because he didn't know what the outcome would be and there was nothing he could do. Then he thought there *was* something: he could decide not to care about the outcome. The worst that could happen was that he wouldn't get his money back – painful, but he'd live with if he had to. It wouldn't be the end of the world. He still had his three greengrocery shops and the rent from the blacks. He could start again and never put his money anywhere so foolish next time. Instead he would get a bank box – another potential liability if the taxman found it. Joey looked on everything in his life in terms of liabilities and assets. Anything that wasn't turning a profit or was costing him money was a liability. His shops and houses were assets, as were his visits to the market when he bought goods direct from lorry drivers. Cath and Brian were assets to the business – question mark over Brian at present; the van was a liability that ate money in petrol, Road Fund licence, insurance, repairs. He wondered if he could hire it out when he wasn't using it.

Word came that the meeting would take place on neutral turf in Kensington, in the public bar of the Devonshire Arms at the end of a little parade of shops across the road from the red-brick St Mary Abbot's hospital. That was ominous, Joey thought, with its casualty department in case things went wrong.

The first thing that went wrong was Cath wanting to come. Joey told her she couldn't.

'I'd have a lot to say to them.'

'I know. That's why you can't.'

'You'll be too soft. You'll let them get away with murder.'

'How will it look, Mum?' Brian reasoned. 'Me turning up with m' mum?'

'It's all your fault we're in this mess,' she said, 'listening to that stupid brother of mine. I thought you had more sense, I really did.'

Brian didn't respond, and an awkward silence hung over the kitchen in Gracie's old house like a pall of smoke from burnt fat.

'He's right,' Joey said quietly. 'They wouldn't take us seriously.'

'They would if I took that bloody cleaver he carries.'

'Weapons are the last thing we need at this meeting.'

Finally his wife accepted that her presence would be too much of a divergence from the norm.

Joey was tense as he and Brian sat waiting for Jack in the Joe Lyons tearoom at the entrance to Kensington High Street Underground station. He watched the white-overalled woman behind the counter pour tea into lines of cups from a large chrome teapot, wondering how many she wasted, how profitability might be improved by pouring it more carefully for customers.

Jack was late, but he turned up eventually with an older man, a boxer called Jimmy Tippet, whose broad shoulders and squashed-in face spoke volumes.

While Jimmy was getting himself a cup of tea, Joey said, 'What's going on, Jack? Why did you bring him?'

'Jimmy can still knock anyone out with one punch. He was a blinding boxer in his time.'

'We don't need anyone knocked out, do we?'

'You think they're just gonna give us the dosh and say, "Sorry, Joey, won't happen again"?'

'We have to keep an open mind about that.'

'It ain't gonna happen,' Jack told him, 'no matter how wide open you keep your mind.'

That worried Joey as they walked down Wright's Lane into

Marloes Road. Before they reached the Devonshire Arms, he did get Jack to agree that Jimmy Tippet should wait across the road, outside the hospital, in case he was needed, rather than coming in set for a fight. Billy Hill arrived and joined Spot, who was drinking at the long, worn bar with two other men, neither of whom was a twin and didn't look as if they'd be much good at negotiating. Charlie Richardson was with Billy and both men ordered orange juice. Joey couldn't see Eddie. There were about half a dozen other customers in the bar, none obviously connected to the meeting. They looked like hospital porters.

Joey's heart sank at Jack's opening gambit: 'Where're them other two mugs?'

'They'll be here,' Spot said, and sipped his whisky. 'How d'you want to play this, Billy? Shooters and chivs on the table?'

That made him laugh. 'Them were days Spotty.'

'He's getting to be a bit dangerous,' Spot said, nodding at Brian.

Joey saw his son puff up with pride, which worried him. It wasn't smart to respond to flattery. Anyone susceptible to it was a fool. He thought he'd taught Brian to be shrewder than that. Perhaps this was a waste of time. Maybe he should cut his losses and write down his son on the balance sheet as a liability. That prospect saddened him.

While they waited for the Krays, Billy Hill and Spot talked about horse-racing, boxers they knew, villains they'd been inside with, how things had changed. When the twins appeared, twenty minutes late, and ordered light ales, it was clear to Joey who was the boss: Ronnie was a bit taller and scowled more than when Joey had last seen him at the Bookers' house in their street. He did most of the talking. Reggie seemed the wiser, more even twin. They eyed up Jack and Brian, assessing what damage they could do and how quickly. Jack and Brian were doing the same.

'Joey,' Billy Hill said, 'do you wanna outline the situation?'

'Yes,' Joey said hesitantly, and knew that was a mistake. 'We have a situation here and it's costing everyone money.'

'We ain't giving any money back,' Ronnie Kray said.

'Let him finish,' Billy Hill told him.

Ronnie didn't. 'As far as we was concerned that's money the Jewboy owed us. He was holding out.'

'Every penny'd better come back,' Brian said, 'or there'll be trouble.'

'There is now,' Spot said. 'That's why we're here.'

'There'll be a lot more,' Jack chipped in.

'And we're just the people to dish it out,' Ronnie Kray said.

Joey caught Reggie's eye, and suspected he was as fed up with this as he was.

'Let's all cool down,' Spot said. 'This is s'posed to be about business. Negotiating. You was a bit out of order nicking all Joey's hard-earned savings, Ron. Be fair, son.'

'No, Spotty, it was *well* out of order!' Ronnie turned to Reggie and laughed. His brother seemed uncertain at first, then joined in.

'Well, the proper thing to do, Ron, is the Christian thing. Give up half the money.'

Joey was unsure if Spot was taking the mickey. 'Think about it, Ron,' he said, 'what all this upset's costing you boys, Mr Spot and Billy. Everyone. There's room for compromise.' As soon as he said it he knew he'd made another mistake. These men weren't capable of reason or analysis. He had made himself seem weak.

'Yeah, we can compromise. We won't whack your places no more. You don't get the gelt back!' Ronnie Kray said.

'You fat fucker,' Jack retorted. 'We'll turn over every one of your gaffs. There won't be a brick left standing. You'll see, you fat iron—'

That was it. There was no going back. Ronnie flew at Jack, fists flying, his brother close behind. Charlie Richardson blocked Reggie with a right hook. When Spotty pulled a chiv, Billy Hill hit him with a bottle. The bowler Spot wore probably saved his life as the blow was deflected on its hard rim before it connected with side of his head and sent him staggering.

Jimmy Tippet rushed in from the street as two customers

joined in the fray – the Krays' boys, Joey realized. One swung a chair and hit Jack across the back. It didn't break as it would have in cowboy films, but sent him headlong to the floor where Ronnie Kray started kicking him. The customer with the chair took another swing at Jack as he caught hold of Ronnie's right foot and tried to pull himself up. Brian hit the chair swinger with a large glass ashtray, cutting him across the top of his eye. Jimmy Tippet purched the other man, then turned back to Reggie, who was as useful as his twin with his boots. Free of Reggie, Billy Hill helped Jack up. They headed for the door with the Krays after them. Jimmy Tippet stood there with his fists up, defying them to come any further.

'What you doing, Jim?' Reggie said. 'This ain't your fight.'

'You know me, Reg. I do like a scrap.' He held the space as Joey slipped out with Charlie Richardson and hurried up Marloes Road towards Kensington High Street. The bell of a police car sounded on Cromwell Road.

Turning, Joey saw the Krays and Spot hurry over the pedestrian crossing and through the hospital gates, less for emergency treatment, he assumed, than cover.

'Wipe your mouth on this one, Joey,' Billy Hill counselled, when he came round to Joey's shop in City Road next day. Brian was there with Jack and Cath. 'I heard from Spotty. The twins are back in their cage. We should let things settle down.'

'That ain't gonna happen in a million years, Billy.'

'We have to let it go, Jack,' Joey said. 'If we don't we all lose.'

'If we do, they'll come and wipe us out.'

'Jack's right,' Cath said. 'You either put them in hospital or prison.'

'Cathy,' Joey said, 'how will any of us make any money meanwhile?'

'They don't need money. They got all yourn, Joey Olinska.'

Joey cringed inwardly at her open hostility. She would take a lot of winning over. 'You weren't there, Cathy. Spot plainly wants the dust to settle.'

'He's finished,' Jack said, and glanced at Billy. 'You got anything different to say?'

'I dunno, Jack,' he said. 'He's still a dab hand with a chiv.'

'He can't control the twins – or anyone else, for that matter,' Jack said. 'He's an old man. He's dead. All he needs is someone to bury him.'

There was a finality in Jack's words that told Joey there could be no peace for anyone until that was done.

SIXTEEN

Acid bubbled up from his stomach, giving him heartburn. Nothing helped, not the Milk of Magnesia he drank by the bottle or the uneasy truce they were experiencing. Brian and Cath were like cats on a hot tin roof. Jack was wound up like a coiled spring. He came to the shop a couple of times a day to make sure everything was quiet. At first, Joey was grateful, but after a while even that worried him.

Jack paced the shop edgily, as if he didn't know what to do with his pent-up energy. He opened and closed the till a couple of times for no apparent reason.

'You still boxing, Jack?' a customer asked.

He ignored her. Or maybe he didn't hear her. Joey wanted him to leave, but he couldn't bring himself to tell him to go.

After about a fortnight, Jack was coming past once a day. In the third week he didn't appear at all, and Joey wished he would. A bad feeling crept through him with the arrival of the dark grey Vauxhall Cresta that pulled up outside the shop even before he saw the Krays get out.

'Mum wants some nice carrots, a nice fresh lettuce and a pound of tomatoes,' Ronnie said, with a bouncy squeak to his voice.

Uncertain if he was being serious, Joey waited. He looked at Reggie, always the more sensible of the two. Neither he nor the third man who was with them gave any clue.

'You're still open, ain't ya?' Ronnie asked reasonably. 'You do sell fruit and veg? Mum wants some nice carrots, a nice fresh lettuce and a pound of tomatoes.' He repeated the words exactly as if he'd carefully learned them.

Joey got him what he asked for, totalled it in his head, then rang it up on the till. 'That's one and four, Ron,' he said, wondering who was kidding whom. He glanced hopefully to the street, thinking Jack might show up, as Ronnie Kray searched his pockets for some money.

'I ain't got a brad on me,' he said. 'When you're as rich as me, you don't carry cash. You got any money, Reg? You, Tony?' Neither had. 'Oh, but you owe us, Joey, don't you? You ain't paid us for weeks for looking after the place for you, have you?'

'Be fair, Ronnie,' Joey said, acid surging into his throat. 'You had all that dosh off Sammy Cohen.'

'That was just compensation for our friend Peter Rachman losing out on them houses you bought.'

'That was just business,' Joey protested. 'Anyway, Spot said half of it should come back.'

'Spotty's an old man. Old men can't tell us what to do, can they, Reg?'

'Not if they ain't got what it takes to back it up,' Reggie said. 'Billy Hill's an old man too. They're both being put out to pasture.'

'I tell you what, why don't I pop my watch to you?' Ronnie pulled off a chunky gold watch and offered it to Joey, who took it reluctantly. 'What d'you wanna give me as a loan on that. A twoer?'

'It's a nice watch. I don't have that sort of money. Not any more.'

'Come off it, Joey. You got bundles still. These little greengrocers are gold mines. A oner.'

Again Joey said no and shook his head.

'You're giving me the hump, Joey,' Ronnie said, no longer smiling. 'Just gimme twenny quid outa the till so I can pay for Mum's bit of gear. She'll be well upset I don't pay for it.'

Joey opened the till and took out twenty pound notes, as if he was pulling out his teeth. He'd rather do that than give these Nazi extortionists more of his hard-earned cash.

'Look at that! You got bundles in there.' Ronnie reached into the till and instinctively Joey slammed it on his fingers, causing the fat man to scream. Reggie and his friend Tony Lambriano rushed forward, barging Joey out of the way to free Ronnie's fingers.

'The little fucker's broke m' fingers, Reg!' He broke m' fingers!' He lashed out at Joey with his left hand, knocking him down, then started to kick him.

Joey covered his face and curled up tightly as the boot went in again.

'All right! That's enough.'

It was a voice Joey didn't recognize, but he felt truly grateful to whoever was. He dared to raise his eyes and saw two burly uniformed policemen in the shop, the Krays regarding them sheepishly.

'He slipped on a banana skin, officer,' Ronnie said. 'I was helping him up.'

'We saw you kicking him. What's this money doing here?' He picked up the pound notes Ronnie had dropped. 'Were they robbing you, Mr Oldman?' He was one of the two beat bobbies who patrolled City Road.

Joey hesitated. Here was a God-sent opportunity to rid himself of this troublesome crew. If he made a vigorous enough complaint they might be prosecuted and sent to prison. But what then? Would he be thought of as a hero among the other neighbourhood shopkeepers or a mug? He was glad to see the police but he didn't want to be involved with them like this.

'Mr Oldman?'

Joey lost his nerve. 'Ronnie popped in to pay me the money he owed me,' he said. 'He gave me his watch to hold as security. Here.' He offered it back to Ronnie.

'That wasn't what it looked like from the street, Mr Oldman,' the policeman said. 'If you want to press charges we'll run these teddy-boys down to the station in very short order, sir.'

That might have persuaded Joey, but Reggie said forcefully, 'We ain't done nothing, have we, Joey?'

'No,' Joey said, and sighed.

*

The police wouldn't give up with Joey. There were lots of complaints about the Krays but no one would stand against them as a witness, certainly no one who was at the sharp end of their demands – they were too scared. Brian could see how frustrated the police were and when a detective called Thorpe pointed out that it would take only one person to convict Ronnie and Reggie, he was almost inclined to help him. If no one did, the twins would go on terrorizing everyone for ever more. Brian remembered this man and was less reassured by him even than Joey was. He'd come to the house once before and done business with Billy Hill.

'I'm sure they were up to no good, Mr Thorpe,' Joey said, 'but not in my shop. I couldn't in all conscience put them away for something they haven't done.'

'You must do as your conscience tells you,' the detective said, and left disappointed.

Brian was disappointed too. He wished his dad would tell on the twins and get them put away. Then he wouldn't have to go out again with Jack and wreck another of their spiels. It scared him when they did that, but he couldn't not go. Something pulled him in – and it wasn't that he couldn't let Jack down. Whenever his uncle showed up and said they were going to give those flash herberts another lesson they wouldn't forget, a spell fell over Brian and he went along with whatever Jack had planned.

Not even Cath tried to stop him. She said she would have liked to be going out and paying them back herself. She wanted them flogged and their fingers cut off to end their thieving ways. It didn't occur to her that Brian might get hurt, that it might never stop, or that it might be wrong. All she seemed to care about was that she and Joey had been robbed of the money it had taken them years to save.

Jack's plan was as bold as it was dangerous. They weren't going to wreck a joint in the West End but in the Krays' heartland. They were going to whack a spiel the twins' brother Charlie ran in a low-rent flop-house almost next to Bow police station.

'You gotta be mad, Jack,' Brian said, as they drove east. 'Right by the police station? What if the cops are protecting them?'

'If they are and we wreck it, that'll finish them. They'll see that nowhere's safe for them.'

Fear rose up Brian's throat. He racked his brain for a better plan. At the very least he needed his cleaver or another gun like the one he'd taken from the West End spiel. The claw hammer he'd brought with him from home seemed inadequate. He prayed the Ford Zephyr they were in would get a puncture or break down – the last place he wanted to have a fight was in that spieler.

'Relax,' Jack said, as he pulled up at traffic-lights on Bow Road. Rain was slanting down and the streets were empty. That was in their favour.

'We'll have the element of surprise. It's the last thing them mugs'll expect. With no one else involved, apart from us, Bri, they couldn't know we're coming – unless their gypsy relations read tealeaves.'

That gave Brian some comfort.

The spieler was so close to the police station that the cops would hear any commotion – the blue lamp wasn't fifty yards away. The house itself was so dark that Brian wondered if this was the wrong address as they sat in the car directly outside. Then they saw a punter hurry through the rain and go inside; soon after, he was followed by another. Each man knocked at the door, which was opened just wide enough for him to be recognized, then let in.

'They'll know us straight away,' Brian said. 'The game's up.'

'They'll know us by the time we're done. Come on.' Jack was out of the car and on the pavement. He didn't look back to see if Brian was following as he went up the short path. Brian got out, the claw hammer at his side, and caught him up. The door was cracked open and a minder peered out to identify them. Alarm flashed across his face as Jack kicked the door, smashing it into him, then pushed on past. Brian was close behind and hit the minder with the hammer. He went down and didn't move. He was so still that Brian briefly panicked – maybe he'd killed him. Then he realized he didn't care: he was committed, with no going back. He ran along the narrow, red-lit hall and into the main room, which was crowded with punters playing cards. Reggie was sitting on a stool at the bar drinking light ale and looking pleased with himself. He had his arm around a blonde woman with sunken black eyes. There was no sign of Ronnie.

'Don't come to our place nicking like that, you ponce!' Jack flew at him before he could respond. The woman screamed, as Brian cleared the bar with his hammer, the bottles exploding. He swung at a man he recognized who came at him, connecting with his mouth, and breaking his teeth. Then he hit another, and a third. Adrenalin pumped through him and suddenly he was Victor Mature in *Samson and Delilah* – he'd seen him at the Bug Hutch as a kid, swinging the ox bone and smiting the enemy. He, too, could take on the lot of them. Some were too scared to enter the fray. He stepped forward to hit another punter, but the man put up his hands. He was trying to escape so Brian hit someone else.

Then someone was tugging at his shoulder and shouting at him. He turned with the hammer raised, but Jack pulled him off balance and they hurtled towards the door. But Brian couldn't accept that what they'd delivered was enough of a lesson. He wanted them all on the floor, screaming and bleeding, but Jack dragged him away. 'You mad or something?' he said. 'You'd have killed someone.'

They scrambled into the car and swerved away from the kerb.

'Did we get the twins? I only saw Reggie.'

'The fat ponce weren't there. I done Reg. He was too worried about the tart he was with to do much.'

'It wasn't enough to stop them, Jack.' Brian knew the twins would come back at them with more force now.

'Look,' Jack said, angling the driver's mirror towards him so that he could see behind.

Uniformed police were running out of the station and into the spiel, their truncheons drawn. 'Perhaps they wanna have a bet,'

Brian said, still not convinced that he and Jack had done enough damage to stop the Krays.

Operating without any long-term strategy, they could only wait for the next round. And for the twins to strike back at them – they had to.

'What's the end game?' he asked, as they drove toward Deptford. He'd learnt such phrases from Tom Driberg. It was part of the government's function to plan, to have a strategy. 'If we want to be guv'nors in the West End we have to know how we're going to take over.'

Jack pulled in to the side of the road and turned off the engine. Both men got out of the car, and went towards a snooker hall. 'We see off Billy Hill and Albert Dimes once and for all,' Jack said. 'That ponce Spot has gone. You ready?'

'What else have we got to do? Wait for the twins to come back at us?'

'They won't do that now. They've had enough.'

'That's a mug's way of thinking, Jack,' Brian said boldly. Jack went white, and he expected his uncle to lash out, but he didn't, perhaps because they were moving through the tables, in a snooker hall above Burton's in Deptford.

'You want to kill the twins? Let's get a gun and and shoot them. Then they'll have had enough.'

Brian didn't respond. He knew what Jack was doing. If he rose to this challenge, they would almost certainly find themselves doing exactly that, and probably getting topped for it. Some little tic in his brain was telling him he could do it, should do it. It was like an itch and he used all his willpower not to scratch it.

'Don't you fancy it, Bri?' Jack mocked. 'Why don't you stay at home and play with yourself?'

'I'll do it,' Brian said angrily. 'Course I will. Anything's better than waiting around for them.'

He ducked under a table lamp and saw Jimmy Tippet. His reputation was solid on his patch in Deptford and he seemed to have no interest in moving up to the West End. 'I'll give you a hand if you need it, Jack,' Jimmy said. 'But this does me down here. A bit of this, a bit of that. I don't really want to be involved. The Richardsons is well out of it now with their scrapyard. Is it worth it? It ain't, really.'

'You scared, Jimmy?' Brian said impatiently.

'It don't make a lot of sense.'

'Then why don't you stay at home and play with yourself!'

'You want some, Brian, I'll give you plenty.'

'Any time you like.'

'You flash fucker. You're a liability.'

'You'll see when we run the West End.'

'West End ballocks. Who cares?'

'I don't know why you bother, Jack,' Brian said, turning to his uncle. 'He ain't interested. Let's go. He don't want to be involved.'

'Let him say, Bri.'

'No one gets hold of nothing if you're all busy whacking each other. Getting a living's what it's all about.'

Brian spun a ball hard against the opposite cushion, scattering the other balls on the rebound, ruining the game. He wouldn't waste any more time on this geezer, he decided. They weren't getting anywhere. He'd go for a different sort of risk. He stalked out of the hall and hopped on a bus to Clapham Common. There was real danger involved here as sometimes the men you approached were policemen after an easy pinch.

The instinct Brian was developing in such circumstances made him hesitate when a tall, good-looking man of about thirty came up to him, having walked the walk and taken a good look.

'Is she going to show up?' he said, catching his eye.

Brian gave him a long sideways glance. What was this handsome man doing here? Was he a cop? No, he argued with himself. After all, he was a good-looking fella too, and he was here because of his needs – and his need to be reckless.

Fighting tension, he said, 'Oh, she's always late.'

'Not exactly reliable, are they? Women!'

'I expect she'll turn up when I've decided to go to the pictures on my own.'

'What you going to see?'

'*Some Like It Hot*,' Brian said – he'd noticed it was on at the Gaumont when he'd got off the bus.

'You like them a bit naughty, do you?'

Not knowing much about the film, and not sure what naughtiness was involved, Brian said. 'It makes a change.'

'Do you have a cigarette to spare?'

'I'm sorry,' Brian said, 'I don't smoke.'

'You're sensible. I keep promising the wife I'll give up. Not easy.'

They fell silent, Brian more convinced by the second that he was talking to a policeman. He knew he should walk away, but he couldn't. Not now.

Both spoke at once and laughed. Brian let him continue.

'I haven't seen you before. You're not a policeman, are you?'

Now Brian was certain he was a copper, so he walked away quickly. He cut through the trees, feeling angry with himself. Hearing the man pursue him, he wished now he had bashed him up, killed him, anything to stop him following. Panic gripped him as he thought of what Jack would say if he was arrested; what his dad would say. The man's fingers gripped his shoulder. Brian shrugged him away violently.

'Get off – that's my girlfriend,' he said, seeing a young woman on the path ahead, smoking a cigarette. As he hurried towards her, the man slowed, but still kept coming.

Brian grasped the young woman's arm. 'Come with me – please. A policeman's following me.'

What she heard he wasn't sure, but alarm swept over her face. 'No, please,' she said. 'I'm sorry. I've never done it before, honest.'

For a moment Brian didn't understand what she meant. Then realized: she was on the game. 'It's all right. Just keep walking.'

She lived in a small terraced house in a street on the north side of the common. Her name was Martha and she couldn't stop shaking when she took him into the ground-floor-front bedsitter. At first, he thought it was because she was cold. The room was like an icebox. 'I thought you were a policeman,' she said. He guessed she was about eighteen – she was long-limbed, with a boyish appearance. A long scar bisected her left eyebrow.

'Have you got a shilling for the gas meter?' she asked.

Brian reached into his pocket, found two and gave them to her. She put both into the slot and lit the gas fire as, through the window, he saw the plainclothes policeman walk past.

'Shall I make us a cup of tea?' Martha asked.

'I don't need anything, thanks. I'll get going soon.'

That caused her some confusion. 'Is there something wrong? It's my first time. I have to get some money or I'll be thrown out of here.'

'How much do you charge?'

'Ten bob. Is that too much?'

'Martha, don't be daft!'

'I'll do you for five,' she blurted out.

'How much is your rent?'

'Fifteen shillings a week.'

He looked round the room and decided she was being rooked. He took thirty shillings from his wallet. 'There's two weeks' rent. But don't ask your customers how much to charge or they'll end up getting it for nothing.' When she made no move to take the money, he pressed it into her hand. 'This really is your first time, then' he said, as another man joined the tall copper outside. They went off along the street together. 'Is there a back way out?'

'Oh, you can do me – I've got to get started somehow.'

Without warning, he was found he was aroused and didn't know why. Perhaps it was relief after the earlier excitement and his narrow escape. Or perhaps it was this girl's boyish looks, accentuated by the scar. 'How d'you get this?' he asked, touching it.

'My brother did it years ago when we were playing with a rounders bat.'

'It suits you,' he told her. Then he realized his greater experience put him in control. It meant she was no threat and he didn't want to risk going back outside yet.

Martha was as inept as a lot of boys he'd known, and so inexperienced that she barely knew what to do. He entered her easily from behind.

'I don't have any protection,' she said. 'Do you?'

But it was too late for that.

Afterwards, she cried, 'What if I get pregnant? You should have worn a rubber johnny.'

He gave her another pound and left, disappointed. Somehow he had imagined sex with a woman would be more fun, as so many people were obsessed with it.

SEVENTEEN

The dullness of his daily routine at the shop forced Brian out at night to search for excitement in risky encounters. At the rate he was going, it would only be a matter of time before his luck ran out, but that didn't stop him.

Just as he was getting ready to close the shop, bringing in the trays of fruit and vegetables on display outside, Alfie Collins, who helped Cath in her shop, raced in as white as a sheet. 'It's Mum! It's Mum,' he said, barely coherently.

'Go! Run home and help her,' Brian said. 'What can I do?'

Alfie shook his head, unable to catch his breath, and Brian realized he was talking about Cath. 'Did she have an accident, Alfie? D'you call an ambulance? Did you?'

'They come and wrecked the place. We tried to stop them.'

Brian ran all the way to Cath's shop. People were crowding the pavement outside and a fire engine was parked in the street. The acrid smell of charred wood hung in the air. 'They attacked her and tipped over the paraffin stove, Bri,' someone said, as he pushed through to the door.

The shop was a jumble of cauliflowers and cabbages, potatoes and carrots. Fruit was strewn everywhere, some of it crushed underfoot in pools of water. The shelves that weren't burnt were wrecked and the till had been upturned, pennies and halfpennies scattered across the floor. Cath was crawling about, with a cut on her head, trying to retrieve the money.

'Mum,' Brian said. 'What you doing? You're bleeding. Why didn't someone take you to the hospital?'

'I've gotta find the money, Brian,' she said. 'They've taken the money. Your dad and me worked so hard for it.'

'It's not important, Mum,' he said, trying to help her up.

'Don't be stupid! They took it. All of it. Why have they done this? Why?'

'The bit of money in the till isn't as important as you.'

Shock seemed to have robbed her of sense. She stared at him vacantly. He pulled her to her feet. 'Get up,' he said. 'Mum, stop this.'

'I've got to get the money. What's wrong with you?' She lashed out, catching him a blow on the side of the head, her eyes burning fiercely. 'It's all your bloody fault, you stupid sod. You shoulda taken care of them bastards. Why didn't you kill them when you had the chance?' She pounded on his chest.

'She's in shock,' an ambulance man said.

Without warning she threw her arms around Brian and sobbed. 'Oh, Brian, I'm sorry, my darling – I don't know what I'd do without you. You must help me get it back. And what about your dad?' She ran out of the door and across City Road.

Brian tore hard after her, ducking and diving through the traffic to which Cath seemed oblivious. She ran all the way to Clerkenwell Road and the greengrocery shop that Joey ran with the help of an Italian man who'd stayed on after the war.

The crowd outside told Brian everything as he raced across the traffic lights at the junction with Farringdon Street. Both front windows were broken and the place had been wrecked.

'They come, Brian. They come,' Giuseppe said.

He saw his dad sitting on an upturned apple box with his head in his hands. Cath got to him first and clasped him to her. Brian could remember few such shows of affection between his parents.

'They got the money, Cathy,' Joey said wearily, 'all of it. Bloom will go crackers. We can't go on.'

'What's he talking about?'

His mother dismissed Brian with an irritable flick of her hand. 'We still got the houses,' she said. 'We'll get cleaned up and start again. Jack and Brian can bloody well pay them back – like they shoulda done before. Them bastards'll get all they deserve.'

A man in a Mackintosh took his pipe out of his mouth. 'Who are *they*, Mrs Oldman?'

Copper, Brian thought straight away.

'Who are *you*?' Cath said.

'Detective Constable Pyle. We'd like to catch the thugs who done this.'

'Teddy-boys. That's all it could be.'

'I wouldn't advise taking the law into your own hands, Mrs Oldman.'

'Well, it ain't no good relying on your lot. Just leave us alone, why don't you?'

The policeman told them where he could be found and left.

'Perhaps we should leave it to the police now,' Joey said, when he had recovered a little.

'Too late for that,' Cath said. 'Look at this mess. Did they take it all?'

'Of course they did. Every penny.'

'I'll strangle them with my bare hands.'

'What money you talking about?' Brian asked.

'I was looking after some for John Bloom.'

'How did they know you had it, Joey?' Cath asked.

'What's going on?' Brian said.

Joey shook his head.

Cath turned on Brian, her eyes boring into him. 'You should top them rotten sods.'

Jack was doing a bit of car-ringing with the Richardsons. There was no phone in the breaker's yard so Brian went across the river to see him. On his way, he stopped at his favourite shop in Smithfield Market to buy another cleaver from the ironmonger. The owner was just closing for his half-day and was reluctant to stay on. 'It's very urgent, Mr Evans,' Brian told him. 'I need it right now.'

'Well, just for you, son.' He went back in and put on the lights. The neon flickered, illuminating dozens of knives, some with eighteen-inch blades. There were saws, too, and cleavers. Brian bought two fourteen-inch cleavers.

When Jack inspected first one damaged shop, then the other, he said little, but his face tightened. Cath and Joey were clearing up, but it would be a long while before they opened for business again. If they ever did. 'We will kill them,' he said, 'and their family and all their friends.' This was all to do with loss of face, Brian realized.

The Richardsons declined to help, even though they had no liking for the Krays. 'We have to honour the agreement we made about the West End.'

'Fuck off, Charlie,' Jack said. 'That was years ago.'

'Well, when you decide what to do, let me know. Me and Eddie, we'll give you a hand there.'

'This is it,' Jack said emphatically.

'You'd best be careful, Jack,' Charlie warned. 'You could set things off with Old Bill.'

'No. They'll all be good as gold.'

Jack asked John Bindon to give them a hand – he knew how to use himself and had no liking for the Krays these days. He promised to find some help and meet them at the Rupert Street carpet joint the Krays ran. Brian wondered if this wasn't a mistake. He didn't know how reliable Bindon was. 'We shouldn't trust anyone with this sort of knowledge, Jack. Especially not Bindon. He used to work for the Krays.'

'He's all right,' Jack snapped. 'He's hated them since Ronnie made him his bum-boy. John'll find some reliable faces to help us. We'll flatten anyone connected with them.'

None of Jack's anger had subsided by the time they turned off Oxford Street in his Ford Zephyr and into Wardour Street. That worried Brian. They needed to be cool and shrewd, as his dad had shown him, not hot-headed. They parked in Old Compton Street, ready for an easy getaway, and walked across the road to Brewer Street, then into Rupert Street to check out the situation. The rubbish of the fruit market had been swept into heaps, which a couple of tramps were picking over, finding bruised apples among the discarded leaves. The spiel was above the family butcher's on the corner of Rupert Court. The place was closed, the front cleaned, the unsold meat put away. A few pheasants hung forlornly in the window. Brian felt like them, unable to escape.

The doorway in Rupert Court that led up to the club was dimly lit and unmanned. Immediately Brian was wary. 'I don't like it, Jack. It don't feel right,' he said. 'Let's catch them somewhere else.'

'It's just early. They don't expect no serious punters yet.'

Whatever argument Brian put forward he knew Jack would find a reason to rush in and do as much damage as possible. He could no more turn back than Brian could refuse to follow him.

'How do we know they'll be here even?' The two cleavers inside his jacket gave him no comfort.

Then he had an idea and grabbed Jack's arm, stopping him. 'I gotta much better plan. Let's go to their house and rough up their family. That'll get the twins so wild they'll come flying back when they hear. They'll be mob-handed.'

'How's that any better for us?' Jack said.

'It means they're drawn away from here. We can double back.'

That made Jack think.

'If we do split them off,' Brian added, 'we could catch them with their trousers down. What d'you think?'

Jack bought it. They walked calmly out of Rupert Court back to Old Compton Street where the car was, and Brian heaved a sigh of relief.

The traffic was light and all but disappeared by the time they turned off Bethnal Green Road on to Vallance Road. A couple of cars and a van were parked in the street where some kids were still playing, even though darkness had fallen. The small terraced houses were quiet. The flickering grey light of television sets could be seen behind the thin curtains at the windows. Not in the Krays' house.

The twins' mother, Violet, was a strong woman who tried to stop them coming in. Jack shoved her back against the clothes tidy in the narrow hall. 'My boys'll bleeding well kill you,' she screamed, as he opened a door and found himself in a bedroom.

'Where're them twins?' Jack asked. 'Hiding under the bed?'

They checked out the kitchen and scullery.

'They don't need to hide from the likes of you, Jack Braden. Or that little iron hoof you got to wipe your snotty nose.' She threw Brian a glance that was filled with hatred.

Brian trembled with fury as he pulled a cleaver from inside his jacket. 'You know what I'm gonna do with this, you old cow? I'm going to cut off their fingers one joint at a time and hear them scream.'

'You and someone's army, sonny,' Violet said.

Brian tried to avoid her as she took a swing at him, but she landed a stinging blow across his face. He punched her, sending her sprawling in the hallway. 'You dirty guttersnipe,' she screeched, as Jack and Brian went up the stairs to the sitting room where the television was on. The twins obviously weren't in the house or they'd have shown themselves by now. The mantelpiece was crowded with trophies from their short-lived boxing careers and photographs of them with fighters like Freddie Mills. Brian cleared the lot with his cleaver, and Violet screamed again as she came through the door. 'You wicked little bastard,' she yelled. 'My boys'll kill you stone dead for that.'

'Yeah, so you said.'

A hammering started on the front door.

'Mark my words! There they are now!' Before they could stop her she ran down the stairs and along the hallway to open it.

It wasn't the twins returning, just neighbours asking if Violet was all right.

'What's this? The Crazy Gang?' Brian asked, as they got downstairs.

'You'd better sling your hook before we set about you,' one of the group said.

'Which one of you's first, then?' Jack said, to an overweight man who smelt of stale lard. 'You?'

No one stepped forward.

'Tell them two fat nancies of yourn we're coming back.'

'Good riddance to bad rubbish!' Violet shouted, as they went out, and slammed the door after them.

Brian was pleased that his plan had worked so well when, less than an hour later, they saw a 2.4 Jaguar and a Rover 90 pull up outside the house. He recognized the bulky figure of Ronnie Kray, who leapt out with six other men and ran into the house, followed by Reggie.

'They're as daft as brushes, falling for that,' Jack said.

'The thing is,' Brian said authoritatively, 'it's family. They can't stand the thought of their old mum getting hurt. We'd have had them and all the rest to fight if we'd have steamed straight into that spiel.'

'Well, now it should be easy.' Jack started the car.

The club was tense, electric with anticipation, none of the people at the tables concentrating on their game and more faces in than there should have been for that time of night. Danger flashed in Brian's mind but he couldn't walk out now he'd got Jack to play this stroke. It was a dance of death for his own mum, and the only way Cath might release her grip on him.

The twins were sitting on stools at the bar, drinking coffee and laughing in the dim, smoky atmosphere, as if they'd achieved something brilliant. How could they – Brian stopped.

'Well, you took your fucking time,' Ronnie Kray said. The people flanking him laughed.

They'd been tricked. Brian knew for certain he and Jack were dead. He thought fleetingly about offering up his cleavers and making it easy for them.

No one expected what happened next.

In a fluid movement Brian pulled out the cleavers and hurled one. It sailed through the room and hit Ronnie square in the forehead, knocking him out. He fell from the stool like a lead weight.

He hoped the rest of his luck would hold up when, with a bellow of rage, he ran towards the bar after Jack, heading straight into the confusion he had caused. Slashing right and left with the second cleaver, he cut a punter's upper arm to the bone. Jack was causing mayhem at the bar and the last Brian saw of him was when he heard Reggie shout, 'Get hold of the fucker. Get hold of him!'

Then something heavy hit Brian on the back of the head and he stumbled forward, dropping the second cleaver. He reached down to retrieve it as blows from fists, bottles and blackjacks boiled down on him. His hand seized the hickory handle and he hacked at the feet and ankles of those around him. Everyone panicked and jumped back as the cleaver lopped off the front of a man's shoe with the toes inside it. The injured man's scream was frightening but then Brian heard an even more frightening one. Eventually he realized it was his own – a wail of pain from the kicks and stabs he was getting. With paralysing shame, he heard himself calling, 'Mummy! Mummy!' He wanted to die there and then.

EIGHTEEN

Two days passed with no word of where Brian was or of what might have happened to him. It was almost more than Joey could bear. His nerves were stretched, his stomach upset. He shuffled about the wrecked shop in Clerkenwell Road with Giuseppe, moving pieces of debris from one place to another, making no impression on the mess. There was no word of Jack either.

Cath was going through the same motions in the City Road shop when Joey called in. He watched her pick up a tattered cabbage and put it down again. 'I'm going to the police,' she said. 'I can't stand this any more.'

'To say what? My boys been missing from home for two days? Oh, they'd be very concerned, Cathy. Who knows? We might get them in even more trouble.'

'Who says they're in trouble?' his wife snapped.

Joey returned to Clerkenwell Road. When a familiar customer came in and looked slowly at the wreckage, Joey started to weep.

'At least you'll get the insurance, Mr Oldman,' the old lady said, as she went out, her leatherette shopping bag empty.

But there was no insurance on any of his shops. He hadn't forgotten to renew the policy but had taken the decision to save the weekly premium. It cost more than fifty pounds a year. In hindsight, he had been foolish. He paid protection of various sorts and insurance was similar, but he had a choice where that premium was concerned.

A policeman paused outside the shop and Joey quaked.

'Mr Oldman,' Sergeant Watling said. His moustache was iron-grey, his stoop pronounced.

Joey watched the man's lips move but he couldn't hear the words, only the sounds of the street through the broken shop window: a rag-and-bone man passing on his horse and cart, a lorry juddering along in a high gear, the gearbox crunching as the driver tried to change down.

'I think you'd better have a seat, old son,' Sergeant Watling said. 'You don't look so hot. If we're not careful, we'll have you in hospital too.' He helped Joey on to the upturned orange box that stood in the corner where the till was.

'Hospital?' Joey said, in a hoarse whisper.

'One of the nurses recognized him, God knows how. The old kyke tailor's daughter. If she hadn't identified him, he might have died without you knowing.'

The situation was deteriorating and Joey couldn't breathe properly. Was it Brian? He couldn't bring himself to ask. He hoped it was Jack, then felt ashamed. But having lived with Brian all his life, he was more his own than Jack ever was or would be.

'I'll get an ambulance for you, Mr Oldman,' Sergeant Watling said. 'Hang on here, old son. I'll nip along to the police box on the corner.'

Joey's bony hand shot out and seized the policeman's arm. 'Who? Who . . . ?' He couldn't bring himself to complete the sentence.

'Your boy, Brian. You went into shock when I told you. You got a drop of brandy here?' He looked at the wreckage. 'Perhaps not. I won't be a mo.'

Joey watched him go, tears clouding his eyes. He was aware that Giuseppe was crouched in front of him, holding his hand like that of a child. 'You'd best get the missus, boss,' he said. 'Go to the hospital.'

Joey clasped the young man's hand so tightly he winced. He couldn't go to the hospital right then, or get Cath. 'We have to clear up the shop first, Giuseppe,' he said, eyes glazing. 'Customers are wanting their veg.'

'There ain'ta no customers, boss. We ain'ta got no stock worth having. Them Kray boys came anda done us. You remember?'

Joey levered himself upright, leaning heavily on Giuseppe. 'Cath'll know what to do.'

'Ain't you gonna wait for the copper to get off the blower?'

Without responding Joey went out of the shop and began to walk.

Cath's wail was enough to stop the traffic on City Road or wake the dead. She aged before Joey's eyes. He reached out to her and pulled her to him. Only in adversity were they so close and he wondered briefly why that was, how they had grown so far apart. Why? He stopped thinking about it. He knew the reason, and he didn't want to go there.

They got a cab to the hospital. 'It's St Bart's,' Joey said again, not sure if he had already told the driver. St Bart's held bad memories for Cath. It was where Gracie had died, where Jack had been picked up and carted back to the army. It seemed like such a long time ago, but it wasn't.

The nurse looked alarmed when they stepped up to the reception desk. Cath said. 'Where's my Brian? Where's Brian Oldman? We're his mum and dad.'

'I'll get Sister. Can you wait?'

Why wouldn't they? Joey thought it a silly thing to say. But people said all manner of silly things when they were upset. He and Cath said silly things.

'Thank goodness you got here,' the large round-faced sister said.

The silver filigree buckle on her wide belt must be worth at least a tenner, Joey thought.

'I'll take you to him. It was lucky Nurse Cohen recognized him or we might never have known who he was.' She led them up the stone stairs that bent round the building. 'Where is he?' Joey asked.

'He's on the surgical ward. He has that many cuts and breaks, it's a wonder she knew him at all. It must have been the most ferocious attack. Who could do such a thing to another human being?' She stopped outside the vulcanized-rubber doors to the ward. 'I should warn you, he looks pretty alarming. He lost so much blood. I don't want to get your hopes up.'

At that, Cath burst into tears. The sister took her hand and squeezed it.

'You mean he's not . . . He's still alive?' Joey could barely say the words.

'I wish we could be more optimistic. I really do.'

'Can we go in now?' Joey asked. He took Cath's arm, as much to steady himself as her.

Cath gave a short, anguished cry as she stepped through the brown floral curtains round the bed, then instantly choked it off. An acid taste clung to the back of Joey's throat, while his stomach churned. He wanted to kill the people who'd done this to Brian. How Sammy Cohen's daughter had managed to identify him he couldn't guess. For a moment, Joey thought they must have made a mistake or someone was playing a wicked trick on them, but Cath stepped forward and reached out to Brian with a terrible longing. The sister caught her arm.

He was bandaged almost from head to foot, with his left leg up in a pulley over the bed. In places blood was seeping through the bandages on his leg, stomach and chest in dark brown patches.

'That's where the worst cuts are,' the sister was saying.

Only his eyes, his nostrils and his lips were uncovered. His lashes were matted and his nostrils caked with blood; a tube of some sort fed into one of the holes above his cut and badly swollen lips. Joey's eyes clouded with tears so he looked away. Then he saw the tube that drained into a bottle under the bed. It appeared to be filling with blood.

'He's not breathing,' Cath said. 'He's not, is he?'

'Yes, he is, Mrs Oldman,' the sister said. 'Just about. I'll get the doctor to come and have a word with you. Perhaps you should send for a few things and stay here tonight.'

*

'Tonight will be his most critical time,' the tall Scottish doctor said, when he had checked Brian's drip and read his chart. 'He has a fever. Our concern is that it might turn to pneumonia. That would be the worst possible thing to happen.'

'This is the best hospital in the world, Doctor,' Cath said. 'Can't you help him?'

'Believe me, Mrs Oldman,' the doctor, whose name was Hemdale, said, 'every possible thing that can be done is being done. All we can do is say our prayers and wait.'

As Joey walked out of the hospital to fetch some things from home so that Cath and he could stay, he felt a terrible foreboding. He would never hold or see his boy alive again. As he walked across the cobbles in front of the main building, tears ran down his gaunt face.

'If Brian dies I won't rest until I've brought about the death or destruction of everyone who played any part in it.'

'You should have done that before it ever came to this, Joey Olinska.' Cath pulled away her hand, got up and left him with Brian. Her shouting at him and abusing him for his inadequacies he could take, but not her silent rebuke.

A bed was available for them on a side ward but neither he nor Cath used it. Instead they stayed at Brian's bedside, watching the comings and goings of nurses and doctors, who told them nothing, only that he was hanging on and fighting.

'He's a strong boy,' Joey said to a nurse, as she changed the drip going into Brian's arm. He wanted to believe it, and that his son was not the sissy Cath sometimes made him when she encouraged him to put on her clothes and makeup. Why did she do that? Why did he allow it? Was he so weak? Why hadn't he spent more time with Brian, taken him to football or gone to the boxing club with him? Where had the time gone? In constantly chasing money. What good had it done him? None. What had he to show for it? Three shops, two of which were out of action now and the houses let to blacks, who he'd managed to hold onto in spite of the damaging Notting Hill race riots. If Brian survived things had to change. He reached out and touched the boy's hand, needing to make contact, if only through the heavy bandages. 'Brian, I don't know if you can hear me. I know I haven't been much of a dad to you. I'm sorry for that, I really am. Please don't go away from us. Please.'

He was stiff and cold, and his eyes would scarcely stay open as he sat propped in the chair by the bed. 'Why don't you try to get some proper rest, Mr Oldman?' a voice said.

It belonged to a black nurse. What might she have heard? 'We call you if there's any change. We call you and your wife.'

'I want to stay.'

'What's happened?' Cath said, waking up with a start.

'Nothing. The nurse just changed his drip,' Joey told her. 'His temperature's still sky high.'

'Does that mean he's getting pneumonia?'

Joey didn't know. So many people had died of it in the war, but now things were different. They had penicillin, a wonder drug that had stopped all that.

'Why don't you get some sleep, Cath? I'll wake you if there's any change.'

'Why don't you? I'll stay with him, Joey. You're done in.'

The thought of lying on a bed, closing his eyes and slipping into oblivion was tempting and he almost succumbed. But if he woke to find that Brian was no longer there . . .

For three days and three nights, Brian's fever raged. Twice, his heart stopped and was restarted. Finally Dr Hemdale said, 'The fever seems to have burnt itself out.' To Joey this felt like a win on the football pools, a real milestone passed on Brian's road to recovery, although he still didn't wake up, there were no fewer drips and no fewer bandages. He noticed that the urine in the bottle under the bed was less bloody – that must be a good sign. He went home to wash and sleep for the first time since he'd gone to fetch his and Cath's things. There, he dreamt that Brian died and didn't say goodbye.

Hammering on the door woke him and he hurried to open it, fearing the worst. The old detective, Inspector Trope, was there with another detective whose name he didn't catch. 'Can we come in?'

'Has something happened to Brian?'

'What could be worse, Mr Oldman?' DI Trope said. 'Them killing your son? They will sooner or later. Is that what you want?'

Joey didn't say anything, but set about making a pot of tea.

'This running feud between your lot and the Krays can't go on or some innocent bystander will get killed. I don't think you'd want that on your conscience.' This policeman seemed decent and reasonable, Joey thought, and genuinely concerned about Brian. 'They still don't know if he'll pull through,' the officer went on. 'I hope he does. A young man like that, all his life before him. What if they'd killed him? Would you let them get away with murder? That's what it would have been, Mr Oldman.'

Murder. The word chilled Joey. They might easily have killed Brian. It was that which finally decided Joey to act. 'It was Ronnie Kray what came to my shop and wrecked it,' he said. 'Him and the thugs with him. Johnny Shannon was the only other one I recognized.'

'Was his twin with Ronnie? I'd like to put them both away.'

'Not that time.'

Joey made a statement, which the second policeman carefully wrote down, sitting at the kitchen table. He then read it back to him and Joey signed it. Now it was done and he felt relieved. He wouldn't be bothered by Ronnie Kray any longer.

'Oh, Joey,' Cath said despairingly, at the hospital later that day. 'What have you started? Do you know what you done?'

'Maybe saved Brian's life,' he said. 'This isn't going to end unless we stop it, Cath. You talk to the cops as well. Let's put both buggers away.'

'You think that'll stop it? Don't be daft. They've got friends.'

'The police said they'd protect us. They will if we help put them away.'

'You ought to talk to Billy Hill about what the police will and won't do. D'you think they're going to sit outside our house the whole while, then escort us to the shops and wait there? I don't think so. Maybe for a day or two. You got to get back to them, say it was all a mistake.'

'They know it was the Krays what did this to Brian. God alone knows what's happened to your brother. The police have heard nothing.'

Joey tried to stay resolute, but Cath's warnings left him feeling less than secure as he looked at Brian in the bed, helpless as a baby, no less vulnerable. He wished Jack was around or that he knew how to contact him. Then, perhaps, he'd feel safer.

NINETEEN

Lying in bed, caught between wakefulness and sleep, Brian slid in and out of consciousness uncontrollably. Once he heard a noise like something had been dropped and a voice telling the culprit to be quiet because 'This boy is dying.' At first the words didn't mean much to him, but then he realized she'd been talking about him. He told himself he didn't want to die, but as consciousness gained the upper hand and he became more aware of tremendous pain he wished would go. Finally, someone said, 'Increase the morphine,' and the pain subsided and he drifted away again.

The first pleasant sensation he was aware of was someone gently moistening his lips with a piece of damp gauze. The nurse leaning over him in her stiff lilac and white uniform was slightly out of focus and all he could see was a glow behind her that made her look like an angel. As she moistened the gauze again, some drops trickled into his mouth. He could never have imagined water tasting so good. 'Am I going to die?' he whispered.

'It was touch and go for a long while,' she said. Her voice was soft and concerned.

'Are you an angel?' he asked, still unable to focus on her.

'Angels wouldn't put up with our long hours and poor pay.' She laughed.

'I can't see you very well.'

'I'm surprised you can see at all after what you went through. I expect we can do something about it. Hang on a mo'.' She moistened another piece of gauze and bathed his eyes. Brian strained forward as much as he could when she stopped, wanting her to go on bathing them as it felt so good.

Still she remained a blur. 'Am I blind?' he asked.

'Can't you see? I'll get the doctor.'

'No. Don't go.' Again he strained forward to see her and fell back on to the pillows, exhausted. He closed his eyes. For how long, he didn't know.

When he came to again, a bright light stung his eyes. Someone was pulling the lids open. 'There's not a lot of papillary function ... Ah, you're back with us, are you? I'm Dr Hemdale. You took quite a bashing, chum. We didn't think you'd make it.'

More days passed as he drifted in and out of time. Occasionally he was aware of Cath at his bedside, and Joey, and at one point even Billy Hill, saying, 'Your dad sorted out them mugs good and proper. What a hero, Brian. Ron looks like he's going away. Serves him right, the fat poof.' The one person who he got no sense of being around was the nurse, whose look and touch was that of an angel. Maybe he only imagined her. Or maybe she was an angel.

'Where's the other nurse?' Brian said, as big Bertha checked his dressings and emptied his urine bottle.

'Don't you want me looking after you, man? Mrs Williams will be in tomorrow. I'll get her to come if you're a good boy and take your liquid paraffin.' She eased the little china measuring cup to his lips and gave him no choice. It was either down his throat or down his front.

It didn't matter that his angel, Mrs Williams, was married. He wasn't interested in her in that way – but something about her made him yearn for her to be near him, touching him.

The angel wasn't Mrs Williams, he discovered, when the latter bustled in and woke him to take his temperature. Her touch, her quick movements, her starched, creaking uniform were quite different. When Cath came in with Joey he said, 'Where's the nurse that was looking after me? The nice one.'

'They're all nice, Brian,' Cath said. 'Even the blackies. There are certainly a lot of those. Your Dad's been round the hospital wards counting them.'

'There was one who was here when I first woke. I thought I'd died and she was an angel.'

'Who?' Cath said suspiciously. 'Leah Cohen? It was her what recognized you.'

'Was it? She was here and then she was gone. Is she coming back?'

'I think our Brian's sweet on her, Cath,' Joey said, glancing at a visitor to the next bed who was lighting a Senior Service cigarette.

'Don't be wet. Brian's not interested in that,' Cath said sharply. 'Not her anyway. I'm very grateful she knew who you was. We were beside ourselves with worry. We might never have known.'

His brain felt as if it was filled with fog. He tried to clear it as he plied them with questions. No one seemed to know how he'd got there. A tramp had found him on the bombsite of St Anne's Church opposite the French pub at the bottom of Dean Street in Soho. He had taken Brian's watch, wallet and money thinking he was dead – at least, that was what he had told the police when they had picked him up. A bricklayer working at the adjacent site on a block of flats had spotted Brian the following day and rung the police. He'd thought it was a body too.

'What happened to Jack?' Brian asked.

'No one's heard a dicky bird,' Joey said. 'Not a word.'

'He didn't do you any favours,' Cath said bitterly, 'deserting you like that.'

'We don't know that he did, Cath,' Joey said.

None of that much interested Brian. He just wanted to see Leah Cohen. 'Can you find out when Leah's coming back on duty?' A mistake, he realized, when he heard the edge in Cath's tone – in his weakened state he was attuned to such nuances.

'Don't waste your time worrying about her. She's not worth worrying about, Brian. There's plenty of other nurses to look after you.'

He let himself drift into unconsciousness. It was the easiest way to rid himself of people he didn't want to bother with any more. They all knew they shouldn't tire him.

Brian was conscious now for longer stretches of the day and he was acutely aware that three days had passed since Leah was supposed to have come back on duty. 'Dad, can you find out why Leah Cohen hasn't been back to see me?' Brian said to Joey as he sat by his bed.

'I think she's been moved to another ward. I saw her emptying a bedpan when I slipped in to see how many blacks were there. There were plenty, and I don't know where they all live. I wish I'd got a few more properties – I should look out for some. I don't care what Peter Rachman thinks, he can't have them all.'

'You got to be careful, Dad. He's well in with the twins.'

'I would've got more if that kyke tailor hadn't lost all our money – if he did. You never know with that sort, Brian, do you? Well, they're not our kind, are they? I don't think your mum's got a lot of time for his daughter. Not after what happened. I daresay it wasn't the girl's fault.'

Brian closed his eyes, hurt that Leah hadn't come back to see if he was all right. Perhaps Cath was right about her.

The bandages and dressings came off, but Brian's strength was slower to return.

'Is something worrying you, Brian?' Dr Hemdale asked. 'You don't seem to want to get well. Are you afraid the people who beat you up will do it again? I don't think that's likely. I think one's in prison, waiting to go to trial. If there is something, we could maybe get the psychiatrist to have a word. These trick cyclist fellows can be quite useful, you know.'

The doctor was examining his right leg where the tendon was ruptured. Brian cried out in pain. 'Sorry,' Dr Hemdale said. 'You're going to need a lot of physio to get that right. Most of the other injuries are making progress.'

'Will my eyesight clear?' Brian asked. He could barely see to read a newspaper. The patient in the next bed, who took the *Daily Herald*, read to him, but all the stories seemed to be about what Harold Wilson and his cronies were doing wrong, how they were betraying the trade-union movement and what an outrage prescription charges were – all they did was feed the greedy pharmaceutical companies. Brian longed for a bit of crime and scandal. His old friend Tom Driberg, who was now MP for Barking, was mentioned quite a lot. Perhaps he wouldn't have ended up in hospital like this if he'd stayed friends with him and gone to university.

The Indian eye specialist turning up interrupted his thoughts. He was careful, but the light from his ophthalmoscope made Brian cry. Finally he said, 'It's unlikely that the damaged retina will recover dramatically, but it should improve a little over time. Meanwhile, glasses will help with the fuzziness. Is there anything you'd like to ask me?'

Brian thought about that. 'Is Nurse Cohen coming back on this ward?'

'I don't know what the nurses' rosters are. Is she nice to look at? Perhaps I could recommend her return as therapy.'

If he did, it didn't happen.

Fed up with political stories, Brian switched neighbours for a different newspaper report. The following Sunday, the old boy read him a story from the *News of the World* about Ronnie Kray going to trial for the arson attack on Joey's shop. There was mention of Jack and the rivalry that existed between them, but nothing about where Jack was now. If they had killed him, no body had been found. After Brian had gone down under the welter of blows, he didn't see what happened to Jack, but he knew it wouldn't be anything good. The thought caused his pulse to race and his stomach to churn and he felt exposed in the bed. He wanted to retreat into unconsciousness again, but he couldn't.

The doctors decided Brian was well enough to go across to the physiotherapy unit and one of the porters, George, came to collect him – mercifully he was a *Daily Mirror* man. The news in it was slanted to the left, but there was lots of crime and scandal.

It was a shock to be taken out of the hospital and across to the physio unit in a separate building. The air outside was dusty and hit Brian like a brick.

Once there, he found moving his limbs difficult: the joints were stiff and his muscles painful. He could only walk like an old man. After the first four days, it didn't seem to be getting any better.

'You're improving,' Mrs Dunphy, the Australian physiotherapist, told him, as she immersed his damaged leg in hot wax to ease the stiffness.

Brian struggled to cope with the state he was in. It hadn't mattered when he was cosseted on the ward but now he was having to cope with the real world, other than through the pages of the *Daily Mirror*, he was sinking into depression. His fifth physiotherapy session was on Monday, the following week, and George was late. 'His mum's died,' the sister told Brian. 'We'll get someone else to take you.'

Nurse Cohen arrived on the ward, pushing Brian's wheelchair. Nervous excitement rose in him. He wanted to ask her where she'd been, why she hadn't come to see him. Then he remembered he was cross with her because of her vanishing trick. He tried to be distant and cool. She, too, was distant, but efficient. She didn't move like the angel he remembered, but like a busy nurse with a lot to get through. Certainly she wasn't a newspaper reader like George. Brian wanted to know what was happening with the *Lady Chatterly* trial but didn't dare ask.

'Why are you taking me?' He tried to sound irritated.

'If you'd rather someone else did, I'm sure I can find better things to do.'

'It makes no difference to me.'

'Do you need help getting into the wheelchair?'

'I can manage.' In fact, George always helped him and Brian wasn't sure how to lever himself off the bed and into it. His arms were still weak. At one time, when he was training, he'd been able to lift himself off the floor with his hands flat down at his sides.

Leah made no move to help as he struggled, just held the chair. When he finally got his legs over the edge of the bed, he put too much weight on the damaged one and cried out in pain. Still Leah didn't help. But when he got himself into the chair, breathless and sweating, it was with a sense of achievement that was entirely thanks to her. The easiest thing for her would have been to lift him as George did.

'There. You *can* manage, Mr Oldman,' she said firmly. 'All it needed was a little effort. We'll expect you to make better progress now. There are people a lot worse off than you who need this bed. The sooner you're out of it, the sooner we can help them.'

She sounded like the forty-five-year-old matron, but looked eighteen, and had made him feel about five years old. He was amazed that he could have been so wrong about her. She turned the wheelchair and pushed him away in silence, apart from the rustle of her uniform. He wanted to ask her all sorts of questions, but hurt pride wouldn't let him. He told himself his mum was probably right about her old man being in on nicking their money and that Leah knew about it too. That idea immediately met resistance. Whatever Cath chose to believe about Sammy Cohen, it was hard for Brian to see how Leah could have been a part of it.

Then they were at the physiotherapy unit, and Leah said, 'I'll leave you in Mrs Dunphy's capable hands. Remember, let's see some real progress.' She strode out, leaving Brian breathless and bereft. Exactly the feelings he'd experienced when Leah hadn't come back to the ward.

Mrs Dunphy helped him out of the wheelchair and on to the edge of a tub of warm wax. He plunged his injured leg into it, which felt good, but he wasn't listening to what she was saying to him. Instead he was thinking about Leah and regretting his missed opportunity. How could he have been so stupid? He should have asked her what her problem was, but that might have been too forward and frightened her. Maybe she was frightened of him, or of the people who had beaten him nearly to death. Perhaps they'd threatened her, he speculated. But why would they? How would they even know where he was? Perhaps Leah had told them and was setting him up for them to come at him again and kill him this time. That was totally stupid, Brian thought. Why did he listen to Cath saying things about Leah? She was evil, the way she put the poison in. He knew just how evil his mum was.

'Brian, are you all right? You're shaking like a leaf and sweating,' Mrs Dunphy said. 'Is the wax too warm?'

'No. It's fine.'

For the whole hour, Brian argued with himself over what he should do about his mum not liking Leah and why he should concern himself about it. When Leah came back to collect him, a smile of pure joy lit his face.

'You must have had a good session,' she said. 'Mrs Dunphy's worked wonders.'

'No,' Brian said. 'You came back. I didn't think I'd see you again.'

'Well, I couldn't leave you here.'

'No, I meant earlier, when you came to the ward.'

'It was only because there was no one else. I certainly didn't want the job. Not after what you said about me.'

'What d'you mean? What did I say?'

'Well, if you don't remember, I'm sure it doesn't matter.'

'I didn't say anything. What did you hear? Was I delirious?'

'You didn't say it to me – I don't think you're that brave. Your mum told Sister Murphy you'd said my presence was upsetting you. That's why they moved me to another ward.'

'No!' He was shocked. 'I didn't say that. I was looking for you, I was, honest!'

'Well, I can't say I'm bothered.'

'I didn't tell her that. I didn't!'

'They why'd your mum say you did? Sister thought I'd done something wrong, or said something I shouldn't have.'

Brian hated his mum for that. He wanted to tell Leah it was his mother who decided for him, but he couldn't bring himself to diminish Cath. Instead he said limply, 'I don't know why she'd have thought that.'

'Don't you?' Leah looked him directly in the eye.

Still Brian didn't know what made him so concerned about Leah's opinion of him. She looked as near perfect as he remembered. Her large dark eyes seemed to see and understand everything, while her olive skin was clear and unmarked. The little he could see of her hair under the cap was thick and dark, shining with vitality. Her body was as slim and agile as a boy's, yet strong enough to lift patients heavier than she was. She moved with the economy of a boxer. Brian jolted forward when he heard her saying, 'It doesn't matter. It just meant I didn't have to meet your mum again. She looks at me so accusingly – like I've done something wrong.'

'She thinks your dad nicked their savings.' It wasn't what he had wanted to say. Why was he defending Cath's behaviour? 'It was all the money they had.'

'That's stupid. He wouldn't do that. He's done some stupid things but he's not a thief.'

'I told her that.'

'It was those men who came trying to sell protection, the Krays. They're monsters.' She spat the word with a vehemence that belied her calm exterior. 'I hate them. Was it them did this to you? It was, wasn't it?'

The thought of the Krays stopped the breath in his lungs, throwing him back to that night in the spiel. He was struggling now as if his windpipe was blocked.

Leah took his wrist to check his pulse, then put her hand on his chest. 'Breathe slowly. Come on, breathe.' Her hand slid down his chest. 'Here. Let your diaphragm go and your lungs will fill automatically.'

Air rushed into him as Leah massaged his diaphragm.

'Tell me how you feel, Brian. I'm interested to know. I really am. I'd like to be a psychologist. There – I haven't told anyone else that.'

Brian closed his eyes. After a moment, he said, 'It's like I'm drowning. I feel I can't breathe so I try to breathe faster, but I just seem to be taking in water, not air.'

'It gets worse, does it, when you think about the Krays?' she asked. 'What else makes it worse?'

Mum hitting Granddad with the iron bar. The words almost popped out. He managed to pull them back, but couldn't stop the shaking that followed. Instead he said, 'I try not to think about it. I feel helpless when I do. I can't help Jack because I'm drowning, like.'

'Was he with you?' Leah asked.

'Yeah, but I didn't see him after he went for them twins. They weren't s'posed to be there. I got hit over the head and didn't get up after that. I don't know what happened to Jack.'

'He came here one day early on. He was injured – not badly.'

'He came here?'

'To see you when you were unconscious.'

'Where is he? Where'd he go? No one's heard from him.'

'I don't know. I'm afraid I don't like him,' Leah said.

Her frankness shocked Brian. Jack had gone against the Krays to get her off the game and he thought she might have at least been grateful. He didn't want to remind her, though, in case she fled.

'He's like the twins,' Leah went on. 'They're the same type.'

Brian waited, scared she was about to bracket him with them too. He wanted her approval. As if reading his thoughts, she said, 'You're different. Very different.'

'How's that?' Brian said uncertainly, in case she knew about him going with men. He was afraid to probe further and again he found himself wondering why. All he knew was that he cared.

'I'll think about it some more.'

After she had returned him to the ward and left, he felt bereft again. It was as if he'd lost an old friend and didn't know how to get them back. The weekend, when there was no physio, no George and no Leah, was the longest yet. The visits from his mum and dad didn't shorten it. On the Saturday, he wanted to ask Cath what she'd said, but couldn't. Finally, on Sunday he got to it after a long silence.

'I didn't say anything much. Why would I bother myself about a little tart like her? She was no better than a prostitute when Jack rescued her. Look how she thanked him! She wouldn't even speak to him. She's no good, Brian, no good at all. I wouldn't concern myself about her.'

Brian looked at his mum sitting at the side of the bed, eating the grapes she'd brought him as though she resented giving away the profits. Her eyes seemed to bore into him, trying to discover something about intentions he didn't even know he had.

'She don't mean nothing to me. Why would she?' he found himself saying and hated himself for saying that. He smacked his head back on the pillows trying to get comfortable, wishing his parents would go.

'I got a line on another house over at Notting Hill,' Joey said. ''S got about twelve big rooms. We could put thirty or forty blacks in there. Maybe a few more, if I can squeeze a couple of extra bathrooms and kitchens in.'

'You don't need to spend any more on them, Joey,' Cath said. 'It's not a bloody hotel. You give too much value. What do blacks care how they live? Any more of them come over, there won't be room for us.'

'As long as there's enough to fill up this house,' Joey said. 'Three quid a week each, we'll do all right. We'll put in a couple of extra toilets.'

'What about all that trouble with them in Notting Hill?'

'I treated my lot okay. It pays.'

'How'd you get the poke?' Brian asked.

'A bit here and a bit there, son. Then the bank came in with a bit for improvements to the shops.' Joey touched his nose confidingly.

'Did you hear from Jack?' He came here.'

'When? Did he say anything to you?' Joey asked.

'I didn't see him. I was asleep. Leah told me.'

'Oh, her,' Cath said, as if Leah's opinion about anything didn't count. 'I think Billy saw him at a racetrack with Albert Dimes. We haven't seen him, have we, Joey?' Joey shook his head.

It was only after they'd left that Brian realized something was wrong. Joey's response was strange; he'd wanted to know what Jack had said, not where he had been. What could he have said that was of such consequence to them? They were hiding something from him, he decided, something that wasn't in his best interest.

TWENTY

Monday came, and physio was on the cards. Brian waited with anticipation for Leah to appear but instead George arrived. 'What's the matter with you?' he asked.

'Nothing. Why should there be?' Brian said irritably.

'You got a face as long as the Mile End Road. 'S not bad news, is it?'

'You don't know what's happened to Leah – Nurse Cohen?'

'She's on the kiddies' ward. I don't think she likes it much.'

'She don't like kids?'

'She likes to get into people's minds and see what makes them tick,' George said. 'A very smart girl, that one. She wants to be a psychologist or something. Always studying.'

'What's wrong with being a nurse?'

'I s'pose she wants to better herself.' George pushed him out of the ward. 'I see your friend Tom Driberg's in some sort of trouble with the Labour Party. Why don't he come to see you, Brian?'

'I don't suppose he knows I'm here.'

'Well, you could give him a tinkle.'

'Yeah, maybe I will,' Brian said, without enthusiasm. What would he want with him now? He'd sooner have a cup of tea with Nurse Cohen than give Tom Driberg a hand shandy.

Tea was over and all there was to look forward to was the long, drawn-out slide into night when you couldn't sleep because you'd slept too much in the day. He dozed as he listened to the auxiliary start along the ward with her rattling trolley, collecting the cups, when he became aware of someone stopping by his bed and pushing away the over-bed table.

'How are you, today?' someone asked, their voice soft and concerned.

The angel was back! Brian was afraid to open his eyes in case he was dreaming and she wasn't really there. Then she touched his wrist to take his pulse and he felt a tingle up his arm. 'You'll make my pulse race, Nurse,' he said, still not opening his eyes. 'Please put me out of my misery and tell me it's you and that I'm not dreaming.'

'You not dreaming. It's Big Bertha, Mr Oldman.'

At that, his eyes flew open. Leah was standing there, laughing. 'Why would your pulse rate go up just because I touch your wrist?' she asked.

She sounded serious, in spite of her laughter. Feeling slightly embarrassed, Brian said, 'I don't know. Why does it?'

'Well, let's see, shall we?' She checked the upside-down watch pinned to her uniform. 'No. It appears to be quite normal.'

'Then why does my heart thump, I feel sick and my throat goes dry whenever you're around?'

'You must be sickening with something. I'll get the doctor.'

Brian shook his head. 'Don't. It's you I wanted to see.'

'I'm just going off duty.'

'Oh, do you have to?' He couldn't keep the disappointment out of his voice.

'I'm coming to take you to physio tomorrow. We're going to get you more active. You've been far too idle these past weeks.'

'I've been ill,' Brian protested.

'You're not any more. So, get a good night's rest. You'll need it.'

With that she was gone. Brian still wasn't sure if she was teasing him. He wanted to call after her to stay, to ask her what else she was going to do besides studying. Was she going out to see anyone? He was scared to ask in case he frightened her away.

'She's a lively one, that girl,' his socialist neighbour said. 'I bet she gets all the doctors' hearts going. And something besides, I'd say.'

A wave of jealousy washed over Brian. He wanted to tell him to shut up. What if she had no interest in him beyond getting his much-needed vacated bed and he'd only imagined anything else?

After physio, and with the help of Mrs Dunphy, Leah made him put all his weight on his damaged tendon. It hurt like hell and he would have collapsed if he hadn't had the two women's support.

'It will hurt at first,' Leah said.

'Have mercy on me. It's killing me,' Brian said.

'How can you take me dancing in two weeks' time if your leg isn't working?' Leah said.

'There's an offer to get any red-blooded patient walking again,' Mrs Dunphy said.

Brian looked at Leah, unaware of the weight on his damaged leg or the pain. All he was thinking about was getting fit and out of the hospital.

Was it possible? Could he be in love with a woman – this woman, this beautiful creature called Leah – when before he had only ever been interested in boys or men? She excited and terrified him as she drove him towards wellness.

Leah came to dominate his waking moments as he was pulled between thinking of how gone on her he was and worrying in case she didn't feel the same about him and he'd made a fool of himself. There was no way he could gauge it. With a bloke you sort of caught his eye and knew by his furtive look or his edginess whether he was up for it. Perhaps it was the same with women, except none of those looks came from Leah. But she wasn't doing anything wrong or illegal. He had only ever seen her in uniform. What would she look like without any clothes on? Would he be more excited than he was now? Could he get any more excited? This wasn't like the tension he experienced with men, so easily released but never truly satisfied.

Lying on his bed, he closed his eyes and let his thoughts go to

Leah, her narrow hands and long, delicate fingers that were made for touching or taking his pulse, for gently bathing his wounds. They weren't made for heaving soiled mattresses or empty bedpans. He didn't want her doing that. He wanted her sitting on the bed, sharing a joke with him.

'I think she's sweet on you, Brian,' his *Daily Mirror*-reading neighbour on the door side of the long ward said like he had suddenly woken up. 'You'd better watch it, son. You know what some of these nurses are like.'

Brian lay back on the pillow and shut his eyes. Leah was there behind the lids, leaning over him, plumping up his pillows, her small breasts pressing into him. He could smell her. It was the fresh-from-the-bath smell of Palmolive soap and surgical spirit. He imagined himself bringing her close to him and kissing her, then undoing her silver-buckled belt, unpinning her starched front, unbuttoning her uniform. In his mind's eye he saw her smooth naked thighs above the black stockings held up with her suspender belt over her pants. One by one he removed them all until she was naked. Then he imagined her slipping into bed beside him. She was stroking him, taking his pyjamas off. Finally they were both naked and Brian felt the touch of her skin against his. He stroked her smooth buttocks as she kissed him, putting her tongue into his mouth. He kissed her back, then harder, moving his body down hers ... kissing her vagina, putting his tongue inside her as the men did in the 8mm porn films they showed in the spiels some days when business was slow. He could almost taste her. His cock grew hard and throbbed as if with a will of its own. Oh, Leah, his thoughts screamed, let me be inside you, let me be a part of you.

He couldn't stand it a moment longer. Easing himself to the edge of the bed he reached for his plaid dressing-gown and pulled it around him to hide the lump in his pyjamas.

'Where are you going?' Bertha said, in her sing-song voice. 'You shouldn't be out of bed.'

'I've got to go to the bathroom,' Brian said. He was steadier on his feet and in less pain. 'Nurse Cohen said I should try to walk on my own.' He stepped round her.

She put out her hand to help rather than stop him. 'I'll get the porter to come and take you, honey.'

''S all right. I can manage. Nurse Cohen said I should try,' he insisted, and moved off, watched by her and the other men at his end of the ward. They all knew what he was up to, Brian was certain, as he went past them. An old boy in the end bed nearest the double doors put up his thumb and Brian went bright red.

He bolted the door as soon as he was inside and reached into his pyjamas. It happened so fast he couldn't believe it was over, but still he wanted more. Leah was off for forty-eight hours and he wasn't sure if he could bear not seeing her for so long, always wondering what she was doing. Two whole days and nights ... Thoughts of Leah, who was still a tantalizing mystery to him, pulled and pushed at him beyond endurance. He ran his thumb over the head of his penis. Soon he was completely lost again, convulsing like an epileptic, utterly out of control when he ejaculated for the second time. What that must be like inside Leah was something he couldn't bear to imagine as his body arched off the seat.

A sharp rap on the door startled him and Leah fled.

'You all right in there, son?' It was George, the porter. 'Giving it plenty, are you?'

Panic rushed through him. George might have heard him. He'd tell Bertha and she might tell Leah. But Leah would understand. She loved him as much as he loved her. She'd understand his urgency.

'I'm all right,' Brian croaked, and pulled the chain, flushing away the evidence in the shiny medicated Izal toilet paper. Still his erection remained. Maybe he'd have to sit in a cold bath.

Brian watched the night nurses work their way along the ward, settling the patients for the night. He worried in case, as they fussed round him, they saw the pole he still had. It just wouldn't die down.

'You all right, Brian?' one asked. 'Can I get you anything?'

He wondered what she'd say if he told her what he wanted.

The more intense the feelings he experienced for Leah the more uneasy Brian became. There was no doubt that he was in love with her, and he was sure she was in love with him, although she'd never said so. Perhaps you didn't have to say it. But what would happen when he left the safe, secure world of the hospital? How would they survive outside, with Cath not liking her, Joey not defending her, and animosity from Jack because he had wanted her for himself?

Jack. Brian couldn't bear to think of him and decided to contrive a way to stay in hospital, safe, with Leah. He was getting stronger every day and the doctors were saying he should think about going home.

On Wednesday afternoon, seven weeks after Brian had been admitted, Jack walked in wearing a new pale grey suit. It had a short, boxy Italian jacket with the wide shoulders that were so much in fashion now. Leah told him about fashion, joking that he'd been in hospital so long everything had changed half a dozen times.

Jack looked fit and well, but there were a couple of scars over his eyes. Brian couldn't remember if they were from his army days. The chunk missing from his left ear was new.

'One of the hounds bit me,' Jack explained, when he saw Brian clocking it, 'during that dust-up in Rupert Street. I was more scared of getting rabies off one of them now.' He smiled tightly. 'You don't seem very pleased to see me, son.'

'Oh, I'm just surprised, that's all. I mean, I didn't hear nothing. Cath and Joey didn't either.'

'Don't be daft. I seen them – I sorted them out cushty. I went and sorted out the twins, too, with Joey. Spotty and the other fella we packed off to Brighton.'

Brian choked back the inclination to vomit as he prayed Leah wouldn't come in and see Jack. He wanted to sink into the pillow, close his eyes, and when he opened them again, for Jack to have gone. Instead he found himself saying, 'What d'you mean you sorted the twins out with Joey? How d'you see them? When?'

'What does it matter? It's all sweet now.'

'I need to know – I mean, fuck it, Jack, I almost died!'

'You're telling me. After that set-to in Rupert Street, we all thought you was a goner. It put the wind up everyone. Your mum and dad went and nicked Ronnie for burning their shop – well, Joey did, the mug. Ronnie was well and truly up the steps. I talked sensibly to them and to Old Bill. We put some notes into Ken Drury, and the twins give Joey back his money they nicked off Sammy Cohen – well, most of it. Suddenly Joey got a loss of memory and couldn't identify Ronnie no more. That wasn't till you was well on your way to recovery. He wouldn't have done it if you'd popped your clogs.'

'Oh, great,' Brian said. 'After what they done to me? I'da killed them the first chance I got. I still will.'

'No. Things are sweet, Bri. We're all being a bit sensible now. Everything is ours – well, half of it. We decided how we carve up the West End.'

'We?' Brian challenged. 'What? You and the twins?'

'Let the dust settle. Then we'll sort them out good and proper.' Jack swept the room with a glance, as is he was searching for someone. Brian knew who and dreaded the inevitable enquiry.

'Where's Leah Cohen? She works here now – Cath said it was her what recognized you. I wouldn't mind giving her one. I expect she's up for it still. Nurse. Bit different from when I first met her.'

Brian's breath was coming in short bursts and he wasn't getting enough oxygen into his lungs. He wanted to tell Jack to back off, but couldn't. The words wouldn't come because he was so angry. Only he wasn't certain if he was more angry at him for speaking of Leah like that or not doing anything about the Krays. Finally he said, 'How did you get out that night? Last I saw, you were whacking the twins.'

'We was set up well and proper there. Maybe it was John Bindon what put the bubble in. I saw him, but he didn't do much to give us a hand. You chopped off Frankie Frazer's toes – d'you know that?'

'Did I?' Brian said, thrown. He remembered swinging the cleaver. 'I knew I did someone. I was just trying to do as much damage as possible before I was done for meself.'

'You did that all right. There's a lot of one-legged villains about now.'

Brian laughed. It felt good.

'I took a lot of hits,' Jack said. 'Then I got a knife at Ronnie's throat. He squealed like a pig – you shoulda heard him. I got out using him as a shield, but I was stabbed. I couldn't have stood up for much longer, I'd lost that much blood. Look.' He lifted his shirt to show a wide scar under his ribs. 'Ronnie got the hump about all the claret over his suit. I just laid low. I went to see that doctor friend of Billy Hill's, Stephen Ward. He ain't a proper doctor, but he's got plenty of penicillin and drugs to kill the pain. He fixed me up fine, let me use his flat in Wimpole Street.'

'Whose idea was it to do a deal with the twins?'

'Joey's. He's shrewder than ever. He said this wasn't doing any of us any good and went with me to see Reggie. The deal was easy done. Reggie's sensible – not like that fat poof. He's crazy that one.'

'I didn't get a thought in all this?' Brian tried to keep the hurt out of his voice.

'We was thinking about you most of all. Joey didn't want them coming back at you. The twins was talking about it, after all the damage you done.'

Brian felt better and laughed again.

'It's all sorted now, Bri. Here, I got you some car magazines.'

Brian wasn't interested in cars.

'Your mum thinks you'll be home in a few days. Maybe you should go to Clacton for a holiday – sea air'll do you good – then a bit of training, get fit again.'

Brian saw him glance up and down the ward again and hoped Leah was taking a patient to surgery or physio. Twice he was on the point of saying something, then found he couldn't. His rationale was that he didn't want to alert Jack to his feelings about Leah in case he told Cath and she put the poison in.

'I got a new drum in Old Compton Street. Handy. I could put a couple of donahs in there if I don't use it. They'd earn plenty. Maybe I'll go and sort out Sammy Cohen's daughter.'

'She ain't like that, Jack,' Brian said, angry again. 'She's a blinding nurse.'

'They're all like that, Bri, given half a chance. She'd earn a lot more than she does here, that's for sure.'

'No! Don't. You hear what I say? Don't. All right?'

'What's it to you?' Jack said. 'She's got a lot of mouth on her, is what I hear. 'S what our Cath says, full of big ideas about what you should and shouldn't be doing. You can't stand for that.' He got up. 'I'd better make tracks.'

After he was gone, Brian lay back and breathed evenly as Leah had taught him. His fears didn't abate.

Along the corridor, there were a number of doors, some to side wards and rooms where they did things Jack didn't want to see or know about. The fifth door he opened was a bathroom and Leah was giving an old boy a bath. She was wearing a rubber apron and thin rubber gloves and was washing the geezer's crêpy skin on his back, which had several large sores that made Jack feel ill just to look at them. He hated anything to do with sickness. 'You can do that to me, if you like,' he said. Leah jumped. 'I'd enjoy having my back washed.'

'You shouldn't be here,' Leah said. 'Sister will be cross.'

'We won't worry about her, will we?'

'Visitors aren't allowed in the patients' bathrooms. It's against the rules.'

'So are a lot of things, Leah. There are too many rules.'

'I don't know where we'd be without them.'

''S right. We'd have nothing to break, would we?'

'You're not supposed to be here,' the old boy in the bath said. 'Nurse Cohen said you gotta leave.'

'Button it, Granddad. No one asked for your opinion.'

'Well, you got it, you cheeky young sod. If I was half my age I'd box your ears.'

That made Jack smile. He pulled on one of the spare rubber gloves in the bathroom, his large hand barely going into it. 'How about coming for a drink or a bite to eat when you get done here?'

'Oh, I can't do that,' Leah said.

'Why's that? Ain't I good enough for you now?'

'It's not that. I have to study. I've got lots of exams coming up.'

'Well, I'm good at studying,' Jack told her. 'I'll help you.'

'Mr Braden, please go,' Leah said.

'It's Jack. Remember? The man who rescued you a few years ago when the Kray twins had hold of you. Or don't you want to remember that?'

He could see how well she remembered it. She pulled off her gloves and pushed past him, looking as if she was about to cry. Tears were the old standby. The get-out. He wasn't going to give up on her, though. He stepped over to the bath and yanked out the plug by the chain. 'We don't want you slipping over and drowning, you old bastard, do we?' he said, then went out to look for Leah.

Houdini couldn't have disappeared more completely and Jack was annoyed, after all he'd done for her. Learning that she was shortly to go off duty he waited outside the main entrance, hoping to catch her. Eventually she came out of the doors and down the steps with two other nurses, each with dark blue capes around their shoulders. She broke her step when she saw Jack leaning against his new Ford Zodiac, then tried to scoot past him. Jack was quicker and caught hold of her. 'Leah, I just wanna talk to you.' The other two nurses gave him a long look and Jack winked at them. They weren't bad-looking either and he guessed he could have had either of them.

'I have to study. If I don't, I won't pass my exams.' She turned across Charterhouse Square towards the nurses' home on the far side.

'I thought you was already a nurse,' he said, sticking close to her but letting go of her wrist.

'I've got a psychology exam at the end of the month.'

'Well, we could still go out. Psychology ain't gonna do you much good, is it?'

'Look, I really can't go. I don't have time.'

'What's that about, then?' Jack demanded, catching hold of her again. 'What? You let half of Hoxton fuck you before I came along.'

Leah tried to pull away, but he tightened his grip. He wasn't going to let go so easily this time. 'Not so fast,' he said, angry now. 'You owe me, don't you?'

'What?' Leah said, fear in her voice. 'Why are you doing this?'

'Why d'you think? Look at you. Why d'you ignore me when I came round looking for you? I saved your life. You'd still be working for them Kray slags if it weren't for me.'

'I'd have killed myself first,' Leah said quietly.

'Then I'd say you owe me your life. What's wrong with you?'

'I can't. I'm sorry. I don't want to hurt Brian.'

'What?' That shocked Jack. He hadn't paid any attention when Cath had remarked that Brian was interested in Leah. He'd thought it was a joke or wishful thinking on his sister's part. She knew how Brian was as well as Jack did.

'You gotta be joking! How's it gonna hurt him? You don't mean nothing to Brian. Believe me, he's not made that way.'

'I think he loves me. I feel the same about him.'

'Brian? Don't be stupid. You ain't going off with him in a million years. He's an iron. You want a real man. You better think about what you owe me. Fancy worrying about that poof.'

'He's not! He's not,' Leah said, and burst into tears.

People passing were staring at them now, and one paused, a tall doctor in a white coat. He'd be gone in one, Jack decided, if he tried to butt in.

'Are you okay, Leah?' he asked, in an Australian accent. 'Is this fellow bothering you?'

'You want me to tell him?'

The menace in Jack's tone was enough, and Leah shook her head.

'Ta-ta,' Jack said, and the doctor started to walk away. Then he came back.

'You don't look too hot, Leah,' he said. 'We'd better get you inside.'

When Jack turned to deal with him, Leah broke free of his grip and ran into the nurses' home. 'You tired of living or something?' Jack said.

'Look, I think you'd better go, matey—'

The sly left hook in the solar plexus was about the last thing the doctor had expected as Jack continued to stare him right in the eye. The blow winded him and Jack put out an arm to steady him. 'Just don't interfere in other people's business.'

With that, Jack walked away, leaving him gasping for breath. He'd return another time and sort out Leah Cohen. What he knew for certain was that he wasn't going to let a donah as good as that waste herself on an iron.

'What's wrong, Leah?' Brian said, in a frightened whisper as he followed her round the ward, trying to help with the teas.

Leah pushed the trolley to the next bed, the auxiliary nurse arching her eyebrows at him in commiseration. Of all the emotions that poured through Brian, confusion was uppermost. He had thought things were sweet between them and couldn't understand why she had turned like this. He could feel himself being pulled down into that emotional pit where he often found himself when Cath was displeased with him. There, fear swamped him and made him breathless without his knowing why, only that it had everything to do with her killing his granddad. Now, sensing the men in the beds watching him as they sipped their tea, Brian was determined not to slide into it.

Instead, he marched after Leah and caught her arm to turn her. As she turned she smacked him across the face, shocking him as never before. There was a clatter of cups on to saucers as the whole ward came to a standstill. This was a lovers' quarrel of such intensity it gripped and fascinated everyone.

'What are you going to do?' Leah challenged. 'Hit me? Threaten me like your uncle Jack did?'

So Jack was the problem, not him. 'What did he say to you?'

Before Leah could answer, Sister's sharp voice penetrated the length of the ward. 'Nurse Cohen,' she said, 'into my office. Now, if you please.'

Leah gave him a withering look before she trudged away. How could she love him at one moment and despise him the next? It was beyond his comprehension. He needed to talk to her, to understand what was going on.

He waited and waited, but Leah didn't return to the ward. He asked the other nurses where she was. No one knew or, if they did, they wouldn't say.

'She's been sent to her room in the nurses' home, Brian,' the ward sister told him, when he dared to ask her.

'Why? She didn't do anything wrong.'

'Well, I believe she's become emotionally involved with a patient. It's causing her to behave in ways she shouldn't on the ward, and certainly not in front of other patients.'

'She didn't do anything wrong,' Brian repeated.

'I'm not even sure she's cut out for nursing. Perhaps she'll settle down when she leaves the hospital.'

This was news to Brian. What could Leah have done that had cost her her job? 'She loves nursing. She's so good at it, Sister. She can't get the sack.'

'That's not the case. She plans to go to university to study psychology,' the sister told him. 'We'll all be sorry to lose her. Meanwhile, she must conduct herself in the way we expect of our nurses. There's no excuse. I only hope Matron doesn't hear about it.'

Life after leaving hospital was something Brian had to face, what it might mean for him and Leah, how and where he might see her again. He was mobile now and knew where the nurses' home was, Leah having shown him on the way to physio. She had even pointed out which was her room. Occasionally patients were seen in the street as they went from one building to another for examinations, mostly in wheelchairs or with a member of staff. Brian couldn't risk going to the nurses' home in his pyjamas and dressing-gown. Anyway, men weren't allowed in it, Leah had told him, not even patients.

His day clothes were in his beside locker for the little excursions he made around the hospital in preparation for his discharge. He slipped his feet into his shoes and wrapped his clothes into a neat bundle under his arm, then slipped off to the bathroom. There, he changed and hid his dressing-gown and pyjamas. As he was coming out, he met fat Bertha, who wanted to know where he thought he was going.

'Don't tell anyone, Bertha,' he said. 'Please. I want to go and find out what's happened to Leah.'

'You had a big row, man,' Bertha said.

'I've got to see her to straighten things out.'

'You can't get into the nurses' home, man. If she won't come out how you gon' explain?'

He waited, hoping she would provide the solution.

'There's a way in through the gardens in Carthusian Street. They don't put no one on the back door. I don't know how you find her room. I dunno where it is.'

'Well, I gotta try.'

Encouraged, Brian set off. He found his way into the grey- and cream-painted building through the garden, but there were four floors and all the doors had numbers, no names. As he wandered along the first-floor corridor a nurse with wet hair, wearing a dressing-gown, came out of the bathroom and caught her breath in alarm when she saw him. She recovered when he told her he was looking for Leah.

'I think she's on the second floor. Room C eighteen, I think. Eighteen or twenty.'

Brian went up the stairs, strengthened by the prospect of reaching Leah and finding out what was going on.

As he rounded the bend at the top he met a middle-aged woman in a grey overall, carrying a large bunch of keys. Her thin lips puckered in an angry grimace. 'What are you doing here? Get out at once before I call the police.'

'I'm looking for Leah – Nurse Cohen.'

'Out! Men are not allowed in here.' She bustled up to him and prodded him with a stiff index finger, driving him back to the stairs.

'I want Leah! Leah!' he shouted. 'Leah, it's Brian!' He stumbled on to the stairs and caught the handrail. He could have punched the woman and knocked her down, but he didn't want to get Leah into any more trouble.

The woman in the grey overall was relentless. She drove him all the way out into the street and slammed the door. Brian stood on the step and rang the bell until at last the door opened and Leah stepped out. 'Leah,' he said sheepishly.

'Brian, you'll get me thrown out. Is that what you want? Don't you think you've done enough damage? I don't want to see you any more.'

'Don't say that, please, Leah. Tell me what I've done wrong.'

Brian waited as Leah let a nurse go into the building. 'I don't think it could work, Brian. I thought I loved you, but I couldn't take on your family as well. I mean, first your mum – that's weird. No, it's not,' she said, after a moment's thought. 'It's classic. A mother not being able to give up her only son and trying to emasculate him. It's really your uncle Jack I can't take. He gives me the creeps. I won't put up with that, and I don't have to. Not now.'

'What did he say?' Brian asked. 'Did he say something about me?' Leah glanced away, making him even more anxious. 'What?'

'He tried to make me go with him because of what happened in the past.' She stopped abruptly, upset, then turned back to the building. 'It doesn't matter. Not any more.'

'I'll kill him,' Brian said, churning with anger. 'Please, Leah.' He caught her arm. 'I love you, I think – I mean I do but, well, it's just that it's never happened before so I don't know what to expect. It's not like any other feeling I've ever had.'

'He said horrible unkind things about you.'

A sinking feeling pulled at Brian's intestines. He didn't want to lie to her but wanted to deny his entire past.

'Is it true?' she asked.

If he told her the truth he'd be finished. He thought about telling her he'd been with that girl from Clapham Common, Martha, as a way of denying what he'd done, but that would have been just as much of a lie. Carefully he said, 'Nothing I did or was matters any more. I've changed. I'm an entirely different person now I've met you. You did that, Leah. I couldn't have become that person without you.'

Leah closed her eyes and nodded. 'He was angry and jealous.'

'God, I want to kill. I feel like going over there and killing him right now.'

'No, you mustn't. You're not like him, Brian, you're not. Just because someone in your family has that taint, it doesn't mean you do. There's a gentle, sensitive soul inside you, I know there is.'

'Please, Leah, can we get some coffee and talk? There's a place on Baltic Street, Divito's. Let's go there.'

'How do you know it?'

'We put a pinball machine in there and looked after it.' He saw at once that telling her this had been a mistake. It had brought her back to Jack.

'Can we go somewhere else?'

Instead they went to Alfie's greasy spoon on Clerkenwell Road. That was a mistake too, Brian realized, the moment they walked in. Three different people greeted him and asked after his mum and dad. Any moment Jack might come in. He sometimes used this place. Without a word, Brian led Leah out on to the busy road. The traffic was struggling east, trying to get through the City and out to the East India docks or further to Tilbury. Finding somewhere quiet to sit and talk seemed a dead loss. As they started back along St John Street towards the hospital Leah took his hand. That one little gesture suddenly made his head swim and gave him hope. He didn't know what to say to convince her of his feelings for her. Instead he laid her hand on his chest where he guessed his heart was. 'Can you feel it?' he said, glad that she hadn't simply pulled away.

'It's like a trapped bird.'

They sat on a bench in Charterhouse Square and watched the starlings flying in to roost, chattering in their hundreds.

'I'm sorry I came into the nurses' home.'

'I'll let you into a secret, Brian,' Leah said, smiling mischievously. 'Nurses do sometimes sneak in boyfriends and most of the wardens turn a blind eye, but you ran into Mrs Suggs. She's a real killjoy. She'll be going off duty in about ten minutes.'

Brian froze, unsure what Leah was saying to him. Did she mean he might sneak in after Mrs Suggs was gone or that he'd have been more successful if he'd waited? Then he got a completely different message, which confused him even more. Leah said, 'They'll miss you off the ward and send out a search party, if we're not careful.'

'I don't care. I just want to be with you.'

Leah smiled and he almost relaxed enough to smile back. Their faces were just inches apart and seemed to be getting closer, which made him so nervous he thought he might pass out. He wasn't sure that he didn't when their lips finally met as if almost by accident. His mind went blank as waves of sensation spread through his body. The traffic stopped and the starlings fell silent as they waited for the kiss to end.

Then he became aware of what was happening in his trousers. He was scared in case Leah noticed it and thought less of him. He didn't know what to do, how to move forward. With boys you just grabbed. Then it occurred to him that perhaps he didn't have to go beyond the bench, beyond kissing.

But Leah said, 'She'll be gone now, Mrs Suggs. You can creep up to my room, but you have to be quiet.'

'Are you sure it'll be okay?' Brian asked, uncertainty bombarding him as his erection grew more and more insistent.

'Yes, really,' she said, her lips so close to his that he could feel her breath as she spoke. He kissed her again and felt the same sensations as before, only now they were more intense because he wasn't taken so completely by surprise.

How they got upstairs without his heart stopping Brian didn't know. He stood breathlessly in her tiny room with its narrow bed, the slender wardrobe, and the table under the window with all her study papers. Leah bolted the door and he started towards her. She put a finger to her lips, then took off her cardigan and they were in each other's arms, kissing hard. His erection stood between them like a guilty reminder of his past. Leah couldn't help but notice it as she pressed ever more insistently into him. He tried to arch his body away from her but she simply moved closer.

'It's all right,' she said. 'It's all right.' She unbuttoned the front of her uniform, just like she did so many times in his imagination, then shrugged it off her shoulders and let it drop to the floor. She stepped out of it and closed on him, her panties over the suspender belt that held up her black darned stockings.

Brian fumbled with his belt and staggered to the bed with her as he tried to kick off his trousers. On it, they kissed harder and for so long they stopped each other breathing. Between them they slid off her panties and Leah unfastened her stockings, rolled them off and undid the suspender belt.

Then it happened like some dark, malevolent stain deep inside him that was waiting to pull him back. Seeing her nakedness, with its black hairs growing up towards her navel like a man, Brian's erection vanished, and with it all the feeling in his body like water running down the plughole in a bath until finally there was nothing left. Short of crying, he didn't know what to do. This hadn't happened with a man, there was never any requirement on his part to sustain feeling for this length of time.

'It's all right,' Leah said. 'Don't worry. It'll come back.'

That didn't reassure him.

His hands explored Leah, tenderly at first, but still he felt nothing. Anxiety caused him to caress her harder as if the actions themselves would squeeze feelings from him. None came, only a deepening sense of panic. His dick lay lifeless now his heart's desire was within reach. What was happening to him? Perhaps he was worried about being caught in her room. No. He was anxious about the trouble she'd be in if she was caught, but it wasn't just that. He felt Leah's delicate hand enclose him and squeeze, as he'd done to himself many, many times. No response. A scream started in his mind and he fought it. Oh, God, why? I'll do anything if only I can. Leah began rubbing him, and he enjoyed her touch, but the anxiety wouldn't go away. It increased and fed itself, like air feeding a fire. Soon there would be nothing left but ash.

'It's all right, my darling,' Leah whispered, as she pressed close to him in the narrow bed. 'It'll be all right. It's easy for girls, but not for boys. I love you, Brian. I love you so much. You're the only man I'll ever love and it wouldn't matter if it never happened as long as I can be with you.'

Tears spilled over Brian's eyelids. He didn't move. He was thinking about the words Leah had just uttered. Tentative feelings emerged, like shoots after a hard winter, but he was scared to acknowledge them. 'I wanted it to be so nice,' he said. 'It's the first time I've ever felt like this with anyone,' he confessed. 'I didn't want to disappoint you like this.'

'You haven't. Really. You haven't. Don't be silly.'

'I'm blubbering like a big soft girl.'

'It's because you think you've disappointed me. That's the nicest compliment you could ever pay me.'

Brian wanted to cry all over again, but his feelings were pushing through resolutely now and he almost looked round, expecting some physical presence to cut them off. Then he was acutely aware of Leah's hands on him. A new fear rushed in: it would all happen too soon and be over before he got inside her. Leah clasped him as he supported himself over her and tried to guide him inside her. The sensation of her touch was at once exquisite and unbearable. Brian screwed up his eyes tightly, trying to gain control of those fierce random feelings which made him scream, No! First the silence of his mind then the cry of terror burst out and straight through the thin walls. 'No!' he cried again and again. Leah's attempts to quieten him were futile. Behind his eyelids he saw *her*, mocking him, telling him Leah was a dirty kyke, a prostitute, no good. He couldn't rid himself of her image, not even with his eyes open. It was *her* who was trying to get him to fuck her. Was he going mad? The image of his granddad flew up at Brian as flesh peeled off the side of his head where she hit him with the iron bar. His mum was saying how she'd give him the same if he didn't do as she told him.

With a terrible scream Brian lashed out with his fist and struck a hard blow on her left cheekbone, then another and another, trying to silence her.

Now there was screaming from outside the room and people were banging on the door, but he went on swinging his fist at her, trying to rid himself of the image as a great pool of stickiness glued his legs to hers as if for all eternity. Then he knew he would never be free.

BOOK 2

TWENTY-ONE

Nicking things was fun. It was profitable and exciting but, most of all, it put Tony Wednesday in charge. He could decide whether he did it or not. Almost every day he nicked something from shops, and sometimes at night he went out nicking from houses or warehouses, slipping out of a window at the orphanage and down the ivy-clad wall.

He lay in bed, listening for the dormitory to settle after lights out. Each night the routine was the same. At nine o'clock the lights were switched off from outside; there was a bit of talk before the room settled, last-minute reminders about tomorrow, a few insults, then quiet. Ten minutes later the brother on duty would look in, walk the length of the dorm with a flashlight to check that the boys were in the right beds, then leave. Staying awake during that time wasn't difficult for Tony. He just lay in bed thinking of how he hated this place, how he'd like to kill everyone in it, especially the thin, rat-like brothers in their brown habits and the fat, overfed nurse.

Slipping out of bed, he went across the room to Micky Lee, who was only thirteen but went out nicking with him. They couldn't take many of the things they lifted back to the orphanage, but clothes and money were easy to hide. The rest they sold in transport cafés and spent the money on the pinball machine or jukebox. Often they sold too cheaply so the money didn't last long.

'Micky. Micky,' Tony said, in an urgent whisper, 'you coming? Mick? Wake up!'

Either scared or tired, his mate wouldn't respond. Tony hesitated only a moment before he decided to go on his own. He'd been planning to break into a men's outfitters on the high street to get some new clobber. He was fed up with hand-me-downs. The brothers were tightwads and didn't spend a penny unless they were forced to. Clothes, the raiment of vanity, were low on their list of priorities. Boys who'd got a place at the local grammar school were bought uniforms, but always grant-aided. Tony had purposely messed up his eleven-plus exam to punish the brothers. He certainly didn't want to have to wear a free uniform that was to be cherished and guarded against damage because another wouldn't come your way until the current one was at least two or three sizes too small.

Going down the ivy outside the window was as easy as sliding down a pole. He tried to go carefully because he'd noticed it was getting worn because he'd used this way out and in so often. The brothers hadn't seen it but, then, they were stupid. Most likely some snitch would tell them about it, and he'd have to find another route.

He made straight for the shops on Kingsland Road. Most were rubbish, with nothing he could take and sell easily – tailors or button suppliers. He couldn't break into the outfitters without Micky's help, so he decided on a large tobacconist's instead. Smokes were the easiest thing of all to sell in a café. Everyone wanted them. They were bulky and difficult to hide, and it wasn't worth nicking just a few packets. He needed at least two cartons. He'd tried lifting a couple of boxes at the back of the newsagent's when he collected the papers early in the morning for his delivery round. He earned twelve shillings a week. It was a drag getting up, especially when he'd been out late at night, but it meant he had a legitimate source of money that explained other cash or things found in his possession. He told the brothers he'd saved up his paper-round money. They were gullible and Tony liked to pull the wool over their eyes. What he acquired now was easily explained by his full-time day job, even though they took most of the three pounds he earned weekly for his keep.

'Fucking hell,' he said, when he remembered he hadn't got the breaking tools. Micky usually brought the crowbar. He looked in the alleyway at the back of the shops for something to force the lock on the window. There was an old packing case with strips of metal, none of which was strong enough to use as a bar. He could go across Kingsland Road on to the overgrown bombsite to look for something. He thought about it, then dismissed the idea. He might get nicked for loitering, like some queer.

Tony tried the door and windows. There was always a chance one would be open.

He'd hardly touched the first window when some geezer shouted, 'Oi! Whatcha doing?' Without waiting to discover who it was, Tony ran along the alleyway, grateful to the man for being so stupid as to give him plenty of warning. Someone less stupid would have crept up and grabbed him. People were so stupid. Tony heard the man's lumbering run slow to a laboured, breathless walk and smiled. He didn't dash out on to the main road in case a cop saw him, but slowed to a walk, wandering the streets of Hoxton, looking for an opportunity. Cars were parked in the streets, some quite smart, but they were a waste of time. Usually all you found were tins of barley sugar and rugs but now and then, during the day, you got a handbag or a briefcase that some stupid person had left on show. Cars were easy to screw, and so were vans. Although Micky was only thirteen he could drive, and a couple of times they'd nicked a car and gone for a spin. It was a big waste of time, Tony decided, with nothing to show for it at the end. If Tony wanted a ride in a car, he could go out with Brother Simon for a jaunt in the country, as the stupid fucker liked to call it. He didn't enjoy what went with it: giving the brother a wank on the back seat.

Crossing Regent's Canal, Tony found himself in de Beauvoir Road, his eyes still darting about for an opportunity. He tried the door to the post office and found it securely locked. The houses here were bow-fronted, late Victorian terraces, and Tony didn't expect to find much. He felt a bit despondent, but he was determined to press on. Most of the windows were dark, people in bed because they had get up for work the next day. He'd be tired at work tomorrow. As a site clerk at a warehouse being built on Leman Street, he'd found a bit of fiddle booking in tradesmen when they were taking days off. He'd got ten bob for that, but knew he wasn't getting a big enough share. Some of the bricklayers earned four pounds a day. Ten bob was okay for a labourer on three quid, but even that was too cheap. He'd ask for 25 per cent in future.

Then he saw his chance, a ground-floor window that was ajar.

He slipped into the shallow front garden, watching owlishly for any sign of movement. He was especially careful because some of these houses had two or more tenants. The ground-floor front was someone's bedroom, but the people in the bed were sound asleep and smelt as if they were drunk. He went through trouser pockets and handbags, finding a total of three pounds, nine shillings and four pence, which made it worth the bother.

In the kitchen he found a strong carving knife to do the gas meter. With the knife behind the flimsy lock it didn't need much pressure to break open the box. He got a load of shillings, about two pounds – he didn't stop to count. As he was about to start up the stairs, to check if the people there were any richer, someone approached the front door and he heard a key scrape across the lock.

For a second Tony froze, then stepped back into the messy kitchen and pushed the door to. What if they wanted a cup of cocoa? The knife was still in his hand. He could stab them. No, that was stupid, he told himself, and put the knife on the dresser. He could hear them whispering. It was a couple.

Then the worst thing happened. The man went up the stairs to their rooms but the woman came along to the kitchen. She opened the door and, finding Tony, screamed, 'Stephen! Stephen!' Tony stepped past her and raced to the door. He flung it open and shut it to delay Stephen.

But the man could run. Tony heard him close behind and he wasn't flagging. Why was the stupid idiot bothering? Tony hadn't nicked anything worth all this trouble. Come on, give up, you stupid fucker.

On and on the man came, relentlessly, as Tony zipped into Shoreditch Park, thinking he might hide with no lights there, but he wasn't far enough ahead of Stephen to make that possible. Now Tony could feel himself tiring and wasn't sure he was going to get away. Panic snatched at him, and he wished he'd kept the knife. No. If he killed someone during the course of a robbery he'd hang. He put on a spurt, lungs burning. He snatched a glance behind him, then wished he hadn't. Stephen was gaining on him.

Tony burst out of the park on to Rushton Street and was bathed in the yellow glare of the gaslights. There was no escape now, and he thought about turning round and whacking the bloke when he felt a hand grasp his shoulder. Tony found some extra adrenalin-driven energy and spurted ahead. It was now or never. A smile started as he heard the man's breathing becoming laboured. Yet still he came on.

As they reached New North Road and the brighter glare of sodium street lighting, he knew the game was up. There were two policemen on the far side of the road, patrolling on foot. Two people running couldn't help but attract their attention. They started towards him, and his pursuer, as if encouraged by this, reached out again and grasped his shoulder, pulling him to a halt.

At the police station, Tony was put into a cell to wait. It wasn't long before Sergeant Watling arrived. He smacked him hard around the head with his open hand, sending him careening off the cream-painted wall that was scratched and scarred.

'Are you crackers? Are you a fucking mental retard?' he yelled, and hit him again, knocking him down. 'Didn't you listen to anything I told you?'

Tony Wednesday knew he could hit him back and make a good fight of it, even allowing for the old man's cunning, but that wouldn't get him out of his predicament. He was completely stupid for getting caught like this. He shuffled away, his back to the splintered wooden bed as the policeman reached down for him. 'Get up before I kick the stuffing out of you. Lord knows what good that'd do! Those priests must have beaten you often enough and still you end up in the nick.'

Without a word Tony got to his feet, keeping an eye on Sergeant Watling's hands.

'How often do they beat you in the orphanage?'

'They don't,' Tony said.

The look Sergeant Watling gave him said he didn't believe him. 'It's lucky for you, son, that the desk sergeant here's an old friend of mine or you'd have been down at Shoreditch magistrates' court in the morning and no telling where you'd end up.'

Still Tony didn't say anything.

'At least you don't yak your head off or, worse, cry,' the sergeant said. 'Maybe you did learn something from me, after all. I'd've thrown you in the canal if you'd been a whiner. So, you like stealing, do you?'

'I don't know, guv'nor,' Tony said. 'It was the first time.'

The policeman roared with laughter. 'Like hell it was, you lying little bastard.' He paused to look him up and down.

Tony was as tall as his mentor, with lean, stringy muscles, a long face and a slightly hooked nose. Sergeant Watling nodded, his anger gone. 'You're not stupid, Tony,' he said. 'Anything but. A disappointment, though. I didn't come down to that poxy orphanage every week with a bag of sweets to see you end up nicked. The fuck I did, sunshine.'

No, Tony thought, you came down to do that fat sister on your Mac on her office floor.

'What you smiling at, you cunning little bleeder?'

'Cunning' was a compliment. Tony Wednesday felt better about what had happened. A broad grin parted his lips and showed his even teeth. He had cultivated a smile like Burt Lancaster's in *The Crimson Pirate*, all teeth, the same as a shark.

'If you wanna be a thief, son, get a licence,' Watling told him.

Tony was unsure what he meant. The old copper always meant something, was always trying to give him lessons. 'What? Like a fishing rod licence?'

That made the sergeant laugh again, and Tony knew for sure then that he was somehow going to walk away from this arrest.

'Wouldn't that be handy? Popping along to the post office and paying over your shilling. No, the police are the only people with a licence to steal – apart from the poxy government what robs from the working man's pay packet every week. You join the police, Tony, you not only get a licence to steal, all the others protect you. Mark my words.' He touched the side of his nose.

'How can I join the police?' Tony said. 'I'm not old enough.'

'A cunning lad like you? You was born old enough, Tony. It's the cadets you'll be joining.'

'What about getting nicked tonight?'

'That's where we take care of our own, son,' Sergeant Watling said proudly, and winked at Tony like he was one of their own already. 'You'll see. We'll get you signed up and you'll have a job for life. Like me.' He put his arm around Tony's shoulders and pulled open the heavy cell door. 'You know what I like best of all about you, Tone?' he said.

Tony waited. The policeman zipped his finger and thumb across his mouth. Tony gave his shark's smile.

'How does anyone come here to get measured for a suit, Sammy?' Jack Braden said, glancing round the untidy, ash-strewn workshop on Theobald's Road. 'I can't believe people come here for a fitting when they can go to smart gaffs like Montague Burton's for half the price.'

'Montague Burton?' Sammy Cohen hissed, careful not to disturb the ash on the Players Weight in his mouth. 'All he could ever cut are those rags the army wears. So, why is it you come here, Jack? Is it to insult me? I made you suits like you were born in them.'

'Yeah, you didn't do bad,' Jack conceded. 'You got a nice bit of Tonik mohair to make me up something?' He was avoiding getting to what he really wanted and let the man run his tape-measure over him, jotting figures on a torn-up cigarette packet.

When he was done and Jack had chosen a halfway decent cloth, he said, 'How's your Leah, these days, Sammy?'

Sammy Cohen threw back his head. 'How would she be after what that animal did to her? So help me, Jack, if I was half my age I'd have gone after him with an axe. Do I care if he's Joey's boy? He should be dead.'

'Well, 's nothing to do with me,' Jack said. 'I always had a soft spot for your Leah, you know that. In fact, I wouldn't mind looking her up, make sure she's all right.'

'Looking her up?' Sammy said. 'So what is she? A film at the picture house that you can just look her up? See what time she's showing?'

'Calm down, Sammy. I'm a friend. It's me, Jack Braden. I saved her from a fate worse than death, remember?'

'Should I forget? A father who had no power to stop his lovely little *Mädchen* being taken by the Krays and put into prostitution? I should go on living.'

'Yeah, well, that's in the past now,' Jack said. 'I'm not like that. All I'd want to do is take care of her, like you would. Where is she?'

'It's more than a year since that monster violated my little Leah. Still she's not well. What he did to her disturbed her mind. She studies all the time, things of the mind, trying to understand what afflicts her. Her teachers are pleased with my Leah. One day she will qualify, find her place in the academies and put all this behind her, please God. One day.'

'Yeah, yeah,' Jack said. 'That's good. Where is she?'

'Did you not hear me? I can't tell you that. You'll be a reminder of her past, threatening to suck her under again. She'll never forgive me if I bring her back to all that.'

'And I'll never forgive you if you don't cough up the address,' Jack said, the raw edge of violence suddenly back in his voice.

'Why don't you and your family leave me alone?' Leah said, when she opened the door of the ground-floor flat she rented on Malvern Road in Bow.

She'd been forewarned, Jack realized. 'I'm not my family, Leah,' he said. 'The fact is, I can't leave you alone. I've waited as long as I could. I wanted you to forget what happened with Brian. He behaves like an animal nowadays. Just give me a chance, Leah.'

She walked back into the flat without saying anything. Jack waited a moment, then decided this was an invitation to come in.

She was as beautiful as he remembered. The doctors had done a terrific repair job. Just looking at her on the sofa in the ratty little sitting room with its hand me down furniture made Jack breathless. There was only one tiny scar over an eyebrow, and her raven hair gleamed with health, like the woman's in the Silvikrin advert on telly. Her breasts were still small, her hands, too, where she clasped them on her lap. Her knees were pressed together, her feet small and neat in black pumps. She was trembling, which made her even more attractive. He wanted to fall upon her there and then and make love to her. Her vulnerability was almost unbearably exciting. How he held back he wasn't sure, but knew he must. How long he could wait he didn't know.

'I love you, Leah,' he said. 'I've loved you from the very first day I seen you in that flat the twins were running. You was just in need of someone to take care of you. I knew I had to protect you.'

'The only way you can do that now is by going away,' she said, without looking at him. 'I want you to go away and never come here again. If you really love me, you'll do as I ask.'

It was all he could do to stop himself lashing out at her. But that wasn't the way to win a woman. 'I can't do that, Leah,' he said quietly. 'You owe me, and it's time I collected what I'm due. I've waited long enough. I'd say there's plenty of interest owing too. Look, it'll be good. I'll get us a nice gaff in Chelsea or the West End, wherever you want to live. I've got plenty of money. It'll be great. Away from all this.'

Leah just stared ahead, eyes blank.

'God, it's a bit of a gaff, Jack,' Bobby Brown said, when he walked into the second-floor flat in the pink brick block on the corner of Park Street and Brook Street in Mayfair. 'How'd you get hold of a gaff like this? You could stick a couple of brasses in here and not know they was there.'

'Stephen Ward had one here,' Jack told him. 'He rents it to me. He thinks he might be nicked soon. He's been involved with some dirty deeds.'

'You gonna put some old toms in here or what?'

'I'm moving in with Leah Cohen.'

'What – the kyke's daughter?'

'Oi, enough of that. He's all right, is Sammy. He thinks the world of his daughter.'

'What's Brian gonna say? He'll go fucking mad.'

'Who cares? I mean, what can he say? He'll get plenty of trouble, if he starts.'

'He can dish it out too.'

'Am I an invalid or something?'

'He's turned into a right wicked bastard.'

'I know. He's getting to be more trouble than he's worth. I shoulda let the Old Bill put him away when they wanted to. But what can you do? He's family.'

'Someone's gonna end up topping him, Jack, the way he shows out all the time. He mugged me right off in the club last night. Called me a no-good ponce. Said I weren't even a good thief. Me? I been a thief all my life. If he don't keep his gob shut I'll end up topping him.'

Jack followed him as he wandered about the flat. There were two adjoining rooms with sliding doors between them, each with windows that overlooked the street. At the end of the corridor there was a study with bookshelves in the tiny recesses at either side of the fireplace. Round the corner there were two bedrooms and two bathrooms, a kitchen at the opposite end of the hall, with a back door on to an iron fire-escape. That was what Jack liked most about the place – a back way out, if anyone unwelcome came through the front door. There was always someone.

'I got the nod from that blagger I told you about,' Bobby said. 'Ronnie Biggs. It's the Glasgow-to-London mail train what's the target. You know me, Jack, I always did like post office goods for getting my indoor money.'

'What's it worth, d'you reckon?'

''S hard to say. Biggsy's been plotting it up and reckons it could be as much as a hundred and fifty, hundred and sixty grand.'

'How many you gonna need to stop a train, Bobby?'

'You gotta be well firmed up, that's for sure.'

'Twelve? Fifteen?' Jack speculated. 'It don't come to a lot between that many.'

'Seven and half apiece wouldn't be bad.'

''S too many involved. You'd end up grassed for sure.'

'Not with you and Brian involved, we wouldn't. No one would dare.'

'I ain't got that many I can rely on, Bobby. You should talk to Charlie Richardson and his brother.'

'Them? You wouldn't end up with a brad. They'd steal the lot and tell you they had to weigh off the Old Bill and half of British Rail. Unless you'd guarantee it for a piece?'

'Well, let's talk to them. See what they think.'

The Richardson brothers sat in their sweaty caravan in their breaker's yard in Bermondsey, then offered the same opinion as Jack. 'I'd stick to what I know, I was you, Jack,' Charlie said. 'You can't go wrong with spielers, can you?'

Something about the way he said it made Jack suspicious, and he wondered if they weren't trying to put him off. 'Good advice,' he said, and got up out of the little armchair that was pushed into the corner. 'Wipe your mouth on this one, Bobby. Come on.'

He started out through the narrow door, Bobby following.

'What was that about?' Bobby asked, as they crossed the littered yard, avoiding the pot-holes that were full of rainwater with an iridescent oil slick.

'I think they'll start plotting this one up themselves now you've told them,' Jack said. 'Where's your pal Biggsy? Let's have a meet.'

They met in a spiel Jack looked after in Holloway. A few blacks used the place, but Jack didn't mind as long as they lost their money like everyone else. The place was quiet, the gambling earnest. He collected the money once a week and didn't need to do much for it.

'How d'you know the train's gonna be carrying that much?' Jack asked Ronnie Biggs, who sat at the bar, leaning on the counter as if he was too tired to support himself.

'We been plotting this one for months, Jack,' he said. 'Plus my pal's got a postal worker straightened. He's been counting the sacks. It's sometimes a mixture of registered packages and old notes being returned to the Mint for burning.'

Suddenly Jack sat up, glancing around in case anyone nearby had heard, but they were all intent on their gambling. He nodded at Biggsy and Bobby to follow him as he went into the tiny office behind a grubby velvet curtain. It was big enough to boil a kettle and make a cup of tea without reaching far, and with three men, especially one the size of Ronnie Biggs, it was crowded. They didn't need to shout. Jack questioned him closely about the notes going back to the Bank of England. That was information worth having and Bobby hadn't had it. He was glad about that or the Richardsons would known about it.

'How do we know when old notes are going back to be burnt?' he asked.

'We don't exactly. Or how much. No one can get that info,' Ronnie

Biggs said. 'But most weeks it goes down. I mean, think about it, Jack, how often notes get handled. Stands to reason it goes each week.'

'How d'you stop a train? Dynamite?'

Ronnie Biggs laughed. 'No. We got someone who can fix the signal. Turn it to red. It has to stop. The driver'll get out and go to the nearest phone, which is about four hundred yards back from the signal. He'd phone and see what's happening. We'll capture him, tie him up, and our man backs the train up to the road bridge. Then our blokes have the sacks over the side and into a lorry.'

'You got it all plotted up, Ron,' Jack said, 'but how many villains d'you know can drive a train?'

'It'll all go off cushty, Jack, we'll find someone,' Ronnie Biggs said. 'We'd all know our whack would be safe with you in. I don't wanna involve the twins – Ron's mad. The hounds'd trust you, Jack. We'd have a right result.'

Jack felt rather flattered.

'Are you completely fucking mad?' Brian said angrily. 'You're not a blagger, Jack, and nor am I. I know what Joey's going to say if you take this to him – and you'll need someone like Joey to sell that sort of money. He'll say stick to what you know.'

'Blagging money off people is what I know.'

'Yeah. Not off trains. This is what you know.' They were in one of their carpet joints in Camden Town. It was carpeted everywhere in red, even the walls and doors. The effect was a powerful assault on the senses. Brian's interior designer had came up with it.

'We ain't gonna get rich here,' Jack said.

'We're getting a living,' Brian told him. 'A good one. I know how to get an even better one without putting yourself on offer – muscling in on other clubs in the West End. Paul Raymond's for one, in Soho. You seen what goes down there? Bundles!'

'The twins look after him in the West End,' Jack reminded him.

'So fucking what? We put up with them for too long.'

'We agreed a truce, Brian.'

'Truces are for old men.'

'Being old,' Jack said, 'means you lived a long while.'

'Either that or you're a coward. You've taken their medicine – up your arse mostly.'

Brian saw Jack tense, but when he made no move he knew he should goad him further. This wasn't about Jack being a blagger – he couldn't care less about that. It was about something that tore Brian's insides apart: him capturing Leah Cohen. He'd sooner kill her and Jack than have that happen.

'Just watch your mouth,' Jack warned.

He wasn't rising, so Brian tried a different tack. 'What's Leah Cohen charging you?'

'I warned you, watch your mouth,' Jack said, and lunged, but instead of hitting him with his signature punch, which his nephew wouldn't have been able to avoid, he seized him by the throat and pulled him close. Mistake. Brian put his forehead on the bridge of Jack's nose and brought his knee up into Jack's groin. Jack crumpled into a ball, and Brian tried to follow through with his knee in his face. His mistake. Jack caught his knee and unbalanced him, then followed through, hitting Brian a series of blows. They sent him reeling into a table and he scrabbled around to stop himself crashing to the floor. His hand fell on a bottle of whisky and he lashed out, shattering the bottle against Jack's shoulder-blade. Jack delivered two stinging blows to Brian's face and would have landed a third if the club minder hadn't stepped in to pull them apart. 'You two fucking mad?' Johnny Shannon said. He was a big fella who'd come over to them from the twins. He wasn't scared of Jack. Everyone in the club had stopped gambling and drinking and was watching. 'This ain't no good for business.'

'You're right, Johnny,' Jack said. 'Good luck. So pack it in, Brian. Get it?'

Brian dabbed his swelling eye with a handkerchief. 'She's still a cunt, Jack, and so are you, for going with her.'

That wouldn't be the last of it. The rage he felt inside wasn't about to die down.

TWENTY-TWO

Leah Cohen walked and talked like a dead woman after her move into Jack's Park Street flat. She didn't care that it was in Mayfair, the best part of London, or that it was spacious. She much preferred her poky little room and the freedom that went with it in Bow. She would only give herself to Jack physically, never mentally or spiritually, because she despised him. When he had forced her to go with him, her first thought had been to kill herself, and it didn't leave her. It was her ultimate access to freedom.

'What do you think?' Jack said eagerly, as he showed her around. 'Look at the fridge – it's the latest from America.'

'Oh,' Leah said without interest.

'It's the business,' Jack said, like a disappointed child. 'I paid a fortune for it. It's got an ice-cream compartment.'

'I'm moving in here because I have to, Jack,' she told him. 'I'll give you what you want, but I intend to go on studying full-time.'

'What for? I'll give you everything you want, Leah. You don't have to work,' he said. 'That's daft.'

'You won't give me the one thing I crave,' Leah told him, 'which is freedom. And another thing. I don't ever want to see Brian, not here or anywhere else. If I do I'll kill myself.'

She had spoken without trace of emotion.

'We won't have him here.'

'Get it over with, Jack,' Leah said coldly. 'Give me a poke. That's what you want.'

'No. No. I want to take care of you,' Jack replied, with touching earnestness.

But Leah wasn't touched. She knew his concern wouldn't last.

He'd lose his temper and the monster would be back. She lay on the bed, hitched up her skirt and pulled down her panties.

Jack protested again that that wasn't what he wanted, but finally, like the animal he was, he climbed on to her, entered her and spent himself, then lay on top of her panting. Leah didn't move throughout the whole procedure, other than to turn her head to avoid his breath. Breath, like kissing, was too intimate. His sex was unprotected, but she didn't care. After Brian had made her pregnant, her colleagues at St Bart's had helped with the termination and tried to talk her out of sterilization, but Leah had been adamant. She'd agreed to talk to the psychiatrist and had continued to see him long after both surgical procedures. Now she hated Jack Braden almost as much as she hated his nephew. She couldn't bear to be in his presence, but was too terrified of him to do anything other than resist him silently and passively. She'd get stronger through her studies. She knew he hoped that in time she'd warm to him but Leah was determined she never would.

'It was definitely Drury, was it?' Jack asked Jimmy Humphreys, as he followed him through the empty club. Without customers, the smell of stale tobacco smoke, beer and sweat hung over the place.

'Oh, it was definitely him, Jack.' Humphreys was thin with a mop of brushed-up hair that looked like he spent a lot of money on it. He was a creature of the night, who ran pornographic bookshops in Soho. 'What am I gonna do? Start paying him for the twins, like he said?'

'Did he get to see the hard stuff you got in the back?' Jack asked.

'He was just letting me know he knew it was there and what trouble I'd be in if I didn't start paying him for protection.'

'You'd better wipe your mouth for now, Jimmy. I'll talk to some different Old Bill.'

'What a wanker,' Brian commented, when Jack told him. 'Why don't we do the job properly and wipe the twins out?'

'If we go round chopping people up, we'll have no friendly Bill.'

'So are we working for the Bill now? You can if you want – be a right mug's game.'

'Take it easy, for fuck's sake. Let me talk to Bill Trope.'

'He's an old man. He's gone. Why rely on him?'

'I can't just move in on that manor like some villain, Jack,' DCI Trope told him, when they met at Theobald's Road. 'Anyway, I'm retiring next week.'

'So we either whack the twins or wipe our mouth? Is that it?'

'There's an Old Bill at the Yard,' Trope said, 'George Fenwick. He might help out if the price is right.'

Later Jack went to see Brian and told him what Trope had said. 'You'd better come along to the meet,' he concluded.

'Why? Has he gotta be whacked?'

'I'm warning you, Bri. You'll end up losing all our business.'

'What can bent Old Bill do?'

'We'll give him a bell and go and find out.'

DI George Fenwick was an open and friendly suit-and-boot man who laughed a lot when Jack and Brian met him in the Shakespeare outside Victoria station. He reminded them that they had history with Drury. 'You beat him up, Jack. Unless he's lost his marbles, he'll want some sort of payback. Especially now. That's what his visit to Jimmy Humphreys's bookshop's all about.'

'He's gotta be an old man now,' Brian said. 'What can he do?'

'A lot. He's just been made my boss at the Yard,' Fenwick told him. 'If he's thrown in his lot with the Krays you might as well shut your shops. But he's probably too shrewd for that. What you going to offer him?'

'What will he want?'

'What they all want, Jack,' Fenwick informed him. 'A little bit towards the pension.'

'Yeah, how big a little bit?' Brian wanted to know. 'We ain't going to start working for Old Bill, no matter how shrewd you think he is.'

'We'd better talk to him and find out what his plans are for all the porn in Soho,' Jack said.

'Can you go into him,' Brian said, 'or are we going to have to put the Krays out of business?'

'I think you should try talking first, Brian,' Fenwick told him.

'Make a meet, if you can, George. Let's see what this newly formed Porn Squad wants by way of a pension.'

'As much as we can get, duck,' was Ken Drury's frank answer when he came to the Rupert Court club a couple of nights later. Jack was now running it. 'Everyone's got to pay so there's no unfair competition.'

'No hard feelings over the past, is there, Ken?' Jack said.

Drury thought about that, then shook his head. 'No,' he said. 'I was out of order. I was a bit green in those days. I'll admit I was coming on a bit greedy then.'

'Well, it's all in the past now,' Jack said.

'That's right, duck,' Ken Drury said. 'Now I'm *very* fucking greedy, because we know down to the last penny what bookshops like Humphreys's make and what that other cunt Paul Raymond puts up to import them. You want to stay in business, you all pay your dues.'

'You can go and fuck yourself,' Brian said, and pulled out a sap to hit the policeman. Jack moved faster, putting a right hook into Brian's ribs.

'Better keep the little iron in line,' Drury warned, 'or he goes away. I'll get George to be the bagman – me, I don't ever want to see you, or that piece of excrement again, not until I'm ready to nick you.'

'That'll be a long, long time, Ken,' Jack laughed.

'Fact of life,' Fenwick told them. 'It'll come some time, Jack. Let's try and put it off as long as we can, shall we?'

After he left, promising to negotiate the best terms he could get with Ken Drury, Brian told Jack he didn't trust the man. 'I don't like him accepting that we gotta go away eventually.'

'He's all right, Bri. Least, he's doing the business with Drury.'

'Yeah, but they might be stitching us up.'

'Then how would they earn anything?' Jack asked. 'Maybe we should test them both – move in on some of them places you reckon are ripe for taking over, see what they do.'

'One that's run by the twins?'

'That's the idea.'

The board meeting was called for two thirty at John Bloom's Park Lane flat. Joey Oldman got there early, intending to advise John in private that they couldn't continue to expand without a sound financial footing. John Bloom treated the company as his own private bank account and was taking too much out for it to be sustainable. The door was opened by a pretty eighteen-year-old with whom he was having an affair. She asked the maid to get them tea, which was served in the dining room.

'Where's John?' Joey asked the other two directors. Neither knew.

'The young lady said something about him going somewhere to secure a loan,' Clive Davis told him.

'Has he?' Joey said, anxiety making his voice rise. 'Who from? He didn't say anything to me about it.'

'You'd only have complained if I had, Joey,' the effusive John Bloom said, stepping into the room. Christine, his girlfriend, came in with him and he fondled her backside in the tight pencil skirt.

Joey could see at once what this was about: a distraction from the business in hand, a familiar tactic. But John's unorthodox approach to money worried him. He had a great talent for making it, but wasn't so good at hanging on to it – not even enough to pay the creditors. They were getting more and more strident in their demands.

'I'm supposed to be overseeing the financial side of this company,

John,' Joey told him, 'and the way you're running things worries me.'

'As long as we go on making it like we are,' Bloom said, 'why should you worry?'

'Because that's what I'm here for. Too much is going out. There's not enough in the bank for rainy days.'

'Well, that's where you're wrong, sunshine,' Bloom said. 'Sir Isaac Wolfson, the merchant banker, wouldn't agree with you. He's agreed to back us with a multi-million-pound loan. That lawyer of yours, Arnold Goodman, helped fix it up.'

That announcement stole the show. Joey's protests over whether the banker was aware of the full picture cut no ice with his fellow directors. They couldn't have been more delighted if he'd announced a multi-million-pound profit and certainly weren't about to support Joey in trying to curb him.

'John, I want you to look at item thirty-nine on the balance sheet, tucked right away down at the bottom,' Joey said. 'Do you want to tell the board what this is?'

'That looks like a dividend I was paid,' Bloom said, offhandedly. 'I needed some money so I brought it forward.'

'But, John, you're taking money out as dividends far in excess of other shareholders. You can't do that. You're treating the finances as your personal bank account.'

'Not really.' John Bloom glanced at Clive Davis.

'The thing is, Joey, other shareholders are holding shares for the beneficial interest of John,' Davis said.

Joey was shocked. 'Is that legal?' he asked, hoping one of the others would know. At the earliest opportunity he'd have it out with Arnold Goodman, the lawyer.

Goodman had rooms on the second floor of a building in Fetter Lane, but his firm didn't spend money to impress clients. The economy of his accommodation impressed Joey.

'Bloom is an undoubted success, Joseph,' Goodman said, 'but

no matter how successful he is, neither he nor any other shareholder can conduct his business in the way he is. Not without disaster.'

'How responsible am I going to be?'

'You won't be held financially responsible – it's a limited company – but the Board of Trade might rap your knuckles for not being more prudent.'

'With John Bloom at the helm?'

'My advice is to get your money out as fast as you can.'

'Then why did you introduce him to that banker?'

'It's what I do best, Joey,' Goodman said. 'Isaac can take care of himself.'

'Perhaps he reads the *Financial Times*. Our shares are priced at more than three pounds each. We'll hit sales worth two hundred grand this year. Bloom thinks there's no stopping.'

'The Board of Trade will stop him soon enough if you don't get this on to a better footing. And if you can't, get out,' Goodman said.

When challenged, John Bloom insisted everything was in order. 'What d'you wanna do, Joey? Unload your shares? If you do, I'll have them. I'll cut you a cheque right now at the full market price.'

Bloom was a persuasive salesman, Joey hesitated for a moment, then nodded. Bloom wrote a cheque on the company account for thirty thousand pounds and gave it to him.

'I'll let you have my letter of resignation and share certificate.'

'No hard feelings, Joey. I'm giving a party at the weekend. I'd like you to come.'

Later that day Joey rang Goodman and told him what had happened.

'Is the cheque going to clear, Joey?'

'This one probably will, but I'm not sure about the others. The washing-machines are breaking down all over the place. He's not paying the service contractors. You can bet he didn't tell Sir Isaac Wolfson that.'

'He'd be a fool if he did,' Goodman said, 'but a bigger fool if he didn't. I'll let Isaac know.'

Joey wasn't much of a party animal, but John Bloom's parties were always full of interesting people and good places to pick up business. Joey left Cath talking to a skinny, good-looking young man who said his name was Davy Jones and that he sang. Joey wondered if he was a busker – he looked like it, in his frayed denim jeans and torn baseball boots, asking Cath if she thought he should change his name. Joey slid away to listen to a conversation a charismatic Indian called Emil Savundra was conducting with a group of men: car insurance was growing at such a rapid rate, apparently, that one could make one's fortune overnight. Such talk always fascinated Joey, but it seemed not to impress his audience who soon moved away. When the Indian went to refresh his drink, Joey followed him.

'I'm interested to know why you think there'll be such a rise in car use,' Joey said, as he poured himself some tonic water.

'You haven't put any gin in that, old boy.'

'I don't drink alcohol.'

'Most wise, sir. We drink far too much. I never did, of course, before I came to England.' Savundra considered his glass, as if he was deciding whether or not to put it aside. 'A huge rise in motor-car use will inevitably follow all the motorway-building Ernest Marples has announced. People fill whatever space is available to them.'

'Perhaps one should form a civil-engineering company.'

'Too late, old boy. The Tories have organized that and parcelled the work out to their friends.'

'So anyone in business should make friends with them,' Joey suggested.

'I'll drink to that,' Emil Savundra said. 'Aren't you Joseph Oldman, John's financial director?'

'Not any longer. I resigned.'

Emil Savundra glanced across the room at John Bloom, then took Joey by the shoulder and led him away from the drinks table.

'A good move, old boy. If you can't check him, leave him. Are you looking for another position?'

'I'm not looking to become anyone's stooge,' Joey said.

That was the start of his relationship with Emil Savundra and the motor-insurance business of which he knew nothing, except that you took premiums against risk and tried to get the customer to reduce that risk. Joey soon discovered that his new business partner wasn't concerned about risk, just as long as the premiums were collected.

Cath was shocked when Joey suggested they become members of their local branch of the Tory Party.

'Is there one?' Brian asked, across the table where they were having their tea.

'We've always voted Labour, Joey,' Cath said.

'Why?' Joey wanted to know. 'We're natural Tories, Cath. We believe in free enterprise.'

'But Manny Shinwell's always looked after us well enough. What would your friend Mr Driberg have to say about it, Brian?' Cath asked.

'I can't think he'd say anything at all, Mum,' Brian told her. 'He doesn't think much of his own lot. He never did. I'll ask him if he comes to the club tonight.'

'Think about it, Cath,' Joey said. 'We might do ourselves a bit of good. Emil Savundra's doing all right.'

It was nearly a week before Tom Driberg came into the club. He brought a high-court judge with him, Sir Aubrey Melford Stevenson, who'd been there before on the lookout for girls. The Tory Secretary of State for War, John Profumo, came too, with his girlfriend, Christine Keeler. They all greeted Brian like old friends, which he enjoyed. Famous people made him feel important.

'Has Mandy been in?' Christine said, in her deep, northern voice laced with Chelsea. 'She's supposed to meet us.' She pointed to the judge, her finger hidden behind her handbag.

'I haven't seen her,' Brian said, 'but she's always late.'

'Well, I don't feel inclined to wait for her, Aubrey,' John Profumo said to the judge. 'I can't stay long at Cliveden. I've an early plane to catch in the morning. Perhaps we should go on and leave a note for her.'

'Bugger that for a lark, Jack,' Melford Stevenson said. 'I'm not going without a girl. I might get sozzled and end up with a boy.'

'You could do worse, Judge!' Brian joked. He cast his eye around the dark, smoke-filled room, looking for a girl he'd seen earlier. She was at the furthest roulette wheel but he couldn't remember her name. With a nod he directed the judge's attention in her direction. 'How about her?'

'Oh, rather,' he said enthusiastically. 'Is she free?'

'I'll soon find out.' Brian stepped across the floor of the club. They encouraged attractive young women for this very purpose.

Heather Knight was her name. She was a pretty nineteen-year-old, perfect for the judge. She raised no objection to being taken to a party, organized by Stephen Ward, at Lord Astor's country seat. 'Will he pay me, Brian?' she asked.

'I expect so, but don't push it. Treat this as a favour to us. You know we'll see you all right.'

'Why don't you and Jack come with us, Brian?' Tom Driberg suggested. Brian knew what his ulterior motive was, but so did Jack, and he wasn't keen on going until Driberg whispered that Ronnie and Reggie would be there. That was a red rag to a bull. The twins seemed to be in Jack's sightline everywhere he turned.

The journey out to Buckinghamshire took about an hour, everyone crammed into John Profumo's ministerial car. Christine Keeler sat on Profumo's lap and Heather on the judge's, and, judging from the sounds they were making, Brian doubted they'd need to get to the party for what they had in mind.

Cliveden was an impressive pile, four storeys high and miles wide, a bit too chocolate box for Brian, but with more bedrooms than most hotels could offer. Even with about a hundred guests partying in the main drawing room, which led on to the terrace, the place seemed empty and the noise echoed against the high ceilings. Profumo and Christine headed straight upstairs, barely greeting their host. Sir Aubrey did the same with Heather. Tom Driberg, accompanied by a much larger, plummier politician, Bob Boothby, made the same sort of overtures to Brian. He wasn't interested in him, nor in Boothby, who also propositioned him when Driberg left to cruise the room. Instead he pulled a young man for Boothby.

'Are you Ronnie Kray?' the young man asked. 'I was brought here especially to meet him.'

'No, but I'll take you to him.' He led him across to Bob Boothby and introduced him as Ronnie Kray.

'Oh, you talk ever so nice, Ronnie,' the young man said, when Boothby turned on his immense charm. After a couple of minutes they were heading out of the double doors to the stairs. Brian smiled. He enjoyed facilitating people like this and understood the kick Stephen Ward got out of it.

They had been at the party for about forty minutes when a trail of guests gravitating towards the billiard room caught Jack's attention. 'What's going on in there?' he asked Ward.

'Oh, I wouldn't go in there,' he said. 'The twins are dispensing medicine.'

Brian laughed. No one could have said anything more likely to provoke his uncle. Jack stepped straight over to the billiard room and threw open the doors.

The Krays were sitting in two throne-like leather chairs, as if they owned the place. George Cornell was doling out more drugs from his bag than the dispensary at Boots the Chemist on Piccadilly Circus. There had been bad blood between him and Jack ever since Jack had whacked him and his mate Bernard Hedges for stealing from his spiel.

'What's he doing here?' Jack growled. 'This is a party for decent people, not slagheaps.'

'How come a whore like you got in, then, Jack?' Ronnie said.

That did it for Jack. He came round the end of the table staring at Ronnie. Everyone in the room was so drawn to the electric tension between them that none saw Jack scoop up a billiard ball and smash it in George Cornell's face, splitting both lips. 'Why don't you keep your goon under control?' he said. 'He's spoiling a good party.'

Ronnie jumped out of his chair, brandishing a machete he'd been holding below the arm. The collective gasp of surprise was nothing to Ronnie's astonishment when Brian stabbed him in the side with his flick-knife.

'Nice to see you again, Ron,' he said, as he slipped out the blade.

He was about to jam it in harder when Jack caught his arm in an iron grip. 'Don't be a mug,' he hissed. 'Not here.'

Brian felt a moment of indecision, uncertain whether to stick the knife back into Ronnie Kray or into Jack. He wasn't sure which of them he hated most. Finally he wiped it on Ronnie's jacket. 'You're not looking your old self, Ron.' The look Ronnie gave him was more one of sorrow than anger. Brian doubted it was a fatal stab wound through all that fat, but he'd have to go to hospital.

'It's time to collect the judge and get out of here,' Jack whispered. 'Fetch the car.'

They left quickly as people edged towards the stricken Ronnie, Cornell and his swollen mouth forgotten.

John Profumo refused to abandon ship, but the judge blessed Jack all the way home for his discretion. 'But where can I take this pretty little poppet now?' he asked, as they neared the West End. 'I can't risk sex in a car on the public highway.'

Brian glanced at Jack and knew at once what he had in mind.

'You can go to my place in Mayfair,' Jack announced. 'You'll be safe there.'

What he'd do with Leah, Brian didn't know or care. Turf her

out for the night, he guessed. Jack thought of himself as a strategist, and cultivating an Old Bailey judge was an insurance policy. Brian hoped they'd never need it.

A few minutes later he told the driver to stop so that he could get out to go to the club. No more than fifteen minutes after his arrival Ken Drury came through the door and dragged Brian outside. 'What are you completely mad, duck?' he asked. 'The good news is Ronnie's going to live. The bad news is, he's angrier than a man with a wasp up his bum.'

'Well, the fat poof knows where I live,' Brian said boldly.

'That's the problem, duck. Trouble means lost income for everyone. We don't want a penny drop in ours. Understand?'

'Loud and clear, Mr Drury,' Brian said. 'So tell the fat cunt to stay out of our way and he won't get any.'

Having moved on from Syd Griffith's level of banking at his local branch of Martin's Bank, Joey found Captain Tyrwhitt most agreeable to talk to about money. He wondered, just briefly, how agreeable this man would be if suddenly he didn't have any money. But, then, how agreeable would Martin's Bank be in such circumstances? Would Tyrwhitt be as susceptible to corruption as the manager of Martin's Bank? Possibly not as he was one of the bank's owners – unless he was benefiting hugely. Tyrwhitt was expanding his tertiary bank and was keen to try and get some of Emil Savundra's business.

Tyrwhitt poured two glasses of sherry in his thickly carpeted Brook Street office in the heart of Mayfair and brought one across to Joey.

'I won't, thank you, Captain,' Joey said.

'Too early in the day? Or won't mix business with pleasure?'

'Neither, really. It doesn't agree with my heartburn.'

'Well, my bank could relieve that for you, Mr Oldman. Some tea, perhaps?' He rang through to his secretary and ordered some. 'We had a close look at Savundra's business plan. You do realize the man's a crook?'

Joey hesitated. 'Perhaps he is. I just want to make sure that if I put money in I'd get more than my fair share out, Captain.'

'Ah, that makes this a different sort of conversation,' Tyrwhitt said. 'Please, call me Charles.' He smiled.

Joey smiled back. He'd come to the right bank after all.

Soon they were talking about how they might get Fire, Auto & Marine Insurance to expand even faster. 'The easiest way, Joseph, is not to have the risk underwritten by reinsurers.'

'Isn't that risky as a business model?' Joey asked. He knew it was and why, but wanted to hear the reasons from the banker.

'It's all about timing. Most of what people do successfully in business is about timing. If you hold on to anything for too long, it inevitably goes down, as a general rule. Perfect timing would be to get out just before the level of claims exceeds income. At the moment Mr Savundra's on a rising arc.'

'He's having his risk underwritten,' Joey pointed out.

'At a large premium,' Tyrwhitt said. 'Remove that premium and the profit arc rises more steeply.'

'It'll fall when the claims start to come in.'

'At the moment he's allowing fifty-seven per cent for reinsurance to deal with them and another thirteen per cent for claims outside the contract. That's a whopping seventy per cent and he's still making money.'

'If he cut the price of premiums by thirty per cent to capture market share and carried all the risk, he could only run for one or two years at full tilt before the level of claims wiped out his profits.'

'Only if he pays the claims,' Tyrwhitt said.

'Joey, you're an out-and-out crook,' Emil Savundra said, when they met in his office in the West End. 'But I like it very much indeed.'

'Between us, Charles Tyrwhitt and I will put in sixty thousand pounds for one year.'

'How will this money be spent?' Emil Savundra asked.

'Mostly on reaching out to brokers,' Joey said, 'so that when car owners go looking for insurance this is where they think of first.'

'What happens after a year, my dear Joey?'

'We'll see how the land lies and decide whether we want another year.'

'You think I can put off paying claims that long?' Savundra asked.

'We'd be disappointed if you can't.'

They had a bottle of champagne in Tyrwhitt's office when they signed the contract. Joey took a glass but didn't drink, preferring to remain clear-headed.

'Here's to the enormous success of Fire, Auto & Marine,' Tyrwhitt said. 'May it never receive a claim against it.'

They laughed.

'May all the claims be small ones,' Savundra said.

'And never settled!' Joey added. They laughed again.

'Charles,' Joey said, when the business was concluded, 'Cath, my wife, is interested in getting involved in local politics.'

'Why? It'll take up all of her time, frustrate her beyond endurance and offer little satisfaction.'

'Then why do people do it?' Joey asked.

'Good question. I haven't really got an answer. For most I suspect it's what they can get out of it. The civic-minded, who'll tell you they want to give something back, they get their kicks that way.'

'You think it's not worthwhile, then?'

'It depends what she expects to be her return. Where are you? Camden Town?'

'Hoxton.'

'Ah, yes. Why don't I introduce her to a good friend I have on Camden Council? I imagine your greengrocery business is being squeezed quite hard by the emergence of the supermarkets.'

'More and more,' Joey said. 'Cath responded to it by selling some groceries. It helps, of course, but we'd need to get bigger so we have more purchasing muscle.'

'Local politics is good for business – it certainly makes getting planning permission for expansion easier.'

'She put in for permission, but there was an objection from a planning officer, a dyed-in-the-wool socialist.'

'The worst kind. Did she bribe him?' Tyrwhitt smiled.

Joey smiled back, but said nothing. The man had taken fifty pounds from her to drop his objection.

'I think I should definitely introduce you to my friend in Camden Town.'

That was Cath's *entrée* to politics.

The rivalry between Jack and the Kray twins was heightened when Brian persuaded Jimmy Humphreys to tell Jack what Paul Raymond's Revue Bar was pulling in every week. He was keen to move in on it and take it over, but he knew the Krays would have something to say about that. He still owed them a big one and they'd get it sooner or later, but Jack seemed reluctant to take them on, even though the hardest man Brian had ever seen had walked through the door. He had finally been released from the army prison where he'd shared a cell with Jack. He was a rock-like black man called Pongo, and he was a man of few words, who clearly thought the world of Jack – and even more when Jack took him into the firm. Brian would have liked his own Pongo and felt a bit menaced by his loyalty to Jack.

The Revue Bar, in the passage between Brewer Street and Berwick Street, was impressive, especially with the classy strippers it employed. When Brian went there with Jack and Pongo and said what they wanted, Paul Raymond, with his coiffured hair and jazzy dogtooth suit, tried to negotiate. 'We don't need any extra muscle, Brian. The twins make sure there's no trouble here,' he said. 'We get the odd drunk who doesn't like the price of the champagne he's thrown down his throat. Our own staff take care of them.'

'We heard you're going to get a lot of aggro.'

'No, definitely not. You apes are not coming in here with your nigger and threatening me,' Raymond said, thrusting his face into Brian's. 'I'm calling Ronnie and Reg. They'll have something to say about this.'

'Oh, there's no need for that, Paul,' Brian said. 'We came to talk, that's all.'

'I thought that would change your mind, you little poofter,' Raymond said, as Brian turned away.

'Oi, don't turn away from me when I'm talking to you.'

Brian slipped a set of brass knuckles over his fingers and punched Raymond in the guts, then again as he doubled up in shock. He kept hitting him, split his eye and lip, aware vaguely that Jack and Pongo were looking after a bit of business with a couple of minders who had weighed in. They didn't put up much resistance.

'That's enough, Bri,' Jack said, pulling him back.

Brian shrugged him off and leant closer to Raymond. 'You still wanna call me nasty names, do you?'

A pathetic croak emerged from the club-owner, which Brian assumed was a 'No'. 'You need some extra help here. Right?'

Another little croak. This time, a 'Yes.'

Two days later the newly-promoted DCI Drury came looking for Jack and Brian. 'It didn't take you long to get up to your old ways,' he said. 'I'm arresting you both for GBH.'

'That's no way to do business,' Jack told him.

'Your strokes are no good for business either.' Drury had three other detectives with him. 'There was a punter you hurt at Paul Raymond's place the other day. You hurt him badly.'

'Get away,' Jack protested. 'He was minding Paul Raymond and attacked us.'

'Either way, you're both nicked, duck.'

'Pongo, call Joey,' Brian ordered. 'Tell him to get hold of his lawyer.'

Jack was outraged and told Pongo to call DI Fenwick.

'Corrupt policemen won't help you, duck,' Drury said.

'That's rich, coming from an Old Bill who's middle name's Hairpin!'

Arnold Goodman came to see Brian at Cannon Row police station, behind Whitehall, and advised him to say nothing.

'Not even to give them my alibi? Brian asked.

'Do you have one?'

'Oh, yes,' Brian said. 'I was with Tom Driberg all day. Go and see him, Arnold. I'm sure he'll agree to help. He's a great one for the truth coming out.'

'Were you involved in that terrible beating?' Tom Driberg said, when he came to Brian's flat in Camden, near Regent's Park.

'If you think that, Tom, why'd you agree to be my alibi?'

'You know why,' the MP said. 'I'm very fond of you and I don't want to see you in trouble. There's nothing I can do to help Jack, though. Drury won't budge.'

'That's because he's corrupt and working for the Krays,' Brian told him.

'If you have evidence of that, I could take it to the Home Secretary.'

'That won't help Jack with bail,' Brian told him. 'Still, a bit of bird'll probably do him good. I can take care of things while he's away.'

Joey thought that a very foolish move and told him so.

'Why's it foolish?' Brian challenged. 'I thought you wanted me to make something of myself.'

'That's all your mother and I want, Brian,' his dad said. 'But not like this. It really is time you got out of this gang nonsense and into business.'

'Why would I do that, Dad? I love this work. I'm running things as I want, now Jack's away. It's terrific.'

'You're being utterly foolish,' Joey told him. 'Arnold said it's likely that Jack will go to prison. You could be headed the same way if you're not careful. That's if the Krays don't kill you first.'

'Oh, you're so amusing, Dad, you should be on *Sunday Night at the London Palladium*. Could be I might top them – no one would miss them.'

'Think about it, Brian. This is your opportunity to get free of all this gang stuff. You might not get another chance.'

But Brian was in his element running things and he wasn't about to give it up. Not even when his mother came to the club and pleaded with him. 'Your dad said business is far more exciting.'

'What? Selling a few spuds? That's a job for old women.'

Without warning Cath smacked him hard in the face, startling Brian and causing Pongo to lift his eyes from the racing paper at the end of the bar in the empty club. Brian raised a hand, indicating there was no need for him to do anything. He wasn't sure if, or at what point, Pongo would come to his aid. They had yet to straighten that out.

'I won't have you being disrespectful about your father, Brian. Not after all he's done for you,' Cath said.

As hard as Brian found it to resist his mother, he stretched every fibre of his being to do so. He wanted to run the club and, by extension, the entire criminal enterprise. He knew he could make a better job of it than Jack.

Judge Melford Stevenson caught him in the club later that night and asked if it would be all right for him to pop up to Jack's flat with his little poppet. He was giving little Heather Knight one regularly now and still hadn't been reduced to doing it in a car on the public highway.

'I should say so, Judge,' Brian told him. 'I'll slip over there and make sure his girlfriend ain't around.'

He could have phoned Leah and told her to make herself scarce but he chose to go there and confront her, suspecting how she'd react.

'I told Jack that if I saw you ever again, Brian, I'd kill myself,' Leah said.

'Good. Why don't you, then? Do us all a favour.'

She fled, taking nothing with her. Perhaps she was going to kill herself and he wondered briefly how she might do it. The river? Jumping under a tube train?

While he waited for the judge to arrive with Heather, Brian poked around the flat. He looked through some drawers and found Leah's underwear. He fished out a pair of her panties, put his thick hand inside them and spread his fingers, then brought them up to his nose. Without warning, he got hard and wondered why. He told himself she meant nothing to him, had nothing he was interested in.

The low clunk of the kitchen doorbell startled him. He returned the panties to the drawer and went to answer it. The judge always used the service alleyway and came up the iron fire-escape so his entrance couldn't be seen from the road.

'Is anyone else around, Brian?' he asked.

'Only me, Judge. I'll be as quiet as a mouse. What Heather's got don't interest me.' He winked at the girl and nodded them through to the spare bedroom.

The judge's lovemaking was quiet. No sound escaped from the room as Brian lay on the bed in Jack and Leah's room, thinking about Leah and why her underwear caused him to get an erection. He drifted off to sleep and woke with a sense of unease, but with no idea what had caused it. He sat up on the bed and put on the light. It was two o'clock.

He got up and cracked open the door. Across the narrow corridor in the lit bedroom, he saw two men plunging a knife through the quilt into the covered figure below. Panic assailed him and for a moment he thought he was having a nightmare and called out to wake himself, alerting the two men, who whirted round in alarm. Without thinking, Brian rushed at them, reaching into his pocket for his flick-knife. The two men came to meet him head on. From the glimpse he caught of them, both seemed familiar but he knew neither. The first slashed at him with the knife, causing Brian to dance back, but the second hit him like a steamroller as he bowled on through the flat to the fire-escape. Brian scrambled to his feet and went after them, but they were well gone.

Creeping gingerly into the bedroom, fearing what Jack would say to him for letting the judge get stabbed, he eased back the quilt over the motionless figure. He stared for a long while at the blood-soaked body before he realized it wasn't the judge.

Sir Aubrey was hiding in the darkened bathroom, crouched between the lavatory and the wall, shaking like a leaf. He let out a shriek of terror as Brian reached down and touched him. 'It's me, Judge. Brian.'

Still the judge couldn't stop trembling. Brian stood with him and looked at the body on the bed. 'I don't know who they were,' he said, 'but I wouldn't think they were after Heather.'

'Me?' Sir Aubrey managed to say.

Brian shook his head. 'I doubt it. Who'd know? Look, we better get you dressed and away from here.'

'Yes, yes,' the judge said, but he was incapable of dressing himself. He couldn't move.

Brian called DI George Fenwick and told him he needed help, then went back and assisted the judge into his clothes.

Ten minutes later the detective was examining the girl. 'She's well and truly dead.' He glanced across the corridor to the judge, who was still shaking where he sat on Jack's bed with a quilt around him. 'What about him? Did he do it?'

'No,' Brian said. 'I think it was some mugs the twins sent after me. They must have followed me from the club.'

'You'd better get him home. We'll take care of the girl,' Fenwick said. 'Will he be able to keep his mouth shut?'

'I'll talk to him.'

Brian took the grateful judge home and put him to bed in his chintzy house, called Truncheons, where he lived with his wife. She was off visiting her sister in Canada.

'You want me to stay with you, Judge?' Brian offered. He saw the alarm on the other man's face and laughed. 'Oh, not like that.'

'I'll be all right. I'll have a brandy and some sleeping pills.'

'Tell me where they are and I'll get them for you.'

When he brought them upstairs, the judge said, 'Brian, I'm so grateful for all you've done. My wife couldn't have faced such a scandal. You're such a sensible young man. If ever you need help in the future, I'll do anything I can.'

Brian smiled. That was one he'd keep safely in his back pocket.

The news of the so-called Great Train Robbery that greeted Jack, who was on remand in Brixton prison, when his door was opened that morning, frustrated him almost beyond endurance. The prison and the whole country was alight with the shocking news that five million pounds had been stolen. It was an unimaginable sum.

'Someone had a nice result there, Jack,' Billy Hayward said to him, as he joined him in the breakfast line. 'You wouldn't mind being a blagger for that sort of money. All old notes, is what they said on the radio.'

Jack was too angry to respond and Hayward moved on to talk to someone else about the robbery of the century. All Jack wanted to do was contact his brief and get him to send Brian in to see him, hoping he had been in on it with Bobby Brown and Ronnie Biggs. The minutes dragged past as he watched the clock, waiting to be called to the legal visiting room. He didn't dare talk openly to Brian on the phone, but waited for him to come in, posing as the solicitor's clerk.

'Where've you been?' was how Jack greeted him, once the screw had stepped outside and closed the door. 'I've been going mental since the news broke.'

'This was the earliest they had a room free.'

'Have we got some of it, Bri? Have we?'

'I haven't seen anything of Bobby since you went inside. I assumed he was pugged up plotting with Ronnie.'

'Well, he'd better have our whack or there'll be trouble.'

'There's trouble already,' Brian told him. 'Tom Driberg came to see me just before I came down here. He said there's going to be really serious repercussions from a robbery this big. He said it's changed the whole socio-ecodynamic of crime.'

'What's that meant to mean?' Jack asked.

'The senior members of the government are meeting to discuss it and so is the opposition. Driberg won't be able to help us any more.'

'What did you tell him?'

'That we weren't involved,' Brian said. 'I don't think he believed me.'

'Great. We get the blame and not the dough. We'd have had that money if I was out. I'm going mad in here.'

'Tell me what you want me to do,' Brian said.

'Go and see DI Fenwick. Tell him to get hold of that witness against me. We'll do something about him.'

'I can't. Ken Drury's got him well pugged-up.'

'George Fenwick'll find him. All we gotta do is straighten him out. S' easy if he's one of Paul Raymond's minders. Take Pongo with you. He'll make him see things different. At this rate I'll end up topping one of the screws just for the hell of it.'

'Take it easy, Jack,' Brian cautioned. 'It's still a hanging offence.'

Jack felt bereft when his nephew walked out of the door, promising to contact the DI at the Yard. He wondered if he would, or if he was enjoying his freedom a bit too much.

Back on the wing, which was single cells that let out on to a corridor, Jack picked a fight with Billy Hayward when he said he'd heard that the Richardsons had backed the Great Train Robbery. Even though he knew it was a wind-up, that Billy and his younger brother Harry 'Flash' Hayward hated Charlie and Eddie, he had to respond. Billy fought back hard and Jack had difficulty putting him down, he was so churned up. Matters got worse when the screws eventually broke it up and they were put behind their doors for forty-eight hours: no contact with other prisoners or their legal teams, no newspapers or radio.

But before his time behind his door was up, Jack was released, the charge against him dropped. The punter he was supposed to have beaten up had withdrawn his complaint, saying he'd made a mistake.

'He didn't make a mistake, duck,' DCI Drury said to him at the gate outside Brixton prison where he and Brian were waiting. 'Some of your lot got to him so it's business as usual. But, meanwhile, stay out of the twins' places. Understood? By the way, you need a shower, duck. You smell almost as bad as your nigger.' He glanced at Pongo, who was leaning against the boot of a shiny new Mercedes. Then he turned away and rang the prison bell. It was all Jack could do not to hit him, and he might have done, if Brian hadn't dragged him away.

'Where's Bobby Brown? Where's our share of the money?' he wanted to know.

'He's disappeared, Jack. We went to his house,' Brian explained. 'His old woman hadn't seen him in months.'

'Yeah, what kind of fanny is that?'

'It's probably true. Ronnie Biggs is gone too.'

'They can't all've gone, Brian. We know who was approached. Find them. Get the info from them.'

'I'm afraid that's not all the bad news,' Brian said. 'The police captured some of the blaggers holed up in the cellar of a nearby farm.'

'They recover the money?'

'Some, not much.'

'Thank God for that.'

Jack grew more furious with each item of breaking news.

'Brian came here!' was how Leah greeted him when he walked into the flat after being absent for almost a month. 'He came here. I told you what I'd do if I saw him.'

'Take it easy,' Jack said. 'He needed to do some business here. There was no choice.'

'What sort of business could it have been that he took the spare mattress and bedding? Something filthy, I'm sure. He's such a degenerate.'

'Leah, Leah,' Jack said, trying to calm her. 'It's all right. I won't let him come again now I'm back.'

Leah was standing in the kitchen doorway not looking at him. She sighed and brushed past him, then walked along the corridor to the spare room. She closed the door. Absence hadn't made the heart grow fonder as he'd hoped it might, but he wasn't about to give up on her.

Manny Evans, the pawnbroker, rang Jack and asked if he could come and see him. He wouldn't say what it was about. Protection, Jack guessed. They agreed to meet at the club.

'I don't want no protection, see,' the pawnbroker said, when he came in. 'I can get that from the police. No, I was asked by a villain if I can move some money out of the country.'

'How much?' Jack said, all his senses alert.

'Too much. Not money I want to be involved with, see. It has to be from the train robbery.'

'Who's the villain, Manny?' Brian asked.

'You won't say it came from me?'

'As if we'd do that,' Jack said. 'There could be a nice little taste for you, Manny.'

'It's a lad called Mark Protherow. I've known the family for years.'

'Agree to meet, Manny. Tell him you got someone who can help.'

Jack, Brian, Pongo and another villain called John Flynn waited in the run-down Ladbroke Arms in Notting Hill. Flynn was carrying a small wooden box with some airholes in it. 'What's in the box, John?' Brian asked, curious. Flynn winked at Jack but wouldn't say.

When Protherow came through the door and saw Jack he stopped, then ran out, but the four of them flew after him. He fled across the road, was almost hit by a fifty-two bus and ran back in blind panic.

'Mark, we just wanna have a chat,' Jack said. 'We wanna help you, son.'

They took him to a house Joey owned around the corner in Blenheim Crescent. The hallway was full of prams and boxes, as if someone was moving in. Brian had keys to all the rooms and found one that a family was moving into. The place smelt of sweat and burnt chicken fat. 'Man,' a tenant greeted Pongo on the stairs.

'Where's the money, Mark?' Jack asked in a reasonable tone.

'What money's that, Jack?'

'What you want Manny Evans to get out the country.'

'I was meeting Manny to sell him a bit of swag.'

He refused stubbornly to talk until Jack, Pongo and Flynn got to work on him. First they beat him and he didn't talk. Then they put his head in a bucket of water and he didn't talk. Then Jack held up the box. 'Do you know what we got in the box, Mark? 'S a rat.' He pulled on a leather glove, reached into the box and grabbed the rodent, which squeaked in terror. 'I'm gonna put it down your shirt, man.'

Brian had a morbid fear of rats. 'No, Jack. You can't do that.'

'Don't be a mug,' Jack said. 'He's got my money.'

'Please, Brian,' Protherow appealed to him. 'Help me!'

'Tell them, for fuck's sake!' Brian yelled.

'I don't know!'

Flynn pulled open Protherow's shirt and thrust the rat inside. Protherow shrieked hysterically and threw himself around like a man possessed.

'Hold him!' Jack shouted at Pongo, but not even he could do that.

The door opened and a woman looked in. 'What you do?' she said, as the rat sprang out of Protherow's shirt and ran through the door between her legs. She shrieked too.

When he had finally calmed down, Protherow told them his money was in the left-luggage office at Victoria station, then gave the whereabouts of another train robber.

'None of us expected anything like as much. I mean, my whack was about two hundred grand. We don't know what to do with it all.'

'I'll show you,' Jack said. 'You'll get a cut, son. Where we gonna find this other blagger, David Crutwell?'

'He's in Canning Town.' Protherow was inspecting his chest for rat bites. 'Look what he done! Look!' he said, directing his anger at John Flynn as if he had bitten him.

When Jack and Brian got to the address in Canning Town Crutwell was gone.

'Eddie Richardson came and took him with some other men. They kept asking where his money was,' his wife told them.

'Did he tell them?' Jack asked.

'He wouldn't say anything. That's why they took him.'

'We'll get him back. Where'd they take him?'

Mrs Crutwell said she didn't know, and Jack believed her. 'They didn't get the money?' he asked.

'What money?' she said. 'He's only got his wages from Silcock's.' Silcock's was a cake-meal factory in Canning Town.

'D'you want us to get David back alive, Mrs Crutwell?' Brian asked.

She thought about that for a moment or two, then nodded. 'He wouldn't tell them. He'd sooner die first.'

David Crutwell's screams could almost be heard at Waterloo station. They certainly weren't muffled by the battered old caravan in the Bermondsey breaker's yard. Nor were they drowned by the grinder that was screeching its way through a girder in the yard. This made too much noise for the operator to hear Jack's car approach.

As they opened the caravan door Eddie Richardson was kneeling on the chest of a man strapped to an old office chair, using a large pair of pliers to pull out his wriggling prisoner's teeth. His brother stood beside him.

'Can I get my aching tooth pulled out?' Jack said.

'Hello, Jack. How are you, son?' Charlie said calmly.

'You got our man,' Jack said.

'That's all right, son, you can have him. He don't know nothing or he would've talked before he lost four teeth.'

'You'd better take him to one of your bent doctors, Brian,' Eddie said. 'Get him fixed up.'

'Well, someone ought to, by the look of him. You sure he didn't tell you nothing?'

Charlie laughed. 'Either that or he's got an exceptional pain threshold.'

'What's that?' Pongo asked.

'Didn't they teach you nothing in the army academy?'

Crutwell could barely walk nor speak as they helped him out to the car. 'I told them, Jack. I told them where it is – the money.'

'Then why were they still pulling your teeth out?' Brian asked.

'Because they enjoy it,' the train robber managed to say.

Leaving Crutwell propped up in the car with a handkerchief to his mouth, Jack ran back to the caravan with Brian, Pongo and Flynn. There, he spotted a five-gallon jerry-can and carefully lifted the lid. It contained petrol, which he poured along the front of the caravan on the ground.

'Charlie! You got about five seconds to put us into the money or we'll burn you alive.'

Charlie slid open the window. 'What? What you done? That's petrol!'

'You ain't nicking our money.'

'Half of it's ours. You came and talked to us first about the blag. That makes it half ourn.'

'You wiped your mouth,' Brian said, and took a cigarette lighter from Flynn.

'Come on. Fair's fair. We gotta have at least half.'

Before Jack had finished his count to five, Brian threw the flaming lighter at the petrol, which ignited across the front of the caravan with a blinding *whoomp!*, causing them to jump back. The Richardson brothers threw themselves out of the door, Eddie jumping clear of the flames but Charlie falling short and hitting the ground, his trousers catching fire. He screamed as Jack and Flynn pulled him clear.

'How about it, Charlie?'

The deal was easily done.

Joey was shocked when Brian broached the subject of moving the best part of five hundred grand in old notes out of the country. 'Are you mad, boy? Every policeman in the country is looking for that money. It can only have come from one place.'

'You saying no, then?'

The coolness of Brian's response shocked him even more. 'You've got to heed Tom Driberg's warning,' he said. 'Get out before it's too late, son.'

'Too late for what, Dad? I suppose we could try to lose half a million in cash through the shops, but it might take a while.'

When Joey had recovered himself, he said, 'There's a safer way. Let me talk to someone.'

That someone was Charles Tyrwhitt at Cotterill and Jenkins.

'The first question I'm obliged to ask, Joseph, is why it needs to go out of the country.'

Joey smiled weakly, uncertain what Tyrwhitt meant. Was he asking if the money was stolen or had he assumed that and asked merely if it had to go. Maybe he was offering a better alternative, but Joey couldn't read him. 'I could tell you it's funds I've avoided paying tax on.'

'Well, no one enjoys giving money to the government. How much is there?'

'Half a million pounds. Possibly more.'

He got it in one. 'That amount can only have come from the Great Train Robbery. Am I right?'

'If you don't ask,' Joey said, 'you won't be lied to.'

'Good.' Tyrwhitt smiled without missing a beat. 'We'll handle it for seventy per cent.'

Joey laughed. 'I think even this crew might baulk at that.'

'It's my best offer, Joseph. I'd advise you to think about it carefully. You won't get better.'

Joey thought about nothing else for the next two days, wondering if he couldn't slip some of it out through the shop. It was a ridiculous notion. He'd be an old man before getting it done, or prematurely old with worry. Then another two train robbers were arrested. That brought Jack round, wanting to know what was happening.

'We're playing a waiting game with the banker, trying to get his price down.'

'Isn't it likely to go up,' Jack said, 'the more villains what are arrested?'

'That's a risk you take in any money market, Jack,' Joey said, as if he was a regular player.

'Then I'd better meet the banker.'

Brian laughed.

'What's so funny about that?' Jack demanded.

'You'll see when you learn who it is,' Brian said. 'You'll probably want to kill him.'

'If you do,' Joey warned, 'you won't get a penny out of the country.'

'Who is it?' Jack snapped.

'Captain Charles Tyrwhitt,' Brian said. Jack turned away with a shrug. Joey was amazed at how relaxed Jack was at this news. Maybe there was hope for him yet.

He was equally relaxed when he met Tyrwhitt in his Brook Street office. It wasn't exactly a reunion of old friends talking about the good old days. Tyrwhitt was polite and charming, as Joey had guessed he would be with any large potential customer, and Jack was disarmed. They talked about boxing, which they both still followed with keen interest, each aware of the up-and-coming young boxers at local clubs. Tyrwhitt was involved in various boxing charities and said how he'd like to bring Jack in.

'How much?' Jack asked bluntly.

'Oh, it's more about giving time than money for someone like you, Jack.'

'The sport's character building,' Jack said, with an air of self-importance. 'Of course I'd get involved.'

They agreed a sixty–forty split in the bank's favour, Tyrwhitt guaranteeing to get it safely out of the country into secure banks abroad.

TWENTY-THREE

Over the coming months as Jack watched the news and saw the Robbery Squad capture more train robbers, including Ronnie Biggs, each incident made him feel ill at the loss of his money. There was still no sign of Bobby Brown. He'd done a runner, living it up somewhere on his share. Part of Jack was pleased for his friend; part of him hated the snide for double-crossing him. When Ronnie Biggs got thirty years – for robbery! – clearly the game was over. There'd be no more shares. Jack blamed Bobby and was determined to punish him.

At a charity boxing tournament Tyrwhitt's bank sponsored, he ran into Ronnie and Reggie Kray. Sparks ignited the hostility between them when Ronnie demanded their whack for the robbery.

'How about you two get in the ring and put on a show for a couple of rounds?' Harry Carpenter challenged them. He wasn't reporting for the BBC but supporting the charity.

'Look at the fat poof,' Jack said. 'He wouldn't go *one* round, even with Reggie's help.'

Ronnie charged Jack, who was ready for him and wasn't worried – even when Reggie got involved. Friends broke it up, but Ronnie went on issuing threats, telling Jack he was going to kill him.

'It looks like you're gonna have to get some help with that, son,' Jack told him.

'Clearly you have old scores to settle with those two, Jack,' Tyrwhitt mused, as he watched them leave.

'Not really. We tend to avoid one another, these days. It's bad for business when we meet up.'

'How sensible,' Tyrwhitt said. 'Do you know someone called Charles Richardson?'

Jack was cautious. 'Why?'

'He and his brother took a lot of money out of a company we loaned it to, built up a good credit-rating, then helped themselves to a large amount of goods and didn't pay for them.'

'That's their game, long-firm operations.'

'The company's going belly up as a result.'

'A fact of life in business, isn't it?'

'Of course,' Tyrwhitt conceded. 'But it's hurting our bank. How would you feel about taking a percentage to get our money back?'

'How much we talking about?'

'Our little bank stands to lose two hundred and twenty thousand pounds.'

'That's a lot of money,' Jack said. 'And the Richardsons would sooner give blood than hand the money back.'

'I don't care how much blood they give, just so long as our money's returned.'

'How much are you offering?'

'Ten per cent was what I had in mind.'

'It'd be worth more than that just to try and get money out of those two.'

After a lot of haggling, the banker agreed on twenty per cent.

'If they just hand it back, Jack, it'll be an easy forty-four grand,' Brian said. 'But why they gonna do that?'

'They ain't – without a fight,' Jack answered.

'You want to fight the Richardsons?'

'Why not? We can't let them or those other ponces rule the roost. We'll go and talk to them,' Jack said.

'Let's hope the Krays go on hating the Richardsons as much as we do,' Brian said.

'You've got to be kidding, Jack.' Charlie Richardson laughed. 'Give back nearly a quarter of a million? The little firm what sold the goods is a limited company. It's a tough world. They couldn't make a profit on them.'

'We're asking you nicely, Charlie.'

'What if I tell you to take a funny run?'

'We'll chop you up and turn you into pig feed,' Brian said, producing a cleaver and swinging it.

'You crackers, son? Totally fucking mad?'

'I wouldn't be surprised. The money either goes back, Charlie, or it's all-out war,' Brian announced.

'You know how that sort of aggro costs everyone, but it's got to be,' Jack told him.

'You can have war any day of the week,' Eddie told them. 'We can put you two mugs away easy – specially with all that trouble you're making for yourselves with the twins.'

That was what Jack had feared they might say. Then he got a shock.

'Let's give back the money to his banker,' Charlie suggested. 'He could be well useful, bruv. That's how Jack got all that train money out. Right, Jack?'

Jack smiled.

'It's pretty clear Charlie's still upset about what we had off that train robbery, Jack,' Brian said, when they'd left, with a firm promise that all the money would be returned.

'What can he do about it?'

'He's an out-and-out snake. He's plotting.'

'You worry too much.'

And he was right. A week later Charles Tyrwhitt called him to the bank and said all the money was back in from the Richardsons. 'It must be the easiest forty-four fraud you've earned,' he said.

'That's what reputation does for you,' Jack said coolly.

'The Richardsons offered to mind me and the bank.'

'What did you tell them?'

'That I'm happy with the current arrangement,' Tyrwhitt said.

Jack was immediately suspicious. Something about the way the banker had responded made him uneasy. He was convinced that some sort of arrangement with the Richardsons was now in place – those two would sooner part with their first-born than money. It had been a mistake to give them access to the banker. He'd have to watch Tyrwhitt the whole time for any indication of betrayal, analyse his every statement.

'I assume you'll want cash?' Tyrwhitt said, breaking into his thoughts.

'In the smallest possible parcel,' Jack told him.

'It'll be done. Look, there's a boys' boxing tournament coming up next month, to be attended by her Royal Highness Princess Margaret. Perhaps you'd like tickets. Joey Oldman and your sister are going, representing their local Conservative Association. They've made a handsome donation.'

'Is that what you want from me, Charles?' Jack wondered if he'd invited the Richardsons.

His wife's tension was painful to observe, and Joey felt it increase the moment Jack and Charles Tyrwhitt walked down the aisle at the Royal Albert Hall towards his seat in the second row from the ring. He put his hand out to reassure her.

'Why's he here?' she asked.

'He helped Tyrwhitt out over a bit of business. Don't fret, Cathy. Charles'll keep him under control.'

'He'd better. I don't want him introduced to Princess Margaret,' Cath said, as if she or Joey had any influence over that. 'I certainly don't want him introduced to Margaret Courtney – I don't want our chairman to know who he is.'

'Stop worrying about it. You're not your brother's keeper.'

'It might reflect badly on me if it came out – and please don't call me Cathy. You know I prefer Catherine.'

Joey stroked her arm to calm her as Jack approached, but she sat rigid. Their conversation with him was equally stiff. Joey was relieved when Tyrwhitt came over with a man he recognized as Lord Boothby, who seemed to know Jack and greeted him by his first name. He spoke charmingly to Cath, who relaxed until he turned back to Jack.

'It's your big moment, Jack,' Lord Boothby said. 'Princess Margaret wants to meet you. She's keen to know how you got into boxing. I said I was sure you'd explain the finer pugilistic points to her as the matches proceed. I've rearranged the seating so you're next to her. Excuse us.' Suddenly he turned back. 'Forgive me, Mrs Oldman, Margaret Courtney said you do sterling work in raising money for the party.'

'I try. This is Joseph, my husband,' Cath said.

'Yes, Brian's parents. Such a charming young man.' He guided Jack along the aisle to the throng gathered around the royal party.

'What will the lady chairman say about that, Cathy?' Joey asked.

Cath was too intent on what was going on between her brother and the princess to reply. She didn't watch a single punch landed by any of the boxers, Joey noticed. Instead her eyes were glued to Jack as he leant in to Princess Margaret, giving a whispered commentary which was making her laugh.

Afterwards Margaret Courtney came up to them. 'My word, Catherine,' she said, taking her arm. 'The princess has gone to Annabel's with Charles Tyrwhitt and your brother in her party. He was such a hit with her. What a dark horse you are. I didn't know you had such a colourful family.'

'Jack doesn't like publicity,' Cath said.

'Well, I expect he'll get a few pics in the tabloids tomorrow. So will we – doing our bit to redirect youth. The evening was a great success. I'm thrilled for you both.'

'We cannot expand the business any further at present,' Joey told Emil Savundra, at their weekly meeting to discuss the financial viability of Fire, Auto & Marine Insurance. He insisted on weekly meetings. Savundra wouldn't have bothered to meet at all, just so long as the money was coming in and he could take it out as he wanted. He conducted his business in much the same way as John Bloom, whose company was now unravelling.

'To expand the business, you need money to underwrite potential claims,' Joey said patiently, for the umpteenth time.

'My dear Joseph,' Savundra said, 'you told me yourself that all we need to do is delay paying the claims until more money comes in. Then we're on a sounder footing.'

'But we're never going to be on a sounder footing or even catch up at this rate,' Joey said, 'much less get ahead. How much longer do you imagine we can hold claimants at bay?'

'Well, let's pay some,' Savundra said. 'We *are* paying some.'

'Only from the premiums we keep taking. There have been complaints from the Board of Trade.'

'I'd like you to meet a gentleman from the board, Joseph, a Mr Alan Carmichael.'

'He'll want some answers to the customers' complaints, Emil.'

'No, my dear Joseph, he'll want a little baksheesh.' He rubbed his fingers together.

'If he does, that'll keep them away from the door a little longer.'

His worry seemed lost on Savundra, whose thoughts simply moved on.

'Meanwhile, I have some government bonds worth about half a mil,' he said off-handedly. 'I'm prepared to put them up as security.'

'You are?' Joey said, taken aback, although nothing was surprising about this man, who stepped dextrously ahead of his creditors.

'They should hold the fort nicely, wouldn't you say?'

'Where are they?'

'Oh, I had the foresight to bring them to our little meeting, Joseph. I thought you would say they were needed.' He produced a thick wad of bonds from a pigskin briefcase and offered it to Joey. Each bore the Treasury seal and signature. They were ten-year bonds issued in 1964 and totalled £540,000. 'There you are,' Savundra said. 'Now you must stop worrying.'

'That's why I'm here.'

'Of course, of course, my dear fellow. But we have a sound business model, you understand.'

'Arguable, Emil. We're still expanding too fast and some of the risks we're insuring are too high. We should tell our brokers to be more judiciour in the risks they underwrite for us.'

'No, no, Joseph. Everyone who can afford a motor-car deserves insurance. Look, you'd better get these bonds into the bank,' he said, signalling the end of their meeting. The chairman of the board had a very short attention span. His prime concern always seemed to be what people thought of him.

A smile two miles wide spread across Tyrwhitt's face when Joey produced the bonds. 'This is excellent, Joseph. It means the bank can now get out with a small profit. My advice to you would be to do the same.'

'Not with collateral like this, Charles. We're expanding too fast and likely to run into problems later, but it's still a profitable business with this amount in hand.'

'We'd better take these to the cashier. Does Savundra have access to any more money like this?'

'He's a man of surprises.'

'As long as none is nasty.'

Business was at such a volume now that Joey wanted Brian to come in with him. He could see how unhappy his son was in his relationship with Jack, especially now Jack seemed to have jumped up the ladder in the social pecking order. 'With the property and the insurance company, there's more than I can handle,' Joey told him.

'It all sounds dead boring, Dad. Anyway I've got a business – the spiels.' He was at their rooms in the top part of the house in Notting Hill for Sunday lunch.

'What sort of business is that? None of it's legal.'

'We got enough Old Bill straightened. Every week they come in and cop their whack.'

'For as long as it suits them. That could change like the wind.'

'So could your business. Especially dealing with that bent bastard Savundra. You gotta be mad.'

'Brian! Don't talk to your father like that,' Cath said. 'You're always saying no to him.'

'It's all right, Cathy,' Joey said. 'We'll let it drop. Young men have to establish themselves.'

'But it's hurtful,' she said. 'Jack Braden might be my brother, but he won't do you any good, not in the long run, even if he did catch the eye of Princess Margaret.'

'I'm sorry, Mum,' Brian said, lowering his head. 'I'm just not cut out for Dad's sort of business.'

'You were so responsive when you were a little boy. I don't know what happened, I'm sure.'

Suddenly Brian looked as if he was about to cry, and Joey felt sorry for him. 'Cathy,' he said, 'let him make his own way.'

When Tyrwhitt called Joey to tell him he had to see him straight away, his voice sounded full of panic, but he wouldn't say why. Joey agreed to meet him at his office. There, he found Tyrwhitt pacing his room. As soon as he walked in, Tyrwhitt burst out, 'Those bloody bonds are forged! Excellent forgeries, but forged nonetheless, the bloody little swindling Indian worm.'

'So Fire, Auto & Marine's worthless?' Joey said. 'I've still got some of my own money in there.'

'Well, on paper it appears to be. However, that doesn't necessarily mean it's entirely worthless – or not until it's known publicly.' The banker stood still and stared hard at Joey. 'We could salvage something, Joseph. You have a growing customer base.'

'But how long will it be before we're found out? We've had so many complaints about unpaid claims.'

'Has Savundra done an accurate claims-risk-premium equation? It would appear he hasn't. His premiums are the lowest available. Much lower than the risk he's insuring.'

'The unpaid claims are mounting. The Board of Trade are pressing us over them,' Joey told him, 'but I might be able to hold them off.'

Tyrwhitt waited for him to continue.

'I'm meeting one of their investigators.'

'Can Savundra get any more of these bonds?'

Joey was puzzled. 'What's the point if they're no good?'

'They're only no good to the observant, Joseph. We could use them to raise cash for your property developments. They'll return a profit.'

It was then that Joey's attitude towards Charles Tyrwhitt changed. He knew he had a lot to learn from him.

Cath was shocked when Joey told her about the bank. She had a peculiar faith in the honesty of the educated upper-middle classes, especially those who supported the Conservative Association financially. 'He raises a lot of money for us,' she said.

'I expect he'll go on doing so.'

'But what if he's caught, Joey?'

'I'm sure he won't be. His kind never are. It's always the mugs lower down the ladder who go to prison.'

Mugs like Alan Carmichael – Joey met him the following day to talk through the liquidity problem of Fire, Auto & Marine, which would only need a little more time to sort itself out.

'How much?' the tall Board of Trade inspector asked, sitting stiff with probity across the cheap desk in Joey's Lombard Street office. With an iron-grey moustache and swept-back hair, he had the bearing of an ex-military man.

Joey tried to guess what he earned in a year. Fifteen hundred pounds was the figure he came up with, tops. 'If you could see your way clear to giving us, say, six months, that would help enormously.'

'Six months is a long time. By then lot of premiums will have been taken in.'

'God willing, all the genuine claims will have been paid too,'

Joey said. 'I believe you have a daughter about to start college.'

Carmichael arched his eyebrows, but said nothing.

'There must be a lot of expense involved,' Joey went on.

'There certainly is,' the investigator said. 'It goes on and on.'

'If it helps, we'd like to make you a loan,' Joey offered.

'A loan, Mr Oldman?' Carmichael said. 'Oh, yes ... a loan. I suppose that would help.'

'We wouldn't be in any hurry to have the money back. Shall we say five hundred pounds?'

The man's stiffness dissolved and Joey realized he could have got the six months for two hundred and immediately asked for it to be extended to twelve. As a sop to his conscience, Carmichael said their agreement rested on the condition that the insurance company didn't discount premiums any further.

That was acceptable to Savundra. He was pleased. But his whole manner changed when Joey told him there was a serious problem with his securities. 'How can there be?' he blustered. 'They're government-backed. I know Wilson's administration is a little shaky but, come on, old boy, it's not likely to fall, is it?'

'You come on, Emil,' Joey said firmly. 'Don't take me for a bigger fool than you thought I was. You know and I know those bonds are forged.'

'That can't be. Look at the watermark.'

'I have. I had an expert inspect it too. The head is the wrong way round.'

Savundra examined one of the bonds. 'How do you know it isn't meant to face that way?'

Joey considered him for a long moment, wondering whether or not he should simply leave. But he couldn't. He took an envelope from his pocket. 'Here's a genuine bond. Yours is perfect in all other respects. I should go straight to the police.'

'I'll go with you,' Savundra said. 'This is scandalous. The brokers who sold me those bonds must be crooks. We should expose them.'

'Do you want to make the call or shall I?'

For the first time ever in Joey's experience, the Indian entrepreneur was lost for words.

'If we do, neither of us will gain. In fact, we'll lose,' Joey said. 'How many more can you get?'

Suddenly Savundra was his confident self again, the smile back on his face. 'How many do you want, Joseph? And what will I get?'

'For now, Emil, what you get is your supposed investment staying in place at the bank and you not going to prison. Meanwhile, Fire, Auto & Marine takes in premiums as fast as it can, discounting where we have to,' Joey said, ignoring his promise to the corrupt Carmichael.

'How do I know this property development you're trying to get us to invest in is sound, Joey?' Charlie Richardson was sitting at the bar in Mr Smith's nightclub in Catford.

'Because I'm investing in it, and so is the bank,' Joey told him. He glanced across the empty, garishly decorated space, which smelt of stale beer and cigarette smoke, as a woman in a checked overall lazily pushed a Hoover over the stained carpets. He hated the place when it was empty like this; he'd have hated it even more when it was full of people, noise and cigarette smoke.

'How do we know you'll raise enough money to develop the site?'

'Easy. It's being underwritten by one point two million's worth of government bonds deposited at the bank.'

'That sounds pretty cushty,' Eddie Richardson said. 'Why not just sell them and use the money instead?'

'They're ten-year bonds with another nine to run.'

The two brothers were thoughtful now. 'So we'd be nine years getting our money back if it went wrong?'

'Business is about long-term investment. Charles Tyrwhitt told me you were looking to get out of long-firm operations.'

Charlie shrugged. 'How much d'you reckon you need?'

'We can get the site in Threadneedle Street for two hundred

and ninety grand. To develop it to a ten-storey office block we need another one point one million, plus about fifty thousand in fees.'

'How many other investors are in?'

'Three. Me, Fire, Auto & Marine Insurance, and the bank, Cotterill and Jenkins. They're putting their clients' money in.'

'What about Jack Braden? 'S he going in?'

'He's not been invited,' Joey said. 'We don't need such an unstable element in this enterprise. Whoever comes in has to be sound enough to stay the course.'

'About right,' Charlie said. 'We could bring some of the dosh back from South Africa if this looks kosher, bruv,' he said to Eddie.

'We don't know what it's gonna be worth, Chas.'

'I was coming to that. Conservatively, two point eight million pounds, when it's finished, with a letting value of a hundred and forty to a hundred and fifty thousand pounds a year.'

'Sounds all right,' Charlie said, nodding to Eddie. 'We'll come in for a fifth. Our brief'll want to take a gander at the bonds you got underwriting the project.'

That prospect put Joey in a spin. If the bonds didn't match up to their expectations, the Richardsons would not be pleased. And they weren't likely to walk away, glad of their near miss. There'd be unpleasant consequences.

'Are you sure the bonds will pass muster, Charles?' Joey asked Tyrwhitt anxiously, as they waited for the Richardsons' solicitor.

'A criminal lawyer is unlikely to know the difference,' the banker said confidently, 'unless one of his clients forged them.'

The intercom on the desk buzzed, startling Joey. Tyrwhitt reached out and gripped his arm, steadying him, then flicked the open switch. His secretary told him Mr Jacobs had arrived.

'Ask him to come in, Sally.' He clicked off the phone. 'We'll soon know, Joseph.'

Paul Jacobs was about thirty and resembled a number of barrow-boys Joey knew who worked the Petticoat Lane market of a Sunday morning. He wondered if he was related to Danny Jacobs, who had a china stall and whose party piece was to throw a whole set of dinner plates into the air and catch them. Like him, Jacobs had a low hairline and eyebrows that met in the middle. That, along with his Italian-style suit and loud tie, did a lot to reassure him. He didn't want tea and seemed positively uncomfortable in Tyrwhitt's plush office. When the bonds came up from the vault, Joey almost smiled as Jacobs went through an elaborate process of examining them, his brow beetling.

'The serial numbers are attached to the paperwork related to the development they're underwriting,' Tyrwhitt said.

'I can see that, thank you.'

Finally Jacobs got up from his chair. 'Everything seems to be in order, Mr Tyrwhitt. I'll report as much to my clients,' he said, and left without another word.

Tyrwhitt smiled elaborately and jiggled his belly with his fingertips in an exaggerated laugh. He wanted to go and celebrate.

Joey declined. He had a lot of work to do before he went home in time to be settled with a tray on his lap to watch *Steptoe and Son* on the BBC.

Cath was out at the local Tory Party headquarters with Margaret Courtney and the committee, but Joey made no arrangements for Thursday evenings when his favourite television show was on. He tried to ignore the doorbell and pretend he wasn't at home, but it was so insistent he decided it had to be someone who knew he would be in. It was the Richardsons and he felt obliged to let them come up to the first-floor sitting-room of the house on Ladbroke Grove, opposite a bombsite that someone had just started to clear for rebuilding.

'He's watching *Steptoe and Son*,' Charlie said. 'Someone said you always watched this.'

'I'd like it to finish before we talk business. Sit down,' he said irritably, and returned to the black-and-white images on the screen.

For the remaining fifteen minutes the room erupted with laughter, none louder than Eddie's. It stopped when the familiar music started and Eddie pulled a gun from his leather bomber jacket and leant over, pointing it at Joey's head. 'D'you think we're just off the boat?' he demanded.

'Of course I don't. You're two of the smartest men I've done business with. What's the problem?'

'You're treating us like out-and-out mugs. You could have taken us into your confidence, Joey. We could have been of great benefit to you,' Charlie put in.

'What are you talking about?' Joey said, his eyes flitting nervously in the direction of Eddie and the gun.

'Them bonds you got stuck up in that fancy bank. Did you think we'd send a mug to look at them? Is that what you thought?'

'Of course not. You're too shrewd.'

'You bet. And Paul Jacobs is one of the shrewdest fellas around. He spotted them right off. I tell you what, Joey,' Charlie said, 'if we'd parted with our dough your missus would be picking bits of your brain off that wall.'

'I don't know what you're talking about.' Joey was unable to resist a glance at the wall behind him – anything to avoid the gaping hole in the gun barrel. 'So tell me.'

'They're forgeries, you tricky bastard.'

'Don't be silly! They're not. They're as sound as the bank.'

'Where'd you get them?'

'They're rock solid!' Joey laughed uncertainly. He didn't know how long he could keep this up or whether it would stop them shooting him.

'Where'd you get them?' Charlie Richardson repeated.

'I can't divulge my source. You can choose to participate in the investment or not, as you—'

'Where the fuck did you get them?' His tone was more menacing now.

'You know me better,' Joey said, trying his last throw of the dice.

'You stupid berk, you don't know *us* at all,' Charlie said. 'Ed.'

Eddie pressed the gun to Joey's temple and cocked the trigger.

'If you don't think he'd do it, Joey, why you trembling?'

'I'm scared the gun'll go off accidentally,' Joey said, trying not to let go of the food he'd eaten earlier.

'Well, I'll say this, son, you're a cooler customer than I took you for,' Charlie said. 'We could do a lot with bonds that good, Joey. What I think is, you're using the oldest trick in the book to get money into a speculative investment. But you know what they say, son, the old ones are always the best. We're talking to you sensible now, Joey. We wanna do some business with them bonds. So, where'd you get them?'

Still Joey held out.

'Okay, one last chance. Tell us where you got them bonds.'

'No.' Joey held firm, believing now that they wouldn't shoot him. They wanted the bonds more than they wanted him dead.

'Gimme that gun, Eddie.' He took it from his brother and, without warning, hit Joey in the mouth, breaking his front teeth.

The shock took his breath away. He tried not to breathe again for fear of intensifying the pain that flooded across his face.

Charlie Richardson was saying, 'You wanna tell us, son, or would you prefer a bit more dental work?'

'You broke my teeth,' Joey mumbled, the pain worsening by the moment.

'I think he wants us to take him to the dentist, bruv,' Charlie said.

A tiny part of Joey's brain wanted to believe that that was where they were going when they pulled him out of the chair and took him downstairs to their car. The pain in his mouth grew more intense on the journey, and he slipped in and out of consciousness. When he came to, he thought he was strapped into a dentist's chair. But dentists didn't strap you in. Finally he realized that the Richardsons had taken him to their breaker's yard in South London. He was tied to an office chair in a new caravan. Charlie was kneeling on his groin, trying to pull out one of his teeth with a pair of pliers. The crunch on the enamel was excruciating. Then there was more pain as the tooth broke, and yet more, if that was possible, as the pliers skidded into his gum. Joey screamed, but with the rumble of trains and a grinder that was operating somewhere nearby no one heard.

'You amaze me, Joey,' Charlie said, almost conversationally. 'You really do. I didn't think you'd hold out this long.'

'Maybe the bonds are kosher after all, Charlie,' Eddie said.

'No. He's holding out on us, the little kyke. Let's do some more of his teeth.'

'You're enjoying this, ain't you?' Eddie said.

'D'you know what, Ed? Dentistry's a missed vocation of mine. Come on, open wide, Joey. No?'

'No,' Joey cried, as he came back to life with tears streaming down his face and pee down his legs. 'No. Please don't. I'll tell you,' he whimpered. He'd survive, and get even with these men. He'd have them either killed or sent to prison.

Brian hammered on the door of Jack's flat, having rushed past the porter and up the stairs. 'Come on! open the poxy door!'

Eventually the lock rattled and Leah was staring at him, shocked.

'Where is he? Where the hell's Jack?'

'You can't come in—'

'Just shut up,' Brian said, and shoved her aside as she announced she was calling the police. Jack came out of the bathroom doing up his trousers. 'We gotta top the Richardsons. They done Dad. They done him!' He ran to the kitchen and grabbed the biggest carving knife he could find.

Jack followed him. 'What d'you mean they done him? Killed him?'

'They pulled all his teeth out, that's what.'

'Get him out of here,' Leah shrieked, as she ran into the kitchen. She hit Brian with an empty vase, smashing it on his shoulder.

'What are you doing? You gone mad?' Jack said.

'Get him out. *Get him out!*' Leah shouted hysterically.

'Shut it,' Jack ordered, but she took no notice and scrabbled in the cutlery drawer for a kitchen knife, then lunged at Brian. Jack caught her with a left hook and knocked her spark out.

'Oh, Leah,' he said, dropping to his knees beside her.

'Worry about her?' Brian said. 'But what about them other slags?' He pulled at Jack's shoulder. 'You coming?'

'What you gonna do? Rush over there and chop them up?'

'I'll kill them. The first one I see is dead and that's a promise – and everyone who helps them. I mean it, Jack.'

'Be sensible about this, Bri. We have to be cunning, wipe our mouths for now. Get them when they least expect it. Look, I gotta get a doctor for Leah.'

'No. You gotta see Dad. You can't recognize him.' Brian was in tears.

'Take a deep breath, son. Think about how we can hurt them most.'

'I'll top them!' Brian said.

'No, that'll only make them dead,' Jack said. 'The way to hurt them is take away their liberty.'

'How do we do that? Grass them to Old Bill?'

'We'll think of something. We will, Bri, so just calm down. Look, I gotta get a doctor. Just stay calm, okay?'

Brian felt overwhelmingly disappointed. This was someone he had once admired and looked up to. Now he was useless. Scared of the Richardsons.

Brian went from club to club, drinking more than he should, trying to plot something devious against the Richardsons but getting foggier and foggier. Pulling the attractive young man with Tom Driberg couldn't have been easier.

'I don't know what good you'll be to anyone in that state,' the MP said petulantly, and went off to talk to one of the women hanging around the bar.

Brian made love angrily to the young man, taking out all his frustration on him. Afterwards he hadn't calmed down at all. 'Who you looking at?' he demanded.

'What?'

Brian lashed out at him. One blow followed another as he attempted to assuage the feeling that smothered him like a shroud. He slammed the young man into the doorframe as he tried to shove him out of the apartment, then pushed him downstairs and on to the street.

'What's going on?' a neighbour said.

'Shut up and go back inside,' Brian ordered.

An hour later he wasn't much calmer when he opened the door to two policemen who had called round in response to a complaint from a Dominic Langham about an assault – Brian hadn't known his name.

'Who?' Brian said. 'Never heard of him.' He stared hard at one of the officers. 'I know you, don't I?'

'I certainly know who you are, sir.'

'What's your name?'

'PC Wednesday. We'd like you to come to the police station and answer a few questions.'

'You gotta be kidding,' Brian said. 'Here.' He tried to give them money, not even bothering to count it.

'You'd better come with us,' the older man said, reaching out to take Brian's arm. Brian landed two punches on him before PC Wednesday hit him with his truncheon, bringing him down.

After Joey pleaded with him, Arnold Goodman responded to Brian's phone call and came to see him at the police station. 'I've had a long talk with the duty inspector, Brian, and I'm afraid I can't get you out this evening.'

'Why not?' Brian said angrily. 'I haven't done nothing.'

'They claim you assaulted, then tried to bribe a policeman.'

'Call Tom Driberg and Lord Boothby. They'll get me out.'

'I wouldn't count on it, Brian. Not tonight,' Goodman said. 'I know how upset you are about what the Richardsons did to your father. For your own safety, you have to stay in.'

'How is Dad?'

'Your mother said they were taking him to the operating theatre to remove his broken teeth,' the lawyer told him. 'Try to stay calm. I'll have someone talk to your uncle.'

The cell at Cannon Row police station was about ten feet long by six wide, the green-painted walls were scratched with names and abuse, and the place stank of vomit and piss masked by Tepol disinfectant. Everything seemed to conspire against Brian, making him even more het up.

The young, good-looking PC Wednesday came in to talk to him. 'You can get out of this easily,' he said. 'All you have to do is give the police something in return.'

'Like what?' Brian said. 'A hand-job?'

He didn't bat an eyelid. 'The Richardsons. Word is, it was them what did your dad. Right?'

'If they did and I could give them to you I would,' Brian said. 'Anything to get out of here.'

'Well, the night is young.' The policeman left the cell.

Brian was sorry to see him go. He liked him.

'I really can't do much for Brian,' DI Fenwick told Jack, when he came round to the flat. 'The best I can do is get some of the charges dropped, but not whacking the constable. Old Bill take a dim view of their own being beaten up.'

'Tell me who to go to, George, and I'll do it,' Jack said.

'There's only one person who might be able to help, and that's Detective Superintendent Slipper.'

Leah appeared in her nightdress, looking like a zombie. Fenwick stared at her.

'Leah, why don't you go back to bed?' Jack reached out to her, but she pushed him away and went into the kitchen.

'Is she all right?' Fenwick asked.

Jack shook his head. 'Is he bent?'

'Slipper? I haven't got any direct experience, only heard rumours. If he is, he won't be cheap.'

'Can you set up a meeting?'

They met on the Embankment, not two hundred yards from Cannon Row police station. The detective was on his own, which Jack took as a good sign.

The first thing Superintendent Jack Slipper wanted to know was who had told him he'd help.

'That don't matter,' Jack said. 'Either you can or you can't.'

'Then I can't. It's that simple.'

'Not even for a lot of money?'

'Give me all the corrupt policemen you know, and your nephew walks away scot-free.'

Jack wasn't sure he wanted Brian out that badly. 'I didn't think you was a rubber heel.'

'Give me some names.'

'Not even Old Bill who work for the Krays,' Jack said, 'and, believe me, I'd like to be shot of them.'

'You surprise me,' Slipper said. 'It's the first time I've come across such honour among thieves. I'm arresting you for trying to pervert the course of justice.' He raised his hand and signalled to some men – detectives, Jack realized, his heart sinking – who ran across the road through the traffic.

Arnold Goodman was uneasy when he came to see Jack, saying the police were intending to proceed with the charge.

'They offered me a deal,' Jack told him. 'They want the names of bent coppers. If I give them some, they won't go ahead.'

'They've got little evidence. I'm sure we'll win in court.'

The following morning Goodman was effective at Bow Street magistrates' court. Jack watched from the dock as he stood up before the stipendiary magistrate and asked for bail as they intended to defend the case vigorously.

'These are serious charges, Lord Goodman,' the magistrate said, causing Jack to turn and look at the overweight brief. He didn't know he'd been made a Lord. 'The police are concerned he might interfere with witnesses.'

'What witnesses, sir? There are none, only the police themselves. I doubt they could be influenced or interfered with.'

'Quite,' the magistrate said, and freed Jack on bail.

When Brian heard about Jack's result, he felt confident that Lord Goodman would do equally well with his bail application when he went before the same magistrate.

'My client has a full defence. The terrible mitigating circumstances of his father being tortured by criminals led to this temporary loss of control.'

'His "loss of control" seems to have stretched over a long period, Lord Goodman,' Sir Michael Stern, the magistrate said. 'I think Mr Oldman must be held in custody.'

Brian stared at the rolls of fat on the back of Goodman's neck, feeling sick and let down. Why hadn't his friends come to help him? They'd deserted him. He felt suicidal as he was taken to prison to await trial.

TWENTY-FOUR

He must be pretty special to be invited on a course at Bramshill staff training college, the inspector at his nick had told Tony Wednesday. Tony had believed that from the start. For him, joining the police was like coming home to the family he had never known, apart from Sergeant Watling. No one said what the purpose of this special training was, only that he'd find out in due course.

Tony Wednesday didn't believe in luck, good or bad. He didn't believe in coincidence either. Instead he thought everything had a purpose. He didn't immediately know the purpose of his running into a young policeman at the college whom he'd fought as a kid at the Festival of Britain street party. He discovered that they had been born on the same day of the year, which put him in competition with John Redvers, who said he remembered him and recalled every detail of what had happened.

'God, you must be the Memory Man,' Tony joked. The others at the induction laughed, but not Redvers. He didn't seem to have much sense of humour. 'You know who he was, don't you? Someone whose dad thrashed him for losing a halfpenny when he was a kid. He never forgot it.'

'I lost my dad in the war,' Redvers said.

Tony nodded. He wasn't going to allow Redvers to siphon off the others' sympathy so he grabbed it back. 'So did I,' he told him. 'Least, he didn't come back after doing his duty. M' mum, whoever she was, dumped me in a doorway.'

'That's right. A beat bobby found you and brought you up,' John Redvers said.

'Well, not quite, but close enough. He used to visit me in St Joseph's orphanage. That's how I came to be in the job.'

'I knew it was you. I never forget a face.'

'Then you must be the perfect policeman,' Tony said, ratcheting up the rivalry. 'What are you doing here?'

'Same as you. I was invited. The police are paying to put me through uni. In the holidays I have to do some practical.'

Sport of some sort was obligatory on the course – the police placed heavy emphasis on physical fitness. Tony chose fencing and learnt quickly. Soon he fenced well, with quick responses. The sport required stamina and mental agility, while the alternative was to risk getting his face squashed playing rugby, which he'd avoided at the Hendon training college. Tony thought a lot of his face and had decided it was worth protecting. Maybe Redvers did too. He fenced, and so far had lost two out of three bouts against Tony.

They were fencing in the gym when an attractive young woman pushed open the double doors and looked in, distracting Redvers, who lost a point. 'Sorry,' she said, 'I was looking for Superintendent Slipper.'

'Oh, Miss! I think this is him,' Tony said, pulling off his mask and indicating Redvers. 'What's your name?'

'Oh, very funny,' the young woman said.

'I like that. Your mum must have had a great sense of humour – 'bye, Oh Very Funny,' Tony said, as she went out. He turned to Redvers, who was staring after her open-mouthed as if he couldn't quite believe she was real. Clearly he was struck by her and Tony saw this as another area of competition. 'I'd give her one,' he said. 'More than one, in fact.'

The young woman pushed open the door again. 'I thought I'd better just check. You're not Superintendent Slipper, are you?'

'No, I'm sorry,' Redvers stammered.

'Oh, don't feel bad about it, John,' Tony said. 'Slipper looks like an old lag. Oh Very Funny couldn't possibly fancy him, not when we're on offer.'

'I like older men.' She made for the door.

'Who should we tell him was looking for him?'

'Oh Very Funny,' she said, and was gone.

In the third week they were summoned to a meeting in a small lecture theatre. The entire assembly comprised twelve young policemen and one young policewoman: Oh Very Funny. When Detective Superintendent Slipper arrived, wearing a suit that hung badly on his long, angular frame, the main instructor shouted, 'Attention!'

'Make yourselves comfortable,' Slipper said. 'It's going to be a long session. Most of you will be wondering why you're here. Twelve young men and one young woman who haven't got as many years policing between them. You're here because the powers that be have decided you're special. They've been watching your exam results, your sports and social skills, your intelligence and policing aptitude, and from that they've concluded you're more than special. In fact, you're exceptional.'

A little buzz of appreciation went around the room as they checked each other out in the light of this information.

'But what to do with this exceptional talent? We're going to harness it to change the face of policing, and the public perception of policing. You've all been selected to go on to the Robbery Squad, even though none of you has nearly enough experience to brush his or her own teeth.' That brought a little laugh. 'Corruption is rotting this institution from the inside, and everyone is the poorer for it. You're coming into my squad because I need a team of officers I can rely on not to have been tainted by corruption, officers who won't have picked up the lazy, easy ways of other policemen. We're not effective against major crims because they corrupt our officers. The time has come to drop the hammer on the Richardson torture gang. They've got away with too much for too long. Even tough guys like the Krays and Jack Braden are scared of them. But by the time we're done with you, you'll be ready to tackle them single-handed.'

He talked for two hours about the Richardsons and their specialities.

The following day they each had a one-to-one session with Slipper.

'It's a tall order for any police officer, much less an inexperienced one, Tony,' Slipper said, over a cup of tea. Tony wondered how many cups he'd drunk during the course of these interviews. 'Without a new *esprit de corps*, the Met is lost.'

'And we're going to be dumped in the deep end to help sort out things, sir?'

'You'll be supported by officers specially chosen from various teams in the Met. They will provide leadership. What we need is incorruptibility, courage, the ability to lead by example. We'll want to know if there's any hint of corruption among the officers you work with. I'll need you to keep your eyes and ears open. If you're not up for this you must say so now.'

'It's why I joined the police, sir.'

'Excellent. That's the way we'll turn the force around, Tony.' He set down his cup and got up. 'I knew your sponsor, Sergeant Watling. I started as a constable on his patch. A good man. How is he?'

'He's retired, sir. He married a sister from the orphanage where I was brought up. She gives him pure hell. He spends every spare moment on his allotment.'

Slipper smiled. Perhaps he knew what he'd missed by staying single.

'Do you want to come for a drink with us, Oh Very Funny?' Tony asked, when he ran into her in the corridor as he left the interview room.

'Who's us?' she wanted to know.

'John Redvers and me. He fancies you as much as I do.'

'But he doesn't have your social skills?' she challenged.

'He was raised by the Plymouth Brethren.'

'What are they when they're at home?'

'They're about four rungs below the vicious brothers at St Joseph's orphanage where I was brought up.'

'Is that meant to make me feel sorry for you?'

'I'd think less of you if it did. It didn't disadvantage me.'

'Could anything do that?' she said.

Tony liked Sonia Hope. She seemed to know her own mind and wouldn't be a pushover – but he'd keep pushing.

'Did you believe all that guff Slipper gave us about being incorruptible?' Tony asked in the pub, testing them.

'Can the police really be as corrupt as he suggested?' Sonia speculated. She drank half-pints of draught lager, so she wasn't expensive to take out, even less so when she insisted on buying a round.

Tony was curiously old-fashioned, even in the so-called swinging sixties, and felt uncomfortable when a woman paid for herself. 'How are we going to get a decent car and holidays on the Costa Packet if there aren't backhanders?'

'He wants people he can trust to help eradicate corruption,' Redvers pointed out.

'Yeah, but that's like trying to eradicate poverty and sickness, John. Nice theory.' He caught Sonia's eye, but her face was blank.

'It's a good principle to work towards,' Redvers said.

'Not as good as being on the RCS, dealing with major villains – that's like being given the keys to the bank. Where's the harm if you look the other way or let a bit of evidence fall out of the folder before it's given in court?' Tony challenged.

'Corruption diminishes us all,' Redvers argued.

'Only if you get caught,' Tony countered. 'You're sounding like the boss. We were specially selected because we're smart enough not to get caught.'

'That's so cynical,' Redvers said.

'We've all heard stories about the RCS. They're the bentest cops of all and we've got to fit right in, snouts to the trough.'

'This is a waste of time and I can't be doing with it any more,' Redvers said. 'Are you coming, Sonia?'

'Er, no. I'll see where his argument goes.'

'I've got some revision to do for college. See you tomorrow.' Redvers pushed away his drink and left. They watched his exit.

Sonia grimaced. 'Poor John. He takes himself so seriously. Couldn't he see he was being sent up?'

'Was he? How do you know?'

'Wasn't he, Tony?' she asked, holding his eyes.

'Perhaps you should have made your excuses and left too.'

'I can decide when I have to go,' she said, 'and with whom.'

'Well, that sounds hopeful,' he said.

'I'm usually a long time making up my mind – even over buying a new pair of flares. I agonize for ages about whether or not I'll go out with someone.'

'Well, as you're already out, do you want to get something to eat?'

'I had something in the canteen.'

'That was hours ago,' he pointed out.

'We could get something,' Sonia said, 'but I'll pay for myself.'

'You know you're going to drive me mad, don't you?'

That was the start of a relationship that never really was. She remained irritatingly undecided while he was naturally uncommitted. What kept him going back – apart from her blonde hair, startling blue eyes, hollow cheeks, kissable mouth and slim body – was that she wouldn't let him have sex with her. The more she resisted, the more he wanted her. He knew that the moment he did he'd lose interest, and perhaps she understood this. The swinging sixties didn't swing, as far as Sonia was concerned.

Maybe the location was the problem. Bramshill House, where the college was located, was a grand Jacobean pile that was enough to give anyone brought up in a normal house agoraphobia. Sonia had been brought up in a council house in Farnborough, Kent, and until she had gone to police training college, she'd always shared a room with her sister. Bramshill was set in hundreds of acres of its own land near Basingstoke, in rural Hampshire, so perhaps swinging Britain hadn't reached it, though they did play

Beatles records in the pub, which was a long walk from the college. And Sonia insisted on paying her share – which was boring.

John Redvers admired Superintendent Slipper and came to see him as a father figure. The older man took a close interest in the development of his protégés, driving out to the college and dropping in on lectures, looking at their written work, listening to their responses in class. His disappearance for two days had most of them commenting on his absence, but Redvers didn't need one of the lecturers to tell him that the guv'nor was in court with Jack Braden. His mother had told him so. Although she had renounced that part of her family with the same force that she had renounced the devil, she always seemed to know what they were up to. She probably knew just as much about what the devil was up to. Again and again she had told John it was his duty to smite evil, regardless of the raiment it came in. Redvers had difficulty with that concept: he instead found himself with a dangerous yearning for his extended family.

Suddenly the trial was over and Slipper turned up the next day, but he was a different man: angry to have seen Jack Braden walk free. 'Unfortunately that's the way criminals are treated nowadays, while the police are rubbished,' he told them. 'They get clever lawyers to cast aspersions on police integrity and juries believe them. We have no one to blame but ourselves. There was a time when a policeman's word stood against any criminal's. With your help we'll get back there. We'll make sure we nail this wicked man.'

He slapped a photograph of Braden to the blackboard and pinned it there. 'Study this. Make him your target.'

Redvers put up his hand – he couldn't stop himself. 'Sir, if a jury found him not guilty, don't we have to accept that?'

'If we could rely on a jury,' the super said dismissively. 'Now study these.' He pinned up photographs of Ronnie and Reggie Kray, the Richardson brothers and members of Jack Braden's gang. 'These are the men we want in the dock. In future none of them is going to walk out of court. We have to do it the right way, the fair way. When you've finished here, you'll each be assigned to one of the teams dedicated to targeting them. Commit their names and faces, with their deeds, to memory. Eat, sleep and breathe with one thought and one thought only: putting these men away where they belong.'

Redvers couldn't eat or sleep. For two whole days he was in torment over what he had to do. Jack Braden was his uncle, Brian Oldman his cousin. He was sure they had committed crimes too numerous to mention, but Jack had been found not guilty by twelve of his peers and Redvers wasn't about to dismiss them or their judgement.

Finally he summoned the courage to speak to Slipper in private. With great difficulty he said, 'I have to leave the squad, sir. I may even have to leave the police. The fact is, I know Jack Braden.'

To his surprise, Slipper was understanding. 'Are you compromised by him?'

'I don't think so, sir.'

'You don't think so? You must know, man.'

'He's my uncle, sir.'

'Well, that's pretty damn compromising in itself, Constable. Do you know anything about Braden's corrupt, illegal activities?'

'No, sir, I don't. My mother and I went to live in Manchester.'

'You're sure about that? You'd need to be more than three hundred per cent certain if I was to trust you on my squad.'

'I'm sure, sir,' Redvers said. 'I know no more than I read about them in the newspapers.'

Even so, it soon became clear that Slipper wasn't comfortable with the situation. 'It's not on your record, son,' he said. 'At some point that information will come out and be used against you. I had such high hopes for you. You're the brightest, cleverest policeman in the whole group, but blood's thicker than water, as they say. I can't allow you to be compromised. I hope you can find it in yourself to go on being a policeman. Coming forward like this indicates honesty and integrity, qualities we're sorely lacking at present.'

As Redvers stepped out of the room tears clouded his eyes. He wanted to get away from Bramshill and this special pool of bright policemen and one woman.

'But why are you going?' Sonia asked yet again, as they watched Redvers pack his bag in his neat and tidy room.

'Something's come up.' That was all he was prepared to say.

'Is it true you've been caught at it, John?' Tony Wednesday joked.

'That's not funny, Tony,' Sonia admonished him.

'Then what's the problem?'

'I really can't say. I'm sorry.'

'Fine. Be a man of mystery. I'll just give Sonia a Chinese burn and make her tell me.'

'I'll have a lot of Chinese burns then – he hasn't told me.'

'Are you leaving the job?' Tony asked. 'Is it because I keep beating you at everything?'

'I'm going back to university,' Redvers said, 'but I promise you, when I've got my degree I'll dedicate myself to putting Jack Braden and his gang where they belong.'

'You'll be lucky!' Tony said. 'They'll be long gone by the time you're done, college boy.'

They walked him down to the main entrance, where the college minibus was waiting to take him to the station. None of them had much to say to each other and for once Tony knew enough to keep quiet. He shook Redvers's hand, then watched Sonia throw her arms round him and kiss him. Not even that loosened him up. He must have been damaged by his church upbringing and Tony felt grateful for the lack of care and love in his own early life – he'd come out relatively unscathed.

For some inexplicable reason they went back up to Redvers's room and stared at the empty bed, the empty bookshelves, missing him already.

'Poor John. I thought he was going to cry. He was very upset.'

'Not half as upset as I'll be if I don't get into your pants before we leave,' Tony said, with casual indifference.

'Oh, you really know how to treat a girl.'

'You're not a girl, Son, how can you think you are?' he said. 'You're a plonk. You know what? If you're not careful the swinging sixties will have swung right past you with your single-minded dedication to catching villains.'

Sonia met his look and held it. Her eyes were fiery and at first he assumed she was angry or upset about Redvers leaving. 'Well, there's a bed here,' she said. 'The key's in the lock.'

Tony turned it with a resounding click.

When her clothes were off and they were naked on the narrow bed Sonia's bravado vanished. It was her first time, she confessed, and he was humbled. Objectively, he suspected he wasn't a good or considerate lover, more a smash-and-grab artist, getting what he wanted and leaving the woman to take what she could *en route*. Now he found himself taking time, touching and caressing her gently, stroking her first with his finger, then with his tongue . . . She came with a pleasure that quickly seemed to turn to anxiety, even terror as she shook like a leaf and cried gently, as if she feared he had caused something to break inside her. Indeed he knew he had, and nothing could put it back as it was before.

Afterwards he felt proud of his achievement, then curiously uninvolved. Soon he was impatient to put on his clothes and leave.

'Where are you going?' Sonia asked.

'To my room. I've got work to do.'

'Tony?'

'The cleaners'll want to get in here.'

The mere thought of what the Richardsons had done to him made Joey's face ache, his head ache, his jaw ache and even the nerve endings of the missing teeth ache with the memory of their being wrenched out of his gums. He had lost four during that torture.

He didn't know how he'd survived them even pulling one out without giving up the information. Someone had once said of him that he'd sooner lose his teeth than his money.

The Richardsons had got to Emil Savundra and now had a package of the bonds, which they were using to leverage investment in South Africa, so Joey couldn't use them as security for his property development. As if this wasn't causing him enough misery, Jack Braden called round most days, reminding him that they had to hurt Charlie and Eddie Richardson. It was as if he was a bit lost with Brian serving six months in Wandsworth for assault. All Joey wanted to do was push him out of the apartment and forget the Richardsons.

'They were way out of order, Joey, and they'll be taught a lesson.'

Shut it, Jack! For God's sake, shut up about those monsters, was what Joey wanted to scream at his brother-in-law. Instead, he heard himself say, 'You'll have to be so cunning about it, Jack. Yes, teach them a lesson, but set yourself up with a perfect alibi first. Otherwise you'll join Brian in prison.' He hoped.

'Like give a party at the club for a retiring policeman?' Jack smiled.

'As long as there are lots of policemen around to swear to your presence.'

'An old DCI called Winston Doodie's retiring. Bill Moody, a Superintendent we slip a bit to on the Porn Squad is laying on a party for him at the club. I'm gonna have a lot of brasses there with their tits out.'

'No, Jack,' Joey said. 'No one's going to admit to being at that sort of party. Make it one you could bring your wife or girlfriend to. Get lots of your high-profile friends there – people like Brian's chums Boothby and Driberg. Then send someone to strike at the Richardsons. Could you get those sort of people there?'

'It'll have to wait till Brian gets out. They'll all come for him.' Jack smacked his hands together. 'We do that pair of mugs, Joey, and I guarantee your jaws'll stop aching.'

*

The visiting room at Wandsworth was choked with cigarette smoke while Jack waited for Brian to come in. No fewer than seven prisoners had greeted him as he walked through, all, he guessed, seeing their status raised when he acknowledged them by name.

Brian was greeted by as many prisoners' wives when he appeared, several offering him bits of the food they'd brought in for their husbands.

'You're popular with the ladies,' Jack observed.

'And why not, when you see what most of them have to look forward to? I bring a bit of sparkle into their lives. Their husbands don't feel threatened by me.' Brian was a good-looking man, and the best dressed prisoner in the place in his navy blue trousers with the neatly pressed shirt and tie.

'What's the food like?'

'Lousy,' Brian said. 'So's the company. But you do have time to think in here, Jack, and that's good.'

'What do you think about?'

'Wanking mostly.'

Jack glanced about in case his neighbours had heard. 'Leave off, Brian. There's kids in here. They'll hear you.'

'You ever read Nietzsche?'

'What's he written? Anything worthwhile?'

'He pointed out that a lot of people will willingly risk their lives in order to promote their power. They'll fight or go to war.'

'Yeah, well, I could've told him that,' Jack said. 'He didn't have to write a book about it.'

'He saw some men as superheroes, ready to die at any age for power and greatness. What does it matter if you die at twenty-seven when you've owned the world?'

'Well, you could enjoy it a little longer,' Jack said and laughed, thinking this was a really smart answer. As far as he was concerned, this was all ballocks, but not as embarrassing as a conversation about wanking.

'What's joy?' Brian was saying. 'Nietzsche said joy and suffering are inseparable. That's what we've got to go for, Jack. Power and greatness.'

'Well we ain't exactly mugs,' Jack said, 'are we?'

'No, but we've got to have the greatest criminal gang in history. Look around, Jack,' he urged. 'It's all here, waiting for us.'

'What? In these old lags? What good're they to anyone? They've all been nicked and they'll go on that way.'

'Not if they've got superheroes leading them, Jack. There's a lot of talent in here, villains who could use some work when they get out.'

'Well, we can give them a few bob to tide them over. We ain't got no work for them.'

'You're missing the point. These blokes self-start. Give them a few quid to tide them over and they're a firm. Our firm. We'll provide the leadership. Look, I'm going to send you someone who'll do the Richardsons for us.'

'We can do them anytime,' Jack said. 'All we do is set up an alibi. I got plans for that.'

'We gotta use someone who can get near to them. Nietzsche.'

'Is that what he's called?' Jack said, with a smile.

'No, Denny Jones. He's going out about two weeks before me. Take care of him and the others I send you. Get ready to lead them.'

Jack liked that idea. Just so long as Brian didn't think it was *his* firm.

Waiting for Brian to get out, Jack gave a number of villains a few quid to get them back on their feet when they came to the club. Then Denny Jones showed up. He was the only one to get past Pongo without being announced. He was as charming as a con artist and as bright as a three-card trickster. He was lean and tanned and wore a suit that fitted him.

'How d'you get that tan?' Jack asked.

'I had a south-facing cell.'

Jack thought he was taking the piss. He didn't like smart-alecs. 'Straight up. I had a top bunk and I'd pull it in front of the window. I had to keep moving in case I got stripes on my boat race!'

Still Jack didn't know if he was joking. 'What d'you do when you're not getting a tan, Denny?'

'Armed robbery's my real game. If it moves and has got money in it, I'll have it. Or try.'

'How come you palled out with Brian? You're not an iron, are you?'

'Leave off. He's a diamond. He pulled me out of a bit of bother with one of the Krays' blokes – George Cornell. Brian's got all them screws running around him like blue-arsed flies. He really knows how to get into their heads. He said you got a bit of bother with the Richardsons.'

'Nothing we can't handle.'

'I'll help you out any time. I hate them.'

'Why? What they do to you?'

'Nothing.' He lit a cigarette and blew smoke, then said quietly, 'They put electrodes on my brother's balls, made him tell them where the dosh he had from a Securicor van was.'

'That's Charlie and Eddie's trademark, all right.'

'When Brian gets out I'd like to help do them for my brother, Jack. For free,' Denny Jones said. 'It won't be long now.'

'Why ain't you dressed?' Jack said to Leah, as she walked through the flat in a crumpled nightdress and slippers, her face bare of makeup.

'I'm not going to your party,' she said. 'It's a bunch of thugs.'

'It's not like that. They're all respectable, these people.'

'Like you,' she countered.

'Yes, like me. The party's to celebrate Brian's release from prison.'

'I can't,' she whispered, on the edge of tears. 'Please don't make me.'

'I want you there with me, Leah. It ain't much to ask.'

She was shaking her head, getting more and more agitated.

Moods came on her like this – one moment she'd be glassy-eyed and lethargic, the next ranting. He couldn't take much more of it. 'I told you, Brian won't touch you, Leah. He won't.'

'You just don't get it, do you?' Leah screeched. 'You don't. You never will.' She ran through the flat, smacking things off tables and shelves, breaking them.

'Stop it!' Jack shouted. 'Just don't give me ache, Leah. Get fucking dressed and make yourself presentable or I'll give you worse than ever Brian done.'

'Why don't you just kill me and make my life easier?'

'For what use you are to me you might as well be dead.'

'Then why don't you let me go?' she screamed. 'Why? Why?'

'Leah,' he said, 'you got to understand. I ain't ever going to let you go.'

Such statements always punched her panic button.

'Then I'll kill myself,' Leah said, and snatched up a shard of glass from a broken vase in the fireplace.

Jack was ready for her and slapped her hard as she turned to him, sending her sprawling across an armchair, tipping it over. He threw it aside easily, grabbed her and slapped her again, then again. 'I'll kill you first,' he warned, and hit her as she tried to fight back. He was on top of her on the carpet, holding her wrists. Her nightdress had ridden up showing her bare legs and panties. He felt immediate sexual desire for her. It was a long while since they had made love. Too long.

'No!' she shrieked. 'No!' She struggled more as he stripped off her panties, forced her legs apart and freed his hard cock from the tangle of pants and trousers. 'No!' she cried, but he wasn't listening. His needs were far more pressing.

'Where's Leah?' Joey asked, as he came into the club – Jack was standing at the bottom of the stairs to greet his guests. Joey was wearing the double-breasted dinner jacket Brian had said his father had bought from the widow of one of his tenants. His new teeth were shiny white to match his shirt. 'Is she here, Jack?' he pressed. 'I've got a message from Catherine.'

'She's not well,' Jack told him. 'And where's Cath? I thought she was coming with you.'

'She's not too good either. She's been overdoing it.'

'But this is Brian's party,' Jack said. 'Margaret Courtney's here – everyone is.'

'She's been working non-stop for the Tory Party, trying to cover the blot Brian made in her copybook. No job was too big or too small for her,' Joey told him. 'She wants him to come and work with me in property development, now, give up the life.'

'Why would he do that? He's got power here.'

'Catherine sees it as a way for him to redeem himself. This is no life for him, Jack. He's not suited to it.'

Jack waved his hand impatiently to shush him as a comedian started to tell a joke about a policeman who had caught two lovers at it in the back of a car. In the hush that fell over the club two voices were heard in competition with the comedian's. They belonged to Denny Jones and Brian, who were having a row for everyone to hear.

'You're not only stupid,' Brian was shouting, 'you're drunk and stupid, and tomorrow you'll still be stupid and probably drunk as well.'

'Well, you're just a fairy,' Denny Jones said, and took a wild swing at Brian, then crashed to the floor.

'Take him to the gents',' Brian told Pongo. 'Put his head down the bog and sober him up. I don't know why Jack wants ex-cons like this around him.'

'Is that what he is?' asked Lord Boothby, who was close by. He was wide-eyed – an attitude he adopted quite often. 'Is he reformed, Brian?'

'Oh, yeah, like me, Bob,' Brian joked.

'Goodness, I hope you've not entirely mended your ways!'

Margaret Courtney came over, drawn to the commotion. 'Are you all right?' she asked. When Brian told her he was, she enquired if it had been too awful for him in prison. 'How might the government improve the experience?'

'The only way they could do that is by going to prison for a short while themselves and seeing what it's like,' Brian told her.

'The way some of them are behaving,' Margaret Courtney riposted, 'it could be for a long while!' Everyone laughed.

'Prison could be counted a success, Margaret,' Boothby said. 'This dear boy was studying Nietzsche.'

Jack caught Brian's eye and slipped out to the toilets. There, Pongo was unlocking the window so that Denny Jones, sober now, could climb out and back unseen. 'You all set, Denny?' Jack asked.

'All apart from the shooter.'

Jack took a .32 calibre pistol tied in a handkerchief from his jacket pocket and gave it to him. Denny undid it. The handle was bound with sticky insulating tape so there'd be no prints.

'They're definitely down at Mr Smith's, are they, Jack?'

'That's the word. They're tryna nick the club off the Haywards. If you can pop them both, Denny, there's a bonus. We'll make sure you got an alibi here. Get back as soon as you can.' He watched Pongo boost the villain out of the window.

The party at Jack's club was in full swing when word arrived about a shooting at Mr Smith's in Catford. Two people were dead.

'Is it our dogs what are down?' Jack asked.

'Someone copped it, for sure,' came Denny's reply over the phone. 'I'm not sure if I clipped the Richardsons. There was a lot of confusion when the shooter come out.'

'They'd get the message, though,' Jack said, feeling elated. 'Come back here as soon as you can.'

An hour or so later the apparently drunken Denny Jones was in the middle of the floor with his arm round Brian, urging Joe Brown and the Bruvvers to sing another number.

At the case conference Superintendent Slipper had called his message was clear: it was time to move against these thugs and take them off the street. 'Get out there and get information,' he told his young Robbery Squad, operating out of Scotland Yard. 'Make deals with criminals if you have to, find witnesses who won't be afraid to give evidence against them.'

The first they found was Denny Jones, named by an informant as the person who had done the shooting. He stated he was nowhere near Mr Smith's at the time. 'I was at Jack Braden's club all night.'

'Then you'll have plenty of alibi witnesses,' DCI George Fenwick said. He had been newly promoted to the so-called 'Porn Squad.'

'Well, someone musta seen me.'

Tony Wednesday decided he was blessed with second-sight. He knew how this would end before it had even started and had said as much to Slipper. As a result he and the superintendent were walking to the House of Lords to interview Lord Boothby.

'Yes, I did see him. I believe I even spoke to him. He's the redeemed convict who had a row with Brian Oldman,' Boothby told them.

Tony Wednesday almost laughed at his naïveté – and such people were helping to run the country. Margaret Courtney and a half-dozen more people supported the alibi that Denny Jones had been at the club all night.

Slipper was frustrated beyond words. 'I wish that lying bugger had shot the Richardsons at Mr Smith's. Wouldn't that have saved the taxpayers a lot of money? They can't keep on getting away with this, Tony. I promise you they aren't going to get away with it much longer.'

Later on, Tony Wednesday was talking to DCI Fenwick, who confessed to having been one of the guests at the club. He offered him the name of someone who might help: 'A villain called Johnny Bradbury. Charlie Richardson sent him out to South Africa to talk to a business rival. Unlike Denny Jones, this one's seen the light. He hasn't any love for the Richardsons.'

'Why tell me?' Tony Wednesday said. 'Tell the superintendent.'

'You're the new élite. He'll believe you and won't blame you if you strike out.'

'Will this villain come back from South Africa to give evidence, Tony?' Slipper asked.

'There's a good chance he might, sir. Unlike Denny Jones, he had a true change of heart. He'll know what they're up to.'

The superintendent thought about that, then nodded to himself. 'Have you got a passport, Tony?'

'No, sir. I've never been outside the country.'

'Well, you'd best get yourself one. We'll go to South Africa, interview Mr Bradbury and drag him back here if we have to.' Suddenly his face was bright in the belief that the case was breaking.

'How come you get to go?' Sonia asked later that evening.

'Perhaps the super fancies me,' Tony said.

'He's not the only one. You might be gone a long while.' She reached out and kissed him. All their sexual activity was initiated by Sonia nowadays. None of it was as exciting as going after crims, as Slipper called them.

TWENTY-FIVE

Although Brian loved the life and the freedom it gave him, Jack's instability that bordered on madness caused him to worry about the future. Could there be any future? Brian wasn't sure what had made his uncle flip, but it was probably that he was popping too many pills. However, when he accused him of taking whatever the head doctors were pouring into Leah, Jack went berserk and they would have come to blows. Without Pongo there to calm him down the situation would have been worse. The stocky black minder was a good, steadying influence on Jack. He didn't say much, but when he did, it seemed to count for something with him.

The call Brian got from Pongo warned him that Jack was on his way round, looking for a gun. Paul Raymond, the strip-club owner, was the object of his fury this time. Brian placed a few objects strategically around the flat with which he could whack his uncle if need be – a leather sap, a truncheon, knuckle-dusters and a meat cleaver.

'You got a gun?' Jack said, as soon as he was through the door. He was as high as a kite. 'You must have.'

'You know I don't, Jack. What do I need a gun for? I like a cleaver.'

'We gotta shoot Paul Raymond. Teach him a lesson. He's cheating us. We'll take him out to Fat Boy's pig farm at Stoke Poges and pop him.'

'What sort of lesson's that if he's dead? He won't earn us a penny.'

'It'll learn others.'

'Calm down, Jack. Okay? Jimmy Humphreys looks after us there.'

'Paul Raymond's doing him.'

'Jack, stop this,' Brian ordered. 'Now.' He glanced at the weapon nearest to hand. A set of brass knuckle-dusters. Not his favourite.

'Humphreys is in with him. He is. Get a gun.'

At first Brian had been amused by Jack's paranoia; now he was increasingly alarmed by it. He was almost as mad as his girlfriend. Pongo was worried too, but he was loyal. All he would say was that Jack was popping a lot of pills. He didn't know what they were. Anything that was around and that people would bring him, Brian guessed.

'We're getting a good pension out of his Revue Bar. It practically runs itself, trouble-free, with Jimmy Humphreys's help.' He watched Jack pacing about. 'Where's Pongo? Is he minding you? Look, I don't want you on the street on your own.'

'Am I one of your girls?' Jack said. 'I gotta find a piece.' He rushed out of the flat.

'Is he cracking up, Brian?' DCI Fenwick asked, when Brian consulted him. The RCS inspector always had shrewd advice. 'If he did shoot Raymond there'd be all sorts of ructions.'

'If he don't get sorted soon I think he might do it.'

'There'd be no help from us if he did.'

'Do you think Ken Drury would do anything?'

'He might, but I doubt it, Bri. He's a lazy duffer at the best of times. Now he's a commander, anything that looks like trouble he steers well away. It's Superintendent Slipper who might cause some aggro. Especially if he manages to nick the Richardsons. Then he'll start looking elsewhere. And the twins might do something to protect Raymond – he gives them money too.'

'Jimmy said he did. That's why Jack doesn't think enough comes our way,' Brian told him. They were in his Camden Town flat, parcelling out money. George Fenwick collected money for a lot of corrupt policemen, including the whole of Drury's Porn Squad.

Jimmy Humphreys screamed and screamed at Jack, begging him not to shoot Raymond when he thrashed through the empty bar after the club-owner, throwing aside chairs and tables and waving a small handgun. Some dancers, practising with their clothes on, stopped, uncertain what to do. Like most people in this netherworld, their instinct wasn't to call the police.

'Jack,' Brian cautioned, coming in off the rain-soaked Soho street with Pongo, 'Jimmy's right. This is crazy.'

'Then we got to weigh him off, too,' Jack said, throwing chairs off a table to get a better view of Raymond.

'The easiest solution is to pay more money,' the club-owner said, putting up his palms, a little leather handbag dangling from his wrist.

That wasn't satisfactory to Jack. In this mood nothing would satisfy him quite like killing the sharply dressed, coiffured Paul Raymond.

'What d'you think you're gonna do? Give us a fiver each and send us on our way?' Jack said, pulling back the hammer and pointing the gun at Raymond's head.

'Jack!' Jimmy Humphreys screamed. 'No! No!'

Paul Raymond crossed himself, then lunged crazily at Jack. It was like a scene from Bedlam, and all Brian could do was duck as Jack fired.

There was a terrified shriek, then hysterical crying. The bullet had hit one of the dancers, who was standing frozen, too scared to move. When the dust settled and the screaming stopped, Brian learnt she was called Rita Webb. The small-calibre bullet had cut through the calf muscle in her left leg. 'Talk about mad, Jack. Good hit! What d'we do now?' Brian asked.

Jack's mood suddenly dropped. 'I don't know. Make sure this monkey pays for a decent doctor,' he said, jerking his thumb at Raymond.

DCI Fenwick had been entirely wrong about Ken Drury running for cover at the first sign of trouble, but he didn't bother to tell Jack.

Two days after the shooting, Drury came in to see Jack at his club. 'Your days are numbered, duck,' he said. 'You can't go around threatening respectable businessmen with guns.'

'Paul Raymond's a ponce and a thief.'

'Jack,' Brian cautioned. He thought his uncle was about to fly at the corpulent policeman when all he wanted him to do was shut up, but that wasn't Jack's way and never would be.

'Let him rip his mouth off,' Drury said. 'It's only a matter of time, duck.'

'And for you,' Jack said, sticking a finger in his face.

Brian saw Drury tense and knew he was ready for a fight. With a policeman this senior that was bad news. Jack had got away with beating him once. He wouldn't again.

'You can't go round protecting mugs like that for ever, not when they're stealing our money.'

'Let me tell you this,' Ken Drury said. 'The Richardsons are about to be nicked over the Mr Smith's affray. When that happens, you're next.'

Jack hooked him in the throat, putting him down.

Brian leapt on Jack to stop him following through – he didn't want him making the situation worse. But Jack threw him off and pressed in menacingly on the policeman. 'You mug,' he bellowed. 'Don't you ever come in here threatening a respectable businessman again!'

'You're a big-headed ponce, that's all,' Drury said foolishly.

As Jack moved in for the kill Brian hit him on the side of the head with the flat blade of his cleaver. He knew then that either Drury had to go or Jack did. George Fenwick was the man to advise on how that could be achieved.

DCI Fenwick was one of a number of policemen who had managed to run as successfully with the hares as he did with the hounds, keeping both reasonably happy. He was on Slipper's special team piling up the evidence on the Richardsons. Commander Drury, as head of the department, kept a watching brief.

'He came in the other day and addressed us about your little firm – Jack's firm, he called it,' Fenwick told Brian.' Said you're terrorizing respectable businessmen in the West End. He advised us to forget certain witnesses who we thought might give evidence against you.'

'Like who?' Brian asked.

'Mostly club-owners. People we'd struggle with. Drury knows them all. I pulled him afterwards to get the full SP. I pointed out it could be well involved, nicking Jack.'

'A lot of Old Bill might have to go as well,' Brian said.

'That's not how Ken Drury sees it. He reckons we can't be nicked. He said, 'Who's going to believe a criminal against the word of a policeman?'

Brian began to think Drury was as mad as Jack – perhaps he was popping a load of pills as well. Believing you were untouchable, no matter what you did, was madness. Maybe now was the time to get out. Get out to what, though? His lifestyle was like a drug habit, one he wasn't sure he could break, even though he knew it was life-threatening. Nietzsche's will to power didn't take account of that, or what to do about the emptiness of life without power and greatness. Beyond his involvement with the firm, Brian saw only emptiness – and it frightened him.

Tony Wednesday knew that nothing happened by chance, and wondered why he had been removed at the last minute from the section of the Robbery Squad he had started with and put with DCI Fenwick's lot. There were whispers that George Fenwick was at it, which would be ironic if it was true, placed as he was in a position of considerable trust. Then he thought about whether it was because Sonia was in his old squad and someone was concerned he'd be distracted, worrying about her. Finally he decided this was a means of testing him. That was Fenwick's style.

'What corrupt policemen do you know, Tony?' Fenwick casually asked, as they strode across the road from Scotland Yard to St James's Park Underground station. They were on their way to Parkhurst prison on the Isle of Wight. He pushed through the barrier and went down the stairs without buying a ticket. He grinned back at Tony.

'Are there such policemen, guv?' Tony said, following his lead. 'I've never met any.'

'Haven't you? Maybe you haven't got your eyes open, son. Superintendent Slipper's got a forty-foot yacht moored at Cowes. We can have a look at it when we get to the island. Or do you think his old mum buys de-luxe Christmas crackers? Then there's Commander Drury. He's so bent they call him Hairpin Drury. Just about everyone who works with him is at it.'

'How could they possibly get away with it, guv?' Tony said, looking for all the world as if he was just off the boat. How much of this, if any, was true? And what was he supposed to do with the information?

'In this job, everyone learns to watch everyone else's back,' Fenwick said.

'Superintendent Slipper brought us in because we're not tainted, sir,' Tony pointed out.

'That's right. Let's see if we can't keep you that way.'

The prisoner they went to visit was a robber called David Crutwell. The hope was that he might give evidence against the Richardsons.

'It's a nice idea,' Crutwell said, in the tiny room used for legal visitors. He was a bulky man in his thirties with a deeply pockmarked face and a large nose, that he picked unselfconsciously. 'I dream of the day they go down. Especially if they come here. They'll get slaughtered, the thieving bastards, along with Jack Braden and his poofy nephew. They steal off hardworking villains.' He sounded bitter.

'I hear they give Old Bill money to stay free while you go down for a long one,' Tony said, glancing at Fenwick.

'Oh, yeah? Which Old Bill? I could use some of that.'

'Won't help you now, David,' Fenwick said.

The con gave the impression that he was thinking about this, then said, 'What do I get out of it? Do I walk?'

'It's not likely, David. You were on that train robbery with Biggsy.'

'Yeah. He's out,' Crutwell said.

Tony Wednesday glanced at the senior detective again, then seized the initiative. 'Give us some names and you could go the same way,' he told him. 'But you'd be on your own, of course, taking your chances with staying at liberty.'

'You helped Biggsy in that way?' the surprised Crutwell said. 'The cunning bastard. He kept well closed up about that.'

'That was part of the deal,' Tony lied coolly.

'Steady on, Tony,' Fenwick said, getting in on the act. 'Let's not promise anything we can't necessarily deliver.'

'Come on,' Crutwell said eagerly. 'Could you get me out?'

Tony waited, but the DCI gave no signal of where he should go next. They seemed to have this con exactly where they wanted him. It was amazing how easily such villains were duped. Then he guessed that if you'd been banged up for a long while, with a lot further to go, you clung to any line that might jump-start your life. He'd feel that way after only weeks in this hole, he was sure.

'You could go like Biggsy – over the wall. Unofficially.'

Crutwell grabbed at the lifeline. 'That'll do me.'

'Just how the hell do you think such a thing might be arranged, Tony?' Superintendent Slipper wanted to know.

'I've no idea, sir,' Tony said, with a smile, 'but if we want to make a real breakthrough on these gangs we've got to be imaginative.'

'We could string him along with that promise,' Fenwick said, 'then not deliver.' They were in Slipper's fourth-floor office at Scotland Yard.

'That would be the last info we'd get from any of them, guv,' Tony said firmly.

'Both games will be equally dangerous,' Slipper mused. 'How valuable is Crutwell's information?'

'He'd be a strong witness against the Richardsons. They tortured him for his share of the train-robbery money. Possibly Jack Braden's outfit did the same,' Fenwick said.

'Then let's play him for all he's worth.'

Suddenly Tony was a major player in the drama, not just someone who carried messages, like most young detectives. On his next trip to the island with Fenwick, he said, 'Let's take a look at the super's yacht, shall we?'

Moored in Cowes harbour with hundreds of other boats, some much bigger, it was less impressive than the DCI had implied. The sleek, varnished mahogany hull, with a small wheelhouse aft and an equally small cabin, didn't seem to offer much comfort.

'It's a racing sloop,' Fenwick explained. 'He sometimes sails with the Duke of Edinburgh and the Tory MP Ted Health.'

'You reckon he's bent, guv?' Tony asked.

'What do you think?'

Right then Tony wasn't about to commit himself. He wanted to see more evidence.

'Did Biggsy get out of prison with this sort of help?' Crutwell asked, as he paced the small room. Apparently the thought of getting out made him restless.

'He didn't put up names,' Tony said. 'He went in to corrupt police officers.'

'Yeah, he got a lion's share. Him and the geezer who helped set up the blag.'

'Who was the other organizer, David?' Tony asked.

'Roy the Weasel is all I know – we all got nicknames on the blag.'

'That won't even get you on to the gardening party,' Tony said sharply, 'much less over the wall.'

Crutwell stopped and stared at him. 'What do you want to know?' he said.

Tony glanced at the DCI, as if seeking his permission. 'How the Richardsons were involved.'

'I don't think they were. Biggsy and Roy the Weasel went to them early on, but they didn't think you could stop a train.'

'How was Jack Braden involved?'

'He was up for it, but got himself nicked. When he went inside they cut him out.'

'None of that helps you very much, David.'

'They swagged our shares off us – give us sweet FA,' Crutwell said bitterly.

'Who did? Braden's lot?'

'No, the Richardsons, the wicked bastards.'

'Did they torture you, David?'

Crutwell closed his eyes, the memory still painful.

On the ferry going back to the mainland, Fenwick joined Tony on the aft deck with two pints of bitter. He said he thought Tony was wise beyond his years in the ways of coppering. At that Tony felt a real sense of pride, as is he'd received an accolade beyond the gongs policemen wore on their tunics. 'I was schooled for it from an early age.'

'Yeah, your dad was a copper, wasn't he?'

Tony said yes, feeling no inclination to correct him as to his relationship with Sergeant Watling. He enjoyed hiding behind wrong details about himself and decided to make a point of never correcting it.

'Who was it you went to see in South Africa?' Fenwick asked. 'Johnny Bradbury?'

'Who?' Tony said. Superintendent Slipper had asked him not to tell anyone. Perhaps the super was testing him through Fenwick.

'The Richardsons have got the ache with Bradbury. They want him to stay shtum,' Fenwick continued. He smiled, and Tony knew what that meant.

For John Redvers law held all the answers. It was precise, objective, unemotional. He'd never been happier than when he was studying at Birkbeck College. In the whole three-year course he didn't miss a single lecture. Now it was coming to an end and he was sad.

Possibly, too, it was coming to an end with Elaine Stone, the law student he had been going out with for two years. Elaine was almost as dedicated to her studies as he was. She was short, with a round face and frizzy hair that she didn't bother to straighten like other girls. Not bothered about fashion, she didn't go in for minis either. There were other good things about her, one being her independence: she didn't want to hang around and distract him.

'What's wrong, John?' she asked, sitting on his bed with her ankles crossed and her knees pulled up to her full breasts.

He pretended he didn't understand what she was talking about, but guessed it was to do with the end of college life and the uncertainty it created. They had made love today, the last Thursday of their final term, not their usual Saturday night. Perhaps that had unsettled her.

'Life isn't very satisfactory,' she said. 'Maybe it is for you.'

'I don't understand,' he said. 'You've got your law degree and it's bar school now.'

'That's so typically male and goal-oriented,' she said, leaping off the bed and reaching for her clothes. 'What do I have to do? Go off to the King's Road, pick up a hippie and shag him?'

He'd missed something here. Had there been a conversation to which he hadn't paid attention because he was thinking about a legal conundrum? 'I don't know what you want from me, Elaine.'

'Don't you? Jesus Christ, we've had this offhand relationship for most of our time at college, but I don't know you, John. Oh, I know your name, how old you are, that you're a police inspector and ambitious. But I don't know what excites you, frightens you or moves you. You seem afraid of emotion.'

'That's ridiculous,' he said, taking offence. 'You're a trained lawyer. Why aren't you more in control of yours?'

'Right now I don't want to be. I want to explode with excitement and passion before I die of frustration. I don't want to get to eighty, look back on my life and find it's full of regrets about things I didn't do, didn't experience and didn't feel.'

'I do feel.'

'Do you, John? What the hell is it you feel? Nothing much for me.'

'Well, what do you want?' Redvers asked. 'Do you want to get married? Is that it?'

'Probably, and probably I want to have children. But only with someone who feels passion, who can experience the moment.'

'That sounds like you don't want to marry me,' Redvers said.

'What if I said let's go out and celebrate, have a wild time? Let's go to the Pheasantry in the King's Road, smoke pot and get squiffy.'

'I'd like to know my results before I celebrate.'

'Oh, I bet you would.'

'Anyway, that's hardly my idea of a wild time,' Redvers said.

'That's my point. After all this while, John, I still don't know what is. Getting a hundred per cent in an exam?'

'I'm a policeman. I can't afford to behave irresponsibly – smoking pot is against the law. You ought to know better than to consider it.'

'Well, maybe. But what's life without risk? I really can't stay with you until we get to eighty, sad and regretful. I'm sorry, John. I'm not going to see you any more.'

'Oh, I see,' Redvers said stiffly. 'But we've just made love.'

'Yes. I'd sort of decided it would be the last time when I came here.'

'Oh, I see,' he said again.

'Oh, I see,' Elaine echoed, imitating him.

When she did that Redvers wanted to slap her. If he did, he knew he'd never see her again. She was too liberated for that. He was rather hoping this wasn't really the end.

'Unfortunately you don't see, John. That's your big problem. All you see is what's directly in front of you. I'm sorry, but it's true.' Finished dressing, She picked up her handbag and left.

Redvers was startled, but made no move to stop her. Maybe he should have done. He'd believed they had a solid relationship – he'd been thinking about asking her to go to Manchester with him to meet his mother. Instead he decided to read some of the case files the police had sent him.

'What do you make of DCI Fenwick?' Tony said, during a break in the music. He was in the 2i's coffee bar in Old Compton Street with Sonia. Freddie and the Dreamers were struggling to make an exit and conversations were starting up, the chink of coffee cups competing with the buzz.

'D'you ever stop thinking about work, Tony?'

'Of course. I couldn't think about it when that group was playing,' he replied. 'But I'm a detective, Son. I look at people and think, Are they at it? Most of them are, of course.'

'You think everyone's got an ulterior motive?'

'Don't tell me you don't?'

'Of course. Why would I? Life's too short.'

'Then why are you a plonk?' Tony asked, using the derogatory term she accepted but didn't enjoy.

'So I could stalk you. Why else?' she said.

'So what do you think of Fenwick?'

'Well, he certainly fancies himself as a lady's man with his high-heeled boots and all that Old Spice aftershave. And the way he sometimes looks at women – "Well, here I am, baby, waiting for you."'

'Yeah, well, that's policemen. D'you think he's at it?'

'Not with me he's not.'

'D'you know what, Son. I think you're a lot shrewder than you crack on,' he said patronizingly.

She didn't come back at him. Instead, she looked away to the little stage where someone was adjusting the sound equipment. 'If I was, why'd I let myself get pregnant?'

A long silence followed. They watched the man trying to position the mikes so they wouldn't obscure the singers.

'Tony?' Sonia said. 'Say something.'

'Why did you?'

'I was crazy enough to fall for an obsessive detective.'

'Can there be any other kind?'

Sonia looked away again.

'So, do you know any reliable abortionists?'

Tony could hear the brittleness in her words, her voice cracking. He wondered if she would cry. 'Plenty. I got a whole book of them. You never know when an abortionist will come in handy.'

'Fuck you, Tony, I'm serious,' she said. 'I'm going to need someone, something.'

'Why would you want one of them creeps poking around?' he asked.

'Why do you think?'

'You didn't answer the question, Sonia.'

'Well, I can't see you wanting to get married,' she said hesitantly. 'But at least you didn't say, "Is it mine?"'

Tony held her eyes until she glanced away. Then she turned back suddenly. 'You bastard. You thought it.'

'No,' he lied smoothly. 'I was thinking you wouldn't be mug enough to go with anyone else, not with me around. You know how I came to be found?'

'The romantic butter-box baby dumped on the orphanage doorstep.'

'Almost. I don't think there was a box – I was just wrapped in an old blanket and left in the street. Nothing so romantic as the orphanage doorstep.'

'At least your mother didn't go with a black man, Tony.'

Tony thought about that. There were plenty of them about after the war – plenty now, and more arriving all the time. He glanced across the coffee bar and saw a black man he was certain was dealing drugs of some sort – purple hearts, probably. He nodded in his direction. 'Do you fancy nicking him? He'd be a pushover.'

'Call in the local coppers if you want. I'm off for the night.'

He shrugged, letting the dealer have a free ride. 'If you can't find an abortionist, I wouldn't want my kid to end up in an orphanage, like I did.'

'Well, I s'pose I could get that old policeman you're always on about to keep an eye on him.'

'Oh, you think it's a boy, do you?' Tony was taken with the idea of having a son.

'I've got a strong feeling about it.'

'I got some bad news for you, Sonia.' He waited. 'Sergeant Watling popped his clogs – kidney failure. Keeled over on his allotment. No one noticed him until that bossy cow he married got fed up with keeping his supper hot.'

'Oh, Tony, I'm sorry,' she said. 'Why didn't you say?'

'What could you have done? Given him one of yours?' Tony said callously. 'As he ain't around I'll look out for the little sprog. I don't want him growing up like me, a bastard.'

'A real romantic bastard, Tony.'

'Well, is that yes? Or d'you want my list of abortionists?'

It was Sonia's turn to keep him on the hook, and he noticed he was sweating. Finally she leant into him and kissed his lips.

'Be your best man?' DCI Fenwick said. 'You sure it's yours?'

That offended Tony, but he wasn't sure why. Perhaps because it cast aspersions on Sonia, or him, with the suggestion that he wasn't man enough for her. Perhaps this was what love was, not some overwhelming rush of emotion. 'Unless it's yours, guv,' Tony snapped back.

'I'd like to have paid a visit. Sonia's a cracking looker.'

'Well, what d'you say?'

'What can I say? I'm your man. Where you going on your honeymoon?'

'Hadn't thought about it. Back to work, I s'pose,' Tony said. 'I can't afford much else.'

'Well, I've got an idea. Why don't you combine work and pleasure?

A pal of mine's got a blinding gaff in Marbella, a villa on a hill overlooking a golf course. 'S got a pool, palms in the garden and orange trees. Sean Connery lives just along the road. You could have a game of golf with him.'

'Where's the collar involved?' Tony wanted to know. 'Do I have to dig the garden or something?'

'Ken Drury went out there a couple of times. You could dig around, see what you come up with. Might help us nick these villains.'

'Is the owner of this place a criminal?'

'Oh, well retired now, Tony,' Fenwick said. 'He's respectable, got a lot of Spanish property he lets. You'll need a bit of money to go away with.'

'What you going to do – have a whip-round?'

'Better than that, son,' DCI Fenwick said, and winked.

He took Tony to a new club in South Kensington that Jack Braden and his nephew had taken from its owner. Like most such places it was very different by day, without customers and noise, booze and pills swilling around. Jack Braden came out to the bar in his shirtsleeves. He was bleary-eyed, unshaven, and looked as if he hadn't slept much. He was about the same height as Tony but putting on a bit of weight now. Still quite handy in a fight, he'd heard.

'George tells me you're the man what's helping put the Richardsons away?' he said.

Tony laughed. 'Well, hardly, Mr Braden. That was mostly down to a bloke called Johnny Bradbury. I was just one of the team who went to interview him and brought him back from South Africa. He was a blinding witness.'

'You're too modest, son. You're the one with the slippery tongue what got them talking, right?'

'It wasn't hard,' Tony said. 'You treat people as bad as the Richardsons did, no one's ever going to have a good word to say for you, not if the circumstances are right.' They had worked hard at contriving the right circumstances; careful preparation paid dividends. He glanced at George Fenwick, who had given them Bradbury, but he said nothing. Tony wondered why.

'That's right, Tony. You treat people royally, they do right by you. You wanna pop through and find Brian, George?' Jack said to Fenwick. 'He wants a word.'

'I need a word with him, too.' Fenwick walked away.

When he'd gone, Braden moved behind the bar. He opened a drawer and started to count some money. 'We like to treat our friends royally. I bet you didn't know Princess Margaret's a friend of mine.'

'I saw you together in the *Daily Mail*.'

'That's right. She's a diamond – supports our boy's boxing charity. Here, there's a twoer, Tony. A bit of spending money for your honeymoon in Spain.'

'Two hundred pounds is a lot of money, Mr Braden,' Tony said, making no move to take the cash.

'See it as a wedding present – George said your new wife's very pretty.'

'Some people might see it as a bribe, me being a police officer.'

'You ain't doing nothing for me, are you?' Jack said. 'I didn't ask for nothing. Only that you have a happy marriage – like me.'

'Do you know a policeman called Drury?' Tony said.

'What is this? A get-up?' He waited. 'Yeah, I've heard of him.'

'Have you had any dealings with him?'

'This is a get-up!'

'He's a very corrupt policeman,' Tony said.

'So someone told me.'

'There'd be a lot of satisfaction in the Met if we could nick him.'

'Tony, you nick Ken Drury,' Jack Braden said solemnly, 'there'd be a lot more than a twoer on the table. He's been the bane of my life – and most other businessmen in the West End.'

'D'you wanna help us?' Tony invited.

'George Fenwick said you was shrewd and ambitious. That's a

dangerous mixture, but I like you, son. I'll ask around. Have a drink, enjoy your honeymoon. When you come back, maybe I'll have something for you. I gotta see a man about a dog.'

Walking to the car, Fenwick said, 'What did he bung you for your holiday, Tony? Anything worthwhile?'

'Was that what was supposed to happen, guv?' Tony said, knowing instinctively that he shouldn't let anyone know what he was getting. 'It's as well he didn't. He's interested in someone nicking Commander Drury. He's been taking money off Braden.'

'I'm sure he is, Tony,' Fenwick said with a smile. 'A lot of villains want to stop effective coppers. It won't happen, son.'

He climbed into the car and started the engine. Tony paused at the front passenger door to glance back at the club, the entrance indicated by a switched-off neon arrow pointing downstairs. He didn't know how he'd nick this little firm but he was determined to find a way.

TWENTY-SIX

Forces were plotting against him. Jack knew it in every bone of his body. Rumours were rife about action the police were planning. There had been such an air of confidence around Old Bill since Charlie and Eddie Richardson were weighed off, each with life. Even those who came in with their hands out looked at him in a way that said, 'You're next, sunshine.' All the while villains, most of whom were robbers, were piling into their little firm getting handouts, getting drunk. Jack wondered when they would see some return on this investment Brian insisted on making. Most of them weren't heavies who could frighten people into paying to be looked after or get rid of the punks who tried to row in. Instead they were men who operated best in balaclavas with sawn-off shotguns. Jack was ready to close down that branch of the firm and sack the lot of them. But each time he suggested it Brian argued that they would come good: they were plotting and would make money.

Right then Jack needed something to pick himself up. He was fed up playing games with Pongo, who was hiding the drugs from him. He hid them from Pongo, then couldn't remember where he'd put them.

When he glanced up from searching the drawers of the little desk in the office, he saw his minder rolling down the narrow corridor towards him to tell him he shouldn't have any more pills. He didn't know why he didn't just sack the black bastard. Then he remembered. Pongo was the only one he trusted.

'Jack!' Pongo said urgently. 'Sammy Cohen's come to see you. He's in the club.'

'What's happened? Has something happened to my Leah?'

'He said it's Leah he's got to talk to you about.'

'I need something for my headache, Pongo,' Jack said. 'Where you put my tablets?'

'It's the pills what are causing the headaches, Jack,' Pongo said kindly. 'You should lay off them, man.'

'What are you, a doctor suddenly? Find them pills before I throw you out on your ear. Where's Sammy?'

He walked out and along the corridor to find the wizened old tailor waiting by the bar in the empty club, looking for all the world like he needed an undertaker.

'What's the problem, Sammy?' He went behind the bar to resume his search.

'Is Brian around?' the old man asked, without preliminary greeting.

'What do you want with him?'

'Why would I want the time of day from him? I wouldn't care if I never saw him again.'

'Well, that's easy,' Jack said, his hand falling on some pills wrapped in silver foil. He couldn't remember what they were but swallowed one anyway. 'Just don't come here. He ain't likely to go over to Theobald's Road. Carnaby Street is where he gets kitted out nowadays.' He felt a rush of something and enjoyed the sensation, losing the words that the man before him was saying. All he saw was the thin, pale lips moving. He brought his mind back to the moment.

'I come here as a father to beg you to let Leah go.'

'Go where, old man? What you talking about? Why would she want to go anywhere? I give her everything she wants.'

'Jack, she has been studying. Such studies. Such a brain. She gets the highest grades.'

'It's a bloody correspondence course.'

'The professor can't give her higher grades than he does already. He said she must apply to Cambridge University. Do I dream this?

I do not. My Leah, such a bright girl. She must go to this great university.'

'I don't want her going nowhere,' Jack said. 'I told her, studying's all right, I don't mind her doing a bit of that, but she ain't going nowhere else.'

'But, Jack,' Sammy Cohen remonstrated, 'she must. This is something she must do. Don't deny my Leah such a chance. I'm an old man. Soon I may die. Let me see my girl happy before I die. Never has she had a moment's happiness in all her life.'

That hit Jack with great force. 'What you saying, you lying kyke? She's happy where she is with me. She is.'

'No, Jack. Not one moment's happiness does she get with you,' Sammy Cohen repeated. 'Every week a father must listen to his child weeping on the phone. Finally I can stand no more so I come here to you to beg you to release my *Mädchen* from this terrible enslavement.'

'You might be old, Sammy, but you ain't too old to get a bloody good hiding, you come here with this ballocks,' Jack told him. 'You can get on your knees, you can lick my feet, do what you like, but she ain't going nowhere. If you don't shut it I'll take the phone out the flat and stop her calling you.'

'I thought this would be your answer,' Sammy Cohen said. 'All my life I've suffered tyranny, this way, that way or another way. I can't put up with this for my Leah. It has to end for her now.'

He pulled out a gun and waved it at Jack, his bony hand shaking.

'Oh, the old gun trick, Sammy.' Jack laughed. The effect of the drug was gone, replaced by adrenalin.

'I don't care what the consequences may be. My pain is nothing now. I can't see my daughter go on suffering in this way. It's more than a father can bear—'

'Where d'you get that little pea-shooter? Ah, look, it ain't even got any bullets in it!' Jack said suddenly.

'What?' Sammy looked down at the .32. 'No,' he said as Jack grabbed for it. A struggle ensued but Sammy wasn't giving it up easily. His bony fingers were locked on to the stock as if they were glued there. Suddenly the gun went off with a deafening report. Jack felt something rip into his shoulder as he punched Sammy in the throat. Brian ran in with Pongo.

'A lot of fucking good you are!' Jack said, in a flash of anger.

'What happened?' Brian said. 'Jack, you're bleeding.'

'The crazy old coot tried to kill me. He got me in the shoulder. I thought the gun wasn't loaded.'

'You'd better get to a hospital,' Brian advised.

'Yeah, that'd be handy. What'll they do – call the cops? Forget it. What's it look like, Pongo?'

Pongo eased the jacket off as carefully as he could, stopping when Jack winced. He was the only person Jack would allow to do anything like this. He held his breath as Pongo tore open his shirt and inspected the small entry and larger exit wound in the upper arm. 'It missed the bone, Jack, but you won't be giving no one a right hook for a while.'

'You'd better have a doctor take a look, Jack,' Brian said. 'I know plenty who are still qualified.'

'Not here, though, Bri. Get me back to the flat. You got any pills for pain?' he asked Pongo.

'No.'

'What shall we do with Sammy?' Brian asked. 'Take him out to the pig farm?'

'Shut up – he's my girlfriend's father,' Jack said, shocked. Despite what Sammy had done he didn't see him as a real threat. He would like to take a few live threats out to Stoke Newington, though, and feed them to the pigs. Yeah . . . No. Stoke Newington didn't sound right. 'Did I say Stoke Newington?' he asked, with a sense of panic, not sure if he had spoken his thoughts, 'I meant Stoke Poges. Throw the kyke bastard out and take me home.'

At the flat Jack found Leah on the phone. She looked surprised and rang off immediately. She was up to something – she'd known about the planned attack, he was sure. 'Who was you talking to?' he demanded.

'Since you keep me a virtual prisoner here, Jack, I'm making the only escape I can through study and intelligent conversation on the phone.'

'Well, not any more. Not after this little upset with your dad.'

'What happened?'

'Any more of it and you'll both end up at the pig farm. And it won't be to get a bacon sandwich.'

'What have you done to him?' Her voice all but disappeared on an alarmed intake of breath. 'Where is he?' She rushed back to the phone, but Jack beat her to it and ripped the wire out of the socket on the skirting board, despite the pain in his arm.

'You don't study any more, you understand? You don't talk to those poxy teachers who fill your head with stupid ideas. Get it? You'd better.'

'I hate you, I hate you so much! I wish my father had killed you.'

'Get her a kitchen knife, Pongo,' Jack ordered. 'Let her have a go herself.'

'Jack, don't do this, man. It's not sensible.'

Jack bellowed at him to get a knife, and Pongo ran to the kitchen. He came back with a six inch blade and hesitated.

'Give it to her.'

Still Pongo hesitated. 'Jack, this is crazy—'

'Do it, you black bastard, or I'll stab you.' He waited for the knife to be placed in Leah's hand. Then he said quietly, coaxingly, 'Come on, Leah, you got the knife. Stab me. Right through the heart.'

He exposed the patch of his chest behind his breast pocket. It was Leah's turn to hesitate. Then, without warning, she lunged at him. Pongo shouted and Jack hit her, knocking her down.

The doorbell sounded and Pongo went to let the doctor in.

Jack reached down to Leah. 'Get up,' he said calmly. 'I'll ask the doctor to give you something to calm you down after he's seen me.'

*

Lying on the double bed with her knees drawn up, Leah was aware of a man coming in. He had a bag in his hand and she assumed he was a doctor. He came over, set the bag on the bed, then sat down and reached for her wrist. Instinctively she pulled it away, but he made soothing, reassuring sounds and took her pulse. 'It's quite erratic,' he said. 'Do you sleep okay? I can give you something if you don't. You'll have a real shiner in the morning. Put an ice-pack on your eye.'

As he talked Leah relaxed a little and allowed him to take her blood pressure. It was seriously low, he told her. He wanted to know about her periods, if they were heavy. One question followed another. She hadn't had a period for months, and it wasn't because she was pregnant. Finally Leah trusted him enough to say, 'I wanted to kill him, Doctor. I would have done if I'd had the chance.' The words were sandpaper rubbing across her tight vocal cords. When he laughed, she knew he wasn't a friend. 'We all feel like that sometimes in relationships,' he said. 'You're suffering from depression. Did you say you're not sleeping well?' He was writing on a pad. 'I'll give you a prescription for the depression. It'll help in the bad patches.'

'Can you give me something to help me sleep tonight, Doctor?'

He seemed pleased to be able to do something. He found a plastic bottle of tablets in his bag, but hesitated before he gave it to her. 'These will sort you out. Don't exceed the dose. They can be pretty addictive.'

After he had gone, Leah lay curled on the bed clutching the bottle. The knowledge that it contained the means by which she could escape into sleep gave her strength. A little later, she got up and went to the kitchen, where Jack was having tea with Pongo, his only friend. What Pongo got from Jack she didn't know, but it had to be something other than money. 'What do you want with me, Jack?' she asked. 'Can you, in God's name, tell me that?'

Jack nodded at Pongo, who got up and went out.

'I can't live without you,' he told her. 'You're with me for life. We should get married.'

'What is it you want from me?' she asked again, as if he possessed the mental capacity and sensitivity to understand.

'I don't know what you're saying,' he said. 'I give you all this.'

'But what is it you want from me? Whatever it is I can't give it to you. Oh, sex, I know you want that. You just take it – you mount me like a dog. I loathe it. Every time you do it I feel as if I'm being raped.'

Jack flew up from the table, throwing his chair aside. 'Shut it, Leah!' he screamed. 'Shut the fuck up or I'll give you another hiding.'

She went back to the bedroom, and heard Jack call Pongo to go to the club. She didn't move for a long time, listening to the emptiness in the flat, the hum of the refrigerator, then the rattle as it shut off. She looked at the bottle of sleeping pills. There was freedom, a few blissful hours of sleep. She uncapped the bottle, put a capsule on her tongue, poured some water into a glass and swallowed. One wasn't enough to guarantee escape. Two might be but three was certain.

The next thing Leah knew, if only vaguely, was that Pongo was calling her name as she slipped into a long tunnel. He was shouting at her to come back, until his voice lowered, his echoing voice said, 'Or should I just let you go, Leah? I know that's what you'd want. But Jack'd go mad if I did, madder than he already is.' Oh, you're so kind, Leah thought. 'None of us can escape him. I'm sorry, girl.'

Leah came round in hospital, recognizing at once the familiar surroundings and smells. She began to cry. Jack was sitting at the side of her bed, telling her she was a silly girl, believing she was crying because of what she'd tried rather than failed to do. He promised he'd make it up to her. 'We'll go on holiday,' he said, 'somewhere really nice. Just the two of us.' It was the last thing she wanted.

You don't get it, Jack. You just don't get it, she said, over and over again, but not a word passed her lips. He never heard anything she said.

Tony Wednesday sat in a Scotland Yard briefing for a raid on the house of a villain named Jack McVitie. He was thinking that the DI wasn't making enough of who this man was. It was believed he might be a witness against the Kray gang. Tony's squad was secretly targeting them, trying to beat Nipper Read's gang at Tintagel House to the punch. There had been a surge of confidence in senior CID officers after the Richardsons' convictions.

A uniformed sergeant opened the door and looked round the room. Tony saw a colleague point him out. The sergeant crept over to him and told him he was wanted at the hospital. Sonia was in labour.

'I'm a copper, Sarge,' he whispered, 'not a doctor.' The detectives sitting close to him chuckled.

The raid on Jack McVitie's drum was easy. For a villain with such a hard reputation, he folded without resistance when they burst in and whacked him with pickaxe handles. Soon he was telling them how Ronnie Kray had given him a hundred pounds on account of four hundred to shoot a former partner in one of his clubs. He'd lost his nerve so Ronnie was now after him. The squad set him up to get more information on Ronnie and Reggie. They wanted them both.

By the time Tony got to the hospital at two o'clock in the morning Sonia had given birth to the baby. He saw immediately that all was not well. She looked a wreck and couldn't, or wouldn't, sleep. She wanted to know what was happening with their baby – something was wrong. Tony looked for a nurse or a doctor. They seemed in short supply. 'They took him away, Tony, and no one will say why.'

'There's nothing wrong with him. He's in an incubator, that's all,' Tony said. Was that where all newborn babies slept? He didn't think so.

She wouldn't be reassured that there wasn't a problem so he

went to find a nurse who could point out his son so that he could see for himself.

In the intensive-care baby unit, the nurse wouldn't say much but hurried off to find the doctor. When he got there he seemed very young and as if he'd been woken up. He buried his nose in the case notes.

'Yes, well,' he began uncomfortably, 'there's a serious problem with the baby, Mr Wednesday. He has what's called a hole in his heart. He's struggling a bit. It's why he's here and not on the ward with your wife.'

'Is he going to survive, Doctor?' Tony asked, shocked, despite knowing hospitals performed miracles every day.

'It's not my case, Mr Wednesday. You should speak to the registrar, Dr Singh, when he comes in tomorrow.'

'Can they operate? You can repair damaged hearts.'

'I really think that's something to talk to Dr Singh about.'

'He's going to die, isn't he?' Tony said bluntly.

The doctor looked ready to run. Tony felt the same. Why couldn't these people be straight with you? He had no idea what he should tell Sonia, but even he couldn't go back and say their son was doing okay.

'Why don't you just switch off the incubator?' he said suddenly, not sure where the words came from.

The doctor's response surprised him. 'That would be best,' he said, 'but we can't.'

'No, I s'pose not.'

Sonia wailed like a banshee when the little fellow stopped breathing at nine fifteen the next morning and the registrar didn't try to revive him. He would have been severely handicapped if he'd lived. Tony felt helpless in the face of Sonia's suffering.

Later, an inept hospital social worker said, 'You're both young. You'll have other children.'

Later still Sonia said, 'I don't want other children, Tony. I want him.'

'I know . . . We've got to think about burying him. Or letting the hospital do something.'

'I don't want that to happen. Not yet,' Sonia said.

When she finally got round to it, she wanted a proper funeral, and invited some family and friends. As he watched the little white coffin, hardly bigger than a shoebox, go into the ground at Nunhead cemetery, where Sonia's nan was buried, he glanced up at the faces on the other side of the grave. A young woman was watching him, Sonia's cousin Alison, and she was showing out to him. Funerals affected people in different ways. At the small reception afterwards, she gave him her phone number.

'I can't work it out, guv,' Tony Wednesday told George Fenwick, 'It's been a month now and Sonia talks like the baby's still around. She can't seem to move on. I mean, it's not as if we really knew him, is it?'

'Women do get attached to them. It's all hormonal.'

'Well, it's time she got over it. She's a pain, moping around.'

'Yeah, well, marriage is like that, Tony. There's always something they've got the hump with.'

A couple of days later Tony called Sonia's cousin for her advice. They met in a coffee bar on Victoria Street. She worked in the Army and Navy Stores.

'Oh dear,' she said, reaching across the table and laying her hands on his. 'You're really suffering, aren't you?'

'It's not me,' he said. 'I just don't know what to do for Sonia.'

Screwing Alison in the back of his Ford Cortina wasn't the solution, but it eased the pressure. He knew he mustn't do it again – at least, not in the car in case they were nicked.

Bobby Brown's reappearance on the scene, stony broke, unsettled Jack, Brian noticed. Until then he had been in a relatively calm period. Jack didn't seem to know whether to treat him like his long-lost friend or to ex him. Then Brian suggested a solution Jack liked.

They took Bobby out to Wilder farm at Stoke Poges, threatening to pop him and feed him to the pigs. Brian found the stench unbearable as he stood with Pongo while Jack backed his old friend up to a huge pig pen, a gun to his head. 'This is it, Bobby,' he said. 'You got to be taught a lesson. You can't have us over like you done and run out.'

'I didn't, Jack. The Richardsons was after my share.'

'So you pissed it all away, gambling in Marbella with Sean Connery. Well, goodbye, you thieving rascal.' As he pulled the trigger he pushed Bobby back into the pig pen while the hammer fell on the empty chamber. Brian and Pongo laughed. So did Jack – and so did Bobby when he clambered out covered with pig shit, hardly believing he wasn't dead. He started swearing.

'It'll be easy enough to find you now, Bobby,' Brian said, and they laughed some more, until Bobby came after them, flicking pig shit at them. They ran.

Jack's paranoia flooded back. He had got over Bobby's betrayal, but now it was Jimmy Humphreys who was the problem. He'd been seen with that dog Commander Drury.

'He's drinking with him, staying close, Jack, that's all,' Brian assured him. 'Someone's got to keep an eye on what's going on.'

'He's betraying us, Bri, that's what, the same as that slag Denny Jones you brought to us.'

'Denny's as solid as gold,' Brian argued pointlessly. 'Bobby would bet his life on him.'

'Well, what about Bobby? We should have done him properly at the pig farm. That's where he's gonna end up.'

'You're just jittery 'cos a few've gone down for long ones,' Brian said.

'I'm protecting our firm. Someone round here has to. We don't want to be doing armed robbery. Makes you too vulnerable to Old Bill.'

'Come on, Jack. It's good business. It is,' Brian insisted. He knew how the figures stacked up, what was taken in the train robbery against what was recovered.

'Not any more it ain't. We're finished with all that. We get plenty from the clubs and a bit of protection. And pills. That's where the dosh is nowadays. We can't let the jungle bunnies nick it all,' he said, although Pongo wasn't five yards away.

Bobby was startled when Brian broke the news. They were set with a few blags, having spent time and money putting them together. 'You know what, Bri? This is all part of Jack's problem. He ain't half gone downhill since I was out in Marbella.' Brian knew it; and that he was the only person Bobby would dare say it to. He wondered how long that would last if Jack kept on like he was.

'I got an idea, Bri,' Bobby said cautiously, glancing around the pub. 'Me and Denny could have this blag, with just you. Sort of start our own little firm.'

'Don't you think Jack's paranoid enough? You know what it would mean if we did and he found out.'

'We could put away a share for him. Your dad could hold it. Think about it, Bri. And he doesn't need to find out, does he?' Bobby said. 'I mean, how long before Jack goes completely barmy and gets us all nicked? This is a real opportunity to make something for ourselves without all that craziness. I mean, you got access to the money outlets as good as Jack, ain't you? Think about it, Bri.'

Of late Brian had thought of little but the inevitability of Jack going down and pulling everyone with him. Against that was Jack finding out they were making one and going totally berserk. You couldn't fight such madness. Or maybe you could. After all, that was how Ronnie Kray was going, getting nuttier and nuttier while his power slipped away. 'I'll think about it, Bobby.'

'Don't be too long, Bri. A couple of them jobs are ready to go. If you don't have it, I could find someone else.'

'Yeah, yeah,' Brian said irritably. 'It's not an easy decision.'

It wasn't. It was something he needed advice on and there weren't too many around he could trust. DCI George Fenwick was an obvious candidate. Brian liked to think that his only loyalty was to money, but he was a copper and he might well come under external pressures, so he couldn't and shouldn't trust him or any other copper. Instead he went to talk to Joey.

The first thing his father wanted to know was how he would handle Jack if he found out.

'There's no reason for him to find out, is there?' Brian said.

'Don't be silly, Brian. You'd be dealing with villains the whole while. How is it they always get caught? By not keeping quiet.'

There was a new energy to his dad that he sensed might relate to Eddie and Charlie Richardson being in prison, the knowledge that they couldn't torture him again. And Brian knew he was right: you'd never get villains to keep quiet when they had something big off. It was their glory and gratification.

'This is business, Dad, and we should run it like that. But Jack's too stupid to see it.'

'Ultimately there is only one way to handle Jack.' Joey paused.

Brian knew at once what that pause meant. His dad wanted him to get there by himself, and he had, but he needed Joey to say the words so there could be no mistake. But when he did – 'You have to let Jack go to prison' – Brian was shocked. The words were cold and sharp, like shards of flint. Fleetingly he wondered whether Joey could dispense with him in the same way.

'If you can handle Jack, I can handle the money. How much are you talking about, Brian?'

'Bobby reckons there's between fifty and seventy grand in each of those Securicor trucks. That's good business, Dad.' He could see his father thought so too.

'Do you need money to set it up?' Joey asked.

'That's taken care of for now. We might need some more later if this little firm gets off.'

'I'll talk to Charles Tyrwhitt – greedy little twit that he is. I'll introduce you as a new client with a new firm.'

'He can keep closed up, can he?'

For the first time in that meeting Joey laughed.

*

Charles Tyrwhitt's narrow shoulders shook with laughter inside the chalk-striped worsted suit. He assured Brian that banks abided by strict secrecy laws that forbade them to divulge their clients' business on pain of their teeth being wrenched out. He and Brian glanced at Joey, who looked as if he was about to black out.

'I'm sorry, Joseph,' the banker said. 'Wrong metaphor.'

'Can we take it that the bank will be interested in getting the money out of the country, Charles?' Joey asked, recovering.

'If we aren't, Joseph, I'm sure you have alternative means,' Tyrwhitt said.

'Cotterill and Jenkins would be our preferred route.'

'Oh, your father's such a silver-tongued flatterer, Brian. Just how hot is this money?'

'Warmish.'

'Well, our charge would depend upon that little piece of information. In principle, yes, we'd love to do business with your new firm.' He shook Brian's hand.

Now Brian had a bigger hurdle to get over. He couldn't easily free himself from his connection with Jack so he decided to give him one last chance. If his uncle said no, he would think about taking up Joey's suggestion. If Jack continued to behave irrationally, the decision would be easier. A little. 'What d'you say, Jack? Did you think about that blag on the Securicor van that Bobby and Denny got set?'

'I told you – I fucking well told you I don't know how many times. It attracts too much attention from Old Bill. Giving people what they want – gambling, a bit of sex – no one minds that. Everyone wants it. It does no harm. Blagging upsets the banks and insurance companies. They come down on the government, what goes after the police, who come down on us.'

'This is silly. It's there now, Jack. Why not let Bobby and Denny have their own little firm?' Brian said. 'We could cop a piece of it.'

'No!' Jack's statement was as emphatic as a slammed door.

*

When Brian went off to meet Bobby and Denny, he was angry and disappointed. By the time the taxi got to the Greyhound pub behind Barker's, he had made up his mind.

'Jack said no. We can't have it.'

'Cushty,' was Bobby's response.

'What d'you say, Brian?' Denny Jones asked. He was married but kept a rented bedsit in one of the grotty streets of Kensington Square where he swagged mysteries.

'If Jack gets word of this,' Brian warned, 'one of us might have to cap him. Can you handle that, Bobby?'

Bobby glanced nervously between the other two. Finally he said, 'Jack's been my mate for as long as I can remember, Bri, but the thing is, I don't know him any more.'

'Is that yes?'

'I'd say so,' Bobby said. He slapped his hands together. 'There'll be no stopping us.'

This time it was news of the Krays being nicked that sent Jack crazy. DCI Fenwick brought word to the club. Their whole firm'd had their collars felt.

'I don't believe it.' Jack grabbed Fenwick by the throat and pushed him up against the bar.

'Straight up. It'll be all over the newspapers in the morning.'

'You're lying. It's a trick to trap us.'

'Why don't we wait and see if they stay nicked?' Brian said.

'The team of Old Bill who pulled them is pretty thorough.' Fenwick made no attempt to free himself.

'What does this mean for us?' Brian knew what Jack was thinking.

'Who do you trust? Trust only those you trust,' Fenwick advised.

'Can we still trust you?' Jack said, pulling a gun and pressing it to Fenwick's head.

Still the detective made no move to extricate himself, perhaps because he could see that everyone in the club, punters and croupiers, was watching. No one but a total madman would shoot someone in such circumstances, and Jack wasn't totally mad. 'With your life. It's me here warning you.'

'Who can we trust, Brian?' Jack repeated endlesly, in the days that followed.

Finally Brian snapped. 'What d'you want me to do? Draw up a list?'

'We have to off someone so people know,' Jack suggested.

'Oh, yeah? That's what that maniac Ronnie Kray thought when he killed Jack McVitie,' Brian pointed out. 'Now they're well and truly weighed off. Got any more bright ideas?'

They pushed into Raymond's Revue Bar, but instead of meeting the doorman they ran into Commander Drury.

'Looks like our favourite corrupt policeman's got a new job,' Jack said. 'Doorman.'

'Two major firms down,' Drury announced, as if it was his personal doing. 'Guess who's next to go, duck.'

'I thought we had a big interest in our mutual well-being, Ken,' Brian said.

'At least someone on your firm's got some sense, Jack,' Drury said. 'What are you two doing here?'

'Same as you, Mr Sticky Fingers,' Jack quipped, 'telling Paul Raymond and everyone the Krays looked after that their business is under new management.'

'Do I get my extra share from you now?' Drury said.

'If you got our well-being at heart, Kenny-boy.'

'I always have when it coincides with mine.'

'The usual percentage, the usual arrangement?' Brian ventured.

'Not any more, duck. It's double bubble now for double trouble. These are dangerous times. I'll get the tallyman to call on you after you've had time to inform everyone.' With that he pushed out of the club.

Brian stood in the foyer and stared after him through the glass doors as he disappeared into the crowd, that was mostly looking for Soho's cheap thrills. He felt nothing but contempt for the man and all his greedy kind. 'We've got to do something about him or there'll be no end to his demands,' Brian said.

'Why bother? We'll just nick a bit more off Raymond.'

'No, Jack. We'll see about putting Drury away.'

'You got anything in mind?'

'That young detective who works with George Fenwick, DC Wednesday. He got some info on Drury when he was out in Marbella.'

Uncertainty ate into Brian as he waited for word of the robbery that was going off. He was going deeper into crime when, increasingly, he wanted to get out. The most successful criminals didn't have a conscience – the Richardsons didn't and neither did the Krays, but look at what had happened to them. Maybe conscience would prevent him ending up the same way. He couldn't face going on the blag, but perhaps that was more to do with cowardice. Letting others do the blagging, when people like security guards, who were only doing their job, might get hurt, made him a double coward.

The telephone startled him, even though he was sitting in his flat waiting for the call. It was Denny Jones. 'We had it off.' That was all he said. Brian put down the receiver.

How Jack found out or suspected who it was, Brian could only guess. He hit the roof. 'How is it that blag's gone off, Brian?' he demanded. 'I said we weren't going to be blaggers. It's too much aggro.'

'Well, we're not the only firm that's active.'

'It was Bobby's blag. The one him and Denny Jones was plotting. Who had it? Did Bobby? I'll kill that treacherous fucker. I shoulda done him when he came crawling back broke from Spain.'

'I wouldn't have thought it was Bobby,' Brian lied.

'We got to find out,' Jack said. 'You're s'posed to be the eyes and ears of this little firm. You're worse than useless. Have I gotta do everything?'

Brian wondered just what Jack thought he did.

A couple of days later he was with Joey at his flat in Ladbroke Grove. His mum was out with some Tory grandees and they were watching Frankie Howerd on TV. 'Is the money safely out of the country?' he asked.

'Who said it was going out of the country?'

'Either way, when can the chaps expect to get paid?' Brian was being pressed by the others, even though the delay in dividing up the money meant they were less likely to become suspects.

'There's twenty-one thousand to come, Brian. That's seventy thousand less our seventy per cent. What do you want done with it?'

'These are villains, Dad. They'll want cash in hand.'

'Which they'll spend in short order and end up broke again,' Joey pointed out. 'Or worse, arrested. Did any of them think about a pension fund? Or a property? Three or four thousand will get them a very nice four-bed semi in Sutton, in Surrey, or a nice terraced house in Wimbledon.'

Brian laughed. 'Is that a joke, Dad?'

'Those men will inevitably go to prison by the law of averages,' Joey said. 'The money could be making them money now for later.'

'Villains don't think like that. If they did, they wouldn't be villains.'

'Then maybe you should think about your future, Brian.'

'With Jack? I'm not sure there is one.'

'Then get out,' Joey said, 'right now, before it's too late.'

'Easier said than done. I'm the one who checks Jack's excesses. Without me he'd get nicked for sure. The only way I'd get to stay clear is by giving him up, Dad.'

'It always comes to that in the end,' Joey said. 'You should think seriously about the means, Brian – something that won't involve you.'

Something was wrong, Brian knew, as Pongo came through the club looking for Jack. There was an urgency about him that he didn't normally display. With him was a villain called Timmy Walsh, whom Brian knew from when they had been recruiting for a blag. He was a getaway driver.

'What's the problem, Pongo?' he asked.

'I gotta talk to Jack. 'S he in the office?'

Brian resisted going after him but nodded Walsh to the bar. Drink was his weakness, he remembered. That was why they didn't use him. 'Give him whatever his heart desires, Ewan,' he said to the barman.

'You always was a gentleman, Brian,' Walsh said, and ordered a large gin and tonic.

'What's got Pongo so worked up?'

'I don't know. I just told him Denny Jones was in the Elephant in Brixton, shooting his mouth off about Jack, saying what a slag he was, how they'd had him over.'

'Did he say how that was?' – anxiety was creeping into his voice.

When Jack raced into the bar from the office in his braces Walsh told him everything he knew. As the extent of the treachery was revealed Jack began pacing hysterically. 'I thought you ought to know,' Walsh finished, like the school snitch. 'I thought Denny worked for you.'

'He does,' Jack said. 'We give him a few quid to keep him out of trouble.'

'He's gonna be well in trouble if he goes on talking about that security truck in Kingston,' Timmy said. 'Well organized, it were. I wish I'd had some.' He glanced at Brian, who winked at him.

'Count your lucky stars you didn't, son,' Jack said. 'Look, slip over and capture him for me, Timmy. Pongo'll go with you. Bring him here. No, second thoughts we'd better take him to the flat. We got respectable people here. We don't want no drunk shouting the odds.'

Bobby Brown joined them, showing his own anxiety, which didn't help.

'Is it true, Bobby?' Jack asked, from the back of the car, as Bobby drove them to the flat.

'He's probably had too much to drink, Jack,' Bobby said, as he caught Brian's eye in the mirror.

'Did he have that Kingston job without me?' Jack asked.

'He's a blagger,' Bobby answered noncommittally. 'That's his game. It's not your line, is it?'

'I said we didn't want that kind of aggro.'

'So what's he gonna do for us, Jack?' Brian asked. 'Sweep up in the club?'

'Yeah, if I tell him to,' Jack said truculently. 'And you, and Bobby.'

'Ballocks to that,' Brian said angrily. 'We've got all this talent doing nothing.'

'Yeah, well, they can fuck off out of it. Most of them are wankers.'

'Blagging's like gambling, Jack,' Bobby cut in. 'It's in the blood. You can't stop it, mate.'

'Was it him?' Jack said, to Bobby. 'Did he have that Kingston job after I said no?'

'What if he did, Jack? What's the diff?'

'You'll fucking well see when I get hold of him.'

When Denny Jones got to the flat he was three sheets to the wind. He tried to put his arm round Jack as if he was his best friend. 'What's this about, me old cocker? Pongo said you wanna talk about my future – got a bit of work, have we? 'Bout time.'

'You ain't got no future, Denny. I can't trust you. What'd you do with the money?'

'Knocked most of it out. The handler only give me four grand. Time you paid a few exes – it's gone.'

'You was robbed,' Jack commiserated. 'Who handled it? What's his name?'

'Come on, Jack,' Denny said. 'I can't do business like that.'

'No, we'll get a bit more out of him for you. You deserve it.'

'This is what I do, Jack,' Denny said. 'I told Brian that, didn't I, Bri?'

'You told me often enough, Denny,' Brian confirmed.

'I mean, I can't go around poncing a living off club-owners and dirty bookshops like you.'

Jack lashed out, hitting Denny with a left and a right, spinning him over a coffee-table.

'That's enough, Jack,' Brian said, grabbing his arm.

But Jack was in full paranoia mode and threw him off, dragging Denny on to his feet. 'Where's the money, Denny?' he demanded. 'Who placed it?'

He hit him again and again. Brian tried to stop him. Bobby did nothing, as if he knew better.

Brian ought to have known better: 'Leave off, Jack,' he said. 'He's on our side.'

'Stay outa this,' Jack told him, and hit Denny again, then again. 'Where's the money? Where is it?' Denny's groans were barely coherent as Jack continued hitting him.

'Jack, stop!' Brian ordered. 'You'll kill him.'

'That's about right, the treacherous bastard. Get up – get up, you dog,' Jack screamed at the limp Denny.

'Jack,' Brian protested, getting between them. 'Enough. He's gone. He's dead.'

'Good,' he said, as Leah staggered in. She was doped, clearly, but conscious enough to want to know what was going on. 'Get out, Leah,' Jack ordered. 'Go back to bed.' He pushed her towards the door, then turned to Brian and Bobby. 'Get him out of here. Take him to the pig farm. Get rid of him. Out, Leah! Get out!'

He pushed her into the hallway and towards the bedroom.

'I can't go in there again,' Leah slurred, as she indicated the sitting room. 'You killed him.'

'Shut up or you'll get the same,' Jack told her.

They carried Denny out to the car as if he was drunk and propped him up on the back seat. At that point Bobby stopped. 'I ain't going out to no pig farm with him, Bri,' he said. 'Denny was a good pal of mine.'

'Shut up, Bobby. I'm not going out there either,' Brian said. 'Denny's not dead.'

'He's not?' Bobby was full of doubt. He leant into the car and looked closely at him. 'Then he needs to go to hospital, Bri.'

'We can't take him there. I know a doctor.'

'Bri,' Bobby said, 'you done brilliantly, son, having Jack over like that. But he'll go fucking mad and kill the lot of us when he finds out.'

'I've been thinking about that,' Brian said, as he started the Jaguar Mark 10. 'We gotta do something drastic about him.'

Bobby nodded solemnly. 'And soon, Bri.'

Not even Jack's oldest friend was prepared to tolerate him any longer. That decided Brian.

'You know why you're here, Inspector Redvers?' Sir John Waldron said, from the far side of his uncluttered desk in the seventh-floor office at Scotland Yard.

It was eight o'clock in the evening. Redvers had heard that the commissioner was a tireless worker, determined to get crime and corruption under control. He glanced at the two senior officers in the room with him. 'I have a pretty good idea, Sir John,' he said smartly.

'We've scored considerable successes against the pernicious criminal gangs who have tyrannized society. One set has proved a particularly difficult nut to crack,' Sir John said. 'Jack Braden and Brian Oldman. I understand you're related to them.'

'It's not something I brag about, sir.'

'I can understand that. You're an exceptional policeman, Redvers – a qualified lawyer who likes being one, I'm told.'

'I do, sir. I find the work very satisfying.'

'Then tell me why or how these particular criminals and their gangs have survived for so long.'

Redvers wondered if he wanted a long, legalistic answer or a more direct response. He plumped for the latter. 'There's only one way, Commissioner. Corrupt policemen are helping and protecting them.'

'I don't like that notion. It leaves a bad taste in the mouth. What's your solution?'

'A hand-picked team of detectives to look at all the officers who have ever had any contact of that sort with these criminals, sir,' Redvers said frankly.

'I thought we had a carefully selected team working on the gangs. You were part of it at one time, according to your record.'

'Yes, sir.'

'You've got more to say than that.'

'I think they got tainted by corrupt officers, sir.'

'Do you have any evidence of that?'

'I haven't looked, sir. It wasn't my place to do so.'

'It's the responsibility of every honest policeman to root out the bad apples,' the commissioner said irritably.

'I was never provided with the resources, sir.'

'Many of the men and women on the squads you'd examine might be wholly innocent, Inspector,' the commissioner pointed out.

'They may well be, sir,' Redvers stated. 'If they are, their reputations would survive any such examination.'

'Would you be able to provide any inside knowledge about the activities of your uncle and cousin?'

'I would hope not, Commissioner. I've had no contact with them since I was a boy. My mother took me to live in Manchester. We didn't even go to my grandmother's funeral.'

The commissioner glanced at his two officers and placed his index fingers together over his lips as he thought about his response. Redvers felt sweat run from under his left armpit to trickle down his side. He wanted to bring his hand to it but didn't dare. For a long, bad moment he thought he was on his way out, condemned by blood. Then he got a real shock.

'I'm going to provide you with resources, Redvers, and the rank. As of now you're a superintendent. Perhaps the youngest in the entire history of the Metropolitan Police. I want you to select the men and women you wish to work with and dedicate yourself to rooting out corrupt police officers. Let's get to work, Superintendent.'

Redvers floated down from the seventh floor. He must he dreaming, he thought. He wanted to share this good news, perhaps even celebrate with someone who wouldn't compromise him. His mother wouldn't be interested and didn't have a telephone anyway. There was Elaine Stone, who'd been much in his thoughts but was not in his life. There was Sonia Hope, or Wednesday, as she now was. He didn't know why he thought of her, but getting together with her wasn't a realistic prospect.

Elaine's phone rang and rang. As he was about to hang up, it was answered by a man. Again, John was on the verge of putting down the receiver, but instead he said, 'Is Elaine there?'

'Who?'

'Elaine Stone.'

She wasn't. She had moved.

The surprise in Sonia's voice shifted to something else. She sounded as if she needed to talk and invited him over. She wasn't the woman Redvers remembered from Bramshill and had been in love with, or had thought he was. She had let herself go. Tony was having an affair, she told him, more than one. Why is that surprising? he almost said, but stopped himself. 'Why don't you go back to work?' he said instead.

'You've got to be kidding, John. With him screwing every skirt that passes the office door?'

'It was probably a shock for him too, losing the baby,' he said, not sure why he was defending him. 'Things like that affect people in different ways. I missed my opportunity. I expect I'll stay on the shelf, or chained to the job.'

'I'm sure someone nice will come along and grab you. Someone as good as you.'

There was a moment when he almost kissed her. They held each other's eyes, and he felt the electricity between them. Then he broke the spell, worried that he was being drawn into something he couldn't handle. He said, 'I'm putting a special squad together to investigate corrupt policemen. You could join it.'

Sonia laughed. 'You should investigate Tony. He's up to all sorts of things he shouldn't be.'

The breath froze in Redvers's lungs. He felt guilty, as if this was why he'd come to see her. Then he collected himself. 'Would you consider coming back to that squad?'

'Oh, I'm sure they wouldn't want a worn-out plonk like me – that's what my dear husband calls me.'

'I'd have you. The choice is entirely mine.'

It was Sonia who made the first move, surprising him. She stepped close and kissed him, then started crying, wiping her eyes and smudging her two-day-old mascara. 'I'm sorry,' she said.

He gave her his clean white handkerchief and she dried her face. Then they kissed again, needily, clinging to each other, as if neither had tasted this particular fruit for a long while.

They made love on the rug in the sitting room, Sonia assuring him that Tony wasn't coming home.

Afterwards he felt guilty. Sonia offered him coffee, which he accepted although he wanted to get away.

As he perched on the edge of the sofa, sipping the drink, made with too much milk and too much sugar, her robe parted, revealing her white inner thighs and he was instantly aroused again. She saw his expression and waited. He set down his cup. Then, uncharacteristically, he put his hand between her thighs and parted her legs. The pleasure he found in her was longer, stronger, the shame that followed much deeper.

Quickly, he made his excuses and left, promising to ring her. The elation that had enveloped him earlier was gone.

TWENTY-SEVEN

Night after night at the club Jack told the same story of how people were plotting against him. The Kray twins getting weighed off at the Old Bailey for thirty years did nothing to calm him. He and Brian would be next. Old Bill was coming after them – and Brian couldn't help but agree with that, although he didn't say as much. It might prompt Jack to kill everyone he believed he could no longer trust, anyone who held information on them that could be sold or traded to the police.

'I'll have to pop Leah,' Jack said, sitting in the near-deserted club.

'Don't talk daft,' Brian said. 'You can't do that. What are you saying?' Suddenly he wondered why he cared. Let him kill Leah and go to gaol. That was the easiest solution to his own dilemma. Jack would certainly be nicked for that, because he'd be emotional and clumsy about it. But Brian found himself trying to argue him out of it.

'She's getting to be a real ache, Bri. She's got too much information about me. She'd give evidence against me at my trial.'

'What trial?' Brian asked mockingly. 'Did you get nicked and didn't tell me?'

'We got to get some more guns. The IRA's got plenty to sell. I been talking to a geezer called McGuinness. He can let us have some.'

Brian knew Jack had been making contact with the Paddies. This was likely to get him and everyone else nicked. Still he felt powerless to leave Jack or the firm. Soon there'd be nothing left, regardless of whether or not he got nicked. Most of the punters seemed to avoid the club now because of his irrational, paranoid behaviour.

Half the time it was empty and the dealers would play to make it look like something was going on. In the face of the starkly obvious, Jack made excuses – the weather was bad or everyone being on holiday, just as Brian made excuses to himself about why he couldn't leave. If it wasn't for the activity Bobby Brown organized with the stream of blaggers Brian had recruited from prison there'd be precious little money to pay everyone their wages each week.

Maybe now was the time to make his move. He could always give Jack a bit of a pension, and Pongo, who would look after him. He needed a respectable, legitimate source of income to provide for his little firm.

Brian went to talk to Joey at his place in the city from where he was developing commercial property. The Lombard Street office was a smallish internal box, with no pictures on the walls, no certificates, just rows of metal filing cabinets and desks, a lamp and some chairs. Yet here Brian was, cap in hand, looking to see if that offer was still open.

'Of course it is. I've kept you a seat on the board,' Joey said.

Brian almost laughed. He didn't even have a window in his office.

'Why the change of mind, son? Don't get me wrong, I'm really pleased – and your mother will be as well. Has something happened?'

'The world's changing, Dad. You adapt or die. Nietzsche.' Brian expected him to ask who Nietzsche was.

Instead Joey said, 'It's more Darwin in the City, son – survival of the fittest. I think you'll do all right here.'

'We've survived all right – me and Jack. Just about.'

'What about Jack? What's he going to say?' Joey asked anxiously.

'He's gone a bit mad. He thinks everyone's betraying him. He'll probably come after me.'

'Well, let's make him an offer.'

Again Brian almost laughed. He couldn't believe it was happening, that he was getting out and, in fact, ahead of the game.

*

'You got to be crackers, Joey,' Jack told him. 'What would I want with all that board-meeting ballocks?'

'It's time you went legit. It makes you safe.'

'All I got to do is threaten rivals.'

'What rivals, Jack? All the other gangs are in prison. The Krays, the Richardsons, even Billy Hayward and Frederick Foreman. There's no one else but you.'

'What about all them blacks taking over that manor in South London with their drugs?'

'How long will it be before you're arrested, Jack?'

'What you heard? You heard something, Joey?'

'No. It's the law of averages, Jack. You and Brian've had a good run for your money.'

'Brian ain't leaving to join you, Joey.'

'It's like a football transfer, Jack. It's business.'

'Forget it. Brian's dead first.'

The blood drained from Joey's face. He knew then that Jack was his enemy and would do all he could to bring him down.

'I knew he wouldn't go for it,' Brian said, as he sat at the kitchen table on the first floor of the Ladbroke Road flat. Despite having a dining room among many other rooms over three floors, Joey preferred eating in the kitchen.

'It's early days, Brian. We'll try the other way.'

'It's the other way that scares me, Dad,' Brian said, with a glance at his mum. 'Jack's not a rational human being. The only way I'll get free of him is if he's dead or in prison.'

Without batting an eyelid, Catherine said, 'Either one is possible.'

Brian turned sharply towards her. The memory of how ruthless she could be and the lengths she'd go to to protect him made him quake inside. He'd probably be safer with Jack. 'I couldn't do that to him, Mum,' Brian said.

'Don't be so stupid,' Catherine said fiercely. 'That's being weak. If you want to survive you've got to be strong.'

'Listen to your mother, Brian. She's got a shrewd head on her shoulders.'

'Maybe I should talk to Leah,' Catherine said.

'Why?' Brian asked. 'That won't do any good.'

'Jack puts a lot of store by her opinion. Look how she's stuck by him like she has.'

Leah's head was hurting. She couldn't marshal her thoughts as she tried to work out why this woman was here. It was some sort of deception. She would tell Jack and get her into trouble. Leah didn't want to help with the Tory Party. She didn't even want to leave the flat.

'You're very pale. You're not pregnant, are you?' Catherine asked.

An almost overwhelming desire to tell this stupid woman about her brother seized Leah. Fighting the urge to speak, she took deep breaths, but still she felt hysteria rising. What Catherine said next stopped her breath altogether. 'Jack's sick, isn't he? He badly needs help, Leah.'

'Don't say that!' Leah shrieked. 'You mustn't say that – you mustn't.' She clamped her hands over her ears and shook her head violently, hoping this woman would be gone by the time she stopped. A sharp slap around the face shocked her.

'He can be helped. We have to try and help him.'

Again, fear and anxiety clutched at Leah. 'Did Jack put you up to this? He did, didn't he? He thinks I'll betray him.'

'No,' Cath said. 'I want to help. Let me.'

'You're trying to trick me, get out of this flat. I'm going to tell Jack everything.'

She ran to the bedroom and slammed the door, leaning her weight against it. There was no key: Jack had hidden them all. Cath was on the other side of the door, trying to coax her out. Leah hated her and everyone else in her family. She hated their strong dark looks and their whiny voices and foul vowels.

How much longer it was before Jack got back she didn't know, but when she heard him she threw open the door and rushed out. 'I didn't say anything to Cath, Jack. I didn't.'

'What are you talking about?'

Leah heard the suspicion in his voice and her agitation deepened. 'I didn't betray you, Jack. She wanted me to.'

Air wasn't reaching her lungs as her breathing quickened. She saw him tense, ready to hit her, and backed away.

'Leah, what is it?'

She fled back to the bedroom. There was no point in leaning against the door – she couldn't hold it against him – so she threw herself on to the bed, listening to the pounding in her ears, dreading what would come next.

There was real risk in his action. It might land him in serious trouble both with Jack and the police if it didn't come off. Ordinarily Joey wasn't a gambler. He liked to shave the odds through thorough analysis. Now he couldn't begin to calculate the reaction of the two policemen. They sat across from him in 'Moma's' unadorned restaurant on the corner of Dean Street and Old Compton Street in Soho and made no reaction.

As Joey finished putting his proposition, 'Moma', the short, well-upholstered restaurateur appeared and put their *zuppa pavese* in front of them. Moma offered a limited menu and was particular about whom she served, but treated those she accepted as members of the family and expected them to show appreciation by eating all the food she brought them. Joey was family because he had done a property deal with her stick-thin immaculately dressed Italian husband.

'You're offering us money to put Jack away?' DCI Fenwick said, when the woman had left. 'Is that a joke?'

'I was never more earnest,' Joey told him.

'Yeah, well, you tell Jack we know his little game, mate.'

'Listen,' Joey said, leaning forward conspiratorially, 'this is in our mutual interest.'

The younger detective, Tony Wednesday, was diligently eating his soup, which pleased Moma. He dabbed at his mouth on the thick white napkin. 'How much information you got on him?'

'Enough. You'll have to do the work. I can't be involved.'

'So you won't be giving evidence?'

'This is a get-up, Tony. Jack's testing us,' Fenwick said.

Ignoring him Joey said. 'I can't give evidence against him, but I'll point you in the right direction.'

'What's this about, Joey?' Fenwick asked. 'You had a tiff with him?'

'Jack can't survive much longer, only he can't see it. Brian can. He wants out of the firm.'

'Well, will *he* give evidence?' Wednesday asked.

'He knows he might have to,' Joey conceded.

'He's well involved,' Fenwick said. 'He might go too.'

'No,' Joey said coolly. 'That has to be part of the deal.'

The look the two policemen exchanged told Joey they were at last taking him seriously. Wednesday stared at him directly. He was younger, less experienced, but instinct told Joey that he was the more dangerous of the two. 'How do you know you can trust me?' he said.

'I don't. But I can't see the profit for you in double-crossing me.'

'Will Brian Oldman give up his uncle?' Tony Wednesday said, as they turned along Old Compton Street. 'I mean, put him away?'

'I doubt it, Tony,' Fenwick said. 'He'd have to give himself up. He's too involved ever to get free.'

'But it's like his old man said. They must know it's only a matter of time before they both go.'

'Villains are never that objective, son,' Fenwick said. 'If they were, they wouldn't do what they do. You got something in mind, you cunning bastard?'

'There's money on the table for doing nothing more than our job,' Tony reasoned. 'Their demise is inevitable. Jack Braden going would be something. No one would worry about Brian. But we gotta be careful, guv. I mean, think how much shit could get thrown at us.'

'It's an attractive notion, Tony,' Fenwick said, 'and it's only a matter of time, of course. How do we make them understand that?'

'Who's the most active Old Bill around them?' Tony asked.

'Mr Hairpin Drury for sure.'

'Jack Braden and the iron haven't got any time for him. If Brian could be persuaded to give Drury up as a prelude to his uncle, Drury might do most of the work for us and pull Jack into the frame.'

'Dangerous, Tony. Ken Drury's too involved.'

'What does that mean? Are you in there as well?' Tony asked bluntly, like he knew nothing of Fenwick's involvement.

'What are you? Rubber heels suddenly?'

'We gotta know to see a clear way through,' Tony said, 'or we'll get our collars felt.' He glanced at Fenwick as they waited for a cab on Shaftesbury Avenue.

'I've had a taste,' Fenwick said, like he was hedging his bets. 'Nothing major.'

Tony nodded, as if he was satisfied that the other man was telling the truth, but he knew Fenwick was no more capable of that than any other bent policeman. Being the bagman for the Porn Squad, he knew how to treat him in future: collect what evidence he could, give nothing.

'Could we control the poison what comes out if Drury's nicked?'

'I'd say so – we get it first.'

Was this bravado, Tony wondered, or self-delusion? No one had more to lose than George Fenwick. 'We'd better talk to the chief before we see Brian Oldman.'

'You trust him, Tony?'

'The DCS? You think Mr Slipper's at it?'

Fenwick shrugged and disappeared into the cab that had stopped ahead of them.

*

If Jack Slipper was bent he hid it well behind the excitement he expressed to be heading up the team that might nick not only Jack Braden but Ken Drury. 'I've heard the stories about Commander Drury,' he said, rubbing his bony hands. 'Will Oldman be prepared to give him up?'

'If he sees it's the way to save himself,' Fenwick said.

'Drury would get us lots of Brownie points,' Slipper said, 'and if he could lead us to Jack Braden I'd be far happier about doing the rubber-heels job. So far there've only been rumours about their joint activities.'

'It's definitely more than rumour, sir,' Tony said. 'Our snout said they did a deal to carve up what the Krays left on offer.'

'If Brian Oldman helps put the collar on Drury and Braden, he'll walk. Guaranteed. We'd beat your blue-eyed contemporary into second place, Tony.'

'Well, we're all working for the same firm, guv,' Tony said.

'Superintendent Redvers has more ambition than most,' Slipper said, with an edge in his voice. 'Plus he has the commissioner's ear.'

'Perhaps he's browning him, guv,' Tony suggested.

Slipper stared at him as though he'd farted, and Tony wondered what he could say to retrieve the situation. DCI Fenwick made no gesture to help. But then the DCS laughed. 'Perhaps that's just what the choirboy's doing. The commissioner's letting Redvers run his own investigation into police corruption.'

The edge was back in the chief's voice. Jealousy, Tony concluded. 'Perhaps we should give this to him then, guv,' he suggested, with apparent innocence.

'What? Piss off!' Slipper exploded. 'Let them what does the work get the glory,' he added, putting on a funny voice.

'You're right, sir,' Tony said. 'Anyway, if we give it to Superintendent Redvers it could go right back to Braden – him being Redvers's uncle.'

'Let's see what we can do,' Slipper said, sold on the move. 'Talk to Oldman. Make a deal.'

*

'That was masterful, Tony,' DCI Fenwick said, as they went along the fourth-floor corridor at Scotland Yard. 'Perhaps we should give this to him then, guv.'

'I wouldn't rely on either Brian or Drury doing the biz,' Tony said. 'We gotta have a fall-back position.'

'Have you got one?' Fenwick said, and pushed him into the Xeroxing room.

'Pull Braden for something in his own right.'

With a plan in mind, they went to talk to Brian Oldman. He wanted to meet away from the club so they walked down Newman Street to the newly opened cafeteria on the ground floor of Bourne & Hollingsworth.

'I won't give Jack up. I can't do that,' Brian said, as he sat at the Formica-topped table and sipped his coffee.

'How much longer d'you think your luck can hold?' Fenwick said, softening him up. 'It's only a matter of time now that the twins have gone. We can't go on protecting you for ever.'

Oldman said nothing, clearly trying to calculate the odds on him surviving.

Tony pushed gently at the open door. 'The Krays thought they were invincible, with so many Old Bill at it. But Ken Drury couldn't help them, nor them poofy lords they had as friends either.'

That seemed to amuse Oldman.

'What's so funny?' Tony asked.

'Ronnie and Reggie getting weighed off with thirty years from Melford Stevenson.'

'Can you wonder, the way they upset him in court, shouting the odds all over the place?'

Oldman smiled again, as if he had some big secret. 'It weren't that,' he said. 'The twins sent a couple of heavies after us at the height of the troubles. They broke into Jack's flat when Melford Stevenson was there, giving one to a little bird I'd pulled for him. We smuggled him out, but we let him know who it was what gave him the fright of his life.'

A smile crept over Tony's face. 'So he finally paid them back. I heard he has a long memory. He's still paying back barristers who crossed him.' He noticed the look that slipped between Oldman and the DCI – it had probably been him who had smuggled the judge away. He filed it at the back of his mind. He had other priorities now. 'What's Jack going to do for you when the time comes? Rely on that judge for a lifeline? He shouldn't count on it, nor on Drury. I wouldn't, if I were you.'

'You and a lot of other Old Bill could go too,' Oldman countered. 'Drury'll pull as many as he can into the frame if he's nicked.'

'That's what we're going to guard against,' Fenwick reassured him. 'We'll sift the evidence to keep you well clear – and us. But your old man said Jack has to go.'

'It may be possible, George,' Oldman said. 'We'd have to be doubly careful. Jack's suspecting everyone of all kinds of things.'

'We've got a plan,' Tony said and winked at him in a familiar way. It involved armed robbery.

Jack understood the words that were being spoken, but not why these two Old Bill were coming to him. It didn't make sense. 'What d'you want from me, George?' he asked. 'There's plenty of blaggers about.'

'Not reliable ones, Jack. Not people I can approach,' the detective told him. 'Look, there's been a vacuum since the Krays' conviction. Either your firm's going to fill it or Old Bill has to. It's the law of physics. You can't have a vacuum. This payroll that goes into the *Daily Express* every week, well, I got in mind to blag it when there's double with the printers' bonuses.'

'I told you, I'm not a blagger. 'S not my game.'

'No, you're an organizer,' Tony said. 'You could get a few others to go and lift it for wages.'

'Well, as it happens I do know a few blaggers.' Jack was flattered. The newly promoted DS Wednesday was a smart lad.

'We could suggest one or two blaggers, too,' Wednesday said. 'Blokes with built-in alibis.'

'Think about it, Jack. With the bonuses, it'll be worth about a hundred grand,' Fenwick said.

'Sounds good enough to eat!' Jack was irresistibly drawn towards it. He'd never liked that Tory paper anyway.

'What is this?' Brian asked, when Jack put the proposition to him. 'I thought you didn't want to do regular blagging.'

'The thing is, Brian, there's this vacuum now the twins and the Richardsons have gone,' Jack told him. 'The law said you can't have a vacuum, so either we gotta fill it or Old Bill will. I'd say we've had enough of them thieving hounds taking the lion's share.'

'Who you got in mind for it?' Brian said.

'You remember David Crutwell?'

'He's a good blagger, Jack,' Bobby Brown said, 'or he was. He's on the island for the train robbery. But even if he wasn't he wouldn't be too happy about getting involved – we nicked most of his money.'

'We looked after it for him,' Jack said. 'That's all.'

'That's taking the piss,' Brian said.

'Even if he was up for it, how'd he get off the island?'

'It wouldn't be hard,' Jack said.

'If he's up to having some, he'd have a perfect alibi. We'd better think about others, Jack.'

'Crutwell will be as good as gold. You'll see. Who's going to go and talk to him?' Jack said.

'We'll get some false ID sorted. Go in as his brief with new evidence for his appeal,' Brian said. 'Be easy enough.'

'Easy-peasy.' Jack was feeling good. Maybe he'd take Leah out for a drink tonight. 'You'd best case the *Express* building first. Make sure it runs in there as sweet as I was told it does.'

Bobby Brown was confused by Jack's 180-degree turn, but accepted it as a symptom of his instability. The mad could be forgiven anything, and Brian wasn't about to take him further into his confidence.

As they stepped into the legal visiting room at Parkhurst prison on the Isle of Wight, Brian guessed Bobby was as uneasy about the enterprise as he was. He had been only slightly reassured that they'd passed inspection at the gate, but now he felt trapped and had no idea how far he could trust the two detectives.

'I can't say I like being in here, Brian,' Bobby said, catching his eye. 'Too many bad memories, son.'

'They weren't all bad,' Brian said, 'were they?'

'For you, maybe. Six months ain't so bad,' Bobby said, 'but try doing a four. And what about thirty years?'

'Doesn't bear thinking about,' Brian said. 'I'd top myself rather than face that.'

'Eyes up!' Bobby warned, as the door opened and David Crutwell strolled in with two screws.

He stopped and looked at the prison officers. There was a long pause.

'Well?' Crutwell said.

'Well what, *Mr* Crutwell?' one screw called Peter Ryman said.

'This is a private conversation between my brief and me about my appeal, *Mr* Ryman,' Crutwell said. 'We don't want no one from the government present.'

'Oh, what a pity,' Ryman said. 'I'll send you in some tea and biscuits, shall I?'

'Yeah, that would be nice, Peter,' Crutwell said. 'Two sugars for me.'

The door banged shut, locked, behind the screws.

'I got your stiff, Bobby,' Crutwell said. 'I'm buggered if I want to work for that slag. I'll see him dead first. You'd be crazy to have it. He'll nick everything.'

'No, he won't. Not this time,' Brian assured him. 'Jack had the hump over the train robbery. It was put to him first but it went off when he was inside. Anyway, I'm running it.'

'What makes you think you can pull one with me while I'm in here?' David Crutwell said.

Brian could feel Crutwell's resistance, but saw he couldn't help being intrigued. 'We can if you can, David,' he said.

'Yeah. Well, how you gonna get me out? This is Parkhurst.'

'Compassionate leave,' Bobby told him. 'Your mum's gonna die.'

'Again? The old girl's been gone about twenty years.'

'You had a visit from two Old Bill a while back about you going over the wall.'

'I'm still waiting for them dogs to come good.'

'This is it,' Brian said. 'They got someone who can switch your records so it says your mum's still alive.'

'I expect them two promisers can bring her back from the dead, an' all.'

'This is perfect for you, David,' Bobby told him.

'They ain't gonna let me outa here without an escort. They'd stick to me like glue.'

'Screws are as bent as any Old Bill,' Bobby said. 'We'd drink them.'

'Well, if you can, I'll have some, Brian. I mean, I'd fuck a pig to get out of here.'

Now came the difficult part. Brian was reluctant to broach it. 'The thing is, David, you gotta come back after the funeral.'

'You're kidding me? Let you guys fuck me out of my share?'

'If you don't, you got no alibi.'

'I'd be on the run – nice bit of dough like I should've had from that train. What's the share?'

'We go halves,' Brian said, still unsure if he'd agreed to go back. 'It splits between those what do the blag and us what handle the hot money.'

'Oh, yeah? And what happens to my cut if I come back here? I get out, I keep running, son.'

That wasn't acceptable to Brian. He got up and signalled to Bobby. Crutwell was a liability – he wouldn't help put Jack inside.

'Where you going? Wait a minute! We've hardly talked.'

'We've talked, David,' Brian said. 'We'll find someone else.'

He reached the door, but before he could ring the bell Crutwell said, 'I can't bring the dough back here, can I? I mean, wouldn't you be worried after that last turn-out?'

'Of course. But that was Jack and this is me,' Brian said. 'We got a bent banker. He gets your share out to wherever you want it to go. Only you get the details.'

Jack was nervous about the enterprise, Brian knew, because he wasn't in control of it, wouldn't be barking the orders. 'You sure this is all plotted up right, Brian?' he asked, for the umpteenth time. He was scared the blaggers would run off with his money. That would be ironic.

'It's our firm, Jack,' Brian reassured him. 'They can't run off.'

'We ain't gonna be there.'

'No, but Bobby is,' Brian said. 'He'll look after things.'

'Yeah, well, I don't trust him either,' Jack said. 'Not any more.'

'Well, then, you have it.'

'Why's that?' Jack challenged. 'So if I get nicked you can take over?'

Brian wondered if Jack knew anything or if he was still seeing phantoms in his drug-distorted mind.

His uncle pressed forward his argument before Brian could decide. 'You think I couldn't? Is that it? What if Bobby does a runner with the money?'

Weary of all this nonsense, Brian was on the point of telling Jack to go to hell. Instead he said, 'Time will tell.'

In some ways Brian wished he was on the blag. He doubted it could have been any less nerve-racking than waiting for the phone call to say everything was done. Minutes ticked by with leaden heaviness.

It went off without any resistance at the *Daily Express* building in Fleet Street. The call from Bobby came through. Brian checked the two envelopes with which he would pay off the two escort screws and took a taxi to the vast underground car park at Hyde Park Corner.

The two prison officers, both out of uniform, were leaning against a car, joking with Bobby and Crutwell when Brian walked down the ramp and across to the bay on the north side. There was a real party atmosphere. Relief, he supposed, that the blag had gone off, that they'd got their prisoner back, that they were going to get weighed off a grand apiece in used. Brian approached without a greeting, pulled out the two envelopes and gave one to each man. 'Expenses,' he said.

One screw wanted to stop and count the money, but the other was too nervous.

After they'd left Bobby and Brian checked the money, then switched it to another car. They locked the beaten-up Ford Popular and stepped back, uncertain about leaving it there. What if it was stolen?

'How much d'you reckon's there? Eighty grand?' Brian asked.

'At least,' Bobby said. 'Might even be over a ton. What you got in mind, Brian?'

'You could do a lot with that sort of money.'

'Not half,' Bobby said. ''S like winning the football pools. You could retire nicely on that and never be found.'

'Well, not quite,' Brian said. 'Two hundred grand didn't go far for you in Spain, did it?'

'Well, you had every ponce in the world charging you double and triple for everything. Every bit of money you changed you lost well over half. You get bundles of pesetas back and it looks like a lot, until a beer costs you a wad, along with everything else.'

'What are we doing here?' Brian said. 'Getting wages – five grand each. Five for David, five for Wally. A grand each for those two screws. We talked about our own firm, and now Jack's having it.'

'This is a wind up, innit?' Bobby said. 'I mean, look what Jack did to Denny Jones just for *thinking* he did that. I'll stick with my five grand share, Bri, if it's all the same to you. While Jack's around.'

'What if he wasn't, Bobby? What then?'

'I'd have to go down the island and visit him.'

Brian laughed. 'I was just testing you.'

'I thought you was, you snake.' Bobby Brown guffawed. 'But if he ain't around, Bri, I'm your man. Know what I mean?'

Brian knew exactly what he meant. Maybe Bobby would be the man to give evidence against Jack after all.

Success went to Jack's head. Suddenly he was bragging about his blag going off like some teenage kid who'd broken open his first gas meter. How long before this information was on the street, with grasses picking it up, was anyone's guess. Not long, Brian was willing to bet.

'What's it matter?' was Jack's response, when Brian challenged him. 'We got more than enough to get Old Bill straightened, we should worry.'

'You can't rely on that. We'll all end up getting our collars felt. Be sensible.' Information on the street leading to Jack's arrest was the perfect scenario, as far as Brian was concerned. But for that to happen, it needed Jack directly involved. How he was going to push him into going on the next blag himself, Brian wasn't sure. Convince him the blaggers weren't trustworthy. The only danger there was Jack running out of control and killing someone.

He watched him now with Charles Tyrwhitt as they congratulated each other on the success of the 'collection'. Something about this man made Brian take an instant dislike to him. He wasn't sure what it was. Maybe the over-confident manner that said he owned everyone he did business with. Most of all he didn't like the way he flattered Jack.

'It was a master stroke,' Tyrwhitt was telling him, 'the organization nothing short of brilliant. Your army training paid off, Braden.'

'I'd say,' Jack said, without even a glance in Brian's direction.

Brian thought of telling the banker how Jack hadn't gone near the blag and couldn't organize a ride at a Butlin's holiday camp.

'The money's safely out, is it?' Jack asked.

'All in Curaçao,' Tyrwhitt said.

'Where's that?'

'In the Dutch Antilles, not far from Colombia,' Tyrwhitt told him. 'It's a tax shelter we use for a lot of our customers.'

'That seems a long way off, Charles,' Jack said. 'Can we trust these people?'

'Of course, they're proper bankers. Your brother-in-law found them.'

'I'm fucked if I trust him,' Jack said, as if Brian wasn't there. 'He's as slippery as an eel.'

Tyrwhitt seemed embarrassed, but not even that brought Brian any closer to liking him.

'I'm sure Brian can vouch for Joseph,' Tyrwhitt said, with a little laugh. 'All of our deals have proved solid and profitable. The bankers out there have done exactly what they promised to do, and more.'

'Joey takes the lion's share,' Jack complained. 'Shouldn't we say how much he gets, Bri?'

'I don't think it works like that, Jack,' Brian said. 'We negotiated eight shillings in the pound.'

'Fucking daylight robbery!'

'You know what the saying is, Jack, when you're dealing with banks like that? Money talks, profit walks,' Tyrwhitt informed him.

'No. We got to get a bigger share, Chas,' Jack told him. 'We done all the collar.'

'It's not going to happen, Jack,' Tyrwhitt said. 'Eight shillings in the pound is an excellent return. Without our connections you'd be lucky to get half a crown.'

What a mug, Brian thought, seeing that Jack still wasn't happy. Tyrwhitt wouldn't move on the price Joey had negotiated, and Jack was out of his depth when it came to dealing with people like him. This world now held a lot more appeal for Brian and he yearned to be part of it.

'Our police contact give us another payroll what's going into the *Daily Mirror*,' Jack said. 'It should be worth about two hundred grand.' He sat there, looking like the king of somewhere.

'We could certainly handle that for you, Jack,' Tyrwhitt said, 'but it would still be only eight shillings on the pound.'

'That's ballocks! You'd be getting a hundred and twenty grand. You'd have to go a bit better.'

'We're supplying safety, expertise,' Tyrwhitt said. 'We have a lot more to lose than you do.'

'We?' Jack wanted to know.

'Look, we might go a little better on the exchange if we had our own offshore bank set up in the Dutch Antilles. If you could guarantee a supply of money like this, it would be worth our while to make such a move.'

'We're getting into this game now,' Jack said. 'You can have all the dough you can handle.'

Brian wanted to speak to his dad on his own, but Jack insisted they saw him together and talked about setting up their own bank in the Dutch Antilles with Tyrwhitt.

'Captain Tyrwhitt is a big-mouthed fool,' Joey said.

'Don't you think I can be trusted?' Jack growled. 'I'm supplying the money so I want to control where it's going.'

'There's no question of that happening. It adds unnecessary risk. The money'll go to safe contacts of mine. That's all you need to know.'

'Maybe you're too involved with this banker, Joey. What's gonna happen if he gets nicked for noncing them boys at the boxing tournament? That's his game, you know.'

'Then you ought to tell him.'

'All I know is we ain't getting enough,' Jack said.

'Is that what you feel, Brian?'

'We could always use a better price – it pays to shop around. You taught me that, Dad.'

'Would you want to shop around?' Joey asked. 'To do so increases your risk. You've got a narrow market for that kind of money.'

'How come you banker-wankers are doing so good out of it, then?' Jack argued.

'Go out and try to sell the money yourself,' Joey said. 'See how long you survive.'

'I know your fucking game, Joey. Get me out the way, you grab everything with Brian here. Family won't mean nothing to me, if you try that.'

'Jack, listen to Dad. This has nothing to do with family. It's business. If we could get a better deal, we'd have a better deal. It'd definitely be risky going out with bagloads of money, and you know it.'

Suddenly Jack switched tactic. 'I don't trust Bobby Brown.'

'Then off him,' Brian advised. 'He's got an awful lot of info on you.'

'Two hundred grand is too much dough to trust him with,' Jack said. 'Look at the way he double-crossed us over the train money. I should have popped him. I'm too soft, me.'

Brian glanced at Joey, wondering if this was his opportunity. 'Then you go after the *Daily Mirror* money, Jack. You do the biz with a sawn-off shotgun.'

'You think I couldn't?'

'I know you couldn't,' Brian said, pushing him further into a corner. 'Just like I know I couldn't. I wouldn't want to try.'

'You're just a coward, Brian. I could do it, easy.'

'Why put yourself on offer when you can get Bobby to take the risk with Crutwell?'

'Two hundred grand is much too much temptation,' Jack said. 'They both think we owe them money. I'm gonna make sure my investment goes where it should.'

'Don't be a mug, Jack,' Brian said, but he couldn't persuade him not to get involved, even if he wanted to.

They hit the security guards as they stepped out of their truck on the loading bay beneath the *Daily Mirror* building in Fetter Lane, taking them by surprise. But that wasn't enough. One guard gave up the bag right away, but the second clung to his. Jack levelled the sawn-off shotgun at him. 'Let it go, you stupid fucker. It ain't worth it.'

'No! No!' the guard shouted, clamping his arms more tightly around the bag. Jack couldn't throat-punch him and grab the money with the bag glued to the man's chest. How the gun went off he didn't know. All he could see was the massive hole in the side of the man's stomach. Someone in a stocking mask was grabbing and pulling him. Someone in another mask was pulling the money sack free. Then they were running, jumping into their souped-up Cosworth Cortina and gunning away. Jack didn't want to look back.

'You stupid cunt,' Crutwell was screaming at him. 'You weren't s'posed to shoot him, you mad fucker. I ain't going back to stir, not now.'

Bobby Brown shouted, 'Course you are, David, or you'll definitely be booked as the blagger what this is down to.'

Jack hunched into the seat, ready for them if they tried anything. He eased back the trigger on the remaining loaded barrel of the shotgun as he heard them whispering about him. What were they plotting? Suddenly the threat was too great. He jammed the shotgun to Crutwell's neck. 'You planning to pop me?'

'Someone should, like you done that guard.'

'He had it coming. He wouldn't let go of the money.'

'Calm down, you mug.'

'Don't call me a mug or you're gone too, Bobby,' Jack threatened.

'Yeah, well, why don't you pop us all, Jack? You ain't got nothing to lose now.'

'You having a go at me?'

Crutwell turned to Bobby as if he was in charge. 'What we gonna do?'

'Let's do the money-drop first.'

'Ballocks to that,' Crutwell said. 'Gimme my whack now and let me out. Stop the car.'

'You ain't going nowhere,' Jack said.

'You try some stir, you mug.'

'Stop the car,' Jack ordered, and the driver pulled over. 'Out you go, but you don't get no money.'

'I'd better,' Crutwell said, and backed out of the car, not taking his eye off the shotgun.

'Don't, Jack,' Bobby said. 'You'll get us all nicked.'

Jack turned, thinking about topping him there and then. When he turned back, Crutwell was running. 'Get going,' he told the driver. 'He'll last about five minutes out there.'

'There was two hundred and twelve thousand pounds,' Joey said, from behind his desk. 'But the circumstances have changed. We can't pay eight shillings in the pound. Not now. More like two.'

'I'll kill you and that pervert Tyrwhitt before I let that happen,' Jack said.

Brian knew there would be trouble – he'd guessed his dad wouldn't want to pay much for this money. He held on to the meat cleaver inside his coat. 'We have to wipe our mouths,' he said. 'Take what we can get.'

'You two are jibbing me. I'll put you both in the ground.'

'No one's rooking you, Jack. Look at the circumstances.'

'You robbing fuckers,' Jack screamed irrationally. 'You dirty, thieving bastards! Two bob in the pound? We killed a bloke. You and your banker friends had better think about that.'

'You sell the money if you think you can without getting caught for murder,' Joey said. 'Believe me, I don't intend to go down for this.'

'What's that meant to mean? You grassing me?'

'Don't be stupid,' Brian said.

After a moment Jack cooled down, came back to the table and sat. Joey could out-think and out-smart Jack in his sleep, but the offer he came up with surprised Brian.

'This is what I'll do for you, Jack,' Joey said. 'I'll give you eight shillings in the pound. But Brian has to be part of the deal. He comes out of your firm and works for me. As of now.'

'So you can both plot against me?' Jack said. 'You think I'm mad?'

'No one thinks any such thing,' Joey said, too quickly.

'You conniving kyke!'

Brian hit him with the flat of the cleaver, knocking him out, which left Pongo to deal with. He was in the outer office and Brian expected him to rush in. He knelt on Jack and put the cleaver to his throat, keeping the pressure on with both hands. Then he called Pongo.

The bodyguard's squat figure filled the doorway.

'You can take him home, Pongo, and give him some Valium or I can cut his throat. What's it to be?'

'You know the answer, Bri,' Pongo said quietly. 'If you did that I'd have to kill you.'

'You could try,' Brian said, appearing more courageous than he was feeling. Pongo scared him. Mostly he balanced Jack's madness and kept him functioning in his worst times, but he was irrationally loyal to him, which made him dangerous.

Brian stepped away from Jack. He didn't take his eyes off Pongo, who came forward and lifted his boss off the floor as if he weighed nothing. Putting his shoulder under Jack's arm he carried him out, talking to him soothingly.

Neither Brian nor Joey said a word until they heard them get into the lift, Pongo still making encouraging noises.

'I'm glad you didn't kill him, Brian,' Joey said. 'It would be terrible to have blood on your hands.'

At that moment Brian realized he didn't really know this man, his father – he seemed capable of any sort of accommodation. Had he forgotten about the guard Jack shot during the robbery? Or Cath killing Brian's grandfather? 'We're not done with Jack,' he said. 'Not by a mile.'

TWENTY-EIGHT

The public hue and cry for David Crutwell, who had escaped from Parkhurst while on compassionate leave, was a five-minute wonder. Outrage at the murder of the *Daily Mirror* guard lasted longer, especially after the reward the paper offered; MPs called for restoration of the death penalty. Jack thought he was in the clear as the investigation was being conducted by the Flying Squad and some of the detectives who had put him into the job. Pongo came to the club every day to see what was happening. Jack rarely did – Brian had barely spoken to him all month.

'He's in a bad way, Bri,' Pongo said. 'He's swallowing more pills.'

'You'd better get him to a doctor, Pongo.'

'He won't go. He said he'd kill me if I tried that. I couldn't go against him. He's scared they'll put him in a nuthouse. And that's definitely where Leah's going to end up. They're so bad for each other.'

'You ought to be a marriage counsellor.'

'Will you come and see him, Bri? I think he'd like that. He won't ask.'

Brian said he would, for Pongo's sake.

When he got to the flat Jack was a mess, wild-eyed with several days' stubble. He'd lost weight.

'It's good to see you,' he said, taking Brian through to the messy kitchen and putting the kettle on the gas stove. Brian picked it up, filled it from the tap and put it back.

'Stephen Ward came to see me, Brian. He warned me about Ken Drury. He's moving in on all our spots, nicking our money.'

'Jack, Ward's dead. He topped himself a few years ago.'

'I'm not mad, Bri,' Jack assured him. 'It was Stephen – he was my landlord. He was in a dream.'

Brian felt only slightly relieved. 'What should we do about Drury?'

'His days are numbered. We'll put the old firm back together, Brian. Be like old times. Remember that fight we had in the Rupert Street carpet joint? It was some punch-up. What about that judge you helped when the Krays sent some muscle to cap you and they killed the bird the judge was doing? What was his name? The judge?'

'Melford Stevenson.' Brian remembered him. He had turned into a particularly vicious hard-liner who'd sent the Kray's whole firm down for life.

'That's him. I wonder who's getting his birds for him now. I'll get myself cleaned up and come down the club, show my face to the customers. They like to know things are all right. They know they are when I'm around.'

'Most of them have gone.'

'We'll get them back.'

'Why don't you see a doctor, Jack? Straighten yourself out. Get some pills that'll help you.'

That set Jack off, accusing him of being in with Pongo and trying to take over the firm. Brian left and went to meet DCI Fenwick, who was still successfully running with both the hares and the hounds. 'Something has to be done about Jack. He's off his head,' Brian told him. 'The thing is, George, if the wrong Old Bill gets hold of him, he'll get us all nicked.'

They were in Fortnum & Mason's tea-room overlooking Jermyn Street. Brian often came there – it was a good place to pick up young men.

'Did Jack pop Denny Jones?' DCI Fenwick asked, surprising Brian: Denny's cover was still good. 'That's what we heard.'

Brian didn't say anything. He was watching a good-looking man in his twenties sitting across the room with his mother. Both were showing out to him.

'We'd have to have some evidence. That *Daily Mirror* shooting didn't get us what we need – unless you want to give evidence?'

Still Brian said nothing.

'Like you say, Brian, it only wants the wrong Old Bill to capture Jack and we could all be in the frame.'

'It sounds like we would be either way,' Brian said.

'You could always turn Queen's evidence, Brian,' Fenwick told him. 'Grab yourself a deal. Our guv'nor would go for that. New identity, new life. It's got a lot to recommend it.'

Brian had thought this meeting was about putting Jack, rather than himself, out of harm's way. 'I don't think that's likely,' he said.

'I tell you, Brian, things aren't looking rosy for any of us right now. I'm thinking of going to Australia.'

'Plenty of bent Old Bill out there,' Brian said calmly, as his stomach churned. 'Look, why don't you nick Jimmy Humphreys? He knows almost every earner Ken Drury ever had.'

'I thought this was about nicking Jack Braden.'

'You gotta have evidence for that.'

'There's a lot of police activity but no results. If we don't nick someone soon a lot of pressure will build up.'

'Excuse me,' someone said. Brian turned. 'I think you dropped this.' The young man handed over a fine-grained leather wallet.

'So I did,' Brian said, pleased.

'Aren't you Brian Oldman?'

'Indeed I am, unless you're a debt collector.'

'I came into your club for a friend's twenty-first a few months ago. Someone pointed you out.'

Brian got his phone number and said he'd invite him round for a drink. He would too. He felt good about that.

Chief Superintendent Slipper was laying out the strategy for arresting Jack Braden, and Tony Wednesday could see he was sick at the prospect of what it involved with so many corrupt policemen. It excited Tony more than he could let on.

'Do you know what this means if it's true about Commander Drury?' Slipper said. 'Corruption at his level is hard to believe.'

'The source is impeccable,' Fenwick said.

Tony wanted to laugh. It couldn't have been more impeccable.

'How can we get to Jack Braden without going after Drury for now?' Slipper asked.

'I don't know if we can, sir,' Tony said.

'I don't want any word to get out about the commander. Find anyone else in the job who's at it and could help us nick Jack Braden's firm. I'll talk to the assistant commissioner.'

They left Slipper's office and started along the corridor. 'It's going to be a very dangerous game, Tony,' Fenwick said. 'Think of all the coppers who'll fall with Drury. It doesn't bear thinking about.'

'Bent coppers, guv,' Tony said.

'A lot'll be unhappy and won't go easily,' Fenwick pointed out.

'That's an understatement. They might even come after us. We need to put someone between us and them,' Wednesday said.

'Like who? What you got in mind, Tony?'

Tony saw a way to get at the very bright policeman who was related to Jack Braden. Despite their kinship, Redvers would be desperate to nick him and Brian Oldman.

'How's that gonna help?' Fenwick wanted to know.

'It's no stretch of the imagination to think how he might help a relative. If we can keep Jack in the frame somehow and let Brian walk, Redvers takes the heat for bent Old Bill,' Tony said. 'He's a complete wolly.'

'Is that why he got promoted like he was?' Fenwick asked.

'He's bright academically. He wouldn't last five minutes on the street, guv,' Tony assured him. 'Let's bring him in on this. He's dead straight. He's the one Old Bill who won't sell info to villains.'

'He could be more dangerous than enough,' Fenwick cautioned.

'Don't worry about it. He'll make us look like Boy Scouts, too.'

Tony laughed. The more dangerous the game, the more he enjoyed it. He loved outwitting both the police and the criminals.

'Why did you want to meet here,' Superintendent Redvers asked, 'instead of in my office in Tintagel House or at the Yard?'

They were on the Embankment opposite the Houses of Parliament. Tony had thought Redvers couldn't record anything there so he felt safe. 'Are you corrupt, John?' he asked bluntly.

'Good grief, I hope not.'

'Well, that's what it's come to that we have to ask. I don't know who else to trust on this. Now, where to start? There's a villain on the run from Parkhurst, who was got out to run the blag on the *Daily Express* and the *Daily Mirror*.'

'He was actually got out of prison for the purpose?'

'And disappeared after the guard was shot. He was supposed to go back but didn't.'

'How was he got out?' Redvers was incredulous.

'A bent policeman helped him.'

'Who is this bent policeman?' He was growing irritable now. Perhaps he didn't enjoy the way the information had to be extracted like teeth.

'It's Commander Drury,' Tony said.

'Oh, how amusing, Tony! Why not the commissioner?'

'Is he at it as well, John?' Tony asked.

'This is hideous. Police commanders don't aid criminals to escape from prison to rob and murder. I'm supposed to take your word on this, am I?'

'I wouldn't,' Tony said, 'not in this climate.'

'How was he got out?'

'Compassionate leave, on both occasions. Check it out.'

A couple of days later when Redvers called him, the excitement in his voice told Tony he had bitten. He wanted to meet and suggested the same place as before.

'I did some checking, Tony,' Redvers told him. 'David Crutwell, one of the Great Train Robbers, had compassionate leave from prison coinciding with both the *Daily Express* and the *Daily Mirror* robberies – for his mother's funeral! Twice. There must have been some jiggery-pokery going on there – especially as his mum died twenty years ago.'

'That's brilliant,' Tony said. 'Brilliant.'

'It gets better. The same two prison officers went with him each time. They were almost certainly in on it.'

'It sounds like it.'

'I'd like you to interview them until they break,' Superintendent Redvers said.

'I work for Chief Superintendent Slipper,' Tony said. 'He guards his patch jealously. I'd have to clear it.'

'I wouldn't have it any other way.'

'DCI Fenwick would be a good man to have on this, John.'

'Good,' the superintendent said. 'Tony, I think perhaps you should call me guv, or sir.'

Jimmy Humphreys was arrested and held, charged with perverting the course of justice. His immediate response was panic. He was obviously looking for a way out. There wasn't one. That was clear to Tony as he stood at the back of the interview room and listened. Detectives were taking him though his statement, while Fenwick was steering him away from things that would involve them. Tony knew he was in safe hands here. It was time to put the next part of his plan in place. He turned to the DCI and whispered, 'I'll warn Jack Braden and the iron.' Fenwick nodded.

Jack Braden was at his drinking club, puffy-eyed and downing pills with Scotch. Tony wondered if he'd live long enough to get to court. Dully, he registered the fact of Humphreys's arrest.

By contrast, Brian Oldman was hysterical when he was told what Humphreys was saying about them. Tony wondered if he was acting or if he really knew what problems his arrest could bring. 'How do I know I can trust you, Tony?' he said.

'That's stupid. I'm here, warning you.'

'It's not hard, being inside,' Jack said calmly.

'Are you insane?' Brian said.

Tony wondered if he was changing his mind.

'You stick to what you're good for, son,' Jack said. 'Let me do the business.'

'The fact is, you don't know you can trust me, either of you,' Tony said, raising the stakes a little higher. 'You wanna trust Superintendent Redvers instead?'

'John Redvers? My nephew?' Jack said. 'What's he got to do with anything?'

'He's being brought in on this because he's got special knowledge of you and Brian.'

'He's my sister's boy,' Jack said. 'That ain't fair.'

'What's the plan, Tony?' Brian said, suddenly calm.

'I'll arrest you. Let you see what we've got. Let you steer us away from anything dangerous.'

'Will your plan work, Tony?' Redvers asked, in the briefing room at Tintagel House. 'It's not the way I learnt detective work.'

'It's WW, guv,' Tony Wednesday said, resenting Redvers every time he had to call him 'sir' or 'guvnor'.

'What's that?' What does 'WW' mean?'

'Whatever Works,' Tony told him. 'They think you're going to help them because you're related.'

'I'd like to see them go down for a very long time,' Redvers said. 'I can't tell you how they've blighted my life. I want to put them away by any means possible.'

'As long as we don't break the rules, guv.' Tony said ironically. That was a statement he intended to tuck away and keep, as a plan began to take shape in his mind.

Tony knew that if he was caught in the evidence store with his hands on evidence in a case he shouldn't touch until he was in court it wouldn't be conducive to career advancement. Being caught there was a stone ginger, he thought as he froze on hearing the key in the door at the shelf where some of the physical evidence against Jack Braden was stored. He considered hiding, but if he was found that would only make matters worse. Bluffing was the best way out and he was good at that. Also, most policemen wanted to believe other policemen.

The door opened and DCI Fenwick stepped in. 'Tony,' he said, startled. 'What are are you doing?'

Tony winked at the Cannon Row duty sergeant who was with Fenwick. 'I'm manipulating the evidence so we can make sure Jack Braden goes where all bad boys go.'

'You're taking a chance, aren't you?'

'That's the way I've lived my life, guv.' The duty sergeant didn't say a word and Tony guessed he wouldn't. Certainly Fenwick wouldn't report finding him there. As he went out Tony wondered what the DCI was up to. He didn't tell him what he had left there.

'Superintendent Redvers,' George Carman said, rising in his seat in number-six court at the Old Bailey, a thick sheaf of papers in his hand. He was a small, agitated man, who looked older than he was, but he dominated the space like few others. 'Can you tell the jury what your relationship is to the defendant Jack Braden?'

Redvers knew he could only tell the truth. 'He's my uncle,' Redvers said.

'Mr Oldman, the second defendant?' Carman asked, glancing at his notes.

'My cousin, sir.'

'Did you say to Detective Inspector Wednesday – in the presence of several other police officers – "I want to put them away by any means possible"?'

He couldn't deny having said it, or something similar. What he didn't know was who on their side had so informed this barrister.

Not Wednesday, or he wouldn't have allowed his name to be mentioned.

'"By any means possible". What did you mean by that?'

'By any legal means possible, of course,' Redvers said.

'There's no "of course" in your statement. Only "by any means possible". Most people would take that to be including any illegal means, Superintendent.'

'I certainly wouldn't contemplate anything illegal.' Having made that statement he searched his brain for anything illegal he might have done that this barrister could dredge up.

Carman turned to his junior and collected a page from him. 'Is this your memo, Superintendent?' He passed a sheaf of papers to the usher, who gave one to the judge and another to Redvers.

He studied it with a sinking feeling as the usher took copies to the jury.

'Can you read it to the court, so we all know?'

The words wouldn't come. Staying silent made him appear guilty. The words were innocent, but out of context they might seem corrupt. Still he couldn't say them.

'Superintendent?' the judge said. 'Can you do as Mr Carman asked?'

'Yes, your honour,' Redvers managed at last. '"You should exclude any evidence that favours the defence's case."'

'Is that how senior police officers behave, Superintendent?'

'We spend a lot of taxpayers' money. We have a job to do, putting criminals away.'

'If you hide evidence favourable to the defence's case, innocent men might go to prison, thus spending even more of the taxpayers' money in the subsequent appeal process.'

'I don't believe innocent men have gone to prison.'

'Just as you believe you should put your uncle and cousin down by any corrupt means?'

Redvers glanced across the court at Wednesday, who was sitting at the back of the prosecution benches with DCI Fenwick. He couldn't read anything in their blank expressions.

'I don't think the answer is over there with your colleagues, Superintendent,' the barrister said. 'Does this sort of practice extend to planting evidence where none exists?'

'No, of course it doesn't,' Redvers said emphatically.

'Then will you look at the exhibit list supplied by the prosecution?' The barrister lifted it and indicated the number in the bundle. The jury looked too. 'Can you see the last two items on the list? Hair from Jack Braden's head found in the getaway car used in the *Daily Mirror* newspaper robbery, and a piece of cloth identified as belonging to Brian Oldman caught on the edge of the door.'

'Yes, they were found in the car that was dumped,' Redvers said.

'Did you add those to the list of finds after the suspects were in custody?'

'No, of course I didn't!'

'Then can you tell the jury why they appeared on the list after it was closed and after the car had been examined? Those two items were added with a different typewriter.'

'Is this difference confirmed by an expert, Mr Carman?' the judge asked.

'Yes, your honour. I have the report here and the expert is available to testify.'

'I'll see counsel in chambers,' the judge said.

'There is no question of falsifying the evidence,' Redvers insisted to his boss at Tintagel House. The assistant commissioner was there too, following the collapse of the trial. Redvers wasn't sure they believed him, but that wasn't the worst part of this, or Jack Braden and Brian Oldman being released – not even being looked at askance by colleagues who suspected him of behaving corruptly. The worst part was being told in the Central Criminal Court by a senior circuit judge that he couldn't manage the rise in criminality by unfair practices and unfair laws, and for that reason he was stopping the trial. That had cut deeply. For now he would have to live with this and suffer his penance, but he wouldn't stop trying to win back the confidence of the commissioner, whom he had unwittingly let down. Neither would he stop searching for a way to bring down the man he suspected of being wholly responsible for his downfall. Eventually Tony Wednesday would be exposed for what Redvers believed he was: a sinister, corrupting policeman.

TWENTY-NINE

Brian hunched himself against the gnawing cold in the empty club, trying to warm his hands by the candles lit along the bar. The miners were on strike and neither the Prime Minister nor Jack could turn the lights back on, though Jack probably had more chance of doing so than Ted Heath. The club wasn't their main source of income, these days, but it provided a good cover. Most of their money came from robbery, and Brian noticed that Jack, having literally got away with murder, was taking all the credit for the blaggers who had found a way to their door. He had conveniently forgotten that it had been Brian's idea to collect villains coming out of prison and give them money to tide them over until they could be put to work. Most of them were without any society to return to. The old tenements and tiny terraced houses of Hoxton, Whitechapel and Bethnal Green had been replaced by soaring high rises.

Neither the miners' strike nor the credit Jack was claiming for the firm was agitating Brian right then. What did disturb him was what they had heard following the arrest of Commander Ken Drury. A lot of bent policemen had run for cover, and George Fenwick had disappeared. No phone call, not even a postcard. Brian feared he had been arrested and was being held somewhere while the rubber heels pumped him dry of information. If that was so, they should put a lot of distance between themselves and Old Bill. But Jack wasn't ready to hear that. Once more he believed he was untouchable.

Now he threw open the door and swaggered across the club, looking ridiculous in an Afghan coat over embroidered flared jeans and a bolero jacket with a medallion on his hairy chest. His shirt was open to the navel. It didn't look right on a forty-two-year-old. Somehow Jack didn't cut it as a fashion icon.

'D'you find Fenwick?' he asked.

'He's nowhere that anyone can locate him. That doesn't necessarily mean he's betraying us, Jack.'

'He's grassing us, I know he is,' Jack said emphatically. 'The snake. We gotta kill him.'

'Maybe,' Brian said wearily, 'but we have to find him first. We got enough problems if these rumours about the filth coming after us again are true.'

'Don't talk daft. They daren't, not after that other chuck in court. Stop pissing around. Find him, and I'll pop him.'

'Well, why don't you try calling him, Jack?' Brian suggested. 'Maybe he'll answer the phone if he knows it's you.'

Jack missed the joke. 'Ask that other snake, Tony Wednesday. He must know where he is.'

Meeting Detective Inspector Wednesday wasn't a problem. He was quite relaxed about it, despite the atmosphere currently surrounding the police. 'D'you want to bring some duck food? I'll meet you by the pond in St James's Park,' he suggested.

Standing on the bridge in his sheepskin jacket, watching the birds, Brian scanned the faces around him for anyone who might be unwelcome Old Bill watching them. He could have picked up any one of a half-dozen men, but for some reason that didn't interest him much lately.

'Greedy fuckers, aren't they?' Tony Wednesday said, startling him.

'Who?' Brian said. 'The birds?'

'You didn't congratulate me on making DI.'

'I don't know if I can afford to.'

The detective gave him a sideways look. 'What's Jack's problem?' He set off across the bridge.

'What's happening with all the Old Bill who got nicked since Drury fell from grace?'

'The rubber heels are sifting through them, doing deals. They're letting most quietly retire. For a while it looked like it was going to amount to nothing more than a headline in the *Daily Mail*—'

He stopped, and Brian turned to him anxiously. This detective liked to get in your head and fuck you that way.

'Our new commissioner, Sir Robert Mark, wants to make a big noise about police corruption. His mission statement is to root it out.'

'Is George Fenwick part of his mission?'

'I heard the rubber heels have got him pugged up somewhere. They know he's been at it for a long time,' Wednesday said. 'The question is, can they prove it?'

'No,' Brian said edgily, 'that's not the question. It's can he hold up to questioning or will he give up names?'

'There's always a chance, Brian.' Wednesday smiled. 'It depends what they promise him, what blood-letting the new commissioner's prepared for. This one might be prepared to pay that price. He's the first in the job who's come up through the ranks.'

'Can you find George? Jack plans to go in and pop him.'

'If he's being held, it could be dangerous.'

'You mean pricy, don't you?'

The detective looked at him, making him feel uncomfortable. 'No, I mean dangerous. Unless you blokes plan to retire. Why not? You must have plenty put away.'

'Jack thinks he can walk on water.'

'He should get together with our new commissioner. Rooting out police corruption would be equally miraculous. I'll ask around, Uncle.'

He was gone with the same stealth by which he'd arrived, leaving Brian more uneasy. He knew somehow he had to get his life on a more secure footing.

*

'Are we doing blags today?' Bobby Brown wanted to know, when he came into the club and lit a cigarette from a candle, his shoulders stooped inside the turned-up collar of his overcoat. 'Or we all becoming ponces nicking a living off porno?'

'Do you want to talk to Jack about that, Bobby?'

'What – and end up in a pork pie? Piss off!' Bobby said, and took another deep drag on his cigarette. 'Jack didn't do nothing about getting the power back on then. I thought he'd have had it sorted by now. Them greedy fucking miners are out of order. They only think about themselves.'

'What's happening about this bank job?'

''S blinding,' Bobby enthused. 'After this one, we can all retire. That's about what I'd like to do, Bri. Get right out. Them safe deposits make it possible, for sure.'

'There might be nothing but pornographic pictures in those boxes,' Brian pointed out. It would be a lot of collar and expense for nothing.

Bobby argued that his source knew it was used as a drop for South American drug money. 'It's worth millions. We have to give it a go, Bri.'

'We'd better talk to Jack. Convince him.'

'We could do it without him. We've talked about it long enough.'

That was an option, and perhaps the best, rather than risk catching Jack in one of his bad moods.

Today he was withdrawn when he came into the club. Pongo indicated that Leah wasn't good. She'd been in hospital a couple of times. Brian couldn't remember if she was in or out now. He wasn't that interested, he told himself.

'How do you know it's drugs money in them boxes?' Jack asked.

''S what my man told me, Jack. That's why he's prepared to pass it across. He hates drugs. His daughter died of a heroin overdose.'

'How does he know? They don't label the boxes – little bit of wedge here, tax fiddle in that one, drug money there.' Jack and Pongo laughed. 'Give us a break.'

'He sees the geezers going to the boxes,' Bobby said, becoming animated. 'Someone puts it in, someone else takes it out. Not just little envelopes neither.'

'All sounds iffy,' Jack said. 'Blagging Securicor and payrolls in the open's one thing. They cut up rough, you let them have it. Going into a bank vault where you can't leg it, that's something else. Look how I done that security guard at the *Mirror* and got away with it.'

Like everyone else close to Jack, Brian was fed up with hearing this. It was arrogant and stupid. 'Bobby'd put the team together,' he argued. 'All we have to do is finance it. Could be we can all retire after this one.'

'Who's talking about retiring?' Jack said. 'You think I should retire? I run the West End now.'

'But you're letting the druggies take over,' Bobby said. 'Nutters out of their heads shooting up in doorways. It's not like the old days, Jack. Women could walk down the street unmolested. They knew you were there to protect them.'

Cleverly Bobby went from insult to blatant flattery, then threw it all away. 'It's madness to let this one go, Jack.'

'You saying I'm mad?' Jack closed the space between them to menace him.

Bobby lit another cigarette from the stub of the last. 'No. It's just a blinding job, Jack. I mean, if you don't want it, I could go after it myself.'

Jack gave a cold laugh. 'You hear that, Pongo? Bobby's starting his own little firm. Over my dead body, son.'

'Jack, listen,' Brian said. 'This could be a real result.'

'It's too iffy. Banks give you nothing but aggravation,' Jack said. 'Take my advice, stick to what you know best.'

'What's that? Muscling old toms for a few quid?' Bobby said.

'It's done us all right,' Jack argued.

'It's ponces' work,' Bobby said.

'You and me are gonna have a right falling-out.'

That was Jack's last word on the matter, but not Bobby's. He persuaded Brian to have another look at the bank on the corner of Baker Street and Marylebone Road. Above ground, traffic roared past while tube trains rumbled past the basement vaults. Brian wondered if that was the way in.

'If he ain't having it, Bri, you gotta decide. I mean, I know Jack's family, but he's an ache. Someone's gonna clip him before much longer.'

'You?' Brian challenged.

'Someone will, Bri.' There was a hint of panic in his voice, as if there was no going back. 'Maybe even take him out to Stoke Poges for the pigs – that'd be a laugh.'

Brian thought about the blag. If it could be done, it should be done. It wouldn't be easy, although it would be easier without Jack. 'Start putting a little firm together, Bobby. I'll take a chance on that drug money being there.'

Bobby went off, swaggering in his high heels and fashionable suit with big lapels. Brian smiled. He was a good villain, for all his mouth.

Jack wasn't at the club when Brian arrived. The electricity was back on but there had been more light when they were only burning candles. One table was busy with a game of pontoon at two quid a point. The house was well ahead, and Brian took that as a favourable sign.

Eventually he tracked Jack to his flat. When he opened the door, he looked like a rabbit caught in car headlights. 'What you doing? You're not s'posed to come here.'

'Who said, Jack?' Brian purposely hadn't phoned ahead. 'Are you the guv'nor or is Leah? Anyway, Mum said she was in the nuthouse.'

'It's not a nuthouse, it's a psychiatric hospital. She's back home and I don't want her upset.'

'I won't upset her,' Brian said, 'if she don't upset me.' He stepped inside. 'Look, I'm having a go at that Lloyds Bank job. I thought

I'd better tell you. I got a real good feeling about this one. I mean, wouldn't it be nice to retire to Marbella with a few million? Money we can go again on without having to get a rate from that wanker Dad's mixed up with.'

'Bobby Brown's going bent on us,' Jack announced.

His continual jumping subject to subject without warning still shocked Brian and he couldn't find an appropriate response.

'Don't trust him,' Jack added.

Holding to his course, Brian argued the case. The blag could be worth two or three million. What was there to trust?

'I have to do something about him,' Jack mumbled. 'I might have to cap him along with George Fenwick.'

Leah came out of the bedroom into the hall in a black nylon negligée that matched the rings under her eyes. When she saw Brian she gasped and dropped tray loaded with cups and saucers. 'What's he doing here?' she asked quietly. 'He wasn't ever to come here. You promised. I told you I'd kill myself, and I will! I will—'

'Leah! Calm down, for Christ's sake. He's going—'

'I'll kill myself—'

'Go on!' Brian shouted. 'You need a knife?'

'He's going. He is – get out of here!'

'You ought to take her straight back in the nuthouse,' Brian said, provoking her. 'She's a bar of Cadbury's—'

Leah screamed and dropped to the floor, grabbing a shard of china. She sprang up with it, threatening Brian.

'Go on, then, you maniac.' He drew back his fist.

'Get out!' Jack yelled at him. 'Get out!'

'Why, when she's so entertaining?'

Leah ran into the kitchen and began to hurl things at the wall.

'Jesus wept,' Brian said, as Jack caught hold of her. Fleetingly, he felt a bit sorry for his uncle, but then he remembered how he had come to be with Leah.

*

Regent's Park was only a short walk from the Baker Street bank, fairly anonymous and safe.

'You're sure he's kosher, Bobby?' Brian asked, as he strode across the grass towards the pond. The speed at which they were walking might get them remembered, but they were late and Bobby was scared the man would go.

'He's sound. He wants to make sure you're the right type.'

Brian didn't like the sound of that. 'What type?'

'Well, not someone doing it for the money.'

Brian pulled up sharply. 'Why are we doing it then?'

'Oh, didn't I mention that, Bri? It's to get back at the drug-dealers who hide money there. That's him.'

The man indicated was in his early forties and looked like a flasher, in a green parka and plimsolls.

'His daughter got hooked. Killed herself. That's why he hates the dealers. Kevin!' Bobby greeted him. 'Sorry we're late. This is my pal I was telling you about.'

'Nice to meet you,' Brian said.

'You're younger than I expected.'

The man introduced himself as Kevin Fleet – probably his real name, Brian decided, as he told him he was Alan Smithson.

'Are you clean living, Mr Smithson?'

'I don't smoke or drink alcohol. I certainly don't go with dirty women.'

'What about drugs?' Kevin asked.

'I wouldn't touch them and I'd advise you not to.'

'I don't. So many young people's lives are ruined by drugs.'

'We see them all over Soho, shooting up in doorways, swallowing pills,' Brian said. 'The police don't do much.'

'They can't do anything, not while the banks are used by dealers,' Kevin said. 'The bank has no real knowledge, of course. Its policy is not to enquire. Otherwise no one would rent security boxes.'

He outlined the profile of some of their clients, how many were up to no good; how the country was going to the dogs; how Ted

Heath taking the country into the Common Market would make matters worse – the man couldn't even negotiate with the miners.

'A power-cut might help us,' Brian pointed out, only to be told the alarm system wouldn't be affected. Kevin Fleet couldn't get them into the bank, but promised a copy of the alarm and vault plans.

'What do you want out of this, Kev?' Brian asked – and almost blew it for them.

'Why would I want anything?' he said. 'I'm not a criminal.'

Brian apologized, calming him. Then, after plying him with as many questions as he could think of, he promised to do all he could to stop the drug-dealers. Kevin hurried away.

Brian doubted this would be a goer. 'What a div. Where did you find *him*, Bobby? In a Christmas cracker?'

'He asked George Foreman if he could get him a gun. He was planning to kill one of the drug couriers.'

'George is involved, is he?'

This was something else Bobby had kept back. George Foreman's presence would make Brian hesitate. There was bad blood between Jack and George, who'd been on the Great Train Robbery and hadn't given Jack a taste. Brian wasn't keen on him either because Foreman had mouthed off in public about his sexual proclivities.

'We can't go without him. He found the blag.'

'Nice one, Bobby. Anything else I should know?'

'There's a lotta collar involved, Bri,' Bobby said. 'George'll be handy. He's strong as an ox. We go in through the Underground. You wanna take a look?'

A tube train roared into the station, drowning what Bobby was saying about the maintenance shaft fifty yards into the tunnel. It was off to the left and ran right under the bank.

As the train pulled out, Brian asked, 'What they going to do? Shut the station for us?'

A lot of work went into the planning, weeks of getting the right information and firming it up. They'd go in as a maintenance crew late at night. Once in that tunnel they'd have to stay until they were done, eating and sleeping there. Finding a reliable thermic-lance operator to cut through the vault floor took time. Charlie Peck, the man they settled on, estimated it would take maybe two days and nights. The big advantage was that there were no alarms in the floor. The disadvantage would be the molten metal and concrete dropping back into the shaft.

All those weeks of work seemed to have been for nothing when Bobby woke Brian early one Sunday morning to say it was off. Jack had captured Terry Lynch, one of their maintenance crew, and poured a lot of Scotch down him, breaking two of his teeth doing it. Eventually he had told him about the thermic-lance man. Now Jack was off on a major rant.

'I can't have none of this now,' Terry Lynch told Brian, when he went to see him, 'not with Jack involved. Look what he done to my fucking teeth, and all that Scotch set m' ulcer off. I didn't mean to tell him nothing.'

'I'll sort him out, Terry. We'll make sure he gets a whack,' Brian said.

'That's not the problem, Bri,' Terry said, 'him having a share. He's not reliable, is he? He's off his head.'

'No. But think how you'll feel when it goes, Terry, and we walk away with bundles,' Brian said. 'We could collect a million apiece in that vault.'

After he'd thought about that for a while, Terry decided to get the best dental job available.

Brian was convinced that this money was his way out of the life. This one job, robbing money from obvious crooks, would set him up to go straight. He talked to Joey at length about how it would be handled. Joey was offering thirty new pence in the pound. 'This is old money,' Brian argued. 'We'd be looking for sixty at least, Dad.'

'We couldn't get the gelt to Switzerland for that,' Joey informed him. 'The Swiss secrecy laws will protect the money once it's there, and only the named holders would have the details. We can't do all that work and pay sixty per cent. Look, come back to the house for dinner – if there's enough power to cook. We'll talk some more about the details. We don't see hardly anything of you, these days, Brian. Your mother misses you.'

'Can't she persuade Ted Heath to settle with the miners?' Brian said.

'Not even the Tory ladies have any faith in him nowadays.'

When they got to the flat his mother wasn't there.

'When did you last have a meal that Mum cooked?' Brian asked.

'She works so hard for the Party,' Joseph said. 'They really appreciate what she's doing. I'm not sure anyone else in the country will, though.'

'I'd say Heath's lot are about as unpopular as they can be.'

Brian and Joey went into the kitchen, opened some tins and continued to talk about money.

'What the hell's going on?' Jack demanded, as Brian walked into the club. 'You cutting me out?'

'No one's cutting you out, Jack,' Brian told him. 'There wasn't any need to bother you, coping with Leah as you are. The thing is, if we're not on for this, we'll miss out.'

'No. We just steam in, nick our share like before.'

'This way we stand to get more and everyone's shtum.'

'With that bunch of nancies you got on it?' Jack said. 'They'd go about two minutes in a tight situation.'

'What? Georgie Foreman, Bobby Brown, Charlie Peck? They're real blaggers.'

'We don't do nothing with Georgie Foreman. He's an out-and-out nonce.'

'You don't have any say in it, Jack, not any more.'

'Yeah? Who said, you fat poof?'

'Everyone's got the pox with you—'

'Who?' Jack demanded. 'What they been saying?'

'You're finished, Jack. Washed up.'

'Bobby put you up to this, didn't he? Look how I walked last time. I ain't washed up!' Jack launched himself at Brian.

Brian could do little until Jack's fury was spent. Then all he could do was dab iodine on his cuts. After that they met only at Brian's flat or in coffee bars.

'He's gone completely potty, Bri,' Bobby Brown announced. 'Look what he done to you. We could wind up Georgie, send him in after Jack.'

'Forget it. We want Georgie at the bank.'

'Well, I ain't having none, Bri. Not if Jack's involved.'

'Well, piss off then,' Brian said irritably. 'Walk away from your share. Fine. We'll work round Jack. He gets his share, but nothing more.'

'We was best mates. Now he ain't worth a rub.' Bobby paused, uncertain. 'How you gonna manage that – work round him?'

'I've set it up with a banker to get all our shares into safe accounts abroad. Neither Jack, the banker nor anyone else can get access to them.'

'Who's doing this? Your dad?' Bobby asked.

Brian remained silent.

'I gotta know. The others'll want to know, especially Georgie.'

'He'll make sure our shares are safe.'

Finally Bobby was satisfied.

They hadn't been in the tunnel for more than fifteen minutes when Bobby complained he couldn't breathe because of the fumes from the thermic lance. He started to panic and Charlie Peck stopped. For a while it looked as if the whole blag would have to shut down. They couldn't get out into the daylight, and if they waited until dark to take Bobby out, there wouldn't be enough time to do the job over what was left of the bank-holiday weekend.

'It's my asthma. What's the point of all that dough if I'm dead?'

'Can't you put a hankie over your mouth?' Charlie Peck said.

'Fuck that,' Bobby said. 'This is asthma, you berk.'

'Well, you'll just have to die, son,' Charlie Peck said, and fired up the lance again. He went back to work, ignoring Bobby's panic. Brian did the same, sending him along the tunnel. The fumes were choking and Brian wondered if any of them would survive. Charlie Peck ought to have anticipated it and organised some breathing apparatus.

The worst part of the operation for Brian wasn't the fumes but the stink of unwashed bodies and shit from where they'd relieved themselves in the tunnel. He was unable to wash or even brush his teeth, and had only stodgy meat pies to eat. He wanted desperately to soak in a bath. The few hours' sleep he snatched were less than welcome because he couldn't shower when he woke up.

Then molten metal fell on Georgie Foreman's arm, burning it as he was clearing away the red hot slag under the hole. He screamed and screamed, frightening Brian, then louder when Brian emptied a bottle of water over it. A great cloud of steam came up. 'Get it off!' big, tough Georgie cried.

When Brian ripped at the cooling slag it pulled away some flesh.

'Jesus Christ!' Charlie said. Bobby rushed over and immediately threw up at the sight of the wound. Brian was the only one brave enough to deal with it. He wrapped a dirty towel around it, then bandaged it with a torn-up shirt. Georgie didn't lose consciousness, but he sweated as he clamped the hand of his good arm on Brian's shoulder, nearly crushing it when the pain was bad.

'We got to get you out of here to hospital, Georgie,' Brian said, 'or you might lose your arm.'

'How we gonna do that, Bri?' Bobby asked.

'We'll just have to take a chance, won't we?' Charlie said.

'And that's the job cattled,' Georgie said. 'Fuck it, I'd sooner have the money.' They all stared at him. 'I mean it.'

In the flickering light of the Tilley lamp Brian nodded. His attitude towards Georgie had shifted dramatically. 'You should get more than your share, Georgie.'

'Let's get in there first, Bri.' He swallowed a handful of aspirins.

Eventually they broke through. And soon after they ran out of gas and the lance stopped cutting.

'You stupid berk, Charlie,' Georgie said, with a flash of irritation. 'Why didn't you get it right?'

'I did,' Charlie snapped. 'Brian said we couldn't carry it all.'

'So we'll send out for a couple of full cylinders,' Brian joked, and the tension dissipated.

They threw a bucket of piss over the hole up into the vault but still had to wait more than two hours for the concrete to cool. Brian glanced at Georgie, who was trying to sleep but couldn't. He didn't want to think about how much pain he was in.

They discovered that the hole through the floor wasn't big enough for any of them to squeeze through, which caused acrimonious recrimination until Brian picked up a chisel and began to hack bits off the side. All this added to their time underground. They knew they had to be out and away in the small hours of the bank-holiday Monday. According to Brian's reckoning, they'd been in there just over forty hours. That gave them less than six to get into the vault and out with whatever they found. It had to be done by wriggling up through the hole. This was especially difficult for Georgie, who could use only one arm, but he was determined to go into the vault.

Excitement rose with each safe-box drawer they cracked open.

'Look at this!' Bobby said, like a child at Christmas opening yet another present.

'What about this, then?' Brian was no less excited.

'Oh, my God, have we had it off!' Charlie exclaimed.

'Didn't I tell you we'd retire?'

'Brian!' Georgie's voice cut through the clamour. 'There must be millions here.' He had found what they assumed was the drugs money. Bundles, it was hard to guess how many. Sixty, seventy, each holding fifty thousand-dollar bills. That was three and a half million dollars!

'Marbella, here I come!' Bobby snapped his fingers. 'Didn't I tell you?'

'You were gonna blow it out. Remember? "I ain't having it with Jack involved,"' Brian reminded him, in a mocking, whiny voice.

'Yeah, well, let's get this down the hole and get out of here,' Bobby said. 'We got enough to live on for the rest of our lives.'

'Leave off,' Georgie said. 'We ain't half done yet. There could be as much again.'

'We're running out of time,' Brian reminded him.

'There's probably nothing but some dirty pictures,' Bobby put in. 'Let's wipe our mouths, Georgie.'

'You can if you want.'

'Look, it's turned twelve o'clock. We can't hang around,' Brian said. 'Start getting the loot bagged up and out into the tunnel, Bobby. We'll do some more boxes.'

Georgie Foreman went at them like a demon, swinging a flogging hammer one-handed, then Charlie Peck used a crowbar to rip them open.

'Bri! What's this lot, d'you think?'

He'd found some sort of bonds. What they were worth Brian couldn't guess. His father would know.

'Are they worth the aggro, d'you think?' Charlie asked.

'If they're not valuable why're they here?' Brian said. 'Bring them. They gotta be worth something.'

'Brian!' Bobby called as he scrambled back up through the hole. 'Tel's on the walkie-talkie. He reckons Old Bill's outside the bank, a carload of 'em.'

'Doing what?'

'They're checking the locks and windows, he reckons.'

'What's that about? The alarms didn't go off, did they?' Now Georgie had stopped, he was ashen, his fleshy face drawn with pain.

'Not a squeak. Terry would've said if they had – unless he's been asleep!'

Brian was struggling against panic. He wanted to run, with nowhere to run to, nowhere to hide. All he said was 'Keep going with the boxes.'

'Are you mad?' Bobby said. 'We can't do no more. I'm off.'

'Just where the hell you gonna go with Old Bill out there?' Brian shouted.

'Well, what if they hear us?'

'How can they down here? Alan!' Brian called through the hole. 'What's Terry saying now?'

'Nothing. He's not saying nothing.'

'Ask what's going on.'

They heard the exchange, the tinny crackle of the radio, the distant voice of Terry Lynch saying the police were back in their car, just sitting there.

'We should've got going when I said,' Bobby complained. 'What we gonna do if they sit there all night and the bank opens? We're stuck down here, Brian.'

The minutes moved slowly as the police sat there. No one spoke, their breathing shallow and quick. Georgie was shivering, while sweat poured off the rest of them like water through open sluice gates at a sewage works. That was what they smelt like too.

Although time was moving slowly, it was moving against them. Bobby was right: if the police stayed, they would be trapped in the tunnel, unable to get out before the bank opened. Brian glanced at the pile of black plastic sacks they had to get away. It would take a while to haul them all through the tunnel. Maybe they'd been too greedy. The bags were stuffed with money, bonds and photographs – Brian wouldn't let them take any jewellery as it was too easily identified, but these men were thieves and had probably lifted some anyway. There was a gap between the early-morning service train that came through around three forty a.m., checking that everything on the track worked, and the first train with passengers at four seventeen. Just thirty-odd minutes to get the twenty-seven sacks out of the service tunnel and across the tracks into the lift shaft to the street where Alan Day's brother would collect them in his council rubbish truck.

Someone's stomach rumbled.

'How you doing, Georgie?' Brian asked.

'I'm all right, Bri.' His voice sounded strained.

After an hour and ten minutes, the police moved off. The men flew into action. In their haste the last sack snagged on the side of the hole and money spilt out over Bobby, who cursed, then started to scoop it into another bag as they lowered Georgie through the hole. His injured arm caught and he yelled, then passed out. Brian couldn't hold his dead weight so Georgie dropped like a stone into the tunnel.

Brian scrambled down after him. 'Georgie?' he said, leaning over to him.

'What the fuck do we do now?' Bobby asked. 'Leave him?'

'Don't talk like a prick,' Brian snapped. 'Get all the sacks out.' He watched them start away.

Georgie Foreman opened his eyes. 'Sorry I'm messing things up here, Bri.'

'You always were an awkward bastard.' Brian grinned, relieved he was still alive.

Neither Brian nor Georgie had made it into the service lift before the four-seventeen rattled into the station with all its lights burning and only two passengers on it. They let it go out, then slowly and painfully climbed the stairs. There was no ticket collector at the barrier as they reached the top. They walked out into the fresh morning air in time to see the dustcart disappear along the service road and on to Marylebone Road to the safe-house.

Elation at being out of the vault and the tunnel almost overwhelmed Brian. He wanted to go home and have a bath but didn't want to spoil the party. Ignoring his loathsome stench he went to the club with the others. Not even Georgie was prepared to miss that. They drank and relived the best and worst moments, which kept everyone high. Although they were tired, no one wanted to leave.

'What a result,' Bobby gloated. 'Didn't I say it would be a result?'

'You should've been there, Jack,' Georgie said. 'It was blinding. Some of the stuff in those boxes – pictures of cabinet ministers stuck right up one.'

'Who?' Jack wanted to know.

'That Lord Lambton and that other geezer from the Lords,' Georgie told him. 'We'll knock them pictures out to the *News of the World*.'

'Yeah, you do that, Georgie. It's about your mark.'

That set off old animosities.

'What's that meant to mean?' Anger flared in Georgie Foreman despite the poor physical shape he was in.

'We'd better divvy up the money,' Jack announced, 'so you mugs don't spend too much at once.'

'Are you kidding?' Bobby said. 'Marbella here I come. Nice house, big pool, a few games of golf with Sean Connery. Cushty.'

'It's all right, Jack,' Brian said. 'The money's gone.'

'What d'you mean, gone? I say how it gets divvied up. Me.'

'Too late,' Georgie told him.

That only made Jack angrier. 'Where is it? Where's it gone?'

'Jack, we're all having a nice drink. This isn't the time, is it?'

'It's exactly the time,' Jack said. 'You ain't taking over the firm, you fat poof.'

'What did you fucking well call me?' Brian retorted, with mock-offence. 'I'm not fat – but a poof? Well, yes.'

That broke the tension and made everyone laugh. Then Jack turned on Bobby. 'What you laughing at?' he demanded. 'Is that what this is all about? Mugging me off?'

'Leave it out, Jack,' Bobby said. 'Calm down, why don't you? We had it off big-time. We had a blinding result.'

'And cut me out!' Jack said. 'We'll see about that.'

He went behind the bar, pulled out a gun and waved it at them.

'Come on, Jack,' Georgie said, 'you're out of order. We're all s'posed to be mates now.'

For a moment Brian thought he was going to try to take the gun off him. He didn't see how – Georgie couldn't have taken a light from him in his state.

'Come on, where's the money?' Jack said.

'You ain't nicking our share. We done all the collar.'

'Who said you get a share, Bobby?' Jack snapped. 'I say who gets a share.'

'The fuck you do,' Georgie growled.

'Yeah? We got a bit of sorting to do, Georgy-Porgy.'

'We all got the pox with you,' Bobby said.

'You thieving mug!' Jack exploded, barely getting his words out. 'You always was a noncing, no-good thief, Bobby.'

'Put the gun down,' Brian ordered.

'I'm a thief, but I ain't a ponce. You let others do all the collar, then ponce their shares.'

'You mug!' Jack shouted, his voice the loudest amid the abuse, competing with Brian's demands for everyone to calm down. No one did. Tempers rose. In the affray, the gun went off. Dead silence followed, until Brian broke it. 'Bobby?' he said. 'Bobby?' He fell to his knees beside Bobby's still form on the floor.

'Oh, fuck. Someone better call an ambulance.'

'An ambulance isn't going to do Bobby much good now,' Brian said.

'Oh, Jack,' Charlie said. 'Why the fuck d'you do that?'

'He was mugging me off. That's what everyone gets who tries it. Just get him out of here – take him up to the pig farm.'

Brian felt as sick as he guessed everyone else did. This had been Bobby Brown's finest hour, a moment of huge triumph the 'no-good thief' would never top. Now he was dead, killed by his oldest friend. 'Forget it, Jack,' he said, standing up. 'You did him, you take him up there. I've had it.' He stalked out, not caring what happened to Jack. Bobby's death made what they'd achieved over the long weekend seem worthless. The others started to leave. Jack was appealing to them, saying they'd get a bigger share, but no one was interested. Jack wasn't controlling the money.

'I can't believe he done that. I can't.' Charlie Peck shook his head as they regrouped in the street.

'This changes everything, Bri,' Georgie said.

'I don't see how. I mean, I feel as gutted as you do about Bobby. His kids'll get his share. This can't change anything.'

'Where you gonna say he is?' Charlie asked.

'He had to go away.'

'But he didn't see them from one year to the next.'

'They still get Bobby's share,' Brian insisted.

'What about our shares, Bri? Shouldn't we just take our whack and split before the wheels come off?'

'That might be best, Bri,' Charlie put in.

Brian assured them the money was safe. In a day or two their shares would be in their nominee accounts abroad.

'What if Jack comes after the dough?' Charlie said. 'I mean, he's completely off his trolley doing Bobby like that.'

'What chance we got if he comes after our shares?' Alan Day asked.

'But he can't get them – he can't,' Brian insisted.

They weren't convinced.

'Why would you expect criminals to trust a banking system, Brian?' his father said, when they met at his office. 'Don't you want to know what your individual shares are?'

'It leaves a sour taste after what happened, Dad.' Brian had grown up with Bobby Brown. He'd known him almost as well as he knew Jack and now he had almost certainly been taken to the farm and eaten by pigs.

'You'd be well advised to stay as far away from Jack as you can. He's completely cracked.'

'How far can you get from a madman when he's still acting like you're joined at the hip?' Brian said. 'What do I tell the others about their money?'

'They're each due approximately eighty grand,' Joseph said. 'That's without the bonds. It was smart of you to bring those. There were four million pounds' worth.'

'What?' Brian was shocked. To think that Charlie had wanted to leave them! 'What will we get for them?'

'If they belong to the same people who put all the dollars there we could pay ten per cent on that sort of paper. But they might not be from the same source.'

'What d'you mean?' Brian asked suspiciously. 'Who else is there?'

'The IRA for one.'

'Well, what are they? A bunch of thick cowboys,' Brian said, with bravado. 'They might manage to kill a few civilians. They'll find us lot a bit different.'

'What if the money belongs to someone even nastier than the IRA?' Joey suggested. 'Someone with a lot of influence – say, MI5.'

'Why would they have that sort of money there?'

'Possibly to bribe government agents. If that's the case, we'd pay a lot less.'

'Well, they won't know who had it. Anyway, Jack can deal with that – he's such a tough guy,' Brian said.

'Those sort of people would take no time at all to go from him to you, and everyone else.'

'The boys'd think I'm trying to rook them. What about the rest of their dough? When can they get that?'

'They can't, Brian. Not in hard cash. Charles has tied it up for five years in growth bonds.'

'Why the hell d'you let him? They'll go mad.'

'Do you know what would happen if you went on to the street with the sort of money and securities you brought here? You'd all be in jail within hours. This job is bigger than the Great Train Robbery. It threatens the stability of society – the whole banking system.'

'But it's all died down,' Brian said. 'There's not been a word about it in the papers for at least three days.'

'That in itself may be worrying,' Joey said. 'Charles thinks those boxes could've contained something connected to someone important in Heath's government. Your mother, of course, would never hear of such a thing.'

'They gotta get something now,' Brian said.

'Interest-free loans from the bank, which they could use to buy a property in Spain. With interest rates currently at twelve per cent that's very generous.'

'They're villains, Dad,' Brian reminded him. 'They won't see it like that.'

Nor did they. Brian met up with Georgie, whose burn had been treated in hospital and had discharged himself. He had elected himself spokesman for the blaggers. They wanted the readies now.

'I thought you had more sense, Georgie,' Brian told him. 'The police already gave Charlie a spin. What if they'd found bundles of dough there?'

'Don't take us for mugs, Brian,' Georgie Foreman said. 'First it's Jack tryna jib us—'

'I'm not. This way you get everything you want, plus security. Think of it like a monument to Bobby. He promised us all we could retire on this one. If you have the readies, you'll be broke within a year or, worse, nicked.'

'I'll take my chances. Who's holding?'

'I can't tell you that,' Brian said.

'It's your old man, ain't it?' Georgie speculated. 'Bobby said he was well connected to some banker.'

'Bobby was a diamond geezer, but he had a big gob.'

'Well, we're gonna see your old man with pickaxe handles,' Georgie threatened. 'We'd do it, Bri. You know that.'

'Give me a couple of days,' Brian said. 'We'll see if we can't uncouple the dough. But I guarantee it won't come back anything like fifty per cent. More like ten.'

'Don't give us that ballocks! Most of it was in old.'

'So wander into a bank and change up great wads of dollars. Or the bearer bonds,' Brian mocked. 'You'd be nicked in three seconds. The same problem if you stick the dough under a floorboard – Old Bill sniffing around.'

'I don't give a monkey's. You slags ain't ripping us off,' Georgie said. 'You'll both get what Bobby got before I let that happen. That's a promise.'

'One you think you can back up, Georgie?' Brian challenged, grabbing his damaged arm.

'Ah, leave off, you bastard!' he roared. 'Leave off.'

Brian released him. After the pain had passed Georgie said, 'I don't care how many Old Bill you got straightened, Bri. If we don't get our money we'll do it. We'll pop you.'

THIRTY

'Detective Inspector Wednesday?' an authoritative voice said, stopping him on the fourth-floor corridor at Scotland Yard as he turned out of the lifts.

'You sound like you're about to feel my collar.'

'Is there something I could arrest you for?'

'I shouldn't think so.'

The man laughed. 'I'm not a policeman.'

'Then how did you get access to this floor in Scotland Yard?' Tony asked. 'Mr . . . ?'

'Smith,' the man said. 'There's nowhere we can't get access to. Is there somewhere more private we can talk?'

'Why do we need to talk in private?'

'There are corrupt policemen about,' Smith said. 'I don't want my business known.'

'Along here,' Tony said. He opened a door and showed him into the stationery store.

'You're investigating Jack Braden's firm and its involvement in the Baker Street bank robbery.'

'An uphill struggle.'

'Because you're corruptly involved with them.'

'Ballocks, I thought you said you weren't a policeman.' He began to feel increasing danger from this man. Ironically he believed that he might be safer with A10, the police who investigated corrupt colleagues. They did not hold clandestine meetings in stationery stores.

'We know how crime gets managed. Silly ballocks – your new commissioner won't change it. We have another interest. Braden's lot took something from the bank that we want back. Bearer bonds.'

'Why don't you ask him for them?'

'Do you think he'd give them to us? If we asked and he didn't, we might have to kill him,' Smith said, 'and that would put us even further away from our property.'

'How much are they worth?'

'A great deal of money. Several millions.'

'Killing Jack Braden might be the best way to spring the bonds,' Tony said. 'Assuming I believe any of this.'

'We'll kill the lot of them to get our property back.'

'Your getting in here doesn't convince me,' Tony said coolly, even though he believed the man.

'You can only play both ends against the middle for so long, Mr Wednesday,' Smith said. 'Then you run out of options. We're offering you more options.'

'Do I need more options, Mr Smith?'

'You're not a fool. A villain called Bobby Brown was in on that bank job. His friend Jack Braden shot him and fed him to the pigs at a farm in Stoke Poges.'

'But I can't get a statement from pigs! What do you want me to do?'

'Help us get back our bearer bonds,' Smith said.

'What's in it for me?'

Smith, who was tall, pink-faced and elegantly dressed in a cavalry twill suit, met his eyes. They showed no emotion. 'Your continued survival.'

'I'll talk to Braden.'

'Do more than talk to him,' Smith said, 'or you might wind up like DCI Fenwick.'

'Where is he?'

'Move this forward with Braden and we'll tell you.'

Tony left Smith to find his own way out and went to see Chief Superintendent Slipper. 'Guv,' he said, 'I got a whisper about a villain who may have been on that bank-vault job. Bobby Brown was right at the centre of Jack Braden's firm.'

'We need some good news on that front,' Slipper said.

'The problem is, the snout who gave it me thinks he's dead, guv,' Tony said. 'Killed by Braden in a row.'

'Even that's something. It could give us the right sort of lever to open them up. Drop whatever else you're on, Tony, and run this one out. Any resource you need – the Home Office is putting pressure on the commissioner.'

'So I heard, guv,' Tony said, and went to the door. Then he turned back casually. 'We heard from DCI Fenwick yet? He once nicked Bobby Brown.'

'I'd doubt if George Fenwick can help anyone, apart from himself,' Slipper said. 'A10's got him pugged up somewhere. They expect him to give them all that Commander Drury didn't. Superintendent Redvers is playing him out in the sticks somewhere. He might let you interview him.'

'I thought Redvers was sent off somewhere after going bent on the Braden trial,' Tony said, a little surprised. He'd heard nothing about him coming back into favour.

'He somehow convinced the new commissioner different.'

'Good,' Tony said. 'I always liked Redvers. I'll talk to him, guv. See if he can help us out.'

At Tintagel House on the south side of the Thames, between Vauxhall and Westminster bridges, Tony found Redvers in the large briefing room he used as his office on the fifth floor. Most of his squad seemed to be in and out of the room. He saw at once that he tended to stoop now and was going grey. Perhaps the job was too much for him – or his new family.

'I heard you got married and had a baby boy, guv,' was Tony's opening gambit. 'Congratulations.'

'Yes,' Redvers said stiffly. 'Warren, we called him. He's three months old.'

'You got a photo?' If any thing could open up the prick, that might. Redvers produced one, whereupon Tony went through the motions of enthusing about the baby and the mother, who didn't look all there. She had a sour expression. 'Nice,' he said finally. 'Lucky you, guv.'

'Strange. I always thought you were the lucky one, getting Sonia,' Redvers said. 'How is she?'

'How would I know? We've not been together for a while. She lost the baby – did you know? A boy. It's strange,' Tony said, picking up on Redvers's expressions and feeding them back to him – it was a trick that often made people feel at ease. 'He didn't live a day, but it still leaves you miserable.'

'Sonia took it badly,' Redvers said. 'Very badly.'

Tony gave him a sharp look. 'You been seeing her, guv?'

Suddenly Redvers seemed wrong-footed and Tony liked that.

'No. I'm guessing. Knowing how she was.'

'Yeah, that's right. We didn't talk about it much – or anything else, come to that. Of course, she managed to blame me. She turned out to be a right fucking pain.'

'I can't imagine that,' Redvers said. 'She was always such fun. I'd've happily swapped places with you.'

Tony gave him another look, causing Redvers to avert his eyes. He knew the man had always fancied Sonia. That he hadn't landed her was just one of his disappointments. Tony suspected his whole life would be full of them. It was always the case with people who were afraid to live. 'She's gone back to the job,' he said. 'Doing fraud investigations. Not much fun there, I wouldn't have thought.'

'Is she with the newly formed Serious Fraud Office?'

'Strange how things work out,' Tony said. 'I always thought she was more suited to you. I was surprised when she chose me. Mind you, you put yourself out of the frame a bit.'

'Was she really interested in me?' Redvers asked, with a bit too much enthusiasm.

Tony switched tack, leaving him dangling. 'How's your investigation going? Finding any bent Old Bill?'

'How many are there – in your experience?'

Tony shrugged. 'I've heard the talk, like everyone else. I can't say I've knowingly met any. It doesn't bear thinking about, guv, policemen in league with criminals. People keep telling me DCI Fenwick was up to those sort of strokes. I find it hard to credit personally.'

'I'm afraid it looks very much like it,' Redvers said. 'We're questioning him hard. You worked with him, and he mentions you quite a lot.'

'Not saying I'm bent, I hope?'

'We wouldn't be having this conversation if he had. It would be good if you could look at some of the information he's giving us,' Redvers said. 'Perhaps give us a steer on it.'

Tony was uncertain if the man was being utterly naïve, in allowing him to look at things he might engineer them away from, or cunning, searching for a way to entrap him. His mind always took him to the latter view. 'Of course,' he said. 'I wouldn't mind interviewing him myself about an inquiry we're pursuing.'

'I'm afraid we can't afford to let him have contact with any serving policemen at present. Isolating him in the country seems to be having the desired effect.'

Tony decided to pursue another route.

He saw Terry Lynch the moment he stepped into the boozer in Hackney. He was telling a story to another villain in the bar. 'So there I was, getting on brilliantly with this girl,' he was saying. 'Talk about form, she didn't half have some. Well, I'm getting stuck right up— Oh-oh, I gotta go.' He'd spotted Tony Wednesday and set his drink down to leave.

'Wait a mo', Terry. What did she do?' the disappointed villain asked.

'Yeah, don't run out on my account, Terry,' Tony cut in. 'We'd all like to hear what she did.'

'I dunno. I forget,' Terry Lynch said, panic in his eyes as they flitted between the villain and Tony.

'Under age – she's a million. Let's go somewhere and talk. You might remember,' Tony said, pushing him towards a quieter part of the bar. 'Through here, Terry.'

'I ain't got nothing to say to you, Mr Wednesday.'

'That's strange,' Tony said. 'You were looking for a thermic-lance man.'

'Are you one, then?'

'I wish,' Tony said. 'I dare say I'd be looking to retirement after that bank-vault job. Cor, wouldn't that be nice?'

Terry Lynch leant in closely to him. 'Look, that was a very well-placed villain I was talking to. He booked you for Old Bill right off. I gotta get well free of you before I can give you anything. Meet me on the far side of the rec across the road. There's a shelter near the swings.'

'You leg it, Terry, we'll fall out,' Tony warned.

'I won't, on my baby's eyesight.'

'You do – you'll have a blind child.'

Terry Lynch was a dedicated family man with five kids he thought the world of and a wife who presumably loved him. Tony knew he could find him any time, but Terry ran no further than the shelter on the recreation ground on the other side of Lea Bridge Road.

'What d'you tell your well-placed villain friend?' Tony asked.

'I said you was looking for an earner so I bunged you.'

'Who was the lance operator who cut the hole in the bank floor, Terry?'

'I don't know that, guv.'

'Tell you what, Terry, I'm a doddle compared to the people looking for you on this one. You took something from the vault that they're not very happy about. These geezers won't mess around. They won't just make you disappear, they'll make your wife and children disappear too. And your parents. Not only that, they'll make you choose which goes first. There'll be nothing I can do about it either.'

Terry Lynch turned ashen. 'Jack Braden's little mob was after one. The iron hoof, Brian, was putting it together.'

'Who did they get?' Tony wanted to know.

'Charlie Peck put his hand up.'

'I don't think so,' Tony told him. 'We gave Charlie a spin. Wasn't nothing there – no Charlie, even.'

'Can you wonder? He's well scared,' Lynch said. 'Them slags ain't given him his whack – or no one else for that matter.'

'Why's that? They tryna jib him?'

'He reckons they gotta wipe their mouths,' Terry said, 'on account of the dough being so hot.'

'Could be right. You think Braden's just whacking him out?' Tony asked.

'I wouldn't be surprised, no-good slag,' Terry said, with feeling. 'Brian promised everyone their dough was safe out the country. No one's seen nothing yet. He didn't do nothing when Jack capped Bobby Brown rather than give him his whack.'

'You were there, were you?' Tony said. He wasn't surprised when Terry didn't answer. 'Him and Jack Braden were best mates.'

'You can't go mates with a maniac like Jack,' Terry Lynch said. 'Jack definitely offed him – I expect it was so they wouldn't have to pay him his whack. He's totally crackers.'

'It would've been simpler to pay everyone. It makes no sense.'

'None at all,' Terry Lunch conceded. 'But, then, why would villains get nicked if they was sensible, guv?'

'Cos people like you grass them, Terry. Where do I find Charlie Peck when he's not at home?'

'He's got a bird he lives with out at Gerrard's Cross – Mo Thompson,' Terry Lynch said. 'He drinks regular in the Packhorse.'

'I need an address, Terry.'

Three armed detectives from the Flying Squad went with him on the raid to Gerrad's Cross. They hammered at the door of the rose-entwined cottage, then rang the bell, and heard a voice: 'All right, all right, keep your hair on!' A good-looking woman with a peroxide bouffant opened it. 'Let me guess,' she quipped. 'You've come to read the gas meter.'

'Where is he?' Tony said.

She scoffed. 'Why don't you tell me? Your lot came and got him out of bed yesterday.'

'My lot. Old Bill?' Tony was shocked. 'What lot? Where were they from? Did they have warrant cards? Search upstairs,' he told two of the detectives. 'He just went with them, did he?'

'Charlie didn't argue with them, which ain't like him. Mind you, who would if they had guns pointing at them?'

'Did you see their warrant cards?' Tony pressed.

'They didn't show me anything,' she said. 'Some of them looked like dayglos. They had that swarthy Mexican look. They said a couple of things in Spanish.'

'What *are* you talking about? How? There are no Spanish Old Bill.'

'That's what it sounded like,' Mo Thompson said. 'I mean, when we was in Marbella looking for a house, that's what all them dayglos sounded like.'

'And armed?' Tony said. 'You'd better tell me everything you know, or think you know. Otherwise you might never see Charlie again – not alive, that is.'

The club where Jack Braden based himself was locked up when Tony Wednesday got there. He rang the bell and finally heard someone come to the door: 'Go away! We ain't open.' It was flung wide open by Pongo. 'Oh, it's you, Mr Wednesday. You should've given us a bell.'

'Where's Jack?'

'In the back room on his rowing machine. He's off the pills now,' Pongo said with pride. 'He's getting fit again.'

'Is Brian with him?' Tony asked, going through.

'We ain't seen him for a few days now,' Pongo told him. 'His dad was here looking for him. I think maybe he's out doing a bit of ironing, Mr Wednesday. Know what I mean?'

'Don't let anyone else in.' Tony went through to Jack, who was in a white polo-neck sweater and shorts, exerting himself on a rowing machine in what he laughingly referred to as his office.

'If I throw a bucket of water over the floor you might put a few knots between yourself and the trouble you got coming.'

'What trouble could I have, Tony?' Jack said, and carried on rowing.

'Don't get cute with me, Jack. There isn't time.'

'Right now, the only trouble I got is with Leah. She's out of the hospital, but she's acting up again. They give her some stronger stuff. Largactil, I think. Makes her well dopey.'

'Either they give her more of the liquid cosh and finish her off or you'd better marry her, Jack, so she can't give evidence against you.'

'Why'd she wanna do that?'

'You're being cute again.'

'Get to it, son,' Jack said. 'Whatever it is, I know it's gonna cost me bundles – it usually does. Sometimes I think I was better off with Ken Drury. He was a greedy fucker, but at least you knew what you was stood in each week.'

'Your firm's been ID'd as blagging that bank vault,' Tony told him.

'Cor, wouldn't that be something?' Jack said. 'I wish.'

'I only know what grasses tell me,' Tony said. 'Now, we can dick around and play games and maybe I can help you out with losing a bit of evidence. But what I can't do much about is these heavies who are looking for their money that's gone missing.'

Jack Braden stopped rowing. 'What's the SP, Tony?' he said, suddenly serious now.

'A man who I think was from MI6 came to see me. They want their bearer bonds returned. What I haven't worked out is if they're tied up with the South American geezers who captured Charlie Peck.'

'Who?'

'Fine. You go on playing games. I'd say those guys were Colombian and they ain't happy bunnies right now.'

'Well, we could whack them the same as anyone else.'

'I'd say those geezers have done a bit of whacking themselves.'

'How close are they?'

'They got to Charlie Peck yesterday. How far behind can they be?'

'How'd they get on him?' Jack seemed puzzled.

Tony wanted to laugh. The world was full of grasses. There was no loyalty anywhere when money was on offer. Villians were so vain. They couldn't accept that someone might break the code.

'I'd pop anyone who grasses,' Jack threatened.

'Like Bobby Brown?'

Another laugh emerged from the putative oarsman. Less certain this time.

'You think Charlie Peck's going to go down with the ship when you didn't even give him his whack? He's gonna give your name and whoever else was involved as fast as he can – especially to those guys.'

Jack Braden got up from the rowing machine and reached for a towel to wipe the sweat off his face. 'Now, you're gonna tell me what it's gonna cost us to make this go away, Tony, are you?' he said.

'I can't make it go away. I can give you a good price for dropping you out of the bank robbery, but the Colombians – they're something else. If you can get them to a meet to negotiate, we can scoop them up. But if they've already met up with Mr Smith, the MI6 man ...'

'We can get them all to a meet and blow their fucking brains out,' Jack said. 'Pop them out to the pig farm. Pigs'll eat all kinds of shit.' He laughed.

'Those guys won't easily be lured into a trap. All we can do is wait for them to find you. They will.'

'I'm gonna be tooled up ready for them,' Jack said. He opened the door and went through to the bar. 'Pongo, where's that piece we got?'

'You sure, Jack?' Pongo said, glancing at Tony.

'You telling me how to run things now? Give it here.'

'Jack?' Pongo said urgently, with more sense than his boss.

'Give it here!' Jack bellowed at him, and snatched the Webley Revolver that Pongo pulled out of a drawer. 'What do you think of that?'

'Dangerous,' Tony said.

'It'll stop any greasy Colombian or MI6 geezer,' Jack said. 'Now, how much do you want for dropping out the firm?'

'Me, Jack?' Tony said innocently. 'I don't do that sort of business. I'll speak to you later. I'll try and get a lead on the dayglos. Be lucky, Pongo.'

Waving the gun around, Jack pretended to take pot-shots at his imagined enemies. The thought of shooting a few more people excited him. 'That was a rare sight, Pongo, an Old Bill not taking money.'

'Why d'you think that was, boss? He's too shrewd to cop a drop in front of witnesses. You shouldn't have offered it like that.'

'Don't tell me how to do business with bent Old Bill!' Jack exploded, but Pongo remained his same placid self and Jack felt a bit foolish. 'Remember that mug Bobby Brown? How flash he got? I'm the guv'nor. Right?'

'That's right, boss,' Pongo said.

'Don't you ever forget it. Lock up. We're going home to see how Leah is.'

At his flat Jack tried to wake her. She was in a heavy sleep, almost as if she was dead. Sometimes Jack wished she *was* dead, and hated himself for it. Life would be easier if she was dead, and after what the detective had advised earlier, he'd probably be safer.

'Leah, wake up. Come on,' he said. 'You take too many of them pills. They can't be good for you.'

'I jus' wan' slee',' Leah said woozily, her words running together. 'Le' me slee'.'

'Yeah, in a little while. Come on, wake up.' He shook her. 'Look, I'm a man, Leah. I want to have children to leave my firm to, and the clubs. That's not too much to ask, is it? Come on, it's not.'

'Tha's righ'.' Leah turned away, her eyes closed again.

'Can I get you anything?' Jack asked. 'A cuppa tea or something? I want to do things for you, Leah. I want to make you happy.'

'I a' happ',' Leah said, drifting off. 'The pills make me happy . . .'

'You just sleep, Leah. I'll sit here with you and look at you. I like looking at you, Leah. I love you. I trust you. I can trust you, Leah, can't I? Being with you's really good, Leah, but I have to know I can trust you, cos you know a bit too much about me, Leah . . . You know I killed people, don't you, Leah? They didn't mean much to me. Not like Bobby. Bobby . . . my oldest friend. When I popped him, that was hard. I trusted Bobby – like I can trust you, Leah. I couldn't trust Bobby no more. He got jealous of me. We took him out to the farm and cut him up and fed him to the pigs. They eat everything, Leah. Did you know that? Every little scrap.'

'Ja',' Leah intoned, 'need sleep.'

Jack watched her drift away again. Then, taking the gun from his pocket, he slowly cocked the hammer and let the barrel roll round with a bullet ready to go. 'Leah, this is what I popped Bobby with,' he said. 'Bang. Shot him stone dead. Just like that. Look, I really do love you, Leah.'

He slid the muzzle to her temple and threaded her hand round the stock. Her small hand barely went the whole way round, but he just managed to get her index finger in the trigger guard.

'Jack!' Pongo said from the doorway, startling him.

'Oi! Why you fucking well sneaking up on me?'

'I came to see if you was okay,' Pongo said, without apology. 'I'm your minder, Jack. I look after you. Right?'

'Yeah, that's right. Just don't creep around.'

He wasn't sure what Pongo had seen, if anything, until he said, 'It do make an awful mess, Jack, that close up.'

'Make some tea, Pongo. We'll save this for them dayglos from Colombia when the filth finds them for us.'

With more and more money coming in Joey was investing large sums in property development. There was security in bricks and mortar. Office blocks were the thing of the future as business was growing. Borrowing at 14 per cent meant he needed a 28 per cent increase in the market, which wasn't possible. Using money from other sources, he could live with 14 per cent while the market was only increasing at 8 per cent. He could survive, but he needed this source of money to continue until he was past a critical mass in his portfolio. Ten office blocks, built and paid for. He had three so far and two in development. The money was still coming his way at unbelievably low rates. He expected it to continue for a little while longer.

His secretary's unusually shrill voice on the intercom interrupted his thoughts: 'Your son Brian is here, sir.'

'Oh, is he? Did we have an appointment?'

'No, sir. He's with some other gentlemen.' Doreen couldn't keep the nervousness from her voice. 'It's very urgent.'

'You'd better send them in.'

The door crashed open and Brian staggered in. 'Dad, I'm sorry!' Charlie Peck was with him and looked as if he'd been beaten. Joey's eyes went behind him to a tall, fleshy-faced olive-skinned man of about forty in a loud sports jacket and Fred Perry shirt. Three more shouldered into the room.

'This is Mr Ortega and his colleagues,' Brian began. 'This is Charlie Peck – they broke his fingers, Dad!'

'This is not important,' Ortega said, and cocked the gun he was holding. 'You know what this is, Señor Oldman? It's a .45. It'll take your head off your skinny neck unless you give us our money. Now.'

'Money?' Joey said, stalling for time. 'What money's that?' His words were calm but his stomach was churning.

'I count to five, *gringo*,' Ortega said, showing perfectly white teeth in a charming smile.

His three men were armed too, Joey assumed.

'Dad, they know!' Brian said urgently. 'They know about the bank raid. Charlie told them everything.'

'If they knew, son, they wouldn't be here. They'd have the money,' Joey said, suddenly seeing a way through and coolly stepping towards it in his mind's eye.

'Give the money or you dead, my friend,' Ortega said. 'One. Two—'

'What is important to you, Mr Ortega? Getting your money or having one worthless person dead?' Joey asked.

'We live with the loss. A lesson to others not to steal from us.'

'Your bosses find such lessons profitable, do they?' Joey spoke evenly, now in control again. 'What will you do after you shoot me? Take the money? I'm not a bank. I don't even have a safe.' He turned to Brian. 'Are you hurt, son?'

'Nothing that won't mend,' Brian said. 'Charlie's in a lot of pain. He needs a doctor.'

'Of course,' Joey said. 'My boy can go. And his friend – are you okay, Charlie?'

'They don't fuck around,' the grey-looking Charlie Peck said. 'I'm sorry, Mr Oldman.'

'Get off to the hospital. We'll sort this out.'

'No.' Ortega stepped forward to stop them. 'They bring the police.'

'Neither of us wants the police in on this, Mr Ortega,' Joey said. 'Their percentage is always too high.'

Ortega laughed, while his colleagues looked confused.

'Why don't you carefully lower the hammer on the gun?' Joey suggested.

'*Vayase!*' Ortega said. 'Get out!'

'Go, Brian,' Joey said. 'Take Charlie to the hospital.'

'You gonna be all right, Dad?'

'Yes,' Joey said. 'We're going to talk business. Go.' He steered Brian to the door, then closed it behind him and Charlie.

'You a cool customer, Señor. A good father.'

'We don't go in for guns much here,' Joey told him. 'They upset the police. I don't think we'll be needing it, anyway.'

'You wanna get me our money now?'

'You're a man who likes giving lessons, sir. You see how vulnerable money is in safe deposits?' Putting it there shows so little respect for it.'

'It gives us easy access.'

'The bank robbers had easy access too. It was neither safe nor legal. How much money do you have coming into Britain a year?'

Ortega laughed again – he laughed a lot, and Joey liked him. 'People pay a lot for that information, Señor.'

'More than you had sitting in the bank vault. Presumably you bring it in by courier. That makes it vulnerable. The courier could be arrested at any point in the journey, the money lost.'

'You got our money safe?' Ortega said.

Noticing that the Colombian had only referred to money, not bonds, Joey decided that the latter didn't belong to the drug-dealers. 'How much did you have in the box?'

'I'm not the book-keeper,' Ortega said. Joey simply waited. 'Three million, forty-five thousand US dollars.'

Joey realized he had been holding his breath.

'The robbers, they find something else, yes?'

'A worryingly large amount.'

'Then maybe we take this for safe-keeping,' Ortega suggested. 'We forget you stole our money.'

'We didn't steal your money. We transferred it to a safer place.'

'Oh, Señor Oldman,' Ortega said, 'I like this description. I will remember.'

'My bank would like to handle your money for you, make it safe for you, place it offshore, put it into legitimate investments that return a good profit.' He could make that happen with Charles Tyrwhitt's help. 'You can't get your money instantly from an investment bank. You simply borrow against your assets.'

'At a price,' Ortega pointed out. 'Why would your English bank want to get involved with our business?'

'We make money work harder.'

Ortega needed to talk to his people later that night in Colombia. He was happy to do that. Before the meeting ended he warned Joey that if they thought for a moment he was cheating them, they'd kill him, his family and his family's family.

Joey wasn't sure who that was. Jack Braden? John Redvers? 'If I were to cheat you there'd be no profit for anyone.'

'I think my boss will like you, Señor.'

'I'll talk to my partners at the bank.'

They weren't his partners, but Joey knew that if they went for this he would demand to become a partner.

Tyrwhitt turned him down flat. He wasn't interested in Joey becoming a partner in Cotterill and Jenkins, but was interested in expanding the bank's international clientele. 'Who are these people, Joseph?' he asked. 'Just how much business would you be bringing here? Is it criminal? You'll appreciate we're licensed deposit-takers. We have the bank's reputation to protect.'

'If you put that question to a lot of your clients you'd come up short, Charles,' Joey said bluntly. He was irritated and would like to pull him off his high horse.

'What makes you think they'd be placing large sums of money with us each month?'

'They have large sums to hide. I have to demonstrate that their money is safe and accessible and is being made to work hard.'

'There's a huge contradiction in that, Joseph,' Tyrwhitt said. 'If you were a banker you'd know that the harder money works the more at risk it is.'

'They'll be most concerned that the authorities can't trace it,' Joey said.

'Something all our clients need to be reassured about. We could hardly function in our offshore capacity if that wasn't a given.'

'Can we handle this much money?' Joey asked.

'We?' Tyrwhitt gave a little laugh. 'That's a little presumptuous, Joseph.'

'Then the next question, Charles,' Joey said, 'is what do I get out of this?'

'We have a good relationship,' Tyrwhitt said. 'We make funds readily available to you.'

'You do. At the market rate. I've brought you good business in turn,' Joey said.

'As a reward for bringing us this business we should think in terms of a bonus,' Tyrwhitt said, 'based on a percentage of the commission we charge.'

'I'd say that was a little presumptuous. I'd like a seat on the bank's board. They'd want security from me. If I'm here I can keep an eye on their money.'

'Things don't quite operate in that way, Joseph,' Tyrwhitt said. 'We're the copper-bottomed guarantee.'

'Get off it, Charles. These people don't observe old-school rules.'

Joey believed Tyrwhitt wouldn't let this sort of money slip away from the bank, and when he said he would talk to his board, Joey knew he'd get what he wanted. The little dance had been Tyrwhitt's way of saving face.

The first thing Brian wanted to know was, did Joey's place on the board mean their money would be safe?

'Your individual shares were always going to be safe,' Joey told him, at the kitchen table in Ladbroke Grove flat while Cath made Cona coffee for them. 'But if the Colombians want all their money back, I'd be honour-bound to return it.'

'The chaps won't be very happy about that,' Brian said.

'You saw how these people operate,' Joey said. 'They knew the exact number of dollars in that deposit box.'

'That still leaves four million from the bearer bonds.'

'At ten per cent, that's four hundred thousand – not to be sneezed at,' Cath said. 'Goodness – we could guarantee to re-elect Ted Heath with that.'

'The bonds might be more trouble than they're worth, Brian,' Joey said.

'Fine. We'd better have them back.'

'No, Brian! This is a generous offer your father's making in the circumstances.'

'We should have put Jack on to those dayglos. He could've whacked them out.'

'Don't be so stupid!' Joey snapped. 'Those people are seriously dangerous. They would kill us all and think nothing of it.'

'Listen to your father. He's a banker, giving you sound advice,' Cath said, with evident pride.

When Brian shuttled between the two of them Jack took a different line. 'Banker?' Jack mocked. 'Sounds like a wanker to me. I told you I shoulda taken care of them shares.'

'Yeah, but the chaps would've ended up just the same – with nothing.'

'Well, they ain't gonna get anything worth a rub now,' Jack said.

'The bit we got coming from those bonds ain't exactly nothing.'

'*If* we get it. If Joey don't jib us with all that cobblers about who maybe owns them.'

'What if they do belong to someone dangerous?' Brian was hedging his bets.

'What d'you want to do? Get Old Bill to steam into the meet Joey's setting up with these dayglos?' Jack said.

'Dad thinks there's a lot more to be made from the Colombians.'

'Yeah, sure. Not for us.'

'How much would Old Bill want?' Brian asked.

'You know what a hungry bastard Tony Wednesday is. 'S not like dealing with George Fenwick. What a gentleman.'

'Did Wednesday find him?' Brian asked. 'Or did he wind up at the pig farm?'

'That would've been the safest place for him,' Jack said. 'The Old Bill ain't found him yet – so he reckons.'

'We'd best wipe our mouths and take whatever Joey offers.'

'I'll talk to him. I need the money. Leah and me is getting married.'

'Oh, yeah?' Brian was startled. 'Where you gonna live? The nuthouse?'

'You shut your dirty little queer mouth, Brian.'

'You gotta be a bit mad too. She's completely crackers.'

'No, she ain't. She's getting well.'

''S not what Mum reckons,' Brian told him. 'She said she's barking.'

'Yeah, well, that cowing sister of mine always hated her.'

'Do yourself a favour – dump the loon.'

'I'm fucking well warning you, Brian—'

'Warn the hell you like. She's an out-and-out nutter and I wouldn't give her house-room.'

'She wouldn't want it with a poof.'

'Not even in a nuthouse!'

That was a step too far, and Jack flew at him. 'You still sweet on her or something?' he demanded, grabbing Brian's kipper tie.

'Interested in that—' Jack hit him in the face. They fought furiously, Brian coming off worst. As they wrestled on the floor, he tried to reach into his pocket for his flick-knife. Had he found it, he would have stabbed Jack. Instead he crawled away, sorry for his remarks about Leah and wondering why.

The invitation to meet with Mr Smith wasn't an invitation: there was no choice. That was made plain by Arnold Goodman, who came to Joey's little office in Lombard Street to tell him. The solicitor hadn't been there before and, with his weight, didn't enjoy having to climb four flights of stairs.

'Who is Mr Smith, Arnold?' Goodman hadn't volunteered the information.

'He almost certainly works for MI6, but I doubt if he or they would ever own to that. I do know he's done work for Harold Wilson so you're in good company. It might be in your interest to meet him. It would certainly be to your cost if you don't.'

That made Joey more than a little curious.

They met in the basement dining room at the Pickwick Club in Great Newport Street. Not a part of town Joey enjoyed; everyone, it seemed to him, was either on the lookout for something or hoping to be noticed in their weird clothes and hairdos. The tall man in cavalry twills who got up from the small table and adjusted his horn-rimmed glasses was good-looking enough to have been an actor – Joey had recognized several having lunch. Smith had little small-talk as Joey searched the menu for something that wasn't too rich. When the waiter had brought their drinks and stepped away, Smith said, 'We understand you were given a parcel from a certain bank vault to dispose of.'

Joey's stomach lurched. Now he didn't think he'd be able to eat anything. What had started as a seemingly profitable enterprise with Brian was turning into a nightmare.

'The fact is, Mr Oldman, that the parcel doesn't belong to the party offering it for sale.'

'You represent the owners, do you?'

'I can assure you the owners aren't the drug cartel who are coming to see you about their missing money. The owners of this particular parcel won't be so tolerant.'

Joey could feel his lungs constricting. 'What is it you want? The parcel returned?'

'The bank where it was kept wasn't reliable. We'd like to make other arrangements for it, possibly with you as part of those arrangements.'

This was a time to be silent and listen. Joey remembered what Arnold Goodman had said.

'There would be an arrangement fee, of course. For this we would require you to make transfers from time to time, covertly and in cash. We'd assist with transport across borders.'

'Do I get to know who I'd be doing this for?'

'I'm sure the Blessed Arnold has already told you,' Mr Smith said. 'Our terms are generous, but you must tell no one of this arrangement. Not the bank's directors or your son. If you're agreeable to it we could be of some assistance to you with Señor Picado.'

'You seem to know a lot about my business.'

'That's the sort of business we're in, Mr Oldman.'

Joey paused. 'I suspect I'm working with the devil.'

'You still have a choice at this point, but if you go forward with us it's a long-term commitment.'

The waiter arrived with the soup. Joey found he could eat without any difficulty, his decision made.

Having entered into his pact with Smith, he felt more comfortable about meeting with the Colombian drug boss, José Picado, at the Park Lane Hilton. Even so he took a long time dressing, choosing his most sober suit. He polished his shoes, then changed his tie four times. He wanted to be businesslike but not funereal.

José Picado was short, round and fifty. He wore a dark suit, so Joey felt confident of his own outfit. Unlike his colleague, Picado had no apparent charm or personality and his face gave little away. This was a man to learn from, Joey decided.

'We like the sound of our money being made legitimate, Señor Oldman,' Picado said. 'So tell me how this will happen?'

'I would wash it in high-yield investments,' Joey said. 'The more at risk it is, the more you earn. Quite a lot can go into property development in London. It's not yielding much at present, but it will.'

'How do you scrub it clean in the first place?' Picado asked.

'By sending it through a series of shell companies,' Joey told him.

'How much you charge for this service?'

'Forty-five per cent of what we take in,' Joey told him. He had thought that too high when Charles Tyrwhitt had suggested it, and, from Picado's reaction, so did he. It occurred to Joey that Tyrwhitt had hoped he'd make a fool of himself, so the Colombians would turn to him.

'This much I could not get with a gun, Señor!'

'What we do is remove all risk,' Joey said, sensing he was digging himself into a hole.

'All risk? Here, there is no risk. Our biggest risk is in shipping the money over,' Picado said. 'Can you reduce that risk?'

Without knowing how, Joey said, 'Yes, we can.'

'How, Señor?' Picado asked earnestly.

Given time, Joey knew he could find a way, but right then he had an idea that would involve Mr Smith and his outfit. However it happened, though, this was an opportunity of a lifetime and he wasn't going to pass it up. 'If I told you that,' he said, 'what use would I be to you? I'm in the business of providing a service. I see you as part of that business.'

Picado did and said nothing. Instinctively Joey knew he should say no more.

'How would you account to us?' Picado asked eventually.

'Monthly, in the normal course of banking practice,' Joey told him.

'We want weekly accounting. Still, forty-five per cent is too much.'

'How much money are we talking about?'

'Our business is most profitable, Señor,' Picado said. 'You are holding as much as we bring here in one month.'

'It's costing you what at the moment?' Joey asked boldly.

Picado laughed. 'Perhaps ten per cent.'

Joey remained as sober as a funeral director. 'Then you don't need the services of my bank. Tell me where you want your money returned to – not Lloyds Bank?'

'Ah, you are most confident. But you have powerful friend, no?'

Joey wondered if he was referring to Smith and Co.

'Fifteen per cent is what we will offer you, Señor.'

That was something in the region of $450,000 a month coming to him or to the bank. A staggering sum, enough to crack the most sober expression. But Joey didn't crack. His heart in his mouth, he said, 'I can't do it.'

'Twenty-five per cent is our final offer, Señor Oldman,' Picado said. 'For this we want complete accounting of when and where our money is moved.'

'We don't do that. We're an investment bank. Our clients trust us to manage their money.'

'Who are your other clients?'

'Señor Picado, you must see us as priests. Your money is like confession. Such information is sacrosanct.'

This was acceptable to the Colombian and he proceeded as though the deal was done. Joey reminded him it was not. The 25 per cent on offer was a long way short of the 45 per cent he had sought. They were far apart still. Finally Joey offered a compromise. A fee of a million dollars a month, regardless of the amount being moved, starting with the current month. Picado found that acceptable provided Joey handled the money in transit. In agreeing to do that Joey hoped he was able to persuade Smith to play ball.

'You will tell us now your method of bringing the money in?'

Slowly Joey shook his head. 'No. First I will talk to my partners.'

'Sí. I like this way of doing business. Pepe,' Picado said to Ortega, who had remained silent throughout the conversation. 'Let's give our new business partner a present. Our finest product, Señor Oldman. Ninety-eight per cent pure.'

'Heroin?' Joey enquired in alarm.

'Heroin is a dirty drug,' Picado said. 'Only niggers take heroin. Cocaine is the drug of choice for the sophisticated user.'

In accepting the present, Joey didn't know what he would do with it. He knew no one who used cocaine and certainly not in such quantity. The only person he could think to give it to was Tony Wednesday. He was sure the detective would find a profitable use for it.

The deal left Joey with two distinctly different problems. The first was a deal-breaker unless he solved it: how to ship the money without risk. He rang Tyrwhitt and arranged a meeting, then called Brian and told him to come to the bank.

Tyrwhitt was amazed that Joey had struck such a deal. 'Can they pay this fee each month?' he asked.

'Can we solve the shipment problem?'

'Can I solve it, you mean, Joseph. I presume you can't?'

'The fees will be coming to the bank,' Joey pointed out, 'not to me personally.'

'Quite so,' Tyrwhitt said. 'There are two options. Bring the money in slowly through a series of shell companies, or more speedily in the diplomatic pouch. Both will cost money, but both are viable. I've a chum at the Irish Embassy I was at Trinity with. We'll solve the problem.'

Satisfied, Joey went to talk to Brian. The secretary had rung to say he'd arrived.

'Is this going to be your office at the bank, Dad?' Brian asked, when the woman showed him in.

'We haven't done that deal yet,' Joey said, feeling slightly uncomfortable. 'Look, Brian, I'm afraid I wasn't able to get anything out of the Colombians for you and your pals.' The words came more easily than he had expected. He watched Brian carefully for any sign of doubt. There was none. He nodded, accepting it. His response was almost touching and Joey found it hard to resist.

'Charlie'll believe you, Dad,' Brian said. 'He was grateful to get his life back. But I don't think Jack will.'

'He's turning into an animal,' Joey said. 'We must find him a bone to gnaw on before he embarrasses us all.'

'That might happen anyway,' Brian said. 'I keep hearing rumours about the police investigating the firm.'

'Regardless of all the money he's given them? That seems like a pretty poor bargain.'

Suddenly they heard a commotion outside the room. Then Jack

burst in ahead of Joey's protesting secretary. Pongo was with him. 'Give us our fucking money, Joey. You ain't robbing us, pal.'

Brian was right. Jack wouldn't accept that there was none and threatened that Pongo would throw Joey out of the window. 'I don't care if you are married to Cath,' he said. 'She'll be a widow.'

'Shall I get the police or Mr Tyrwhitt?' the secretary said.

'Maybe they can get here before Joseph hits the pavement,' Tyrwhitt said, coming into the office. 'I'll handle this, Yvonne. Braden, let's be reasonable here, shall we?'

'I'll be reasonable, Charlie old boy,' Jack said. 'Either you slags come up with my dosh or you can go down for all them porno films of little boys you got.'

'What? This is an outrage,' Tyrwhitt said. 'I don't know what you're talking about, man.'

'Just give him the money, Charles,' Joey said. 'All of it. The consequences will be entirely his.'

'What consequences? What ballocks is that?'

'How long will it take to get his money?' Joey asked. 'A month? Ten days?'

'We mustn't allow the bank to be blackmailed by these thugs.'

'Make it ten days,' Joey said. 'It's the best we can do, Jack.'

After a great deal of indecision Jack decided to accept the ten days' delay, provided the sum included the South American money.

What he could do to render Jack harmless in ten days Joey wasn't sure, but it was better than having Pongo drop him out of the window on to Brook Street.

'Someone has to put that oaf in his place, Joseph,' Tyrwhitt said, after Jack had left, with Brian placating him. 'Does one really want this sort of business?'

'Times are changing, Charles. Money no longer cares who owns it.'

'We have rather more old-fashioned values,' Tyrwhitt said.

'Not many clients earn you a million dollars a month. I think the board would have something to say if you turned it away.'

'How will you deal with your brother-in-law?'

'Discreetly, Charles. With no reference to the bank.' Still Joey had only a vague idea. It involved Detective Inspector Wednesday and would prove costly, but he could live with that.

'How do you think the game is being played, Superintendent?' Sir Robert Mark, the commissioner, asked pacing his seventh-floor office in the tower at Scotland Yard.

'If it's not played fairly I don't enjoy it,' Redvers said. He had on his best suit – a navy blue hopsack he had worn for his wedding. He had ironed his shirt that morning especially for this meeting. 'It doesn't seem right, sir.'

The commissioner's dark eyebrows rumpled in a frown. 'Would you prefer that the canker infecting the Met is left untreated?'

'I'd prefer it to be removed by straight policing, not deception.'

'You have to recognize in such games of double-bluff when you step over the line and where you have to stop,' Sir Robert said. 'Perhaps you don't feel capable of recognising that line.'

'I'd back a straight policeman against a corrupt one any day of the week. It's the only way to win, sir,' Redvers said. 'You asked for my honest opinion, you got it.'

'I appreciate it, Superintendent. I feel it's now or never for the decent men and women in the job. We have to root out this pernicious evil. I understand you're a religious man?'

'That was how my mother brought me up, sir.'

'Good. It's a sound starting point.'

For a moment Redvers thought the commissioner was going to ask him to pray with him, and was relieved when he didn't. That wasn't a part of his education he had developed and he knew that what had been forced upon him by the Plymouth Brethren wasn't likely to accord with Sir Robert's conventional Christian beliefs. He admired the commissioner, for having come up through the ranks, and for his courage. It was for that reason he had agreed to take on this assignment, although he doubted he had the guile to bring it off, and was terrified of disappointing him. 'I thank you for your faith in me, Sir Robert.'

'I looked through the records of a great many officers both inside and outside the Met to find the right man. I hope you are he. I'm convinced you've not been tainted by corruption, despite the many rumours about you.'

Leaving the commissioner's office to take up his new job as acting head of A10, Redvers still wasn't sure he was the right person for the task ahead. More and more lately he had found himself turning to God for help, unable to break himself of the firmly entrenched habit of praying on his knees. That was where Detective Chief Inspector Peter Robertson, his second-in-command, found him when he stepped into his office at Tintagel House without knocking.

'Oh, excuse me, sir,' the DCI said. 'I didn't mean to intrude.' He stepped out of the office and closed the door to wait there. Redvers could see him through the frosted glass in the door. No mockery, no embarrassment. Redvers knew at once that he had the right man to help him bring down DI Tony Wednesday and his army of evil policemen.

THIRTY-ONE

The new place they bought for themselves on Stanley Gardens, round the corner from Ladbroke Grove, was a whole house. It cost a hundred grand. Notting Hill was coming up, the black renters having been pushed northwards. This was a home suitable for a banker, Cath said, where she could hold local Tory Party committee meetings.

'Do you like this material, Joseph?' she asked. 'It will look good in the sitting room with chairs to match.'

'I prefer to leave it entirely to your good judgement, Catherine,' Joey told her. He was pleased that she was enjoying selecting the furnishings. 'You've got an eye for all that, even my suits. I like this.' He picked up a piece of plum velour.

'Yes,' Cath said. 'Perhaps for the chairs in your study.'

'Jack is a serious liability.' He followed her into his study, the raised ground-floor room at the rear of the house overlooking the garden.

'Why on earth would he want to marry Leah Cohen? I don't know what Margaret Courtney will think,' Cath said. 'She so enjoyed his company. To say nothing of Princess Margaret.'

'It might embarrass you with the Conservative Party,' Joey said. She still hadn't given her emphatic endorsement for his strategy to deal with Jack. Perhaps she couldn't forget blood.

'What about the invitation to his wedding? He might get suspicious if we refuse.'

'This young detective is very efficient.' Joey sighed heavily as he thought about Tony Wednesday. In the long-run he might prove more dangerous than the South Americans. 'Hopefully he'll take Jack down before the ceremony.'

The tour of the new house over, he went off to his office at the bank. The detective was happy to come there as it was 'off his manor'.

They were pushed for space in the Brook Street premises in Mayfair and Joseph's office was little more than a broom cupboard but, unlike his Lombard Street office, it did have a window, albeit on to the well of the building. Around one o'clock each day the sun peeped in briefly. He enjoyed the sparse space, believing anyone impressed by big, smart offices was a fool. It was what he delivered that mattered.

'What do you expect me to do about your brother-in-law, Joey?' Tony Wednesday asked, leaning against the wall, hands in the pockets of his Gannex mac, one leg bent up, the foot flat against the new white paintwork.

'It would be best if he was off the scene.'

'How that's achieved, d'you think?'

This policeman always required you to spell things out. Joey obliged. 'I'd prefer it was prison.'

'Then you'd better give me something to help nick him.'

'I can't believe you don't have plenty of evidence, Inspector,' Joey told him. 'I daresay you've got information on all sorts of people – me included.'

'If that was the case, why wouldn't I nick them?'

'Presumably it's more profitable not to.'

'You're a shrewd man, the sort who'll end up owning everything. I like associating with such people.'

'You're the one most likely to survive.'

'Then let's see what mutual benefit there might be in putting Jack down. The trick is to do it without hurting your own interests.'

'Might this help?' Joey opened the drawer in his small, leather-topped desk and pulled out his present from Señor Picado.

'What is it?'

'I'm given to understand it's ninety-eight per cent pure cocaine.'

'Do junk heads go a lot on that?' the detective asked. 'I thought most of them want heroin.'

'The more sophisticated, less addictive personality prefers this.'

'No such thing on the drug scene, uncle. I'll ask around, see who wants it – maybe the Richardsons.'

'Aren't they serving life sentences?'

'There are others in the family business I'm helping get started.'

'That must be gratifying for you, Inspector.' If the detective caught his irony he didn't react, but Joey didn't labour the point. 'When can we expect action on Jack?'

'We'll tuck him up quite soon.'

'You'd have no difficulty getting Leah to give evidence against him.'

'I'll keep it in mind.' The detective slid the large bag into his raincoat pocket.

Coming into the squad office at Scotland Yard, Tony was dismayed at the inactivity. Then he remembered it was diary day. Once a week detectives surrendered their daily log for the DCI to check. Less than the required contemporaneous record, it was a last-minute scramble to remember who had been doing what and when. As a DI, it was Tony's responsibility to check the diaries before they went to the DCI.

'Guv,' a detective said, from across the room, as he picked up a diary and tried to read the spidery scrawl, 'a detective from A10's looking for you – DCI Robertson.'

'Caught me at it, have they, Derek?' Tony said.

'They'd have to get up early, guv. He left his number.'

When DCI Robertson answered his phone he suggested they meet for a cup of coffee, which puzzled Tony. This wasn't standard procedure with A10. Perhaps they wanted something from him. Robertson was based at Tintagel House so they agreed to meet in the Shakespeare at Victoria. With no idea what the man looked like, Tony was alarmed when a large ginger-bearded man of forty approached him at the bar and said, 'Hello, Tony. I'm Peter Robertson.'

'What are you drinking?' He tried not to show his surprise.

'Pint of bitter. I keep telling myself I'll give it a miss at lunchtime – the job doesn't do you any favours.'

'The sixty-four-thousand-dollar question, Peter: how d'you know me?'

'We've been on obo with Jack Braden's firm, looking for corrupt detectives. We filmed you coming out of his club twice.'

'Was I sober?'

'I didn't think you'd admit it,' DCI Robertson said.

'Caught on film, Peter? It'd be pretty stupid to deny it.'

'Did you know we've got George Fenwick pugged up?'

'I thought he'd emigrated to Australia. What are you telling me? He's bent?'

'He's not admitting it. He said you'd be worth a look.'

'I'd be sorry if he'd gone bent,' Tony said. 'He taught me a lot about coppering.' He gave the DCI a look to see how this was going down. The detective seemed uncomfortable and Tony wondered if he wasn't simply being decent and warning him.

'Is George all right? I mean, he's not gone mad?'

'He's well looked after.'

'What about his freedom?'

'At the end of the day he may get it. Some of our people've got him in a nice hotel out at Henley-on-Thames, costing the taxpayer a fortune.'

'There are one or two things I'd like to check about Jack Braden,' Tony told him. 'There's a chance we can collar him. My guv'nor's desperate to do that. George might have a couple of useful names.'

DCI Robertson waited, as if he was unsure of his next move. He drank some of his beer and put the glass on the bar. 'Do you want the name of the hotel?' he said.

'Not if it'll embarrass you.'

'It won't if the source doesn't come back to me.'

Back at the Yard Tony went straight to see his boss to try to make his reason for being at Jack Braden's club official. With the times and dates from Robertson he simply altered the diaries to make sure he recorded the visit. 'Is the chief around, Mary?' he asked the secretary.

'He's on the phone,' she told him. 'He's just finishing.'

Slipper saw him and waved him in as he dropped the receiver back into the cradle. 'Assistant Commissioner Virgo,' he said. 'I sometimes wonder if he's not at it. What's the story, Tony? Is Jack Braden coming for that bank vault?'

'Finding what puts him there is the problem.'

'The pressure's not slackening,' Slipper said. 'If we get them this time, we'll never let them go.'

'We need to get closer.'

'What do you suggest?' Slipper asked. 'Join his gang?'

'Ideally. But the rubber heels watch his every move, trying to identify corrupt cops. They clocked me on camera visiting his club,' Tony said, 'so now I'm a suspect. It doesn't make you want to try very hard.'

'If they don't leave us to do the job,' Slipper said, 'it won't get done. I'll talk to the assistant commissioner. I know what he'll say. It's coming from the commissioner. We're going to get this done, Tony. Just get as close as you can.'

With that instruction from his boss duly noted in his diary, plus the earlier entries, Tony believed his arse was covered.

Suspecting A10 might have a wire on Jack Braden's phone, and his nephew's, Tony sent a note to the club in a black cab. London cabbies were always reliable.

'What's going on, Tony?' Jack said, as he strolled through the Italian café on Kingsway in jeans and a suede jacket. Music from a jukebox competed with the hiss of steam from the coffee machine and the clank of thick china cups. 'What d'you wanna meet in this poxy place for?' he said, running a hand through greying dark hair. 'You can't hear yourself think. Oi, turn that racket off,' he shouted to the man behind the counter.

'Jack, calm down,' Brian hissed. 'Listen to what Tony's got to say. Leave the music,' he told the waiter. 'It's good.'

'Is that what you call it?' Jack groaned. 'Look at the state of the country – we got over a million unemployed. They should bring back National Service.'

'Why's that, Jack?' Brian quipped. 'So you can go back on the run?'

Jack seemed not to hear. 'We should get them lazy bastards off the dole and down the mines. Our taxes are paying for all that.'

'When did you pay any tax?' Tony asked.

'What are you? A tax inspector or a police inspector?' Jack said.

'I might not be a DI much longer. George Fenwick's talking to the rubber heels out in the Crown at Pigshill in Henley.'

That made Jack pay attention. 'He's definitely there, is he?'

'He's helping them, saving himself.'

'Treacherous git!'

Tony watched his square jaw tighten, his right hand curl into a fist.

'Old Bill are watching the club, Jack,' Brian said. 'They might have it bugged. That's why Tony wanted to meet here.'

'I'll remember to smile and talk proper.'

'Jack, you'd better take this seriously.' Brian hunched over the table, looking straight at him. 'Wake up, man. That's why Tony's here – to help.'

'Help himself to a few more quid from us?'

'Listen to his plan. It'll work.'

Jack waited for Tony to speak, plainly irritated.

Tony sat back in his chair and made him wait a little longer. Then he said, 'The idea is, we nick you with a great show of publicity.'

'Fuck off. You think I'm gonna let that happen?'

'It worked a treat last time we did it.'

'But I'm getting married!'

'Jack!' Brian hissed, chin jutting forward. 'Hear him out, for fucksake.'

Tony watched Jack clock the skinny waitress, who looked a bit like Twiggy. She brought them cups of white coffee. They watched her walk away before anyone spoke again.

'You go up the steps, then, like last time, we let you get a chuck in court,' Tony announced, as if it was a result.

'How's that gonna be guaranteed?' Jack was focused now. 'They might not wear it.'

'There'll be an embarrassing lack of evidence,' Tony assured him, and gulped some coffee.

Finally Jack took a deep breath. 'Well, I can't go on the run. I'm getting married.'

'Congratulations. Do I get an invite?' Tony said, and smiled as he wiped his sweating hands on his trousers. If Jack stood for this, he realized, he'd stand the prick.

When he got back to the Yard two rubber heels were waiting in his office. They were sifting through his papers, reading his diary entries. One was DCI Robertson.

'How you doing?' Tony said, like they'd never met.

'Not so good, I'm afraid,' the DCI said. 'It's always painful to me when I have to arrest policemen.'

'Did you ever think about changing your job?' Tony's exterior was cool, but his mind was in complete turmoil. He couldn't see a way through this.

'We're arresting you on suspicion of perverting the course of justice, Inspector. You're not obliged to say anything, but anything you do say may be used in evidence against you.'

'Is this a joke?'

'If it is, son,' DCI Robertson said, 'no one's laughing.'

At that moment Tony became aware of the total silence in the squad room. No one said a word. The typewriters had fallen silent, and even the phones had stopped ringing. The world seemed to be waiting for Tony's answer and for the first time in his life he didn't have one.

*

Feeling as thin and drawn as she looked, her eyelids heavily painted with liner and lashes heavy with mascara, Leah was dressed like a doll in the peach-pink silk corset dress with a heart-shaped bodice, chosen for her by Jack. She hated the way she looked, and felt trapped in this civil wedding ceremony, teetering on her white peep-toe stilettos. She wanted to run, but was unable to break free. Her thoughts were murderous, yet she couldn't save herself. Maybe the pills Jack had given her to calm her down were stopping her. They made her feel like giggling. Then she realized she *was* giggling, despite how she felt. Fear could make you laugh . . .

'Leah!' Jack hissed. 'This is serious.'

Nothing was more serious than the loss of control Leah felt. She couldn't even ask what he was doing to her. He was saying he would honour and cherish her, which wasn't true. Own, imprison and torture her were more like it, and still she could do nothing about it.

'You have to make your declaration now, Mr Braden,' the registrar said. 'Read the words on the card, but put your own name in, and you put your name, Miss Cohen, where appropriate.'

Leah was an intelligent, rational person and this official was treating her as though she was sub-normal. Why couldn't she stop herself going along with it? Perhaps she wasn't as intelligent as she'd imagined . . . But intelligence had nothing to do with what was happening at Caxton Hall.

'I call upon these persons here present to witness that I, Jack Donald Braden, take Leah Rosamund Cohen to be my lawful wedded wife.'

Leah giggled again. People were waiting for her to do or say something. She wasn't paying attention.

'Leah,' Jack prompted. 'What about it?'

What about what? All Leah wanted to do was break out of the shell that imprisoned her thoughts.

'You have to say the contracting words, Miss Cohen,' the registrar said, 'or I can't pronounce you man and wife.'

'Yes,' Leah said. 'Why don't we get the bloody thing over with?'

The words came out in a roar, shocking the registrar, causing him to step back.

This was a nightmare Jack was caught up in. Leah was having a breakdown before his eyes and he wasn't even sure that he was properly married and safe. Now Pongo was at his side hissing urgently, 'Jack!' and pulling him away. 'Brian's outside. Tony Wednesday's been nicked.'

'Don't talk silly. Where is he?'

'I dunno,' Pongo said. 'He didn't say.'

'No, where's Brian, you fucking ignoramus?'

'He's outside in the car.'

Turning back, Jack signed the register hurriedly, his hand shaking, and ran out of the register office. 'What do you know?' he said, climbing into the car.

'An Old Bill called to warn us,' Brian told him. 'What should we do? Go on the trot?'

'Leave off,' Jack said. 'I just got married.'

'Yeah, that must be worth staying around for!'

'You shut your fucking mouth, Brian.'

'Think about it. He's been nicked and the filth are closing in on us. We're nto gonna get any help in court, much less a chuck.'

'Maybe he ain't really nicked. He's too cunning.'

'Tell that to a donkey,' Brian said, 'and he'll kick you.'

'I'm sorry it's come to this, Tony,' Superintendent Redvers said civilly, as he stepped into the small, musty-smelling interview room at Cannon Row police station. Neither Scotland Yard nor Tintagel House could accommodate prisoners. 'I thought your career would have ended somewhat differently.'

'Oh, has it ended? How's that?'

'You being arrested like this.'

'That's funny, guv. I thought we still had old-fashioned things like evidence and trials,' Tony said.

'Yes – yes, I'm sorry. I'm getting ahead of myself.'

'You've done brilliantly, guv. I heard you got made acting head of A10. You must be the youngest ever appointed. And we all thought you were a wolly. Definitely a bit naïve.'

'But honest,' Redvers said.

'Well, I wouldn't know about that. What if you were arrested for no good reason? Would that be the end for you?'

Redvers laughed. 'Why would I be arrested?'

'Who knows? Helping your cousin Brian Oldman and your uncle Jack, I suppose.'

'That's ridiculous!' Redvers said defensively. 'Don't try that one. Someone already has and it didn't wash. I haven't been helping them. I haven't!'

'You don't have to convince me, guv. I'm only saying what a lot of coppers believe; that you helped them in the past and probably still do. I didn't say I believed it.'

'It's nonsense.'

Tony could see he was rattled and hoped he'd make a mistake of some sort that would give him a lever to prise open a hole through which he might escape.

'DCI Fenwick gave us information about your involvement with criminals,' Redvers said. 'It will be backed up with solid evidence.'

'George Fenwick went bent, did he? Is that what you're telling me?' Tony was nothing if not consistent. There was no way he'd admit to anything.

'He's deeply implicated in corruption,' Redvers told him. 'He said you were too.'

What was Fenwick doing? Trying to save himself? How many names was he prepared to put in the frame? The DCI must have known his DI would have covered himself, made sure no tag ends of evidence were left to implicate him.

Fenwick himself had taught him that. When Redvers cited his putting criminals into the *Daily Mirror* and *Daily Express* payrolls, Tony's anxiety increased. Could there be evidence against him?

Was Fenwick a lot more slippery than he'd imagined? Had he been collecting evidence without him even suspecting? It was possible there was something on him fitting up criminals as a favour to Jack Braden ... Despite this, Tony said boldly, 'You believe a self-confessed corrupt policeman rather than a hard-working copper?'

'You were observed having contact with known criminals.'

'Well, you can't nick them if you don't,' Tony said. 'All contact is noted in my diary. Unless Fenwick's got times and dates when we met them that I didn't note. Has he?'

'That remains to be seen,' Redvers said noncommittally.

'You should bring on your evidence,' Tony challenged him, 'or talk to Chief Superintendent Slipper. He'll give you a steer.'

'Are you refusing to make a statement, Inspector?'

'Don't be a wolly, John,' Tony said, with great force. 'I just made it. To say more might jeopardize sensitive operations. I mean, how do I know you aren't helping your cousin and your uncle?'

'This is ridiculous!' Redvers said, and glanced at the other two policemen present.

'I find it just as ridiculous that *any* policeman would go bent,' Tony said, without a ripple on the surface. 'That's not why we come into the job. Or are you saying the job corrupts us?'

That gave Superintendent Redvers a moment of uncertainty. He hesitated. Tony seized it and worked his pry bar. 'Could you talk to Chief Superintendent Slipper, sir? I can't say I enjoy being nicked. What I do enjoy is nicking bad people, seeing them put where they belong.'

Tony thought he detected a faint smile on DCI Robertson's lips and wondered if he'd gone too far.

'Keep an eye on him, Chief Inspector,' Redvers said. 'No phone calls or contact with anyone.' With that he went out, slamming the door. A long silence followed. Looks ricocheted about the room. For a while no one said anything.

'Nice one, Tony,' DCI Robertson said finally. 'Sit tight and you'll do.'

'Yeah? What I don't know,' Tony said, 'is whether you're the most cunning fucking detective I've ever met or the most helpful.'

'Time will tell. There's a phone. You know how to get an outside line. We'll be across the corridor.'

He nodded to Sergeant Daly and they went out. Tony picked up the phone and dialled, wondering if it was bugged.

'Chief Superintendent Slipper, please,' he said, when the phone was answered. 'It's DI Wednesday, and I need to speak to him urgently.'

Still smarting from being told by the arrogant Tony Wednesday that they all thought him naïve, a wolly, John Redvers wondered who 'we' included, whether that was how Sonia had seen him. The one small consolation was that she had seen through Tony. Now he was angry as he walked along the corridor with Chief Superintendent Slipper listening to what he was saying about Wednesday, deciding the man was allowing his feelings to cloud his judgement.

'I've never liked coppers who police policemen,' Slipper said. 'I suppose someone has to do it when they occasionally stray.' He glanced sideways in Redvers's direction. 'Tony Wednesday is entirely right in what he told you, John,' he went on. 'I'll stand by him in the face of any charge.'

'The problem is, sir,' Redvers said, 'he didn't tell us anything much. That's not what I expected from someone in his position.'

'It's a highly secret operation we're conducting. We can't do it in the open, not without alerting major crims.'

'Are Jack Braden and Brian Oldman two of them?'

'I can't even tell you that,' Slipper said. 'We hand-picked every officer on this operation. I don't know anyone on your team, Superintendent. You can understand Tony's reluctance to tell you anything in view of who you're related to.'

Redvers felt his cheeks smart as his anger deepened. He felt guilty, even though he'd done nothing to compromise himself as a policeman. In the face of such unbridled support from a senior officer, he knew he'd be foolish to pursue DI Wednesday without solid evidence, but he was determined to do so none the less. 'I'm not likely to tell those two anything,' he said, 'and I came clean about my being related to them, sir. The commissioner knows.'

Chief Superintendent Slipper nodded. 'You've certainly got the wrong man in Tony Wednesday. Check his diary against what Fenwick or any other treacherously corrupt policeman said about him. You'll see.' He stepped into the lift.

Redvers didn't join him. He took the stairs and walked back to Tintagel House.

There, he found DCI Robertson and told him to release Wednesday with an apology.

'Did something happen I should know about, guv?'

'It seems he's not corrupt,' Redvers said.

'Phew!' the DCI responded, with exaggerated relief. 'That's all right, then.'

'Are you sure Wednesday knows the whereabouts of DCI Fenwick?'

'Oh, yes.'

'Then watch him like a hawk. I want the evidence on film when Wednesday approaches him.'

'You sure he will, guv?'

'The only way he can guarantee his continuing existence is by persuading Fenwick not to give evidence. He'll go there. Not today, maybe, but sooner rather than later,' Redvers said, and went into his office.

Jack didn't stir as the car pulled up outside the block of flats in Park Street. He sat hunched in the back, wondering what to do about Leah.

'Jack?' Pongo said, turning from the driver's seat.

'What?' Jack said, snapping out of his reverie. He wasn't convinced everything was safe now, even though Tony Wednesday was back on the street taking care of things. Life would improve after they'd dealt with one last detail. He glanced at Leah, wrapped in his long Afghan coat. He wasn't sure if she was asleep or lost to medication. 'Look, I'm gonna stay in with her tonight and watch telly,' he said. 'Slip out to that pub in Henley. See if you can catch hold of George Fenwick. Give him the time of day. Box a bit clever, Pongo. Don't get seen.'

'Yeah, I got a kitchen hand's uniform, Jack. When d'you ever notice a black kitchen worker?'

'You be careful, Pongo. Be terrible if you got yourself nicked. Pug up somewhere afterwards. Give yourself an alibi.' Jack meant what he said to Pongo. He didn't often tell him how much he valued him, but Pongo's loyalty meant everything to him. He got out of the car and pulled Leah after him.

The long, continuous ringing of the doorbell was somehow incorporated into his dream, and when Jack woke alone on the sofa in the sitting room he thought the sound was on the telly. He'd fallen asleep watching *Sunday Night at the London Palladium*. Now it was two o'clock and he was cold and stiff, the flickering screen hissing and the doorbell still ringing.

'All right, all right, keep your shirt on.' Jack got up and switched off the gogglebox, then went to the door. The police shoved it open and pushed in the moment he slipped the catch.

'What's this? The Police Benevolent Fund collection?' he said, when he recognized DI Wednesday.

'Jack Braden, we have a warrant to search your flat,' Wednesday told him formally. 'We'd prefer to have your co-operation, but we'll manage without it. Through there,' he told his men.

'Well, you could have done this at a reasonable hour,' Jack complained. 'My wife's not well. She's asleep.'

'We'll be as sensitive as only policemen can be, Jack. We won't disturb her – unless she's lying on something she shouldn't.'

He winked at him and Jack tried to read what that meant, guessing this must be part of the get-up they'd arranged.

They hadn't been searching long when one of the detectives said, 'A shooter, guv.'

It was sitting in the coffee-table drawer.

'This the one you shot Bobby Brown with, Jack?'

'Guv!' another detective said, coming out of the bathroom. Jack followed them. A large plastic-wrapped package was taped under the lid of the cistern.

'What's this?' Jack demanded, a sick feeling flooding his stomach.

'It looks like a large bag of cocaine,' Wednesday said, opening it. He dipped a wet finger into it. 'It tastes like a large bag of cocaine.'

'You planted that!' Jack screamed. 'You planted it.'

'Don't talk daft, Jack.' Wednesday smiled. 'We're detectives, not gardeners.'

There was chaos in his parents' house, which they were trying to get straight after their recent move, but Brian felt safe there – a lot safer than he did at his flat, waiting for the police to arrive as he knew they would now that Jack had been arrested.

'Can you trust Wednesday, Brian?' Joey asked urgently, as if he was about to offer some alternatives.

'What choice do I have, Dad? He's promising us a deal.'

'There's always South America,' Joey told him. 'Ortega would sort you out.'

'I couldn't stand the heat,' Brian joked. His father didn't laugh. 'Tony said it would be rough, then get better. Mind you, I don't care about Jack staying in the frame. If I get clear of this, I'll become a businessman. I mean it, Dad.'

'You will get clear. Lord Goodman will get you the best defence money can buy.'

Now that the deed was done Brian was having doubts about the detective running the show. If he didn't come through, his solicitor would have to come up with a lot more than money could buy. He felt sick and helpless at the thought of prison, even on remand.

He was struggling to convince himself that going to court was the best option.

'Are you seriously telling me, Superintendent, that no police officer, other than your men, approached DCI Fenwick while he was in your charge?' Assistant Commissioner Virgo asked.

John Redvers felt more uncomfortable than he had at any other time in his entire life. He could only guess at what these men in the commissioner's seventh-floor office were thinking. He didn't want to go there.

'We watched him virtually twenty-four hours a day, sir,' Redvers replied. 'No one approached him. We're certain of that.'

'He just got up that morning and decided all he'd told us so far had been a lie? He wasn't got at, and he certainly couldn't tell them the truth that they'd been planning to entrap DI Wednesday. If he did it would look as if he'd perverted the course of justice. Is that what you're telling us?' Virgo said.

Glancing at the commissioner, who wasn't saying anything where he stood at the window with his back to the room, Redvers sighed. 'There's nothing suggests otherwise, sir.'

'Extraordinary. Absolutely fucking mind-boggling. He was our ace. I think you all must have been sleeping and let the fairies get to him.'

'No one was sleeping, sir.' Redvers insisted as he became increasingly worried by the commissioner's continuing silence. It was clear there wasn't going to be any help from him. This was so different from his previous visit when he had been handed the keys to the kingdom. Without a word being said, Redvers knew he had failed the one person who mattered most. His scheme had backfired. Encouraged, as he believed he had been, by the commissioner to use subterfuge to entrap Tony Wednesday, he had done so against his better judgement. There was only one way to conduct yourself with crooked policemen or anyone else: by being as straight as could be. If he took nothing else from the Church his mother and cruel stepfather dedicated themselves to, it was that. This was his payment for not keeping to the straight and narrow way.

He tensed as Sir Robert Mark turned slowly from the window, weary with disappointment, his face as dark as a thunderous sky.

'We've expended huge amounts of time and money investigating corrupt policemen,' he said. 'Did you think you could achieve in weeks what hundreds of detectives failed to do so far?'

'I will break this firm within a firm, sir,' Redvers said, trying desperately to claw back a scrap of respect.

'Meanwhile, Assistant Commissioner Virgo is going to assume personal responsibility for your department,' Sir Robert said. We'll start doing deals with corrupt officers, giving them immunity from prosecution in exchange for information. But not Fenwick. He has to go to prison. That's all.'

Redvers felt as if layers of skin were being stripped away from him. As he went out of the office into the anteroom, he might have burst into tears but for the three secretaries who avoided looking at him from their click-clacking typewriters. This was worse than any punishment Wilfrid Ford, his stepfather, had meted out. He hurried away with no idea how to recover what had been taken from him.

'That was a blinding bit of news, Jack.'

Jack turned in the breakfast queue at Brixton prison, where he was on remand with Brian, as John Bindon approached him. Bindon was resting from his acting career, having been caught with dope in his possession. He managed to be best friends with everyone because he'd been on telly a few times. 'That bent Old Bill suddenly going the other way was like someone answered your prayers,' Bindon said.

'I thought it was a joke.' Jack liked Bindon, even though he was unreliable. 'They're always coming up with sick jokes.'

'All you need now is him saying how you was fitted, Jack.'

There was no word from Pongo about how he'd got to George Fenwick to make him turn. Jack assumed he had got clear and was pugged up somewhere or taking care of Leah.

'What's happening, Brian? Did you hear?' Jack said, going into his nephew's cell with a mug of tea. That was all he could face for breakfast.

'How would I know?' Brian said. 'I'm not sure I believe what happened with Fenwick. There was a man out to save himself.'

'Maybe that's what he did,' Jack said. 'Where's that snake Tony Wednesday? Let's get him down here and ask him.'

'Be sensible. He won't come near us now,' Brian told him. 'He said that at the start, Jack.'

A screw came to the door. 'Brian, your solicitor's here.' He saw Jack. 'Oh, and you, Mr Braden.'

In the legal room, sitting forward in a chair that was fixed to the floor, Jack asked, 'Did you get in touch with that detective?'

'Lord Goodman did,' the lawyer told him. 'He'll only talk to you in a formal interview with your solicitor present. Whatever he promised you, Jack, I don't think it'll happen.'

'What's going on?' Jack demanded.

'Calm down,' Brian muttered.

'The police are going back to court to ask for an extended remand.'

'Not good news. It wasn't what we agreed to.'

'The circumstances have changed, Brian. The kilo of cocaine found at Jack's flat – traces of it were in one of the Baker Street safe-deposit boxes that were robbed.'

'Fuck, no! That's a fit-up! They're fitting me up!' Jack bellowed. 'I'll kill that snake Tony Wednesday. I wouldn't have drugs at the flat. 'S madness.' He looked at Brian and the lawyer.

'He's made quite sure you're tied in to the Baker Street bank robbery,' the solicitor said.

'I wasn't there,' Jack said. 'Tell him, Brian.'

'He wasn't in on the bank robbery,' Brian said.

'What you gonna do about that?' Jack snarled.

'The solid piece of evidence the police have against you, the cocaine, says otherwise, Jack,' the solicitor said. 'The cocaine.'

'Something very dodgy's going on, Arnold,' Joey said in the lawyer's Fetter Lane office. 'I'm sure it's the cocaine I was given by the Colombians. I handed it to DI Wednesday.'

'That's monstrous if it's true, Joseph.'

'One kilo. Ninety-eight per cent pure. It was a present for our doing business together.'

'Unfortunately we can't use that in evidence,' Goodman pointed out, 'even if we were inclined to.'

'No. But I'll make it plain to Inspector Wednesday that if anything happens to Brian I won't rest until he's destroyed.'

'What about your brother-in-law?'

'He can go to hell on a bike.'

'Then let me talk to Wednesday again and see what I can negotiate for Brian,' Goodman said.

'I want him out of the messy business he's been caught in,' Joey said. 'He'll be safe in the property business with me.'

Tony Wednesday laughed as he stood in the vast reception area at Scotland Yard, listening to the fat, oily lawyer. He knew his reputation for cunning, and the political and royal circles he sometimes moved in, and felt flattered. But his was legendary. Tony felt safe meeting him in this public space, knowing he couldn't get into trouble over it. 'We've been after Jack Braden and Brian Oldman for far too long, sir,' he reminded him, as if Goodman needed reminding. 'We're unlikely to let them slip from our clutches now. The evidence is all there.'

'Is it? Like the kilo of cocaine?'

The smile vanished from Tony's face and his jaw tightened. He wondered what the tricky bastard was saying.

'Presumably Jack Braden's more important to you than Brian.'

'He's definitely the prize, but Brian's done some pretty diabolical things in his own right.'

'Such as?' the lawyer enquired.

'We can't discuss that here. We do need to put Brian away, despite his dad – we get all sorts of threats from the families of villains.'

'I'm sure Brian's done nothing in his own right that can't be overlooked for a price,' Goodman said.

Tony met his gaze, watching him raise his thin, black eyebrows and pull his chin into his neck. Now they were getting to the nitty-gritty of this visit. He'd never have believed Joey Oldman would have the stomach for violence.

'It would depend on how big a price, and how many were involved in the overlooking,' he said. It was early days so he could drag out any such negotiations. The more evidence he put in place, the more he could get for dropping Brian out. He knew just where he'd go to get part of it. Leah Cohen, or Braden as she now was, would be down for a visit in hospital.

'Can I help you?' asked the young woman behind the reception desk at Friern Barnet psychiatric hospital. Somehow she didn't seem like a receptionist, in tight blue jeans and a skinny-rib roll-neck sweater.

'I'm Detective Inspector Wednesday,' he said, twisting his head to read the nametag that was sideways on her left breast – Clair Hammill. 'I've got an appointment to see Dr Bloomsbury.'

'Yes. You want to talk to Leah Cohen.'

'Doesn't she use her married name – Braden?' Tony enquired, as if he knew nothing about her.

'No. She hates being called that. I'm the psychiatric social worker in charge of Leah's case.'

'How is she? Well enough to talk to me?'

'Well enough to give evidence against her husband, is what you really mean, don't you?'

'Yes. I like people who come right out and say it straight, instead of the sly avoidance we usually get.' He gave her a big smile and waited. She turned away, but looked back when he said, 'What do you do in your spare time, Clair?'

'Excuse me, Inspector?'

'I'd like to have a drink after work with someone as straightforward as you,' Tony said, with a boyish grin.

'My boyfriend might have something to say about that.'

'Not if you don't tell him.' Tony watched her come out from behind the desk, admiring how the jeans hugged her shapely hips, her jumper showing off her breasts.

She met his eyes again with a determination that made her interesting rather than beautiful. 'You like what you see?'

'I can't pretend I don't.'

'I'll try to find Dr Bloomsbury.'

She went off across the oak-panelled hallway and disappeared down a corridor.

Dr Andy Bloomsbury was stoop-shouldered, around thirty-five, and wore a yellow corduroy suit and a red-and-white spotted bow-tie. Tony followed him to the dayroom where Leah sat staring out of the window at the expanse of mown grass outside. She didn't move as they approached her and Dr Bloomsbury introduced him. He turned back to Tony. 'She suffered a complete breakdown after her husband's arrest. We're treating her for schizophrenia.'

'Leah, will you look at me?' Dr Bloomsbury said. 'How are we feeling this afternoon?'

'Why do you talk down to me like that, Dr Bloomsbury?' Leah said, turning, but not looking at them. 'As if I'm a child. I'm not. I know almost as much as you.' She turned away, agitated now, and stroking the window with her fingertips.

'Calm down, Leah. No one's patronizing you.'

'It feels like that. It always feels like that. Leah, do this, Leah, do that. Rewards for good behaviour, punishment for bad. I know a lot. I've been studying for a long time.'

'We have to understand,' Dr Bloomsbury said, 'that intellect can't always reconcile our emotional states.'

She turned to face them. 'But you've got my diagnosis wrong, Dr Bloomsbury. I'm sure you have.'

'We'll talk about that another time, Leah.'

'I'm not schizophrenic. It's a depression-induced psychosis.'

'Let's discuss it elsewhere, Leah,' Dr Bloomsbury said firmly. 'Inspector Wednesday wants to ask you some questions.'

'Yes, I know. You want me to give evidence against the man who forced me to marry him – and his nephew,' Leah said. 'Clair told me. I hate that man – I'll never call him my husband. I was his prisoner. He held me against my will. I hate him and his nephew. Brian Oldman's just as bad. Both of them are psychotic. I want to give evidence against them. I want to see them in prison for the rest of their lives.'

'If you're up to it, Leah, I'd like you to tell me what you know,' Tony said.

'Yes,' Leah said. 'I can't tell you what a relief it was when they were put in prison. I'll do anything to keep them there.'

'With your help I'm sure we can make that happen, Leah,' Tony told her. Leah thanked him again and again, anxiously wringing her hands. He doubted if she'd hold up in the witness box, but decided she would be the means by which he would relieve Joey Oldman of a decent wedge of money.

THIRTY-TWO

Brian's arrest, in a blaze of publicity, on charges of murder, extortion, ABH, and his remand to Brixton prison incensed Joey beyond words. Despite the promises DI Tony Wednesday had made, he felt a deep unease about what might happen to his son. He could live with it, but his wife couldn't. She had taken it badly, especially the publicity. She turned, almost overnight, into a different woman. She had aged, and retired from the world. He urged her to see the doctor, even though he knew the man could do nothing. Her concern for her position in the Tory Party overlay her anxiety: she was sure she would be ostracized both socially and politically. Ironically, the number of phone calls she received about party business increased, but any of those might have been from the curious gathering gossip.

There were other things to talk about besides Brian's incarceration. Thinking he could win a popularity contest against Arthur Scargill and the miners' unions, Ted Heath had called a snap general election and lost. Not even that distracted Cath. Her usual confidence was gone. She needed to be active, so they went to see Lord Goodman. He told them that the police seemed to be piling everything on to Brian and Jack, which didn't help.

'Bribe them,' Cath ordered. 'We know they're all corrupt.'

'The charges are too serious,' Goodman reiterated.

Joey wondered if he hadn't become too much part of the establishment since he'd been ennobled. 'How long is Brian likely to be in prison?' he asked.

'If he's found guilty on even a quarter of those charges, it's likely he'd attract a life sentence.'

Cath let out a cry. 'No!'

Joey knew exactly what she was thinking. It was the start of her fight back, and he was glad, even though nothing had changed: it meant he wouldn't lose her too.

In the cab back to Stanley Gardens, she said, 'I can't let this happen. Brian doesn't deserve the same treatment as Jack. He hasn't done anything seriously wrong.'

'Nothing as bad as Jack, I'm sure.'

'You'll have to negotiate with that detective, Tony Wednesday. There's John, Alice's boy. Perhaps we could ask her to get him to help Brian.'

'That's unlikely,' Joey said. 'You haven't spoken to Alice since your mum died – or her boy, come to that.'

'Well, I'm going to invite him to tea,' Cath announced. 'It's time to see how he's turned out.'

'Let me try with Tony Wednesday first. He's more at the centre of this,' Joey told her. 'Go to your nephew if all else fails. Look, drop me at the bank – I'll try to see Wednesday today.'

When Joey rang him DI Wednesday said he was too tied up to meet today but, when pushed, he suggested the tea bar by Chelsea Bridge. Then, on a cautionary note, he added, 'Come alone, Mr Oldman.'

Joey wouldn't have dreamt of taking anyone with him. As he put the phone down his secretary, who had come with him from Lombard Street, said on the intercom, 'Mr Tyrwhitt's asking if you've got a moment to spare.'

'Later this afternoon,' Joey said.

'He's here now, sir,' Doreen said. 'He said it's urgent.'

'Then ask him to come in.'

Charles Tyrwhitt was in managing-director mode, armoured in his double-breasted worsted suit. 'Joseph, we must talk. Unpleasant as it is, we're concerned that this business might affect the bank.'

'I haven't time at the moment, Charles.'

'This is important, Joseph.'

'It really will have to keep,' Joey said. 'I've got a meeting with an important client. I'm sorry.'

'The bank can't risk any sort of scandal.' Tyrwhitt pursued him out of the door.

Joey didn't stop to argue. He wouldn't risk missing the detective.

The tea bar on Chelsea Bridge seemed an incongruous place for a business meeting, even of this nature. Joey watched DI Wednesday get two cups of tea and a KitKat, then join him, traffic roaring past.

His cup was thick and chipped. Joey had developed a liking for fine china and tea from a silver pot. 'I can understand your caution in the circumstances, Mr Wednesday. I told my senior partner I was off to meet a client, which I hope you will be by the end of this meeting. Let's stand by the parapet.'

'In case either of us decides to jump?'

'The traffic noise presumably prevents us trying to record this.'

'These are dangerous times. A lot of policemen are being forced to resign under this commissioner. What is it you want, Joey? As if I couldn't guess.'

'I want you to keep your promise to my son. I'll pay for whatever help you can get him.'

'Not Jack Braden as well?'

'He's got to take his chances.'

'He's well and truly in the frame.'

'With the help of the cocaine I gave you.'

'What did you think I'd do with it? Sell it on the street? I'm not that sort of policeman.'

'You're clever, Inspector,' Joey said. 'Tell me how you can help my son.'

'He's kept bad company for too long. We all knew it was only a matter of time. He's well overdue.'

This told Joey the price would be high. Within reason, he wasn't concerned about that. What he did want was a guarantee, not just vague promises to leave out some of the poison so Brian didn't get such a long sentence.

The five or six years the detective suggested was a big improvement on the expected fifteen to twenty in a maximum-security prison, but for Cath's sake Joey wanted more: he wanted his son to walk out now.

'Not for all the money you can lay your hands on, Joey.'

'You don't know how much that is.' He wondered what Wednesday would say if he told him it was several millions.

'You're making it sound more and more attractive.'

'I want Brian to walk free of this.'

'He's had one stroke of good luck in DCI Fenwick recanting like he did. He was a major witness for the Crown. Now, if Jack's wife were to decide to kill herself . . . She could do them both a lot of damage.'

'Perhaps between us we could talk to her,' Joey suggested.

'I already did.' Tony Wednesday smiled. 'How do you feel about Detective Superintendent Redvers?'

'Brian's cousin?' Joey said, unable to hide his surprise.

'His squad's forcing the pace on this,' the DI said.

'Perhaps he's trying to exorcize the taint of blood.'

They sipped their tea, and watched flotsam appear from under the bridge and float away down the Thames. 'How would you feel if we set Redvers up so it appeared he helped Brian get an acquittal?'

'What would you need? More cocaine?'

'Something has to be done about Jack's wife . . . I could talk to her doctor – if you've got the money. I'm sure he could use it. All the stress can't be helping Leah.' The detective screwed up his KitKat wrapper and threw it into the river. 'Jack stays in the frame.'

'How, if Leah doesn't give evidence?'

'Your son has to lolly him up. Then the court would see Brian's a reformed character, if nothing else.'

'I'll go and see him,' Joey said. 'He might resist that.'

'It's his choice,' Wednesday said, as an articulated lorry drove past, throwing out a cloud of choking diesel fumes. 'Let's talk about money.'

That was Joey's favourite topic. They arrived easily at a deal, which made the detective lick his lips. He'd move heaven and earth to collect what Joey had promised him.

'You got a visitor, Brian,' the red-headed screw said, from the door. Brian had left it open because he couldn't bear being closed in, and he stayed in his cell because he didn't want to mix with other remand prisoners – they assumed you were like them and shared their values. Brian wanted to establish himself as independent of Jack, but it was difficult because his uncle spent most of his time here – and was sitting with him now. Jack had never been one to suffer his own company: he needed someone around to tell him he was the man. Plenty in here were still prepared to do that.

Brian wasn't down for a visit. 'Who is it?' he asked.

'Your solicitor, I think.' The screw winked.

'What does he want?' Jack asked. He was jealous of anyone's visits, especially Brian's legal ones. 'What about my visitor, Clive? Where's my Leah?'

'I ain't had no request from her yet, Mr Braden,' the screw said, and nodded Brian out.

When he got to the legal visits room Brian understood the screw's wink. 'How did you get yourself in here?' he asked his dad.

'I gave the jailer some money.'

'You couldn't give him some more to let me run, Dad? I'll go as crazy as Jack, with much more of this,' Brian said.

'Your lawyer thinks there might be a way out for you.'

Brian grinned and thumped the table with a clenched first. 'Not before time, Dad.'

'You have to think of yourself,' Joey said.

'What d'you think I've been doing? I should never have gone back with Jack after I got out of hospital.'

'You give him up and save yourself.'

Suddenly Brian's bounce was gone. His dad didn't know what he was saying. He couldn't give evidence against Jack, as much as he hated him.

'If you go to prison for twenty or more years it won't help Jack, or save him a single day of his sentence. We'll negotiate with him, put some money aside for him. Look, I had a meeting with that detective, Tony Wednesday—'

Brian laughed scornfully. He might have guessed. 'It's him that's fitting us up, Dad!'

'I know it, and he knows I know it,' Joey told him. 'That doesn't help. Arnold's had some fruitful discussions with a member of the attorney general's staff. If you give evidence, the charges against you will be dropped.'

'Dad, I can't,' Brian said, on the verge of tears now. 'Do you know what that would make me?'

'Yes. A free man. Try thinking of your mother instead of yourself. How will it look to her friends in the Tory Party? They don't know what a decent man you are. Think of me, my business interests. I'm coming under pressure at the bank. It'll make no difference to Jack and he'll have money.'

'I'm sorry, Dad, I can't go that way.'

'This is stupid, Brian,' Joey said, with a flash of impatience. 'You got yourself into this mess. You were warned again and again to get away from that man. We're moving heaven and earth to pull you out of this and you still throw it in our faces.'

'You don't care what doing that would cost me!' Brian shouted. 'Just so long as you and Mum aren't inconvenienced! Well, piss off – I'll make my own way!' He leapt out of his chair and rang the bell.

Back in his cell he paced angrily. If he did as his father wanted, he'd be tainted as a grass, regardless of what Jack might or might not have agreed to. Briefly he wondered why he cared what criminals thought of him, and came up with no answer. He just did, and that disturbed him even more. Perhaps he would never escape this way of life.

Joey was hugely disappointed by Brian's response but he didn't tell Cath. Instead he went to see Lord Goodman. This setback wouldn't deter him. 'Such a stupid boy, Arnold,' he said. 'I wanted to shake him, knock some sense into him.'

'We can't live their lives for them,' Goodman said. 'The detective, is he still keen to help?'

'He wants Brian's evidence against Jack, plus some cash. I can try increasing the cash.'

'Do you trust him?'

'No, but with a large sum of money coming his way, I think we can rely on him.'

'I made some enquiries about him. He's recently been under suspicion himself. Someone as corrupt as he is will have made mistakes. We could get word about him to the commissioner's internal-investigation team. It's risky, of course.'

'*Anything*'s worth trying.' Joey sighed wearily. They were grabbing at straws. 'What about your help on the prosecution team?'

'They could only do that if the police agree to back off.'

'Let me talk to the detective again,' Joey said. 'I'll promise him the earth.'

The first thing Tony Wednesday wanted to know was whether he could deliver the earth, especially as Joey couldn't persuade his stupid son to help himself. Joey could tell him only that a lot of money was available, which certainly kept the detective interested.

The meeting place was to be St Jame's Park, an improvement on Chelsea Bridge, with all its pollution, but as he was about to leave the bank, Wednesday rang and told him to wait. He'd ring him back about where to meet. An hour later he showed up in Brook Street unannounced. Another of his precautions: it meant no trap could be set for him. Joey admired the man's survival instinct.

'Money is all I can offer. A great deal of money placed in an offshore account.'

DI Wednesday laughed, his greed almost palpable. 'We've been working on Jack and Brian for a hundred years!'

'But Brian's nothing,' Joey stated bluntly.

'He's done his share.'

Now the detective seemed nervous. Perhaps he was human after all, responding to something in his fatherly appeal. More likely it was money. Joey knew how deeply it could affect people – some would do absolutely anything for it.

'Twenty grand is what it'll cost,' Wednesday said. 'Used notes in small parcels.'

'You'd be better off with it out of the country.'

'Where I can't see or get to it? Forget it.'

'Brian has to walk free.' Then Joey realized he should have negotiated harder: DI Wednesday moved the goalposts.

'The twenty's just for me. Others'll have to have a dip – Chief Superintendent Slipper'll probably want more than that.'

'How much more?'

'That depends how involved he is. He's well greedy.'

'Brian must walk free,' Joey told him again.

'That's the object, but I can't guarantee it.'

'My son has to walk free.'

'I've got to know the money's safe,' Wednesday said. 'I'm putting myself well on offer here.'

'It couldn't be safer in God's pocket,' Joey assured him. 'I'll talk to a colleague at the bank. The money will be safe.'

'Who's the colleague?' Wednesday asked suspiciously.

'Let me talk to him first. I'll arrange for you to meet.'

As soon as the detective had left, Joey rang Charles Tyrwhitt. He agreed to meet on neutral territory – the bank's boardroom. The twelve-foot-long-polished walnut table was too big for the room. Tyrwhitt sat at the end reserved for the chairman as he listened to what Joey told him. Resistance showed in his fidgety little actions.

'I don't see how we can help him, Joseph,' he said eventually, his index fingers pressed together under his chin. 'In fact, I'm sure it's not the sort of business this bank could undertake.'

'Arms-dealers, drug-dealers, anyone with any other sort of crooked business deal but mine.'

'You're being emotional, Joseph.'

'I certainly feel it. My son's liberty's at stake. He could go to prison for a long, long while.'

'"If you can't do the time, don't do the crime", as the old saying goes,' Tyrwhitt said pompously.

'There might come a day when I remind you of that, Charles.'

'I doubt you'd have cause, old boy. Everything here is above board. We pass our bank inspections with flying colours.'

'I know we do,' Joey said formally. 'I wouldn't have come on to the board if that wasn't the case.'

'Yes, well, there's a question mark over your position now,' Tyrwhitt told him. 'I don't wish to add to your current problems, old boy, but dare we risk the bank's clients being embarrassed?'

'Of course not,' Joey said accommodatingly. 'The lurid publicity following my son's arrest – and my brother-in-law's – was embarrassing.'

'Braden was a thoroughly bad lot in the army.'

'He still is,' Joey said. 'Some of the things he acquires for certain members of the bank's board might cause us even more embarrassment if it came out.'

Tyrwhitt averted his gaze, probably because he'd understood Joey's veiled threat. 'The simplest solution is for you to resign, Joseph. Sever all connection with the bank.'

Joey recoiled. He hadn't seen that coming. Recovering himself he said, 'What if your dealings with Braden were revealed in court?'

'What? Tyrwhitt blustered. 'All we do is share an interest in boys' boxing clubs. We help with fund-raising – Princess Margaret supports us.'

'If you say so.'

Tyrwhitt tried another tack. 'I could force your resignation through the board.'

Joey laughed. Not something he did often. 'That would be to risk me taking my clients away. Especially Luis Picado.'

'Oh, no. No, no! That's not how banks operate.'

'It's the way I operate, Charles. I'm currently managing eight million dollars' worth of assets for Picado. They've delivered two million pounds in fees. I don't think the board would cheer at losing that.'

'Clients will soon realize you don't have the experience to handle those amounts safely on your own.'

'They don't want safety,' Joseph said. 'Picado's more concerned to come out clean. That's why he's prepared to pay.'

'Yes, under the auspices of the bank,' Tyrwhitt said firmly.

'Then force me to resign. I've already talked to each of my clients.'

Colour drained from the MD's face. 'You're quite ruthless,' he said, then seemed lost for words. Perhaps he was suffering some sort of heart-attack. Joey made no move to help him. Eventually he said, 'I suppose that's to be expected, with your background.'

Joey shook his head, unconcerned. 'I'd like you to handle DI Wednesday's account details.'

That was a further shock for Tyrwhitt. 'Why me?' he said.

'That way all our secrets will remain intact.'

Joey knew this wasn't the basis for an enduring relationship but, then, he wasn't expecting it to last. Charles Tyrwhitt would learn just how ruthless he could be.

'Get one thing straight, Chas,' Tony said, across the table in Whites. 'I never want my name on any of the documentation, nothing that can track back to me. Understood?'

He smiled and ate some soup. The Tory gentlemen's club was a disappointment. He hadn't recognized any famous politicians among the thirty-three men he'd clocked having lunch there as he had followed the waiter to Charles Tyrwhitt's table. He had guessed why they were meeting there and found it funny, especially as the food wasn't better than he'd had at the orphanage.

'Joseph has explained all your needs, Mr Wednesday.'

'Shrewd fella,' Tony said, wondering why Joey had passed him on to this banker. Perhaps he was afraid of some sort of double-cross.

'Do you have much business together?' Tyrwhitt asked casually, waving to a man at another table.

'Look at me, Charles. Ordinarily I deal strictly on a cash basis. I've been persuaded there's a safer way. You're going to introduce me to it.'

'Nominee accounts in the Cayman Islands.'

'How do they work?'

'Quite simply,' Tyrwhitt said, 'your account's held by a nominee who is not traceable to you. Your interest is returned to the nominee. Your name never appears. You pay no tax on interest or dividends.'

'Cash never has my name on it either,' Tony said.

'Sometimes it can prove embarrassing. Our way is safer.'

'Is Joey Oldman good for all he said he is?' He didn't expect this man in his starched cutaway collar and regimental tie to give him a straight answer, but he was in the business of asking questions.

'His son in prison is embarrassing,' Tyrwhitt said. 'How do you propose to get him out?'

'I'm paid for results, not explanations.'

Tyrwhitt relaxed visibly. 'A secretive man,' he said. 'I think we're going to have a profitable relationship.'

The trial at the Old Bailey was less than a week away and nothing seemed to be happening that suggested it wouldn't go ahead. Brian felt sick at the prospect. The possibility of a long prison sentence weighed heavily. He couldn't sleep, couldn't eat and, with a constantly upset stomach, he was losing weight. He knew it would be easier to kill himself than spend years locked up.

Now he was relying on Jack, instead of the other way round,

visiting his cell on the smallest pretext to ask about things to which his uncle couldn't possibly have an answer. After supper one evening, he said, 'What's happening, Jack? Is anyone doing anything? Our trial starts Monday. You blink and we'll be away.'

'You got the old man with all the gelt,' Jack reminded him. 'I thought he was doing something.'

'You got DI Wednesday,' Brian said. 'Isn't he putting himself about?'

'He's Old Bill. I can't see him doing fuck-all.' He seemed resigned to his fate. 'Look, I ain't heard from Leah. I thought she'd at least write. D'you think she's ill, Bri? She must be, I'd say.'

'I don't think I can do this, Jack. I can't take it.'

'She must be ill. The hospital don't say nothing when I phone up.'

The bell signalling lock-up sounded and Brian was assailed by blind panic.

The summons he got was of the drop-everything-and-run kind. It alarmed Tony Wednesday. 'Where's the fire?' he asked, stepping into his boss's outer office.

'You'd better go in.' The chief superintendent's secretary nodded him through.

He tried to read from her expression whether he was in trouble but got nothing, so went into the office. 'Guv?'

'You know David Morse from the DPP's office?' Slipper said, indicating the man sitting at the desk.

Tony waited.

'We've lost our judge in Jack Braden's trial,' Morse said.

'What?' Tony said. His shock left no room for relief. 'We can't have.'

'He's been struck down with a virus. He can't run this trial.'

'How long's he gonna be off?' Tony looked to his boss for an answer.

'For ever, as far as Braden and Oldman are concerned,' Slipper said. 'He's not coming back.'

'That can't happen, guv. We might not hold on to our witnesses. Some of them are very nervous.'

'We can't risk postponing the trial,' Morse said. 'The DPP's looking for another judge.'

'He won't have read the papers. The delay could be months.'

'We'll buy him a book on speed-reading,' Morse joked.

No one laughed.

'You'd better talk to our witnesses, Tony.' Slipper sighed.

'Do you think DI Wednesday arranged this?'

'If he did, he didn't do us any favours,' Joey's lawyer told him. 'The new judge is Sir Aubrey Melford Stevenson. He's a hard-liner or, in the parlance of villains, a right wicked bastard. He won't give an inch.'

'Could the detective have engineered that?' Joey said, indignation rising.

'I hardly think that's within his competence, Joseph,' Lord Goodman said. 'Melford Stevenson's known for his extreme bias towards the police. It could possibly give grounds for appeal if he goes true to form.'

'If it goes that far, Arnold,' Joey said gloomily, 'it's a lost cause anyway.'

'We must expect the worst.'

Suddenly the pressure was off and, for the first time in weeks, Brian relaxed. 'It's a real result,' he told Jack, pacing excitedly around his cell.

'This judge owes us, all right,' Jack said, 'but will he weigh on?'

'Of course,' Brian said. 'I'll get Joey's brief to send him a note. We pulled him clear when the Krays killed that little brass Heather he was doing in your flat and George covered it up. That's why he loves the Old Bill so much. No, he's well involved. We can expect a right result, Jack.'

Brian felt positively cheerful.

THIRTY-THREE

Their trial began with the judge coming unexpectedly through the door to the bench, taking the clerk by surprise. Belatedly he called, 'All rise.' Those present shuffled to their feet as Sir Aubrey Melford Stevenson, in his purple-trimmed black robes, took his seat after bowing to the barristers. He glanced across the well of the dark oak-panelled court, first at Brian, then at Jack without recognition. Curiously Brian felt disappointed, even though he knew there could be no acknowledgement. If the judge was going to help them, the last thing he would do was give any sign that would reveal their relationship.

'Will the prisoners in the dock please stand?' the clerk instructed, as everyone else sat and turned in their direction.

'Jack Braden, you are jointly charged that on or about the ninth of March 1973 you did murder one Robert Brown and unlawfully disposed of his body by cutting it up and feeding it to pigs at Wilder Farm, Stoke Poges, Berkshire. You are further charged that between June 1969 and April 1973 you did assault one Leah Cohen with intent to do grievous bodily harm—'

'That's ballocks!' Jack cried out. 'It is!' He appealed to the spectators. 'I love her.'

'Mr Braden,' the judge said evenly, 'you will have an opportunity to refute these charges in due course. Until that time please remain silent. Mr Clerk?'

'Further, you are charged that on or about the weekend of the tenth of September 1971 you did break and enter bank premises in Baker Street, London, and remove from the safe deposit boxes various items and money of unknown value and quantity.'

'Not guilty,' Jack said.

'Mr Braden,' the judge said, 'you'll be advised when to respond to charges. Last warning. Mr Clerk?'

The clerk went through exactly the same process with Brian who, feeling the terrible pressure of unanswered accusation, understood why Jack had interrupted. His inclination was to do the same. If they let these things go without protest the whole court would see it as an admission of guilt. It was all he could do to keep quiet as his barrister got up to address the court.

'With respect, my lord,' George Carman QC said. 'I represent the second defendant, Brian Oldman. I would like at this point to move that all the charges against my client be dismissed as there is insufficient evidence to sustain any of them.'

'I won't hear your argument at this stage, Mr Carman. This will be something for the jury to decide,' Melford Stevenson said.

'With respect, my lord,' Carman persisted, 'I fail to see how any juror of whatever competence could follow the charges, much less, one assumes, even more complicated evidence. We have been more than an hour reading the charges alone!'

'With interruptions, Mr Carman,' the judge pointed out.

'Quite,' George Carman replied. 'My point is that Mr Oldman, my client, has been lumped together with his uncle and accused merely by association.'

'That is something for the jurors, Mr Carman.'

When he got up to speak, the diminutive prosecutor, Sir Donald James QC, could barely see over the lectern in front of him. Brian was puzzled to know why he used it, if it caused him problems. Perhaps because it made him look small and less aggressive. He laid into Brian and Jack for more than an hour and a half as he outlined the case, saying how their deeds were so terrible, so despicable that even policemen hardened by years of experience in crime blanched to hear of them. 'They lured their oldest, most trusted friend out to a remote pig farm, knocked him out and fed him live to pigs—'

Jack jumped up out of his seat and grabbed the rail of the dock. 'That's a lie!' he said. 'A wicked lie!'

Brian wondered what Jack was disputing, the killing itself or that they'd got the details wrong about how Bobby died.

'Mr Braden, possibly this is a lie. It's equally possible that the prosecution will be tripped up on it. Meanwhile, you will remain silent until it's your turn to speak,' the judge said. 'You have a very competent team of defence lawyers. They will speak on your behalf. Sir Donald?'

Sir Donald James continued to outline the evidence the prosecution would present of robbery, extortion, torture. The catalogue of 'criminal depravity' seemed endless. Brian knew that a lot of the details were wrong and wondered if the witnesses he was promising to produce were witnesses to anything at all. He felt cheered by the inaccuracies.

The first prosecution witness was a shock. Brian had expected it to be a policeman, but it was David Crutwell, who had survived precisely seven weeks on the run after the *Daily Mirror* robbery – out on another daytrip from Parkhurst!

He said who he was, where he currently lived, and that he was in Parkhurst for having taken part in the so-called Great Train Robbery. With the Bible in his hand he swore to tell the truth. Brian was keen to hear how he would try to keep himself out of it.

'Mr Crutwell, can you tell the court what your relationship is with the two men in the dock?' Sir Donald said.

'Oh, we ain't related. We just done a bit of work together.'

The spectators laughed and Crutwell looked round as if he was about to take a bow.

'What line of work were you in?' Sir Donald asked.

'I was a blagger – a robber – until I reformed.'

'What brought about this reform?' Sir Donald asked.

'Killing the security guard when we was robbing a payroll at the *Daily Mirror*. That was it. I didn't sign on for that.'

'You never thought this might happen when you were going about your criminal enterprise with a sawn-off shotgun?' the judge questioned.

'You don't,' Crutwell said. 'Course you don't. You think the threat's enough. Usually it is.'

'Who shot the guard at the *Daily Mirror* robbery? Do you know?'

'I was there,' Crutwell said. 'I seen it with me own eyes.'

'Is that person present in this court?' Sir Donald asked.

'He's up there in the dock. Jack Braden.'

'What?' Jack protested. 'You lying slag.'

'You have already been warned, Mr Braden,' the judge said, 'one more uncalled-for comment and you'll be removed to the cells. Sir Donald?'

'Thank you, my lord,' Sir Donald said, with exaggerated politeness. 'Mr Crutwell, you're quite certain it was Jack Braden who killed the guard?'

'He popped him, all right. Poor bastard had no chance.'

'Mr Crutwell,' the judge asked, 'have you been threatened or made promises to give this evidence?'

'I'm doing a twenty for robbery,' Crutwell said. 'If they give me another twenty for saying the truth I couldn't not say it.'

'Did you know a man called Bobby Brown?' the prosecutor asked.

Brian saw Jack sit forward, tense, anticipating what was coming. He didn't feel inclined to offer support, but guessed that in his calmer moments Jack probably regretted what he had done to his one-time close friend.

'Bobby? Course. A diamond. It was him what came down to see me in Parkhurst. He recruited me for the *Daily Express* and the *Daily Mirror* payroll robberies.'

'Do you know what happened to Mr Brown?' Sir Donald asked.

'Yeah. Jack capped him for being mouthy,' Crutwell said.

'Can you translate that for the jury?' the judge asked.

'Jack knocked him out,' Crutwell said, 'then took him down to the farm at Stoke Poges and fed him to the pigs.'

'Were you there when this happened?' Sir Donald asked.

'I was there when he whacked Bobby, then give the orders to take him out to the pig farm.'

'What exactly did he say?' Sir Donald asked.

'"Take him down to the farm." Everyone knew what that meant. The only way you come back is as a piece of bacon. No one wanted to take him, cos Bobby was well liked. Jack took him himself.'

'Did Braden have anyone to help him feed Bobby Brown to the pigs?' Sir Donald wanted to know.

'You only have to heave him over into the pen,' Crutwell said. 'I mean, Jack's a strong fella. Bobby wasn't exactly big.'

'But someone did help him. Who was that person?' Sir Donald turned to look at Brian in the dock.

Bizarrely, Brian felt his cheeks turn hot, even though he had been accused of doing something he hadn't done. He had no idea why Crutwell was telling it like he was, other than to distance himself from the shooting. He had seen the witness statement, read how Crutwell had lied and said he had taken Bobby out to the farm with Jack. That was probably more the work of the police than Crutwell.

'Who helped to feed Bobby Brown to the pigs?' the prosecutor asked again.

'I wouldn't know anything about that,' Crutwell said.

'Oh, come now, wasn't Brian Oldman involved?'

'I don't know.'

Brian perked up at the change of story.

'Just a minute. In your statement you said Mr Oldman was there, helped tie up the victim and carry him out of the club.'

'Yeah, well, I was that cheesed off at the little poof,' Crutwell said, glancing at Brian. 'I just stuck him in as well.'

'Let me get this perfectly clear,' George Carman said in cross-examination. 'Mr Oldman did not, as far as you know, carry Bobby Brown from the club and take him to the pig farm for disposal?'

'No. He had nothing to do with Jack popping Bobby. He wouldn't.

He was arguing with Jack not to. He was always arguing with Jack, trying to stop him. It was murder being around them.'

'Brian Oldman tried to stop Jack Braden killing Bobby Brown? Is that what you're telling the court?' Brian's defence counsel asked.

'Oh, yeah,' Crutwell agreed. 'He said Bobby was his best friend. He shouldn't hurt him.'

'I didn't! I didn't!' Jack yelled. 'You lying slag! I didn't kill Bobby.'

'Take him down,' the judge said. 'You'll stay in the cells for the rest of the day.'

He was hoping to slip in and out of the Friern Barnet hospital without being noticed, and Clair Hammill was the last person he wanted to see, but she'd caught him now, bang to rights, calling his name as he crossed the entrance hall. He turned as she approached briskly along the corridor. 'Have you just been in to see Dr Bloomsbury?' Clearly she knew he had.

'I needed to check a couple of facts about Leah Cohen's movements last year,' he said.

'Why didn't you ring me? I could have given you those – I've been the most present person in her life since she's been in and out of here. What did you want to know?'

'It doesn't matter. It's done now,' Tony told her.

'Were you going to call in and say hello?' She seemed hurt. He hadn't expected her to react like that. It was boring. 'I'm a bit pushed, Clair,' he said. 'I gotta get back to the Bailey.' Having done what he needed to do, he wanted to get away. People in the nut-house scared him.

'What you came to check must have been pretty important.'

'You ought to have been a detective, Clair,' Tony told her, with one of his most charming smiles. He saw her soften.

'I'm used to asking questions.'

'And getting answers,' Tony said. 'Look, I'll call you later.'

'Will you?'

'We'll go for a drink,' Tony promised.

He gave her a quick kiss and felt resistance – perhaps because they were in the main entrance hall of her workplace.

Each time he entered the patients' cold, unheated dayroom Leah noticed that Dr Bloomsbury did so as if he expected to be attacked, his small eyes darting about, checking where the threat might come from. She watched as he stayed close to the wall, then ventured across the room when he saw only one other patient and a nurse. If ever she had her own patients, Leah knew her approach would be different. She'd try to respect them as people, rather than viewing them as a collection of neuroses.

'Good book, Leah?' the doctor asked, adjusting his green corduroy jacket. He was wearing matching green suede shoes.

'It's on parapsychology.' She hoped he'd share her enthusiasm.

'I doubt it would be very useful,' Dr Bloomsbury said. 'It wouldn't be accredited to your course, you know.'

'Yes – but it's interesting,' Leah said, trying to broaden the discussion, but Bloomsbury looked away, not interested. She moved on quickly. 'It's hard to concentrate. I keep thinking about the trial.'

'Yes, it will be disturbing to you,' he said. 'Members of staff have commented on how troubled you've been.'

'Oh, no,' Leah said, with slight panic. 'I haven't . . . I mean . . . I just want to get the facts right.'

'Are we being as self-aware as we need to be, Leah?' the doctor asked, in a quiet, apparently kind tone.

Something was wrong. The feeling she got from him was just the opposite. 'What?' she asked.

'Believing you're not affected by all this? What must we do to progress and get out of here?'

'Develop self-awareness,' Leah said firmly. 'And I am. Every day I observe things about myself.'

'Yet you say you're not disturbed by this trial.'

'No, I'm not. Am I?' Uncertainty was pressing in.

He paused. 'I'm wondering if it's such a good idea your giving evidence, after all.'

'I must. It's my duty,' Leah said, as a mixture of emotions rushed at her, fear the most prominent. She really wanted to appear – it was the only way she would finally be free.

'Is it, Leah?' the doctor pressed. 'Are we sure this isn't the means of getting back at your husband?'

'No. I mean, yes,' Leah said, then didn't know where she was. Words came out that she couldn't seem to control. 'I want to hurt him for all he did to me. I hate him. I hate him.'

'Is that a progressive response, Leah?'

'It's self-aware,' she said. 'I do hate him.'

'What conclusion does this hatred bring you to?'

'I want to hurt him. I hate him so much I want to kill him.' Great waves of emotion poured out of her. 'I hate him so much. I hate him–' Her fingernails were digging into her palms. She was trying to punish herself for being so stupid and saying such things, but couldn't stop herself.

'Calm down, Leah,' the doctor was saying, signalling to the nurse, 'or we'll have to give you something. Leah, calm down!'

'Fuck you! I have to give my evidence and end this. I'll kill myself if I don't. I'll kill myself – I will! I will!' she was screaming now.

'Nurse, could we have twenty mils of Largactil?' Dr Bloomsbury called.

Terror overtook Leah and she flung her arms around wildly as the doctor and nurse tried to hold her. She would be lost for a long while if they gave her this drug. The psychosis would return.

'No! No!' she screamed. 'I want to give evidence. I want–'

Then there seemed to be a lot of staff around her, all talking at once. They held her down and she felt the needle in her vein. Almost immediately, she slipped off a high ledge and was falling into a tunnel that got darker and darker the further she fell. Soon she would reach the bottom and when she got there she knew she would be dead.

*

When Brian saw Tony Wednesday in animated conversation with the junior prosecuting counsel he became curious. The reason was soon clear.

'My lord,' Sir Donald James said, rising in court, 'my next witness was to be the wife of the first defendant. Regrettably Mrs Braden has suffered a relapse. She is unable to attend court.'

'Is this a temporary state, Sir Donald?' Mr Justice Melford Stevenson asked.

'Dr Bloomsbury, her psychiatrist, can't be sure. However, he doesn't feel her recovery is likely to be swift. He fears any appearance in court could prove detrimental.'

'Can you proceed without this witness?'

'My next witness isn't available, my Lord,' Sir Donald said. 'He has to come from Spain.'

Brian looked at Jack to see what he made of that. Denny Jones was the most likely candidate and it was odds-on he'd provide Jack with as big a shock as Crutwell had.

Travelling back to Brixton, all Jack could talk about was Leah. 'She's ill, Brian,' he said, through the vent between the compartments in the prison van. 'That's why she didn't come to see me on remand. They could have let me know.' He went on and on about her, boring the pants off Brian. He stopped listening and stared out at the streets. Rain was falling steadily as they headed south over London Bridge, passing people hurrying to catch trains, all of them free, apart from the ball and chain of a mortgage, the shackles of family and a job. Brian would have traded places with any of them. Briefly he turned his attention back to Jack, who was still on about Leah. Some hope. The only place he was likely to see her was in the witness box, giving evidence against him. If he couldn't grasp that, he must be pretty dim. Brian was depressed to think that he had been so influenced by such a stupid man. Here he was, riding back to prison with him instead of being free.

'Clair, am I going mad?' Leah asked, running up to her psychiatric social worker as she came on to the ward looking for her. She was in a blue winceyette nightdress and an old dressing-gown, her black hair lank and unkempt. Her skin felt as if it was crawling. She didn't know if this was really from lack of washing or part of the drug-induced psychosis. She didn't know how long she had been like this, but it seemed weeks.

'Everything's fine, Leah,' Clair Hammill assured her.

'No,' Leah protested. 'I can't get this fog out of my head. I'm supposed to go to court and give evidence.'

'The court excused you. Dr Bloomsbury said you weren't well enough,' Clair said. 'He gave you something to help you stay calm.'

'I saw that policeman with him – the one who came to the flat to talk to Jack. That was why Dr Bloomsbury drugged me. He wants to stop me giving evidence.'

'Leah, does that make sense?' Clair asked.

'They don't want me to give evidence,' Leah insisted.

'Why's that, Leah?' Clair asked. 'Is it logical?'

'Don't you see? The detective's working for that monster. He doesn't want me to give evidence. He's trying to get him off.' It was so clear to Leah. Jack had told her so often that the police would do anything for him as long as he paid them. She should have cottoned on to when the detective had come to see her, promising that Jack and Brian would go to prison for ever. 'That has to be the reason,' Leah said, believing she'd given Clair a clear explanation. 'Why else would Dr Bloomsbury drug me?'

'Leah, think about this rationally.'

'I am. I don't want any more drugs,' Leah told her. 'I was reading about the psychosis that drugs like Largactil cause. I don't want any more. Then I can give evidence.'

'I'll talk to Dr Bloomsbury,' Clair said. 'Ask him to reduce it.'

'He won't, Clair. Please don't – he's part of the conspiracy.' Leah was becoming even more agitated, and although she was aware of what was happening, she couldn't stop.

'Calm down,' Clair said. 'I'll ring the detective and see if I can't get him to talk to me.'

'You won't join his side and become part of the conspiracy?'

'I promise I won't.'

Going back to the Yard to catch up on paperwork after court was the last thing Tony Wednesday wanted to do, but it was the only way to stay on top of things. Other major crimes were being committed – blagging from Securicor trucks ferrying money around the country was the fashion with villains. It didn't stop because Jack Braden and Brian Oldman were in court. Criminals never learnt from the mistakes of others; the dimwits rarely even learnt from their own.

One of the phones on his desk was ringing. Tony hesitated. He wanted to go out and eat, maybe pick up a bird – there were plenty available. He didn't want to get caught up with some criminal intelligence he'd have to deal with. Not tonight. Concerned that he might be losing his edge, he picked up the phone.

'This is Clair,' the woman said firmly. 'You didn't call me.'

'But I've been thinking about you,' he lied, pleased to hear from her. 'I've been flat out in court, chasing witnesses, thanks to Leah Cohen not showing up.'

'She's not well,' Clair said, her tone softening.

'I thought perhaps she couldn't face giving evidence. A lot of people can't.'

'You're not angry with her?'

'We're solid enough without her. Those two will go down, all right.'

The silence that followed was like an accusation. He could almost hear Clair wrestling with her conscience, in conflict about something. He waited, letting her do the work. Then she surprised him. 'Would you like to make love to me, Tony?'

'What d'you think?' he said. 'That's an offer no man could refuse. Your place or mine?'

*

'Wow!' Tony said afterwards, sinking back on the bed in his tiny fifties-built flat on the corner of Dean Street and Old Compton Street. 'That was better than a poke in the eye.'

'How bloody romantic!' Clair said irritably. 'Perhaps I should try poking you in the eye – see if you come. I didn't.'

'That's because you're a hard woman to please.'

'No, you're just a selfish bastard.'

'You really get to it,' he said. Sonia was the only woman who had ever spoken to him in this way – when they were breaking up. He wasn't really in a relationship with Clair so it couldn't be breaking up. 'Is it your psychiatric training that makes you so blunt?'

'When I told you about Leah your reaction was really strange.'

'Was it?' Tony said.

'You didn't ask how she was, if she was going to get better in time to give evidence.'

'So?' Tony asked. 'We can get by without her.'

'It's a human response,' Clair said. 'She's a key witness.'

'She won't be able to give evidence, will she?'

'You seem to know she won't,' Clair said. 'How is that?'

'Clair, what the fuck are you saying? Is this about not getting your rocks off?' he asked. 'Or is everyone working in mental health paranoid?'

'Is every policeman corrupt?' she answered. 'I think you know more about this than you're letting on. You got at Dr Bloomsbury – the little shit – didn't you?'

'You're as mad as Leah is,' Tony said. 'Too much time around the toons.'

'Then you must be as corrupt as Jack Braden – too much time around crims.'

'You know what, Clair? I was planning to go again. But I think you'd better fork yourself off.' It was a joke that didn't work.

'Fuck you!' She smacked him around the face. Tony almost hit her back, but instead he caught her behind the neck and pulled her mouth to his. She resisted at first; then her lips softened. He'd go again before he took her out to dinner.

Disbelief spread across Jack's face, when Dennis Jones was called to give evidence. He stared, mouth open, dribbling slightly. Denny was tanned and healthy-looking, but Brian noticed his clothes were frayed, as if he wasn't prospering in Marbella.

He told the court how Jack had robbed honest, hard-working blaggers, promising to handle their money, which he then stole; he told of how he tortured them to get their dough; of how he had challenged Jack about holding out on their shares and Jack had beaten him to death, as he'd thought, then ordered Denny's body taken to the pig farm.

After this, the prosecutor sat down, looking fairly pleased with himself. Brian watched his brief get up. George Carman had a sour face as though he was suffering from an anxiety attack. He glanced first at the tiny Sir Donald James, then the witness.

'Was Brian Oldman involved in stealing any of this money from other criminals, Mr Jones?'

'No,' Denny said emphatically. Throughout the examination, Brian listened in amazement as Denny refused to name him as a party to anything.

'If it wasn't for Brian I'd be a goner. He was the only one with the guts to stand up to Jack. When he couldn't, he'd trick him, like he did when he told Jack I was dead, then sent me to Spain with a nice few quid.'

Brian glanced at Jack, whose expression of disbelief had frozen on his face. 'I always liked Denny,' Brian whispered, by way of apology.

'Mr Jones.' The judge looked up from the notes he seemed to be writing the whole time. 'In your statement to the police, you named Mr Oldman as being part of every criminal act Mr Braden was allegedly involved in. Why is that?'

Denny laughed. 'Well, when you're in a Spanish police cell and ain't had a decent cup of tea for days on end, nor likely to, then some Old Bill from England come and treat you like you're best mates and tell you this person and that person was involved in this and that, you think, Why not? You tend to say whatever they want to hear.'

'But, Mr Jones,' the judge reasoned, 'you subsequently made a statement to that effect.'

Denny Jones nodded. 'The thing is, they're treating you like a human being suddenly and you don't want it to stop, know what I mean? Old Bill badly wanted to nick the two of them, not just Jack.'

He glanced across to the dock and winked at Brian.

Brian felt the same wave of warmth towards Rita Webb, the stripper shot by Jack at Raymond's Revue Bar. She was next to give evidence for the Crown.

'Jack and Brian often came to the club to demand money off Paul,' she said. 'Well, Jack did the demanding. Brian didn't do anything really.'

'Did Mr Raymond give them money, Miss Webb?'

'Oh, he had to pay Jack or he'd have put him out of business,' she said.

'Can you tell the jury what happened on that day in April 1968 when these two men shot you?' Sir Donald invited.

'Oh, Brian didn't shoot me. It was Jack.'

'Just tell the court,' Sir Donald said irritably.

'They come into the club around eleven o'clock in the morning with Jimmy – Jimmy Humphreys,' she explained. 'Paul – Mr Raymond – was rehearsing us girls. Jack was angry and crashing about, Jimmy was telling them how Paul – Mr Raymond – couldn't pay more. They wanted more. Mr Raymond said no. Jack Braden aimed the gun at me and said unless Mr Raymond give him a bigger share of the profits he'd shoot me. Then he did.'

'What was your relationship with Paul Raymond, Miss Webb?' John Mortimer, Jack's QC, asked.

'I was a model.'

'Were you having sexual relations with Mr Raymond at the time?'

'My lord, is this relevant?' Sir Donald James was out of his seat.

'Mr Mortimer?' the judge asked, clearly enjoying the line. Brian recalled the strokes the judge had got up to with some of the girls he'd pulled for him.

'I suggest she was having sexual relations with him, and is still, so is prepared to lie about the incident,' John Mortimer argued.

'Well . . .' the judge hesitated '. . . don't stray too far.'

Mortimer didn't stray anywhere off the question of sex, arguing the club owner was having it with any number of his strippers.

George Carman followed a similar line when he cross-examined the witness. 'Were you having sex with Paul Raymond at the time?'

'That doesn't make me a bad person,' Rita Webb screeched.

'Of course it doesn't, Rita,' Carman soothed her. 'But to lie about it in court could make you liable to a prison sentence. I'm sure you don't want to go to prison, so think hard about this next question. Are you certain Brian Oldman was there when you were shot? Or could it have been someone else?'

Rita Webb stared across the well of the court to Brian, who stared back. She glanced at the judge, then back at Brian, who was holding his breath. 'I really can't remember,' she said. 'I just assumed he was because he's Jack's nephew.'

Brian sucked air into his lungs noisily as if he'd been held under water, causing the judge to glance at him. 'I think that's a suitable moment,' he said, and rose for the day.

As they emerged from court Lord Goodman took Joey's arm. 'The prosecution are struggling to make a case against Brian,' he whispered. 'We should keep our fingers crossed.'

'I daren't even think about the possibility,' Joey said. He was aware of points being made in Brian's favour, but was unsure how they added up for the jury. Whenever he dared sneak a glance at them, they were stern-faced and full of the onerous duty with which the judge had charged them.

'Your money was wisely spent on that policeman, Joseph,' Goodman continued, in a low, conspiratorial voice. 'Now, it might be advisable to have Catherine in court for Brian's defence.'

'Oh, I don't think she could bear it.'

'Seeing his loving, supportive parents in court, especially two such pillars of society, might sway the jury.'

'I'll talk to her.'

'Oh, Joseph, no. No,' Cath said. 'My nerves couldn't stand it. I'll do anything for Brian but that. Not on public display. I couldn't.'

'Any damage to your standing in the Party will have been done by now, Cathy,' Joey said.

'Please don't call me that. You know I dislike it.'

'I'm sorry.' His apology was sincere, but he was tired. Life with his wife was wearisome. She was so obsessed with appearances that he couldn't even watch his favourite television programme in case it was thought common. 'Think about it. It might even do you some good in the party, standing by him, especially if he's found not guilty.'

'Leah, wake up. I need to talk to you.'

'What? What is it?' Leah said, startled. 'I wasn't really asleep. I was dreaming about my childhood. I haven't dreamt since I've been here.'

'That's good,' Clair told her. 'Look, I want you to get up early in the morning, ready to leave the moment I come for you.'

'Dr Bloomsbury said I'm not ready to be discharged yet.' Leah wanted to get out of the hospital and return to studying, but was afraid to in case she had another breakdown.

'I spoke to Sir Donald James, the prosecutor at the Old Bailey,' Clair told her. 'He said if I could get you to court he'd put you into the witness box to give evidence, even though the prosecution case is closed.'

'Can I?' Leah was suddenly excited by the prospect. 'Will they really let me?'

'Sir Donald's spoken to the judge,' Clair said. 'He's perfectly amenable to your interrupting the defence case.'

'What about Dr Bloomsbury? He'll say I'm still not well.'

'We'll leave before he gets here. He has a clinic at the West Middlesex first thing anyway. Go back to your dreaming. Don't talk in your sleep or tell anyone.'

Sleep was impossible, and Leah was scared that excitement would so exhaust her she'd be too tired to give evidence against her husband and Brian. She kept looking at her watch on the side table. The digits didn't seem to move. She heard the dawn chorus and saw the sun come up over the buildings beyond the grassy area outside her window.

'Goodness, you're up early, Leah,' the night nurse said, as he did the medications before he handed over.

'I've got a big day, Robbie,' Leah said, wanting to share her excitement.

'Something important happening, pet?' Robbie asked, stopping the drugs trolley.

Caution swept over Leah, dampening her spirits. 'No. I mean, Clair said I mustn't tell. I mustn't . . .'

'Does Dr Bloomsbury know?'

'Please don't say anything to him.'

'That's cool, pet,' Robbie said. 'Look, why don't you go and have your your shower?'

'I've had one,' Leah said.

'Then get yourself some breakfast.'

Leah could feel his eyes on her as she went along the corridor towards the dining hall. She willed herself not to look back. If I do, she told herself, he'll tell Dr Bloomsbury.

Clair appeared on the ward in a skirt with a matching jacket instead of her usual jumper and jeans. 'Are you ready, Leah?'

'Yes. But Robbie tried to find out where I was going. I didn't tell him.'

'Good. The little sneak would report you to Dr Bloomsbury.'

They started out of the door, but Clair pulled her back. 'I'd better sign you out or they might send a search party.'

Leah waited, on edge, as Clair went back, opened the daybook on the front desk and wrote in it. 'There. Come on. Quickly.'

They hurried out through the front door into the bright sunlight. It seemed like freedom to Leah. After her appearance in court she would be free. As they started towards the main gates a Land Rover drew up and the familiar figure in the corduroy suit got out.

Leah felt the tug of panic, but Clair's grip on her arm steadied her. 'Keep walking, Leah,' she said, steering her past Dr Bloomsbury, who was locking his car.

'Clair, where are you going?' he asked.

'We're only going for a walk!' Leah blurted out.

'You're both looking a bit smart for that.'

Clair stopped and looked at him. Leah couldn't. 'We're going to court. The judge needs Leah to give evidence.'

'Oh, does he? Well, even if he sent a court order, medical orders override it. Take her back.'

'No,' Leah said. 'I've got to give evidence.' Breaking free, she ran hard, but didn't get further than the front gate. She was brought back, kicking and screaming. They sedated her again, pushing her back into that dark tunnel.

Sitting in court all day, listening to the things people were saying about Brian, the eyes of jurors constantly flicking in her direction to see how she was responding, was an ordeal for Cath. She acquitted herself well, often crying. What Joey didn't know was whether the tears were genuine or a performance for the jury. She wasn't given to crying.

'I hope the jury was impressed,' she said, as they left the building. 'I'm sure no one in the Tory Party would be.'

'You'd be surprised,' Lord Goodman told her, his deep brown eyes twinkling. 'A caring mother? That's the impression the jury have retired with.'

'How long might they take?' Joey asked. For the first time since the trial had begun, eight weeks ago, he felt weary. He wanted it over so he could sleep.

'I don't think it will be quick,' Goodman said. 'Go home.'

'My Colombian clients are in town. Can you drop Catherine, Arnold?'

In Joey's office Luis Picado sat stiffly, the smile on his tanned face at odds with his words and posture. 'You're causing us problems, Joseph. Big problems.'

'What can I do?'

'You're not concentrating. If you screw up, my friend . . .' he didn't finish the sentence. 'This court case has been a strain, no?'

'Yes. I fear the worst.'

'Maybe we could do something about the jury,' Picado said, 'or this judge.'

'Bit late for that,' Joey said. 'But business is good. Your investment has increased substantially.'

Picado nodded. 'We make more money than we can easily dispose of.'

'Your money is washed quite clean. We are diversifying out of gilts into a more risk-prone area.'

'What we need to know is that you can handle this if your son goes to prison,' Picado said. Joey knew that if he couldn't, he shouldn't go on acting as their banker. Brian's trial was a distraction, but so far it hadn't hurt his business and soon it would be over.

'There's a more important question, Joseph,' Tyrwhitt said, when Joey discussed moving the Colombians' money out of government securities and into a higher-risk portfolio. 'Are you competent to operate in these money markets? You need to be alert to even the slightest shimmer. A sneeze could cost them their fortune.'

Joey resented this line. He had only consulted him out of courtesy. 'I can cope,' he said arrogantly. 'It's time our bank moved forward and embraced the modern world of finance. We're being too nannyish in our approach. There's a lot of money to be made here.'

'Or lost.'

Joey nodded coldly and left the MD's office. Tyrwhitt's nose was out of joint because an immigrant greengrocer from Clerkenwell was taking Cotterill and Jenkins into the late twentieth century. He was determined to do it.

'Won't he send the police after me?' Leah said, glancing round the top deck of the bus. She was trying to identify Dr Bloomsbury's Land Rover, certain he was following them.

'I think your recovery depends on you giving evidence,' Clair said. 'I'm prepared to take the risk.'

Leah took her hand and squeezed it, still not quite believing that Clair had got her out with no one noticing.

When they stepped into the reception area at the Old Bailey, Clair went up to the desk. 'Where's Jack Braden's trial taking place?'

The policeman didn't need to check the list. 'Court number five,' he said. 'But I think it's all over.'

'We have to hurry, Leah,' she said.

The policeman stopped them. 'Do you have business with the court?'

'She's a witness. She was delayed.'

'I'll ring the clerk.' He reached for the phone.

'It's all over bar the shouting.' The clerk was a ponderous man who repeated things slowly, as if they didn't understand.

'But I have to give evidence,' Leah said urgently.

'It's all over bar the shouting. The jury's retired.'

'Isn't there someone she can talk to?' Clair pleaded. 'She was stopped from giving her evidence.'

'Oh! The judge might want to know about that.'

To Leah, the judge seemed a cold, unfeeling man, but he was cultured and not unkind. He sat opposite them in a wooden chair in his room, which was decorated with police memorabilia, and listened carefully to what she said about Jack.

'Is there evidence that you were kept from coming here?'

'Dr Bloomsbury stopped me. He said I was too ill.' Leah saw at once he wasn't convinced. 'I saw him talking to the policeman who I saw with my husband.'

'If you're suggesting the police behaved improperly I'd need something exceeding substantial to bring the jury back. I'm sorry. I can see how important it is to you, Miss Cohen. But I believe your evidence would have made no difference to the verdict. You'll see.' He nodded, bringing the meeting to a close. All hope drained out of Leah.

The court was tense with anticipation as the jury came back in at ten forty. The foreman stood erect and delivered guilty verdicts on all counts against Jack. He waited without moving, as if he had expected nothing else.

Now Brian feared the worst. His mind went blank as the clerk turned to him. What would a long prison sentence mean for him? He would kill himself. Why didn't all prisoners feel that way? Perhaps they did.

'Not guilty.' The words were a foreign language he didn't understand. Not guilty? Was that what he'd heard? Or had he imagined it? His mind jumped at every gasp that came from spectators. Then it was all over. Not guilty on each charge. Was that possible? Or was he still asleep in Brixton, dreaming? Jack was gripping the dock rail, shaking, saying, 'Leah!' Maybe he was dreaming, Brian thought. If anything suggested as much, it was Leah Cohen being there.

'This is an extraordinary result,' Melford Stevenson was saying. 'I can't believe we've listened to the same evidence.'

No! Brian's thoughts screamed. You should be on my side after all I did for you! He forced himself to listen to what the judge was saying.

'The police must thoroughly examine their methods.' He glanced away from the jury to the dock. 'Jack Braden, you have been found guilty of the heinous murder of your one-time best friend, a boy you grew up with. You murdered him over money. Although throughout his entire adult life he was a criminal, possibly he could have been redeemed. I will retire to consider your sentence, but you can expect nothing but a very long time in prison.'

'No!' Jack shouted, 'You can't do that! You owe me, you slag! You owe me for the tarts we got you – for pulling you out of trouble! You owe me!'

Brian's heart thumped. Suppose this started an investigation into their getting girls for this judge and the verdict was set aside? He wasn't clear yet.

'Take him down,' the judge said, ignoring Jack's protest.

George Carman was on his feet. 'My lord, might Mr Oldman be released?'

Brian's heart stopped altogether as the judge fixed him with a stare. 'I suppose that must happen, Mr Carman. Mr Oldman, I will watch you very closely indeed when next you appear before me.'

Brian had no opportunity to speak to Jack before the screws ushered him out of the dock and through the court. Then he was in the lobby and free, people pressing in on him, slapping him on the back. Reporters were there, asking how he felt about the result. The crowd was almost suffocating. This must be what it was like for a pop singer. He barely saw the slim figure that flew across the lobby, bursting through the throng, with the sheer force of surprise and smashed him around the face, shouting, 'You bastard! You should be in prison, too, for what you did to me!' Before she could say more, hands were dragging Leah away as she continued to struggle and protest.

He wanted to yell after them to leave her be. Instead he watched her disappear, still in a daze, realizing now, too late, that he would liked to have spoken to Leah, but he wasn't sure why. Then she was gone, and other people were demanding his attention. A tearful Cath was kissing and hugging him. Joey was clapping him on the back. None of what they were saying registered. Journalists were repeating their questions.

A set of familiar angry faces appeared in front of him, DI Wednesday at their head. 'You might have got a terrific result,' he was saying, 'but you're going sooner or later. We'll have you, uncle.' He gave him a slight wink before he was pulled away by his colleagues.

'Bad loser,' Joey commented, trying to steer him away.

Brian looked sharply at his dad, attempting to grasp what was going on. He turned back and found himself facing his cousin John. 'The judge was right. It was an astounding result,' Redvers said. 'But right now we're interested in identifying the policemen who helped you.'

'Good luck, John,' Brian said, his old confidence returning. Then his dad was pushing him towards the exit, ignoring the clamour.

THIRTY-FOUR

John Redvers needed to summon a lot of courage before he found enough nerve to go and see Sonia Hope, who had reverted to her maiden name after her divorce from Wednesday. He wrestled with the notion for days before deciding he should telephone her. When she agreed to meet him, he asked himself if this was an excuse to follow up on his feelings for her rather than strictly business. He still wished things had happened differently between them. He'd never leave his son Warren, or his wife for that matter, but there was little between him and Carol, either emotionaly, physically or spiritually.

'Why did you come to me, John?' Sonia said, standing opposite him with her arms folded, in the office she shared with several other police officers, none of whom were there. 'What is it you want?'

Redvers hesitated. The folder he'd brought with him was sticking to his sweating palm. He felt mean and somehow dishonest even to be thinking about his plan. 'I don't really know, Sonia,' he said feebly.

'You seem like you want some sort of absolution.'

'Oh, do I?' This wasn't the Sonia he used to know. This Sonia was hard and abrasive, perhaps because now she had to survive in a mostly male world.

She shrugged with the air of someone who had better things to do.

'I wasn't aware that I was behaving in any particular way,' Redvers said. 'I don't throw my weight around. Is that what you mean?'

'No. You're acting as if you've been caught doing something you shouldn't. Is that why you're in A10?'

'I don't feel guilty about investigating corrupt policemen.'

'It can be lonely in the job,' Sonia admitted. 'You don't have many friends, apart from colleagues. Do you have any friends, John?'

'I get the distinct impression you feel uncomfortable with me being here,' Redvers said. 'You've every right to be, I suppose. I behaved badly, just leaving as I did. I'm sorry.'

He watched Sonia move out from behind her desk and go across the room to switch off the photocopier. As she did so, she caught a pile of papers, which fell to the floor. Redvers went to help as she stooped to pick them up.

'It's all right,' she said, pulling them away from him.

He eased back but didn't get up, enjoying their closeness, even though she wasn't friendly. Suddenly she stopped what she was doing and looked at him. He flushed.

'Why didn't you come back to see me when I was having such a bad time?' she asked. 'You can't know how much that hurt. I thought you were someone I could rely on.'

'I'm sorry, I shouldn't have come here.'

'Probably not.'

He wanted to say he had been scared to go back, scared of getting involved but he couldn't bring himself to. Instead, he got up with her. Sonia threw the papers on to another pile.

'Is this all the space your team has?' he found himself saying.

'I'm quite clear about what I do,' she said. 'I've got nothing to hide. I do understand the relentless job most policemen have to do. I understand why sometimes they don't follow the rules.'

'You think I don't?' he said. This really wasn't the conversation he wanted to be having with her.

'I doubt it, John. You have to be in that space with nowhere to turn.'

Suddenly her eyes widened and she pulled back. Perhaps she'd read something on his face. He knew he had to say something. Slowly he nodded. 'When I was at my first station, I was still studying. I was aide to CID when we nabbed a dealer. We'd watched him selling. The flat was empty when we searched him.'

'You put some on him?' Sonia said.

'The detective did. The dealer got three years.'

'It sounds like he deserved it.'

'He was stabbed to death in prison.'

'And you've been trying to unpick your guilt ever since by arresting those who stray,' she mocked.

'I'm sorry I troubled you.' He turned to leave.

'You didn't,' Sonia told him. 'Neither did you tell me why you came here. Are you so used to deception you feel you can't be straight about anything?'

That stung him, making him less sure of his next move. 'I thought as you weren't part of general policing in this financial-irregularities outfit you might have an objective view on starting an investigation into Brian Oldman. He shouldn't be free.'

'The jury didn't take that view.'

'They didn't have the whole picture.'

'And you do, John? Is that what you think?'

'Wrongdoing on the part of policemen allowed Oldman to walk. There can be no other explanation.'

'Perhaps you should stop for a moment and try to get some objectivity,' Sonia said. 'The job makes us all a bit obsessive. One major criminal walked. The other went to prison. Result.'

'Tony helped him walk,' Redvers said suddenly.

'Is that why you came here?' She was clearly astonished. 'You want to know if my ex is capable of being as corrupt as that?'

There was hurt in her voice and he knew she was lost to him. He pressed on regardless. 'I know he is.'

'Perhaps. But you'll have to get up very early to catch him.'

'He'll make a mistake. He may have already.'

'We all make mistakes,' she said. 'We have to try to live with them. Please leave.' She turned away and picked up some papers off her desk.

'Sonia, I just wanted to say . . .' he began. 'I'll leave you with that.' He slipped a buff folder on to her messy desk. It was the evidence he'd assembled on DI Wednesday and Joseph Oldman. He hoped it wouldn't turn up on Wednesday's desk.

Three days later, summoned to Assistant Commissioner Virgo's office on the fifth floor of the tower, Redvers wondered if Sonia was angry about what she'd read in the papers he'd left her and had informed on his being a party to planting the drugs dealer. But it soon became clear, with Chief Superintendent Slipper present, that the head of the Flying Squad was put out at his suggestion that detectives had helped Brian Oldman walk.

'The Flying and Regional Crime Squads put in a lot of work on Brian Oldman,' Commander Virgo was saying. 'Why the fuck would they let him walk?'

'I believe a lot of money went down.'

'If that's the case, what makes you think you might be able to put him back in the frame?'

'Especially as you've not been doing regular police collar,' Slipper added.

'It's still investigative work, sir.'

'How do we know it wasn't you who helped him?' Slipper asked.

'I wouldn't do that,' Redvers said vehemently, aggrieved that they were taking this line.

'Never done anything wrong, Superintendent?' Slipper asked bluntly.

Convinced now that Sonia must have said something, Redvers remained silent, but colour crept up his neck.

'You must know how difficult it will be now to convict Brian Oldman,' Virgo said. 'You couldn't not.'

'I'd still like to try, sir.'

'That's something we'll have to take a view about,' Virgo said. 'The job's not about you, son, or what you want.'

'I'm an honest, efficient policeman, sir.'

'You've been responsible for getting rid of a few corrupt officers,' Virgo allowed. 'We're all grateful.'

'I've got two commendations from the commissioner,' Redvers said, standing his ground.

'You wouldn't be the first from your lot to join the opposition.'

'I resent that,' Redvers said, getting up out of his chair. The two men did the same, as if afraid they had a fight on their hands.

'Calm down. It was an observation. No one's condemning you. Look, we'll discuss this in private and let you know. Any further thoughts, Jack?' Virgo turned to Detective Chief Superintendent Slipper, who shook his head.

Stepping out of the office, Redvers swayed as if he was about to fall over. He felt like giving up, getting out of the force altogether, but if he did that he knew he'd be finished, condemned as the man who had perverted the course of justice and set Brian Oldman free. How ironic would that be? He had started this investigation and he was determined to press on. He'd get Oldman, whatever his bosses said.

Tony Wednesday watched Chief Superintendent Slipper work the room after the briefing he'd given on some targets who were robbing security trucks and money in transit. He always spoke personally to each of his detectives, especially before a raid.

When he got to Tony he said quietly, 'Our commissioner's planning a new strategy that won't exactly endear him to detectives or put many villains away. He's making uniformed branches and CID interchangeable each time anyone goes up in rank.'

'You gotta be kidding, guv?' Tony was about to take his board to become a DCI.

'Detective sergeants have to go into uniform to become an inspector and vice versa. The idea is that it stops us getting too cosy and corrupt,' Slipper said. 'Perhaps he has a point.'

'It'll destroy all the relationships we build up.'

'We're supposed to pass on those contacts. If you want to stay in CID, Tony, pull out of your board.' He turned away.

The briefing was over and Tony went to collect and sign for his gun and bullets from the armourer.

Slipper caught his eye and nodded him out of the door. In the long, neon-lit corridor, he said, 'I heard from Assistant Commissioner Virgo that they're putting Redvers back in uniform.'

'Is he getting promotion, guv?' Tony asked, keeping the satisfaction out of his voice.

'There was no evidence that he helped Oldman, as such.'

'I thought Redvers was close to the commissioner.'

'Obviously not close enough.'

Still Tony resisted smiling. Instead he let anger show. 'So Brian Oldman gets another free ride – the bent bastard!'

'Not quite,' Slipper told him. 'The squad's been asked to keep a watching brief. If he so much as spits on the pavement we'll have him. I'll leave you to organize that, Tony.'

'Thank you, guv,' Tony said, and went to join his men.

Queen's 'Bohemian Rhapsody', which dominated the charts, was on the hotel Tannoy system as Brian walked across the terrace, aware that one of the two older women lounging by the pool was watching him. He'd taken a nice tan and had worked out a lot getting fit during the four weeks he'd been there.

'Excuse me, Signorina,' he said, in a mockingly heavy Italian accent, 'the gentleman on ze beach, him say you likea some company.'

'Oh, what gentleman's that, then?' Catherine asked, from behind her large Biba sunglasses, now a bit outdated. She was lying on a lounger by the pool at the Grand Hotel.

'I zink ees name Brian,' Brian said. 'I zink 'e your brother, Signorina, no?' She loved to play these games.

'No,' Catherine said. 'I don't think I know anyone of that name. What's your name?'

'It Bruno, Signorina. From Napoli.'

'What are you doing in Rimini, Bruno? Are you a waiter, by any chance?'

'I'm going mad with boredom,' Brian said, in his normal voice.

He was bored just sitting around the pool, reading, or sitting on the beach, reading, pretending for his mother's benefit to be interested in the bikini-clad girls. There were things going on in London that he felt he should be part of.

'Put some oil on my back. I don't want to burn,' Catherine said.

Brian did as she asked, knowing how she loved being on show with him, letting people believe they were lovers. She was fifty-five now and putting on a little weight, although she denied it. She wouldn't allow herself to be seen in a bikini, even though Brian encouraged her, but she dyed her greying hair, keeping it inky black. Finishing with the oil, he said, 'We'd better get a bit of lunch – miss the rush.'

There was never any rush at the Grand, with three restaurants, mostly serving fish, which Brian didn't like.

'Are we going on the coach trip afterwards?' Catherine asked.

'Would you mind if I didn't?' Brian said, having made an alternative arrangement with a young waiter.

'Oh, baby, aren't you feeling well?'

'I thought I'd stay in and take a look at those books Dad gave me. I need to understand a bit about the principles of business if I'm going to work for him.'

'You're not going to work for him, Brian,' Catherine said firmly. 'You're going to work *with* him.'

'What's the diff?' Brian said.

'There's all the difference in the world. You'll be his partner. Your father's really excited about it. He's waited such a long time. Try to be a bit enthusiastic, Brian.'

'I am, Catherine,' Brian told her. 'I'm forgoing the excitement of the coach trip to study business plans.'

'It'll be worth it. You'll have fun. And you'll ease the strain on your father. His health's not what it ought to be. All that business with you and Jack didn't help.'

There she was again, whacking him down, not letting him forget. 'Wear flat shoes for the trip this afternoon,' Brian said tightly.

Catherine sat up and kissed him on the mouth. 'I love you so much. I'd've died if anything had happened to you.'

'Well, thankfully it didn't.' Mentally Brian prised off the tentacles. 'Come on, let's get lunch. Then I can read those books and pay Dad back.'

Brian hadn't been in his junior suite five minutes when there was a rap at the door. His pulse quickened in anticipation of seeing Bruno, the twenty-something waiter, with a long, angular body he clearly spent time working on. He shifted on the large bed and called, 'Come!' and giggled. Nothing happened.

He leapt off the bed to wrench open the door. 'I said come— Oh, where's Bruno?' A young, curly-haired waiter with a white tunic buttoned to his throat gazed at him with large soulful eyes. He was so deeply tanned he might have been an Arab. 'You ordered mineral water, Signore.'

'I thought Bruno was bringing it.'

'Bruno he say you like me, Signore.'

'I like Bruno,' Brian told him.

'Yes, Signore. You like Franco more.'

'What's your story, Franco? You trying to pay your way through college? Or have you got a widowed mother and young sisters?'

'No, Signore,' Franco said. 'I like what we do. You like?'

'What exactly do you have in mind?'

Franco walked in and closed the door. He put the tray down, reached out and took hold of him.

'Oh, yes, that feels nice, Franco.' He sighed: 'I like it.'

The young man came closer and kissed him, then more passionately and Brian became lost to the experience. 'You'll do,' Brian said.

Brian could have spent the rest of his holiday with Franco, never leaving the room, never getting off the king-sized bed.

'You like Franco better than Bruno?' Franco said.

Alarm bells rang – was this a set-up? – but just then Brian didn't care. He certainly didn't notice the door open or his mother breeze in. 'Are you working hard, my—'

'Knock!' Brian screamed. 'Bloody well knock!' She was retreating. 'I do have a life!' he yelled. The door slammed behind her.

'You idiot!' Brian turned his fury on the boy. 'You didn't lock the door!'

'You angry with Franco, Signore?'

'Get out of here, you little poof! Get lost! No – wait. Here.' He grabbed some money and thrust it at the boy. 'Put yourself through college or something.'

'Will the signora tell the *carabinieri*?'

'I think she's had enough of the police to last her a lifetime.' Brian pushed him out of the door.

The clank of cutlery on china as Brian ate dinner with his mother was nerve-racking. Each was determined not to speak first. Brian knew he would break the silence – she could always wear him down. When he was a kid she sometimes wouldn't speak to him all day long if she was angry with him. He was no less affected by that now.

'Aren't you going to talk to me, Cathy?' he said, provocatively using the name that irritated her.

'Please don't call me that.'

He goaded her further, reminding her of the past she chose to pretend didn't exist. 'Billy Hill used to call you that. And Nan.'

'I'm sure it's just a phase you're going through,' she said. 'You'll grow out of it. Most boys do.'

'Mum, I'm nearly thirty-five,' Brian pointed out. 'I've been in this phase all my life, as you well know.'

She wouldn't look at him but cut her food precisely, placing it in her mouth one morsel at a time. Finally she met his eyes. 'What about that girl you were besotted with?'

'Leah Cohen? Well, you helped me bring off a miraculous escape.'

'I don't know what you're saying, Brian. I really don't. Look, you'll grow out of it,' she said. 'I know you will.'

'Your former leader hasn't,' Brian said. 'Ted Heath's hardly a boy.'

'What nonsense, Brian. I've met him. He's such a gentleman.'

'I mean, half the party's that way. The half that went to public school, at least.'

'The sooner we get you back to England and hard at work with your father, the sooner you'll forget this boy nonsense. We mustn't say a word about it to him – it would be too upsetting. It'll be our little secret.'

'Mum . . .' Brian stopped. The burden of secrets he shared with her was too much. His thoughts strayed to Leah Cohen, and how Catherine would react if he went after her again.

'I'll ask the hotel to change our tickets and get us on a plane first thing tomorrow,' she was saying. 'The next day you'll start work with your father. I've had enough of this foreign muck anyway.'

Her cutlery hit the plate with a clunk and she pushed her chair back.

THIRTY-FIVE

Starting work, even though it was with his dad, was like starting school, and Brian approached it with the same unease. Meeting new people, who would be working under him but understood much more than him meant he wouldn't be in control. He hated that.

When he had been in the firm with Jack, the whole world had known who he was. In the offices in the converted house in South Kensington, he was little more than a glorified office-boy. He didn't even know enough about pop music and fashion to have a decent conversation with the people who worked there. They looked grey mostly, and spotty, and he didn't fancy any of them. One of the young women, June Sorrell, showed out to him, so Joey made her Brian's secretary. A fairly quiet thirty-year-old, she wasn't half bad-looking, and she was keen to help. Brian was grateful for that.

'Plunge in at the deep end, son,' Joey said, as he settled in the office. He laughed, clearly pleased that Brian had arrived. 'Unless you prefer to start as a tea-boy.'

'That would be handy,' Brian said. 'What, for five quid a week?'

'The seven properties we're developing are over-extending us a bit, especially that block there.' He nodded across the street at a vast row of tall, stucco-fronted houses that ran all the way to Cromwell Road. 'I don't want it pulling us down if it goes wrong. We might have to do something about it.'

'Is it going to go wrong?' Brian asked, sensing excitement.

'The more profit you make, the more risks you have to take, son,' Joey told him. He smiled, as if he was enjoying instructing him. 'We're going to put it all through some limited companies, which you will control.'

'Like long firms?' Brian wanted to know.

'Hardly. You collapse those and disappear with what you've stolen. We're not stealing anything, just protecting ourselves. I'll get Arnold Goodman to explain everything to you when you sign the company papers. I want you to understand what you're getting into, Brian.'

'It's all legal, Dad? Right? Above board?'

'Yes, of course. But also you have to understand that all business is either corrupt or exploitative. If people want something, you've got to exploit someone to get it for them, or cheat them out of it.'

Suddenly Brian felt uneasy. 'The thought of doing villainy and getting caught, Dad ... I promised myself I was never going back to prison.'

'It won't happen, son,' Joey assured him. 'I'm really pleased you're with me. We'll make a fortune and no one will be able to touch us.'

Perhaps he was being dense, but the way Joey's solicitor explained the principle behind these front companies, and what was involved for him, didn't leave Brian any the wiser. Instead of saying he didn't understand, he nodded and pretended he did, intending to ask June Sorrell later.

'You won't own the assets of these shell companies, Brian,' Lord Goodman said. 'All the equity in them will belong to your father's holding company. It will appear that they've made an investment in your developments. You have day-to-day responsibility for all the properties in your portfolio. But, like all stock-market-quoted companies, you'll be answerable to the shareholders.'

'That's Joey – I mean Dad,' Brian said, glancing at his father. 'What's going to happen?'

'Nothing – not with you in charge, son,' Joey explained. 'You'll make the decisions concerning the properties. Seeing insurance is kept up, deciding whether the building is to be maintained or allowed to fall down.'

'Why would we want that if we're not collecting the insurance like in the old days? We're making everything strictly legal now. Right?'

'Of course. But if the buildings are falling into a serious state of disrepair the council will have less concern about us pulling them down and putting up office blocks.'

'I've obviously got a lot to learn,' Brian said.

'I'm sure you'll soon get the hang of things under your father's tutelage,' Lord Goodman told him.

'One thing you can't do, son,' Joey said, 'is sell any of the properties without the agreement of the shareholders. Is that clear?'

'As mud,' Brian said. 'Who are the shareholders?'

'My company and the bank, principally,' Joey said. 'The properties are held against the loans we've taken out. Their values will go up ten- or twenty-fold when we get planning on the site.'

'Your father's made sure everything is legitimate now, Brian.'

'Excellent. I'd've topped myself if I was doing thirty like Jack. I mean it.'

'Arnold believes the police are keeping you on an open file. They'll be alert to everything we do.'

'They can't nick me again?' Brian said, his mouth suddenly dry.

'Not unless you break the law,' the lawyer assured him. 'I have some mandates for you to sign.' He took him to the adjacent office where a vast array of company and bank documents were laid out. Unused to legal papers, Brian signed without understanding any of it. He'd get June to tell him what they were.

'That was easy enough for my twenty-five grand a year!' Brian joked, as they stepped into the street, still feeling slightly confused.

'There's a bit more to it than that,' Joey explained. 'There's a planning officer from Kensington I'd like you to meet. You should make an appointment to see him on the site we're trying to get change-of-use on.'

'What's the story?' Brian was hoping he wouldn't have to threaten him.

'The Council want some of that block we're planning to develop on Cromwell Road to stay as dwellings.'

'What's wrong with that?'

'There was a lot involved in getting those properties emptied, Brian. It'll reduce the profit if we're forced to make some into houses. There'd be upgrading costs, and we've still got the cost of those with sitting tenants. We need a hundred-per-cent change-of-use to offices.'

'What will you do about the sitting tenants?'

'Nothing,' Joey said sharply. 'That's for you to deal with. Get them out – with the lowest possible cost to us.'

The planning officer, Simon Hatfield, seemed keen to get out on the site, where he complained about the pressure they worked under in cramped offices. He was a shy, under-confident, wet-behind-the-ears kid just out of university. Brian knew straight away where this was going as they stumbled through two houses in the worst state of dilapidation.

'What do you intend for the site, Mr Oldman?'

'Who's he?' Brian joked, looking around, puzzled. 'Oh, me. I thought for a moment you were talking to my dad.'

'Your company owns the site, doesn't it?'

'Why don't you call me Brian so I don't think like my dad?'

'One of my colleagues said he's a tough customer.'

'Yes, he had a hard time in Austria under the Nazis,' Brian said, not knowing what had happened to Joey back then.

'Did something bad happen?' Simon asked, with genuine interest.

'He won't talk about it,' Brian said.

'They wiped out all the Jews and the homosexuals,' Simon informed him earnestly. 'Hitler was probably a repressed homosexual.'

'Well, he probably never knew what he was missing,' Brian said. He waited, watching Simon closely. He knew what he'd meant. 'Most of Dad's family got wiped out,' he added.

'Oh, poor man. That must have been so terrible.'

'Yeah,' Brian said, knowing he had him now. 'Shall we go on, then?'

The dilapidated houses smelt musty with decay and gas seepage. 'Mind yourself,' Brian warned. 'There's floorboards missing.'

They didn't venture far through the houses before Simon said, 'Perhaps I've seen enough.'

'They're all pretty much the same.'

Brian turned back, meeting the young man's eye. 'I've got a better idea.' Without warning, he reached out and grabbed Simon's cock, which was pushing against his suit trousers. 'Oh, what's this?'

Simon laughed nervously. 'I'm sorry.'

'Do you know what you want to do with it? I do.'

'I'm sorry,' Simon said again. 'Was I that obvious?'

'Not really,' Brian told him kindly. 'You sort of get a feeling about people, don't you?'

'You seem to have scored a hit with Simon Hatfield,' Joey said, at one of their weekly meetings to discuss the progress of their developments. 'He rings the architect all the time with helpful suggestions.'

'I keep pumping him for information,' Brian said. 'He really likes our plans for across the road.'

'Your plans, Brian,' Joey reminded him. 'Unfortunately, Hatfield has the least experience so the least influence.'

'The really difficult one is called Zac Swindles. Simon reckons he's got the most influence because of his experience. All the councillors listen to him.'

This Joey knew, but he didn't tell Brian – he didn't want to discourage him – hoping he'd soon be bringing him things he didn't know. He had done well with Simon Hatfield – he didn't want to know how.

'Your mother and I are going to Monte Carlo for a few days. Do a bit of shopping in Nice, get some sun.'

'It'll do you both good,' Brian said. 'Mind you, it's a bit extravagant, the way you always go on about expenditure.'

'No, it's an investment for the future. We won't show it on the books, of course. The deputy chairman of the planning committee and his wife are coming with us. Claude Dobbs will return all sorts of dividends.' Joey smiled. 'I won't be asking him for anything for myself.'

With sterling taking a hammering under Wilson's Labour government, staying in the Hôtel de Paris on the square in Monte Carlo was an extravagance, but Joey wanted to turn Claude Dobbs's head with what might be available to him.

'This is the life, Joseph,' Dobbs said, joining him at the casino bar. 'Do you know who I just saw at the *chemin-de-fer* table? The new James Bond – the actor who plays him, Roger Moore. He looked just like he does in the films. He was throwing money down so fast, I couldn't keep up.'

'Did you win anything?' Joey asked, sipping a glass of orange pressé. He'd been in love with the idea of this place ever since Brian had first told him about it. The sad thing was that evening dress was no longer the rule.

'I won a few bob,' Dobbs said, 'but not at *chemin*. Too fast for me. Norma and Catherine are doing well on the roulette table. Yes, this is the life, Joseph.'

'You deserve to have a little more of it, Claude,' Joseph said. 'You work hard enough. I don't suppose the ratepayers appreciate how hard.'

'I don't suppose they even know what I do.'

'There you are. Take a little for yourself, otherwise you'll get to retirement and be full of regrets.'

'You're a good man, Joseph, generous to a fault. I'm glad I've got you as a friend. Not many appreciate us like you do. I know we said we shouldn't talk business, but I see nothing but benefit from this scheme you're promoting.'

'I do have a bit of a holding in the property company developing it, Claude,' Joey said.

'You live in the borough. You happen to think that an office block on Cromwell Road will be good for Kensington and Chelsea.'

'I'd certainly take space there if they get it through.'

'I can't see the planning committee saying no. We wouldn't even have to go to the full council – not if we're unanimous.'

'Do you think you will be?' Joey asked.

'The report that young planning officer made on those houses said they're pretty uneconomic,' Claude Dobbs told him. 'I'll do the rounds of the planning officers when I get back. Get them lined up.'

'Shall we see how the ladies are doing? Perhaps well enough to buy us dinner. My son told me about a marvellous restaurant that Tom Driberg, the MP, showed him down here.'

Despite Claude Dobbs's best efforts there was a hiccup in Planning. The committee wasn't unanimous so it looked set to go to the full council, much to Joey's irritation. Catherine was even more annoyed. 'Are you telling me all that expense of the trip to Monte was wasted?'

'Nothing of that sort is ever wasted,' Joey said. Delay wasn't defeat, even though it was costing them a lot of money.

'It's not right,' Catherine complained. 'How can just one planner hold up a scheme that will bring jobs and benefit to the borough?'

'We heard how influential Zac Swindles is. Unfortunately councillors listen to him. That's what they pay him for, after all.'

'You've got all this money tied up in Brian's companies. You have to get planning permission. Did you try bribing Swindles?'

'So far he's resisted every approach. Maybe he's holding out for something really big.' He believed everyone was biddable: it was only a question of finding the right price or what moved Zac Swindles.

'What about Brian approaching him?' Catherine suggested.

That shocked Joey. 'We'd have to be careful about strong-arm tactics. Swindles is likely to go to the police.' He didn't want to think about the alternative approach Brian might offer.

'Well, what about one of your police contacts? Can't one of them do something to stop this little bugger holding things up?'

Finding a pressure point through the police was an option he would consider only as a last resort as it was likely to cost him even more money. He'd explored Catherine's political contacts, but had found them of little use. They were too preoccupied and in disarray, tearing themselves apart over the leadership crisis. Catherine supported Margaret Thatcher, but those most likely to help in this situation, Joey knew, were in the embattled Heath camp

With economic pressure increasing by the day, mostly from his own bank, he was forced to approach the police. Tony Wednesday seemed pleased to hear from him and was happy to meet, but his taste in venue was more expensive. Instead of the tea bar on Chelsea Bridge he suggested the Mirabelle in Mayfair.

Joey doubted the detective had used the basement restaurant for such meetings before as the ceiling was low and the tables too close together for privacy. At twelve-fifteen, though, there were more waiters than customers.

'Why is this Swindles geezer holding out?' Tony Wednesday asked, from across the table nearest the door, towards which his eyes constantly darted. 'Can you believe he's not at it with a name like that?'

'If he was, the planning permission would sail through.'

'Perhaps you're not offering enough, Joey. You trying to get him too cheaply? How much is he standing you out of pocket?'

'If we don't get permission and have to restore the houses with sitting tenants . . .' Joey shook his head. It was almost unthinkable. 'I'll either be broke or back running a greengrocery shop. Sometimes I wish I was, son. Life was so much simpler in those days.'

'I know how much,' DI Wednesday said. 'The kind of dough you must be making.'

Joey waited. He knew what was coming next.

'What do I get for my trouble?'

'If you could pull Mr Swindles on board, we'd make it very worth your while, Mr Wednesday.'

'I'd still like to hear a figure, Joey.'

Joey watched the policeman eat his pasta. He was reluctant to name a sum in case it failed to satisfy the man.

'What if he can't be rendered amenable? Would it do as well if he was put out in the cold? Nicked?' DI Wednesday said. 'So, what figure do you have in mind?'

Swallowing hard, Joey said, 'Five thousand pounds.'

'I don't think you can be serious about this planner.' The detective pushed away his plate. 'What's five grand to you?'

'In cash, it's a great deal of money.'

'You're taking the piss, uncle. You must have spent that sort of dough taking the council bloke and his wife to Monaco.'

Despair rolled over Joey like a damp winter fog. He didn't bother to ask Wednesday how he knew about that trip, but obviously he was thorough and worth every penny of what he would ask.

'How much do you want, Mr Wednesday?'

''S easy. Something what reflects its real worth to you.'

Tony could see that the fifty thousand pounds to which the banker had agreed was painful, but he didn't care. He would give value. He always did. Under the Met's new rule, taking promotion meant going back into uniform, so he would never be promoted, and he didn't intend to exist on a DI's poxy pension when he retired. In addition to the money, he told Joey he wanted nominee shares in his property company.

'Oh, is that all?' Joey blanched. For a moment, Tony thought he was going to get up and leave and took it as a good sign when he didn't. 'You're a greedy man, Mr Wednesday.'

'You knew that when you rang me,' Tony said. 'D'you have another way to go?' His silence, Tony assumed, was tantamount to admitting he didn't. 'I need five grand expenses, in marked notes, for my plan to work.'

'Why marked notes?' Joey asked.

'That's for me to know,' Tony said. 'Just be ready with my fifty large on the result.'

His first stop was to a petty thief he'd once nicked. Tony got him to break into the self-righteous Zac Swindles's Mini Traveller, from which he stole a camera, a sheepskin jacket, a pair of gloves and a compass. Tracking the reported theft, recovering the missing items and returning them to a grateful Zac Swindles had been an easy result for the police at Kensington nick, they told Tony, when they gave him a Xeroxed copy of the signed-for list. This he passed to a forger, who owed him, and had him impersonate Zac Swindles, setting up several bent bank accounts. The money that went into them appeared to come from three people whose planning applications he was supporting.

Tony didn't think too hard about who he should use to investigate Swindles.

Sonia, his ex-wife, was a little surprised by his phone call, but not displeased when he suggested they meet.

'How are you, Son?' he asked, in her small Holborn office.

'Well, I'm not a superintendent yet,' she replied, leaning back in her chair. He noticed she was still in good shape, had kept her figure. Her breasts pushing invitingly against her jumper as she stretched. Her blonde hair showed a bit of grey and she looked tired, but he'd have given her one right there, even with her colleague at the other end of the room.

'We used to talk about that at college. Ten years to super.'

'John Redvers made it, all right,' Sonia pointed out.

'I heard he went bent for his cousin,' Tony said, not letting her get away with that.

'I doubt it. He never had enough imagination to be corrupt.'

'You gonna get there still, d'you think?'

'I'm a woman. When have we prospered in this job?'

'You're smarter than most men, Son,' he said. 'And better-looking.'

'You still know the right buttons to push, Tony.'

He smiled, remembering the good times. 'You seeing anyone?'

'Nothing serious. All the good guys stay married. You?'

He shook his head. 'I expect I'll end up a lonely old fart, talking about the good old days. D'you want a drink?'

'Maybe,' Sonia said. 'First, tell me why you're here.'

He laughed, as if he'd been caught out. He expected no less of her. 'You don't change, Sonia. Right to the point.'

'Well, I'm pretty sure you don't change either, Tony.'

'I got a tip-off about a bent planning officer in Kensington and Chelsea,' Tony said. 'He's supposed to be well at it. Putting plenty of money away.'

'Sounds more like something for Kensington nick.'

He nodded again, his eyes fixed on her. 'That wouldn't have given me a reason to see you.'

'Oh, Tony.' She sat back, as if caught off-guard. 'Perhaps you are changing. But you didn't bring me a bunch of geraniums – like the ones you swiped from someone's window-box!'

'God, don't you forget anything?' he said. Her remark seemed to suggest she was ready to drag up any and all of his past misdemeanours in their other life. 'Do you want me to give this to Kensington nick? I can.'

Sonia shrugged. 'I dare say we can take a look – after all, if we can't trust public officials, Tony, who can we trust?'

'That's right,' he replied.

She agreed to have dinner with him and they took a taxi to Le Bistingo in Old Compton Street. He was thinking it would be an easy move for them to slip from the little bistro to his flat, but didn't push it. The wine and food relaxed Sonia and she softened, telling him she'd seen John Redvers, who had come looking for her opinion of him.

'I hope you told him I was the worst low-life.'

'He already knew that, Tony!' She laughed – by way of apology, he decided. 'What he really came about was your relationship with Brian and Joey Oldman. He thinks you helped get Brian out of all those charges at the Bailey.'

'Who does he think I am? Fucking Houdini?' Tony said, suddenly uneasy. He no longer felt like swagging her back to his flat. Sonia was too smart not to join up the dots if he nicked Zac Swindles and learnt it was Joey and Brian's development he was objecting to. She'd get there sooner if he tried to take the case back from her.

'Are you okay, Tone?' she asked, touching his hand across the squashed-in table.

'Yeah. I still feel a bit peeved about that slimy little queer walking like he did.'

'We might not get him,' Sonia confided, 'but we could nick his dad. We're looking at Joey Oldman and his relationship with a crook called Savundra and Fire, Auto & Marine Insurance. They left thousands of motorists uninsured.'

'Well, give him a kicking for me.'

'It's a slow burn, that one.'

Sonia seemed surprised when he put her into a taxi and said good night.

The Fraud Squad might have been slow in moving against Emil Savundra and Joey Oldman, but they weren't in going after Zac Swindles and nicking him for corruption. The clear trail Tony had left for them made it easy. It was time for him to get his money from Joey and make ready to run at a moment's notice in case Sonia twigged the connection.

'Oh, nice office, Joey,' the detective said mockingly, looking about the sparsely furnished room. 'What did this stand you in to furnish? Three quid?'

'I don't need fancy ornament,' Joey told him. 'It just announces to clients you're wasting their money on your comfort.' He waited, but remembered DI Wednesday was good at waiting, too.

'Zac Swindles has been suspended. All his cases have been handed to other planning officers. His name is dirt with the council. He'll stay nicked and you'll find it's plain sailing on your planning applications now.'

'Excellent.' Joey said. 'As soon as we get it, you'll be paid.'

That brought an icy chill to the room, like opening a freezer door.

'You can take a flying fuck, Joey,' Wednesday said angrily, catching him by the lapels of his Savile Row jacket. 'I got rid of the obstacle. Now I get paid in full.'

'Not until planning is granted.'

The policeman thrust his face close to him, menacing him. 'That wasn't the deal.'

'But I haven't got that sort of cash.'

'Then you shouldn't have gone shopping,' Wednesday said. 'Pay me or you're up the road.'

'You can't threaten me like this!'

'Listen, you tight-arsed kyke,' Wednesday said, pulling a small cassette player from his Mac pocket, 'and listen good.' He pressed the start button. Joey's voice was uneven and crackly at their Mirabelle lunch asking for help.

'Oh, my God.'

'You still wanna jib me?' Wednesday said. 'Get my fucking money. I'll wait.' He dropped into a chair and folded his arms.

Joey almost ran to Charles Tyrwhitt's office. The MD was on the telephone but ended his call abruptly. 'I need fifty thousand transferred to a nominee account right away,' he said, with urgency just short of panic.

Tyrwhitt got up from his leather-covered desk. 'Are you all right? You look quite ill.'

'Shelling out large sums of money affects me in that way,' Joey said. 'Detective Inspector Wednesday's in my office. He's removed the major obstacle to planning consent on Cromwell Road. I had intended paying him on the final result. He has other ideas.'

'He's a man who knows what he wants. You'd better sit down in case you fall down. I'll deal with Wednesday.'

Joey felt an intense pressure on his stomach, a burning sensation just below the sternum and was glad to sit down rather than go back in to deal with the detective. He couldn't forgive him for recording their conversation and knew he could never trust him again.

Tyrwhitt returned. 'He's gone,' he said. 'He wants the money in a nominee account in Switzerland. He's learnt about the unbreakable Swiss secrecy laws. We've painted ourselves into a corner with him.'

'Can we draw down the money for him?'

'Why not? We're there, after all, Joseph,' the MD said accommodatingly.

'Fifty thousand is a lot of money,' Joey said, still smarting. 'What is it? The equivalent of four years' salary for that policeman?'

'With the bank rate at eleven per cent and borrowing at four above base, a prolonged delay would cost you more.'

'Pay him,' Joey said petulantly.

'I told him there would be a delay in the money getting to Switzerland. We'll try to extend that.' Tyrwhitt smiled, as if he'd pulled off something good. 'Clearing planning is a huge relief, Joseph. You're running so close to the penalty if you don't complete. Now you can, with confidence.'

'Provided the bank comes in with the rest of the money against the properties.'

'We can now.' He leant down to the intercom. 'Sally, bring in the Cromwell Road file.' He released the switch. 'It's still at four above base.'

'I'll get Brian to come in and sign the papers.'

'What about those last sitting tenants? Will you pay them?'

'The freeloading gits. Not a penny.'

'Five thousand pounds each is a small amount by comparison.'

'There's a dozen or more of them,' Joey pointed out. 'Those

parasites hanging on to their squalid little bug-holes are no bar to planning now. I have two and a half million tied up in this, Charles, every penny I've got. I'm damned if I'm shelling out more to have those scroungers leave.'

'The development value of the buildings will be five or six times their collective value, Joseph. Fifteen million pounds. Did you ever expect to be worth that amount?'

'Oh, yes. Close the deal.'

La Colombina d'Oro in Dean Street remained Joey's favourite restaurant, both for the food and its lack of ostentation. He celebrated there with his wife.

He smiled when he saw his favourite planning-committee member pass the window and enter the restaurant. 'Are you going to join us?' He was expecting good news on the planning application before the committee.

'Claude, are you all right?' Catherine asked, concern in her voice. 'You look quite ill.'

Now Joey could see that Dobbs was ashen.

'Can I have a word, Joseph?' He was barely able to get the words past his lips. 'Outside.'

'What is it, Claude? Tell me!' Anxiety snatched at Joey's stomach as he hurried through the tiny entrance to the pavement, Catherine following.

'Have you closed the deal?' Dobbs asked, in a deathly whisper.

Was the man losing his memory? Of course they'd closed. Brian had signed all the papers, transferred the money. The forty-six house and the lease on a church were now theirs.

'All planning applications are suspended pending a full investigation.'

Joey saw his lips move, but couldn't comprehend the words.

'The police found another bank account belonging to Zac Swindles. He's accused everyone else in the department of being involved in corruption over planning.'

'No. No!' What felt like sharp knives buried themselves in Joey's intestines. 'You told me our application would sail through the council tonight.'

'It was supposed to. Instead the chairman made this announcement.'

A stricken cry came out of Joey and Catherine grabbed him, but he collapsed, clutching his stomach.

Just then the restaurateur came out to see what was happening. 'Call an ambulance! Please!'

Removing the ulcers left Joey with a somewhat reduced stomach and internal clips holding together what remained. He didn't care about that or the discomfort. All he wanted was to get out of hospital and back to work in the hope of retrieving something of what was lost. Unless he did, everything would be gone.

'What you *will* lose is your life,' Catherine said. 'You're barely out of the operating theatre.'

'This *is* my life,' Joey said, exasperated. A wave of pain washed through him, and he screwed up his face until it had passed. 'What's Charles saying about the block?'

'He's found a buyer of sorts,' she said. 'A housing trust. They're prepared to pay a quarter of a million.'

That brought another wave of pain, which was nothing to do with his stomach. There was trickery going on, he was sure. Tyrwhitt would be making a chunk of money somehow on this deal and Joey could do little to prevent it.

When Brian came in he brought no good news. Tony Wednesday was angry that he hadn't got his money. 'I told him we didn't get planning permission. He's threatening all sorts.'

'He'll just have to wait,' Catherine said, as though it was an option. She was very shrewd, but emotion made her incredibly stupid at times, Joey thought. It made them all incredibly stupid.

'He'll cool down,' Brian said. 'He'd sooner have the money, even if he does have to wait.' He glanced away. 'A couple of other detectives came to the office, asking about the planning applications we've got in on Cromwell Road and the one on King's Road.'

'Perhaps that Tony Wednesday sent them,' Catherine said.

'I wouldn't think so. One was a woman.'

Joey looked at him, not following his logic. 'What did they want to know?'

'What dealings we've had with members of the planning committee and the council.'

'Is that all? Nothing else?'

'They took copies of our planning applications—'

'You gave them to them?' Joey said, helplessness flooding through him. 'What about that housing trust? Is it genuine?'

'I've been making enquiries. I haven't got an answer yet.'

'I'm sure Tyrwhitt's rooking me. I'll be wiped out if I have to sell at that price. I've got to get up.'

'Let me handle this, Dad. We can always reapply for permission when the dust settles.'

Joey's despair deepened. 'With interest rates as they are? I'd bleed to death faster than I would have done from the ulcer.' He lay back for a moment to get his breath. Talking was exhausting. 'We might be better off having a fire, Brian.'

'Burn them for the insurance?' Brian seemed shocked. 'Are you kidding me?'

'Be careful, Joey Olinska,' Catherine warned. 'Those detectives asking about planning applications might put two and two together.'

She rarely called him that, these days, as if she wanted nothing of their past. He could see tension in her face and touched her hand to reassure her. 'I'm sure it's just part of their enquiries into widespread corruption in the council. It'll go away. As Brian said, we can reapply.'

Two days after Joey returned home, Detective Sergeant Sonia Hope called to see him. 'We're sorry to trouble you so soon into your convalescence.' She perched nervously on the edge of an armchair in the large ground-floor sitting room, a buff folder on her knees. 'Do you know a Mr Swindles from the RBK and C planning office?'

'Through developing property, Miss Hope,' Joey said, 'I've got to know most of the planning officers, including Mr Swindles.'

'He claims you've bribed some of them,' Sonia Hope told him.

Joey laughed, which hurt his stomach.

'If only life were that simple,' Catherine said from his side on the chesterfield. 'My husband would never do such a thing.'

'Does Mr Swindles have any evidence to support his claim?' Joey asked, his attention on her folder. He wanted to know what it held, what she was adding to it.

'He's produced little to date.' She made a note.

'How long is your inquiry likely to last?' Joey asked. 'It's going to hold things up. No permissions are being approved.'

'You don't have any applications in currently.'

'Our son does,' Catherine said.

Immediately Joey wanted to call back her words and knew somehow he had to mitigate them. 'My bank invested in his developments,' he informed her.

'Which is his company?'

'Stonehouse Investments Ltd.'

'Are they connected with the disgraced Labour MP John Stonehouse?'

'He was on the board at one time but no longer.'

'Did you pay for Claude Dobbs and his wife to go to Monte Carlo earlier this year?' she asked, without looking up from her notes.

'I did not,' Joey lied evenly, knowing he had covered all those bases. 'We did see Claude and Norma there. They were staying at the same hotel.'

'Which hotel was that?'

'The Hôtel de Paris.'

'Isn't that rather expensive, sir, for a man on Mr Dobbs's salary?'

'He told me he saves up for a yearly treat. He likes to splash out for four days. It makes him feel like James Bond. In fact, I believe he encountered Roger Moore there.'

'You didn't buy his tickets for him?'

Joey shook his head. 'I've answered that.'

'Your tickets and his were purchased in cash from the same travel agent in Kensington High Street.'

'Is that surprising? We're in the same borough.'

'I'm sorry, Sergeant. This is all rather tiring for my husband,' Catherine said.

'Yes, I do apologize, Mrs Oldman.' Sonia Hope got up.

Something about her body language told Joey she wasn't done yet. He was ready for her as she turned at the door.

'Do you know a Detective Inspector Wednesday?'

For a long moment Joey stared at her, his heart racing. 'I'll remember him all my life. He tried to put my son in prison. Don't tell me he was just doing his job. I believe he went way, way beyond what a policeman should do to secure a conviction.' He allowed his anger to surface. 'What is the purpose of this line?'

'Your name's been linked with his in an allegation that you perverted the course of justice.' Her vivid blue eyes held him.

Struggling to his feet, Joey said, 'What nonsense! I've never heard such rubbish. Whoever came up with that needs his head examined.'

'Maybe,' she said, and departed.

Joey steadied himself against the sofa. He felt exhausted and angry. Tony Wednesday himself must have sent this woman as a warning. He knew he had to get back to work, regardless of what Catherine said, and sort out his current financial tangle. He knew what he had to do. He'd transfer funds from the Colombian accounts to Brian's companies. It was a high-risk strategy, but it would be only temporary and would stabilize him. Without financial stability he had no power.

'The base rate has gone to eleven and a half per cent,' Charles Tyrwhitt said, coming into his office. Joey had known he would be his first visitor on his return to the bank. 'We need you to do something about the two point five million you have out,' he said. 'With interest at four above base you'll soon be looking at three million. The matter's made worse by those loathsome squatters who've moved in.'

'I'm taking steps to have them evicted,' Joey said.

'If you can get them out,' Tyrwhitt said, 'I've got some Arabs who'll buy the lot off you discreetly.' Joey met his eyes with a question. The MD squirmed, as if he was embarrassed. 'For a little under two.'

'That's better than that housing-association offer. Still it's too cheap, Charles.'

'But beggars can hardly be choosers, old boy. With the crippling cost of money, you're risking exposing the bank.'

'Hardly. Give me a few days and I'll be fully in funds.'

'How?' Tyrwhitt's eyes almost popped out. 'Did you rob a bank?'

Moving as fast as he could, Joey went down to the basement vault. It was built of steel and concrete within an existing room. The airtight door, with a time-lock, was left open during office hours. He went to his own filing cabinet and unlocked it to get the portfolio he kept for Luis Picado. Then he got a serious shock. The trading sheets recording purchases and sales were gone. They must have been filed in the wrong section. He riffled through the rest of the files in all three drawers. They were nowhere to be found. With rising panic, he searched again and again. Only three people held the key to his cabinet: himself, the MD and their chief cashier, John Lockhart.

Joey found him at his desk in the back office on the ground floor. He was an affable Liverpudlian who, with the fame of the Beatles, had allowed his accent to creep back. He had a great mop of hair, the envy of many men of his age who were losing theirs. His usually open face was now like a closed book.

'Where are they?' Joey demanded. 'Where are the transfer sheets for the Picado account?'

'I'm sorry, Mr Oldman,' Lockhart said. 'I'm sorry.'

'Tell me where they are, John.' His voice rose with anxiety. Finally, he grabbed hold of the cashier to shake an answer from him and found himself creasing in pain. John Lockhart helped him into his own chair, then leant close to him. 'The MD took them,' he whispered. 'He had a run on some of his traded positions and needed to support them for a few days until they came good.'

'And?' Joey was barely able to ask.

'They didn't come good, I'm afraid, sir.'

Joey could have punched the man, or had his job off him for letting that happen. No one was supposed to dip into another's client account without permission from either the client or the manager. Joey had given no such permission and he knew Picado hadn't. But shouting at Lockhart would do no good; Tyrwhitt could be persuasive and Lockhart knew too much for Joey to toss him out on his ear.

'You stupid cunt,' Joey screamed at Tyrwhitt as he stepped into his room. 'You stupid, stupid, fucking cunt.'

'There's no need for that sort of language, old boy.' He got up and quickly closed the door.

'How much can you put back?'

Tyrwhitt shook his head. 'I was hoping to make it all good before you got out of hospital, Joseph. I might have done, had you not been such a workaholic.'

'How much can you put back?' he repeated and saw, from the expression of helplessness on Tyrwhitt's face, that it didn't amount to much, if anything. 'Do you know what you've done, Charles? Those fuckers kill people. They won't just kill you. They'll kill me, too.'

At that moment the fight left Joey. The walls were closing in on him, reducing his options to one. Arson. Meanwhile, he would have to talk to Luis Picado. If he didn't, and the Colombian learnt how cavalier they'd been with his money, he was dead.

THIRTY-SIX

For two nights running the violence surrounding the attempted eviction of squatters from the Cromwell Road properties made the top spot on the BBC's nine o'clock news. On the third night it was the second item, and on the fourth, Shirley Williams was saying more housing should be provided by the government for the homeless – a real vote-winner. The housing minister wasn't available. With the squatters now firmly entrenched, the Arabs had backed away from any purchase. Brian felt incensed as he watched the television in his recently acquired maisonette on Mount Street, situated above an antiques shop.

When the doorbell rang he went to let Catherine in. She came up and walked past him, looking into each room on the entrance level as if she expected to find someone there. 'Are you on your own?'

'Well, Father Christmas certainly ain't here, Mum.'

'Don't say "ain't", Brian,' she admonished. 'You got to speak so nicely when you spent time with Tom Driberg. Pity you ever gave up those contracts – even if he is an old poof.'

Brian stared at her coldly. 'D'you wanna check the rooms upstairs?' he asked.

'Oh, Brian, we used to be so close.' She put an arm round his waist to steer him through the apartment.

'It's called growing up.'

'It doesn't mean you grow apart.' She went upstairs and stopped at the kitchen doorway. Cups and pans were piled up. 'Look at this mess. We must get you a cleaner.'

'Mum,' he said firmly. 'I use everything, then I clear up.'

'Your father's sick with worry about those squatters. Did you see that ridiculous Shirley Williams on the news? As if she's their answer to Margaret, God help them.' She waited. 'Could any of your friends get them out?'

'I don't do the rough stuff any more, Mum.'

'It would still be legal – there's an eviction notice. Your father would pay them well.'

'All that publicity was a beacon to squatters everywhere. Every day more turn up. They're let in, then the doors are barricaded again.'

'The filth and squalor they're living in doesn't bear thinking about. All the internal doors are being taken off, skirting boards ripped out to burn for heating and cooking.'

'Well, we turned off the gas and electricity,' Brian told her. 'Let them do what they like. Let the building fall down.'

'Don't be stupid,' Catherine said sharply. 'It's costing your father a great deal of money.'

'And what about me?' he said, then thought about the situation. 'John Bindon'll have people who could do that for us. He owes me one. More than one.'

John Bindon seemed embarrassed when Brian found him in the snooker hall in Lewisham – perhaps because of his outrageous lies, or because he was too respectable for his company now. He now got semi-regular roles playing tough guys in films and on TV. Being an actor gave him some legitimacy. The life, with long stretches out of work, suited him. 'What exactly you got in mind, Brian?' he asked.

Brian spelt it out. 'It's a choice between killing you, John, for talking to the press like you did or just killing you for fun.'

'What could I do?' Bindon whined. 'It was business.'

'That's what this is.' Brian laid it out. 'It's legit.'

'It still gets you a wad more bad publicity,' Bindon said, as if suddenly he was Brian's adviser.

'Not what I've got in mind. We get a bunch of the hounds to get in like squatters. Then we turn into complete maniacs and take over the place.'

'Terrific!' Bindon said. 'We'll enjoy that. And get paid!'

Wearing ragged, unwashed clothes that made him itch just to be in them, Brian was admitted with Bindon and welcomed by the squatters. Others Bindon had recruited appeared throughout the day. Picking fights was easy enough. Bindon touched up a couple of the women, propositioning them. He didn't care who he had sex with, or what sex they were. A big, bearded hippie, with greasy hair and smoke-darkened skin, came after him. 'Hey, man,' he said, giving him plenty of warning, 'what d'you say to my old woman?'

'I offered her a quid for a blow-job,' Bindon said provocatively. 'But, looking at her, she ought to throw you in as well for that sort of money.' The man smouldered with rage until Bindon hit him with a piece of doorframe he was using to poke the fire. That put him on his knees. Then Bindon kicked him. His old woman jumped on Bindon and he hit her with his elbows. Other squatters piled in, but they weren't a match for fight-seasoned villains.

It took about three hours to empty the houses. Some of the squatters tried to hide, but Brian and his crew searched room by room, house by house. Afterwards, he wanted to be certain they were gone. 'Let's go through and make a final check.'

'It's all empty, Bri,' the exhausted Bindon argued. 'We done it. The lads are paid off. Cushty.'

'You and me should go through again,' Brian said. Something about Bindon's ready insistence had made him suspicious. 'That's how you get paid, John.'

Almost immediately Bindon found some people hiding in the roof space off one of the attic rooms. They wouldn't come out. 'If you don't come out,' Bindon said, 'I've got some hungry rats in a box. I'm going to send them in now.'

'Please don't. I can't stand rats,' a woman said. 'We're coming out. Please don't hurt my children.'

After a moment an attractive hippie woman appeared with a short teenage boy, who seemed cripplingly shy, and two girls of eight and six. Good-looking kids, Brian thought, noticing one was of mixed race. 'No one's going to hurt you,' he said.

The woman, who was dusty from the roof space, seemed vaguely familiar, but he couldn't place her. The boy was clinging to his mother, while the youngest girl was crying.

'It's all right,' Brian said. 'We haven't got any rats. But you can't stay here any more.'

'We haven't got anywhere else to go.'

'That's not my problem.'

'What's your name?' Bindon asked, obviously interested in her.

'Martha. We're not doing any harm. Honest we're not. We got thrown out of our flat because we couldn't pay the rent.'

'You on your own in there, apart from the kids, Martha?' Bindon said.

'Yes, there's no one else,' she said. 'The others all left.'

'Where's their father?' Brian asked, nodding at the kids.

'Which one?' Martha laughed nervously. 'They've all got different dads. All long gone.'

'Oh, you put yourself about, then.' Bindon smiled at the children, who clung tighter to their mum as she brushed a cobweb off her eyebrow. Then Brian saw the scar cutting through it and suddenly remembered who she was: his first heterosexual experience from Clapham Common all those years ago. He wasn't about to remind her, but he looked a little closer at the boy to see if there was any likeness. 'John, get this done,' he said, as the youngest child pulled at Martha's sleeve.

'Mum, I'm hungry,' she said.

'Okay, we'll get you something soon,' Martha told her, then turned to Brian. 'Please let us stay. Social Services will take the children if we leave.'

'We can't have that, Bri, can we?' Bindon said.

'I'm sorry, it's not an option.'

'Look, let them stay here tonight, Bri,' Bindon said. 'I'll find somewhere safe for them.'

'No, John.'

'Fuck me, Bri, you can't let her lose her kids.' He turned to the woman. 'You fuck up, Martha, or let anyone else in here, I'll come back and personally give your little ones to Social Services.'

Not wanting any emotional involvement with this family, this left Brian frustrated and angry. He turned away.

'You'd better get in there and keep quiet.'

'Could you come back with a bit of food, maybe?' Martha said.

'I'll come back and see you – I'll get a bit of weed too.'

Brian strode out of the room.

'What are you doing, John?' he said, when they were back on the pavement. 'Taking me for a fucking wolly? You'll pop back there and slip into her. I know what you're up to.' Curiously, he found himself irrationally jealous.

'I'll get them out, Bri. Stand on me.'

Brian stared at the rogue. 'I think I know her,' he said, and told him what had happened.

'You think that boy might be yourn, Bri? Bit unlikely, innit?'

'Yeah, probably.'

'D'you wanna slip back into her? You might be AC/DC after all.'

'I'll pass. Look, let's make them buildings secure, Rubber Johnny,' Brian mocked. 'After you get your little puddle out, find the biggest padlock you can. If anyone gets back in there, I'll murder you, you fat fucker.'

'It will be done, Bri – Scout's honour.' Bindon pulled huge padlocks and hasps from the back of his old Range Rover.

Sitting in the front passenger seat waiting for him, Brian thought about Martha and her kids. She hadn't fared well and was still unable to pay her rent. 'John,' he said, as Bindon heaved his large frame behind the wheel, 'when you get them out, find them a cheap flat somewhere. I'll put up a bit of rent.'

'What's this? You going straight?'

'Just do it, you fat bastard.'

Bindon laughed and started the engine.

*

'It's done, finally,' Brian said, when he called round to see his dad at Stanley Gardens. He was seriously worried about him. None of their financial troubles had ended with the emptying of the buildings. Now he was waiting for the Colombians to arrive, only they wouldn't say when that would be or what they had in mind.

'At least the buildings can be sold as a vacant lot now,' Brian said. 'If we can get your money back for them, it'll be okay. You could go into the market and get some of Picado's dosh back.'

'Where are the buyers for the buildings?' Joey asked. 'With all the bad publicity the Arabs won't come within a mile. Planning permission seems as far away as ever. None of my people on the council will even talk to me.'

'I could go and see Simon Hatfield. See if I can get something out of him. Stop worrying, Dad. There's always some sort of solution.'

'It might have been better, Brian, if the squatters had burnt those houses to the ground.'

Brian looked at his dad, hunched up on the sofa with a blanket around him like an old man, and realized that he was serious. He didn't want to go there.

'Is the insurance all up to date?'

'Of course,' Brian snapped. 'We had to pay an extra premium when we got squatted.'

'What are you two hatching between you?' Catherine said, coming in with a tea tray.

'Nothing,' Brian said guiltily. 'Just talking about the damage the squatters did. I'll catch Simon Hatfield after he finishes work.' He knew where he sometimes went for a drink – the Britannia, a pulling pub on Allen Street in Kensington.

'I really can't help you, Brian,' Simon said, sipping a glass of Hirondelle. 'The squat bust didn't help your case with the council.'

'That's long gone and forgotten.'

'Not by the council. They think you put the squatters in to get rid of the sitting tenants.'

'That's idiotic! You'd have squatters instead.'

'Well, the council's going to sit tight and not make a decision until the outcome of the corruption inquiry.'

'That could take years!' Brian felt a deep sense of injustice.

'If they do that,' Joey sighed wearily, as he took a short constitutional around the unkempt communal gardens with Brian, 'we bleed to death.'

'Well, I don't think we should try the insurance route. It's madness, Dad. We could end up inside.'

'We have to do something before Luis Picado gets here. A fire would run right through those buildings. Especially with half the internal doors missing.'

'What if someone was still in them?'

'You said they were empty.' They stopped by a large tree. Joey was out of breath.

'Are you okay, Dad?'

Joey brushed aside his concern. 'Do you know anyone in that line of work?'

'No,' Brian said sharply, 'I don't. I won't do it.'

'Oh, well, it was only an idea. Just in case. If the worst came to the worst. I'm sorry. I shouldn't ask you.' He looked as if he was about to cry.

'It's all right. I know what you're up against. It's just the thought of you ending up inside. It slaughters me. You wouldn't survive.'

Joey nodded sympathetically, holding on to the tree, looking desperately ill. Brian couldn't stand it.

'Look, there is a bloke, Roger Smith,' he said reluctantly, unsure why he was telling him. 'Jack used him to burn one of the Krays' gaffs. It's not exactly a recommendation. Let's think about this, Dad. How will there be any insurance money if arson's suspected. Then you'd have nothing to sell.'

'If I don't end up dead first, Brian.'

The raw edge of fear in his father's voice scared Brian. So did the thought of going to prison again.

'Maybe I could talk to this man. You wouldn't need to be involved. I wouldn't allow it. Is he any good, this Roger Smith?' Joey asked. 'No one suspects anything when he starts fires do they?'

Brian waited, uncertain, hoping his dad would understand the risk. He didn't know if he was more scared for his dad or himself. 'Give me his number,' Joey rasped. 'Just in case.'

Brian checked his book and read it out. Joey's hand shook as he took the number and Brian knew he couldn't let him do this. 'You're in no state to talk to anyone. I'll talk to him.'

'I promise you, son, you won't be involved. But I just need to know I have a way out if push comes to shove.'

Brian met the asthmatic arsonist Roger Smith at a pokey little pub in Peckham High Street, South London, where lorries and buses clogged the road with diesel fumes, making it the worst place for an asthma sufferer.

'I don't do that sort of work no more, Bri,' he said. Brian felt relieved, until he saw him smile. 'I did a three in the Scrubs. They taught me a trade.'

'Oh, yeah?' Brian said. 'What's that?

'Sewing mailbags. There've been no end of opportunities. I tell you what though, son, I don't ever want to go back inside. I was seriously abused by niggers.'

'Why?' Brian asked, irrationally angry. 'You weren't a nonce.'

'They was running the wing with their drugs, and I had to have a little bit – to help my asthma. I wanted to kill myself when I got out. The only thing that stopped me was Mrs Thatcher – she's good news. She'll get rid of them. I thought Enoch Powell was going to do it for us.'

'You ought to talk to my mum,' Brian said. 'She's a big fan of Mrs Thatcher. But can she win an election?'

'Well, no one's going to vote for Callaghan's fucking lot again,' Smith said vehemently. 'You sure all them houses are empty?'

'It's just an option, Rog.'

'No harm taking a look – see if it can be done.'

They parked in Grenville Place and walked round the block. With a large bunch of keys, Brian opened two padlocks and released two great steel hasps on the door. As they stood in the wrecked hallway and peered up the stairs, Brian thought he heard someone running. Could it be that Bindon had taken his money and done nothing about Martha and her kids?

'Did you hear that, Rog?' he asked.

They stood and listened to the silence.

'Probably rats.' He sniffed, his nostrils twitching. 'You definitely got rats here, Bri. No one could live in this shithole, that's for sure. Are they all like this?'

They picked their way carefully through several of the buildings, stepping over rubble where squatters had knocked out walls for more communal living. Eventually Smith announced that the whole block would catch easily enough.

Back on the street he said, 'That church still in use, Brian?'

'Not by me it's not.'

'If someone was to do this, the way to go is to start it in that church, let it flash up into the building next door. Some of them churchgoers get very careless with the votive candles.'

'What're they?' Brian asked.

'What the greedy fuckers light when they pray for money and things. We'd give it a bit of assist. Maybe leave a few gas taps open – them squatters'll get the blame.'

'No, we shut the gas off.' Brian was still looking for obstacles to this rotten plan.

'Well, everyone'll reckon the soapy bastards put it back on again,' Smith said. ''S easily done. The trick would be to kick it off in the morning rush-hour.'

'Would anyone be around lighting candles in church at that time of day?' Brian asked, knowing nothing of the habits of the faithful.

Smith stopped and wheezed. 'You'd make it so the wax pooled from overnight. It'll go when it gets to temperature. If someone arranged for a lorry to jack-knife on Cromwell Road and block it . . .' Brian gave him a questioning look when he paused and tried to suck in air '. . . fire engines'll take longer getting there. More damage, more insurance money. There's definitely no one in the buildings, Bri?' he said again.

Brian closed his eyes and shook his head.

'One last thing, who owns it now?'

'My company. Why?'

'It has to be kosher, Bri. The insurance paid up to date? Those insurance companies are dead tricky with big claims.'

'Like I said, Rog, Dad's looking to find another way first.'

Although he recognized what Joey was up against, Brian remained adamant that burning the church and all those houses was too risky. He wanted to find another way to solve their problems. He thought about June Sorrell and the others in the office, all working for wages, none of them knowing about any of this. That was what normal people were like, Brian realized: they worked for wages, got on with their lives, never did much wrong. Why couldn't he be like them? At the end of all his thinking, he was no nearer a solution.

'Are you sure this man's reliable, Brian?' Joey asked.

'Are villains ever? There must be another way,' Brian said.

'You find it, then,' Joey said sharply.

Brian waited, his uncertainty increasing. 'My name's on the insurance. Look, why not let me have one more shot at pulling this out of the fire, so to speak?'

Charles Tyrwhitt was startled when Brian walked into his Brook Street office, past the protesting secretary.

'Why don't you be a good girl and get us a cuppa tea?' he said.

She glanced at her boss. 'That might be best, Sally.' He nodded.

Brian closed the door. 'What's the very best we can get for those buildings without planning permission?'

'At the current state of play, old boy, the best any sale would cover is interest.'

'Hopefully the market will improve.'

'The bank is not in the hope business, old boy,' Tyrwhitt said, leaning back in his chair, his hands folded over his comfortably round belly. 'The fact is, your companies are broke. The bank might have no choice but to foreclose and take what it can get.'

'Or you come up with what you stole from the Colombians.'

'You'd better leave before you find yourself in the hands of the police,' Tyrwhitt said. 'You can't come here making criminal threats.'

'What did you think was going to happen? We'd just let you steal all that money without taking action?'

'It wasn't stolen. Oh, no. It was in a high-risk account your father was managing. In his absence I managed it. Risk is what it suggests, old boy. Now go.'

'The Colombians take a very different view, Charlie, old boy. You dipped your beak without permission.' Brian leaned across the desk, his face up close to the banker's. 'Either their money comes back or you're stone dead the moment they get here.'

Tyrwhitt's lip started to tremble and his breathing quickened. 'I can't get it – not just like that. It'll take time.'

'You haven't got time.' Brian stepped back. 'Don't mess about, Charlie. The money has to come in, or it won't just be you who gets killed. They'll top your wife and your children, your mother too.'

Brian enjoyed telling his father about his meeting with Tyrwhitt, and seeing Joey laugh, even though it hurt his stomach. 'The thing is, though, Dad, it's not going to get the Colombians back their money.'

That brought Joey back to earth with a bump.

'The only thing we can be certain of is Charlie-boy not going to the police.'

'We may have found a way forward, Brian. Your mother talked to Keith Grove, the chairman of the council. He's offered to help.'

'He can really help us break the planning deadlock?'

'He's going to whisper in a few shell-like ears,' he said, 'knock some heads together. He's confident we'll get this through at the next committee meeting, provided there are no more skeletons in the cupboard.'

'Great,' Brian said, relieved.

The phone by his bed rang like an alarm. His first thought, at three o'clock in the morning as he woke alone, was that something had happened to his dad.

'You used me, you rotten shit,' a voice said down the line. 'You lousy bastard! You used me!'

Finally Brian realized it was Simon Hatfield and wondered if he was drunk. 'What are you talking about, Simon? We had a good time.'

'You got what you wanted and then you ignored me!'

'Have I got what I wanted? What was that?'

'The planning committee's going to allow your office development – but they won't if I can help it.'

'What've you got in mind, you nutter?' Brian was alarmed. 'Don't do anything stupid.'

'You'll see!' The phone was slammed down.

Tomorrow he would dig Simon out and discover what his problem really was. Tonight he was too tired.

'Joseph!' Catherine's hysterical voice rose up the stairs. Joseph heard his wife hurry along the hallway and up to the first-floor sitting room where he was watching a rerun of *Steptoe and Son*. 'Is the house on fire?'

'Keith Grove's just told me the planning application's been

stopped. One of the planners claims Brian bribed him.' Catherine was breathless.

'Who was it?' Joey thrust himself out of his chair.

'Simon Hatfield. I phoned Brian but he's not answering.'

'Keep trying. I'll get round there.'

As his taxi drew up outside the Mayfair flat, he saw Brian walking along the street with a bag of food. Joey told him what had happened. 'Is it true?' he said. 'Did you bribe Hatfield?'

'No, of course not. Why the hell would I? He was all for the scheme.'

'Well, he's scuppered our chances now, good and proper. We're down the drain, son.' He turned and started to walk away, his head in his hands.

The wail of klaxons from fire engines, ambulances and police cars filled the air and went on and on endlessly. Traffic piled up on the Cromwell Road and along the M4 to Heathrow.

Anxiety clutched Brian like bony fingers. He tried not to let it take hold, telling himself again and again that this was coincidence, a genuine accident. It had to be. As the property owner he was called to the site to talk to the fire chief and local police. The buildings had been empty, he assured them, and prayed that that was true.

It was around lunchtime before the blaze was finally under control and firemen could get into the buildings. Then the worst happened. They found the first body, a man's, then another. Next they discovered two children, then a mother and child entwined, someone said.

Brian felt angry, betrayed and sick. Had he met John Bindon right then, he would have murdered him for leaving them in the building. He wouldn't go to look at any of the bodies, telling the fireman he couldn't identify anyone as there had been no tenants in any of the buildings. Who those people were, or how they had got there, he didn't know.

In fact, Brian was almost certain he did know who some of them were, but he couldn't trust himself to speak about it, certainly not that he might have known the dead woman and had possibly fathered one of her children. Would they take blood and do tests? If he said a word to anyone it would all come out.

On the radio the reporter was saying. 'It is now confirmed that six people died in the Cromwell Road fire, three of them children. Their mother was believed to have been hiding with them in the building, which, less than four weeks ago, was entirely cleared of squatters. It seems the fire may have been started by a prayer candle, left alight overnight in the adjacent church, which ignited escaping gas from taps thought to have been left open when the squatters illegally turned the gas back on, almost destroying the entire block.'

Brian shut off the radio to answer the phone. At first he thought a heavy breather was winding him up, then realized he was hearing an asthmatic wheeze. His instinct was to put the receiver down immediately. He could almost feel the agitated state Roger Smith was in.

'Bri, it's me. Did you see the news?'

'I've been listening to it all day,' Brian said. 'Sickening.' He was still in shock. The image of those young children with dirty faces clinging to Martha haunted him. She had been a protective mother and he knew he should have done more. He was as much to blame for their deaths as if he'd torched the buildings himself. He wanted to ask Roger Smith if he had done it, but was afraid to, especially on the phone. Was there any way he could have not been involved?

'I've been on the golf course all day, Bri. I thought you said the building was empty. You said—' His voice became a wheeze again.

'What are you saying?' Brian didn't like the arsonist's tone. This was going somewhere he didn't want it to go.

'What the fuck d'you think I'm saying?' Smith wheezed. 'Three little kiddies died and their parents—'

'D'you think I don't know that?' Brian said sharply. 'Look, we're not having this conversation.'

'You said them buildings was empty!' Smith wheezed.

'They were!' Brian shouted, trying to push back his fear. 'They were. Look, what are you trying to say? It was an accident, a tragic accident. That's all it could have been. I'm hanging up right now.' Brian put the phone down, pressing his hands on it, defying it to ring again. Those sharp fingers of anxiety were snatching at him again, getting a purchase and dragging him towards a well of guilt and utter self-loathing.

More and more of Tony Wednesday's day was spent in the hateful administration that supported detection, so when something turned up in which he felt a personal interest, he allowed it to draw him away.

DC Baldwin, one of the detectives working on the long-term Brian Oldman investigation, put his head round the door. 'Guv!'

He got Tony's immediate attention.

'I've just been listening to yesterday's intercepts on Brian Oldman's phone. There's something you should hear.'

Tony got up and followed him to the squad office. There he listened to a breathless voice say, 'You said them buildings was empty. You fucking well said.' Then Brian: 'It was an accident. A tragic accident.'

They went through the entire short conversation repeatedly, getting what they could from every inflection. By the end Tony knew he had Brian Oldman where he wanted him. He snapped off the cassette player. 'Who's the other man? Any idea?'

'D'you think he set the building on fire, Guv?'

'Be handy. We'd have Clever Clogs by the ballocks. Try to identify the caller. D'you think he was disguising his voice?'

'I don't think so, Guv. He sounds like he's got asthma. My uncle's like that.'

'Find him. There can't be too many asthmatic fire-raisers –

unless we nick your uncle.' He took the tape out of the machine and looked around for a spare body. 'Peter!' he called. He wanted some checks made before he went to see Brian Oldman.

Tony watched Brian's face closely as he played him the tape. The rock-hard mask he wore convinced him he was on to something, far more than if he had been affected by it. He shut the tape off. '"Bri, it's me ..."' – he said imitating the asthmatic. 'When we identify him, you're nicked, uncle. Unless you want to tell me who it was?'

'I don't know,' Brian said. 'He sounds like that bloke on the Schweppes advert off the telly.'

'You're going down for a long, long while,' Tony threatened.

'Well, that might sound good, Tony, but I don't know anything about those buildings being burnt,' Brian said. 'All I know is what the fireman told me. Someone left candles lit in the church and gas leaked out of those houses where the hippies had left it on. Now we're well out of pocket.'

'You killed those squatters, no doubt about it. It was an insurance job, down to either you or your old man or both. I don't give a fuck. Nicking both of you would do me. It would make my day, punk.' Doing an impression of Clint Eastwood in *Dirty Harry*.

'You're crackers,' Brian said evenly.

Tony heard the tension in his voice, saw in his body language the nervous little fissures he would eventually open and exploit by playing him off against his father – especially with what he'd found out about their true relationship.

The warning phone call Joey received from Brian didn't give him time enough to prepare himself for the policeman's onslaught. No amount of time would have been enough.

'Those buildings don't belong to me, Mr Wednesday,' Joey said lamely, stepping behind the desk in his office. 'They belong to companies Brian owns.'

'That's not what he said,' DI Wednesday told him.

'Oh, it's all in the register at Companies House.' Joey felt tension spread up from his stomach into his diaphragm and wondered if it was affecting his speech.

'You think I'd come here without doing my homework, Joey? How do you plan to wriggle out of this one? Offer me five grand to look the other way, then knock me like you did before? Fifty grand you owe me, you cheapskate kyke.'

'What are you suggesting?,' Joey said, fearing the treacherous detective might be recording this.

'We had a pretty clear understanding of what was s'posed to come my way – 's okay, I'm not recording this one.'

'There will be a great deal of money coming from the insurance claim on those properties.'

'Not one penny, uncle,' Wednesday stated. 'Not one penny when the insurance company learns it was a criminal enterprise. But, then, we can't trust you anyway when it comes to paying, can we, Joey? You're a jib merchant.'

'How much? Just tell me how much.'

'You killed a mother and her three kiddies. You think I'm gonna take money? No amount is enough not to see you two go down at last,' the DI said. 'That would give a good few high-up Old Bill great satisfaction. I'd be an out-and-out hero. The way people feel about what happened, they'd lynch you if they knew.'

In a suddenly cold, flat voice, Joey said, 'Fifty grand? In cash. Up front.' It was a lot of money, but then he was bargaining for his very existence.

'Is that the fifty you still owe me, Joey?' Wednesday mocked. 'Or a new fifty? I'd be a right mug to go along with that after the last time.'

'No. It'll be payment in advance,' Joey said. He paused as the detective thought about that. Then he tried to take the high ground: 'But then how do I know you'd be able to deliver?'

DI Wednesday laughed scornfully, and Joey saw at once that

he'd confirmed everything for him. 'How you going to get the money when the insurance company comes up with arson?'

'Why would they?' Joey challenged. 'It was a tragic accident. Nothing more.'

'In your dreams. The insurance dicks will see arson.'

'They won't. How?'

'Because the cheapskating rats don't like parting with their money. Three million's a lot to part with.' He gave a little commiserating shrug and waited. Joey waited too. 'There's no possible way out for you or Brian. You're both going down the road. You could blame Brian, say *he* set the buildings alight because he couldn't cope, he was ticked off with you. But then your company's the principal financial stakeholder, it stands to collect and you're in financial schtook. How bad does that look for you?'

Joey wanted to believe this was solely about price, the detective's negotiating strategy. 'Look, I'll pay you a hundred grand to make this work,' he said breathlessly.

'That sounds all right. But no. Not even for that sort of dough, Joey. It's time.'

The detective's words haunted him. For Wednesday to turn down that sort of money made Joey's arrest inevitable. He fled to Mr Smith to see if he could help. He said he would look into things, then rang him two days later. They lunched at Soho's L'Escargot, even though Joey couldn't abide the thought of eating snails.

'Help is available, Joseph,' Smith said matter-of-factly, as he slipped the slimy mollusc into his mouth. 'However, the only possible way to keep you out of it is for Brian to go to trial.'

'I can't have that,' Joey said emphatically. 'I really won't. I promised he wouldn't be involved.'

'Presumably you need to collect the insurance money?'

Joey looked away.

'Think about it. If it's criminal damage by your son, the insurance is still valid and you can collect as the beneficial interest holder.'

'I can't do that to Brian. I'll take my chances.'

Smith took off his horn-rimmed glasses and polished them with a corner of the tablecloth. 'The fact is, Joseph,' he said, 'you've become too useful to my employers for them to allow that to happen. The service you render us at the bank is vital to the national interest. We can't risk losing you.'

'Then get us both out of this mess.'

Mr Smith tweaked another snail out of its shell and swallowed it, then shook his head. 'That would cause a scandal Mr Callaghan's government couldn't afford. The whole country's looking for a guilty party. It must be your son.'

It was an unbearable dilemma for Joey. Finally, he managed to whisper, 'How long would he have to go to prison for?'

'Depends how good his lawyers are!'

'We'd get him the best money can buy.'

'I'm sure if he were to plead guilty to manslaughter, we could have someone talk to the right judge in his club,' Smith said. 'Help him to see the national interest here. No more than six years is what I think we could guarantee.'

'Oh, dear God,' Joey murmured. 'This will kill his mother.'

But six years was a reasonable bargain and Brian was still a relatively young man . . .

THIRTY-SEVEN

Joey found it very pleasant to be sitting on the pale blue brocade sofa with its intricate pattern of gold and silver thread, one of three in the sitting room of the suite at the Dorchester Hotel in Park Lane. Having tea with his host, who had a great fondness for English tea, was the scariest experience of his life. The cups were of thin china, the sandwiches and slices of cake dainty. Luis Picado was in a short-sleeved Fred Perry shirt and immaculately pressed chinos. At any moment Joey thought he might be killed. He didn't know how they'd dispose of his body. Room service?

'You have been working hard on our behalf, Joseph,' Picado said, pouring himself more tea. 'I knew it was the right decision to let you go back to work to restore our funds.'

'I couldn't have done that without the additional money you put up,' Joey said. 'That was an act of faith I appreciated, Luis.'

'Neither of us would've gained anything if I'd listened to José and killed you.' He glanced across at Ortega, on another sofa. The other man smiled, showing a mouthful of large, white teeth.

'Thank you for your confidence, José.' Joey tried to sip some tea.

'But then we have to consider your powerful connections and how this helps us. This is business. Nothing is personal in business.'

Joey still didn't know when they were going to get to whatever they had planned for him. Perhaps it was nothing after all. Perhaps they were scared of Mr Smith and Co. The waiting was unbearable.

'Is the situation improving for your son?' Picado took a slice of cake that broke before he got it to his mouth. Swiftly he caught the falling piece.

'He's in prison awaiting trial.'

'The police or the judge, they can't be reached?'

'Unfortunately not. There's no movement anywhere.'

'Your police and judges are so hypocritical. They need money, they should take it,' Picado said. 'This is causing you much personal grief.'

Joey arched his eyebrows. 'I'd rather be in his place.'

'A noble sentiment, but a waste of time. Here you can do him more good than he could do for you.'

That was like absolution, but still Joey felt uneasy.

'Are you keeping a close eye on our money?'

'Every penny is carefully monitored, then checked at the end of each day. Only my chief cashier and I now have access to the portfolios.'

'What are your plans for our untrustworthy Señor Tyrwhitt? Are you going to kill him?'

This was the purpose of the meeting. Joey panicked, not knowing how he'd go about getting such a thing done, now that Brian and Jack weren't available. Wednesday was an obvious source, but he couldn't even imagine how much that would cost. 'No,' he said, suddenly inspired. 'I intend to take a leaf out of your book, Luis.'

'A leaf? I don't understand,' Picado said.

'I'm going to kill him but not with a bullet.' Joey was confident now. 'I shall destroy his bank, leaving him penniless. That will hurt him so much more.'

'Excellent!' Picado turned to his compatriot. 'You see, José? Sometimes there are better ways to kill people.' He turned back to Joey. 'This will take how long?'

'I don't know. But it will be done and you will see the result.'

Picado sipped his tea and nodded. For the first time since Charles Tyrwhitt had raided the portfolios Joey felt able to relax a little.

There were no other prisoners in the van bringing Brian from Brixton prison, just three screws. He was handcuffed to one, another held a transistor radio to his ear, with the tinny sound of Abba singing 'Knowing Me, Knowing You' coming out of it, while the third drove them across Blackfriars Bridge to Ludgate Circus. Brian sensed that people in the street were stopping to stare as if the van displayed a big placard announcing who he was: child murderer. He didn't want to look for fear of meeting their eyes and seeing the hatred. It came at him all the time from the other remand prisoners in Brixton. Several had tried to scald him with boiling tea, some of whom were guilty of far worse than him. Telling them he was innocent made no difference. The three children and their mother were still dead. Coming to trial at last, was almost a relief. Now he could prove his innocence.

As the prison van turned off Ludgate Hill into Old Bailey, he could see a crowd of people outside the Central Criminal Courts. The officer cuffed to him told him to steady himself as the van slowed and protesters surged past the police cordon to bang on the vehicle. They were shouting abuse and calling for the return of capital punishment. Their hostility frightened Brian. The police did nothing to stop them. He was hugely relieved when the van reached the Old Bailey courtyard and the gates closed.

'We feel the same,' a screw said, and hit him as they went into the cell below the court.

'Oi! I saw that,' another screw said. 'That's no way to treat him. Do it like this.' He punched Brian in the kidney. 'I got kids of my own, you murdering bastard.'

There was no relief from the pressure when, twenty minutes later, his barrister, George Carman QC, arrived with Lord Goodman's man, Kevin Wheeler. Brian had made a statement declaring his innocence, and would never stop repeating it. 'I didn't start that fire and kill those children. I didn't.' He had been saying this for the past five months, but still wasn't sure even now if Carman believed him.

'You've seen how big the crowd is outside the court, Brian,' his barrister said, treading out his cigarette end and lighting a fresh Benson & Hedges. 'It's an indication of the strength of public feeling.'

'That's what they want, don't they, my mum and dad? They want me to plead guilty, spare them any embarrassment.' Brian felt crushed, especially knowing what he believed were the true circumstances of the fire. He didn't know why Catherine was letting this happen. Yes, he did. But he didn't want to think about that.

'Brian,' Wheeler said, 'we've been over this.'

'Go and ask Joey why I'm here and not him! I'm not pleading guilty. I can't. I won't.'

'I really don't know what's going on between you and your father, Brian,' Carman said. 'I'm simply advising you on the best position to take. We might yet negotiate this down to manslaughter.'

'You know what, George?' Brian said. 'I thought you were a fighter, but you're a defeatist wanker. I think I could do better without you. In fact, I'm sure I could. At least the jury will hear me saying straight up I didn't kill those kiddies.'

'Brian, we didn't choose Mr Carman with a pin. Think carefully about this,' his solicitor said.

'That's all I do in my cell, Kevin – when I'm not avoiding scalding water. I told you I didn't do it,' Brian said emphatically. 'Either you believe I'm innocent or you can get lost.'

'I've never offered less than my best, despite what you may feel,' Carman told him stiffly. 'However, it's my duty to clients to advise them of their best interests as far as I see them.'

Anger at the betrayal pressed in on Brian. 'My best interests lie with you asking Joey Oldman what happened. My fucking father!'

But he knew Lord Goodman wouldn't let these lawyers do that. He would always protect Joey's interests, Brian realized, come what may.

Number-two court was jammed. There wasn't a spare seat anywhere. Even all the legal benches were full with barristers who had no part in the case ducking in to watch. The hostility that had pressed in on Brian for months was no less prevalent here as George Carman rose in the hushed room and said, 'It is with regret, my lord, that I have to inform the court I am no longer representing Mr Oldman.'

Brian met the eyes of the judge, Mr Justice Melford Stevenson, who was hearing the case. Had he got it by accident or had someone else arranged it?

'A lot of time has been spent on this case, leading to several delays,' the judge pointed out. 'Is there no way you and your client can be reconciled?'

'Regrettably we cannot, my lord. Mr Oldman is adamant. He no longer wishes me to represent him.'

'What a pity, Mr Carman. I had looked forward to having you before me. You're released.' The judge's gaze fixed on Brian again as the barrister collected his papers, bowed and left. Brian felt uncomfortable under the man's scrutiny. Was this payback time, after all? It was too much to hope that he'd deliver the same sort of result as before.

'In a case as serious as this it is not only advisable but essential that you have adequate legal representation, Mr Oldman. Do you have an alternative barrister in mind?'

'No,' Brian said clearly. 'I plan to represent myself.'

Surprise rippled around the court.

'That is an option you have the right to exercise,' the judge said. 'It is a course you'd be unwise to take. I must try to steer you away from it or risk a miscarriage of justice. I'm going to adjourn this case for a week to let you take further advice. Don't hesitate to contact my clerk if you're having difficulties.'

'All rise,' the usher called. As Brian got up and started to turn, one of the screws in the dock tripped him, causing him to stumble down the steps.

'I've had all the advice I want from lawyers,' he told Wheeler, back in his cell. 'Tell Goodman to talk to the real guilty party.'

'Do you know who that is, Brian?'

'I know, all right, so I'm not pleading guilty to anything.'

'The simplest thing would be to tell the police.'

'Which particular bent copper should I talk to?'

'There must be some who aren't corrupt.'

'Yeah, like the judges and lawyers!' Brian said angrily.

'That's a cynical view.'

Brian's anger didn't go away. 'Telling any of them wouldn't do me or him one bit of good.'

'Look, I'll go on helping all I can,' Kevin Wheeler said. 'I owe Lord Goodman that much at least.'

'Forget it. I'll do without your help – and his.' He turned and rang the bell for the prison officer. The meeting was at an end.

When the screw came back from showing the lawyer out, he opened Brian's door and stood there, his fat belly bursting through his tunic buttons, one of which was missing. 'You think sacking your brief will help? The court'll help you if you do it on your own, of course, but that ain't gonna do you any good. You're dead meat, you murdering fucker.' He stepped back and slammed the door.

Brian closed his eyes and took a deep breath. He had never felt more alone in his life. It was going to be a real uphill struggle.

Catherine's nervous, edgy movements told him exactly what Brian's incarceration was doing to her. She was avoiding expressing her feelings. There was no way she could interpret this crime as Robin Hoodism or entrepreneurship, as she had some of Brian and Jack's past deeds. The death of the children and their mother had shocked the nation. Catherine was increasingly tired, working too hard, refusing to ease up. It was the only way she could stay ahead of the tide of ignominy that was threatening to engulf them.

'How can he possibly manage his own defence, Arnold?' she asked, in their upstairs sitting room, nervously moving her teacup around in its saucer.

'It's a complicated case, Catherine,' Lord Goodman said. 'He really won't be able to stay on top of it on his own.'

'He's such a foolish, headstrong boy at times.'

'The judge will bend over backwards to help him. He'll probably declare a mistrial, at which point Brian might take legal advice.'

'The nightmare of bad publicity will never end.'

'What about this other nonsense Brian's dragging up for his defence?' Joey said.

After a long pause, Lord Goodman said, 'There is a risk that the judge will let things through to the jury that might not ordinarily be allowed.'

'That's silly,' Catherine said. 'The press will tear at us like hyenas. What's got into Brian? He's thinking only of himself.'

'It won't do anyone any good if he tries to drag me in,' Joey said. 'Is there any way we can stop it?'

'Not now that he's sacked his barrister. I could send a note to the judge suggesting Brian's fuelling a family feud with this.'

'Yes. Stop it from going any further,' Catherine ordered.

His wife couldn't bear being shunned in the street by people who were normally friendly, and when Margaret Courtney, who had become deputy chairman of the Tory Party, asked Catherine to call on her at Party Headquarters in Smith Square, Joey assumed it was curtains. 'It may not be the boot,' he ventured. 'Margaret's made of the same tough stuff as Mrs Thatcher.' He admired Margaret Courtney. She worked in banking and possessed a fine mind. He found her easy to get on with. He decided to go along and support his wife at their meeting. 'We'll show the world we've got nothing to be ashamed of. We believe implicitly in Brian's innocence.'

'He is innocent, Joseph, isn't he?'

'I'd be the first to condemn him if I thought for a moment he'd done such a wicked thing,' Joey said evenly.

In her office Margaret Courtney was expansive and ebullient, and insisted on showing them round the elegant Georgian house even though they had been to Smith Square before. There was scarcely enough room for all that was going on – even the first-floor shadow cabinet room was stacked with filing boxes.

In her cramped office, adjacent to the chairman's, she said, 'You will realize, perhaps better than anyone, Catherine, what our prospects are. There's now a real chance we'll be elected with Margaret Thatcher as prime minister.'

'Catherine's worked tirelessly for that,' Joey said quickly.

'So have you, Joseph. We all appreciate what you've both done.' Margaret Courtney hesitated. 'But with this trial attracting such adverse publicity it's wondered if perhaps you shouldn't step down from the finance committee – you must be so occupied.'

'That suggests we're guilty of something,' Joey said. 'We're not. Neither is Brian.'

'You know how narrow-minded people can be. Do you want to risk the Tories losing the election?'

'Brian's trial has barely started,' Catherine argued, colour coming back to her face. 'We're confident he'll be found not guilty. I refuse to abandon the party I love.'

'I feel I'm behaving like Judas bringing you here.'

'Not your finest hour,' Catherine said sharply, causing Joey to shrink back. He wondered if this was the right approach. His wife pressed on: 'No one's more keen than we are to get Margaret elected. Joseph and I will work and work for that – it'll distract us from this other wretched business.'

'We'll do a lot of fund-raising,' Joey added. He laughed. 'Who won't open the door to us in such circumstances?'

It was an offer the cash-strapped deputy chairman couldn't refuse. 'Then might I make a suggestion?' she said. 'When you came to Britain your name was Olinska. Why not revert to that? We're much more proud of our origins nowadays after all. It makes us more pluralistic, and that's the sort of society Mrs T wants to sponsor, one in which everyone has equal opportunity. You could be at the vanguard.'

Catherine sighed as if she had been separated from a great pain. He felt the same sense of relief.

'And what are those origins?' Charles Tyrwhitt asked, when Joey informed the bank of the change for letterheads and incorporation certificates. 'Polish?'

'No. A little town in Austria, north of Linz.'

'It's a good idea going back to basics,' Tyrwhitt said superciliously. 'We all know where we are then. Some of our friends in the Dutch Antilles and Jersey might be reassured.'

'What possible difference could it make?' Joey was growing increasingly irritated with the man, whose arrogance plainly made him believe he'd escaped the wrath of the Colombians scot-free.

'Margaret Courtney's right,' Tyrwhitt persisted. 'There will be a taint if Brian's convicted. It would inevitably come here. Our clients couldn't bear to be put under the spotlight.'

'Most of them have done far worse than Brian.'

'The difference is that a lot of them have either been elected or seized power with an army behind them.'

Joey was finding it difficult to bide his time. He was waiting for the right opportunity to bring Tyrwhitt down and grind his face in the dirt. 'And you, Charles? Should we be concerned about any possible taint from your peccadilloes, were they to become public?'

'What are you talking about?' Tyrwhitt stiffened.

'For the sake of the bank, let's hope it remains a strictly private matter or the Tory Party might find your money too risky. There goes your longed-for knighthood.'

'Nothing's further from my thoughts!' Tyrwhitt protested. 'I have to congratulate you, Joseph. It was a coup, hooking Mrs Marcos. Do our Colombian friends want anything for the introduction?'

'Their money properly looked after,' he said tartly.

'Will you go out to oversee the transfer of Mrs Marcos's money?'

'It won't happen till after Brian's trial.'

'That could cost us a lot in interest and fees.'

Joey merely stared at him.

'Well, yes, of course,' Tyrwhitt said uncomfortably. 'I dare say the lady can afford to live on credit for a while.'

The balance of power had shifted. Tyrwhitt was still called managing director, but Joey was delivering the big-fee clients. He would wait for the bank to become almost totally dependent on them, then wreak his revenge.

Brian refused to budge from his decision to represent himself, and thought the judge fair as he issued a warning to the diminutive prosecutor not to take advantage of the defendant-in-person.

Brian listened to Sir Donald James's blistering list of offences, stating the evidence he would bring in support of each indictment. This culminated in the murder of three children, whom he named, holding up photos of each, giving them a clear identity for the jury, reminding them of how short their lives had been as a result of Brian's actions. Brian saw again the dirty little faces, which were permanently printed in his mind's eye. As Sir Donald spoke of how dedicated their mother had been, despite her addiction to drugs, Brian glanced at the jury. Some were looking at him, others were close to tears. How would he ever persuade them to believe him?

At the end of the opening, the judge said, 'It isn't usual practice for the defence to lay out its case at the beginning of a trial, but it might help both you and the jury, Mr Oldman, should you wish to do so. The jury can infer nothing, should you not choose to.'

'Yes, I would like to.' Brian stood up from the wooden chair in the dock and gathered his notes. They were difficult to manage without a table to put them on. It took him a long while to work out what he might say, with everyone waiting and staring at him. He shuffled and reshuffled the pages before him, then abandoned them. He had wanted to write a great speech like the ones Perry Mason made on television, but he wasn't any good at writing, and what he had come up with sounded nothing like Perry Mason. He wanted to be straightforward and clear, not oily like most lawyers.

'Basically, what the prosecution has stuck up about me is a load of ballocks,' he found himself saying. 'Give a dog a bad name and all that. That's all the prosecution and the police are doing. It is,' he insisted. 'You know the old saying, "Throw enough muck at someone and some of it's bound to stick"? Well, that's what all this is. Only none of it's going to stick. I'm not trying to lessen or make what happened to those children seem unimportant. It was terrible. But it wasn't me who did it. I didn't. The police know who really did it, but they're taking money off him to keep him out of the frame. What I'll try to do in my defence is get out of them who this person is. I'll answer every charge ever made by every corrupt policeman who speaks against me. If you don't believe all policemen are corrupt, you've got to be blind, deaf and dumb.'

Some of the jury burst out laughing. They were probably as tense as he was, Brian thought. But they could go home at night, instead of to a lock-up where knives and pans of boiling water were a constant threat. Brian wasn't sure if he could survive this trial, but he was going to have a good try.

At the end of the opening arguments, the judge told the pressmen, 'I'm lifting reporting restrictions as this case has aroused such public interest. However, I expect you to report fairly and to respect the privacy of both the defendant and the witnesses.'

Depression was drawing him into its undertow like a dangerously random river current and Joseph seemed helpless to stop it. Catherine couldn't bear to attend court. Instead he gave her a sanitized version of events, witnesses, surprises, setbacks, making it all seem less hurtful than it was. He wasn't sure if he could go on attending, seeing the damage done to Brian while he inflicted so little on the witnesses. His assaults on their integrity were like peas hitting armour. Even at this late stage he knew he had to redouble his efforts to deliver some sort of assistance to his son. Cautiously he arranged a meeting with DI Wednesday.

'What sort of help do you think I can give him, Joey?' the detective asked, as they moved away from the Central Criminal Courts into Newgate Street, looking for a bar that neither the police nor the barristers used. 'A file in a cake so he can make a break?'

Joseph gave him an uneasy look, remembering how this policeman had once trapped him. 'You're not recording this?'

'You pulled me from the court.'

He was somewhat reassured. 'Some of the magic you produced last time would do it.'

'Yeah, but we had Jack Braden in the frame to take the stick.'

'I'm still prepared to pay a lot to get Brian some help.'

'I like the sound of that, Joey. What else can I do for you?'

Joseph hesitated for only a moment. 'Our MD has an unhealthy interest in children.'

'A paedophile?'

'No actual contact,' Joseph explained. 'Mostly pictures.'

'They're as bad. What do you want me to do? I could bust him or run him over in my car. Neither gets Brian off the hook.'

'No.' Joseph sighed resignedly. 'I'd like chapter and verse on Tyrwhitt. I don't want the bank damaged.'

'There's a lot of those dirty bastards at it, some in high places. He'll get a lot of protection.'

'There would be five thousand pounds for the right sort of information.'

'You must want him badly. And he obviously feels the same way about you.' Wednesday laughed. 'He hired a private investigator to make enquiries.'

That shocked Joseph.

'Most PIs are ex-Old Bill,' Wednesday explained. 'This one knew we'd have a lot on you with Brian in court. He approached one of our skippers, who told me. Everyone's paranoid with your nephew Redvers still breathing.'

Joseph tried to read the policeman, almost afraid to ask what Redvers might have given him.

'Where's the value to me?'

'In other words, what am I prepared to pay?' Joseph said.

'For another five grand we feed him a load of cobblers.'

The deal was easily done, payment upfront. Joseph made the detective another offer. If ever he retired from the force, he'd take him on: he'd make a shrewd banker.

As if to distract himself from what was happening in court, Joseph quadrupled his fundraising efforts for Margaret Thatcher. No door was closed to him, not in banking, business or legal firms. All wanted to know one thing: was Margaret Thatcher electable? A banker at a party Catherine hosted thought a woman prime minister rather unConservative. Joseph persuaded him she would put the Great back into Britain and help them on the way. The man's bank committed five thousand pounds to the cause. Joseph pushed for ten. 'And another ten from you,' he added.

'That's a lot of money,' the banker complained.

'This lady will give us a lot of value,' Joseph assured him. He burnt with such passion he gave scarcely a thought to Brian.

Margaret Courtney came to see Joseph at the bank, rather than summoning him to Smith Square as she usually did these days. After Doreen, his secretary, had shown her in and gone to get tea, she kissed him on the lips. 'You wonderful, wonderful man,' she said enthusiastically. 'I didn't think you'd go at it with such ardour. Your fundraising has left everyone standing. Cecil Parkinson's delighted. At this rate we'll be out of debt for the first time in years.'

'Well, at last we have someone worthwhile.'

'No question,' she said. 'And Margaret so appreciates all your efforts. She and Cecil would like you to join one of her kitchen suppers – just as soon as Brian's trial is over,' she added.

'Regardless of the outcome?'

Margaret Courtney took his hand and squeezed it. 'What you'll discover about our leader, Joseph, is that she's not only appreciative but totally loyal. How is he doing?'

'Not well. They're into the third week of prosecution witnesses. Mercifully, most of them no longer make the front pages.'

'It'll get better, you'll see. It always does.'

Brian had won only one argument so far and that had been about where he should conduct his case. The judge conceded that he needed a table in the dock, but was reluctant to agree that he should be allowed on to the legal benches where he could more easily accommodate the papers and books he was accumulating. Brian argued that if he wasn't given the means by which to conduct his defence adequately and he lost, he might have grounds for appeal. The judge took his point and invited him on to the benches. That brought a protest from the prison service on security grounds.

'You can sit on the bench behind Mr Oldman,' the judge said.

'And act as my junior,' Brian quipped.

Everyone but the screws laughed. He paid for it later back at Brixton. He was turned on to a corridor where the hot-water urn was and a villain associated with the Richardsons scalded him.

Along the front bench from Brian, Sir Donald James sorted papers. By now Brian knew his gestures. This one – searching for and adjusting his glasses – meant that something unpleasant was looming.

'If it pleases the court,' he said, 'the prosecution's next witness needs to give evidence behind screens.'

'No, Judge!' Brian said, leaping to his feet. 'That's not fair. This is the fourth witness they've swung on me in this way. It's impossible to cross-examine them when I can't see their eyes.' It always tickled Brian that the barristers sat down whenever he got up. He rarely did when Sir Donald stood up.

'This witness goes in fear of his life.'

'Would the jury leave, please?' Melford Stevenson said.

Brian was still standing as the usher shut the door behind them. Sir Donald pulled off his wig and sat down. The judge waved Brian into his seat. 'I do understand the problem, Mr Oldman,' he said, 'but the court owes a duty of care to witnesses and the police. We have to be alert to their safety.'

'I'm one man, Judge.' Brian got up again. 'I'm in custody. How can I harm anyone? To suggest I can is prejudicial.'

'His point is well made, Sir Donald. How does the witness feel his life is in danger?'

'Mr Oldman might be in custody but his reach is long. The police feel there are criminals still beholden to him.'

'If you tell me who they are,' Brian said, 'I'd be grateful.' He couldn't think of a single one. 'I've rejected that way of life completely.'

'We have seen evidence of the despicable treatment Mr Oldman's received at the hands of fellow remandees,' the judge said. 'That hardly indicates a supportive network of criminals. We'll have this witness without screens.'

'But, my lord,' Sir Donald protested, 'the police promised he would be protected.'

'Yes, Sir Donald,' the judge said. 'Ordinarily I'm sympathetic to the police but it's not the witness who is on trial.'

'In a sense he is, my lord,' Sir Donald said.

'I have ruled,' the judge informed him. 'Hopefully the witness has a concern that justice must be done.'

There was a long delay, and then, protesting a great deal, John Bindon was brought in. He'd put on weight, Brian noticed. 'This is not fucking right,' he was saying, 'going in the open witness box. What if I get killed?'

'I understand the police have offered you protective custody,' the judge said, 'and if you don't stop this, you'll be held in contempt of court.'

'That's better than being dead from stupidity, man,' Bindon said, and stopped suddenly, seeing Brian on the front bench. 'What's he doing down there? You a brief now, Bri? Cushty.' He spoke as if they had met casually on the street and Brian almost smiled. He wondered how easily the police had found him when he couldn't.

When the court settled down and John stopped performing, Sir Donald mentioned that Bindon held the Queen's Award for diving into the Thames to save a man's life. Brian watched the jury. They were impressed. He must remember to tell them that Bindon had thrown him in after a row.

'Mr Bindon, when the defendant first approached you for help with his properties on Cromwell Road, what was his object?'

Brian shot up. 'He couldn't possibly have known that.'

'Well, I knew what you told me,' Bindon said. 'You wanted help getting rid of the squatters.'

The judge waved Brian down.

'Is that your line of work?' Sir Donald said. 'I thought you were an actor.'

'I am. Haven't you seen me on telly?'

'Does emptying houses of squatters require acting skills?' the QC asked.

'I'd been out of work. Brian knew I was a bit skint, but handy, like.'

'By which you mean you're a good fighter?' Sir Donald said.

'I've done a bit.'

'Were you expecting resistance from the squatters?'

'Well, you gotta be prepared to have a fight. But we had a smart plan. Go in as squatters ourselves and pick arguments with them. They were gone in no time. Cushty.'

'Every last one?' the QC asked.

'Well, I thought so,' Bindon said. 'But squatters're as slippery as eels. You get them out of one room and they slip into another. There were a lot of rooms.'

'Did Oldman know that some of the squatters might have been avoiding you?' Sir Donald asked.

'He knew some of them avoided us. He said the only way to get them out would be to smoke them out.'

'Were those his exact words?' the prosecutor asked.

'Well, I didn't have a tape recorder but I'm an actor. I—'

'You're a liar, John,' Brian screamed, unable to hold his silence. 'A rotten fucking liar and a rotten actor.'

'Mr Oldman,' the judge said, 'as frustrating as it must be to listen to what you believe are lies, it is in the certain knowledge that your turn to cross-examine will come. Please refrain from calling out.'

'That's it, Bri,' Bindon mocked. 'Be a good boy or get done for contempt.'

'Remain silent until spoken to, Mr Bindon,' the judge ordered, 'or you certainly will be.'

'Tell the court what happened next to eject the remaining squatters,' the QC asked.

'Brian said to turn off the water and gas to the buildings,' Bindon said, as Brian tried to hold down his rage. 'We done the electrics too, but they somehow got them back on. Well, then Bri didn't get his planning permission so he was in schtook with money. That was when he started talking about torching the place. Did I know anyone—'

'Liar! You bastard liar,' Brian blurted out.

'Mr Oldman, remain silent or be removed to the cells,' the judge said. 'The choice is yours.'

Reluctantly, Brian sat back and took a deep breath.

'Sir Donald?'

'Was the defendant asking you to find someone who could burn the buildings for him?'

'That's what it sounded like,' Bindon told him. 'It's not my game. I'm an actor, not an agent for arsonists.'

That was the touchpaper for Brian's rage. 'You're a dirty, lying bastard,' he shouted. 'I'll kill you! I'll kill you!'

'Enough, Mr Oldman,' the judge said impatiently. 'We will adjourn for ten minutes while you regain your composure.'

Tony Wednesday smiled as the guards dragged Brian out through the door by which the witnesses entered. He quickly followed, wanting to catch the star witness. John Bindon came through the door, his eyes darting everywhere, but seeing nothing. He jumped in alarm when Tony grabbed him. 'John! You done well there, son.'

'I got the right hump with this. For tuppence I'd be off.'

'You'd get yourself nicked. You've got to play it out now.'

'But there's nothing else to say, is there?'

'Not really. But the silly ballocks gets his turn to rant and shout at you now.'

'I don't want too much of that.'

'Here, take these. They're beta-blockers. They'll keep you calm.' Bindon grabbed the pills and swallowed them.

Out in the lobby, Tony ran into Superintendent Redvers. 'I didn't expect to see you here, guv,' he said.

'We've got a case in court number five – a big drug-dealer,' Redvers said, with pride.

Tony had no idea what made honest policemen tick. Redvers would eventually leave the job with a pension and have to take another in security to make ends meet. 'A drug-dealer in leafy Kent? Are there such people?'

'We've got a few slimy rocks you find them under. How's it going with your case?'

'I'd say we're winning,' Tony said.

'After what happened at his last trial,' Redvers said.

'It's all about percentages, really. Win some, lose some and live with it.' Tony wondered who was kidding whom, and why he was here. Redvers wouldn't be taking the drug-dealer through court.

'That family still brings the taint of corruption to my door,' Redvers went on. 'The way they get prisoners out of Parkhurst to do robberies – a whole new investigation into corruption among the prison staff is long overdue.'

'That sounds like an old battle.'

'Maybe. In my over-enthusiasm to get Brian I rather missed the target. We'll get the father, Joey – or Joseph Olinska as he's now calling himself.'

'I hear he's getting very grand in political circles,' Tony said. 'That could make him too big a target to go after now.'

'There's only one way to eat an elephant,' Redvers said. 'One bite at a time.'

'Have you got the means to take the first bite?'

Redvers just looked at him, making him feel uncomfortable.

Tony wondered if even now the superintendent was giving him some sort of warning.

'Guv,' a detective said, as he approached them. 'Brian Oldman's apologized to the court. The judge wants everyone back.'

'Thanks, Adam.' Tony started towards him, then glanced back at Redvers, who didn't move. He nodded for him to come too, as if they were close colleagues.

Before starting his cross-examination Brian sat on the bench and read some papers. He'd learnt this trick from the prosecutor. Everyone's eyes were on him. Still he made no move.

'Mr Oldman,' the judge said finally, 'do you intend to cross-examine Mr Bindon?'

'I'm waiting for him to look at me, Judge.'

'Regrettably, that isn't something we can order,' the judge said. 'If he doesn't it's for the jury to make what inference it will.'

'Mr Bindon, will you look at me?' Brian said, rising. He waited some more. 'John. Look at me.' Bindon hesitated, then turned to him. 'Now take a hard look at my face. Do you know me?'

'Of course I know you,' Bindon said. 'I've known you all my life, ever since you was tied up with that rotten murdering Jack Braden.'

'You don't know me, do you? You don't really know me. If you did, you'd know I didn't burn that building and kill those kiddies, whose mother you were having sex with, you degenerate,' Brian said angrily.

'Mr Oldman,' the judge said, 'you must ask questions.'

'Yeah, that would be handy,' Bindon said.

The judge gave him a sharp look.

'Okay, John. When those rotten corrupt coppers offered you a deal, you just stuck my name up, didn't you?'

'No one's offered me a deal, Bri. Why would they?'

'Cos you left those people in the building for a sly shag when you should have emptied it,' Brian shouted. 'That's why, you degenerate drug addict.'

'My lord,' Sir Donald said. Brian assumed he had stood up, but it was hard to tell.

'Yes, Sir Donald, I know. Mr Oldman,' the judge said, 'I am trying to be fair to you, but you must ask questions of witnesses.'

'Why, when he's lying through his teeth?' Brian said.

'I ain't lying,' Bindon put in.

'Mr Bindon, you will answer only when spoken to.' The judge turned back to Brian. 'Try to tease out the possibility of his lying with questions. Trust the jury to decide.'

Brian nodded. He checked his notes, which told him nothing. He looked up suddenly. 'How many times did you slip in to have sex with that mother – while her children were watching?'

'What?' Bindon said, shocked. 'What you talking about, Bri?'

'You know,' Brian said. 'Isn't it true you like to have sex with women while their children are in the bed?'

'You rotten, grassing bastard.'

Supremely confident now, Brian said, 'It's true, is it not?'

'You're off your rocker, pal, like your crazy uncle. I don't know what you're talking about.'

'Yes, you do, John, don't you? And now the jury knows,' Brian said. 'Isn't it true that Social Services were chasing this mother and those children because of the abuse you were subjecting them to? Keeping them in those squalid conditions like sex slaves, giving them drugs—'

'No, no,' Bindon said. 'Don't talk like a cunt!'

'Mr Bindon!'

'You told me you was having a bit of bother getting the squatters out and wanted help. That's all I did. I didn't know you was gonna torch the place.'

'You're a liar,' Brian said angrily. 'A sex predator and a liar.'

'Me? What about you and that woman—'

'Just about right, you fucking grass,' Brian shouted, cutting him off.

'Mr Oldman,' Melford Stevenson admonished him, 'I won't have that language in my courtroom.'

'That's it, baby,' Bindon said. 'Behave yourself or we'll get some matches and burn you up.'

'Mr Bindon,' the judge cautioned, 'that's enough. Mr Oldman? Do you have any other questions?'

Brian looked at his notes and became resolute. 'Mr Bindon, what is your relationship with the notorious gangster Ronnie Kray, who's now serving life in prison?'

'What?' Bindon said, taken completely by surprise. 'I don't have nothing to do with him.'

'Is it not right you were one of his bum-boys?'

'Me? You're the biggest iron on the block, Brian.'

'That doesn't make me a bad person,' Brian said effeminately, making the jury laugh and rattling Bindon more.

'Answer the question, Mr Bindon. Did you or did you not have a sexual relationship with the notorious fat slug Ronnie Kray and through him reach some of the highest echelons in society?'

There was a long silence from the witness box. Brian knew he had the jury's total attention now. All eyes were on John Bindon.

'I met Princess Margaret, if that's what you mean.'

'No. Let me ask you again. Did you have sex with Ronnie Kray?' Brian picked up a paper as if about to offer it in evidence.

Finally, Bindon said, 'Yes. I'm ashamed to say I did.'

'Good,' Brian said. 'Is it true to say that Ronnie and Reggie Kray hate me and my family?'

'Well, come on, Bri, be fair. 'S not without cause, is it? You done them up like kippers.'

'Isn't it also true that as a result of your relationship with Ronnie Kray,' Brian went on, 'you burnt those buildings to pay me back for your ex-lover?'

'No, that's rubbish,' Bindon said. 'Don't be stupid.'

'Isn't it also true that, in so doing, you killed two birds with one stone, so to speak? You saw the means of ridding yourself of the problem you were having, both with the woman you were having sex with and Social Services?' Bindon was shaking his head but Brian forged on, feeling he was on a roll. 'You maliciously set fire to those buildings, despite knowing that that wretchedly abused family was hiding there, as a means to spite me and my family, didn't you?'

'No. No, that's ballocks. That's ballocks,' Bindon appealed to the jury. 'It is.'

'Well, there's twelve of my peers,' Brian said, turning to the jury. 'We'll have to trust them to decide, won't we?' He turned back to the jury to look at each of them. As he met their eyes he said, 'Look into my heart and know I didn't kill those children, or anyone else.'

'You're the one who fucked her all those years ago and give her a nipper,' Bindon said, leaving the court breathless.

'Is this some clever game they're playing?' Redvers said, as they left court. 'Brian's homosexual, we all know that.'

Tony Wednesday smiled uneasily. 'We'll surprise him yet.'

Redvers looked at him questioningly.

'If he was the father and the jury believe he killed them . . . Have you got something for us, guv?'

'We picked up a rumour that the bank came in short with drug-laundering money. Joey's in trouble.'

'Why don't you go after the bank?'

'For what? More egg on my face?'

'There must be some sleaze-bag drug-dealers who can lead you to him,' Tony suggested.

Redvers laughed. 'It's not their money the bank's handling.'

Tony saw the tall, stooped figure of Detective Chief Superintendent Slipper enter the lobby and stop. 'Excuse me, guv,' he said, 'I want a word with the skipper.'

'If you hear anything about Joey . . .' Redvers said.

'Of course. We're all on the same side.'

'What's he doing round here?' DCS Slipper wanted to know, when Tony joined him. 'I thought we'd kicked him off the patch.'

'Still looking after his family, I shouldn't wonder.'

'He always seems to be around when corruption raises its head.'

'Is he looking at bent Old Bill again?' Tony asked.

'Not that I know. But the rubber heels are all working overtime.'

'Well, as long as we stay a few steps ahead, guv.'

'It's no joking matter, Tony. The commissioner wants to get the job done before he goes. Retirement isn't to be an option for anyone they catch.'

'That might make Old Bill think twice before he dips his beak.'

'He's bringing in more detectives on a massive outside investigation,' Slipper said. 'I don't think any of them will have much sense of humour.'

'It'll slow down hard-working coppers again, guv,' Tony said. 'Redvers let something slip about his uncle's bank fronting drug money.'

'I expect we'd find more than enough if we could get warrants,' Slipper said. 'Have we got enough to get a warrant? The Home Office wouldn't be amused if we started looking in banks. We might find too many dirty secrets.'

'Does the name Charles Tyrwhitt mean anything to you, guv? He's Oldman's partner at the bank. We learnt a DS on the Porn Squad's been getting nasty videos of kiddies for him. We dug up a stack of evidence. Times, dates, even what he paid for them.'

'Don't you have enough of your own work, Tony?'

'It's all connected, guv. My instinct tells me it could open up that whole corrupt world of banking.'

Slipper waited.

'We could keep it, pick away at it quietly. I've got a feeling that sooner rather than later it'll get us into that bank and expose Joseph Oldman.'

'I'll trust your instinct, Tony,' Slipper told him. 'Be very discreet. We don't want you nicked by those coppers. I'll cover your back.'

Tony nodded. He'd laugh all the way to the bank.

*

In the cell, as he waited for the van to take him back to Brixton, Brian had a visit from Daniel Pocket, one of Lord Goodman's clerks.

'His lordship wants to know if there's any way we can help you, Brian.'

'What's happened? My mum and dad suddenly got a guilty conscience?'

'I don't know what this feud's all about, Brian.'

Daniel Pocket was a decent sort of bloke and Brian felt bad about giving him a hard time. He was his only contact with the law firm and always wore the same cheap grey pin-striped John Collier suit.

'It's about Joey letting me take the rap for something I didn't do.' The fury boiled up again. 'Why d'you think they're not in court?'

'His lordship said it's because they're active on Margaret Thatcher's behalf. He's got half our office fundraising.'

'I thought he supported Labour?'

'He reads the wind – like your folks, I dare say.'

'I didn't come off too well in court today.'

'I wouldn't say that, Brian. You made mincemeat of Bindon. Some of the jury will definitely be thinking he might have done it for the reasons you said. That was clever – a barrister couldn't have got away with it.'

'Is that right?' Brian felt slightly cheered.

'The thing is, you must hammer it home when you close your case,' Daniel Pocket advised. 'Bindon won't be there to shout back. Make a note to remind the jury what a despicable creature he is. Emphasise he's a drug addict who kept that poor mother squatting in your buildings for his own sexual gratification, then was prepared to get rid of her when Social Services were closing in on him.'

'Did he?' Brian said, surprised. 'I made that up.' He met Daniel Pocket's eye and saw disappointment. 'Well, he probably did. He's got no morals. He'd fuck a Wimpy, if he was hard up – boys and girls, anything that moves.'

'All that helps,' Daniel Pocket said. 'I assume there was no truth in what he said about you being the kid's father?'

Brian said nothing.

'Keep pushing Bindon's connection to her. When you get back to Brixton make lots of notes for your closing argument.'

That was real encouragement, and Brian even started to believe he might walk away from this. Which would leave the question of what to do about the real culprit.

Some prisoners at the remand centre had heard about the drubbing Brian had given John Bindon and the atmosphere was slightly easier. One or two faces even spoke reasonably to him. As Brian was queuing to get his supper another prisoner, Tony Barry, who had been convicted with the Krays, approached him amid the clatter of crockery and complaints about the crappy food.

'I heard how you got on today. Sounds brilliant,' Barry said. 'They should serve you in your cell now.'

'The way this lot treat me I wouldn't risk what they might put in my food, Baz,' Brian said.

'How's it going up there, d'you think?'

'You have your moments,' Brian said, grateful for this friendly conversation. 'Then they knock you back and it's about as bad as you expect.'

'But is it going to get any worse?' Barry asked. 'Has the Old Bill got any nasty surprises?'

'Well, that's the nature of a surprise,' Brian told him. 'How would you know?'

'Could be they're pleasant ones, Brian.' That puzzled Brian. He felt a bit uneasy, but didn't know why. 'I got a message for you from Ronnie Kray. He said he's got a way to help you out.'

'He has?' That was a surprise Brian hadn't expected.

'Yeah. It's this, you slippery poof. Die!' Brian felt the impact of what seemed like a punch before he felt the blade burying itself in his side. Pain shot through his body and the plastic tray he was carrying fell to the floor with a dull clatter. The last thing he heard before he collapsed was Tony Barry saying, 'Now it can't get no worse.'

He opened his eyes briefly as the siren wailed, and felt as if he was floating, which he knew meant he was dying. He was in an ambulance and someone was saying, 'He's losing a lot of blood – I'm not sure he'll make it.'

'Good,' a figure in a dark uniform said. 'After what he's done, everyone in Brixton wanted to do the same.'

Brian was slipping into unconsciousness, not wanting those angry words to be the last he heard.

'Well, don't try it in my ambulance, chum.'

Joseph got out of the taxi with Catherine a long way short of St Thomas's hospital, on the Thames Embankment, knowing journalists would be waiting. Negotiating the labyrinthine corridors to find Brian's ward was difficult – someone with a notebook seemed to be hanging around in every corridor they turned along.

'Excuse me, Sister,' Joseph said, to a woman in uniform outside the ward. 'Where's Brian Oldman?'

'Are you relatives?' she asked, in a West Indian accent.

Joseph hesitated, but Catherine said, 'No, family friends. Can you give us any information?'

'I'm not supposed to say – there're journalists snooping around.'

'Is he out of danger?' Joseph asked.

'Will he be all right?'

Perhaps the sister read something in Catherine's anxiety. She relaxed her guard a little. 'The blade punctured the main artery to the stomach, but he comfortable now. He asleep.'

'Could we see him – just for a moment? Catherine pleaded.

'The police guard him,' the sister said.

'Joseph?' Catherine begged. He knew what she was asking and, as painful as it was, he said no. Leaving the hospital by a side entrance, which brought them to the steps near Westminster Bridge, she said, 'Joseph, I don't know if I can live with this – he's still my son.'

'He's stable. You heard the sister. What more can we do?'

'I'm his mother. It's not the same for you.'

'We're surviving, Cathy, despite that boy having done his worst.'

'But why is he in so much trouble, Joseph Olinska?' she said accusingly. 'You pulled him into property development.'

'Think how full of praise Mrs Thatcher is for us,' Joseph said calmly. 'Would she be so grateful if we linked her to this? Do you think she'd be saying, 'I'm so grateful to Joseph and Catherine for all their hard work'? This pain will pass, Cathy. We pray to God he's proven innocent. The pain'll pass and we won't be damaged.'

Meanwhile, Joseph knew, his wife would mourn the loss of her son. Her politics were a sort of replacement. He prayed they would go on being so and that they would go on surviving.

THIRTY-EIGHT

All category A prisoners in Parkhurst prison on the Isle of Wight got an hour's association each day when they could wander around the fenced-in yard regardless of the weather. They could talk, smoke, tell lies to each other, remember their glory days. Few did. Mostly they talked about appeals pending or lost. A number didn't talk at all. Jack Braden could have fought with any of them. The Kray twins had been there for a while, but now only Reggie was. The Richardson brothers had shown up with members of their various gangs. Mad Frankie Fraser and some of the train robbers were there, two of those Jack had nicked money off. Mostly they'd learnt to tolerate one another and live with an uneasy truce.

Settling into the long prison term had been difficult. All he had thought about at first was paying back those who had betrayed him; then he had thought about being an old man when he got out, about escaping, or killing himself if escape wasn't possible. Finally, he had settled.

Another bout of depression closed in over Jack when he heard about Brian, and he spent a lot of time in the gym. Working out physically kept him from thinking.

With Brian out of hospital it was time to send a message to Ronnie Kray to let him know how well he was doing. He could see Reggie ahead, going around the circuit. As a category A prisoner, the same as Jack, he didn't have many opportunities to mix so Jack had to take a chance. He overtook a couple of lifers and fell into step with Reggie. The lifer he was walking with was the dark, scowling Harry Roberts, in for killing three policemen in Shepherds Bush back in 1966. He stepped away – that was the rule.

'Brian's recovered all right, then, Jack?' Reggie said pleasantly.

'He's a strong lad, Reg. His trial's just resumed. The prosecution's trying its worst with witnesses who should have been dead and buried.'

'That's what they done with me and Ron,' Reggie said. ''S why we got whacked like we done. Same judge an' all.'

'How's the other half doing, Reg?' Jack asked solicitously. 'I expect it's tough for him in Broadmoor, is it?'

'Them rotten slags give him too much Largactil, Jack,' Reggie told him. 'Ron's only a bit depressed. He should be in here with me, so I can look after him.'

'He was well enough to send a nice message to Brian in Brixton.'

'He's a thoughtful man, Jack.'

'Yeah. Well, here's a nice message back for him.' Jack thrust a blade hard into the small of his back and slipped away before Reggie Kray collapsed.

Farnborough police station, just along from the hospital on the A21, was one of the furthest reaches of the Metropolitan Police. There was plenty of crime around, but most of it was dealt with by St Mary Cray or Bromley. Superintendent Redvers encouraged his men to be more ambitious than the local car thief or creep. He had two working full time on Joseph Oldman, or Olinska. None of his men had been in the job when the Krays went to prison, much less had any contact with them. But they enjoyed talking about Reggie Kray's near fatal stabbing as they sat in his first-floor office waiting for their visitor to arrive.

'The knife missed his liver by a fraction of an inch apparently,' DCI Peter Robertson told them.

'It was as well Jack Braden wasn't aiming for his heart,' DC Toby Ryan said. 'He'd still be trying to find it.'

'They're so gone with drugs nowadays,' the DCI said, 'it's not like prison any more.'

'The screws are mostly supplying them.'

'It sounds like you're putting your hand up to do something about it, Toby,' Superintendent Redvers said, coming in with Sonia Hope.

'Got nothing else to do, guv.'

'I've asked Sergeant Hope from the fraud office in Holborn to join us because they've been looking at Joseph Olinska, too. What is said here goes no further. Sonia?'

She glanced nervously at Redvers, then at the other two detectives. Redvers wanted her to sound confident and was concerned at her hesitation.

'Joseph Olinska. Arguably, he's an important financial link in the drugs supplies,' she began, and glanced at Redvers again. He had told her to let it out or not as she saw fit. 'We believe the money comes in by courier in diplomatic bags from Colombia via Panama, France and Ireland. We think the Irish prime minister Charles Haughey is involved. In fact, we know he is.'

'That makes it nice and easy, Sonia.' Peter Robertson laughed. He was a big man with a ginger beard and had put on weight since coming south with Redvers. The waistcoat of his three-piece suit was tight against his stomach. He looked at Sonia as if he fancied her, and Redvers felt irrationally jealous.

'That's not where they're vulnerable, that's for sure,' Sonia said. 'The money's cleared here and goes out through high-risk investments, such as property developments.'

'Where are you suggesting he's weak?' DCI Robertson asked. 'Is he in fact weak?'

'He's weak, all right, Peter,' Redvers cut in. 'This man tries to cover absolutely everything. That means he's hiding more than most.'

'But what's he hiding?'

'We know he's involved with the Picado drug cartel by the money trail. Luis Picado comes over from Colombia for meetings with Olinska fairly regularly. Unfortunately we can't get near enough to know what's said. We certainly can't raid the bank on what we've got.'

'Neither can our little team, Sonia,' Redvers said, 'but we want to try to help.'

Sonia waited a moment. He met her pale blue eyes.

'Am I missing something here?' Robertson asked.

'No – no,' Redvers said quickly, and looked away.

'Why are we getting involved in this?'

Again Redvers glanced at Sonia, and nodded her on.

'We picked up information that suggests Joey Oldman – I beg your pardon, Joseph Olinska – might have been behind the fire on Cromwell Road that's currently at the Bailey.'

'A fire in Chislehurst Caves might be more our line.'

'Can that be so?' Ryan said. 'Haven't they got a witness saying it was Brian Oldman? That actor John Bindon?'

Redvers wondered when Sonia would get to her revelation. 'If it was Olinska, Toby, think how vulnerable he'd be.'

'Well, it would be handy, guv.'

'Why do you think he was involved, Sonia?' Robertson asked.

She hesitated and glanced at Redvers, as if for reassurance. He was encouraged by that. Finally she said, 'We picked up an intercept a while back. Olinska was calling a man with bad asthma. They talked about torching those buildings.'

'Christ!' DCI Robertson said. 'Why's it taken you so long? The trial's almost over.'

Sonia looked at the floor. 'The phone tap was unauthorized.'

'I can see why you'd keep it quiet,' DCI Robertson said. 'Policemen are being sent to the firing squad for less. Who was the asthmatic?'

'We didn't identify him,' Sonia said. 'It just got pushed aside with the volume of work, until we started looking at Olinska. If it helps, we think the call was to somewhere in South London.'

'Well, that narrows it to about three million people, Sonia.'

'I'm sorry,' Sonia said. 'We could have buried it for ever.'

'Not you, Sonia,' Redvers said, then went on. 'We'd better find the asthmatic, and fast, Peter, before he gets buried too. He might just provide us with a way into that bank and Olinska.'

When the meeting broke up, Redvers drew Sonia aside. 'That was very brave of you, especially as we've got this outside lot of police from Dorset crawling all over us with Operation Countryman.'

'I trust you, John. I want your investigation to succeed. I don't mind if you get to Olinska first.' She looked up suddenly and caught him watching her. 'Would you have nicked me in your previous incarnation?'

The easiest thing would have been to lie, but he couldn't.

'You would have done, wouldn't you? We work for months, even years, on an investigation and it goes nowhere. Policemen get impatient, John. You see some of these people quoted in the *Financial Times* but you know they're bent. You just know it.'

'That's not the same as proving it. Still, I meant what I said, Sonia – about you being brave. I'm glad you brought it to us.

'Well, who else is there? I certainly wouldn't trust Tony with it.'

Redvers was thrilled to hear this. It was as though he had passed some test he hadn't known he was taking.

'We'll find the asthmatic man,' he promised. 'If Joseph was involved in burning those houses, we'll prise him right out of the rat-hole at his bank and gut him.'

The call he took from DCI Robertson was possibly a warning. Tony still wasn't sure whether the man was straight but he was sufficiently concerned to check his airline ticket – first class to Australia. If anything went badly wrong for him he'd be on the next available flight. Meanwhile, he didn't like the impression Brian Oldman was making in court. The jury might prove perverse and believe his story. He was going to try to get in one other witness – even at this late stage: Braden's wife, Leah Cohen. He'd go and see her at the hospital. She might even have something on Joey.

His main concern, as he drove up to the Friern Barnet hospital, wasn't how to get Joey Oldman into the frame but how to keep him out of it.

As he waited in the hospital lobby, shrinking away from the strange characters shuffling through, the last person he wanted to see came in with a gang of doctors. It was hard to tell most of them apart from the patients, in their jeans and T-shirts. Seeing him, Clair Hammill broke away from the others. 'What are you doing here?'

'Policing's such a madhouse, these days,' Tony said. 'I'm trying to get a room.'

'If it's that bad why don't you give it up?'

Humour wasn't her strong suit, he remembered. 'Someone has to put the bad people where they belong, Clair. It's not easy – sometimes it's almost impossible – but it needs doing.'

'You're probably right,' she said. 'Is that why you're here?'

'I need to talk to Leah Cohen.'

'She's not here,' Claire said proudly. 'One of our success stories. She's a psychologist at the West Middlesex.'

That made life easier, not dealing with crazies, they scared him. Anyone that out of control did. The best place for them was locked up – the thought of that scared him, too. Probably it was to do with being locked in the cupboard in the sister's office at the orphanage, or worse, the dark, dank room in the cellar with the vaulted ceiling.

Disturbed people bobbed in front of him as he strolled with Leah Cohen across the grassed area between the huge red-brick wings of the vast Victorian psychiatric hospital in Ealing. Why weren't they under lock and key? 'I hardly knew the Oldmans,' she was saying, 'but my ex-husband sometimes hinted at what Joey was up to.'

'Like what?' Tony asked.

'Nothing specific. Mostly Jack was jealous of him.'

'Did you know Brian's on trial for murder?' Tony said.

'I do read the newspapers, Inspector.'

'The problem is, it looks as if he might get off again. Another witness might alibi him. A criminal, of course.'

'Did he do it?' Leah asked.

'We believe so,' Tony said. 'He's clever, and the jury aren't seeing him for the monster he is.'

'He's that, all right,' Leah said. She stopped and looked at him. 'There was a time when I believed you were part of their gang.'

'A lot of corrupt policemen were,' Tony said. 'You don't survive for long in the job if you are corrupt.'

Leah nodded. 'You want me to be a witness?'

He shrugged apologetically. 'Well, I wouldn't want to set you back.'

'I'm stable these days, Inspector. I tried to give evidence before, you know, but I was too late.'

'I'd talk to the prosecutor to get you in this time.' He smiled reassuringly, one eye on the mad people.

'With respect, my lord.' Sir Donald James had got to his feet at the start of the day.

Brian was only on the second day of his defence and he was running out of witnesses. Although he made the jury laugh he felt he hadn't put up much of a case. It had been easier attacking prosecution witnesses. He was still thinking about calling Joseph and accusing him of the arson, but wondered if that would really help or just put them both in prison. Now the prosecution wanted to bring in another witness. Brian's ears pricked up. That might give him an opportunity to attack.

'At this late stage? Without notification?' the judge said.

'The witness has been seriously ill,' Sir Donald explained. 'Now she is fully recovered.'

'You can object to a witness being sprung on you, Mr Oldman,' the judge informed him. 'The prosecution has supposedly closed its case.'

'Would objecting do me any good?' Brian said, getting another laugh. He smiled, enjoying his moment. 'I don't know anything about this.'

'That's the nature of surprises,' Mr Justice Melford Stevenson said.

'Why should I worry when I haven't done anything?'

'Then you may introduce your late witness, Sir Donald.'

There was a low buzz of anticipation as the usher went out of the door and returned shortly with Leah Cohen. She approached the box across the hushed courtroom, glancing at Brian, who leapt out of his seat. 'No, you can't. She doesn't know anything.'

'Mr Oldman,' the judge said, 'the court has agreed to hear Miss Cohen's evidence.'

Brian sank back into his seat, aware that he had signalled to the jury how important she was. If he protested any more, it would only make matters worse. He wanted to put his hands over his ears and shut out her words.

'You are Leah Cohen, formerly Mrs Jack Braden?' Sir Donald was saying to her gently.

Leah replied, in a calm, steady voice, that she had had no choice but to marry Jack. He'd terrified her, threatening her and her father. 'He kept forcing drugs on me, which disturbed the balance of my mind following the violent end of my relationship with Brian Oldman. It got progressively worse during my marriage to Mr Braden. It was a living nightmare from which I couldn't escape. I had to be hospitalized.'

'Would you describe your relationship with the defendant, Brian Oldman, as intimate?' Sir Donald asked.

'I thought I was madly in love with him. I now know I was suffering a serious mental disturbance at the time and had attracted someone who was in an even worse mental state – psychotic, in fact.'

'Miss Cohen,' the judge said, 'are you sufficiently detached to give an unbiased professional opinion?'

'I'm a practising clinical psychologist,' Leah said.

Brian was aware that the judge was looking in his direction. 'Mr Oldman, do you wish to object to this line of examination?'

He shook his head.

'You must be careful not to overstep the mark, Sir Donald.'

'My lord,' the prosecutor said. 'Ms Cohen, what characterized the defendant's disturbed mental state for you?'

Don't say it, please, don't say it, Brian thought, as Leah took a long moment to consider the question.

'When we first tried to make love,' she said at last, 'he thought I was his mother and tried to kill me. He hated his mother who had dominated him all his life.'

'How did he attempt to kill you, Miss Cohen?'

'With his fists. He beat me, then tried to strangle me. People at the nurses' home, where I was living at the time, broke down the door.'

'Was the defendant charged as a result of this grievous assault?'

'He was. But then I had a complete breakdown and couldn't give evidence. The charges against him were dropped.'

'Now that you have fully recovered your health and qualified as a psychologist,' Sir Donald said, 'how would you categorize the defendant?'

From the front bench Brian watched Leah turn and gaze at him for a long moment. She was still good-looking, with her boyish frame, small breasts and high cheekbones.

'Immature, out of control.' Her words grabbed his attention. 'He was like a child who wanted to destroy anything he couldn't make work.'

'Can you expand on that, Miss Cohen?' Sir Donald asked.

'If he couldn't understand or control something or someone, he felt compelled to destroy it or them,' Leah said.

'Is this always an angry, emotional response?'

'No. Sometimes it's cold, calculating and ruthless.'

'Miss Cohen,' the judge asked, 'are you giving this opinion as an expert or as someone who was intimately involved with the defendant?'

'Well, I did know him intimately,' Leah said, 'but I'm trying hard to give an opinion as a professional.'

'Then please tell the court, Miss Cohen, in your professional opinion, was the defendant capable of setting fire to those buildings, regardless of squatters being inside them?'

Without hesitation, Leah said, 'No. I wouldn't say he was.'

A roar erupted in the court, everyone seeming compelled to comment on what she had said. The clerk called for silence. When it was restored, Sir Donald came back. He tried without success to unpick what Leah had said, but she wouldn't move from it. Brian sat and stared at her, his emotions spinning in a vortex.

'What the fuck is your game?' Tony asked, as he caught Leah coming through the witness door. He spun her round. 'Why did you say that? I thought you hated him.'

'I do. But the prosecution asked for my professional opinion. I gave it.'

She pulled away, and Tony didn't try to stop her. He had decided she was still fucking mad.

'Guv! Guv!' DC Brian Baldwin hurried through the door.

'What is it? 'S the building on fire?'

'Not half, guv. We found the asthmatic fire-raiser. We missed him before because it wasn't on his CRO sheet that he was asthmatic. Plus he'd gone out to Marbella for about six months to play golf.'

'Long game,' Tony said. 'Why'd he come back to this poxy climate?'

'For a hospital appointment.'

'Thank God for the NHS,' Tony said. 'Let's see him.'

Numbness settled over Brian where he sat on the scarred bench in the court cell and mulled over what Leah had said about him. He could scarcely believe it. He'd thought she'd murder him. Daniel Pocket, the brief's clerk, was almost dancing for joy as he lit a cigarette. He offered Brian one, and his little silver hip-flask. 'That'll fucking well teach them not to sneak a late witness on to the list like that.'

'She did me a lot of good, though, didn't she?' Brian said.

'Brian, she couldn't have done you more good if she'd reached over and kissed your dick.'

'I can't understand why she said that, though. Not after what I did to her.'

'I can,' Daniel Pocket said. 'Because you didn't do it. You're not capable of doing such a wicked thing.'

Guilt clouded Brian's elation. What he had done was find Roger Smith for his dad and he'd ignored the possibility that those little kids and Martha were in the building when he'd taken the arsonist to see it. Instead of checking himself that they had all gone, he'd relied on a degenerate like John Bindon. He began to massage his head. 'I shouldn't have let it happen,' he found himself saying. 'It's all true. I did do that.'

'What are you saying, Brian?' Daniel Pocket drew on his cigarette and forced smoke out through his nostrils. 'Don't say anything.'

'I did all that Leah said I did.'

'Are you going to cross-examine her? I don't think you should. In fact, you should close your case.'

'I don't think I can, Daniel,' Brian said. 'There's a lot I need to ask her. I haven't had a chance. In court she has to answer.'

'Think carefully about this, Brian. If you don't cross, the last objective impression the jury will have of you is what she said.'

But Brian wanted direct answers to direct questions.

—

'Ms Cohen, how long were you married to the notorious gangster Jack Braden?' he asked. Until now he had assumed it was to pay him back and keep him at a distance but always in sight. 'Ms Cohen?'

He waited, telling himself it wasn't pain that was dulling her eyes. He glanced at the judge.

'Miss Cohen, you must answer the question directed to you.'

'He's trying to cause me as much pain as he can.'

'But you chose to give evidence against him,' the judge told her.

'He knows,' Leah exploded. She turned to Brian. 'You know every painful moment of it. You were his partner in crime. I was suffering mental and emotional torture.'

'So, it wasn't a good marriage?' Brian ventured. He wasn't enjoying seeing Leah suffer, but what she was saying meant everything to him.

'It was loathsome. I hated his touch, his smell. I loathed being near him. He wouldn't even let me study,' Leah said. 'I wanted to blot out every moment – and I did, most of the time, with prescription drugs, until I suffered a drug-induced psychosis.'

'As a result you became a patient in a mental hospital?'

'I would have spent every moment of my marriage there to escape him.'

'Can you say why an intelligent grown-up like you would marry such a person?'

'He forced me to,' Leah said. Emotion was welling up in her and shutting off her breath.

Brian knew he should stop, but he couldn't. 'In this age of women's lib, you were forced to marry?'

Her words came out in a painful, staccato fashion. 'You know, Brian. You know what that monster was like. After what you did I was so vulnerable. He scared me to death with his threats—'

'So you blame me for your rotten marriage?'

'That was the start. My plunge into madness was almost entirely due to you—'

'Your relationship with me did that?' Brian continued to pick at the scab to see it bleed. He couldn't help himself.

'At first, no,' Leah said. 'Then I felt sorry for you.' She was getting her breathing under control, staring at a fixed point at the back of the court.

'Ms Cohen, please look at me. Is that all you felt? Sorrow?'

She shook her head. 'At first you were so vulnerable. I even thought you were sensitive and caring. As I nursed you in hospital I fell in love with you. You were the first man I'd ever loved, the only man—' That shocked Brian. He fell his legs going wobbly and gripped his lectern. 'You hurt me so much. I loved you so much. When you rejected me as you did I wanted to die. I tried to kill myself several times. I wanted to see you dead. What you took away from me I can't ever get back.' Tears ran down her face and she made no move to wipe them away.

Standing at the front bench, Brian swayed slightly and held on to the lectern to stop himself falling over. All the hurt he had done Leah he thought the whole while was part of her madness. Only now was he beginning to appreciate the depth of the hurt. He didn't know how he could change that, and it left him full of self-loathing. He found he couldn't go any further. He thought of an argumentative point, that in blaming him, her evidence had become merely the means to pay him back, but it slipped away. At that moment, he realized he was still in love with Leah.

'You've got to be joking, Inspector,' Sir Donald James said urgently across the Formica-topped table in the court canteen. 'The defence has closed its case. We can't call another witness. Read my lips. We cannot call another witness.'

Tony stared at the tiny barrister and said, in an even tone, 'This isn't *just* another witness, not like Leah Cohen. Roger Smith is a material witness to fact.'

'Then why on earth didn't you bring him forward before?'

'He's been abroad for the last six months.'

'I grant you, having the arsonist saying under oath that Brian Oldman paid him to torch those houses is pretty powerful stuff.'

'I know the judge might refuse him, sir,' Tony said, 'but I'd feel so bad if we didn't at least try. Suppose we don't and Brian goes not guilty? It's possible, the way he's been playing to the jury.'

'I just hope you've briefed him better than you did Ms Cohen.' The QC got up decisively.

The judge heard his argument away from the jury. Brian surprised everyone when he got up and said, 'No, I've closed my case. To let a new prosecution witness in at this stage would be seriously prejudicial. It could give grounds for appeal.'

Someone was giving him sound advice, Tony thought, and glanced at the spiv-like clerk sitting next to the screws.

For a moment it looked as if the judge was going to deny the argument, but he said, 'I'm going to take this on advice. I'll adjourn for one hour.'

When he came back, he quoted chapter and verse on the law. The witness was in.

Tony sat at the back of the prosecution benches and watched wheezy Roger Smith in the witness box. 'Brian asked me to burn them buildings,' he was saying. 'I enquired if the insurance was all up to date. He said he wasn't bothered about that, he just wanted to pay his dad back.'

'Did you know what their feud was about?' Sir Donald asked.

Smith glanced at Tony, who avoided eye contact.

'The answer isn't over there, Mr Smith.'

'He was furious at Joey. He'd recently found out that he wasn't really his dad.'

That brought a gasp from Brian. Tony had thought it might. It had only just been confirmed. They had looked at Brian's blood and that of the dead children after what Bindon told them. None was Brian's child, but they found also that Brian and Joseph weren't blood-related. It was too great a shock to Brian, and Tony worried that the jury might think so too for it ever to have been a motive.

'I have blood reports on both Joseph and Brian Oldman,' Sir Donald said. 'They show they aren't related.' The judge accepted the reports and Brian was passed copies. He didn't look at them, Tony noticed, but seemed to be in a trance. Smith's deal, a light prison sentence for manslaughter, was dependent on him keeping Joseph Olinska out of the frame.

'Can you tell us what transpired next between you and the defendant?'

'We walked the walk,' Smith wheezed, 'checked the building. I told him how I'd do it. I asked was he sure the buildings were empty. He told me over and over they were. 'S sickening what happened. 'S hard to live with. Never again.'

Watching the faces of the jurors, Tony was confident they'd bought this.

The only surprise was that they took so long, having gone out just before the lunch recess after the closing speeches, when Brian had declined to say anything, totally defeated by this betrayal.

The judge called them back into court at ten to four. 'Is there any likelihood that, with more time, you will reach a verdict tonight?' he asked them.

'Well, I think so, sir. We're quite close to it,' said the foreman, a milkman with the Express Dairy. He straightened his buttoned-up suit jacket.

'Very well,' the judge said. 'Return to the jury room. We will await your deliberations. There is no time constraint.'

The fund-raising dinner at the Dorchester Hotel was the biggest event Catherine and Joseph had ever organized. It helped distract them from persistently nagging thoughts of Brian's trial. To meet and welcome the guests, most of whom were in tails and black tie or ballgowns, was gratifying, especially as they each paid a minimum of a hundred pounds a ticket; Luis Picado had bought two at a thousand pounds each, which promised an introduction to the future prime minister. Joseph suspected he was disappointed that she was a woman. Many famous names attended and an equal number of famous faces. The press corps camped outside and, for once, it wasn't trying to target Joseph or his wife.

Catherine was in her element. She might have been born to it, Joseph thought. She was radiant in her long purple evening dress, with thousands of sequins. He was certain she had no concern for Brian just then. When he saw his new assistant, June Sorrell, weaving her way through the ballroom towards him, wearing a more tense than usual expression, he knew the jury had arrived at its verdict.

'I'm so sorry,' she whispered, close to his ear. 'The jury found him guilty on all six counts of murder.'

The shock sucked his breath away. He tried to steady himself, feeling every one of his organs attacked at once. Catherine caught his eye and came over to him, smiling.

'The judge gave him two life sentences to run consecutively,' June said. 'Thirty years.'

'Oh Joseph,' Catherine murmured, the smile still fixed on her face, 'he'll be nearly seventy before he gets out. We probably won't be alive.'

'He can appeal,' Joseph mouthed, so as not to fracture the party atmosphere with such brutal news.

He saw Catherine stiffen, her smile not relaxing at all. He turned. Margaret Courtney was between them, wearing a figure-hugging satin dress and beaming, as if the party was her personal triumph. In a way, it was, he thought. It reflected so well on her and she had kept them in the fold.

'Joseph, Catherine,' she said, linking her arms through theirs. 'Margaret would like you to join her table as a special thank-you for all you've done. We're ready to win the general election.'

Glossary

ache   annoying person or situation
at it   behaving corruptly

bint   girl
blinding   (as in, result) really good
blow, take a   a rest
bluey   five-pound note
bomp on   to register (daily) at the docks for stevedore jobs
brad   a worthless nail (not a son)
busies   policemen
buttonmen   policemen

cap   kill
carpet joint   illegal gambling club, a bit smarter than a spiel
cattled   finished, slaughtered
charver   'fuck'
chavvy   baby
chiv   cutthroat razor
chuck, a   thrown out of court
claret   blood
coco, I should   not likely
Colchester nod   headbutt in the face
collar   work, graft
cozzer   policeman
cushty   very good, pleasant

deuce   two pounds
diamond geezer   good bloke
donah   girl
drop out   not charged, let go free

drum   place, gaff, room

feel a collar   arrest
funny run   dismiss a foolish proposal

gelt   money
German bands   hands (rhyming slang)
get up   an arrangement, ruse, subterfuge
ghost   move stealthily without warning at night
ginger beer   queer, homosexual (rhyming slang)
groin   ring

hampton   'hampton wick', prick (rhyming slang)
have it on one's toes   run away
head   drug addict
house-to-let   bet (rhyming slang)

Irish apricots   potatoes
iron hoof   poof (rhyming slang)

jankers   fatigues (army)
jib   cheat

kate   Kate Carney/Kearney, army (rhyming slang)
kite   cheque

laundress   prostitute
lolly up   inform

merry-hearts   tarts (rhyming slang)
mugged off   made a fool of
mysteries   women

nausing   sickening pain (as in nauseating)
nonce   despicable person into low-life crime (especially child
   molesters)

obo   observation (police)
off   to kill
Old Bill   police
oncer   one pound note
one and a kick   one shilling and sixpence

pongo   a black person
pugged up   hidden safely

roaf   shilling
rook   cheat
rozzer   policeman
rub   wank
rubber heels   policemen who investigate other policemen

sap   mug
schmutter   clothes
shikseh   non-Jewish girl
shmeeze   relaxation
shop   inform on
shtum   quiet, buttoned up
spiel/spieler   illicit gambling joint
stone ginger   a certainty
swag   steal, run off with (silverware and gold)

tealeaf   thief (rhyming slang)
tom   'tomfoolery', jewellery (rhyming slang)
tosheroon   half a crown

whistle   'whistle and flute', suit (rhyming slang)
wipe your mouth   accept your losses
wolly   naïve policeman

ACKNOWLEDGEMENTS

My thanks to Jon Riley, Nick Johnston, Liz Hatherell, Hazel Orme, Rebecca Hughes Hall, Prof. Gary Slapper, and Martin J. Walker, without whom it might have been a lesser book. And many lawyers, who spoke off the record, and the corrupt policemen and ex-criminals, who can't be named because of the iniquitous double-jeopardy laws, but without whom there may not even have been a book!